ALL ALONG THE WATCHTOWER
THE ACADEMY

TOM DOUGHTY

Names: Doughty, Tom, 1949- author.
Title: All along the watchtower / Tom Doughty.
Description: First Stillwater River Publications edition. |
Pawtucket, RI, USA : Stillwater River Publications, [2022]
Identifiers: ISBN: 978-1-958217-31-3 | LCCN: 2022911701
Subjects: LCSH: Military cadets--United States--History--20th century--Fiction. |
United States Naval Academy--Fiction. | Families--Fiction. | United States--History--1961-1969--
Fiction. | Revenge--Fiction. | LCGFT: Military fiction.
Classification: LCC: PS3604.O9251 A45 2022 | DDC: 813/.6--dc23

ALL ALONG THE WATCHTOWER: THE ACADEMY

CHAPTER I
THE BRIGADE RETURNS

The soft, white clouds formed a moving background to the green, copper roof of Macdonough Hall. The Severn River flowed its casual way to the Chesapeake Bay on the other side of the building. Further yet was a dense, tall wall of inviting, lushly green trees that hid the rifle range from view. Macdonough Hall seemed to be trying to force the river and trees into submission by jutting its massive stone strength into a dominating position that blocked the view for dreaming midshipman eyes. However, the river and trees made furtive appearances on either side of the structure.

Macdonough Hall represented the kind of architecture characteristic of the Academy. The buildings were huge granite blocks that overshadowed everything near them. They weighted down the earth like massive mausoleums lording it over the humble, mute messages of the surrounding, less worthy, tombstones.

Bancroft Hall, from which I looked at the scene before me, was another massive creation. This was where the midshipmen lived, two to a room. In each room were two large, beige-painted metal desks facing each other, that looked so solid and heavy that they certainly would have plunged into the burning depths of the earth had not the indomitable, forceful strength of Bancroft Hall supported them. They served to divide the room into two halves. On either side were the bunks. My bunk was on the same side as the shower and sink. Bob's bunk was on the side that had the walk-in closet that held our dirty laundry bags and M-1 carbines.

1

I caught glimpses of the sun flashing off the Severn and mused, *Thales; all things are water.* That had come from a Greek philosophy book, an introduction, which I managed to finish prior to my coming to the Academy. A sense of doom gripped me as I watched the passing clouds and thought, *As fleeting as an autumn cloud. Yet, something must be eternal.*

I heard someone enter my room. For a moment I considered not responding, but quickly turned about, stiffening into attention and sounding off, "Midshipman Sorensen, 721260, sir!"

"Chin in, chest out, Sorensen!"

"Aye-aye, sir!"

"I said, 'Chin in,' mister!"

"Aye-aye, sir!"

Before me stood Budge, one of the upperclassmen in my squad. He was six inches shorter than me with narrow, black, predatory eyes that looked up from a soft, fleshy face. He had curly, dark brown hair, a receding hairline, and a reddish skin tone like a first-degree burn. His body seemed to be coated with a layer of thick subcutaneous fat, reminding me of the soft, impressionable flesh of the bedridden paralytics I had cared for during my high school job, an orderly at Meantacut Hospital. I remembered shifting a patient from his right side to his left side to avoid bed sores and seeing my hands imprinted half an inch into the patient's flesh.

"What's for noon meal, Sorensen?"

"Sir, the menu for noon meal is meatloaf..."

"You mean elephant turds?"

"Yes, sir. Elephant turds cooked in a rich, brown gravy, mashed potatoes, hot buttered lima beans, white and whole wheat bread, custard pie, milk and tea, sir."

"What's for dessert?"

"Custard pie, sir."

"Are you sure about that?"

"Yes, sir."

"Let's find out."

I could hear a fast shuffling jog called chopping, required of plebes while traversing the corridors of Bancroft Hall. Plebes were required to chop down the middle of the corridors, the sides being reserved for the walking upperclassmen. Budge stepped out of the room. I heard, "Hovedo!"

The sound of running stopped. "Sir?"

"What's dessert for noon meal?"

"Apple pie, sir."

"Carry-on."

"Aye-aye, sir."

Budge was back in the room as the sound of Hovedo's footsteps faded away. A particularly pleased look flickered across his face. "Did you hear that, Sorensen?"

"Yes, sir."

"Hit it for ten."

"Aye-aye, sir." I threw myself into leaning rest position to do ten quick push-ups, keeping my arms wide to make them easier. I counted out loud, "One, sir; two, sir; three, sir; four, sir; five, sir; six, sir; seven, sir, eight, sir; nine, sir; ten, sir!" When they were completed, I jumped onto my feet and snapped back into attention.

Budge leered. "Did I tell you to get up, Sorensen?"

"No, sir."

"Hit it for ten more."

"Aye-aye, sir." Again, I went through the routine, this time staying in leaning rest and calling, "Sir, request permission to come aboard, sir!"

"Permission granted."

I jumped to my feet and stood at attention. Budge was about to leave when he stopped short to turn halfway around, "By the way, Sorensen, come-around."

"Aye-aye, sir."

"Are you pissed at me?"

"No, sir." It was important not to show emotion.

"Don't lie, Sorensen. You're as red as a beet. Are you pissed off?"

"No, sir."

"I know everything you're thinking, Sorensen, everything. It shows all over your face. Do you know that?"

"No, sir." I knew that the other plebes were getting as much harassment as I was. If they put up with it, so could I.

"It does, Sorensen. Come-around."

"Aye-aye, sir."

"Come-around."

"Aye-aye, sir."

"Come-around."

"Aye-aye, sir."

"How many's that?"

"Four, sir."

"Good. Let's make it an even five."

"Aye-aye, sir."

Budge left. I glanced out the window, sighed, then sat down at the desk to shine my shoes. I wasn't sure whether I should feel resentment or not. If anything, I had undirected anger. It was vague since I was unable to focus it on anyone or anything. I couldn't blame Budge for doing his job. After all, he was an upperclassman; other plebes got harassed by their upperclassmen. Budge, however, targeted me personally. Why? Did I remind him of someone he hated or, like a predator, did he smell the Heights on me?

I wrapped my shoeshine rag about the index finger of my right hand. I opened the Kiwi polish tin, put water into its cap, then dipped my finger into the water, followed by the polish. Placing my finger onto the toe of the shoe, I moved it in small, vicious circles until I became absorbed into its rhythm.

Budge ordered me to add the five come-arounds to the plebe come-around board. This was a blackboard with a list of the company plebes on it. Next to each name was a row of Xs, each representing a come-around which was used as punishment and was either a fifteen-minute workout in the morning from 0600 hours to 0615 just before morning meal or a half-hour workout in the afternoon from 1700 hours to 1730 right after the required sport. Either workout counted as one come-around. Some plebes had as few as five after their names. Like me, some had over twenty. I made a mental calculation. I had twenty-two come-arounds on the board; add the five just gained and that gave me twenty-seven. I calculated that, at two come-arounds per day from Monday through Friday and one on Saturday, it would take me two and a half weeks to work them off, providing I received no more. The real problem was that during plebe summer, there were two second classmen in each company of thirty plebes. With the return of the Brigade from summer training, there were now three upperclassmen for every plebe.

The Brigade had been back for only a couple of weeks but already the battle lines were forming. I saw that Banfield was about to go. It might take a little longer with Seitzer, but he would go, too. The day before, during come-around, they were on all fours doing the bear crawl while wearing the long, heavy, black winter overcoat in the hot Maryland weather. Their faces looked flabby, as though they both were about to cry. I had expected some evidence of rage, but both were too immersed in passive endurance to feel outrage. The bottom line: they weren't midshipman material, however that was defined.

I put away my everyday class shoes and picked up my "grease" shoes, worn only at noon meal and special functions. I enjoyed the mechanical movement of my hand gliding smoothly back and forth over the shiny black of the shoe. At times, I wetted the end of the rag with my tongue, dipped it into the tin for more polish and continued rubbing. I was amazed as the thick, muddy polish from the can metamorphosed into the glow that made the wearer of such shoes look so sharp.

Dave Husaby, who was the plebe watch for that day, interrupted the work. The plebe watch had a desk that was in a central location of the corridor so that he knew who came into and out of the company area. The watch was excused from his regular routine so that he could perform the duties of sorting the mail and taking and delivering messages. He was granted carry-on for the day and could walk through the halls without chopping and eat without bracing up.

Despite having the striated arm and leg musculature of an old man, minus the pot belly, Husaby reminded me of my grandmother because of his round face, pixie nose, light gray eyes, and weak chin. He paused in the doorway and gushed, "Lieutenant Gardiner wants to see you, Sores! You're the only plebe in the company he's seen all day! You must really rate!"

I responded with a reserved, "I guess," knowing that to be singled out wasn't necessarily an honor. I was relieved when Husaby returned to his duties. Ever since plebe summer, Dave's presence made me nervous. One day, I had been two seconds late for a formation when Dave had been the attendance midshipman. I witnessed the pencil pause above the roster but wasn't sure if Husaby had marked me down as late. During the indoctrination briefing that followed, I was careful to sit next to him. I laughed when Dave laughed, looked attentive when Dave looked attentive. Our eyes met in mutual agreement over some fine points the speaker had made. With each laugh, each look, I collapsed into myself, smaller and smaller, until, at the end of the briefing, I asked Husaby not to mark me late. He answered patronizingly, "We'll see." I bit my lip, silently swearing never to degrade myself to a classmate again. I wished I had taken the five demerits of the average Form 2, a chit filled out by a senior midshipman used to process and punish more serious offences. For each demerit, I was required to march or exercise for an hour. That would have been better than allowing myself to be humiliated.

I decided to wear White Uniform Alpha to see Gardiner. White Uniform Alpha was the white, pajama-like outfit with the flap at the back of the neck, a black necktie that formed a large *v* in the middle of the chest, and the small officer's cap. When I was ready, I stood before the wall mirror, looking for any glitches in my uniform. I placed my index and middle finger along the bridge of my nose to make sure that the visor of the cap was the regulation two fingers width above it. I buffed my class shoes, then chopped to Gardiner's office. At the door I took off my cap, holding its crown against my leg while my right hand was splayed in the hat rim in the proper midshipman manner. Knocking briefly, I took one step inside the room and sounded off, "Midshipman Sorensen, 721260, reporting as ordered, sir!"

We exchanged salutes. "At ease, Mr. Sorensen. Be seated."

"Aye-aye, sir."

I sat before the small, dark, unassuming, almost furtive man. The officer fumbled with some papers on his desk, then said, "I'm sorry we were unable to grant your request to go to your sister's wedding. We feel that you will miss too much training."

"Yes, sir." My mind raced to the upcoming schedule prepared for the midshipmen, running from hour to hour for the whole week. The only training scheduled for the requested three-day leave was six hours of marching on the parade field, an exercise I could easily miss. It irked me that I had gone through the proper procedures, filled out the proper chits, only to be rejected for such a trite reason, six hours of mindless marching.

"I've been looking over the records from this summer. I see that you've had a bit of difficulty." Like a bobblehead, I nodded my head yes a couple of times but couldn't see where I suffered from any real problems. The lieutenant continued, "You lead the company in demerits. You have a total of twenty. I know it doesn't seem like a lot, but they can add up without your noticing."

"Yes, sir."

"I see that you were the first to get a Form 2."

"Yes, sir."

"It says here, 'For conduct unbecoming a midshipman.' What did you do?"

"I spilled some tea on Midshipman Second Class Roark, sir."

"At noon meal?"

"Yes, sir."

"What'd you do? Spill a few drops while pouring his tea for him?"

"Not quite, sir."

"What'd you do? Spill the whole glass on him?"

"No, sir. I spilled the whole pitcher on him, sir."

"The *whole* pitcher?"

"Yes, sir."

Lieutenant Gardiner sat back, putting a hand before his mouth, doing his best not to laugh. His features had lightened. He asked, "What was he wearing?"

"Dress whites, sir."

"Dress whites." I watched Gardiner as he tried to imagine the scene. "Roark has quite a temper, doesn't he?"

"Yes, sir." During meals, the second class sit at one end of the table while the first class sit at the other end. The plebes nearest the ends pour their drinks for them. I had been sitting at the second class end when I lifted the pitcher to pour iced tea into Roark's glass. The pitcher was badly designed; a small indentation on its rim served as a spout. When the pitcher was tilted, the water gushed out of it, making it difficult not to spill it. Since the pitcher was full and heavy, I spilled some tea onto the table. Roark, dressed in his finely tailored whites, jumped back. The second classman yelled, his mouth two inches from my left ear, "Sorensen, you piece of shit, you spill any of it on me and I'll have your ass." I got nervous, spilling more and more tea in a one-to-one correspondence with Roark's violent language; the more Roark roared, the more I spilled. Finally, the pitcher maliciously jumped from my hand and the tea cascaded down the front of Roark's once immaculate uniform.

7

In a rage, Roark yelled that he wanted me to bring him a Form 2, then he left in a huff to change his uniform. I didn't know what a Form 2 was but Larry Bemes, my roommate from the summer, told me that a Form 2 was given for offenses that equaled at least five demerits.

Gardiner shuffled the papers on his desk, trying to keep from laughing. I didn't see anything humorous but tried not to show my annoyance. The officer studied the material before him, then continued, "According to your plebe reports, you're below average. It means that you'll have to work harder to become a good midshipman."

"Yes, sir."

Gardiner sat back, this time chewing the end of a pen. He considered me for a moment, then said, "I guess you'll do all right."

"Yes, sir."

Suddenly, the officer stood up, snapping a salute while I quickly did the same. "You're dismissed, Mr. Sorensen."

"Aye-aye, sir." I chopped away. That was the first and the last time I had a conference with Lieutenant Gardiner.

When I reached my room, I found my roommate, Bob Valdres, sitting at his side of the desk, back to the window and facing the door. A look of contempt and surprise ran over his face as he rushed to the small bulletin board by the door that had our class schedules on it. Hands on hips, feet shoulder width apart, Bob faced me and, with a sneer in his voice, asked, "What are *you* doing here?"

"I didn't have class today. The prof's sick. Why?"

"Shit! Now where will I go?" Bob paused in indetermination, then returned to his chair to study. I sat at my desk to study physics. The tension, which I tried to ignore, was immediate as we faced each other over our desks. I read $S = 1/2 \ Gt^2$, followed by its explanation. Unconsciously, I started rocking back and forth on the heels of my chair. Although I pretended not to notice, I became aware of Bob pointedly glaring at me. Valdres picked up a pencil and started tapping it on his desk's surface. Knowing that Bob was trying to annoy me and doing a very good job of it, I picked up a pen and started clicking it in and out, in and out. Bob responded by kicking the leg of his desk. An increasing tempo developed on both sides where the clicking, tapping, and knocking in all its forms became more vicious, more passionate. With amazing insight, I lifted a heavy, metal paperweight. I let it drop two feet onto the desktop where it crashed with a startling, jaw jarring bang. Bob's kicking became so furious that he half lifted himself out of his chair for more power and leverage. I dropped the paperweight from a greater height onto the floor, but the dull, disappointing thud that resulted wasn't nearly as effective as the brittle sound of dropping it onto my desk. I was stumped on how to outdo Valdres when it occurred to me how absurd this was. Feeling foolish, I put on my cap, took my text, and headed for the library to spend the last period before noon formation.

I hesitated, like a caged animal that pauses when its cage door is finally lifted, before taking the plunge into the corridor. I hoped to make it to the library without becoming the victim of some upperclassman's ire. I chopped down the middle of the corridor. The highlight of the Academy year was the Army - Navy game. For this reason, all plebes called, "Beat Army!" whenever they turned a corner. As I turned toward the ladder (Navy talk for stairway) on my way to the first deck (more Navy talk for the first floor) I called, "Beat Army, sir!"

My thoughts, however, were with Larry Bemes when, at the end of plebe summer, Bob Valdres appeared at our room to ask me to be his roommate for the coming academic year and I answered yes. After Valdres chopped away, Bemes turned startled eyes onto me.

He said with concern, "I think you better find another roommate."

I asked, "Why?" to which my friend answered, "Because there'll be trouble."

Again, I asked why, but Larry wouldn't explain himself. Since I believed in the innate worthiness of all midshipmen, I smiled at Larry's foolish caution. Events were proving that he had been right.

Bemes had given me one other piece of advice, which I had also failed to capitalize on. Again, it was at the end of plebe summer when the plebes were signing up for the mandatory fall sports. Larry said, "I think you should go out for either fencing or crew. They're the only sports not recruited for, so you'll have a good chance to get onto the team tables."

Each midshipman was required to take Naval engineering and science courses in addition to his other major. When he graduates, he receives a science degree in English literature or management or whatever major he chose. My schedule was full already, twenty credits not counting mandatory military events, come-arounds, and E.D. (extra duty), so I didn't want to add the extra pressure of an intercollegiate sport. I answered, "Larry, I'm not a hero. I want to get by as easily as I can. I don't want to spend time or energy doing anything more than is required. I'll stick with the intramural sports."

To my later dismay, Bemes had been right. Most of the harassment took place during meals when the upper class and plebes got together. At company tables, the plebes braced up—"chin in, chest out, mister!"—while sitting on two inches of their chairs. Then the upperclassmen asked them their rates, which were lists, paragraphs, and sayings that they were required to memorize. The upper class also ordered them to do any number of things for the sake of pure harassment. At the team tables on the other hand, the plebes were granted immediate carry-on and suffered no harassment at all. They were a protected class when they were in training and when their sport was in season.

My emergence from Bancroft Hall was accompanied by a sense of relief, accentuated by the coolness of the slight breeze off the Chesapeake Bay and a pleasant dance of sunshine upon a suddenly bright world. At this time of day, the library was nearly barren. This was sanctuary. No one would bother me here. I sat at the first table that presented itself. Slouching down, I stretched out my legs and picked up my physics book. Soon, the text was lying flat on the table while I was sitting erect and pressing my hand against the tabletop. *If matter is made up mostly of space, then why doesn't my hand go through?* I knew the answer. *Because of electro-magnetic forces. But what is that and why?* Everything was a miracle to me, some ineffable sense that we are surrounded by mystery.

My inquisitive nature was both a blessing and a curse, sometimes sending me down a rabbit hole of random thoughts. Too often I stood before the Viking sword in one of the library display cases or before a map, any map, in a magazine, feeding myself with pleasurable minutia while sacrificing valuable study time.

* * *

It was almost noon when I left the library. Formation was outside. While the main body of midshipmen formed up on the yellow bricks in front of Bancroft Hall, small outcroppings of mids formed up on the red-tiled terraces away from tourist eyes. The twelfth company belonged to the latter grouping. After the plebes had run from chow call, where a handful stood in the corridors calling out the menu and uniform for the coming meal, the upperclassmen hurriedly straggled in, in an increasing order of rank, until the first class arrived to complete and fully organize the company. Today there was no inspection so the mids as a group felt relief. Not even the second classmen hunted down their favorite quarries. The smell of the earth and sky made the day sweetly calm.

A few short orders were given that started the columns of midshipmen moving smartly into the dining area. Ordered chaos broke out immediately upon their passing through the double doors leading directly into the mess hall. The shaved heads of hundreds of plebes bobbed like buoys in an angry sea as they chopped to their assigned tables. Once there, they stood at attention, eyes in the boat, looking straight before them, while they waited to see what the upperclassmen were going to do. The only acceptable movements among the plebes were at the first and second class ends where the plebes were busy pouring drinks.

Each table comfortably sat twelve midshipmen, generally four plebes, three or four youngsters, three or four second classmen, and two first classmen. The attitudes displayed by the different classes made interesting contrasts. While the fourth classmen—or plebes—froze at attention with worried looks on their faces, the third classmen—or youngsters—were carefree and playful. They had just made it through plebe year and were still too happy to take life seriously. They were the traditional friends of the plebes and were supposed to help them when they saw tragedy in the making. The second classmen were the disciplinarians of the organization. They were to see that the plebes were properly trained in military matters as well as developing the approved character traits that make good midshipmen. An officer had to be able to work under pressure, so the second class provided that pressure for the Navy's future officer corps. An officer had to have a good memory and an eye for detail, so the second classmen forced the plebes to do heroic feats of memorization and punished them for the slightest infringement of regulations. The first classmen—firsties—were the highest rank in the Academy hierarchy. They had less than a year to go before they graduated as commissioned officers. They were an indolent nobility, indifferent to what happened to their most base subjects, the plebes.

Their primary focus was deciding the kind of car to buy, cash, upon graduation.

From my position of "chin in and chest out," I could see Banfield, Husaby, and Carnevale at the next table. Banfield sat at the seat of doom at the second class end. His hurt, blue eyes and protruding nose hung on a face that made a feeble attempt at arrogance. Husaby stood next to him, chin sinking into invisibility, complexion pale, frightened, looking like a renegade grandmother. Carnevale was third in line with his soft brown eyes set in an expressionless face. I couldn't see the fourth plebe, but knew that it was Seitzer.

The bell sounded for "seats." In one massive movement, the Brigade sat and began eating. The plebes were careful to sit on their regulatory two inches of chair, knowing that by the end of the meal they'd have slid their buttocks to cover perhaps six inches of the chair. They sat stiffly, braced up at attention, while the second classmen plied them with questions. At my own table, Bob was being asked his rates. At the request of Midshipman Second Class Mower, Valdres gave the menus for evening meal and morning meal. Unfortunately, he had neglected to tack on 'sir' at the end. 'Buns' McMunn asked, "Valdres, why didn't you say 'sir'?"

Surrounded by the noise and pandemonium from the other tables, Bob responded with the formula from *Reef Points 1968-1969* which every plebe was issued. "Sir, 'sir' is a subservient word surviving from the surly days in old Serbia when certain serfs, too ignorant to remember their lord's names, yet too servile to blaspheme them, circumvented the situation by surrogating the subservient word "sir," by which I now belatedly address a certain senior cirriped, who correctly surmised that I was syrupy enough to say sir after every word I said, sir."

While listening to this recitation, I watched the activities at the next table. The usually kind, quiet Roderigues told Banfield to spread a wad of peanut butter about an inch thick between two slices of bread. The second classman looked at the conglomeration, told Banfield to add more peanut butter, then ordered him to take a bite. He added, "Never mind. Jam the whole thing into your mouth." The plebe followed orders and began a truly Herculean effort. He took great, striving chews, jaws distending and clamping with a tremendous effort. Banfield's eyes watered. His nostrils flared like a running horse as he struggled for air.

His Adam's apple bobbed up and down as he tried to swallow and gagged. After some time, Roderigues said with evident disgust, "Spit it out, Banfield." The plebe bent over his plate, letting the huge brown and white wad ooze from his mouth. The wad declared its existence simply because of its repulsiveness, a wet and leprous turd. A murmur of revulsion arose among the mids while accusing eyes looked at Banfield. Roderigues said, "Cover it with your napkin." The plebe did so, but the shroud barely covered the body. Carnevale's eyes sought and met mine as a moment of recognition passed between us.

The Academy food was excellent. However, meat loaf was reviled by the midshipmen. One of the disillusioned second classmen, staring at his plate, said, "Bemes, tell everyone that the food is poisoned." Without a thought, Bemes hurled himself from his chair. He stood with his knees bent and legs wide apart, body doubled backwards. Grabbing his throat, Larry cried, "Arg! Arg! Don't eat the meat loaf; it's poisoned! Don't eat the meat loaf! Arg! Arg! It's poisoned!" His body slowly sank to the floor, his face grimacing in agony. A firstie said, casually, "That's enough, Bemes," and just as casually, Larry returned to his place at table.

The show was impressive. It was meant to be humorous and was taken as such. No one was hurt and no one was humiliated. It earned Bemes a lot of respect. He always did the right thing at the right time. Had Valdres or me received the same order, we would have stood at attention and yelled, "Sir, don't eat the food, sir. It's poisoned sir. Sir, don't eat the food. It's poisoned, sir." Thus, Bemes duly won the admiration of his peers and of his superiors.

Budge, who could barely contain his joy at Banfield's efforts and Bemes's performance, turned to me. "Sorensen!"

"Sir?"

"The football team!"

"Sir, the football team is, sir," I made a mental picture of the team, much as I had seen it on the most recent roster posted at Macdonough Hall and recited each position, "Quarterback, number twenty-three, Whitaker, class of '69, sir; left halfback, number eighteen, Gold, class of '69, sir; right halfback, number fourteen, Carney, class of '70, sir; left end, number twenty-one, Edwards, class of '71, sir; right end, number thirty-one, DelSesto, class of '70…"

As I was completing the roster of the team, I could see that Mower and McMunn had become interested in the chase. Mower was light-haired, fair, and had the habit of blinking to excess. He had the youthful, blithe look of Christmastime choirboy pin-ups. "Buns" McMunn was like Mower in his mannerisms, although he didn't have the habit of blinking like Morse code receivers. They were both of moderate height, but McMunn was much the heavier. Buns had dark brown eyes that never looked anyone squarely in the face. Like a rodent, he seemed to be always alert, even when relaxed.

Mower asked, "Sorensen, who won the Rose Bowl last year?"

Up to that time, I had never watched a football or a baseball game in my entire life and gave the routine answer, "I'll find out, sir."

"Who won the Super Bowl?"

"I'll find out, sir."

Buns joined in. "Who won the Indianapolis 500 last year?"

"I'll find out, sir."

Buns: "Who's Mickey Mantle?"

"I'll find out, sir."

Mower: "Who's Ted Williams?"

"I'll find out, sir."

I was warm from the mounting tension. All eyes were upon me. Mower asked, "Sorensen, why don't you know any of these things?"

I gave another stock answer, "No excuse, sir."

Mower blinked several times in quick succession. "I really want to know."

How could I explain to them that I didn't like team sports, anything with a ball? When I was twelve and living in the projects, I was walking to school when a gang of boys my own age stopped me and asked me who I was rooting for in the World Series. My father was a Red Sox fan, so I answered, "The Red Sox." The gang leader said, "We're Yankee fans." They charged me, lifted me up so my back was to the ground and my stomach curved toward the sky. They pulled up my shirt and gave me, in school yard slang, a "pink belly" where they slapped me repeatedly on the stomach until it was pink. It wasn't meant to hurt, or they would have been punching me instead, but I got the point: Red Sox bad, Yankees good.

When I was in the eighth grade, I was going to my social studies class and was going down a stairway when I saw my sister Beth and two of her friends, all three special needs children, trapped in the stairwell by three boys on the football team. They pretended to be apes, scratching their armpits and calling, "OU—OU—OU." As they danced before my sister and her friends, they called, "Retard! Retard!"

I was small for my age until my growth spurt in my junior and senior years of high school. Each boy was a head taller than I was, but I was furious and ran to her defense. With a weak smile, she scooted past me followed by her friends, humiliated. With their victims gone, the boys dispersed in the opposite direction except for one who tilted his head to one side when he saw me. I pushed him and screamed, "LEAVE MY SISTER ALONE!" Not a second passed before a teacher was between us, stopping any further contact between us. He wanted to know what the problem was. I kept yelling, "He teased my sister! He teased my sister!"

The teacher said, "Okay, that's enough. Go to your classes."

From that moment, right or wrong, a football team to me was another kind of gang. It was a visceral reaction, instinctual; I couldn't help myself. How could I explain this to the Naval Academy and to the cogs of a machine, midshipmen like Mower?

I opted to give my second-best reason, something he might understand. "Because they're not important, sir."

"What do you mean they're not important?"

"Sir, there's no absolute truth here, nothing significant to learn in any way. If all the baseball and football players disappeared off the face of the earth, nothing significant would change. It would be no great loss. If all the farmers, carpenters, plumbers, or workmen who build our roads and buildings disappeared off planet earth, we'd be screwed. At the end of a game, what is accomplished? One team wins, another loses. It really doesn't matter which team. Does it lead to a cure for cancer or putting a man on the moon? Is the world changed for the better?"

Cutting off Mower's response, Buns said, "Everything changes, Sorensen. I'm not what you call an absolute truth, but does that make me unimportant? We can't always be searching for what you call truth or working towards a better world, can we?" I bit my lower lip. Buns continued in a friendly, quiet voice, "You should know about sports. They might not be important to you, but you can go anywhere in the world, meet people, and you'll have something to talk about. It's an avenue of communication and from there you can work to other things, the important stuff. Understand?"

"Yes, sir."

Mower added, "I want you to memorize all the team names of the NFL. and the American and National Baseball Leagues. Got that, Sorensen?"

"Yes, sir."

The meal was then dispatched in relative calm. As Budge was leaving, he turned on Bob. "Valdres."

"Sir?"

"What's that grease stain on your shirt?"

"I'll find out, sir."

"You do that. Meanwhile, come-around."

"Aye-aye, sir."

After the upperclassmen left the table, leaving the plebes behind waiting for dismissal, I thought of the events of that meal and of the many meals of the last couple of weeks. Valdres and I, again, took all the abuse at the table. Bemes warned the Brigade of poison, but that was meant in fun. Other than that, it had been two weeks since either Bemes or Bragg, the other plebe at our table, was asked anything at meals. I had yet to see either of them at a come-around since the return of the Brigade. Soon, they would both be safe at the team tables, leaving Bob and me behind to soak up even more abuse.

I had a study hour after the meal. I decided that I'd better find the answers to the questions that the second classmen asked. They were due by evening meal. Diels was a sports buff. He'd know most of the gouge (information). I would check with him first.

* * *

School work always came easy for me. I was an avid reader. However, I still had to learn how to take good notes and how to study. After an afternoon of clock watching in my English and calculous classes, I dropped my books off in my room, changed into gym gear, and chopped to Carnevale's room. Dave Husaby, Carnevale's roommate, was standing over a *Washington Post* that lay flat on his desk. He informed me that Paul would soon be there and asked if I wanted to sit and wait. I said sure. As Dave skimmed over the newspaper, he conducted a small monologue. He whined in the precise, sophisticated accent of a private school, "There's a Rothko exhibition at the National Gallery this weekend. Boy! I'd like to see that!" After a brief pause, "Van Gogh is my favorite artist, although I must admit to a particular fondness for Millet and Gauguin. Durer is good, too. His *Horsemen of the Apocalypse* is great. It's so medieval." He glanced at me. "Are you familiar with that work?"

I shook my head no.

Husaby hummed to himself, "Bop, bop, bee, bop." Slowly he turned the pages of the newspaper, then, "God! Look at this!" He lifted the paper, folding away one side, and showed me a cliché photograph of a cat hanging by its chin and paws, struggling to maintain its grip on a clothesline. "I love cats. They should allow them here. Whenever I see kittens playing, I imagine one to be Hector and the other to be Achilles, fighting before the walls of Troy. I've even named my own cats Hector and Achilles."

When he reached the travel section, Husaby said, after giving the paper a tap, "This is one place I'd love to go, the Louvre. Ever been there?"

"No."

At the entertainment section he asked, "Have you seen what's playing at the movies this weekend? *2001: A Space Odyssey* is playing at the Bijou."

"Is it any good?"

"*I'll* say. The score is from *Thus Spoke Zarathustra*."

"You've seen it?"

Dave straightened into an erect posture to look scathingly at me, eyes burning with anger. "Only the beginning. I would have seen the whole thing if it wasn't for the goddamned niggers!"

I smiled at the incongruity of such a strong prejudice; the last word sounded so foreign, so wrong, coming from the thin lips of the sophisticated, liberally educated Dave Husaby. I asked, "What happened?"

"Oh, they were having a riot the night we went to see it. Just as the movie was beginning, we all had to leave the theatre."

"What was the riot about?"

"Oh, I don't know, something ridiculous. They were running around destroying things the way they always do."

17

"Dave, people don't riot just for the hell of it. There must have been a reason."

"There wasn't any reason. You know how those people are." Dave resumed reading his paper.

Soon, Carnevale burst energetically into the room. Without pause, he said, "I got a joke for you guys." He tossed his books aside. "Why did the midshipman beat off in the cornfield?" Both of us looked at him in silence, waiting for the punch line. "So he could be the cream of the crop!" Groans followed.

As he changed, Paul continued, "Boatman told me that he read a story where a pedestrian was killed by a dime tossed off the Empire State Building. It went right through his head. All day I kept asking myself why it was *him* that was killed and not someone else." He pointed at me. "Why not you?" He pointed at Dave. "Or you? Or, for that matter, me? Why was it him?"

Dave said, "Pure chance."

"Maybe, but then I thought that from the very beginning of time the Universe was so ordered that that particular man would be walking beneath that particular building at that particular time to be killed…"

Dave finished for him, "By that particular dime."

"Right. I think that's incredible."

"What's so incredible? It's the natural course of events. Somebody had to be there."

"But why *that* guy?"

I joined in, "I'll tell you something *I* think about. Why am I me? Why am I Mike Sorensen instead of Paul Carnevale or Dave Husaby? I mean, I have a personality, whatever it is that makes me *me*. Why isn't that personality in someone else's body instead of mine?"

Dave laughed. "No wonder you're always in trouble, Mike, questioning everything like that and thinking weird shit. You're always looking for a reason, but sometimes there isn't a reason. Sometimes things are the way they are because that's the way they are. Why did everyone blame Banfield for that disgusting show this noon meal? After all, Roderigues was the one who told him to jam the sandwich into his mouth. As far as I can see, they blamed him because they blamed him. Things happen because they happen."

I said, "That's too easy, Dave."

18

Paul slipped on his sneakers and the two of us chopped out the door accompanied by Husaby's wish that we have a good jog. We hurried to the nearest exit. Upon reaching the outside, we sensed Bancroft Hall watching us. The relative security found beyond the door was nothing in comparison to the security at our destination of Hospital Point. We passed Michaelson Hall and proceeded to cross a small arched footbridge over a wandering, slowly moving stream. On the other side was a field of short grass with the Severn River on one side of it and the hospital, fronted by a copse of cool, green maple trees, on the other.

Although I had heard a lot about the areas of the country from which the midshipmen were collected, I had yet to hear a mid talk about his family. Perhaps it was the rigorously Spartan atmosphere of the school that forbade intimacy. Perhaps it was the fear of exposing any weakness. I never knew which mids had sisters and brothers and who were from one-parent families. Even my closest friends were silent on the subject.

Carnevale had spent most of his life in Japan, so he told me about the Ainu while I told him about New England dairy farms. In our transit over the bridge, Paul asked, "Did you ever see pictures of the arched bridges in Japan, the ones that look like rainbows?"

"Yeah."

"Do you know why they're arched?"

"I have a feeling you're going to tell me."

"Because the Japanese believe that evil spirits will have difficulty negotiating the bridge and will be left behind. They keep slipping on the steep grade while the people make it over."

The windows of Bancroft Hall, like the eyes of Argus, stared at our receding backs, trying to pierce through them, its demons trying to follow us across the bridge. I knew that Carnevale thought the same thing.

We looked into the calm motion of the water below. Although we were participating in a required activity, our sport being intramural cross-country, we were fortunate in that we both enjoyed running. For me it was a prayer, a union with unknown, mysterious forces, life expressing itself through motion.

Our feet swished through the grass of the field. Some dust was raised but stayed below our knees due to the passiveness of the air. Our first class coach, St. Amand, met us and told us in his quiet way to run a mile or two on our own, then call it a day. We immediately fell into a fast jog, doing an occasional sprint as the mood hit us. We ran in step with the warm air expanding our lungs, giving us strength. The sun's light and resulting heat made us sweat, every pore alive with sensation. As our muscles warmed, the world became benign. Everything was as it should be. Life was so good!

When our run was finished, we headed back to Bancroft Hall. Because we were on an intramural team, we would still have to attend come-around. When I reached my room, I found Bob already in gym gear. Neither of us gave the other a greeting. However, a feeling of camaraderie formed between us, like a brotherhood of victims, as we waited despondently. Shortly before 1700 hours we chopped to the room shared by Mower and McMunn. We stood at attention outside the door while Bob occasionally checked his watch until the few seconds to 1700 had passed. Meanwhile, I read the plastic nametags in the aluminum holder fastened to the door. Beside Mower's name, an advertisement cut out of a newspaper was taped to the door, reading, "...mower is known for high quality performance." Next to McMunn's name was a sentence that had been cut to delete a brand name and carefully taped together again. It read, "I eat Buns every day." I looked surreptitiously about me. Since the return of the Brigade, neither Bemes nor Bragg had attended a single come-around. Once they were on the team tables, they would be untouchable. At exactly 1700 hours, Bob pushed aside the heavy wooden door. We took one step inside and sounded off.

Mower was the only one in the room. He, too, wore gym gear, but wore flip-flops instead of sneakers. Rubbing the sleep from his eyes, he said, "Let's go to the main corridor." He strolled down the side corridors with his plebes chopping behind him like two row boats in tow. Once the three of us were in the main artery, Mower said, "Hit it for twenty-five." Bob and I slammed onto the floor to do our push-ups, counting them out loud.

"While you're down there, give me fifty sit-ups."

Done.

"Crab walk to the end of the corridor and back." Mower walked beside our struggling figures. "C'mon, you pussies!"

Finished.

"All right. Sprint to the windows on the far side and back. GO!"

We did the sprint. As the time for come-around was being eaten away, more and more plebes appeared with their upperclassmen barking orders. The plebes jumped, bent, moaned, and groaned to the quick, frantic movements of a bevy of exercises. It was bedlam at its finest. The strain was intolerable, aggravated by the knowledge that this was punishment. I looked up to see Hovedo, who was on crew, chop through this maze of prostrate, exhausted bodies. He seemed not to notice his compatriots. His stride was light and fresh.

At one point, I was surprised to find Jerry Holmes, the company's only black, doing push-ups next to me. Jerry was also a jock and would soon be on team tables. He, too, was almost never seen at come-arounds. We were both in leaning rest position when, suddenly, I felt a heavy weight on my back. I heard screaming and realized that Holmes was writhing on top of me with a dislocated shoulder. At first, I thought of moving out from under him, but rejected that idea in favor of maintaining my position. Three upperclassmen led Jerry to the dispensary. For Bob and me, there was no break in the come-around. The turmoil continued.

After half an hour, we returned to our rooms. My arms were so fatigued that, momentarily, I was unable to lift them above my waist. I rested a few seconds, thinking of the little trick that Larry Bemes had taught me. Crossing my arms in front of me, I took hold of either side of my sweat-soaked T-shirt. By an effort of will, I lifted my arms up and over my head, and my T-shirt slipped off by following their lead.

Bob had chow call, which gave me ample time to get ready for evening meal. I had looked up the answers to the questions asked me at the previous meal. Now I proceeded to memorize them. I was certain that I had forgotten some of the questions but relied on the upperclassmen themselves to have forgotten them. During evening meal, they were too preoccupied with eating and the coming evening of study to worry too much about the incompetence of a plebe. Besides, I had so many come-arounds that they ceased to be an effective threat. I decided to attend every come-around that presented itself and save myself from the futile efforts and worry trying to catch up. Only a Form 2 could really hurt me, and they were given for greater offenses than forgetting a handful of arbitrary questions.

I heard Bob's drone coming from the hallway, "Sir, you now have ten minutes to evening meal formation. The menu for evening meal is sirloin steak, baked potatoes, succotash, hot buttered rolls, milk, and iced tea! The desert is Boston cream pie, sir! The uniform for evening meal is White Uniform Charley! Formation is outside, sir!" I heard some mumbling and Bob's response, "Boston cream pie, sir."

A moment passed and Bob was in the room buffing his shoes, straightening his cap and necktie. Uniform Charley was the same as Uniform Alpha except that the officer's cap was replaced by a sailor's cap with a blue rim encircling its outer edge. Bob wore his cap at a rakish angle that gave him a jaunty appearance. He rushed out again. "Sir, you now have five minutes 'til evening meal formation…" Bob had a strong accent that changed the "ch" sound to "sh" and vice versa. He also used "th" instead of "s" in certain words. Although I hadn't heard anyone ridicule Bob's accent, the general impression was that my roommate wasn't sharp in good midshipman fashion. Good midshipmen were, by and large, cosmopolitan. Traits coming from highly sectionalized areas of the country were regarded as indicating a certain amount of inferiority. Even Boatman's and Seitzer's strong Southern accents told against them. This impression could cause a plebe a lot of trouble. At the three-minute chow call, I donned my cap and chopped to formation.

As expected, evening meal passed in relative calm. Budge had me do an around-the–world. This consisted of the plebe standing at his place at the table, successively facing all four directions, and yelling as loudly as possible whatever was required of him. This time, I called, "Sir, I don't know who Carl Yastrzemski is, sir! Sir, I don't know who Carl Yastrzemski is, sir! Sir, I don't know who Carl Yastrzemski is, sir! Sir, I don't know who Carl Yastrzemski is, sir!" I was humiliated; Budge was overjoyed.

A few of the upperclassmen at a neighboring table, including the effete Lackning, snickered. Yet, I could console myself that other plebes had done around-the-worlds at some time or other. Mine wasn't an isolated event. Among so many fallen angels, what was one, more or less, to matter?

* * *

That evening it was my turn to go to the library. The hostility between Valdres and me was so extreme that we both recognized the necessity of such an agreement. As I was getting my books together, John Boatman stepped into the room. He was from the swamps of North Carolina. His physical appearance contrasted sharply with that of Valdres. The Mexican American was short and muscular with broad shoulders and powerful arms. With the addition of his black, narrow set, almond shaped eyes above high cheekbones and large aquiline nose, he could have posed as a model for an Aztec pictograph.

John, on the other hand, had laughing sapphire eyes, light brown hair, and jagged, pointed features. His skin was a delicate white, a prime candidate for skin cancer. He had a habit of sucking in air through clenched teeth which sounded like a hiss, "sle." Sometimes the "sle" sound produced was used unconsciously by him when he was trying to make a particular point. He always seemed a little sad, even when laughing. He greeted, "How do, Mike?"

"Hey, John."

"Valdres kicking you out of the room again?"

"No, no. We agreed to take turns going to the library."

"Sle, why don't you get a book on the Alamo so you can read all about Bob's ancestor or, I should say, his supposed ancestor?"

Bob had been sitting at the desk reading. Now, he was glaring at the Southerner. John continued, "You know, Valdres, if there'd been a back door, there wouldn't have been an Alamo."

Bob slouched in his chair giving John his best "what-the-hell-do-you-know" look. He looked totally relaxed, but I knew that my roommate was seething beneath that calm exterior.

"Anyway, Mike, the reason I came over was to borrow your slide rule."

"Sure. What happened to yours?"

"Kaufman borrowed it."

"Oh, Kaufman lost his."

"No, Mower borrowed Kaufman's."

"Then Mower lost his."

"No…"

"Never mind, John, you can use it."

"You won't need it tonight?"

"Naw."

"Thanks." Boatman left carrying away my slide rule.

Bob picked up a pen that had been lying on the desk and threw it down violently. He said, "It pisses me off when someone talks like that about the Alamo. I mean, those guys died for what they believed in. It's…it's sacred. And I'll tell you something else: most people think that there weren't any Mexicans at the Alamo, but that's wrong. The Mexicans of Texas fought for independence just as much as the Gringos. They *died* for their beliefs." I glanced at my roommate, inwardly pleased that John had gotten a rise out of him.

I found my next reading assignment for English, *Huckleberry Finn*. The cover of the paperback captivated me. It depicted a boy in ragged jeans and a straw hat, sitting on the bank of a river. Everything in the picture except the boy and the river was a bright green as though they were engulfed by the green of nature. One had the impression that the existence of the river depended on the boy and vice versa with the green serving to unify them into a whole. I saw myself as that boy sitting by the Mighty Mississippi, watching its smooth strength flow to the sea while a green peacefulness pervaded every atom of my being. It was a life I would have loved.

By the time I was ready to go to the library, the evening had darkened. I left Bancroft Hall and then the night caught me. It was so quiet. I sat on the granite steps from Bancroft leading to the library. I leaned my torso against a stone rampart. The rock was cool. More importantly, it was solid, so much so that only time or the machinations of man could destroy it. It was impervious to almost everything, an approach to the sublime. Let come what may, to be a piece of stone was ideal, a complete denial of feeling, an absolute indifference.

I might have been there for half an hour, an isolated entity, when my reveries were disturbed by the gravelling crunch of footsteps. Out of the dark appeared an upperclassman in the white uniform and blue armband of the watch.

"What are you doing, plebe?"

I rose to attention. "Sir?"

"What are you doing?"

"Thinking, sir."

"Out here?"

"Yes, sir."

"What do you think libraries are for?"

"Thinking, sir."

"So what were you doing here?"

"Nothing, sir."

"Were you playing with yourself?"

"No, sir!"

"Carry-on then."

"Aye-aye, sir."

As the watch and I walked in opposite directions, I heard, "Hey, plebe!"

I stopped at attention. "Sir?"

"Is there anything wrong? You know, a problem or something?"

"No, sir."

The dark separated me and the upperclassman. Now I heard a voice coming from deep shadow, "Carry-on."

Once inside the library's startling illumination, I set about my studies. I worked for a restless hour, then took a short walk to the book stacks, forced myself to return to my place to study for another half-hour, then decided I needed a break and wandered into the magazine room.

CHAPTER II

THE WEEKEND

I knew where the water was deep with just enough chill to make the warmer pockets that much more pleasurable. Alternately, I floated and treaded water, pleased with the knowledge that I could do this for hours. My mind's eye flowed with the pond water into a small stream that weaved its way to the Blackstone River, which, in turn, ran to the Atlantic. The ocean pulled at me with the stream serving as the umbilical. I was a wanderer thinking of home. I was having a real communication, a union with the sea and primeval life. Only circumstance found me a land animal instead of a sea creature.

That was how I remembered my swimming before my arrival at the Academy. It had almost been a religious experience. Now, as I clung to the side of the Academy pool, I saw how foolish I had been. The intense pleasure that I previously experienced became a test of endurance. The only good thing about swim class was that it must eventually end, the only boon that death gives to the living.

Every lesson began with a mass shower that chilled me to the depths of my soul since a cold draft continuously raged throughout the shower area. At that moment, a tug in my bowels forced me to go to the lavatory to relieve myself. Then, short, quick steps took me to the poolside as my skin erupted into a welter of goose pimples.

Each plebe was cold and anxious. The better swimmers had passed the qualifying swim and were excused from classes. The less gifted were left to improve their techniques. Although there is a limit to the amount of water one can swallow, I was convinced, from personal experience, that the limit approached infinity. The classes were graded and the anxiety of failure, especially in the eyes of peers, was all-pervasive.

I found myself clinging desperately to the side of the pool like a sailor washed overboard clinging to a raft in frigid Northern seas. I had been in the water for half an hour and my arms were still a scrawny blue verging on a heavenly white. I discovered that, when sufficiently cold, teeth really do chatter. The only time my body approached warmth was when I was swimming heavily. A dangling plebe next to me claimed, bitterly, that the former class found a thin sheet of ice on the pool. Another plebe complained that it was heated in the afternoon for the swim team.

A German accent called from the diving board, "Okay, you hotdogs, odd numbers, *go!*" For a split-second I smiled. I liked this instructor. Then I pushed off the pool wall, struggling to beat my classmates to the other side of the pool and back. God, how I hated to swim! The pleasure of water had been taken away from me.

* * *

My lively step indicated what mood I was in. Today was Saturday and I looked forward to the coming weekend. As soon as I entered the room for my last class, I retreated to the back and chose a seat next to the window. I adjusted the shade to see the Severn River across Michelson Field. It was a calculus course required for all midshipmen. The students came to attention as the professor, a Navy lieutenant j.g., stepped into the room and immediately granted us carry-on. When I sat down, I shifted my position partly toward the river, partly toward the front of the class. While the professor's voice droned with figures and formulas, I wondered what the upper reaches of the Severn were like. I saw myself on a raft, wearing a straw hat and blue jeans and smothered in a comfortable green. I copied everything down that the prof wrote on the blackboard. I had always been good at math and decided to sit down later to decipher the numbers and symbols. Meanwhile, my mind drifted to Southern belles sitting on plantation porches, cool and sweet in the fierce heat. I'd never had trouble with math before. I'd work these problems out later. My own Southern belle would love me as we sat on the porch swing, holding hands. Of course, I'd have to leave her. That was the price of adventure. She would cry large pearl-drop tears down alabaster cheeks as I bid her farewell, she in her white silks, me in dirty jeans and with bare feet. We were too different. Destiny would lead me away. I heard the chalk trace its confused way across the blackboard and was brought out of my trance and back to stark reality. I copied the figures.

After class, I rushed to the company area to get ready for noon meal formation. There was considerable activity due to anticipation. Many of the upperclassmen had weekend leaves, so they were happy. Since the plebes wouldn't see them for two days, we were happy too. The mood was infectious, spreading throughout the Brigade.

Noon meal formation passed without any problems for anyone. Even chow call, today was my turn, was accomplished without glitches. Since today was Saturday, the plebes were not required to eat in their company area, so I found myself in the human flotsam, all of us looking for a table with no first or second classmen at it. Generally, the tables with only youngsters at it gave the plebes instant carry-on. At the worst, they played a game called baseball. The plebe chose a topic and tried to stump one of the youngsters by asking him questions on that topic. If he managed to do so, the youngster asked the plebe a question on the same topic. If the plebe answered the question correctly, then he got carry-on. If he gave the wrong answer, the game continued.

Because of the weekend leaves, the number of first and second classmen was greatly reduced. Since the third class tables were in high demand, the first and second classmen had to recruit plebes for their own tables. They stood at the ends of the tables and scanned the drifting mass of chopping plebes. Sporadically, one pointed to a plebe and yelled, "*You!*" and the plebe was hooked and landed, like a trophy trout, at that table.

I looked for a likely third class prospect when I spotted a table with only black mids at it. The plebes already had carry-on, which made me resentful toward them. After all, why should they stick together like that and be granted carry-on because they were black? I saw the black first classman surveying the plebes. His mannerisms and the expression of his searching eyes reminded me of my best friend, Kenny, serving in Vietnam. I did my best to sink inconspicuously into the crowd and refused to make eye contact with the first classman who, I suspected, was looking right through me. My eyes darted to the firstie to assure myself that I had made it past him, undetected, when our eyes touched. "*You!*" My heart sank. I'd never get carry-on. I'd be the only white there, so they'd keep me braced up and would harass me to make my meal as uncomfortable and as unpleasant as possible. They'd make me pour all the drinks just to have a white man serving them. I stood at the only empty seat and called, "Permission to come aboard, sir!"

The first classman responded, "Permission granted." A minute passed during which I waited for the onslaught to begin. The firstie said, "Mr. Sorensen."

"Sir?"

"Carry-on."

"Aye-aye, sir." I relaxed. I noticed that the drinks for the upperclassmen hadn't been poured. Although I was in one of the middle seats and the plebe to my left was supposed to fill the glasses, I thought that being the only white at the table, I was expected to fill them. I took the tea pitcher and one of the glasses and was about to pour the drink when the plebe to my left took them away from me to pour the drinks himself. Although I was not included in the conversation at the table, I was both pleased and relieved not to have been excluded from the benefits of my peers.

* * *

That afternoon I had to work off the last hour of my latest Form 2. I was annoyed that Budge had written me up in the first place. Every morning, ten minutes before reveille, Valdres and I took turns sneaking into Budge's room to close his window. That way, Budge and Kristin slept with fresh air in the room yet got up in comfortable warmth. As the autumn nights became cooler, it became imperative that neither of us forgot his turn. Unfortunately, I forgot one morning. Budge came raging into our room and ordered me to bring around a Form 2. What bothered me though was not the Form 2 but that neither Bemes nor Bragg was ordered to close any windows. Only Valdres and I performed that duty. I couldn't blame my peers for their good fortune, but I felt increasing resentment toward Budge. He knew it and did not care.

There were two activities, called extra duty (E.D.), used to work off the demerits from a Form 2. The one least used was marching on Farragut Field. The plebes were required to dress in White Uniform Charley with white leggings and bayonet belts. They carried M-1 carbines with which to perform the manual of arms in between their marching routines. I hated this more than exercising. It was dirty, tiring, and resulted in the loss of valuable time due to the subsequent cleaning of the white bayonet belt and leggings. The worst part was that the drills were monotonous and boring. The mids were kept busy enough so that they couldn't pass the time daydreaming, but not busy enough to make the time pass swiftly. One hour seemed like days.

I was relieved to find out that E.D. for that day would be exercising. Generally, the exercises were the easy ones like toe touches and jumping jacks with a handful of the more difficult exercises added only for variety. Wearing my gym gear, I chopped to the battalion sign-in desk on the first deck where my name was one among a long list of the damned on a computer print-out. I was greeted by a couple of plebes who I often saw at E.D. The same faces kept appearing, so much so that we'd joke amongst ourselves and, gradually, were forming a kind of negative elite. These were the plebes that the upperclassmen had a particular dislike for and hadn't yet been able to "run out."

The plebes formed a double row, standing in the "at ease" position with their legs shoulder width apart and their hands clasped behind the small of their backs. We were relaxed and confident of a relatively easy afternoon until the E.D. runner made his appearance. He was a second classman who had gotten into trouble and had to work off his own demerits. Immediately, thirty plebe hearts sank. The second classman walked up and down before the ranks of plebes. He never once looked up. He was unhappy, brooding, injured. He wanted revenge for his plight. The second classman went into the battalion office. A plebe on the back row whispered, "Christ! Another Hamlet! How many of these guys do they have in this place?" Hamlet reentered the corridor, called out the plebe names, and marked them off on the computer printout. He then led us to the nearest exit.

We lined up on the terrace in two rows of fifteen plebes. With his eyes fixed on the ground before him, the second classman strode back and forth in front of the us. With a deep scowl on his face, he said, "Hit it for seventy-two!" We threw ourselves onto the ground to do the seventy-two push-ups, keeping our arms wide so that we could complete them. Staying in leaning rest, we waited for the next exercise. Hamlet didn't say a word. Minutes passed. The plebes started to sink slowly toward the earth. We did our best not to "bag" it, to take it easy on ourselves, since none of us wanted to be considered a "pussy." Even the strongest plebes sank to the point where their bodies were an inch or two above the ground. My triceps were on fire. Sweat dripped off my chin to form a small pool beneath me. I couldn't take much more. A desperate plebe called, "Permission to come aboard, sir!"

Hamlet answered, "No!"

All the plebes started watching Hamlet with intensity. Whenever his back was turned, the more exhausted of them let themselves collapse onto the ground for a few seconds of rest before forcing their arms to hurriedly push them up as soon as it looked like Hamlet was about to turn around. The agony continued, seemingly forever, then Hamlet ordered, "On your backs!" We shifted onto our backs. "Leg raises. Fifty and count them out!" The plebes lifted their legs fifty times. On the last one, Hamlet said, "Keep them up! Six inches off the ground!" This was the worst exercise. After a couple of minutes, my stomach was on fire. The groans from my companions told me that they, too, felt their stomachs burning. A couple of unconcerned midshipmen walked through our prostrate forms. The minutes dragged on slowly. A second classman passed, saying, "This isn't exercise. This is torture." He went on his way. Hamlet wasn't moved. He brooded upon the wrongs he'd received. Then he said, "Push-ups." The ordeal began all over.

I was relieved when my hour of E.D. was over. I knew that most of the plebes would be spending another two hours with Hamlet. With every drop of sweat, with every moan, with every wearing pain, I thought of Budge. I envisioned Budge's wicked, bemused smile set in his reddish, soft face. Yes, Budge would think Hamlet was very, very funny.

* * *

I took a long, silent look at my grim surroundings. It was night. Among the nicely cut grass and the dark forms of the shade trees were the tombstone teeth attesting to hundreds of lives and deaths. Bodies of children, women, and old men deteriorated just a few feet underground, humanity itself grotesquely rotting into dust. I thought how I might have loved these people. Perhaps the perfect woman, my Dulcinea, was here. I would never know. I would never be cognizant that she once walked the earth and laughed much as I walked and laughed right now. I heard the passion of her lovemaking, heard her weeping at some little hurt while I tenderly comforted her, leaving the big hurts to die in time. Her fingers reached tentatively for my hand and the tenderness of our touch was stronger than all the threats and dangers that life, destiny itself, could muster. A slight movement from Matt Helmsley distracted my musings. He nonchalantly sat on a gravestone while I stood next to him.

He said, "I wonder what's taking Danny so long."

We looked toward the streetlight under which he had disappeared. Both Matt and Danny were my drinking buddies. We enjoyed carousing with one another, but since we had little else in common, weren't too often together during the rest of the week. I asked, "Did you ever wonder about all the people buried here, about all their adventures?"

"Not really."

"Just think. The perfect woman might be buried right here."

"Good. I'll dig her up and fuck her. I can't believe how horny I am. In Nevada I always had pussy and here I am at Annapolis wasting my youth away. At least in Nevada if some broad didn't give it to you, you could go to a whorehouse."

"Did you ever go to one?"

"Sure."

"What's it like?"

"Well, the girls line up and you choose one. Some of them aren't half-bad either. The girls never cum, or almost never, except once I had a girl who seemed to be enjoying it as much as I was. After I was done, we just kind of laid there. I knew a guy who was given ten bucks by his buddies and brought to a whorehouse on his eighteenth birthday. That was the first time he got laid."

"Damn! How about you? When was the first time for you?"

"When I was sixteen, some friends of my father were staying over, and they had a sixteen-year-old daughter. I was sleeping on the couch in the living room. I got up to get a drink of water. When I got back, the daughter was lying on the couch, kind of smiling. I went, 'Eeyow,' then I jumped her bones. That was the first time."

"Damn!"

Matt stood up. "I wonder what's taking Danny so long." I smiled to myself. Although my friend had regular features, he was far from being well proportioned. His body was too long and situated on legs that were too short. He also swung his arms oddly when walking so that I kept seeing the body of a Tyrannosaurus Rex with Matt's head capping it.

A rogue wind rustled among the branches of the trees making the cemetery seem lonelier than it already was. Matt asked, "How was E.D.?"

"Tougher than usual."

"Was Banfield there?"

"He's always there."

A few brown, dead leaves from the turning trees hurdled past us. They were difficult to see and accentuated the impalpable darkness. Matt took his seat again. Our voices seemed to drown in the dark. Matt asked, "Do you think you'll ever get off E.D.?"

"Oh, sure. Today was my last hour. I've only got thirty demerits. Budge has hit me with a few Form 2s, but he spends most of his time giving Bob and me come-arounds. Unless he gives me another Form 2, I'm in the clear."

"That second classman in my squad, Hooker, is crazy. I mean that he's really crazy. Take a good look at his eyes sometime and you'll see what I mean."

"Yeah, well, he's better than Budge and the boys." A rank bitterness entered my voice. "At least in your squad *all* the plebes get zonked. In mine, only Valdres and I get nailed. Bemes and Bragg get to skate. They might be sharper than Bob and me, but they're not *that* sharp. No other plebe knows his rates as well as I do. They don't have to. Budge has me giving my rates every day, all of them. Who else does that? And what really goads me is that Bragg is the biggest bagger in the valley, but he's good at hiding it."

At that moment they saw the figure of Danny "Snowman" Calhoun with his swaggering stride cross the brief space of light beneath a streetlamp. His beefy build, light skin, and flaxen hair, combined with his being from Alaska, earned him the nickname "Snowman." Matt stood up. "Shee-it! I thought you'd never get here!"

Snowman chuckled. "Have a little faith. I got three pints from an old black guy. I gave him an extra two bucks. We have enough left to buy each of us a large soda."

The night made our faces look as though we were wearing thin veils. A chill ran up my spine, so I looked behind me. I said, "Next time I'm waiting under a streetlight."

Danny smirked. "Afraid of ghosts, Mike?"

"I'm a little spooked, that's all."

"You're crazy."

We found a Burger King. Each of us bought a large soda, drank half of it, and poured brandy into the remaining half. Then we walked the main streets of Annapolis taking deep drafts of the brew in the lit areas while pouring in more brandy when the shadows thickened.

Danny and I indulged in a game that we frequently played. Snowman asked, "Suppose you're lost in the woods…"

I cut him off, "Not likely."

"I said *suppose* you're lost in the woods. You're near a stream and you have a can opener. What would you do?"

Automatically I answered, "I'd flatten the can opener and use it as a fish spear."

"Very good."

"Now I have one for you. Suppose you're lost at the same stream…"

"Not likely."

"The point is well taken. Suppose you're at the same or perhaps at another stream and you notice a lot of rocks along it. What do you do?"

"I'd make a fish trap."

"How?"

"First, I'd use the rocks to make a big box in the middle of the stream. On one side of the box, I'd make an opening in the shape of a *v* pointing in. Then I'd walk down the middle of the stream and drive the fish into the box."

I approved, "That's it."

Our walk led us to the waterfront where we could enjoy the sweet, salty smell of the Chesapeake and the smooth shimmer of a dead moon on a near dead sea. We sat on the wooden pier feeling the pleasant roughness of the splintered wood beneath us. I bent over to run my fingers through the slime of the refreshingly cool water. A large piece of Italian bread floated by. It must have recently been thrown in because I could see that it wasn't soggy yet. I reached to touch it. My hand shot back as I jumped to my feet. "A snake, I touched a snake!" The others stood up. I reached a hesitant hand toward the bread. All three of us kept staring at the black ink of the water.

I queried, "Fish?"

I cupped my hand, dipped it into the water, and brought up a small killifish. It was barely struggling to stay alive. I said, "It must be blind. I can't imagine a fish allowing itself to be manhandled like this."

Danny said, "It's probably the gasoline and all the other crap they dump into the water. It's probably sick."

I tossed the fish back into the water. The night settled upon us. The moored craft rubbed against each other, promising thrilling activity to those with a knowledge of sailing. I was looking at a dead world that held such a great promise for life. It was like looking at a seed, hard, contained, and very much alive. The sea, the boats, the moon, three drunken midshipmen, it was romantic. In attempting to describe this uncanny sensation to my friends, I managed to convey only a mass of indistinct gibberish.

Danny responded with a good-natured laugh while Matt sat in a silent stupor. I then began singing one of my favorite songs, pronouncing the word "early" like "er-lie" and changing one word. I sang, "What do you do with a drunken Sorensen? What do you do with a drunken Sorensen? What do you do with a drunken Sorensen er-lie in the morning?"

Curfew was at midnight. After we pretended to assault and capture a few of the watercraft, using imaginary rifles and throwing imaginary hand grenades, we decided to return to base. Before leaving, Danny urinated into the water and declared, "I claim thee in the name of the United States Naval Academy. Amen." Matt and I watched him with total indifference as we swayed in inebriation. Suddenly, to all appearances, we were perfectly sober. Without another word, we quickly marched to Bancroft Hall, by habit falling into step, signed in, and went to our separate rooms.

* * *

The next morning, Dave Husaby, Danny Calhoun, and I walked to the first deck of Third Battalion to make church formation. We had volunteered for town services to avoid the hateful march to the Academy chapel amidst the upperclassmen of our own company. There was much less of a chance of getting a Form 2 or a come-around by going to church in town.

It irked me that church attendance was mandatory. An individual's relationship with God was personal, having nothing to do with formations and, perhaps, not even with church. Although I was a practicing Episcopalian, I was a touch pantheist. God was an old wagon road cutting through the tall, thin, New England woods, or a piece of moss clinging to one of the many small boulders making up the gray stone walls lining the fields no longer existent, made by hands a long time forgotten. It was an emotional experience sometimes achieved in church ritual, but always achieved in nature.

Ten midshipmen were at the formation. It was informal, no inspection, hardly a counting of heads. Two youngsters had taken the rear of the marching column as they moved out in pairs. Subsequently, they disappeared at the first turning of a corner of Bancroft Hall. Danny gave his customary chuckle. So far, we had been faithful in attending church services because of the coffee hour discussion held afterwards. However, when a scion of the church decided that the discussions should focus only on religious topics, we decided to terminate our church attendance. We three renegades intended to march into the church with the arriving group of mids and leave immediately with the departing group.

Our column halted outside the main entrance of the church. We heard the final hymn of the previous service being sung and soon the doors swung open. We rushed into the building, trying to catch the mids leaving through the side door. That's when we spotted the upperclassmen standing Cerberus-like at the exit, attempting to catch escapees. We had to pass along the pews at the rear of the building and that was where Husaby lost his nerve. His knees weakened and he plunged into a pew, threw himself onto the knee cushions, and pretended to pray, eyes closed, hands clasped as he searched for peace and tranquility. I was impressed at how natural and saintly Husaby made his sudden conversion seem.

I hesitated, but Danny was adamant. "Let's hurry up. Let's make them think we're part of the group that's leaving." I caught up and was equally impressed by Danny's coolness. Being careful not to meet anyone's eyes, we lurched through the exit and lined up with the departing group.

Two youngsters from our own church party had also made it through. Danny smiled as he exchanged a triumphant glance with me.

In the relative security of a marching column where two men formed one unit in a long line, Danny asked, "Did you hear about the new plebe board?"

"No. What about it?"

"A review board has been set up with first classmen on it. They're supposed to protect plebes from undue harassment. Any plebe with a grievance is free to go to them to present his case. Do you think anyone will use it?"

"God help the plebe who does. He'd have the whole Brigade on his ass. It'd be hell on earth for the poor sucker."

"He could always resign."

"And be called a pussy."

"And be called a pussy to boot. I figured it was a bunch of crap. I wanted to see what you thought of it."

Now I offered my own bit of gossip. "Did you hear about the firstie who turned in his roommate?"

"No. What'd he turn him in for?"

"I don't know, a sloppy uniform or something like that. Anyways, he found a turd in his laundry bag."

"Human?"

"Yeah, human."

Danny scoffed. "That's what you get for bilging a classmate. It'll get him rank though. Those guys always end up being Midshipman Brigade Commanders."

As we marched through town, we passed several cars that were parallel parked. An old woman with wild white hair sat in one that was boxed in. She jammed her car into forward and rammed the car in front of her. Then she put her vehicle in reverse and smashed the car behind her. She rocked forwards then backwards, alternately smashing into the cars on either side of her. A tittering laugh ran down the column.

I asked, "What's sulfur shelf?"

"Chicken of the Woods. It's a shelf mushroom that's red with a yellow border. It's yummy. It tastes like chicken."

"You've eaten it?"

"Yeah. Have you?"

"Yep."

Danny thought for a while, then asked, "Suppose you were in the woods, and you ran out of candles, kerosene, and whatever else you normally use for light. What would you use as a substitute? You have an animal carcass with you."

"You could use the fat of the animal for oil. You could use that for a makeshift candle."

"What would you use for a wick?"

"Strips of leather from its skin."

"Good guess, but no prize." Danny waited a minute. "Give up?"

"Yeah."

"You'd make the wick from sinew. The strips of leather were a good guess, though."

Once on Academy grounds, the file broke up. The first classman leading the small formation didn't bother to call a halt to dismiss them formally. Instead, he saluted and called, "Dismissed," without breaking stride. The church party dissolved like a drop of milk in a glass of water, each mid going his own way. Danny went back to his room to "catch some zees" while I went to breakfast. Unlike other Academy meals, Sunday breakfast was relaxed. The upperclassmen had taken human form.

As I walked through the chow line, a black cook slopped a white glob onto my plate. I asked, "What's that?"

"Grits. Put some gravy on 'em. You'll love 'em."

I said dubiously, "Okay."

"Jus' try 'em. Thas all. Jus' try 'em."

Once at the table, I put a spoonful into my mouth. It was great! Imagine! To have been alive all these years and to never have tasted such a simple delight. I shoveled the rest into my mouth and could only wonder what other wonderful surprises life had for me!

After breakfast I returned to my room to find Bob sitting at the desk in the regulation dark blue bathrobe. As soon as I entered, my roommate stood up disconsolately, sat on his bunk, took a side-glance at himself in the wall mirror, then stood up again and left the room without comment. As I watched, I tried to guess his mood. When he left without any acknowledgement of my presence, I assumed that he was in a bad mood. From my closet, I pulled out my white leggings and bayonet belt which were dirty from last Wednesday's E.D. where, after classes, I marched an hour in Farragut Field with other miscreants to work off one demerit. Bob returned as silently as he had left, hands in his bathrobe pockets, and thrust himself onto his bunk with the back of his head against the wall.

I started to wash my gear with soap and a pink scrub brush when Bob said, "I was thinking that, if for some reason I got kicked out, it really doesn't matter. Just to be here at the Academy is an honor. The worst midshipman here is still among the elite. That's why so many famous men were midshipmen at some time in their lives. Even if they flunked out, they were still the best."

Bob sat on the edge of the bunk. He opened a desk drawer to retrieve a plastic bag of what looked like rabbit scat. He nibbled at it when he held the bag out to me. "Want some?"

I took a handful. "What is it?"

"Pinion nuts."

I ate a few.

"How do you like them?"

"They're good."

Tossing the bag to me, Bob said "Here. Take the whole bag. My mom can send me plenty more."

"Thanks."

Sitting back against the wall, Bob continued his musings. He said, "Back home in the desert, I used to shoot around the dirt roads on a small trail bike. At night it was bad because the parkers would hear me coming and suddenly flash on their high beams so I couldn't see. If I was at a turn, I'd sometimes go flying into the mesquite." He moved to the edge of his bunk. "Here. I'll show you a picture of home."

Again, he reached into the desk drawer. He pulled out a small photograph and showed me an adobe hut surrounded by a mass of sunlight and sand. Bob and an older man stood before it in work clothes. My roommate said casually, "We had a cow." I didn't see any grass and wondered if the cow ate sand. It was such a stark contrast to the lush New England fields that I was used to.

I said, "That's nice, Bob. Is that your dad?"

"Yeah."

I did my best to wring out the thick fabric of my leggings and bayonet belt. As I was hanging them in the shower to dry, I noticed the writing on my belt buckle. "Fidelity" was printed in an arc at its top while "Obedience" was printed in an arc at the bottom. I then understood one of the required rates. Whenever an upperclassman asks, "What's up?" the plebe must respond, "'Fidelity' is up and 'Obedience' is down on our bayonet belt buckles, sir!" I hadn't heard that formula repeated since plebe summer except once when Budge asked it of me.

Bob was again on his bunk with his back against the wall. Although his face was toward me, his eyes were glued to the reflection of himself in the mirror. His speech became animated, "My grandfather killed three bandits. They were robbing him, and he went for his gun. He killed all three. I look at him now and I can't believe it. He's so old and crinkled that it's hard for me to believe that he did something like that. I keep thinking that he's always been old and crinkled. I can't imagine him as a young man."

I put a touch of Brasso on a rag and, without taking off my belt, applied it carefully to my belt buckle. Bob continued what was a soliloquy. "I got robbed once when I was in Houston. I had taken some side streets and was lost when I heard two guys following me. One came up to me really fast and, before I knew it, I had a knife against my throat. I gave him my wallet and they let me go. They were both Hispanic. I went up one block and found a well-lit street with hundreds of people walking on it. I couldn't believe it, just one block away. Some of those guys wear boots that have spikes in them. They click their heels, the spikes come out of the toes, then they kick you with them."

I was only half listening, preoccupied with my own thoughts about my family. Bob was quiet for a moment, then asked, "Did you ever watch *Star Trek*? I believe that stuff will really happen someday." Sitting tensely on the edge of his bunk, he looked squarely at me. With prophetic finality, he said, "Mankind will travel in outer space. With the immensity of space, man will have to develop new means of transportation. I can actually see spacecrafts disappearing and appearing again millions of miles away in a kind of space-time warp." His eyes were glowing with fervor. "It has to be, just like airplanes, steam, and sailing ships. Whenever mankind has needed something like that, whenever there was an impassable barrier, something has come along to solve the problem. In the future, that problem will be interplanetary, interstellar travel. Mike, I can see this; I actually can see this."

I was looking down at the white bucks I had worn for church formation. There was a black smudge on the in-step. I reached under the sink for the white shoe polish and dashed some of it onto the smudge, dooming it to white oblivion. I, too, could see spaceships dancing in cloudless black, surrounded by pins of light. I was quiet, brooding over the coming hour. I said, "I have to call home. See you at noon." I then chopped to the first deck to make my weekly call home.

* * *

I entered a room enclosed on three sides by wooden telephone booths from which came a gabbling of voices, some in laughter, others in anger, but all muted and confused with the surrounding noise. I dialed home. When my mother answered, I spoke in a deceptively soft, quiet voice to convey to her strength and calm. I was immediately disconcerted by the pleading tone that entered her voice. She was a strong personality and the weakness she'd been recently manifesting alarmed me.

"Hi, Mom."

"Hi, son, I'm glad you called. You know that this is the highlight of my week."

"How's everybody?"

"Everyone's doing good."

"How's Beth?"

"Good. She's been having a hard time with your dad's death and all."

"That was eight months ago!"

"Yes, but your sister has no sense of time. To her, it happened yesterday. The doctor said she had a nervous breakdown."

"From what?"

"I don't know."

I could hear her sniffling. "Are you crying?"

"No, I'm okay. Cora found Beth in the yard a couple of weeks ago. She was standing by the trash barrels and wouldn't come into the house. I was at work."

"Why was she at the trash barrels?"

"I don't know." I heard my mother softly crying as she tried not to be heard.

My mind searched into the past when my sister, six years older than me, used to attack me when she was upset but not necessarily upset with me. I asked, "She's not hurting you, is she?"

"No, no, nothing as bad as that, but she's behaving something awful."

"What's she been doing?"

I heard a sob. "She's...been screaming a lot. The doctor has her under medication. They think she saw something or maybe something happened to her, you know, maybe Peter next door."

A moment of silence. "Are you okay?"

I heard my mother take a deep breath as she composed herself. "Yes, I'm fine."

"So, what happened? You might as well tell me because I'll worry more now if you don't. I already know that something's wrong.'

"It might be nothing. It might be that your father's death triggered something in her. I don't know what to do. I have nowhere to turn to."

"What about Cora and Buddy?"

"They have their own families."

"Mom, I'm four hundred miles away at a school that eats up all my time. I can't do anything from here. Buddy lives two miles away."

"He's busy with his own family."

"Uh huh." I changed the subject. "Any news from Ken?"

"I got a letter from him. It's pretty bad. One of his friends got shot in the mouth. Ken was standing right next to him. It was night and the other man lit a cigarette. He's pretty shook up about it."

"At least he's still alive."

Mom's voice became energetic as she said, "Those Canada geese are back at Diamond Hill. They're gorgeous. Your dog chased after them, but they swam to the other side of the pond."

"Yeah, according to the Audubon Society they're making a comeback."

"Laporte is starting to build on Lauman's farm. The old man would be turning in his grave if he could see what they're doing."

A twinge of quiet, subtle grief gripped me. "That's too bad. I love that farm."

"Do you remember the large round thermostat in the kitchen? It broke so I had it replaced, but the replacement is a small rectangular thermostat, so I tried to get matching paint for the wall only it didn't match and now I have a big ugly spot around the thermostat. The whole wall will have to be repainted."

"Mom, Kenny and I have already painted your house, the whole house, inside and out. Can't Buddy paint that one wall?"

"He's too busy. He's so intelligent that he doesn't notice the little things like that."

"Okay, I'll paint the wall when I'm on Christmas leave. I have to go."

"Son, you're going to call next week, aren't you?"

"I don't know."

"But your calls mean so much to me."

I sighed. "All right. I'll call next week about this time."

"Thank you, son. I love you."

"I love you, too. Bye-bye."

"Goodbye, son."

I rubbed my chin. *Had Mom told me everything?* I left the babbling behind me to return to my room.

* * *

That afternoon I took a small walk through the town, thankful that it wasn't a football weekend. Otherwise, I'd be marching through Annapolis between parallel rows of civilian spectators. Budge would have me counting each step taken on the way to the stadium. In the normal course of events, I'd lose count because of the great number of steps. Inevitably, he would ask, "How many, Sorensen?" and I would make the best guess possible. Once at the stadium, I'd run onto the field to form a gauntlet for the team to run through as they ran from the locker rooms. I would do my best to look enthusiastic for a sport I didn't like, jumping up and down in feigned excitement, hoping that Budge was watching the show. Then followed two desperate hours of cheering on a losing team. If Navy won, the plebes got carry-on for the next three days. It happened once.

The town was pleasant. I wandered from shop to shop, looking at the attractive gewgaws made for the tourists. Turning a corner, I bumped into Hovedo who was accompanied by his parents and younger brother. I controlled my surprise as introductions were made. Gus Hovedo was a midshipman ideal: big, strong, handsome, gifted in every way. His parents, however, were diminutive. They were short, dark, feeble, and looked as though they had stepped off a turn-of-the-century immigrant steamer two minutes ago. It seemed inconceivable that their loins could produce such a complete man as their son. Gus' smiling bravado was in marked contrast to the shy effacement of his family. The little brother remained reserved, inconspicuous. I wondered if he'd be the same kind of man as his brother. After a brief exchange, we parted, and I found myself thinking of Gus who was a real mystery. He liked aircraft and ships, metal and machines; this was beyond my imagining.

In my mindless wandering through town, I became aware of a row of books sitting before me. I was in the children's section of the bookstore where my thoughts gravitated to the past right after my family moved to the Plat. I had bought a stamp book of cats, ostensibly for myself, but really for Beth, so that I could ask her to paste the pictures, the stamps, in the places where they belonged in the text. When she was done, we started to read the book together.

She read it slowly, word by painful word, out loud, "LIONS...ARE...LA...LA..."

"Large."

"LARGE...CATS....THEY...LIVE...IN...AF...AF...AFRICA."

"Very good." Then I exaggerated a Spanish word and added, "EXCELLENTAY." Both of us smiled. A year ago, Cora, Beth, and I had gone to a Peter, Paul, and Mary concert where a drunk woman kept calling, "Excellentay!" after each song.

"THEY...LIVE...IN...FAMILIES..."

"Very good."

"CALLED...PR...PR..."

"Prides."

I heard a knock on the kitchen door. I left Beth and opened it to find Doug Carey, one of the neighborhood boys, straddling his bicycle and, oddly, holding his hand before his mouth and looking toward the ground. I heard, "A bunch of us are having a touch football game and we want you to play."

"No, thank you."

"If you don't, we're going to beat you up."

It was an idle threat. By the time my family had left the Heights, I had been in half a dozen schoolyard fights (five draws and one bad loss), hid in the dark as a gang walked through our neighborhood shooting out kitchen lights, and had two teenage boys threaten to cut off my balls while flashing a switchblade in my face. I wasn't afraid of anyone in the Plat. "Then you'll have to beat me up," and I closed the door and returned to our reading.

My wayward path led me to the Bijou. Checking my watch, I discovered that *2001: A Space Odyssey* was about to begin. I bought a ticket, sat in the middle of the theater, and prayed that the world's tallest man wouldn't sit in the empty seat right in front of me with only seconds before the movie began. For fun, I chose a character during the first five minutes of the movie with whom I could identify. Then, whatever the character did, it was really me doing it. Hopefully, he would be the hero, but if the character turned out to be a villain, well, that wasn't good. I chose one of the astronauts, but, to my dismay, Hal, the spaceship's computer system, killed me at the beginning of the movie. *Yeah,* I thought, *that's something a machine would do.*

When it was over, I decided to return to Bancroft Hall to see how Bob was doing with the football poster. A ritual was performed every Sunday evening preceding a football game conducted the following weekend. Each plebe room had to make a poster purporting to support the Navy team for the coming game. They were presented to the company's upperclassmen for judgement. The plebes lined up in the corridor holding their posters before them and listening to the jibes of their superiors. Hoots and howls echoed down the corridors, especially when the plebes with a particularly gruesome poster were ordered to throw it onto the ground and stomp on it. I had made the last poster and thought it reasonable and fair that Bob should make the one for this week. Certainly, my roommate would have begun it and I could help finish it. When I reached our room, I found my roommate sitting sullenly at the desk with belligerently folded arms.

Bob asked, "Where have *you* been?"

"In town. You haven't done the poster?"

"No."

"You haven't even started it?"

"No."

"Goddamn! We got to get *something* out there even if we have to stomp on it! It's better than getting fried with a Form 2!"

I searched my locker and found some poster paper. I tried to think of a witty saying or idea, but my anger at Bob kept me from thinking clearly. I could see that Valdres was aware of our plight, but his mind, too, was infertile. By evening meal nothing had been accomplished and afterwards we wouldn't have enough time. When the time arrived to present the posters, we two fugitives turned off our lights and listened quietly. We heard the upperclassmen mumbling in the corridor as they milled about the posters. We heard chuckling as a pair of plebes was made to stomp on their work. The group was dispersing when a voice asked, "Hey, where's Valdres and Sorensen?" Immediately, the overhead lights flashed on revealing a welter of bodies crushing the doorway. Bob and I stood at attention amidst the unbelieving eyes of the upperclassmen.

We were brought before our squad's ruling first classman. He moaned, "Why do you guys keep screwing up?"

We answered in unison, "No excuse, sir!"

"I'm giving you two hours to make a poster. If you don't have one by then, I'm writing you up. Now get going.'

"Aye-aye, sir."

Desperation forced us into ingenuity and camaraderie. I had moleskin in my locker. Since the opposing team had a panther for a mascot, I suggested that we do something like "skin the panthers." Bob rigged a little pulley system while I cut the shape of a mountain lion out of my moleskin. In half an hour the poster read "SKIN THE PANTHERS" while the pulley system lifted the moleskin from the underlying outline of a panther. The first classman was pleased, commenting that we might have gotten carry-on had it been done on time. I thought, *not hardly*.

CHAPTER III
THE CLASS A OFFENSES

It was during Wednesday noon meal that the plebes were told by word of mouth that there'd be a spontaneous pep rally that evening. Inwardly, I groaned at the loss of an evening's worth of study time. Budge would be sure to ask me if I had gone and I wanted to answer in the affirmative. The difficult part would be to put a sparkle in my eyes, a smile on my lips, and a thrill in my voice when I made the admission.

Yet, I found a certain comfort at the rally as I rushed to the courtyard in front of the rotunda. Most of the mids, almost all of them plebes, wore pajama-like trousers, T-shirts, and sneakers. A veil of darkness surrounded the bluster, noise, and the false promises from a losing team as though the rally was being conducted in a bottomless well. To move a yard or two from the milling crowd was to become aware of the dead stillness that encircled it. The shadows were almost tangible to the touch and soothed my inner turmoil.

I saw the lanky figure of John Boatman cheering near me. He was hopping from one foot to the other and howling. When he saw me, he hooted and howled again, hopping with a quickened pace. He said cynically, "It's a great pep rally, isn't it? It's great making a fool of yourself for a bunch of losers." Boatman howled some more.

I said, "You're the first plebe from our company that I've ever seen at one of these things."

"You can be sure Seitzer and Banfield are here along with the other 'chosen' ones."

I waited for the massive cheering to subside. A football player stood at the top of the steps leading into the rotunda. On either side of him projected ornamental brass cannons. Standing in a well-lit area, he began to speak. I faced John. "I guess you haven't heard."

"Heard what?"

"Banfield resigned."

"Run-out, you mean."

"Resigned. That slimy freak Lackning went from table to table shaking hands with the second classmen as if he was the one who ran him out. He's not even in his squad." John howled as the others cheered the words of their football idol. Out of the corner of my eye, I could see a first classman watching us. I continued, "I hate that weasel. There's something hideous about him."

"I wonder about that guy myself."

The first classman approached us. "You gentlemen don't seem too interested in the pep rally." My friend and I stood at attention. "What company are you from?"

I answered, "We're both from the twelfth company, sir."

"Who are your second classmen?"

"Midshipman Second Class Budge, sir, Midshipman Second Class Mower, sir..."

"That's enough. Tell Mr. Budge that you didn't find the pep rally interesting."

"Aye-aye, sir."

"Both of you."

Boatman said, "Aye-aye, sir."

As the firstie walked away, I said, "Sorry I bilged you, John."

"That's okay. It was my fault just as much as it was yours." After a moment, he asked, "Are you going to report yourself?"

"Yeah, but I'll leave you out if you want me to."

"All right."

I scanned the immediate area to see if the firstie was still watching us. He was nowhere to be seen. I said, "Budge has a new trick."

"What's that?"

"He makes Valdres and I hold up the plates for seconds." This referred to another responsibility of the plebes. Whenever a table ran out of a particular food, a plebe was required to hold its dish at arm's length over his head. A Filipino steward would then replace it with a full plate. I continued, "Bragg is at team tables, Bemes is about to go, but if we run out of something, and Bemes holds up the plate, Budge orders him to give it to Valdres or me, then *we* don't get to eat until the plate is taken away. I have to give Bemes credit though. He tries to second-guess Budge to give Bob and me a break. He tries to do his share, but Budge won't let him."

"He's Budge's golden boy, huh?"

"I don't think so. I think Budge has it in for Bob and me, especially me. He seems to hate me, but I don't know why. He must have a reason."

"Yeah, he has a reason, and the reason is that he's a jerk; that's the reason."

"But there has to be a reason why he hates me."

"Mike, why does there always have to be a reason? Why can't someone be a jerk because he's a jerk? Why did Hitler hate Jews?" John's voice became excited as he sucked air in through clenched teeth; his hand and arm movements became animated. "Sle, maybe he hated Jews because he hated Jews. I don't know, but I do know that there's no excuse for behavior like that, reason or no reason, and sle, I don't think Budge has any excuse either. He's just a jerk."

"In another situation, he might be a really nice guy."

"Hitler once cried over a dead canary. He was a nice guy, too, but he was still a jerk and, sle, so is Budge. What I don't understand is why you're defending this creep."

"I'm not defending him. I want to know why he behaves the way he does."

"I told you; because he's a jerk, period!"

I was comforted that my friend felt so strongly about my situation in the squad. The midshipman mob started to move toward the superintendent's residence. The noise brought him, his wife, and their fat, twelve-year-old son onto the porch. They waved to the mids. Instinctively, I reacted against the man's arrogance. The super walked with his nose literally stuck in the air. I was much more aware of and impressed by his admiral bars than by the man himself. The super addressed the mids. There were responding cheers. Only a handful of plebes near the porch could hear him, but everyone was quick to take the cue from the front ranks, cheering when they cheered, quiet when they were quiet. Finally, those in front turned toward Bancroft Hall followed, like a herd of sheep, by the others.

John Boatman was still at my side. I said, "I got a busy day tomorrow beginning with swim class in the morning and ending with a cross country race in the afternoon. I've only got one free period in between."

"Ouch!"

The accumulated fatigue of the past weeks exhausted me. "I'm already tired just thinking of it."

Once near Bancroft Hall, the plebes looked towards the windows above them. Occasionally, a water balloon was hurled from a darkened window, most often splashing futilely onto the pavement, at times hitting the target plebe. The two of us chopped to our company area. Thinking, *I might as well get it over with*, I chopped directly to Budge's room. I knocked, opened the door a crack, and called, "Permission to come aboard, sir!"

"Yeah, come on in." I sounded off, then stood quietly at attention. Although it was Budge's and Kristin's room, Mower sat behind the desk. The second classman asked, blinking with wonder, "What is it, Sorensen?"

"Sir, a first classman told me to tell you, I mean, to tell Mr. Budge, that I wasn't interested in the pep rally." I could have bitten my tongue off for having ratted on myself, but I was honor bound not to lie.

"Why? What'd you do?"

I thought how much Mower looked like a little boy. "Sir, I was talking to a classmate."

"Where? Outside?"

"Yes, sir."

"You *were* at the pep rally, right?"

"Yes, sir."

"The whole thing?"

"Yes, sir."

"I don't see any crime in that. I'll take care of it. You don't have to tell Budge. Take off."

"Aye-aye, sir." A wave of gratitude surged through me as I chopped to my room.

* * *

Like so many coconuts floating in exotic seas, the heads of fifty plebes tossed in the cold water of the pool, snuffling and snorting with strangled breathing. They were supposed to take off their white trousers while in water over their heads, knot the legs, fill the legs with air to make a temporary float, then place the float between their legs for buoyancy. The better swimmers had already completed the exercise and stood at the poolside, wearing their wet, white jumpers and blue bathing suits with their wet trousers in their hands. Casually and without interest, they watched their bouncing compatriots trying to accomplish the same feat. There were two methods used to inflate the trouser legs. One was to flick the trousers over the swimmer's head, so that the air rushed into the legs. The other method and the one less used was for the swimmer to take a breath of air (several times), entirely submerge his head (several times), and inflate the pant legs like a balloon. Since the exercise was graded and timed, the last band of swimmers became frenetic in their efforts to pass while the instructor, standing on the diving board, called out the seconds remaining. When time was up, a dozen disgruntled midshipmen were still in the water. I was among them.

The class continued. Wearing everything but socks, shoes, and their caps, the plebes had to swim fifty feet underwater starting from a dead stop. When my turn arrived, I did the surface dive. The class had been advised to go deep so I went directly to the bottom fifteen feet below. Kicking my arms and legs as fast as I could, I hoped to hold out until I hit the opposite wall. My clothes weighed me down and saved me the effort of trying to stay below the surface. I was caught in time. No matter how hard I kicked, I didn't seem to be moving. My lungs were about to explode, yet I was immersed in liquid that seemed to refuse me mobility. I let out some air to relieve the pressure. It helped a little, but, again, my lungs demanded air. As always when I struggled in water, I thought how terrible it must be to die by drowning, the futile battle in ageless depths, gasps for air resulting in water filled lungs, and the floating stillness of death itself. I let all the air out of my lungs and hoped to be carried the rest of the way by momentum and guts. I saw a long, discolored, gray mass that appeared to be fifteen feet away. I was determined to reach it. In less than five feet, I touched the wall and shot to the surface, sucking in a deep breath. The instructor called, "Pass!" then marked it in his ledger. I got out of the water to rest for my second try at the inflation test.

The dozen midshipmen who had flunked were brought to the other end of the pool, squishing with every step they took. Upon command they jumped into the water, slipped off their trousers, knotted the legs, and set about to inflate them. I lifted my arms to flip the trousers over my head but found myself sinking instead. I tried this four times before deciding to attempt the other method. I took a deep breath, submerged my head, blew into the trouser legs, then came up to see the results. They were meager, certainly not worth the unpleasantness of burying my head underwater. For a moment, my attention was caught by the back of a mid's head. The hair was dark and streaked in wet clumps looking very much like drowned rats seen floating in harbors. I resumed my efforts, trying to achieve success with the overhead flip. By now, only two other plebes were in the water with me and soon they were hauling themselves onto the edge of the pool, having accomplished their tasks. My efforts doubled. I was the last mid in the pool. Class was dismissed. As the plebes were filing to the showers, a voice muttered, "C'mon." More midshipmen stopped. Cheering for me—the last man— erupted. The more vehement it became, the more I tried not to disappoint them. Their hearts were with me. I *had* to make it. The seconds clicked away. I wrestled with the air and water, trying to force them to do my will. The instructor started to call off the final seconds. The cheering intensified; I kept flicking my arms over my head. The recalcitrant trousers flopped in front of me with no air in the legs. Finally, the instructor called time. I heard a massed "Aw" and saw shoulders shrugged and casual waves of disappointment. I was the only one who hadn't passed.

* * *

I was bending over, holding my sides, and breathing heavily. It seemed as though all creation didn't have enough oxygen to fill my lungs. Moscowitz, a youngster from my own squad, took first place while I had taken second. Since we were on the same team, I accepted this with indifference. The next runner from our team to come in was Paul Carnevale. He placed tenth. I was still weak on my feet when Paul came in, but now I was upright, hands on hips, arms sticking out like butterfly wings. Paul joined me. We knew that we lost the meet on points alone. As we were about to return to Bancroft Hall, our first class coach hurried up to us and said, "We lost, but you guys ran a good race. Tell your upperclassmen that I'm granting you carry-on."

Paul said, "Sure thing." The two of us walked a few paces when Carnevale asked, "Are you going to ask for carry-on?"

"Why bother? Budge would only find some reason to take it away. Even when we win, I don't get carry-on. Why should I get it now?"

"I haven't placed under tenth yet and I've gotten carry-on every time. It doesn't seem fair."

Quickly and bitterly, I said, "Of course it isn't fair, but who's going to ask for justice? Not me!" When I became calmer, I asked reflectively, "Did you ever wonder how you'd explain running to an invalid?"

"I don't know. I've never run to an invalid."

"You know what I mean. How would you explain to an invalid the pain you experience when running? How would you approach it?"

"Maybe you could find an analogous experience that the invalid had and then you could compare them."

"I suppose. But it wouldn't be the same, not quite. How would you explain the stomach cramps or the dizziness at the beginning of a race?"

"But Mike, we're all like that. How could I ever make you feel exactly what I'm feeling right now? We're all isolated."

I looked at the dust of the field being disturbed by our tramping feet. "I guess you're right."

Once in my room, I prepared my uniform for evening meal so that I could change quickly into it right after come-around. As I did so I memorized my rates. I became more and more despondent as come-around time approached, especially since I deserved carry-on and knew I wouldn't get it.

Earlier that day, I had gotten a box of gedunk (food) from my mother containing a variety of treats like chocolate covered almonds and cookies. Before leaving for classes, I opened a package of Oreos and said to Bob, "Feel free to grab some of these." Now I reached for the same package and was immediately suspicious of its lightness. Looking inside I saw one cookie sitting forlornly at the bottom, the last survivor of a gustatory raid. My hand made a doubting exploration and substantiated my most dire fears. Only one cookie left. Just then Bob returned from yard patrol craft exercises. I was about to remonstrate with him but decided against it since I didn't know if Bob ate all the cookies out of spite.

Valdres said, "Goddamn, I've never peed so much in my life. I'm not used to cold weather and the colder it gets, the more I pee."

I already had my gym gear on and waited for Bob to change into his gym gear. When he was ready, I said, "It's about that time," and the two of us chopped to Budge's room. We entered, sounding off in unison. Budge sat majestically behind his desk, smiling. He said, "Sorensen, do you have something to tell me?"

"No, sir."

"Moscowitz was here. He said that you took another second place. He said that your coach granted you carry-on."

"Yes, sir."

Budge's smile broadened like that of the Cheshire Cat. "Well?"

"Sir?"

"Aren't you going to ask me something?"

"No, sir."

Budge's smile lengthened. "Why not?" I kept silent, then he insisted, "Why not, Sorensen?"

I was aware that Bob had taken a keen interest in the events before him. No matter what the plebes thought of one another, the one plebe would want the other to escape come-around. Bob's presence was mutely supportive. Budge said, "Wait outside, Valdres." When he was gone, the second classman asked, "Why aren't you going to ask for carry-on, Sorensen?"

"Because you'll only take it away, sir."

Budge's eyes twinkled. "That's no reason not to try. Now, don't you have something to ask me?"

"Sir, request permission for carry-on."

"Do you know your rates?"

"Yes, sir."

"Okay, give me the football team."

I did so.

"Give me the menus for evening and morning meals."

I did so.

"Why didn't you say 'sir'?"

I rattled off the paragraph.

"Give me five items from this morning's newspaper."

Done. I was immensely pleased with myself. No other plebe in the company knew his rates as well as I did. It looked as though I might get carry-on after all.

"Who's the Midshipman Brigade Commander?"

"Midshipman First Class Chris John, sir."

"Who's the Midshipman Deputy Brigade Commander?"

My mind went blank. I knew the answer, but nothing appeared to my mind. I tasted the name on the tip of my tongue. If only it would come out of the darkness that sat before me. My stomach turned as Budge waited expectantly. The second classman locked his fingers together and rested them on his stomach. He leaned back, the picture of contentment. I said, "I'll find out, sir."

To all appearances, Budge was calm, but the mirth in his eyes belied the appearance. "Sorensen?"

"Sir?"

"Come-around."

"Aye-aye, sir."

I wanted to scream my rage as Budge led Valdres and me to the main corridor. Paul Carnevale was walking to the head. Our eyes met briefly in understanding and sympathy. Moscowitz peeked from his room. His mouth dropped open when he saw what was happening. Valdes and I joined a group of plebes that were already being run. They were doing sprints, each plebe running every other race. Between races, the plebes were ordered to run in place with the upperclassmen yelling for them to keep their knees high. As I was running in place, feeling resentment and outrage at Budge, I noticed who was *not* there. Bemes was not there. Bragg, the biggest bagger in the company, was not there. Hovedo wasn't there. Schein wasn't there. None of the company studs were there! It was always the same people, picked on by the same upperclassmen! I was always tired, as were all the plebes there. We were being worn down as water wears away the toughest rock. It wasn't right. I *deserved* carry-on. I looked at Budge with his layer of soft tissue beneath a reddish skin the texture of a catfish's belly.

Bob and I had been alternately running sprints and running in place for fifteen minutes. Small pools of sweat marred the floor where an unfortunate plebe had been taken to one side to do a particularly difficult exercise. It was hard for me to believe that this was considered training instead of a bizarre perversion of punishment. I looked at the scattered bodies throughout the corridor. I listened to the protesting grunts and the distorted frenzy about me. *Like a war between ants*, I thought. *All this energy wasted. All observed by an unfeeling god.*

Suddenly, a bright light entered the corridor in the form of happily smiling Buns McMunn. He was feeling *great*! He felt robust, strong. Why, he bet he could even beat the runner Sorensen in a sprint! I ran in place as the other midshipmen cleared the area. McMunn and I lined up at an imaginary starting line. Mower, who had come in with McMunn, said, "Buns, whip his ass."

Budge called, "Go!" and we were off. McMunn took an immediate lead and maintained it to the end of the corridor. I was three feet behind when Buns touched the end wall before turning around and, starting back to the finish line, he yelled, "*C'mon, sweetheart!*"

I revolted at the implied familiarity. I was angered that I was losing, especially since I was so tired to begin with. I said under my breath, quietly voicing my defiance, "Fuck you."

McMunn hadn't heard the words, but a first classman, who happened to be standing near his open door, did. Even before the race had ended with Buns the easy victor, a hush had settled on all activity. A figure said, "Reedy wants to see you, Sorensen."

"Aye-aye, sir."

I chopped up the corridor, not quite sure what was happening. My eyes kept hopping from figure to figure, trying to guess from their faces what this sudden heaviness implied. When I reached Reedy's room and sounded off, the first classman offered me a seat. Reedy then closed the door and sat opposite me.

"Relax, Sorensen."

"Aye-aye, sir."

"I heard what you said to McMunn."

"Yes, sir." I looked at Reedy's long, slim figure, newly filled with seriousness and compassionate understanding.

"Why'd you do it, Sorensen?"

"He told me to 'come on,' sir." I was ashamed to admit that McMunn had called me sweetheart. It was so vile.

"So you swore at him."

"Yes, sir."

"You've committed a serious offense and I can't pretend that I didn't hear it."

I was dumbfounded. Admittedly, I had committed an offense, but I couldn't comprehend why it was so serious. They were only words. I hadn't murdered anyone. Where was the crime?

"Sorensen, as soon as you go through that door, you're fair game. McMunn and the other second classmen are going to come down hard on you."

"Yes, sir." I still didn't understand.

"Do you have any questions?"

"No, sir."

"Bring a Form 2 to my room after evening meal."

"Aye-aye, sir."

As I was opening the door, Reedy said, paternally, "Sorensen."

"Sir?"

"Good luck."

"Thank you, sir."

Upon my passage through the doorway, I am immediately struck by the change in atmosphere. It's like falling into a nightmare, charged, brittle, the ever-present angst of being hunted moment by moment. The shadows are darker. The other midshipmen are indistinct forms, none of which I recognize. I hear voices. "He said what?" "To McMunn?" I don't hear the answers. When I reach my room, Bob is ready for evening meal. He stands before the mirror and puts the finishing touches to his uniform. Nonchalantly, he says, "You're in for it now."

"I know."

Bob is about to leave for chow call when McMunn bursts into the room, pounding the already open door as though it blocked his progress. His buttocks are propped up in solemn dignity like a

Hamadryad baboon. Mower, dragged along in tow, follows McMunn's dark, heavy form. Their mannerisms are so much like Captain Kirk and Mr. Spock that I would have laughed had I not been the alien about to be annihilated. Both plebes sound off while the two upperclassmen descend on me like dogs hounding a woodchuck. They gyrate and scream, drowning each other out, while I wonder if this is really happening. Surely, a mistake has been made. In a flash, they leave only to resume the assault at meal. I brave it, still not fully comprehending what is going on. So far, nothing has happened except that the harassment is a little more severe.

After meal, I chop to my room to be stunned as I turn into the doorway. Everything I own, the contents of my drawers and locker, my books, mattress, sheets, clothes, have been thrown onto the floor in the middle of the room. A photograph of my mother and father is lying face down in the shower. Slowly, I pick it up, wipe the now cracked glass on my sleeve, and replace it on my desk. My things had been thrown into a huge pile that would take the rest of the evening to sort and put away in good midshipman fashion. My clothes would have to be properly folded, my gear put in the proper places. I wouldn't be able to study, a serious omission in a school with such high academic standards. I envision every study hour being eaten like this. It is then that I clearly see what is about to happen. I know that the storm has begun in earnest.

Disheartened, I find a Form 2, sit at my desk, and in the name slot I write in anger "Diogenes Laertius." I don't know who Diogenes Laertius is, but I read the name somewhere and it stuck. Then, with a sinking heart, I tear it, throw it into the trash, and correctly fill out another Form 2.

It takes three days for the Form 2 to be processed, during which time the Academy changes uniforms from summer whites to winter blues. I am subjected to an assortment of attacks. I find my room torn apart two more times. Bob helps me clean up the first two times but grabs his cap and goes to the library the third time. McMunn has me wear a poster saying, "I SWEAR AT UPPERCLASSMEN." I am ordered to wear it, front and back, whenever I am in Bancroft Hall. This is particularly humiliating since the whole Brigade can see what a fool I am whereas before, that knowledge was limited to the company. Fortunately, that lasts only two days. At meals Mower and Budge swoop down on me while Kristin and McMunn watch. They continuously ask me fruitless questions, often up to twenty, which I am expected to remember and have answered by the next meal. The questions focus on automobiles and sports, two areas that I am especially weak in. Now, instead of dropping me for ten push-ups, since I am from the class of '72, they frequently drop me for seventy-two push-ups. If I forget anything, I am ordered to collect seventy-two pieces of that item. They are collected from other plebes during my free hours and during the evening study time. The collection is left outside McMunn's room for his approval and returned to the plebes during my next available study hours. I collect handkerchiefs, a kind of brace for ties called spiffies, and nametags.

At noon meal of the third day, I am braced up, being pumped full of questions. A rhythm builds up where I thoughtlessly respond with, "I'll find out, sir," to every question asked. It is almost a chant when Budge asks, "What's your name?" The question is unexpected and causes me to pause. Before I can answer, Budge says, "Sorensen, around-the-world! Tell the world you don't know your own name!" I see myself standing at the table, facing all four directions consecutively, and yelling, "Sir, I don't know my own name, sir!" It's too much. I'd be denying myself. Budge repeats, "Sorensen, do an around-the-world!"

"Aye-aye, sir."

I hesitate.

"Sorensen, do an around-the-world! Tell them that you don't know your own name!"

I couldn't betray myself. I couldn't deny my own identity. I tense up, expecting the worst. "No, sir."

Budge becomes animated. "Sorensen, I'm giving you a direct order! Around-the-world!"

"No, sir."

"I order you to do an around-the-world."

"I won't do it, sir."

Budge pauses, puzzled. I already have one Class A offense against me. This would be the second.

"Sorensen."

"Sir?"

"Bring around a Form 2."

**

I pick up a pencil and a scratch pad to calculate my immediate future. I committed two Class A offenses. That gives me 120 demerits. Including the forty I already have, that makes a grand total of 160. 180 demerits would see me discharged from the Academy. I had already worked off the forty demerits for previous offenses. One hour of E.D. on Wednesdays if there was no p-rade (Navy for parade—marching in formation before a review board) and the three hours on Saturdays would give me four demerits worked off per week, at least until it got too cold for the p-rades. I would have to restrict as long as I hadn't worked off my demerits. That meant that I would have to be always in my room when not at a mandatory event such as a class or the required sport. 120 demerits divided by four per week yielded thirty weeks of restriction. Thirty weeks divided roughly by four weeks per month yielded eight months. I run through the months: October, November, December, January, February, March, April, May. I'd be restricting for the rest of plebe year. I put my pencil down as a sullen despair grips me. What had I done so awful that I merit this kind of treatment?

My life changes drastically. In addition to the time spent in my room, there is the addition of official harassment. When the other plebes are having weekend liberty, I make formation at the Battalion Operations Office every hour on the hour from 0800 hours to 2200 hours. Uniform inspections are held at these formations, but the midshipman officers generally sympathize with the offenders and the inspections are cursory. On very rare occasions does anyone come to my room to verify that I am there.

Secondly, my own upperclassmen have access to me at all hours of the day. I have nowhere to run to or to hide.

Thirdly, my already difficult relationship with Valdres intensifies. Now, I am always in the room except when I break restriction to collect nametags and the like. After a week's worth of restriction, our fragile camaraderie devolves to the point where we'd only help one another when it is necessary. When getting ready for formation, we still check one another's uniform for lint, and we still tuck each other, which consists of folding the back of the other man's shirt while he is wearing it in such a way that the front of it is tight and free of wrinkles.

Only two things do not change. I still skip church and I still make my phone calls home.

CHAPTER IV
THE NIGHTMARE CONTINUES

Initially, with the exception of trashing my room, the hazing isn't as bad as expected, but overnight it increases by a catastrophic amount. Budge confirms my name is on a computer printout outside of the Battalion Operations Office. The listing gives the number of demerits a mid must work off before being back in the good graces of the establishment. Budge sees that both of the Form 2's have gone through. He takes this as an official sanction for any actions he might take against me. He has a new purpose in life, a new mission. He decides to run me out of the Academy. I start living in the immediate present, moment to moment.

I am studying in my room when Budge crashes in. I snap to attention, sounding off while at the same time the second classman is screaming, "Chin in! Chest out! You've had it way too easy, or you still wouldn't be here, scumbag! Memorize all the coaches of the Academy teams! You should know them anyway!"

"Aye-aye, sir." Budge leaves the room.

* * *

Swimming gives way to boxing, which is much rougher but with a lot less muscle fatigue. My arms no longer hang limply from exhaustion, but I take a lot of beatings. Too often the three-minute bouts become two-man brawls.

I learn a valuable lesson in my first boxing class. I put on the leather gloves and headgear, wet with sweat from the previous class and stained from years of use. As suggested by the instructor, I pair off with a mid within ten pounds of my own weight. We do the warm-up exercises, practice the punches and blocks, do a little shadow boxing. My partner is a handsome blond-haired, blue-eyed idyll straight out of Olympus. He says to me, "If you take it easy on me, I'll take it easy on you." I agree. That day, each pair fights one three-minute round. My partner and I get into the ring and wait for the bell. It sounds, CLANG, and my partner is throwing haymakers all over the place. Hard, fast, wild punches fly at my head, trying to score a knockout. Fortunately, the first couple of punches miss from which I take my cue. Enraged at this breach of faith, I fight back as hard and violently as I can. The fight becomes a brawl.

***

I live each day as it comes. Each E.D., every come-around, every class, each meal, all are ordeals to be overcome as they appear. There is no tomorrow.

I am chopping down the center of the corridor, a furtive animal, a rabbit harried by hounds. In the everyday process of academy life, I must frequently pass through a corridor lined with the rooms of upperclassmen. At any moment, out of the rows and rows of doors, Budge, Mower, McMunn, any upperclassman wanting to deride a plebe, might suddenly appear, ask inane questions, and drop me for ten, or if the upperclassman is having a bad day, drop me for seventy-two. Whenever I'm chopping in the company area, my eyes go from one open doorway to another in expectation of seeing a figure step forth for the sole purpose of flushing me out and humiliating me.

Buns spots me in the corridor. He calls, "SORENSEN, wear ten T-shirts beneath your uniform for evening meal!"

I stand at attention at the sound of McMunn's voice and respond, "Aye-aye, sir." Confused, I obey the irrational order.

***

62

It's breakfast. I am filling second class glasses. Budge's eyes, gloating with pleasure, scan my uniform for glitches. Unable to find any, he comes in from a different angle. "SORENSEN!"

I come to attention. "Sir?"

"The football team!" I see that Budge is really enjoying himself. I'm a little disturbed by his attitude, but I had checked the updated roster the day before at Macdonough Hall. I am confident of my response.

"Sir, the football team is, sir, quarterback, number twenty-three, Whitaker, class of '69, sir; left halfback, number eighteen, Gold, class of '69, sir; right halfback, number sixteen, Carolla, class of '69, sir; left end, number forty-one, Fiore, class of '71, sir; right end, number thirty-one, DelSesto, class of '70..."

Budge interrupts, "What class is DelSesto in?"

"Seventy, sir."

He rejoices, "You're wrong, Sorensen!" He grins, "I saw him last night. He's been dropped from the class of '70 to the class of '71 because of grades. Come-around, Sorensen!"

Chagrinned, I answer, "Aye-aye, sir."

Why does Budge hate me? I refuse to let him run me out!

* * *

I am rushing to class. I burst from my room to hear Budge's voice from the end of the corridor. "SORENSEN, hit it for ten!"

"Aye-aye, sir!" I drop for the ten push-ups. He calls, "Stay in leaning rest until I tell you to get up!"

"Aye-aye, sir." The second classman leaves. Minutes pass. I am aware how the seconds are slipping by. I try to maintain my position, but I am weakening. My arms are burning. I call upon my reserves of will power to fight the pull of gravity. I hate to show weakness, especially before someone I can't respect.

The second classman reappears, calling, "Where are those nametags I told you to have outside my room?"

I push myself into a good leaning rest position. "I'll find out, sir."

"Come-around."

"Aye-aye, sir."

Budge pauses. "Where were you going just now?"

"To class, sir."

"Class? You got an eight o'clock?"

"Yes, sir."

"Hell! Why didn't you tell me? *Go!*"

I run out of Bancroft Hall and am late for Spanish class. The professor looks sardonically at me as I enter the classroom to take my seat. He says, "It is the policy of this campus that I'm to report all midshipmen who are late. After all, this is a military institution." I cringe. Too often the civilian professors think they're admirals. Giving me a glance full of contempt, he continues, "However, I will overlook it this time."

After class, Bemes, who is also taking Spanish, approaches me to say, "You've got to sharpen up, Sores. This is the second time you've been late. Next time he'll report you, sure as I'm standing here."

"Yeah, but it wasn't my fault. Budge dropped me for ten, then left me in leaning rest."

"How about the first time?"

I shrug my shoulders. My wandering eyes land on a copy of Rembrandt's *The Polish Rider*. The painting is of a medieval hunter on horseback. It has a pristine freshness that appeals to me. In the spare minutes before and after class, I'd often stare at it, absorbed in its dynamics. I say to Bemes, "I love that painting. I feel like I'm the rider."

Larry takes a quick glance at it and passes judgement "It's out of proportion. The horse is too small for the man."

"I like it all the same."

* * *

"Sorensen, how's the cow?"

I pick up the carton of milk to look inside. I know that I'm expected to repeat a memorized response from *Reef Points*. I deliver the formula "Sir, she walks, she talks, she's full of chalk. The lacteal fluid extracted from the female of the bovine species is highly prolific to the second degree, sir."

"Translate that for me."

"There are two glasses left, sir."

"Good. Pour me a glass."

"Aye-aye, sir."

"SORENSEN, what's up?"

From *Reef Points:* "Fidelity is up, and obedience is down on our bayonet belt buckles, sir."

* * *

Every minute of my free time is spent on meaningless chores devised, primarily, by Budge with a couple of additions by Mower and McMunn.

Mower and Budge are both at come-around. I am running every sprint while my classmates run every other race. There is barely a pause between each race, yet Budge manages to squeeze in an order. "Sorensen, you've got to win three out of four races, or you'll get a Form 3." It's somewhat of an idle threat. The only difference between a Form 3 and a word of mouth come-around is that the Form 3 is recorded on paper and is thereby made official. Although Form 3s are sometimes given for good service and an appropriate reward, they are generally given as punishment. I win nearly every race.

During one of them, I am pitted against Bob Valdres. We get the "GO" and I take an immediate lead with my roommate right behind me. Bob takes the lead at the far end when we turn, and I wonder if my roommate touched the wall. While passing the watch's desk, I hear a thud and see Valdres stumble. I pass Bob to win the race. As I run in place, I watch Valdres take gigantic, collapsing steps. The injury looks severe. Budge, disgruntled, walks away while Mower, standing next to me, screeches, "C'MON, VALDRES, MOVE IT! STOP BAGGING IT!" He turns toward me. "I thought Valdres is part Indian."

"He is, sir."

"I thought pain didn't bother them."

Miraculously, his injury cures itself, and Valdres trots toward us.

There's ten minutes left of the come-around. Budge rejoins us long enough to ask Mower to help him with a math problem. Since our second classmen are leaving, Bob and I should be relieved. As the second classmen turn their backs on the plebes, Budge is careful to spit out, "Valdres, you're dismissed. KEEP RUNNING, SORENSEN!"

I had expected something like this, so it doesn't upset me. I would have been more surprised had Budge left without a parting shot. While my roommate chops back to our room, I join another group of sprinting plebes.

Hooker, another second classman and one that I dread, stops me. He stands with his hands on his hips. His wildly frightening eyes watch the retreating figure of Budge. He shakes his head in disapproval as I realize that he had watched the whole show. I think, incorrectly interpreting his mannerisms, *God, what now?*

Hooker says, "Belay that last order. Take off."

"Aye-aye, sir," and I rush away, afraid that the wild man will change his mind.

* * *

"Sorensen, why didn't you say 'sir'?"

"Sir, sir is a subservient word surviving…" and I give the rest of the formula.

Where do I deserve senseless persecution? I become more determined. *I WON'T let them run me out!* I don't want to shame my family.

I am learning fast about midshipman honor. In boxing class, my partner is the same weight as I am, but much shorter and stockier. We're practicing left jabs and the corresponding blocks. I throw a left jab, and my partner blocks it. After several repetitions, we reverse positions. It's my turn to block left jabs. My partner connects with a right cross, throwing all his weight behind it. I am caught completely off guard and am nearly knocked off my feet. I scream in outraged surprise, "What d'you do that for?" My partner shrugs his shoulders and shakes his head as though he's as surprised as I am. We continue the exercise. I am much more wary of my partner, half expecting a repeat of his assault. It certainly wasn't an accident, yet I don't understand why my partner would have done that to me. For the next three days my jaws are misaligned. During that time, I am unable to fully close my mouth.

* * *

I am running to formation. I see a ladder (Navy talk for stairs) before me, use it, and am stopped at the other end. A firstie calls, "Plebe, what are you doing using a youngster ladder?" I then remember that only youngsters and above can use the smaller, inconspicuous stairways.

Realizing my mistake, I answer, "Sir, I thought …"

"You thought? Who gave you the right to think, mister?"

I stiffen into position. "No one, sir."

"I suggest you learn where the youngster ladders are."

"Aye-aye, sir."

"Carry-on."

"Aye-aye, sir." I chop away, considering myself lucky to have received only a verbal reprimand.

* * *

It's evening. I am chopping to Bemes' room to get an assignment. I hear Budge. "SORENSEN, hit it for seventy two!"

"Aye-aye, sir."

* * *

E.D. becomes a kind of tormented joke. Since it's the same plebes being fried all the time, it's the same faces that I see at every session. Three other plebes are there as often as I am. Among them is the slow moving, heavy set, badly coordinated Rissa, also from the twelfth. I empathize with him. Perhaps Rissa is having it as badly as I am. At least my own excessive demerits come from two Form 2s whereas Rissa is getting his demerits five at a time with all the hassle that comes with it. With a certain amount of pride, we refer to ourselves as The Runners.

* * *

It's three o'clock in the morning. The plebe watch went to bed long ago. The corridor is dimly lit. There's no movement, just the stillness. I chop to the head, occasionally breaking into a defiant walk. On my way back, I stop at the bulletin board, standing sharply at parade rest. I relax, look at the come-around board, and see the x's after my name that run to its farther end, a kind of infinity since it will never end as long as I'm a plebe. Only Rissa has as many just as Rissa is the only other plebe in the company who makes every E.D. I hear a quiet voice behind me. "Sorensen." It's soft, ephemeral. Surprised, I turn my head just enough to see Lackning's quasi-feminine features at my ear. Immediately, I brace into attention. Lackning croons, "Do you ever think you'll get off of come-around? They'll see that you never get off and do you know why? Because you're a fuck-up. You don't belong here, you and your buddies. It's too bad we only have a year to get rid of filth like you." His taunting voice is sweet, sickeningly sweet, like a drink with too much sugar. I recoil. Silence consumes the corridor. I'm not sure where Lackning is, so I turn my head slightly and catch the second classman gliding away. The soft voice says, "Carry-on, plebe." I don't answer, hoping and not hoping that Lackning notices this breech of respect.

* * *

During restriction I can spend my weekday evenings at the library, so Bob and I continue to take turns going there to avoid each other. Consequently, there is no room check which means that I can spend that time without fear of being caught in the collection of '72 of the many articles demanded by my superiors and in finding the answers to the multitude of questions pumped at me during meals. I constantly fall behind in my schoolwork and make determined efforts to catch up during the weekend restriction.

The civilian "admiral" teaching my literature course hits the class with a spot quiz on *Billy Budd*. I hadn't read the story so when one of the questions asks, "What is the Nore?" I answer, "an obscure part of the rigging of a ship." I fail the test. The next day I find a brilliant red *x* at the top of my quiz. The professor, reminiscent of a degenerate Benjamin Franklin, says in his deeply resounding voice, "It's obvious that some of you haven't been reading the material. This time I'm only going to record your grade. The next time, I'm going to report you to your company officers." It would have been kinder had he threatened to cut off our hands. The threat works. I keep up with my English assignments, but my physics, chemistry, and calculus courses suffer because of it.

* * *

It's a free period during the day and I am required to stay in my room. I'm reading when Valdres flushes into the room, drops his arms in exasperation, saying, "Are you here again?"

"What do you mean 'am I here again'? You know that I can't leave the room except for classes and required events. Of course I'm here."

"You wouldn't be if you didn't screw things up all the time."

"Look who's talking. I'm the only guy who'd room with you. Remember? *You* asked *me* to be your roommate."

"I didn't know you were such a loser."

I stand, pushing my chair back with the force of my legs. I shuffle toward Valdres and am about to swing when I catch myself. Instead, I shoulder him. My roommate stares at me, eyeball to eyeball, and says, "I'll never throw the first punch. If there's a fight, you're the one who'll have to start it. I'm not going to get kicked out for something stupid like that."

I turn away, "I'll be damned if I'm going to do it."

A sullen silence reigns.

* * *

"SORENSEN, ARE YOU BAGGING IT?"
"No, sir!"
"ARE YOU A PUSSY OR SOMETHING?"
"No, sir!"
Why are they doing this to me? I won't quit because of THEM!

* * *

69

The company is going to have a communal come-around. The twenty plebes with come-arounds gather for the morning run. The previous evening McMunn had said to me, "Sorensen, they'll be running you guys a couple of miles tomorrow. Whenever you take a corner, even if it's in the middle of a field, I want you to hit it for ten, then catch up to the others, and hit it for ten at the next corner, then catch up again and so on. Got it?"

"Yes, sir."

Roderiques, lean and handsome, is in charge. He, too, is a long-distance runner, so the pace is steady and rhythmically fast. At the beginning, I take my expected place at the head of the pack. We reach a turn, and I drop for ten push-ups. I rack them out, then sprint to the head of the column. Again, we make a turn, I drop for ten, then sprint to catch up. I am nearly at the head of the group when another corner is reached, and I drop for ten. Each time it becomes more difficult to catch up with the leaders. Eventually, I fall behind and am satisfied in managing to stay with the stragglers when I again must hit it for ten. Roderiques comes to the rear and watches me, then he returns to the front.

A straggler, Dave Husaby, stops to gag. He has the dry heaves and I remember Larry Bemes telling me that Husaby fakes it so that he can bag running. It's a convincing show and confirms what Larry, who never seems to be wrong, told me. I drop for ten.

I sprint and am with the pack again. Rissa, who doesn't have enough coordination to clap his hands, is struggling even more than me to stay up. His run is a plodding, jolting jog accentuated by deep, powerful, gasps for air. With each exhale, Rissa curses, "Oh, those bastards." He inhales deeply, exhales, then repeats, "Oh, those bastards." Amused, I smirk.

Roderiques has come to the rear again. He asks me, "Why aren't you up front with the rest of the runners?"

"No excuse, sir."

We come to a turn, and I hit it for ten. Roderiques stops to watch. When I come up, he asks, "What are you doing?"

"Orders from Midshipman Second Class McMunn, sir. I have to do ten push-ups at every corner, sir."

Roderiques grimaces, "Forget that order. I'm running this come-around, not McMunn."

70

"Aye-aye, sir."
Together, we sprint to the front of the pack.

* * *

I receive gedunk from home. When I open the package, I find homemade cookies. The last batch had been so hard that I couldn't bite into them, and I threw them away. I nibble at the edge of a cookie. It is soft and not bad tasting. I eat it and begin a second. I bite into something hard and discover a large piece of glass. My mind searches my mother's kitchen where she does her baking. One of the cabinet drawers is used as a utility drawer and contains tape, wire, a hammer, a flashlight, screwdrivers, and other odds and ends. Could a piece of broken glass have come from someone working on the kitchen counter and forgetting to clean it up? I throw that cookie away and bite into a third. I hit a screw and my mouth fills with the flat, bland taste of metal. My stomach turns and I gag. I throw all the cookies into the trash and ask myself, *what the hell's going on back there?* Briefly, for some odd reason, I think of my brother.

* * *

My classes are forgotten. I attend them faithfully, as do all midshipmen, but my energy and thought are absorbed into my efforts to combat the hazing from my second classmen.

The company is massing down the ladder toward the mess hall when McMunn asks, "SORENSEN, are those your grease or class shoes?"

I answer, "Class shoes, sir."

"This is noon meal. You're supposed to be wearing your grease shoes. Wait for me in your room after meal. Leave your shoes on."

"Aye-aye, sir."

I wait in my room. Grease shoes are a mid's best pair of shoes to be worn only at noon meals and special functions. I thoughtlessly answered what appeared to be a harmless question. I really didn't have a distinctive pair of shoes since I was careful to keep both pairs in good condition.

71

McMunn arrives with Mower and Budge at his heels. From their mannerisms, it's evident that Buns has come up with an especially clever idea. He's carrying a soccer ball. He tosses the ball into the shower and calls, "Play ball!"

The other two upperclassmen snicker when I ask, "Sir?"

"Go into the shower and play soccer. With your shoes on."

"Aye-aye, sir."

I stand in the shower and kick the ball. The upperclassmen mock me, ordering me to kick it some more. My shoes get horribly scuffed as I carry out the command. I spent a lot of time shining my shoes. I would spend much more time repairing the damage. I keep my head down. Had this assault come from Budge, it wouldn't have taken me by surprise, but McMunn, except for the first couple of days, had never been vindictive like this. My eyes water while the upperclassmen act as if they are at a party. I see the ball scuffing my shoes and am thankful that the inside of the shower is dark. I'm afraid they'll call me out into the light and see my eyes watering. McMunn retrieves the ball, and they leave as I lean heavily against the shower wall.

What if all this effort is wasted, that everything is meaningless?

* * *

Budge's voice rasps, "SORENSEN!"

"Sir?"

"Be in my room in dress blues in two minutes. GO!"

I run to my room, change uniform, then run back to Budge's room. I am barely inside when the second classman yells, "Uniform Charley. GO!"

I rush to my room and change. On my return, "Full dress blues! GO!"

Back to my room, change, and return. "Full dress whites! GO!"

This last time, Budge is looking at his stopwatch. He looks me over carefully to make sure the uniform is complete and on correctly. He says, pleased, "A minute and a half for that last change. Not bad. By the time I'm through with you, I'll be able to blink, and you'll have changed."

"Yes, sir."

72

"Take off."

"Aye-aye, sir."

* * *

"SORENSEN, why don't you resign?"

"NO, SIR."

* * *

"SORENSEN!" Budge's voice is a gruff monotone. He's about to say something he thinks is particularly funny. "Hand me your plebe kit."

"Sir?"

"You heard me. Give me your plebe kit." I am confused. "You're required to carry one. Do you have one on you?"

"No, sir."

"Have seventy-two in front of my room tomorrow morning."

"Aye-aye, sir."

Budge smiles. As our eyes meet, I almost burst out laughing. A plebe kit is a converted sewing kit in which the plebe carries needles, thread, a slip of blank paper, a dime, a pen, or anything else that an upperclassman might need. I have not seen one since plebe summer. No one carries one. It's like an officer pulling out an 1816 copy of the Army regulations and asking a soldier for his musket. The soldier answers, "But, sir, I don't have a musket. I've got an M-16." Later, the soldier giggles and dies before a firing squad for breaking regulations. I have a couple of free periods that day. I break restriction to collect the kits. They are ready in the morning.

I can't think. I need a rest.

* * *

I meet my first real live comic book hero with a real live comic book hero name, Captain Courage of the USMC. He is a big man sporting a recon haircut, almost to the point of being bald. His stentorian voice echoes off the walls and fills the gym. Courage has black belts in both judo and karate and is one of the few subjects that Bob and I agree upon; if you're in a foxhole, he's the man you want to be with.

Courage takes over the boxing classes. When the plebes see him, they're gripped by despair. They know that they'll be doing a lot of fighting.

My sparring partner is a short man with a million muscles making up in weight what I take up in height. Fortunately, we're the last pair in the ring. Courage has the class fight two three-minute rounds for that day. I see from the clock that only three minutes remain in the class and that I'll only have to fight one round. The bell rings and my opponent pummels me mercilessly. I try to block and make a futile effort at retaliation, but my opponent likes the taste of fresh meat too much to allow me to respond effectively. Time is relative. I start living an eternity. I raise my gloves and sink my head, turtlelike, between them and take the beating. I peek at the clock. The seconds seem like hours. My body sways under the force of the blows as I think how little protection headgear really gives. Finally, the bell rings for both the round and the class.

Captain Courage enters the ring and says to me, "Why are you letting a small man like that beat you when you have the reach on him? He shouldn't be able to touch you let alone give you a hammering. I want you to fight another round and I want both of you fighting!"

My heart collapses to my toes. At the bell I make a weak gesture of bravado, sink my head between my gloves, and let the conquering Achilles pound me like dough. This time I don't watch the clock. My only goal is endurance in a world of eternal punishment. But, alas, all good things must come to an end. The bell rings and I am still breathing. Courage is disappointed and shakes his head back and forth. Humbled, I escape to the showers. My tongue explores my upper lip tasting a sticky, salty fluid. Blood. My lip is split.

* * *

"SORENSEN!" Sorensen, Sorensen, Sorensen, always Sorensen when the upperclassmen want someone to deride. I hate that name. Every time I hear it, there is always some kind of pain involved. It has such an ugly sound. It means "fool".

* * *

I am in Kristin's room. I like him because he's a quiet, sensitive man. Whenever I am being grilled by the other second classmen of the squad, he stays to one side, looking at the floor, hands clasped behind his back. I had always liked him. The second classman asks, "What do your parents think of you, Sorensen?"

"I'll find out, sir."

"Do they know you're a fuck-up?"

"I'll find out, sir."

"You must have some idea. What does your father think?"

"He's deceased, sir."

Concern crosses Kristen's face. It's pudgy with a rubbery texture and sits behind horn-rimmed spectacles that make him look oddly mechanical. "When did he die?"

"Last February, sir."

"You can go, Sorensen."

"Aye-aye, sir."

That evening the flak is light. They've let up and I realize that the other second classmen must know of my father's death. However, the next day I am called into Kristin's room. The second classman says only one thing before dismissing me: "Sorensen, if you think you can use your father's death as an excuse to bag it, you're wrong. Get out of here!"

I am devastated. Every day is a battle in which my forces are annihilated. I greet each morning with dread. Heart rending anxiety, a sharp, bitter sadness, has me in its grip. Only one month has passed since the beginning of restriction, a lonely, hard month.

* * *

I am watching the antics of a second classman at another table during evening meal. He sees me. "SORENSEN!"

"Sir?"

"Are you looking at me?"

My eyes shift to the front. "No, sir."

"Are you calling me a liar?"

"No, sir."

"Then you must have been looking at me."

I hesitate because I know what is coming. The upperclassman repeats, "You must have been looking at me."

"Yes, sir."

"You queer for my body?"

"No, sir!"

* * *

It's early evening. I am sitting in a study booth in the corner of the reference section of the library. I stretch my arms, feeling the soreness in my muscles. My whole body is overtaxed. It begs for rest.

I pick up my physics book. This is one of the few study periods I have had in which to work. It's important that I study as much as possible while I have the time. I read, "Practicaluseof the highdirectivity gain available inanartificially dielectric rod antennanasused in television receivingantennas."

It doesn't make sense. I shake my head vigorously. It makes me more alert, so I reread, "Practicaluse of the highdiectivity gainavailable in artificially dielectricrod antennas has been used intelevisionreceiving antennas."

It still makes no sense. I'm too tired. My mind is dragging so I put the book down to give myself a small break. In a moment I'll feel better. Reading the graffiti on the desk where a disgruntled mid had written, "There is no such thing as gravity; the earth just sucks," perks me up a bit.

I pick up my physics book for another try. With considerable effort, I concentrate to slowly read, "Practical use of the high directivity gain..." My head nods onto my chest. When the book falls from my hands, I snap awake. My mind seems stunted, as though I'm in shock. I start again. "Practical use of the high directivity ..." My head nods. The book falls. I know that I can't afford to lose another evening of study, but exhaustion claims my body. Its demands must be met. I cross my arms, placing them on the desktop and snuggle my face into the crook of one of my elbows. I take a deep breath and feel myself sinking deep, deep, deeper onto the desk and am sound asleep before I fully exhale. My last conscious thought is that I must study.

"SORENSEN, what's an Irish pennant?"

From *Reef Points*: "Sir, an Irish pennant is an unseaman-like dangling piece of line or clothing, sir."

* * *

I'm at evening meal, braced up, butt resting on two inches of my chair. Mower and Budge are taking turns grilling me. Mower blinks a dozen times as he says, "SORENSEN, find out who the last five people to break a world record for the mile are."

"Aye-aye, sir."

Budge asks, "What's the Fosbery Flop?"

"Sir, it's a new way of doing the high jump by going over the pole with your back facing the ground."

Without pause, Mower says, "The record for the pole vault has just been broken. Find out who did it and how it was done."

"Sir, it was done using a fiberglass pole."

"Who did it?"

"I'll find out, sir."

The harassment continues while I wait to eat. During a pause I cut a piece of steak.

Mower: "Who won the Grand Prix?"

Me: "I'll find out, sir."

Mower: "Find out about the Indianapolis Five Hundred, too."

Me: "Aye-aye, sir."

I am about to put the piece of steak into my mouth when Budge rages, "DON'T EAT WHEN UPPERCLASSMEN ARE TALKING TO YOU!"

Aye-aye, sir." I put my fork down.

Mower: "What's Hamburger Hill?"

Me: "Sir, Hamburger Hill is a hill in Vietnam where the fighting has been particularly fierce and bloody, sir."

In the pause that follows, I touch my fork. Budge asks, "Who's the Prime Minister of Canada?" I am still holding my fork, so he angrily adds, "SIT AT ATTENTION WHEN AN UPPERCLASSMAN IS TALKING TO YOU!"

"Aye-aye, sir." The hand holding the fork descends, empty, to my side. There is another pause. My hand touches the fork. Budge sees this and says, "You should know who the Prime Minister of Canada is. They're a neighboring country. SIT AT ATTENTION, SORENSEN!" Again, my hand goes to my side as I wonder when I will get a chance to eat.

When everything seems quiet, my hand sneaks its way to my fork, but Budge is again talking to me. "What would you think of someone who didn't know who the President of the United States is?" My hand drops to my side. I now know that Budge has no intention of letting me eat. A plebe is not supposed to eat when an upperclassman is talking to him, and Budge has made this rule his latest weapon. I try a couple of more times to eat, but each time he interrupts me.

For three days I eat almost nothing until I get a chance to go to the Academy store where I buy boxes of chocolate and cookies to eat. A couple of days pass during which I receive gedunk from home to add more brownies and more candy to my food list. This time the cookies are good. My only real meals are on the weekend when I float away from the company area. My weight catapults from 189 pounds to 169 pounds.

Finally, a youngster standing opposite me as we are waiting for "seats" during evening meal looks at me appraisingly and, with a great deal of perplexity on his face, says, "Sores, you've lost weight."

"Yes, sir."

"How much?"

"Twenty pounds, sir."

Mower is shocked, but Budge's face wrinkles in a smile. He says, "Sorensen, I've got something that'll put the weight back onto you. Fill your plate with food. Here, have more corn. Take a larger piece of meat than that; nothing but the best for our plebes." Budge helps me fill my plate to overflowing. A mountain of food sits before me. After "seats" is given, Budge says, "You've got a minute to eat it. *Go!*" Cheering erupts from the second classmen. After a long minute of jamming food into my mouth, Budge yells, "*Time's up!*" I return to my brace. This scene is repeated at the next meal but afterwards, I am allowed to eat at every meal.

I become even more determined. *I'm not going to leave this place because of them!*

* * *

"SORENSEN." My stomach turns. Every time I hear my name it means trouble. "SORENSEN." It's Budge.

"Sir."

"Around the world. Tell them that you swear at upperclassmen."

I stand up at my place at the table, my face screwed up in hurt embarrassment, and I do Budge's bidding. When I sit down, he asks, "Why didn't you say 'sir,' Sorensen?"

"Sir, 'sir' is a…"

"Put 'sir' in between every word."

"Aye-aye, sir. Sir, 'sir,' sir, is, sir, a, sir, subservient, sir, word, sir, surviving, sir, from, sir, the, sir, surly, sir, days, sir…" and the routine goes on and on and on.

I'm so tired.

* * *

"SORENSEN." A momentary nausea like I used to get before a fight with a bully grips me. "SORENSEN." I hate that name. Every time I hear it, I want to spit. "SORENSEN." Budge smiles. "Hit it for ten."

"Aye-aye, sir." I carry out the command.

"Hit it for ten more."

"Aye-aye, sir." I do so.

Budge follows this routine for some time; ten push-ups, then ten more. Finally, he asks, "Do you know how many push-ups you've done?"

"No, sir."

"Seventy." He smiles and I go down for two more push-ups. "DON'T DO ANYMORE! THAT'S A DIRECT ORDER!"

I count as loudly as I can, "ONE, SIR, TWO, SIR! SEVENTY-TWO PUSH-UPS, SIR!" I have disobeyed another order. It's another Class A offense and will boot me out of the Academy. I wait, not really caring, for the expected order to bring around a Form 2.

Budge says, amused, "Get onto your feet, Sorensen." I stand at attention. "Why'd you do that? Do you realize the power I have over you? I can make you do almost anything I want you to do. Do you think an admiral could drop a seaman for seventy-two push-ups?"

"No, sir."

"Do you think an admiral could do a tenth of the things we've done to you to his lowest command?"

"No, sir."

"Then why did you disobey that order? When you're surrounded by people with this kind of power over you, you don't disobey them."

"No, sir."

"Then why did you disobey me?"

"I'll find out, sir."

"Do you know what I'm going to do to you now? I'm going to run you so hard that your sweat will come out in drops as large as this pea." For emphasis Budge picks up a pea that had inexplicably found its way onto his desk. He holds it directly in front of my eyes. The scene is so melodramatic, and the pea is so incongruous, that I start chuckling. Instead of the expected irate anger, Budge starts chuckling, too. We are both on the verge of hysterical laughter, so the second classman quickly says, "Get out of here." I don't get fried.

* * *

For chemistry class, I must balance the reaction when ammonia is exposed to oxygen at elevated temperatures and nitric oxide and water result. I set up the equation for the reaction by writing, "$NH_3(g) + O_2(g) \rightarrow \ldots$" My mind fails me. I have done this a dozen times. I know I can do it. I write on the other side of the arrow, "$NO(g) + H_2O(g)$." Now I must balance the equation. The atoms on one side of the equation must equal those on the other side. I count, then pause. I am *so* tired. I've been run hard all week and now I'm expected to think in a body craving rest. In addition to this, my mind is cluttered and confused by all the claptrap Budge and Mower have me memorizing. I rewrite, "$NH_3(g) + O_2(g) \rightarrow NO(g) + H_2O(g)$." *I must balance this equation.* It's simple to do, but I am exhausted. I place my pencil down, lean forward, rest my chin into my hand like the bronze sculpture, *The Thinker*, and close my eyes and spend half an hour hovering between sleep and wakefulness before I make another attempt at the problem.

* * *

"SORENSEN, how did a fuck-up like you get into this place?"
"I'll find out, sir."
"I'm going to run you out!"
"NO, SIR!"

* * *

It's evening meal and the order for "seats" hasn't been given. I sense a body very close to me, standing directly behind me. I hear a whisper and recognize the person behind me is Lackning. He croons, "Sorensen, wouldn't you like to punch McMunn in the nose?" The second classman comes closer, angling his face so that I can see it out of the corner of my eye. Lackning taunts, "Sorensen, wouldn't you like to take a swing at McMunn?"

I know that I am being bated, but I don't know how to stop it. I truthfully answer, "Yes, sir."

Lackning enlarges his voice for the whole company to hear. "Hey, Buns, did you hear that? Sorensen wants to fight you!"

McMunn asks, "You want to fight me, Sorensen?" Buns outweighs me by at least fifty pounds and is easily twice my strength.

"No, sir."

Lackning says, "But you *would* like to punch him, though. I mean, you *would* like to beat the piss out of him?"

"Yes, sir."

"Then you want to fight him."

"No, sir."

"Wouldn't you like to punch him right in the nose?"

"Yes, sir."

"Wouldn't you like to see him bleed?"

"Yes, sir."

Lackning calls, "Hey, Buns, the fight is on! SORENSEN wants to meet you in the ring. We'll set the fight for an afternoon sometime this week!"

Word spreads of the fight. I want to back down, but the more the word spreads, the more I am cemented to this act of futility. I don't want to shame myself. No one asks me for verification. It is assumed that Lackning told the truth.

Two days pass. The whole company is excited about the fight. I know that I must enter the ring and receive a beating more severe than any I have ever gotten. I'll be slaughtered. The bout is set for the next day. At the evening meal prior to it and before 'seats' is given, Buns puts an affectionate arm about my shoulders. He says quietly, "Sores, I'm not going to fight you."

Relieved, I answer, "Thank you, sir."

"You know that I would kill you."

"Yes, sir."

"So I'm not going to fight you."

"Thank you, sir."

Buns returns to his seat.

Almost two months. An eternity. Life takes on an isolated horror. An unbearable sadness dwells beneath the smooth surface.

"SORENSEN, the Brigade officers!"

* * *

If only I can make it through plebe year, I'll be okay. If only I can put up with this a little longer, just a little longer.

* * *

Rissa resigns. For the second time, Lackning goes through the ritual of shaking hands with all the second classmen during meal. I know that he would do the same for me and I resent it. I will not give Lackning that pleasure. When I return to my room, Valdres is sitting despondently at his desk. Bob asks, "If you get kicked out, where will you go?"

"I don't know. Probably home first, then I don't know."

"I think I'd enlist in the Navy."

I shudder. "Not me. I couldn't bear taking orders from these guys, especially from someone who'd been my classmate."

"I like the Navy. It's where I belong, no matter what I do."

I refrain from comment, afraid that I might explode and say things that I shouldn't say.

* * *

What's happening? Where is it all leading? Why wasn't I born someone else, someone besides Mike Sorensen, company clown, the buffoon? Why couldn't my soul be in another body or have another identity? I look at myself and know that I'm a fool. If only I could be someone else, anyone else but Mike Sorensen.

* * *

A sonorous voice intones, "You take the integral and put it here, then you add the differential, here, then you work the problem out." Thereupon, the young officer writes his musical numbers on the board in figures of magic and incomprehension.

Carefully, I copy the figures into my notebook, not understanding a word. I'm sure it's all very important, very important, as my head starts to nod, and my eyes close when Gus Hovedo knocks me awake. Immediately, I sit rigidly upright, thank my buddy, and, for Hovedo's sake, make a valiant effort to stay awake. I'll flunk this course and it's so important, so very important, and my mind begins to float into other worlds to be startled again by the ever-vigilant Gus Hovedo. My friend pleads, "C'mon, Mike, stay awake." The struggle ends when the class is dismissed. I don't think that the professor noticed me.

Eventually, I decide to get some extra instruction (E.I.). I make an appointment. Maybe, if the prof likes me, I'll pass. I attend the E.I. and solve all the problems given to me. I make no errors. The next day, the same problems are on a test. I flunk it.

Everything is so heavy. I'm not sure how much longer I can last.

* * *

I am pacing my mile run, feeling the stretch of my long legs as they pull against the fullness of the earth. It's early November. The air crisply filters into my lungs like a drink of cool water down a parched throat. All of life pulses in the rhythm of my run. Carnevale is somewhere behind me, and I catch a glimpse of Moscowitz in front. I couldn't begin to guess where the other runners are; somewhere out there, bits of dust related to me through this race. *Pain.* It's ever present in every earth-eating stride just as despair is always present, especially if I give myself time to think. *That's why it's important to keep moving. That's why faith is so important; so one can say "I am" and know all will turn out well. But then there's Budge, Mower, and McMunn. They've taught me a lot. Goddamn them!*

That day I take my eighth second place, Moscowitz having taken nine firsts. In the previous race, I had placed fourth. As always, I stagger about in a near faint, sometimes bending down with my hands on my knees. A short while later, Carnevale crosses the finish line in thirteenth place. He seems fresh although he's breathing heavily. Without waiting for the results, we start walking toward Bancroft Hall when our first class coach catches up with us and says, "We lost, but I'm still giving you gents carry-on."

Carnevale comments, "Well, that's one of us that'll get it."

"What do you mean?"

"Mike hasn't gotten carry-on since the beginning of the season."

"Is that true, Mike?"

"Yeah, it is."

"Why?"

"Because I swore at one of them."

"Oh."

Outraged, Carnevale again speaks up. "He wasn't getting carry-on even before that!"

"Why?"

"Because a second classman named Budge has had it in for him since the return of the Brigade."

84

"Okay, I get the picture. Today's Friday, so you'll at least get a break from that jerk tomorrow."

"No, he won't. The second classmen of his squad wait for him in the cafeteria to razz him at Saturday noon meals, too."

The coach's eyes flare with anger. His facial muscles tense as he says, "We'll see about that!"

The next day, after noon meal formation, the three demoniacs are waiting for me inside the mess hall doors. When I step through them, they pounce on me like harpies when St. Amand, the coach, interrupts them to say, pointedly, "Mr. Sorensen will be eating with me today."

Budge pipes up, "He's in our squad and we'd like him to eat with us."

With obvious, contained rage, St. Amand takes three steps toward them to reiterate, "Mr. Sorensen will be eating with me today. Do you gentlemen have any objections?" The last, more threat than request, has the desired effect. The second classmen flutter away in consternation. The firstie turns to me and says, "You have immediate carry-on. If those guys ever screw you again, you let me know."

I say, "Okay," but I know that I won't accept the offer.

When next I eat with my company, McMunn says, "Sorensen, how do you like hiding behind the skirts of a first classman?" I don't answer, but from the tone of Bun's voice and the reactions of the others, I realize that they're afraid. Unbelievingly, I consider this situation. My three harpies are afraid. They're afraid of a first classman they don't even know! They, the inquisitors, the monsters, are afraid! After all they put me through, it's suddenly revealed that they, the mighty, are cowards. Although they still have power over me, I see how weak they really are.

* * *

SORENSEN, SORENSEN, SORENSEN! With every calling of my name, I wish I was someone else, anyone else, except the newest pariah, Seitzer. Even Husaby is a better man than I am. A whisper sounds through the corridor. I think it's coming from a youngster's room. "I don't know whether Sorensen is the bravest man I ever met or the craziest."

* * *

I dream. *A long-robed figure who I know is Thomas Aquinas appears before me. He speaks, "There is an order to things, a necessary proportion that cannot be violated without harm."* He disappears as I scream myself awake. Bob's questioning voice calms me, and I fall back to sleep.

* * *

I sit in the upper reaches of Michaelson Hall, waiting for the young officer who looks so much like a Greek statue. He is to give me E.I. in calculus. Already, I know that I will understand the prof, nodding yes in recognition of everything he says. I also know that for some unaccountable reason, I won't retain any of it. I sit in an overstuffed, comfortable chair and notice how peaceful it is here. I wonder if I'd get caught if I took a catnap. I look at my watch as the precious minutes pass. The E.I. is at 9:00 a.m. Twenty minutes have passed since then and I grieve at the loss of precious time. At 9:25 I decide to leave when I see the professor walk through the outside doors without noticing me. I am about to follow the officer into his office but decide to use the prof's lateness as an excuse to leave. It's apparent that the professor has forgotten the appointment while I have the never-ending ordeal for acceptance.

Later that day I attend math class, hoping that the officer has forgotten me. Directly after class dismissal, I am cornered by the professor before I can make a discreet get-away. He asks, "Mr. Sorensen, where were you this morning?"

"Sir, I was in the lounge at the appointed time, sir." Politely, I refrain from reminding the officer that he was over twenty minutes late.

"I didn't see you."

"I was there, sir, but decided to leave after I had waited a few minutes, sir."

"Look, I don't know what the story is, but I have a hunch that someone is giving you the run-around back there in the Hall. When you make an appointment, you keep it!"

"Aye-aye, sir."

I am disheartened and embarrassed as the officer turns to leave. Gus, an unwilling witness, looks hurt and concerned. He says, "C'mon, Sores, get on the ball."

I stare at the floor. "Yeah, I'll try." We walk together back to Bancroft Hall.

* * *

Budge asks, "Where's your nametag, Sorensen?"

I wince as I respond, "I'll find out, sir."

"Collect seventy-two."

"Aye-aye, sir."

As soon as possible I start my search for the necessary nametags, chopping from one plebe room to another. Early in my endeavors I come across a swarthy plebe whose whole being exudes Middle Eastern beatitude. With a magnificent sweep of his right arm, like a sultan out of *The Arabian Nights*, the plebe uncovers a whole box of nametags and says, "Here are all you need." At a glance, I see a wealth of nametags and not only from the class of '72, but also tags from '71, '70, '69, and even one from '68.

I ask, "Do you think they'll accept these?"

With a subtle smile of Semitic wisdom, the plebe reasons, "Why not? They asked for seventy-two nametags and there are at least a hundred here. Did they specify a class?"

"No."

"Well, there you are."

I think of the hours of study time I can save. It's worth the risk. "Okay, I'll use them."

Although Budge had given the order, the hazing is done ostensibly for McMunn, so the next morning I leave my collection on the floor outside of Buns' room. It isn't until evening meal formation, however, when I see the results of my risk taking. My heart plummets when I see a youngster wearing the '68 tag. I listen to the tittering of the upperclassmen, reminiscent of the excitement in a school of fish when a pebble is tossed among them. McMunn is not amused. I hear that god-awful name "SORENSEN!"

"Sir?"

"Where did you get these nametags?"

"From a classmate, sir."

"Return them. Now, here's what I want you to do. You're to collect seventy-two nametags from the class of '72, seventy-one nametags from the class of '71, seventy from the class of '70, and sixty-nine from the class of '69. Got that?"

"Yes, sir."

"In addition, you're to tell every upperclassman that you ask for a nametag why we're doing this to you. I'm sure they all know who you are already, but we want to make sure."

"Yes, sir."

Again, my study hours would be taken from me. Later, during evening meal, McMunn amends, "Sorensen, don't bother with the class of '69, the other classes will do fine."

The academy has a tradition called spooning. When an upperclassman approves of a plebe, he shakes hands with the plebe and from that moment on, the two mids are on a first name basis. The plebe is to regard the upperclassman as a friend and a protector if need be. Academy formalities, such as the plebe bracing up, are suspended between them.

I discover that, indeed, I am well known throughout the Brigade. Most of the midshipmen in the class of '70 tell me to leave without giving me a nametag. A handful drop me for ten. Some even spoon me.

Nearly all of the class of '71 are gleeful and spoon me without hesitation. A typical scene goes like this. I knock at a third-class door and enter, reciting, "Midshipman Sorensen, requesting permission to come aboard, sir!" I stand, braced up, as I wait for a response.

The two third classmen are surprised. One says, "What do you want?"

"Sir, I'm collecting nametags from the class of '71, sir."

"Why?"

"Sir, I've been ordered to by my second classmen, sir. I was also ordered to tell you that I swore at one of them, sir."

"Oh, we heard about you." Both youngsters break out laughing. "What did you say to him?"

"Sir, I said, 'Fuck you sir.'"

"Let me get this straight. You said, 'Fuck you, sir.'"

"No, sir. I said, 'Fuck you,'" I pause "sir."

"Oh, you said, 'Fuck you,' without the 'sir.'"

"Yes, sir."

The third classman considers, mouthing the words "fuck you," then, with energy, he exults, "Goddamn! That takes balls! Here's my hand. My name's Bill."

The other third classman holds out his hand, too. "My name's Jonah. Anytime you need anything, just drop by."

"Sure. Okay. Thanks."

I get spooned so often that I lose track of who is spooning me. A few days pass during which I haven't yet collected the required number of nametags. One evening meal, McMunn quietly studies me, then asks, "Sorensen, what's happening when you ask the upperclassmen for their nametags?"

"Some of them drop me for ten, sir, some won't even speak to me, and some spoon me, sir."

"Do you get spooned more often than not?"

"Yes, sir."

"A lot more often?"

"Yes, sir."

McMunn thinks for a moment, then, "Sorensen, forget about the nametags."

"Aye-aye, sir."

As a parting shot, McMunn says, "Memorize last year's winners of all the Bowl Games."

"Aye-aye, sir."

***

I lean back in my chair, putting my hands behind my head. I think of the photographs of prisoners of war doing the same thing. It seems so natural and familiar that I briefly wonder about reincarnation and whether, in a former life, I had been a prisoner of war or was all this just imagination?

It's Saturday night and all the mids not on restriction, with an occasional exception of a mid with nowhere to go, are on town leave.

The noises from the corridor are rounded and soft, having lost their sharp edges in its empty spaces. The smallest sounds echo and carry to the furthest reaches of the building. A shuffling walk, the clicking of a ball point pen, serve to accentuate the solitude, one man unconsciously pointing out the absence of many.

At times, an upperclassman drops in to talk. I snap to attention, and I am immediately granted carry-on. The upperclassman starts to talk about incidentals that eventually lead to his own problems and anxieties. The odd midshipman not in town has reasons for not being there. He fumbles through words to work through a problem, made greater by the surrounding silence. My own reaction is always courteous, but fringed with foreboding since, after all, this is still an upperclassman.

For the most part, though, I spend this time valiantly trying to catch up with my studies.

* * *

"SORENSEN!" A sea of uncertainty sweeps over me. Any second is sufficient to smother me in anxiety. Nearly three months of restriction have passed. It's been a slow death into a solitude as deep as the ocean and no one realizes how slowly time can ooze like blood from a festering wound. Come-arounds become nearly intolerable. Budge, my usual tormentor, times my sprints with a stopwatch to make sure I am not bagging it. Average time: thirty seconds.

A fatal day arrives. Mower has me for come-around. As we enter the corridor, I notice that it's empty except for Mower and me. "Okay, Sorensen, hit it for twenty-five." While doing the push-ups, I listen, waiting to hear other plebes being run. The second classman continues, "On your back for fifty sit-ups." I expect other plebes to show, knowing that surely someone else must have gotten into trouble. Mower orders me to do the same number of leg raises. Hearing no noise at all, I take a furtive look about the corridor. *No one. Not even Seitzer.* "On your feet. Squat jumps." *No one.* I do the exercise until my legs are burning and lungs are heaving. "Okay, that's enough." *Alone.* "Run in place." Mower watches, then forcefully orders, "Quit bagging it! Bring your knees up! Higher! Higher!" I'm the only plebe in the company area being run. "C'mon, Sorensen, let's see some action! My grandmother could do better than that!" Mower picks up momentum. "On the floor! Crab walk! Go!" He has a stopwatch and is timing me. With my back toward the floor, walking on all fours, I waddle down the corridor. Mower becomes more energetic. "Let's go, SORENSEN! Move! Move! Move!" I listen. *Nothing.* I look around me. *No one.* "C'mon, ya pussy! Stop bagging it! Do you think you're on vacation?" I do my best. "Faster, SORENSEN! Faster!" I push myself. We pass a stairwell. No sound is floating up from the floors below; not even the plebes from the other companies are being run. "SORENSEN, I'm giving you thirty seconds to reach the far bulkhead! GO!" I'm the only one. "MOVE, SORENSEN! MOVE!" I scuttle faster. I listen. *Alone, absolutely alone.* My eyes water. *Am I that bad?* I fight the tears, but a sob betrays me. A couple of tears bubble from my eyes. Mower starts back in surprise. I sob again. I continue the crab walk as the second classman stands still, eyes wide with watching. The heavens fall. Still crab walking, I start sobbing uncontrollably. Mower is stunned. "Get up. You're dismissed."

I run to my room, thankful that Valdres is gone. I think that at that moment, I could have been broken. I reason that Mower will tell both Buns and Budge. They've seen me weaken and at evening meal they'll come in for the kill. They'll win of course, but this time I'm going to oppose them. I don't know what's going to happen, but I'm sure it'll be extreme.

At formation, I go unnoticed by the upperclassmen. I wait. They'll get me at the table. I take my place and wait. My guts are exposed, and they'll try to finish me off. I wait, but nothing happens. No one, not even Budge, says anything. A silence, almost a solemnity, descends upon the table. Apparently, I've been given a reprieve. I wait. Nothing. The second classmen lose their chance for victory.

The next morning, I am ordered to give the football team, the news, the menus for the next two meals, and Mower orders me to memorize a list of the current world record holders of the track and field events. I am relieved. I still have enough status to merit persecution. I am still their enemy. Budge even finds a small black dot on the crown of my cap and tells me to rig a new one. That means that I will have to buy a new cover and spend an hour replacing the old cover with it.

* * *

The termination of the cross-country season approaches, the last race being the invitational Brigade Cross-Country Championship. Although it's open to all midshipmen, mostly intramural runners show up. The length of the course has been doubled. We'll be running an unfamiliar race. Paul Carnevale nods his head in the direction of a strange plebe standing to one side and brooding like a fallen Titan. He says, "See that guy over there? He's the one who's going to win this race. He's from the team tables."

"He must be good."

"You bet."

A hundred midshipmen are at the starting line when a starting gun is fired, and they move ahead in one mass. I sit back in the pack, indifferent to who will win the race. Any effort on my part is futile. Nothing will change. The winner, if a plebe, is to get two weeks of carry-on. Budge would never allow that.

In a few minutes, I am in my stride. I feel good. The movement is the important thing, the stretch of the legs, the healthy working of the lungs. To enjoy the moment, I imagine myself, first, as a Peruvian Indian bringing the Inca knotted messages of a crucial battle. Then, I'm a Watusi warrior, tall and strong with a magnificent headdress. My pace quickens. I become nervous as I see myself as a soldier in Vietnam running for my life. I pass a handful of mids. I look behind me, expecting to see Viet Cong. Instead, the foliage blocks my view. I run faster and pass more mids. Fear grips me. This war game is too real, so I block the images of Vietnam from my mind. Soon, I pass Carnevale who always takes an early lead before fading. Paul exhaustedly murmurs, "Keep it up, Mike." I'm a Mohawk Indian, no, a settler running from the Mohawks. I stretch my legs further, passing more mids. I see Moscowitz in front of me and wonder what our standing is. The Titan is behind the third classman, but I see that he is fading and will die before I reach him. The Titan is passed. I now stride in step with the youngster. We're two messengers who must get through enemy lines. If one falls, the other must make it. The survival of hundreds of brave men depends on us. Moscowitz is the leader, but the pace is uncomfortably slow for me. I pass the third classman, knowing full well that the first man is the one most liable to be killed. Now I start playing cat and mouse with the youngster. Every time Moscowitz quickens his pace to overtake me, I speed up. I keep Moscowitz six feet behind me. After several attempts, the youngster becomes discouraged. I take a comfortable lead and resume my normal pace. A Rolling Stones song pops into my head and I adjust my pace to it as the refrain keeps repeating itself over and over.

I can't get no—satisfaction. I can't get no—satisfaction, but I try, and I try, and I try, and I try.

Running around a clump of bushes, up and over a small knoll, I see the finish line. I scan the crowd of waiting midshipmen for exhausted runners. I don't see any. *I must be first! There are at least a hundred mids in the race. Could I have passed that many?* Looking behind, I see that I have a good lead. Out of habit, I do a finishing sprint, thinking, "*Too much energy; I could have put more into the race.* There are congratulations, but the excitement is low key. After all, it's still only an intramural race.

I wait for Carnevale who comes in fifty-sixth. As soon as Paul catches his breath, we return to Bancroft. I am supposed to receive two weeks of carry-on. I expect none. Budge gives me a week's worth.

Three days after the race, I am called into the Battalion Office. As soon as I enter, Lieutenant Crawley, an elderly, rotund man, greets me. The officer shakes my hand and says, "Good show, excellent. You've taken a first and how many seconds? Relax."

We both sit. The lieutenant picks up a pad and pencil, poised for my response. "Um, I don't know, sir. One first, a fourth, and eight second places." The officer jots the figures down. I then correct myself "Excuse me, sir. I made a mistake. It was seven second places." The officer scratches out his original figures to make the correction. He sits back, smiling, and is about to speak, when I say, "Sir, I'm pretty sure I took eight second places." The lieutenant sits up and is about to make more corrections when I say, "No, seven second places, sir." The officer sits back and is now looking critically at me. He twirls his pencil and smiles at me. I never felt so tired in my life.

The officer puts a good face on it. He replaces his pad and pencil and says, "Let's say that you took a lot of second places and one first for the championship."

"Yes, sir."

"Keep up the good work."

"Aye-aye, sir."

"You're dismissed."

As I am chopping to my room, I try to figure out what my record is. *I'm such an idiot.*

* * *

Saturday nights take on a new meaning. Restriction keeps me pinned to my room. The corridors are so quiet they seem devoid of life. I have come to love the solitude and would feel violated should the Brigade crowd my silence. I have accepted my role as pariah, but sense that I have touched a chord that the other midshipmen are not aware of. I've been forced to look into myself. The dreaded emptiness I feared for so long has become a friend and ally.

CHAPTER V
CHRISTMAS LEAVE

s the winter settles in and the long lines of white going to class become long lines of black, I start to spend an increasing amount of time at Mahan Hall instead of the main library. Mahan is a much older building with a comfortable, dusty smell filtering from the stacks of old books. It has a multitude of nooks, crannies, and small doors placed at odd angles in the corners, giving the impression that strange and wonderful things could be found beyond them.

I especially like the walk to Mahan Hall. The winter air is pleasantly brisk and the sparsely lit walk through the dark of early evening is like a path through a romantically enchanted land, large, heavy trees on either side of a yellow-brick sidewalk with ghostly steam oozing from subterranean heating pipes. The chapel is always well-lit and is sparkling white, bound to earth by the huge black anchor lying in front of it. It is an immense, pure, apt symbol of immortality. The figurehead of Tecumseh is at the Bancroft Hall end of the walkway. Whenever I pass the stern figure, I am careful not to look at him, preferring to subject this symbol of the Naval Academy to benign neglect. Once past Tecumseh, the walk becomes immensely enjoyable.

Midway to Mahan Hall and fronting the chapel is the Mexican Monument, an obelisk that serves as a memorial to four midshipmen who were killed at Vera Cruz during the Mexican War. I try to imagine the sense of tragedy which their deaths must have caused, the family mourning, the authorities sympathizing. In my mind I hear the speeches, how they were the pride of the Academy, the best the country had to offer. They had such promise. They would have done great things, all four of them. But I know better. I envy them their early deaths. One of them might have been an incompetent fool, but a piece of shrapnel made him a hero instead. Their premature deaths forestalled any defeats that may have awaited them. They need not ever prove themselves worthy. Their battle was over before it began whereas I still have my battle to face. I read the names again, Clemson, Hynson, Pillsbury, Shubrick. They are only names, a piece of rock with printing on it. Yet, I couldn't help thinking, *they were damned lucky, though, damned lucky,* as I see myself flunking out of school and, in disgrace, being propelled into the Vietnam War.

Once at Mahan, I rummage through the rows of ancient books, enjoying their smell and the texture of their aged covers, like so many worn lives turning to dust with me trying to catch them before they disappear forever. The magazine rack is so poorly stocked that I am not even tempted to daydream my way through it. Unfortunately, my imagination finds an outlet in the many ship models lining the passageways. They had been constructed from bits of bone and wood by prisoners of war in the time of "iron men and wooden ships." The pulley systems on these replicas work. I spend hours before these models, wondering what life aboard them must have been like. I imagine seeing a man keel hauled and watch another man braid the leather cat-o-nine tails that would later be used to whip him. I remember how I felt when I was whipped. I pause. I see my outstretched arms flung up as though trying to embrace the sky. My head hangs limply backwards over a back seared with the red zigzag stripes from the whip. I remember how badly my back burned. I think, *there I go again. This can't be real. It must be my imagination, but then, why is my memory of it so vivid?* Meanwhile, with every voyage thus taken, my grades sink lower and lower.

* * *

When Christmas leave arrived, the midshipmen from Rhode Island decided to fly home together. With excitement static in the air, the mids packed for home, the plebes carrying large, overstuffed bags and the upperclassmen carrying only overnight bags. The handful of Rhode Islanders piled into a taxi, talking animatedly of what they planned to do.

When they reached the airport, they ran to the long lines for their flights home.

I found myself increasingly uncomfortable in large crowds. Half a year ago, I saw masses of people as containing promise and vitality, hidden Einsteins and Shakespeares waiting for the chance that would bring them to the forefront of history and thought. Now, I distrusted these masses since I knew that among their inconspicuous numbers were people like Budge, Mower, and McMunn who were only too ready to explode in vindictive arrogance. I had yet to meet an Einstein, but I had already met a Budge.

My brother, Bartholomew (Buddy), picked me up at T.F. Greene Airport. He gave me a reassuring handshake that failed to convince me that all would be well. The physical make-up between us was nearly identical except that I was light featured with straw-colored hair and greenish brown eyes while Buddy's hair was a rusty red above sparkling blue eyes accentuated by his darker skin tone. He was much the larger of us two. Our mannerisms parodied one another. We both had the habit of crossing our arms, belly slightly extended, hips thrust forward, when standing for any length of time. We both had long strides and swayed our arms and shoulders when walking.

The first thing I noticed after bag pick-up was the sharp, cutting cold and the deep snow. It was dark and the parking lot lights, spaced to seem isolated, were apt images of forlorn hope. My brother drove and was full of questions that I answered with "all right" to keep him from finding out how badly I was doing. Then, he discussed his own work in cancer research. He told me that great intellectual revolutions were taking place in science and that he intended to be at the forefront.

When the conversation lagged, he asked, "Did anybody hassle you at the airport?"

"What do you mean? The Hari Krishna guys?"

"No, the draft dodgers, the war protesters."

"No."

"You're lucky." A deeply bitter tone entered his voice. "When I came back from Vietnam, a good-looking woman, young and beautiful, gave me a paper bag and when I looked into it, it was full of dog shit. I went to war thinking I was a hero and came back in disgrace. Believe me when I tell you that had there been a land bridge between the United

States and Vietnam, there would have been another crossing of the Rubicon."

As we approached the more familiar roads that I had traveled hundreds of times, Buddy said, "I wish you were in Vietnam with me. You would have done well. When I planned ambushes, I needed someone like you to tell me if I missed something or to give me help."

I found his confidence in me embarrassing and murmured, "Thanks."

He picked up on the tone of my voice and added, "You have an aptitude for things like that. Things like that don't bother you."

The closer we got to Meantacut and the Plat, the more wooded the landscape became. The yellowish car lights cut a tunnel into the dark with the ice-encrusted snow lining its lower edges. Thin, gray tree branches reached down from above. Both of us were lost in thought when my brother resumed, "Mom lets me read your letters." Immediate shame and outrage filled me, but I kept quiet. "You've got to stick it out. I know you think you're failing the Academy and us, but maybe the Academy has failed you." Buddy snickered. "I can't believe you're flunking out. *You!* Of all the people in the world, you're the last one I'd expect to flunk out of anything."

"Well, it happens."

The conversation faded to be replaced by casual, incidental comments from minds wading deeply in their own reflections. Buddy said, "Beth might be beating on Mom, but I'm not sure. I remember what she used to do to you when we were kids, before we left the Heights. Boy, you had it rough."

I looked at my brother and saw his sharp silhouette outlined by the dark window. Beth was six years older than I was; when she was twelve years old, I was six and small for my age. "It didn't bother me, not nearly as much as everyone thinks it did. We used to fight about once a week and that gradually petered out as I got older, especially after we moved to the Plat. We had our moments of kindness too."

Buddy dropped me off at the front of the house and, once I had my bag, he left too quickly for me not to notice the fugitive way in which it was done. It was then that I saw that neither the driveway nor the front walk had been shoveled. More aggravating still was the knowledge that tomorrow morning, I would be shoveling a foot of snow for at least an hour instead of relaxing and enjoying my stay. I giant-stepped to the breezeway door as cold and snow invaded my low quarter shoes in wet clumps and my uniform was soaked up to my knees. Mom was at the door, waiting to receive me. "Hi, son, it's good to see you. We've missed you so much."

I sighed. "I guess Buddy is too busy to shovel the driveway."

"I'll call one of the neighborhood boys."

I said what I knew my mother expected, "No, I'll do it."

Overjoyed, Mom said, "It's so good to see you, son."

When I entered the kitchen, the family's dog, a Weimaraner given to my mother by a neighbor, was ecstatic, jumping up with his forelegs hitting my chest and nearly knocking me off my feet. I was happy to see the dog and scratched him affectionately behind the ears. I crooned, "It's good to see you, sure it is. You're a *good* boy." After a minute of this, I said, "Okay, Baron, let me by." I stumbled and pushed my way past the dog.

Beth was standing at the far side of the kitchen table, both wanting to greet me and waiting for me to notice her. As I walked past her on my way to drop my bag in my bedroom, I said, "How ya doin', Beth?"

"Okay."

I tried to notice any difference in her. She had gained weight from her medication. Other than that, she seemed no different than before I left.

I threw my bag onto the floor and changed into my heavy winter clothing. I decided to clear the driveway tonight before it had time to freeze and to unpack the following day. Mom called through my door that Cora would be in tomorrow afternoon to see me. She added, "Ruth's pregnant."

I called back, "Who's Ruth?"

"You know. That girl."

"What girl?"

"The blonde."

"Mom, there are fifty million blonds in the world and I'm sure they're all wonderful people. Which one do you mean?"

"The one going out with Darren."

"Darren who?"

"Seltzer."

"I don't know any Darren Seltzer."

Mom thought that I was intentionally aggravating her. "Yes, you do! He was an orderly at Meantacut Hospital the same time you were! He used to work in intensive care!"

"I don't know any Darren Seltzer and I don't *want* to know any Darren Seltzer. I don't know every orderly in the universe. How am I supposed to know who he is? He's just a name to me."

"Well, I thought you knew him."

"Well, I don't."

When I was fully dressed, I made a search for my gloves. While doing so, my eyes alighted onto a small plastic figurine, an antelope that Beth had bought me years ago. It had been one of my favorite toys even though its antlers had snapped off within the first week of possession. The animal had a slender, muscular build that I found beautiful. It occurred to me that it must have cost my sister a child's fortune to buy it. I picked it up and was flooded by memories of me and my two sisters walking miles from the project to Main Street to buy coloring books and other children's treasures. I remembered our long walks and how wonderful it was to spend the day together. I found my gloves and left to shovel out the driveway and front walk.

* * *

The following afternoon, Cora and Buddy and their respective families visited. Cora was married to a Polish American factory worker named Stanley. He and I were opposites but worked well as a team. Whereas I was an insatiable reader, Stanley was good with his hands. He knew more about the habits of trout than I would ever know. However, he lacked my finesse so that when the two of us went fishing, I always caught the limit after my brother-in-law led me to the trout, whereas he never caught the limit. It was inexplicable why he liked me so much. Even before marrying my sister, he always gave me gifts for no other reason than to give me gifts.

Buddy's wife, Anne, was from Newport and was presumptuous in that she considered herself better educated and better bred than the Sorensens. She had married an upwardly mobile, charismatic, Marine

100

Corps captain and found herself among the children of factory workers. She was educated in Europe and liked to salt French words and phrases into her conversation for the benefit of her ignorant brethren. Physically, she was short and petite with what seemed to be a subdued Asian look due to multiple national origins, in that she had black hair, high cheekbones, olive shaped eyes, and a forever tan. She wore thick black glasses that made her look like a fourth-grade schoolteacher.

The whole family wanted to know what Academy life was like and how the youngest son was doing. They gathered in the living room. I sat in a chair that had a broken support so that I couldn't lean back on it. While Cora's two children and Buddy's two played in the middle of the floor with a box of my old toys, the adults sat in a large circle formed from the couch and three chairs. I told them about the harassment, Budge, and my restriction, wondering if my voice and body language were conveying to them how bitter I was. My mother continually interrupted me by frequently repeating, "We're so proud of you, son." She beamed with happiness. No matter what I said about the Academy, she still thought it was a wonderful place and an honor for me to be there.

Buddy, not to be outdone, joined in with his own stories about Marine Corps training. He told of a recruit who had been caught by his drill sergeant eating ice cream. The sergeant ordered him to put the ice cream into his pocket. When enough time for it to melt had passed, the drill sergeant had the recruit retrieve it from his pocket. Since the recruit had a cold, the ice cream had been absorbed by a much-used handkerchief that was, by chance, in the same pocket. The recruit held up the handkerchief and asked, "What do I do now, Sarg?" to which the sergeant answered, "Suck it off!" Buddy told the story with such relishing humor that everyone laughed. He added, "It sounds much worse than it was. It was harassment, but everyone saw the humor, even the guy who ate the ice cream. No one means to hurt you, Mike. Someday, you'll laugh about all this stuff yourself."

I said, "The harassment at the Academy isn't meant to be fun."

Mom said, "Son, you feel this way because you're still going through it. When it's over, you'll look at it differently."

"Hasn't anyone been listening to me? You don't know what that place is like, or you wouldn't say these things. What am I doing, talking to walls? Don't believe everything you see in the movies or read in the papers."

Throughout the discussion, Anne sat demurely, quietly reading a *Psychology Today* magazine that she had brought with her. Stanley and Cora sat listening and offered no comments. When the group split up, Anne perked up to offer her own comment. "Mike, we're so proud of you." I was unable to read from her expression whether she was being satirical or not. After several combinations of goodbye, she and Buddy left for home with their two daughters.

Stanley and Cora lagged behind with their daughter and son. While Mom was at the door waving goodbye to Buddy and Anne, Cora faced me and said, "Mike, you do what you want to do. We're all proud of you, but if you want to leave that place, don't let anyone con you into staying."

Her husband added, "The way I look at it, you only have one life to live, and you should live it the way you want to."

When the visitors had all left, I asked Beth to make me a coffee. I did this so that I could tell her that she made the best coffee in the world, the best that I ever tasted. It made her happy which, in turn, pleased me. I then sat in my favorite corner of the couch, pulled out of my rear right pocket a paperback copy of *Heart of Darkness* by Joseph Conrad and began reading. I was careful not to put the book down or to let the dog see me daydreaming. Otherwise, Baron would know that I could be approached for petting and, since the dog had no limits, the dog would mercilessly rub against me, all eyes and loving tongue, and all my efforts to read would become futile.

The family reconvened on the afternoon of Christmas Eve. Cora, Buddy, and their families gathered to share in the holiday abundance of turkey, cranberry sauce, mashed potatoes, gravy, squash, pumpkin pie, and the joy of people genuinely fond of each other. Buddy's personality towered over the others with its vivacious glow. He always said the right thing at the right time while I tended to say things just a little off skew and never elicited the right response.

As was to be expected, excitement ran high, and a small crisis developed when everyone except Beth and I migrated into the living room. I remained behind to snack on walnuts and slowly sip my coffee. Beth, meanwhile, was clearing the table. The television and talk in the next room were loud, making the kitchen seem like an oasis of calm. My mood was becoming more and more contemplative.

When it was time to put the turkey away, Beth put it into a large white plastic Tupperware container. She forced the bird in, then closed the lid. It popped up, so she shifted the bird and pressed down the lid again. It popped up.

With a nutcracker, I crushed a walnut with a loud CRACK! Beth started and I saw that she was annoyed by the noise. Again, she pressed down the lid, then let it go. It came up with a loud POP! She cursed, "Darn it!" Becoming passionate, she mauled the bird into an acceptable shape and pressed down on the lid. POP! I placed the nutcracker down onto the table's surface.

I sipped my coffee and saw that even this soft noise bothered her. She fought the bird. I took another sip which animated her. "OOOOOOOOOO, this stupid thing!" She pounded the corpse with her fists. She pressed down on the lid. POP! I placed my coffee cup onto the table.

When the situation was about to peak, I said, "Here, Beth, let me help you with that." When I stood up to help her, she became quiet; the raging seas of a moment before became a placid lake. I bent a few of the bird's joints and then successfully closed the lid. I was mutely impressed since I hadn't thought that the turkey would fit into the container. I said, "See? It's not so difficult," then I left to join the others in the living room.

At 10:00 that evening, the family started getting ready for the Christmas Eve service which began at 11:00 p.m. I donned my full-dress blues and admired the tight fit. My shoulders were wide, my hips and waist narrow, and the uniform accentuated these good points. I wondered if the double row of brass buttons cutting down the front of the black uniform were garish, but the family assured me that I looked splendid. Flash bulbs snapped in the increasing commotion. I heard a familiar refrain from my childhood when I heard Cora yelling, "C'mon, Buddy, quit hogging the bathroom!" while the Scrooge on television was in a similar panic at seeing the ghost of his dead partner. Buddy answered Cora in his high, screeching giggle just as Marley wailed mournfully and rattled his chains. This was a momentous occasion for all of us. My family saw in my uniform the visible and outward sign of success. They, as a group, were "getting up in the world."

We piled into two cars filled with pleasant anticipation like children running to their Christmas presents. Mom and Beth rode with Cora and her children, Stanley having remained at the house, while I sat in the back of my brother's car with their two children. Anne neglected to pull up the seat in front of me, but I didn't mind although my long legs were curled nearly to my chest. The thick winter clothes, the packed bodies, and the warmth of the car contrasted with the empty bleakness seen outside the protective cocoon of the car.

Fifteen minutes later we arrived at church. The desolation of the dark, cold streets made the warmth and light of the church that much greater. My entrance into church was a small triumphal march. Like Caesar, I marched down the aisle with my small army behind me. Childhood enemies proffered hands that weren't open to me half a year ago. To them, I was well on my way to power and success. I did my best to be politely proper. I was careful not to trip on the thick rug on my way to communion. Everyone could see how graceful and handsome I was. Mr. Rota, an Academy graduate from forty years ago, was crying.

Uncharacteristically, the family took a pew in the middle row and toward the front. I attributed this innovation to Anne since she and Buddy had only recently moved to Meantacut and become church members. As soon as the service began, I was immersed in nostalgia and tradition. I loved the Anglican mass with its archaic language reaching into the past.

It wasn't long, however, until I became aware of some unusual behavior. In the pew directly behind us was a young lady of about my brother's age. She sat with an elderly woman and two young men who I thought must have been her brothers. Occasionally, she leaned forwards to talk with a great deal of loud whispering to someone in my own pew. I sat between my mother and Anne. On Anne's other side sat Cora who, oddly, sat between Buddy and his wife. Cora seemed annoyed at Buddy who I discovered was the object of the whispering. Like salt and pepper, the children were sprinkled among the adults.

It was obvious that I was expected to know the young lady, but I couldn't recall who she was. At one point, she leaned towards my mother and said, "You must be very proud of your sons."

Likewise, Anne was behaving in an unusual way. She clung to my arm as though we were special friends, compatriots with deep secrets between us. Continually, Anne whispered to me. I couldn't hear what she was saying but nodded my head "yes" as though I could and hoped that she would soon leave me alone to enjoy the service.

Trying not to be noticed, I glanced several times behind me. Initially, I hadn't seen clearly enough to make any judgements, but the walk to and from the altar for communion revealed an exceptionally attractive woman with golden hair and a well-proportioned body. Her breasts, legs, and hips were full while her waist was narrow. Her face was beautifully handsome without a blemish. A dimpled smile served to decorate her smiling eyes. She looked healthy, intelligent, and happy. Anne made a poor showing next to her. The two women made me uncomfortable.

After an hour and a half, the service ended, worship giving way to the excited electricity of the holiday. I caught several of the milling parishioners taking subtle glances at me. The girls in their teens were thrilled which in turn thrilled me. Buddy whispered at the back of my ear, as though I was thinking it instead of hearing it, "It's like being a stud bull, isn't it?"

* * *

I spent Christmas Day reading on the couch. Occasionally, I'd go to my bedroom to read while Beth watched a Christmas special on television. My sister was happy, so I didn't have to move too often. When Beth wanted to watch TV, she'd sit near me so that when I looked up, she'd be directly in my line of sight. I took the hint and, since my sister was considerate enough to keep me supplied with coffee, I, in turn, looked through the *T.V. Guide* to let her know when the specials were on. I left the room to her, knowing that she'd relinquish the room back to me once the show was over.

Snow had fallen during the night which justified a small ritual that I performed once the family moved to the Plat, which was adjacent to Lauman's dairy farm. After every snowfall, I left birdseed at favored places in the woods. I no sooner decided to take a walk when Baron crawled halfway onto the couch and put his head tenderly onto my chest.

105

I asked, rhetorically, "How do you know? What gives me away?" The dog looked at me with his large, loving, amber eyes. "You think you're going along, huh?" Baron pressed his head against me. "I think it's sickening the way you suck up to me when you want to go out." The dog licked my hands. "Well, all right. Let's go." Using me for a starting block, the dog leapt into the middle of the room, dancing joyfully.

The snow, an accumulation of several snowfalls, was thick and heavy. I bundled up so that I looked twice as large as I really was. I slipped a couple of ten-pound bags of birdseed into a knapsack and started for the woods. The snow was deep, and I was forced to take huge ungainly strides, the rhythm of which was interrupted when Baron, who was following me, stepped on my heels. The two of us worked our way into the fields and woods of the farm. At key points, such as a favorite clump of trees or a small break in the woods, I left small piles of seed for both the squirrels and birds. At one spot I found the remains of a feeder which, like all the other feeders and birdhouses that I had built, was destroyed by the callous boot of a passer-by, maybe a hunter, maybe a farmer. I had camouflaged my best birdhouse with a covering of bark, but that fell to a hunter's shotgun, just as a feral cat I had befriended was also gunned down.

As I continued my journey, my exertions heated my body until it was comfortably warm. I took off my gloves and undid the top button of my coat. Exulting in every step, I imagined myself as the strong man surviving in the wilderness, a mountain man and the spiritual brother of Davy Crockett and Daniel Boone.

I climbed a small hill decorated with thin, gray maples, their arms lightly waving and brushing invisible air currents. Pockets of stunted oaks reminded me how poor and rocky the soil was in this area. Bullberry vines scratched against my trousers and the thick growth of blueberry bushes tried to trip me up. A fat roosting ruffed grouse catapulted from a thicket, wings whistling as, with the dexterity of a fighter pilot, it weaved its way through a maze of branches.

The hill was the back of an abandoned quarry. When I reached the hill's ridge, I was on a cliff overlooking the quarry on the other side. The wind had freed the ridge from its layer of snow so that Baron and I moved freely. As the dog ran along the cliff top, I looked ahead of him for patches of ice that might hurtle the dog over the edge. Satisfied that the dog was safe, I looked at the land below me.

The black rock of the iron ore quarry contrasted well with the white snow and gave the boulders sharp, irregular outlines. In level areas, the snow was covered by an almost imperceptible shiver of gold caused by meadow grass that managed to grow between the crushed rocks and reach above the layer of snow. Further out was pastureland, divided by stone walls lined with maple, oak, and hickory trees. In the corner of one of the fields grew a copse of wild cherry trees topped by winding strands of wild grapevines. Every summer in late August, I perched in the cherry trees and feasted on cherries and Concord grapes until I could eat no more while Baron spent the time flushing up quail and ring-necked pheasants that hid in the raspberry bushes that lined the stone walls. I could see a thin black line haphazardly cutting through the fields and knew it to be a stream where the cows watered and where I had caught spotted turtles. Nearby was a cow pond where Bobby Greensweit claimed to have seen Danielle Bissette skinny dipping.

This good land warmed me and made life beautiful and well worth living. It had been sold to a developer named Steven Laporte. When asked what he intended to do with the property, he answered, "Speculate." The bright orange surveyor's tape hanging from the limbs of the trees and bushes filled me with foreboding. I was unable to imagine houses and asphalt roads in the place of these fields.

I walked to the point where the cliff peaked. The air was crystal clear, the scene below me pure. I thought, *this must be how an eagle feels; this must be what it feels like to be blessed.*

* * *

The days following Christmas were in sharp contrast to those spent at the Academy. They were days of casual activity. In the mornings Buddy picked me up, drove to the University of Rhode Island where he was involved in a research project, and left me in a carrel to study chemistry from a self-help book. The afternoons were spent with walks in the woods and weightlifting. The evenings were for short chilling walks to Cape Cod Creamery for coffee, reading, and watching the young waitresses.

Anne was a frequent visitor when only Beth and I were home and Mom was working at Meantacut Hospital as a nurse's aide. She was constantly fluttering about the house. While never actually doing anything, she was the one person in the house who appeared to be the busiest. At times I wondered what she was doing there.

One afternoon, I was in the cellar lifting weights. I had worked up a good sweat in the two hours I'd been exercising. Anne came down for a couple of minutes to search through empty boxes and crusty, dried out paint cans. I stopped exercising and awkwardly stood, bare-breasted, wondering if I should put on my T-shirt. My sister-in-law hummed her way through the large room, smiled at me, then skipped up the stairs. As soon as she was gone, I finished my workout, annoyed at the interruption.

I went upstairs to treat myself to a glass of grapefruit juice and to go to my room to rest. While walking through the kitchen, I slipped on my T-shirt, expecting to find Anne, but she wasn't to be seen. Once in my room, I stretched on the bed belly down to enjoy the pleasant tiredness of a good workout. I would have fallen asleep had I not heard a noise behind me. Turning my head slightly, I saw Anne out of the corner of my eye. She pulled back, saying, "Oh, I'm sorry. I didn't know you were here."

Not changing position, I responded, "That's all right." I heard the crinkling of the bedsprings in Beth's room, which told me that she was lying down. I closed my eyes and would have fallen asleep except that I became aware that Anne hadn't left my room. She was standing by the bed and watching me. Raising myself partially into a sitting position, I asked, "Am I in your way?"

"No. No. Stay where you are. I have some cleaning to do in the kitchen." After she left, I closed the door.

* * *

I spent a lot of time observing Beth. Something was askew at home, but nothing occurred to enlighten me. I watched her heavy body sway soundlessly through the kitchen to finish the quart of soda opened that morning by Mom. When Beth thought that I wasn't watching, she'd haphazardly glide into one of the bedrooms to make a brief search and then glide silently out after I gave an intentional warning cough to tell her that I was nearby. If Mom and I were having a conversation, Beth sat mutely between us, eliminating herself as a topic. Should Mom and I be in a room with the door closed, I would suddenly open it to find Beth a few feet away preoccupied in cleaning the area or straightening out the stacks of paper on the nearest level surface. Then she'd walk noiselessly away. Yet, these were old habits, certainly annoying, but nothing to worry about.

Now, however, she talked to herself which she had never done before. I would hear mumbling, a long pause as if waiting for an answer, then more mumbling. She seemed to be talking to someone and it sent chills through my spine. I'd hear, "Mike's back from school...I like it when he's here...Because I feel safe...He's my brother," and she'd forcefully nod her head yes as if strongly agreeing to something said to her. At other times her words and sentences were all jumbled together, becoming indistinguishable. They'd erupt from her faster and faster until I entered her room to ask, "What did you say, Beth?" She'd look down on the bed and say, "Nothing." Then she'd be quiet for an hour or so.

One evening while Beth was bathing, Mom and I were watching a *Leave It to Beaver* rerun. During a commercial, I asked, "Why does Beth talk to herself?"

"I don't know."

"I don't see why you're always so upset on the phone if all she ever does is talk to herself."

Mom gave me a pleading look but said nothing as I collapsed into an overwhelming sense of inadequacy. She wanted help and I wanted to give it, but I had to know what was wrong before I could respond. Verging on absolute despair, I demanded, "Look! Spit it out! What's the problem here?" I waited, frustrated by her silence. She opened her mouth, but the words lost themselves before they made intelligible sounds. I couldn't make sense of it. I heard my sister wallowing in the tub as I waited. Finally, I crossed my arms and turned my attention to the Beaver. "Never mind."

Beaver's father was so wise and his mother so understanding. They didn't smell or burp or do any of the human things. They always knew what to do, unlike my own parents who had often made mistakes.

Today's episode was one I remembered from before plebe summer. Wally was buying a new suit and his parents were wisely guiding him into making the right choice. How would Ward and June Cleaver have handled Beth? How would they have handled her one and only date, a boy named Steve? He, too, had been mentally challenged. Steve's brother had driven him to the house and, while Beth and her "date" watched television, the brother and my mother talked at the kitchen table. I had wandered from one room to the other, curiously watching. Beth and her date didn't speak at all. Neither did they hold hands or seem even aware of one another. They were too shy. Eventually, the evening died as did the date and the two brothers left for home. The next day after school, Beth sat by the telephone waiting for a call from her beau. The whole evening, she waited, leaving her phone watch only to go to the bathroom. During supper, she took her plate of food, placed it on the counter next to the phone, and ate there. When it was too late to expect a call, she went to bed. The next day she followed the same pattern, and the next day and the next. For two weeks she waited expectantly, hoping that a thread of wire and electrons would connect her with romance. She sat hunched on a kitchen chair and waited. During the third week, she started to heave heart-rending sighs. She would leave the phone fifteen minutes at a time, but always returned for a vigil of two or three hours before leaving again. I had nothing to say or any hope to offer. After the fourth week, she gave up hope and her silent vigil ended. The call never came, and no one ever mentioned the date.

Now, years later, I wondered what Ward and June would have done. Undoubtedly, Beth would have learned some profound lesson about shattered hopes and unfulfilled dreams. She would have become a wiser and better person for her patience and suffering. I imagined Ward saying, "Beth, we all must accept our defeats. You'll understand this when you grow up." I thought, *maybe, but it still hurts.* How would Ward and June have handled the bullying she and her friends received at school?

* * *

Before I returned to the Academy, Beth gave me one last surprise. I was in my room reading when the quiet of the house seemed unnatural. Mom was at work, but my sister was home and there should have been *some* noise. I went into the kitchen. It was dark since it was late afternoon of a winter's day. I flicked on the lights and found her sitting at the table and crying. I asked, "What's wrong?"

She said, "I'm different."

"What do you mean?"

"I'm different. I'm not like the other kids. I'm not like you and Buddy and Cora."

"So? Do you think we're better than you?" I waited for a response. When it didn't come, I continued, nodding my head toward the window, "Do you think anybody out there is better than you? You're crazy if you do. There's nobody *better* than you." I became angry and knew that I was no longer talking only of Beth but of myself as well. I defended us both. "There's nobody *better* than you. They might think they are, but they aren't. In fact, I suspect that you're better than ninety-nine point nine nine percent of them!" I boiled with rage. What right had Budge or *anyone* to do that to me? *Who are these creatures? Where do they come from?* "Do you know how much that is?" She shook her head no. "That's a hell of a lot! Now let's see if there's anything good to watch on TV."

As we went into the living room, I added, "Beth, if I could choose anyone I'd want for a sister, you're the one I'd choose." Although she was a little happier, I certainly wasn't.

* * *

The day before my return to the Academy was somberly dreary due to a mixture of rain and sleet that had been falling all morning only to be replaced by freezing cold toward the afternoon. Baron and I stepped out under the icily frigid, clear sky to spread our bounty of birdseed for the last time.

The rain had melted most of the snow, so the walking was easy and enjoyable. The starkness of the landscape, the thin gray trees, the withered yellow grass, the bare stone walls, filled me with a warmth that could hardly be expected from their harsh appearance. The barrenness signified the promise of spring, a dormant potential waiting for the right moment to burst forth in all its splendor.

The first mile the dog and I stayed in the fields. Then I decided to take a shortcut through a patch of woods. I made a small detour to look at a sapling. From its shiny gray bark, I knew it was an American chestnut. Its diameter was about three inches. It rose vertically for four feet before it cut sharply into a horizontal line. At that point, shards of wood jutted up like a scream from sharp, ragged teeth. I touched the jagged, white edges. Taking a closer look, I saw small lead pellets and plastic wadding wedged into the wood. I guessed the weapon to be a twelve-gauge shotgun at a range of two feet. "Nice shot," I grunted and resumed my course.

As I approached a stone wall, I stopped short, causing the dog to run up to me to find out why I had stopped. Amazed, I stared at the stand of trees before me. Each tree, every branch, was coated with ice as though the copse was in the land of fairies. I reached out and touched a branch. With a slight gasping noise, the ice clattered to the frozen earth. I knew that soon the sun would reach these shadows and the wind would begin to blow and cause this balanced beauty to disappear. I could end it all now by simply walking through and disrupting the order of the branches. It would save me fifteen minutes. Besides, there was no one else to see this. I said to Baron, "Let's go around," and we circled around the doomed, soon to perish crystal forest.

* * *

On the way to T.F. Greene Airport, I said to Buddy, who was driving me there, "I call home every Sunday and it's becoming brutal. Sometimes Mom cries when she tells me how hard it is to control Beth, but other than Beth talking to herself, I don't see any big problems. You don't think she's going after Mom, do you?"

"Maybe. I don't know."

"I get really depressed after each call, but when I tell Mom that I want to cut back on the calls, she practically begs me not to, that it's the highlight of her week. It's really tough, but I figure that as long as Baron is there, Mom should be pretty safe."

Buddy asked, "What happens when he's outside?"

112

CHAPTER VI
A BID FOR FREEDOM

Metal and exhaust fumes characterized my progress to the Naval Academy. First, there were those of the car that took me to the airport. Next, there were those of the aircraft itself and, finally, the metal and smell of the bus from D.C. to the school. Add the noise and hurry in conjunction with my apprehension and the trip was an understandably unpleasant one. With my gradual approach to school, I saw more and more midshipmen coagulating at the points of transport. Generally, the mids teamed up in small groups of three or four, often with complete strangers with the only thing in common that they were all midshipmen. I knew that eventually I would join one of these groups. During the shuffle from one place to another, I saw a plebe who had grown a goatee. I was envious of such ripe fruit since I had yet to grow a real whisker. Shaving every morning was a requirement at the Academy, so every morning without exception, I ran a safety razor over the bare chin of my face, knowing that at any time I might be asked if I had shaved. What amazed me though was that the plebe was able to return that way. Not even God could save me from upper class fury should I return sporting a goatee.

Once at the Academy, I noticed a distinct difference in the behavior of the upper class. The Christmas holidays fulfilled them somehow, making them happier and less vindictive. I was no longer a focus of hate. They asked me for my rates and let it go at that. It would have been a simple matter to give me the handful of demerits that would have propelled me out of school, but no one espoused that cause. I thought that maybe I had proven myself, yet the doubt remained. I still couldn't relax. I needed positive proof that I had shaken off the hounds.

In the middle of January, two changes took place at the Academy. The first was a reprieve from working off all the remaining demerits for Form 2 offenders. A British admiral was visiting the school and announced to the Brigade during noon meal, "I would like to thank you, as representatives of the United States, for all you have done for the British Isles and for all you are still doing for us. Above all, I would like to thank you for all you do for our daughters." Raucous laughter seethed through the midshipmen ranks. The admiral continued, "In honor of this occasion and because of the friendship between our two countries, I have requested and been granted the ability to give all Form 2 offenders a reprieve. There will be no more restriction and what you call E.D. for past offences."

There was general rejoicing from the upperclassmen and smiles on the faces of the plebes. However, I felt no joy. I had been under restriction for over three months and, although I appreciated the gesture, the damage had already been done. Restriction became more of a habit than a punishment and my bitterness intensified in the coming months once I had time to think things out. I was indifferent to the admiral's generosity.

The other change that took place was the rotation of upperclassmen in each squad. Bob and I were assigned to the second classmen with the worst reputations. Diels, Hooker, and Deichgraber were all bad, but Kruke was insane. Like Hooker, he had wild, excitable eyes that sent chills down plebe spines. I knew that Budge, for all his vindictiveness, was no match for Kruke in pure madness.

* * *

One day, shortly before the takeover, Diels and Deichgraber enter our room. Diels has a weak smile topped by a pair of small, beady, snakelike eyes. He exudes a certain reptilian emptiness and is as personable and captivating as a salamander.

His roommate, Deichgraber, is a funereal figure. His head hangs like a vulture's head. He is unpleasantly grim, even when joking, and he always wears a scowl. He speaks softly, distinctly, and with a low whine.

114

Immediately, I sense the change in atmosphere when the two second classmen enter the room. The plebes sound off. Deichgraber cut it short by giving Bob immediate carry-on but leaves me braced up at the window. He walks up to me and pulls me bodily so that we are both looking out of the window. The second classman sneers, "You're a fuck-up, Sorensen." I remain quiet, so Deichgraber repeats, "I said, 'You're a fuck-up, Sorensen."

"Yes, sir."

"You pull any of that shit like you pulled on Budge and the boys and I'll have your ass."

The nightmare is there, waiting for me. *Was it all to start again?* My eyes water as I respond, "Yes, sir."

"Are you crying, Sorensen?"

"No, sir."

"Don't lie to me, Sorensen. Are you crying?"

"No, sir." *How much more can I take?*

"I could get you on an honor offence. Now, are you crying?"

Tears well in my eyes. "No, sir."

Deichgraber faces Bob. "Valdres, you see what a fuck-up your roommate is?"

"Yes, sir."

Diels watches, amused, but makes no sound. As the upperclassmen are leaving, Deichgraber calls over his shoulder, "Carry-on, Sorensen."

"Aye-aye, sir."

When they are out of the room, Valdres turns on me, "I can't wait 'til we change roommates!"

I continue to look out the window of the stone monolith of Bancroft Hall. I think, *I can't either.*

* * *

From that moment on, the harassment for me all but died out. It's as though having lived through the plague, I gained a certain amount of immunity. Having survived plebe summer and the brutal harassment of my first semester, I had gained a little reprieve.

Diels hardly existed for the plebes, and Deichgraber limited his harassment to chow call by making the plebes in his squad continually repeat the menu. He'd stand directly in front of the worried plebe and stare at his lips as he blurted out the menu, uniform, and place of formation. As the days progressed, Deichgraber and the plebes became more familiar with one another and the chow call devolved into a contest to see who could keep from smiling first, Deichgraber or the plebe. Despite the friendliness of the game, the plebe was aware of the second classman's power and never crossed the line to friendship.

Diels, on the other hand, would enter our room, say something cryptic like, "Russians eat a lot of cabbage," then just leave. He was like a disembodied spirit searching for a place of rest.

Kruke's only aggression towards me was to have me get a recon haircut (Navy for a severe brush cut). Although I complained to the other plebes about getting a recon, I was inwardly pleased since my brother, Buddy, had the same kind of haircut in the Marines. Only Hooker took an active interest in the plebes and focused most of his attention on me.

* * *

Although the members of each squad had been shuffled to form new units, Bob and I were still roommates and, as such, in the same squad. That situation had not changed at all. I did my best not to show hurt when I asked Valdres what the yellow blocks on his schedule meant. He answered, "Those are the periods you're out of the room." So, at the very start of the new semester, the hostility between us was resumed.

When John Boatman visited me, the first words to escape his lips were, "Oh, I see you're still with the wetback. I had hoped that maybe he'd died over leave, but no such luck." Bob sneered at the Southerner. John's eyes sparkled with merriment as he continued, "Is Valdres telling you about his ancestors?" Then without waiting for a response, he added, "Oh, I believe they fought at the Alamo all right, but the question is, which side?" Bob jumped up while Boatman waited for the Mexican American to assault him. After a moment of hesitation, Valdres violently swept up his cap, slammed it onto his head, and, glaring vindictively at John, stomped out of the room. The Southerner stood solidly on his feet,

116

smiling, as he listened to Bob chopping down the hall. Then he said, "I guess that got rid of him."

"John, you shouldn't antagonize him like that."

"Why not? He deserves it."

"For all his faults, he's still my roommate and he's suffered a lot of collateral damage because of me."

* * *

My second classmen posed another problem. They were new personalities, and I didn't know what they expected of me. Except for Hooker, they took only cursory interest in the plebes. As soon as an opportunity arose, Hooker gave me a come-around. My heart took a nosedive, and I knew that I had another savage, unknown quantity to confront. That evening I arrived at his room wearing gym gear. During the first semester I had witnessed Hooker brutally running Seitzer and assumed that it was now my turn. I entered the room and sounded off. The second classman was sitting lazily in a chair, dressed in a T-shirt, white trousers, and a pair of shower shoes. He had curly blond hair, a heavy build, and a mischievous demeanor. The power underneath the soft, relaxed muscles reminded me of the pictures I'd seen of the child-god Bacchus.

Kruke was bent over the sink, washing the top of his cap. He was nearly half the size of Hooker. His nervous mannerisms made me wonder how he had made it this far. Kruke straightened his back and turned to look appraisingly at me and spit out venomously, "Look at that bum! Just look at that lousy bum! He ought to be run out! He's just like Seitzer!"

Hooker puckered his lips in consideration, then said with sibylline calm, "No, he isn't."

"Yeah, he is. No better than Seitzer! They both oughta be run out!"

Hooker kept eyeing me. "He's nothing like Seitzer."

Kruke resumed washing his cap while Hooker looked speculatively at me for a good five minutes. Finally, he asked, "What kind of grades do you have?"

"Bad, sir."

"How bad?"

117

"Very bad. I'm flunking, sir."

"What's your cume?"

"One point five, sir."

Hooker paused, then, "Do you fall asleep in class?"

"Sometimes, sir."

"Budge ran you pretty hard, huh?"

"Yes, sir."

He rubbed his chin in thought. "From now on you come here for come-around. Don't go anywhere else."

"Aye-aye, sir."

"Bring your books and syllabi with you."

"Aye-aye, sir."

From that moment on, I was forced to have my assignments completed, not for class, but for Hooker. I was afraid that, should I bag it, the second classman would turn on me and treat me as Seitzer had been treated. Every day I went to him for come-around and submitted to a question and answer session based on my schoolwork. If he was satisfied, the second classman marked an "OK" on the syllabus next to the assignment. He was always satisfied with me because I was afraid of the consequences if I went to come-around unprepared. The deep pit into which I had been thrust was now getting shallower. I began to hope.

Hooker had his own theories of education that he tried to impart to me. When I complained that I didn't understand the material that I was reading, he said, "Don't worry about not understanding it, the professor will clear it up. Do the assigned work and let things follow their course. Besides, I think you worry too much about grades. You're so busy trying to figure out what to do to get a good exam grade that you're missing the whole point of education: to learn. If you learn the material, the good grades will come of themselves."

I stood at attention during the whole come-around, but I saw the borders of another world. He continued, "I hope you realize that the more you read, the better off you'll be. When you come across a reference to, say, Rutherford, you'll know who they're talking about."

The second classman sat on the end of his spine with only the upper half of his back touching the back of his chair. "If you're reading a particularly difficult author, stick with it. Each writer has his own language that the reader must learn. The first time you read an author, he might not make any sense. The second time, he'll be a little clearer, and the third time, he'll be as clear as glass.

"And let your unconscious or whatever it is work for you. I remember when I had to read John Locke for my philosophy course. I thought, 'Man, this boy don't make no sense,' but the next day I was talking to someone, and I quoted him. It was then that I realized that my mind had deciphered him without my even being aware of it."

Hooker was pleased with his small lectures. He'd ask me if I had any quizzes and prepared me for them. Later, he wanted to see the grades. They were getting better.

After a month, he said, "See? Learning isn't so bad. It only takes a little application. In fact, it's kind of fun, isn't it?"

I murmured, "Yes, sir."

"You don't seem too sure. What's wrong?"

"Well, sir, I really don't think I'm learning anything."

"What do you mean you're not learning anything?"

"Well, sir, I'm learning a lot of things like formulas and things, but they don't seem to have any meaning. It seems like such a waste."

"What do you mean it's a waste? By saying that, you're saying that everything is meaningless and that's just not so. It's all related. Take math. You might think it's irrelevant, but everything you do, every move you make, can be broken down into mathematical formulas from sending a man to the moon to picking your nose."

"Yes, sir."

"Chemistry. That formula for celluloid I had you memorize. Here." He lifted the cover of his desk blotter. "This is celluloid. So are the negatives of photographs and the reels of movies. There's celluloid going to the moon with every space shot. It's all in that formula. It's all part of a working whole."

"Yes, sir, but there's something else, something that's lacking."

"Look. I don't care if you think that something is lacking. You can worry about that once you have satisfactory grades. Then you can afford to," he paused, then stressed cynically, "contemplate the Universe if you want to. Until then, do your work, okay?"

"Aye-aye, sir."

* * *

119

With one exception, my professors for the spring were a nightmare of boredom. It wasn't that I was bored with the subject matter; the professors seemed bored with it. They were bland creatures who, like deep-sea fish, lived in a colorless world. The exception was my English professor, Lieutenant j.g. Brinton, who replaced the constipated monolith of the first semester. He had raven-black hair topping an intelligently Hollywood-handsome face from which peered clear, compassionate eyes. Although he was from Georgia, he betrayed no sign of an accent that would indicate his Southern birth. More importantly, he seemed to be discontented, a victim of a huge disillusionment. At odd moments, such as when he read poetry or spoke of values, a hurt look invaded his fine features as a halfhearted smile traced its way across his face. Once he even said, "I'm going to resign from the Navy when my commission is up," which confirmed his apparent discontent and made his students wonder why anyone would give up such a promising career.

Even more so than Hooker, Brinton seemed to have the key to unknown vistas and had built himself a magnificent structure of knowledge. He, too, saw everything as being related and life as a continuum, a great chain of being. Peter, Paul, and Mary became a part of the continuum of poetry coming from Medieval England and prior to that from the short, hacking poetry of the Anglo-Saxons. Brinton also had the distinction to be the only Naval Academy professor to give me a compliment, telling me that my writing style was like that of Hazlitt, an author we had read for class. He suggested that the class read Loren Eisely's *The Immense Journey*. I did so. The only flaw I found in the man was one that only I would have considered a flaw, he could talk sports.

Toward the middle of the semester, Brinton suggested that the members of the class see the movie *Charley*. Saturday afternoon was the only chance I had to see it, but, unfortunately, it conflicted with an important lacrosse game against a university I never heard of. I weighed the chances of an upperclassman asking me if I'd gone to the game and decided, since it was Saturday and I wouldn't see my own squad until Sunday night, that I'd catch the movie.

The plot of the film is of a retarded man who becomes a genius after an operation but who later reverts to his former life when the results of the operation prove to be temporary. With every word spoken, I was reminded of Beth. Along with Charley, I touched the pathos of her situation as well. The movie deeply disturbed me, especially the last image of Charley on a swing with his one-time girlfriend watching him.

After the movie, I returned to the Academy in a profoundly reflective mood. At evening meal, I floated and found a table with a couple of third classmen presiding over it. One of them looked pointedly at me. The youngster asked, "Mr. Sorensen, did you go to the lacrosse game today?"

I stiffened my brace. "No, sir."

"What event did you attend?"

"None, sir."

Alarm in his voice. "None?"

"No, sir."

"What did you do?"

"I went to see the movie *Charley,* sir

A quiet rage. "Brace up, mister."

"Sir, I am braced up, sir."

"Are you questioning me?"

"No, sir."

"Are you being a wise ass?"

"No, sir."

"Pull in your chin."

"Aye-aye, sir."

"Farther."

"Aye-aye, sir."

"Stay that way for the entire meal."

"Aye-aye, sir."

The other youngster said, "I didn't go to the lacrosse game either. Are you going to make *me* brace up?"

The first youngster looked at the second youngster with accusing eyes, then turned toward me to reiterate, "Stay braced up! Got that?"

"Yes, sir." I pulled my chin into my neck as far as it would go while doing my best to look worried. The first youngster, to show his contempt for renegade plebes, gave the other plebes at the table immediate carry-on without questioning what event they had attended. Sullen hostility formed a pall over the group of mids. No one spoke and as soon as the first youngster was done eating and left the table, the second youngster gave me carry-on, but the meal was nearly over by then.

* * *

I shared a physics class with Larry Bemes, the finest midshipman material the Academy offered. I was proud to be seen with him and pleasantly surprised when Bemes started walking to classes with me. I'd hear him chopping down the hall, calling a touch louder than the other plebes, "Beat army, sir," whenever he squared a corner, then his tall figure would block the doorway. "Ready?"

When I looked at Bemes' freckled face, I'd smile to myself, remembering a small incident from plebe summer when Bemes, Fred Meade, and I were roommates. Shortly before a room inspection, the three of us had been spot checking the blinds, drawers, and shower area for any sign of dust when Roderigues marched peremptorily into our quarters. Without pause, the second classman pulled a desk drawer out, took it off its runners, and placed it on the desk. Then he ran a white glove along the runners and revealed smudges of black grease that we had missed. This gave Roderigues an excuse to rant and rave about how sloppy the room was. As he looked for other signs of dirt in the otherwise spotless room, Roderigues stopped and stood squarely in front of Meade. He said to him, "I want you to tell me by evening meal how many freckles Bemes has on his body. Count them with your tongue." Roderigues resumed cursing and searching. He left but was back in five minutes. He said, "Meade, belay that order about the freckles."

Together, we chopped out of Bancroft Hall. Once outside, Bemes always fell into a large, distance-eating stride. He carried himself like a jaunty old sea dog, swaying his shoulders from side to side as though he was on the deck of a rolling ship. When we met officers, Bemes' salute always snapped. If he was questioned, his answers were abrupt and to the point, like a stiletto right to the heart of the matter. I loved to walk with him and, like Pinocchio, imitated his stride and swagger. When I was with him, I felt like a lion. Sometimes he took a hard, evaluative look at the sky, and said, "Looks like rain."

I then held out my hand, rubbed my fingers together, and said, "Feels like rain."

He sniffed. "Smells like rain."

Flicking my tongue, "Tastes like rain."

Turning his head to one side, "Sounds like rain."

Then we said in unison, "Naw, but it's really going to be a *fine* day," and both of us would burst out laughing.

* * *

As the days deepened into spring, the earth began to blossom. Mockingbirds were busy singing while the huge tulip trees fronting Bancroft Hall began to burst with leaves. Wednesday afternoon p-rades where the whole Brigade marched to Worden Field recommenced as did classes on the yard patrol craft. The Academy changed from their dark blue uniforms to whites, making my world visibly lighter.

On the day of the uniform change, I went to Hooker's room for come-around still wearing gym gear although I expected to study. I entered the darkened room in time to see the second classman plunge from his bunk to the sink to vomit blood. I stood in startled attention until Hooker turned toward me to garble, "I've had my wisdom teeth pulled." His hands cupped either side of his swollen jaw. "Is your work done?"

"Yes, sir."

"Okay, take off."

I left the room and, in transit to my own, decided to visit Boatman with the extra half-hour just given me. As I was chopping to my destination, I spotted Boatman and Seitzer standing in the middle of the corridor, wearing only their jock straps. Before each plebe was a squash ball piled high with shaving cream. From what looked like a starting line, a double row of upperclassmen mostly, surprisingly, third classmen, formed a gauntlet fifteen feet long ending at a towel serving as the finish line. I had no idea what was about to happen, but whatever it was, I knew it would be good.

I hopped into Boatman's room where the door and the events taking place in the corridor were angled in such a way that I could see them without them readily seeing me. The plebes stood with their arms hanging limply by their sides, heads hanging despondently, eyes on the verge of tears. The whiteness of their bodies glowed under the harsh artificial lights, reminding me of skinned fish.

The group of youngsters fidgeted in anticipation. They whispered excitedly to one another until one of them yelled, *"Go!"* Immediately the two plebes squatted onto the balls, amidst the enthusiastic cheering of the youngsters, and tried to jam them, without using their hands, into their buttocks. Both squirmed furiously, flopping about the floor like dying sunfish. I chuckled. Finally, Boatman extended his long legs before him, putting more pressure onto the ball. When it was positioned exactly where he wanted it, he tightened his buttocks, crooked his legs like a grasshopper, and slowly, ever so slowly, got onto his feet. He rightly concluded that any movement of his buttocks would cause the ball to abort. Therefore, he stiffened his legs, tightened his butt, and tried to hop, stiff legged, to the finish line. All this was done to the background of the upperclassmen frantically waving their arms and screaming for their favorite. John hopped forward, but halfway to the towel the ball dropped with a thick thud. Again, I chuckled. John paused expectantly, wondering what to do, when a youngster yelled excitedly, "Hey, Boatman, do you know what you have to do now?" He stood still. "You have to begin all over!" Peals of delight hurtled from the upperclassmen as John made fists of his hands, his face lifting agonizingly towards the ceiling, his entire body straining at the humiliation, an Atlas having dropped the earth.

I chuckled, being as quiet as I could be. John was brought back to the starting line to, again, squat onto the ball. I laughed. I could see the mute anger, frustration, and shame on the scarlet, haggard faces of the plebes. Their muscles seemed flaccid. The flesh on their faces hung. Their movements were halfhearted, stilted efforts as though they were dead men brought back to life. I stifled a guffaw and walked to John's shower stall where there was no chance of being seen and exploded into uncontrolled laughter. I was laughing so hard that my stomach hurt. I crossed my arms and bent at the waist to relieve the pressure. I peeked out of the room at Seitzer and Boatman, returned to the shower stall, and laughed as the tears streamed down my face. I looked again only to go back into the shower stall and cackled until I couldn't breathe. It was the funniest thing I had ever seen. Yes, I was happy now. This was proof positive that I made it. Two months ago, that might have been me out there. I was no longer a target.

By the end of the come-around neither plebe managed to cross the finish line with his precious cargo. When they were released, Boatman angrily ran into his room to be greeted by a much-bemused Sorensen. I said, "Hey, John, that was quite a show you put on."

Boatman turned his fury onto me. "Don't you *ever* mention that again!" I warded off the anger with a shrug of my shoulders and made a discreet exit.

Seitzer resigned and returned to the shacks of Appalachia. The following day, Lackning, who hardly knew him, went the rounds of upperclassmen, shaking their hands in victory.

While watching these shenanigans, I had made an important decision; I decided to leave the Academy, and I danced with relief. The more I thought of it, the better I liked the idea of departing from that hated place. The only difficulty was admitting to myself how very much I really did hate it. It seemed like sacrilege, but the uniforms and glory weren't enough for me to hide my true emotions.

The following weekend, after our initial greetings over the phone, I said with deliberation, "Mom."

"Yes, son."

"I've been doing a lot of thinking."

"About what, son?"

A pause. "I want to resign."

"What do you mean you want to resign?"

"Just what I said. I want to leave this place."

"Why?"

"I hate it here."

"But in your letter, you said that you had made it."

"That's right. I've made it. I've proven myself, and now I want out."

"But you've come so far. Think of what you'd be giving up."

"What?"

"Your whole future."

"Bullshit. I hate it here and I want out! You don't know what it's like here."

"But you've got such a little way to go now."

"I don't care. I don't like it here. I'm not happy here and I want out."

"Promise me one thing."

"What?"

"Before you do anything, wait until I talk to your brother."

"Why? He's not my father. I don't see what he has to do with any of this."

"Just promise me that one thing, okay?"

I smelled the trap. Then, hesitantly, "Okay."

"Promise me you won't do anything until I get back to you. Do you promise?"

I considered a moment, praying for a sudden insight that would help me escape the web. Instead, I answered, "Yeah, I promise." Already, I knew what the outcome would be.

A few days later I received a letter from my mother telling me that she and Buddy would be down to visit me the following Sunday. When they arrived, I was pulling First Regimental watch as a runner (messenger). Midshipman Second Class Kristin was the midshipman officer in charge of the Regimental Office. Lt. Earling was the Officer of the Day. I had known that I would be on duty that day but hadn't filled out the proper chits to be relieved. I knew that, had I done so, the Academy authorities, the Machine, would have denied it. Now, I was forcing the issue and was calling their bluff. If Earling excused me for the day, all well and good; if he did not excuse me, it was one more example of Academy callousness. Either way, I couldn't lose.

I had already pulled two hours of watch and was in my room during a scheduled break when I received a note telling me to report to Lt. Earling, ASAP. I hustled into my uniform and quickly walked to the Regimental Office. Upon my entrance, I sounded off while a chill ran down my spine. This was the first time I met Earling. Before me sat a composite of Scrooge and Sad Sack. Earling looked like a satire, crunched over his desk, chits and forms piled on either side of him. Staring at the officer's balding, domed head, designed to ward off all original and intelligent thought, I wondered with a dreadful shiver what kind of home life can such a man have.

Earling looked up and said, "Your folks are here."

"Yes, sir."

"Did you know they were coming?"

"Yes, sir."

Earling fidgeted and took a sharper look at me. "Did you fill out the proper chits?"

"No, sir."

"Why not?"

"No excuse, sir."

"Did you know that you would have to fill out some chits?"

"Yes, sir."

"And you didn't?"

"No, sir."

"Why not?"

"No excuse, sir."

"You must have a reason."

"No, sir."

Earling glared grimly at me. "Where are you from?"

"Rhode Island, sir."

"That's how far from here?"

"Four hundred miles, sir."

"And your folks drove all that way?"

"Yes, sir."

"And you didn't bother to fill out any chits?"

"No, sir."

Earling paused to study the plebe before him. "Send Midshipman Kristin in. You wait outside."

"Aye-aye, sir."

I delivered Earling's message, thinking how much Kristin's face had the rubbery, rounded look of a toy baby doll with as much expression as that doll. I couldn't help but like what I thought was his quiet reserve. While the second classman was in Earling's office, I observed the other plebes working at the large, room-length desk cluttered with phones and logbooks. They were aware that something was happening, and no one seemed surprised. A couple even smiled at my blank, uncaring face. When Kristin re-emerged, he said, "You can take off, Sorensen. You've got 'til evening meal. Lt. Earling wants to see you before formation."

"Aye-aye, sir."

I turned to leave, but Kristin stopped me. "If it was me, Sorensen, I wouldn't have let you go!"

Since I was relieved of duty, I chopped to the rotunda. Once through the double doors that hid the interior of Bancroft Hall from civilian eyes, I settled into a fast walk that carried me to my mother and brother who were standing spellbound in the middle of the impressive rotunda dome. Buddy greeted me with a handshake and a sad smile. "How're ya doin', Kid Mike?"

"All right."

My mother gave me a bear hug, looking very worried as she greeted me with intensity and feeling. "Hi, son."

"Hi, Mom. Let's get out of this dump. Let's talk somewhere off base." I led the two of them in a fast retreat from Bancroft Hall. Once at the car I said, "Plebes aren't allowed to ride in cars."

Mom pulled back and said, "Then we'd better not take it."

I snorted. "No, let's take it. I don't think we'll be seen as long as we stay out of Annapolis itself. I don't want to go into town because I don't want to see any middie-pukes."

"Middie-pukes?"

"Yeah, that's what midshipmen call themselves, middie-pukes."

"Are you sure we should take the car?"

"Honestly? I don't care if I get caught or not."

We all sat in the front seat with Buddy driving. My brother suggested, "I spotted a rest area on the way in. Maybe we should go there to talk."

I rejoined, "That's fine with me."

The rest area was nestled between the arms of the highway, one going to and the other from Annapolis. It overlooked the Academy which, from a distance, looked like the fabled Camelot. Struck by its beauty, I found it hard to believe that I was associated with it in any way.

Buddy stayed in the vehicle while mother and son walked to a rampart facing the school. We disturbed an elderly couple sitting in their 1969 red Mustang. Both had bluish gray hair and were dressed in the blue jeans and T-shirts of their younger contemporaries. They didn't look like a married couple, there being nothing sedate in their mannerisms.

With motherly concern, Mom asked, "What's the matter, son?"

Out of the corner of my eye, I saw the man bend over his partner, leaning toward the center of the car and jacking up the radio. Jimi Hendrix formed an accompanying background to our conversation. I half listened to the Dylan song as Jimi sang, *There must be some kind of way out of here…*

Talking over it, I said, "I want out; that's all."

"Why, son?"

"I hate the place."

There's too much confusion; I…

"Look how beautiful it is."

"Beautiful or not, it stinks."

None of them along the line…

"You'll be quitting if you resign."

"What's wrong in leaving a place, quitting if you like, if you hate it?"

During the guitar interlude, Mom continued, "You'll be haunted for the rest of your life for this—this—failure."

"I doubt it."

"Is there anything good about the Academy? Can't you find something good about it?"

"Yeah, some of the guys are great, but the place itself is rotten." The aging Romeo jacked up the sound of his radio in his effort to drive the Sorensens from the overlook. *NO REASON TO GET EXCITED…*

Annoyed, Mom raised her voice so she could be heard by me. "DIDN'T YOU TELL ME LAST WEEK THAT YOU MADE IT?"

…THAT FEEL THAT LIFE IS BUT A JOKE…

"THAT THEY WEREN'T GOING TO DO ANY MORE TO YOU?"

The knight in the Mustang turned down the car radio to argue with his ladylove.

"Yeah, that's right."

Mom asked, "So why do you want out?"

"Because I hate it! Don't you understand? I hate it there. I have nothing more to prove. You don't know what it's like. You wouldn't believe the crap that goes on in there. All that beauty and prestige you see is bought at a price."

The knight in the red Mustang jacked up the radio yet again in another effort to drive us off. *ALL ALONG THE WATCHTOWER, PRINCES...*

Mom raised her voice again. "YOUR FATHER WOULD HAVE BEEN SO PROUD OF YOU." I waited for the tears, but, to my surprise, she walked away. I heard our car door open, a few mumbled words, and the firm step of my brother crunching on the gravel.

SLAM! The people in the red Mustang opened and slammed a car door as a statement of outrage at the disturbance my family and I caused in their lives. Failing to drive us away with loud music, they gave us one last, spiteful look and left the rest area with squealing tires and plumes of exhaust smoke. Their sudden departure made the resultant silence seem uncanny, as though a natural order was disturbed by the lack of abrasive noise.

"Kid Mike, what's the story?"

"I hate that hellhole!"

"Is it the hazing?"

"Yeah, it's the hazing, among other things."

"Damn! If only it was me instead of you going back, I'd show them. If only we could exchange bodies for a while, I'd show them what a real military man could do!"

At first, I wondered if he was serious, then I saw the visionary sparkle in his eyes. A smile cracked my lips. "What the hell could *you* do?"

"For one thing, I wouldn't show any emotions. I'd take the best punch they had and never even wince." *Is he joking?* "Remember Valhalla? How the gods and heroes feasted, knowing full well that they were doomed to destruction, how they were determined to die fighting?"

"I've already died fighting. I've had it with Budge and his pals."

"C'mon, Mike. Don't let them drive you out."

"They haven't driven me out. I'm leaving voluntarily. I want nothing to do with the place."

"Mike, we can be the first. You and I can start a whole new tradition. From this moment on, all male members of the Sorensen family will become Marines." Buddy clenched his fists like Scarlet O'Hara. "We must endure!"

I chuckled. "So must a rock. Boy, are you full of crap!"

"But it's glorious crap."

Now that I was laughing, Buddy knew that the battle had been won. It would now be an easy matter to manipulate the recalcitrant midshipman. He shot the determining bolt. "Do me a favor. Stick it out until you finish the semester. Then you can decide what you want to do."

"You mean that you and Mom can decide what I want to do."

"You don't have anything better to do. What's another couple of months?"

"They can be an eternity, but I suppose you're right. I've nothing better to do, at least right now. Who knows; maybe I'll even come to like the place, but I doubt it. I'll do what you want me to do, but I won't like it."

"I'm not asking you to like it, just to give it another try."

"Okay." I was overcome by a sense of doom. I got the message: don't resign, no matter what.

During the entire conversation, I had been looking at the white, granite bastions of the Academy. Maybe I was wrong about it. Maybe I wasn't seeing the whole picture.

The rest of the afternoon was spent sightseeing along the shore roads of the Chesapeake. Shortly before evening meal formation, I returned to Bancroft Hall and reported to Lt. Earling. After we had exchanged salutes, the officer asked, "Mr. Sorensen, how was your afternoon?"

"Fine, sir."

"You realize that you left us a man short, letting someone else do your job for you."

I thought, *I could almost give a shit*, but answered, "Yes, sir."

"Did you make any decisions when you were with your parents?"

"Yes, sir."

"And what was that?"

"I decided to stay, sir."

"Oh, I see. Do you like it here, Mr. Sorensen?"

"Yes, sir, as well as can be expected, sir."

"What do you mean by that?"

"I like it here, sir."

"Yes, well, you're dismissed."

"Aye-aye, sir." We exchanged salutes and I was out the door as quickly as possible. From the hall clock I saw that I had less than five minutes to make formation. I snapped into a fast run but covered only ten feet when the three-minute bell rang. Moving as fast as I could, I lunged up a youngster ladder, realized that I was breaking a taboo, and retraced my steps to resume my run to another ladder. I was almost at formation when the bell sounded. As I hopped into line, Kristin leaned slightly forward of the squad line so he could see me and said, "Where've you been, Sorensen?"

"Lt. Earling kept me, sir. I was barely out of his office when the warning bell rang, sir."

Meal passed without more ado, but afterwards, an alarmed youngster ran into my room. "Sorensen, you better write everything you did after leaving Earling; I mean everything! Kristin gave him a call and Earling says that he gave you plenty of time to make formation! They're gonna try to get you on an honor offence!"

I shook my head unbelievingly. "I don't know. I just don't know."

The youngster waited as I did as he suggested. I gave my testimony to the youngster and began studying, annoyed by the incident, but oddly unconcerned about its outcome.

An hour passed after which Kristin came into my room to angrily throw my report onto my desk. The second classman said, "Sorensen, you ought to know by now where the youngster ladders are!" He was about to leave but stopped short to add, "I was going to tell you what Lt. Earling said about you, but never mind. It would hurt you too much."

I couldn't care less what Sad Sack had to say about anything. However, the subtleness of Kristin's attack, the cryptic insinuations from a second classman that, despite previous experience, I liked, did hurt. Kristin scored another hit, making me feel even more inadequate in the face of overwhelming odds than I ever felt before.

CHAPTER VII

THE LAST DAYS OF PLEBE YEAR

My spring sport was squash. Carnevale and I had signed up for it since it wasn't recruited for and, therefore, would have fewer stars. Again, we were on an intramural team. The intercollegiate teams had been organized the previous fall, and we were no match for the plebes who already had half a year's practice. We walked to the courts together, practiced together, and walked back together. During a match, we waited until our respective games were over, count the wins and losses, and leave the courts to the echoing roars of competition.

At first, I saw squash as just one more unpleasant duty required by the Academy. I went through the form of playing and felt sorry for the mids who tried so hard to win. Often, I played a little softer, made a few little mistakes, to let my opponent win. The only games I tried to win were the ones where my opponent was so bad that losing would be disgraceful. Then, at such times, my opponents claimed that I went crazy and made a terrific comeback to capture the win.

Soon, I started playing my own private games in the court. I liked to play close to my opponent, staying in front of him until the last moment and depriving him of free movement and a good view of the ball. I enjoyed throwing my opponent off balance by hitting the ball at odd angles and with unexpected force against the walls.

As the season wore on, I found myself spending more and more of my time in the muted banging and stifling heat of the courts. It was the one place, other than the library, where I could be safely alone during my off-duty hours. Once I closed the door of the court, the Academy ceased

133

to exist. Although I continued to practice with Carnevale and, at times, with Boatman, I preferred practicing alone.

* * *

In the remaining months of the academic year, the relationship between the upperclassmen and the plebes changed. In preparation for Hundredth Night, the first classmen started to run the plebes. Hundredth Night was the evening of the hundredth day before first class graduation when the firsties become Navy ensigns or Marine Corps 2nd lieutenants. On that evening, the plebes get to run the first classmen in a half-hour reversal of authority. In anticipation of this event, however, the firsties took over the harassment of the plebes. It was one-on-one where one plebe asked one firstie to "Come-around, Mister!" and the two became embroiled in one-upmanship.

Initially, the important thing was the timing. If the plebe asked the firstie out too soon before Hundredth Night, the upperclassman would have that much more time to run him. If the plebe asked his firstie to come-around too late, another plebe might grab him.

As Hundredth Night approached, excitement ran high. I decided to order Roger Wallace, a firstie from my fall semester squad, to come-around. Wallace was an easy-going, inoffensive upperclassman whose most distinguishing characteristic was that he lacked the aggressive bitterness of far too many mids. He was lanky, and a boyish innocence exuded from his clear, baby-like eyes. Hundredth Night was meant to be fun, so I chose a man I could enjoy harassing and being harassed by. One evening meal, I took a full glass of water, threw the water into Wallace's face, and said, "Come-around, mister!" in a gruff voice. The first classman hardly reacted. He said, "Okay. See me for every come-around until Hundredth Night."

The more courageous and imaginative plebes used more convincing methods. Larry Bemes, during evening meal, spread his hand with a huge glob of mustard and ketchup, then slapped his man unexpectedly in the face, almost making the firstie swallow his fork. At the same meal, Boatman committed the most daring feat. He took two full, quart-sized milk containers and poured the contents onto his target's head. The plebes trembled in fear as Boatman made a mad dash for the ladder, followed by a sopping wet, enraged, first classman and the hoots and jeers of that man's compatriots.

Unusual sites became common in the area. The first classmen reigned during the day and had the plebes doing ridiculous things. The plebes retaliated at night. Meade, who was sitting at the first class end and filling their water glasses, had asked Bloom to come-around by placing a mouthpiece into his water glass without the firstie noticing until he was halfway done drinking the water. Protestations that the mouthpiece was never used did the plebe little good. At the next come-around, the handsome, muscular Meade appeared wearing only a jock strap, a tie, and a gray fedora. He carried a large brown suitcase with articles of clothing sticking out of it. For half an hour, he hurried up and down the corridor and stopped every couple of feet to yell, "What time is it? I'm late for my train! Can anybody tell me what time it is?" Then he scurried off to repeat the performance ten feet away. The following morning, Bloom appeared at formation wearing shoes that had been polished with white to look like Buster Brown saddle shoes.

Wallace and I were more urbane. Neither wanted to seriously hassle the other, so it remained low key. Occasionally Wallace came to my room to make a little trouble, but it was meant in good fun. Even when the firstie had given me a minute to take off my dress blues and take a cold shower, I felt no resentment. I started to undress, but in my hurry, I jammed my belt tighter and couldn't remove my uniform in time. The firstie counted out the passing seconds, then ordered me, with my uniform still on, to shower standing on my hands. If Mower, McMunn, or Budge had ordered the same thing, I would have been outraged and hurt. With Wallace, I thought only of the strangeness of having the water run up my body instead of down and how heavy my clothing had become.

My own retaliation was ineffectual. The few times I snuck into Wallace's room, the firstie's roommate woke up, wandered about the room until he found me, and asked me in a sleep befuddled voice, "Sorensen, what are you doing?"

I always answered, "Nothing, sir."

The roommate always answered, as though nothing unusual was happening, "Oh, take off then." I would slink out of the room and Wallace's roommate would collapse, unconscious, back onto his bunk.

Since nothing was ever mentioned about these escapades, I didn't think that the roommate remembered them.

During one of the come-arounds, I lost a ski race. Another plebe and I were brought into the john. On one wall were four urinals with deep bowls. Each plebe mounted two urinals by jamming each of his sneakered feet into one the bowls. The object of the race was to be the first to flood the urinals to overflowing by repeatedly flushing them. Looking like two mad skiers, we started furiously flushing. Despite the encouragement of Wallace, I was badly beaten. My urinals were only half filled when my opponent had successfully flooded his. Wallace said, "Here, Sorensen, I'll show you how to flood these freaking things!" He mounted the urinals and in seconds he had them flooded. "See? Make sure your feet are jammed in tight and you can't lose!"

During another come-around, Wallace had me shower with my sweatshirt and sweatpants on. Then he had me bring him my dirty sock bag and a pad lock. As I stood by, water dripping profusely from my sweat clothes, the firstie opened a window at the end of the corridor, snapped the padlock onto and through the netted sock bag, then threw it out of the window and onto the pavement four stories down. He turned to me and said, "You better get your socks."

Squishing with every step, I ran down the four flights, retrieved my sock bag, and was on my way to the company area when a first classman stopped me. "Plebe, what company are you from?"

I stood at attention with the dripping water forming a small pool at my feet. "Twelfth company, sir."

"Who did this to you?"

The first classman's voice was authoritatively probing, making me suspicious of his motives. Wanting to protect Wallace, I answered, "A first classman, sir."

"What first classman?"

"Midshipman First Class Wallace, sir."

"From your company?"

"Yes, sir."

"Does he do this often?"

Alarmed, I answered, "No, sir. It's only for Hundredth Night, sir."

"You tell Mr. Wallace that a member of the plebe board saw you and might pay him a visit sometime soon."

"Aye-aye, sir." I ran to Wallace to tell him what had happened. I liked the first classman and had already decided that if there was an investigation, I'd try to downplay the harassment, which was only meant in fun anyway.

As I was telling Wallace about the first classman, I saw how afraid he was of the plebe board. It was then that I realized how real its power must be. *Perhaps,* I thought, *I should have reported Budge to the plebe board.* I envisioned doing so. It certainly would have cooled Budge down, but the thought had barely formed itself when I realized that the other second classmen would have turned on me, including Hooker, and my life would have been even more unbearable. I concluded that, no, it wouldn't have worked.

Wallace and I were both relieved when enough days had passed to indicate that he was in the clear.

When Hundredth Night finally arrived, all the plebes were being run at 1630 hours instead of the usual 1700 hours when the roles reversed, and the plebes got to run the first classmen. The workout was intense, certainly as difficult as any that the second classmen had given; yet the plebes were fresh and often laughed. The closer to 1700 it got, the more frenzied the first classmen became, ordering the plebes to do pushups, sit-ups, and sprints. Offers were made. "Sorensen, I'll let you go now if you agree not to run me at five."

I paused in the middle of a pushup. "*No, sir!*"

Exactly at 1700 hours, the plebes stood up and ordered the first classmen to hit it for sixty-nine, their graduation year. Now the firsties had to go through their last and final come-around. I hated uniform changes, so I ordered Wallace to run through a series of them, always making disparaging comments with a lot of stomping and bluster. During one of the changes, I went to my room for shaving cream. When Wallace returned, I asked him his rates. Wallace blinked a dozen times, then said. "S-s-s-sir, the f-f-football team, s-s-s-sir, quarterback, n-n-n-number thirty-f-f-f-four, John Wa-Wa-Wayne, class of s-s-s-seventy; goalie, number twenty-one, C-c-c-clint EEEEastwood, class of '34; wa-wa-wa-water boy, number forty-one, Charles B-B-B-Bronson, class of one; defensive end, number three, Lee Ma-Ma-Marvin, class of '81,... "

"That's enough, mister. Five articles from the newspaper!"

"Sir, *The Washington Post* reports that this year's plebes are pathetically anal creatures and are a threat to national security, boo hoo, boo hoo, sir! A second article states that the first classmen are the finest examples of manhood since the ancient Greek Olympics, particularly one Roger Wallace, aka, The Man, sir! A third article states that Midshipman Fourth Class Sorensen has a smile like a snarling binturong…"

"What's a binturong?"

"A badger like animal from Southeast Asia, sir. Well, more like a weasel, sir, a big weasel that climbs trees. It's hideous, too, sir. Sinfully hideous, like a plebe, sir."

"Enough! What's the Academy chain of command?"

"It has a prehensile tail, sir."

"What's the Academy chain of command?"

"I thought you might want to know that, sir."

"Very good. The chain of command."

Wallace gave a nervous flurry of his hands. "Duh, I don't know that one, sir. Duh, I'll find out, sir. Duh, no excuse, sir. Duh. Duh."

"I really hate to do this, mister."

I filled Wallace's cap with shaving cream. I had not intended to put it onto the first classman's head, but a nearby youngster had a camera and I decided not to miss the photo opportunity. I jammed the cap onto the firstie's head.

As a final act of retribution, the plebes decided to have the firsties do carrier landings. They were ordered to collect their mattresses and pile them at the end of the corridor. Meade ordered Bloom to get his atlas. Bloom did the first carrier landing. Meade gave me the huge hard cover atlas. I yelled at Wallace, "Bend over, mister!"

"Um, aye-aye, sir."

I called, "IGNITION!"

Wallace responded, "Ignition on, sir!"

With all my might, I slammed the atlas into firstie's butt and yelled, "LAUNCH!" Wallace spread his arms like wings, roared like an aircraft, and hurtled himself onto the mattresses. I handed the atlas to Boatman. It was harmless, but I remembered how much it stung, like getting hit with a board, when I had done carrier landings.

This was the last assault on the first classmen. When the come-around was over, the Academy resumed its normal course of events.

Hundredth Night marked a turning point at the Academy. An almost audible sigh resounded through the school. Plebe harassment became incidental.

* * *

One Saturday afternoon in early May, I wandered the Academy grounds, captured by a tremendous sense of well-being. For the first time since the beginning of school I was caught up in my studies. With my hands stuck confidently, unmilitary, into my pockets, I strolled along the sea wall of Farragut Field, thinking that the world was a grand place to be in. To my right was the Chesapeake Bay with its gently modest waves while to my front was the Severn River, as romantic and tantalizing as Moon River. As I approached Santee Basin, I saw the small sailing craft with their midshipman crews readying for a vigorous afternoon.

I paused to look at the rows of new 1969 cars lining the length of the yard patrol craft docking area. Each vehicle belonged to a first classman who dipped into his Naval Academy bank account, automatically kept for him by the school, and was paid for in cash. Standing in a fresh glow of newness, the cars were apt symbols of the graduating body who would soon become the Navy's most promising officers. I imagined owning one of these cars, knowing that it would immeasurably increase my popularity, as would be the case if I owned the newest and best stereo at the school.

While my mind was busy making a recording studio of my room and taking Matt Helmsley and Danny Calhoun for rides in my futuristic computerized car, I backtracked through the library. As I walked over the tiled floor, I noticed how its variously assorted squares looked like city blocks from the air, the white squares being white neighborhoods and the black being black neighborhoods. The green squares could be parks. Then I changed my mind. Such a city would be too congested and not worth living in. People needed open spaces for good mental health. It would be better if the white squares were city blocks of any racial or ethnic group, the black squares farms, and the green squares forest. I looked over the pattern of tiles on the floor and decided that a place like that would be a good place in which to live.

It was then that I shook my head vigorously as though to fling these thoughts out of my head. No more daydreaming for me if I could help it. It had already cost me too much study time. As I left the building, I decided to head for town.

On my way to the main gate, I joined Larry Bemes and Charley Bragg who were also going into town. I said to Bragg, "I saw your match against Penn State. I bet you were relieved when your opponent got hurt right away."

"Why? My parents were in the audience. I wanted them to see me wrestle."

"But you won without a fight. I think that was a lucky break."

"I wanted to fight."

They passed two youngsters from my squad. One said, "Ah, The Good, The Bad, and The Ugly." He paused significantly, then added, "Sores is The Ugly." We all chuckled.

Soon afterwards, Bragg separated from us and said, "I'll see you guys later. I've got to see my townie."

Bemes turned toward me. "Shall we hit the ice cream parlor?"

Much flattered, I jumped at the offer. "Sure thing."

"I've got to get myself a townie. This single life is for the birds."

"What about your girl at home?"

"Oh, she's my regular girl, you know, the girl I'll probably marry. A townie's just a temporary loan."

"Shit, Larry, that's dishonest."

"What's dishonest about it?"

"Using someone like that."

"I've got my needs, Mike."

"Everybody has needs. That doesn't mean you can go around hurting people."

"Who says anybody's going to get hurt? The townie's taking a chance. After all, I might end up marrying her instead of my girl back home. Besides, we might both have a real good time."

"I don't know, Larry. It kind of stinks to me. That's something Bragg would do, not you."

When we reached the ice cream parlor, Bemes held open the door and, clapping me on the shoulder, said, "Sores, give humanity a break, okay?"

We ordered hot fudge sundaes and filled the gaps between mouthfuls with conversation. Bemes said, "I haven't heard you talking to yourself for a long time."

"Talking to myself?"

"Yeah, thinking out loud." Bemes mimicked, "'I wonder how this belt goes on.' 'I wonder how I'm supposed to Brasso this belt buckle.' That kind of stuff."

"I gave that up. When I moved in with Valdres, I discovered that he knew even less than I did, so my wondering out loud did no good. You and Meade seemed to know so much."

"It used to drive me nuts."

"I wasn't sure of myself, that's all."

"I've thought a lot about you lately, you and Bragg." Bemes shook his head. "I don't know about that boy. There's something wrong with him."

"What does he have to do with me?"

"Bragg is a real bagger. He's been AWOL at least three times. He's always riding in cars. Did you see that string of puke running down the middle of the ladder in the company area?"

I nodded yes.

"He did that. He's done a thousand things a thousand times worse than anything you ever did, yet you're the one they always fried while he skated, and do you know why?"

"Yeah, because he's a jock and you know how jocks get to bag it."

Bemes hesitated. "Mike, I'm a jock."

I grimaced. "Sorry. I wasn't thinking. But you're not a jock. I mean I don't regard you as one. You don't behave like a jock."

"Okay, Mike, I get the point. But that's not the reason. The big difference between you and Bragg is that he never gets caught. You do. You stub a toe and they put you on death row. He murders someone and gets a congressional citation. Mike, you've got to learn to hide things better. It doesn't matter what you do as long as you hide it or at least make it look good."

"I never thought of it like that, but you might be right."

"Might? *Hell*."

We finished our sundaes and continued our walk through town. As we passed Bell Telephone with its rows of telephones in its storefront window, I asked. "Would you like to hear something perverse?"

"All right."

"In Guatemala there was a revolution. When they interrogated a captured guerilla, they wrapped a phone line around his balls then rang the phone." I chuckled. "Every time the phone rang, zoom, an electric shock ran through his balls."

While I was laughing, my friend became solemn. A few steps were taken, then Bemes said, "During my year at NAPS they took a whole group of us through the attic of one of the classrooms. They showed us a bird's nest. Above it was the adult bird and its chicks. Someone had crucified them by nailing them to the back wall."

This time I was solemn as I realized how Larry must have viewed my story. I asked, "You don't think that *I'd* do something like that, do you?"

"No, but you should be careful of the way you talk. A person who doesn't know you might misjudge you."

I pointed to the graveyard of a church. "You might be interested to know that there's a Lawrence Bemes buried there."

Larry didn't show the slightest curiosity, so I continued talking. Wishing to exonerate myself, I said, "When I was a kid we lived in the projects. It was supposed to be a bad place, but I liked it there. At any rate, there was a dog named Benji that belonged to one of the neighborhood kids. One day a bunch of us found it in a hole, dead. Someone had hanged it with a hangman's noose. The owner was one of the tougher kids, but when he saw his dog, he started bawling. I remember that dog. I was about eight. I couldn't figure out why anyone would want to hurt him. He was such a friendly dog and perfectly harmless. I found other dead dogs. I know this sounds weird, but I think there was a serial killer of dogs in the neighborhood."

Soon, we found ourselves on a dead-end street that terminated on the water. Bemes placed a foot on the sea barrier, crossed his arms on the raised knee, and looked out over the water, the perfect picture of seamanship. I made a conscious effort not to mimic my friend although I couldn't help but admire his style.

Just then, a passing motorboat swung into a sharp U-turn to come in for a closer look at us. In it were two young ladies with smooth, rounded breasts bulging from their scant bikinis. They had well proportioned, well-tanned bodies with long, finely shaped, slender legs. Both had long auburn hair and delicate features that never saw a blemish. They decided to dock their craft where we two mids were standing. While one of the women raced the engine, the other made a futile attempt to push aside the debris of floating boards, paneling, and Styrofoam cups. Minutes passed. I wanted to help and looked questioningly at Bemes. Since Larry maintained his pose, I decided not to act. When they were six feet away and looking more and more like starlets in all their youthful flesh, I suggested, "Let's jump for it."

Without moving a muscle, Larry said, "Wait 'til they get here."

Unfortunately, the debris was too thick. I thought about skipping across on the floating boards but thought of the humiliation I'd feel if I ended up waist deep in that filthy water. I kept waiting for a response from my friend, but it never came. No words had been exchanged between the two groups. Disgruntled, the women gave up and raced away, leaving me to wonder why Bemes had not thought of some way to reach them. We returned to the Academy with my mind full of bulging breasts, long legs, and unquenchable yearning.

* * *

The school semester wound to a close. The midshipmen had already volunteered for their summer assignments. For youngster cruise, I chose the Atlantic crossing to Europe. As the days brightened, so did the midshipmen. Within a couple of months, a fourth of them would be Navy ensigns pulling duty with the fleet or Marine Corps 2nd lieutenants training at Quantico. Ninety nine percent of the graduating body would be married within a year. Everyone got a six-week summer leave. I took my leave after the cruise.

Twelfth company found itself in second place in the Brigade competitions. It was an accident. No one kept track and everyone was surprised. The ranking was based on the company's performance in marching, class rank according to grades, athletic achievements, and anything else that could be categorized and measured. The plebes were indifferent to the outcome since they would get only an extra evening off to spend in town. The upperclassmen, however, stood to gain a weekend leave, so they took the competition to heart.

As the competition neared its final days, valiant efforts were made to get the company into first place. A blood drive was being held to which it was strongly suggested the plebes should donate. To avoid any residual harassment, I went to the library, where it was being held, during a free period to make my contribution. I had never donated blood before, so I found the rows of prostrate bodies lying next to blood filled plastic bags daunting.

While a medic was checking my blood type, I watched a first classman give a third classman a Form 2 for having holes in the soles of his shoes. The firstie had seen them when the youngster was prone and donating his blood. With a paper cup of orange juice in one hand and the Form 2 in the other, the youngster sat on the edge of his cot, shaking his head in disbelief while his face turned a brilliant crimson. I would have laughed, but I was filled with foreboding about my own donation.

By chance, Roderigues and Husaby were also there. The three of us were given adjacent cots with me in the middle. The mids were placed on the cots so that the feet of one mid was level with the heads of the mids on either side of him. Roderigues nodded toward the youngster with the Form 2 and said, "Now *that's* what I call rinky dink."

Husaby and Roderigues received their needles first. My own needle was on the point of insertion when Husaby's body contorted, and he went into a convulsion. The corpsman on his other side tried to hold the needle arm down which had started to curl upon itself. Two more corpsmen entered the fray. Still, Husaby's arm curled, lifting all three men.

Roderigues sat up on his cot, eyes bulging, lips quivering, fighting an impulse to rip his needle out and run for it. He closed his eyes, snapped his face away, and said, "Don't look at it."

I was sitting up on my elbows and making my own calculations. How would it look if I simply walked away? Unlike Roderigues, I watched the whole thing, patiently waiting for whatever horribly gruesome thing would happen next.

Amidst the strained yelling, a fourth corpsman joined in. At first, he, too, tried to restrain the arm, but to no effect. He released his grip and pulled the needle out. Immediately, Husaby relaxed, and the struggle ceased. He lay on his cot, thoroughly exhausted. A corpsman said, "Nerves."

I felt weak and knew that I must be deathly pale. A moment later, a corpsman inserted a needle into my arm. I felt the pinch. Instead of leaving right away, the corpsman squatted next to my head and asked, "What type of blood do you have?"

"O-positive."

"O-positive. That means that everybody can use your blood. They need it badly in Vietnam. You're doing a great thing for your country and the men in Nam." I glanced at the corpsman, then returned my gaze to the ceiling. The corpsman continued, "Have you any friends there?"

"My best friend. And my brother went there too."

"Then those are the people you're helping, your buddy and your brother." I felt better and the corpsman left me.

That evening at meal I saw both Husaby and Roderigues, but neither of them mentioned the incident. Kruke asked me if I donated blood that day.

"Yes, sir."

"How about you, Valdres?"

"No, sir."

Kruke roughly asked, "Why not? Don't you have any team spirit?"

"Yes, sir."

"Why didn't you donate blood then?"

"No excuse, sir."

"You bet your ass there's no excuse! You're a real piece of shit to let the rest of the company win the competition for you!"

The company placed second.

* * *

My last watch for that academic year was pulled at Batt. Ops. Marine Captain Huisinger was the officer of the day, and Midshipman

Second Class Roderigues was the midshipman officer of the day. Again, I was primarily a messenger, a duty I liked since that meant long walks to strange, new buildings. In addition to this, the day was youthful, fresh, and sunny.

I began the watch with my usual mistake. I was filling in a logbook and attempted to discreetly erase an error. Roderigues called me into the office, casually pointed out the erasure, and told me to hit it for seventy-two. I fell to the leaning rest position. Generally, when doing such a high number of pushups, a plebe placed his hands as wide as possible to make them easier. This time I kept my hands shoulder width apart because I wanted to see what I could do. Using my best form, I rapped out the seventy-two pushups, struggling on the last ten. The second classman, sitting in a slouch, watched my efforts, gave me permission to come aboard, and said, "Damn, Sorensen, they were good pushups! You've really gotten strong!" I knew the rest of my day would be easy.

When my break came, I went to bed for the sole luxury of sleeping during the day, an activity forbidden all plebes except those on watch. After my nap, I shined my shoes and returned to my post where I was ordered to see the captain. As soon as I entered his office, the Marine said, "Jesus Christ! You look like you haven't slept for years!" He handed me an envelope. "Bring this to Brigade Headquarters. After that, you're dismissed. Get some sleep for Christ's sake!"

As I left on my errand, I thought that I should inform Roderigues about Huisinger's order but thought better of it. The second classman would be sure to take my free time away from me. Besides, if I was missed, Roderigues would find me.

After a pleasant walk across Academy grounds, I entered a small white building that looked like someone's home. As soon as I handed the envelope to a Navy lieutenant sitting in a diminutive office, he jumped at me as if he was about to hit me. Lifting a *Newsweek Magazine* to the level of my eyes, he held it there. The cover showed the defeated, disillusioned face of Commander Bucher who surrendered the *USS Pueblo* to North Korean patrol boats earlier that year. The officer jammed the magazine so hard into my face that my nose and cheeks stung. At the same time the officer raged, "See that? Some Naval hero, huh?" He pulled the magazine away from my face, but still held it up in front of me. He continued vituperatively, "What do you think of him? I'll tell you one thing. I don't much like the Naval Academy and that's a fact, but I do know that an Academy graduate would never have surrendered like that!" The officer threw me a salute, the sweep of the arm missing my face by an inch. The officer spat, "Dismissed!"

I hadn't had a chance to speak one word. In the hallway I let out a deep breath of relief. A painting there halted me in mid-stride. It was of two Viking ships colliding in a fiord, their armed crews engaged in hand-to-hand combat. The dynamism of the mountains, rough water, and battling warriors filled me with awe. I, too, hated the Academy, but an Academy man would not have surrendered.

* * *

That evening at formation, a youngster from twelfth company passed us in civilian clothes. He grinned, then laughed and waved to us. He had been before the Academic Board and this appearance confirmed the decision of the Board to discharge him. Another youngster standing behind me said, "It hurts more than it shows." My own cume was 2.25. I was safe so far.

* * *

The festivities of June Week began on Monday. This was the final week of plebe year when the plebes become youngsters, the youngsters become second classmen, the second classmen become firsties, and the firsties become ensigns or 2nd lieutenants. For most of them, this was lasting moment of celebration.

Although the mids weren't allowed to leave academy grounds, they were allowed to have visitors. Cora and Mom made the trip from Rhode Island and found lodgings in a nearby motel. Early in the afternoon, they met me in the rotunda. I informed them that I couldn't leave base and could not go into town. In an abortive attempt to entertain them, I took them to the chapel where they expressed admiration of its beauty, then to the small naval museum. Half an hour later, they were ready for more. I admitted, "I don't know where to take you. You've already seen everything worth looking at."

I led them to Memorial Hall, stopping at each monument along the way to eat up time. Then I led them to a bench beneath the large tulip trees fronting Bancroft Hall and to one side of Tecumseh. Like a bad field commander, I was stumped where to lead them next. It was hot and getting hotter. Sweat was dribbling down all our faces and patches of it were cloying our armpits.

Then an idea occurred to me. Inside Bancroft Hall, in an inconspicuous corner, was a small coffee shop called Steerage. I remembered it from having gone on an errand there for Deichgraber. It was a hangout for upperclassmen. Hoping against hope that visitors were allowed there, like a forlorn Moses, I led them to its doors. For a moment I paused. I didn't want to make a mistake and be publicly humiliated in front of my mother and sister. I took a deep breath and stepped boldly inside. I was relieved to see other visiting relatives and their midshipmen sons, some of whom were plebes, in the handful of booths. No one looked up at our entrance.

Cora said, "Geez, this is really nice. Why didn't you bring us here in the first place instead of letting us cook outside?"

I shrugged my shoulders. "I don't know." Then I apologized, "I didn't mean to keep you in that hot sun so long. I've only been here once before. I didn't know we could use it." However, I knew the real reason. Even though I had not been run out, the months of brutal harassment made me too afraid to act, like an abused dog. Budge had destroyed the boy named Mike Sorensen.

The remainder of the afternoon was spent in Steerage. Cora and Mom were happy, and they did most of the talking. When evening meal approached, I informed them that I had to make formation and couldn't see them until the next day. I added that if they stood in front of Bancroft Hall, they could see the main body of midshipmen march into the mess hall. I strode to the door leading directly into Bancroft Hall. I waved once, pushed through the entrance, and sprang into a fast jog.

* * *

The following morning, I met Mom and Cora again at the rotunda. I was wearing the informal White Uniform Charley, which was the all-purpose uniform that looked like pajamas. I explained to them that

I'd be participating with the rest of my classmates in a ritual held yearly at the Herndon Monument. Every spring as a symbolic act, the plebes climbed the twenty-foot obelisk to top it with a plebe cap. It signified the end of plebe year and the beginning of youngster year.

I led my sister and mother to the monument where we sat on a bench facing it. I was disturbed that they should be so thrilled by the surrounding midshipmen. I saw that, to them, each mid was a white knight, handsome, intelligent, strong, honorable, charming, and in every way the best. To me, it was just another façade like the majestic façade of Bancroft Hall. The plebes gathered around the monument with their camera-carrying families who formed a thin, happy perimeter about us.

It became obvious that my fellow plebes were disgruntled. Mom and Cora turned questioning eyes upon me. I explained, a little confused, "The monument is supposed to be greased." I turned to a passing mid. "Classmate, what's happening?"

With chagrin, the plebe said, "The academy maintenance people complained about the clean-up. The monument won't be greased this year."

The whole of the class of '72 felt cheated. They had earned this rite of passage and now it was denied them. The upperclassmen on the outskirts of the crowd smirked with pleasure. It was as if *these* plebes weren't worthy enough to place a cap on the pinnacle of the monument. It was like saying that the class of '72 was inferior to the other classes. As expected, the ritual no more began than the twenty-foot spire was capped by the nearest handful of plebes, giving the rest of them no chance to participate.

To save face, one of them yelled, "Hey, guys, let's start our own tradition by jumping into the Michelson Hall reflection pool!" Wanting to at least feel that they were part of a momentous occasion, the mass of newly made youngsters, myself included, stampeded to the pool to hurl themselves into its water. Our friends and relatives eagerly followed, snapping photos while we did our best to be celebratory in a disappointing situation.

Afterwards, still in my wet uniform, I found the bench beneath the tulip trees where, for the first time in months, I totally relaxed. Stretching my legs before me and clasping my hands behind my head, I talked to Mom and Cora about the small, incidental things that had been happening to me. With my mother on one side and my sister on the other, I had a strong sense of well-being. I said, "I think I saw a catbird last Sunday. It was all gray except for a small, black patch on the top of its head. That's a catbird, isn't it, Mom?"

"Yes, it is. We used to have lots of them in Pennsylvania."

"I've never seen one before; it *does* sound like a cat when it sings. I guess you'd call it singing."

There was a lot of activity in their vicinity of any number of plebes rushing to pockets of excited relatives. Mom asked happily, "Son, do you know any of these midshipmen?"

"Some of them."

"Cora, I bet you wish you were a few years younger and single."

"You bet! I might kidnap one of them and drag him back to Meantacut with me. All these guys are real hunks!"

"Son, wouldn't it have been nice if your sister could have married a midshipman, maybe one of your classmates?"

I shook my head no. "Not really." Then, abruptly, I changed the subject. "I saw a Chesapeake Bay retriever the other day. It was with a water spaniel. I thought it was funny to see a Chesapeake Bay retriever on Chesapeake Bay. I was with a couple of plebes from my company when I spotted them. When I told them what kind of dogs they were, one of the plebes made a wise crack, but I didn't catch it. I thought, 'Yeah, that's just like the Naval Academy.'"

After a pause, Mom said, "The grackles are back."

Cora spurted, "I hate those things! They're ugly!"

I said, "C'mon, Cora. They're beautiful. How can you say they're ugly?"

"They're big, black things that eat up all the food for the other birds!"

"But I love their color—bluish black—and they sparkle in the sun, almost like floating gasoline. Besides, by the time they come north, there's more than enough food lying around."

"I don't know. I just don't like them."

The next hour was spent talking. Nothing profound was said, no truths revealed. It was a comfortable hour spent by three people very close to each other. At the hour's end, I said, "I have to go to noon meal now. After that I have to go to the commencement for the first class. I won't have time to see you afterwards since I must have my gear stowed in storage tomorrow morning and I'll need this evening to pack. So, I guess it's goodbye for now."

I hugged and kissed them, feeling a bit awkward by this public display of affection. I left them by the bench and walked past the hard, unrelenting face of Tecumseh.

* * *

The commencement consisted of a horde of white uniforms marching to the football stadium to listen to the Secretary of State give the commencement address. Afterwards, the degrees were handed to the first classmen who, in a matter of minutes, would be either Naval or Marine Corps officers. I withdrew into myself, making a mental list of all the things I should pack and what I'd need for summer cruise. Gus Hovedo sat next to me and gave a running commentary on the events taking place before us. I responded to his comments perfunctorily, "Yeah. Yeah."

Only one event served to pull me out of my reverie. At the end of the ceremony, the firsties threw their caps into the air and put on their new officer insignias and caps. Suddenly, one of them was hoisted onto the shoulders of his compatriots. He laughed and waved joyfully as members of his class loaded him down with dollar bills, one from each officer. This was the anchorman, the man with the lowest grades in his class who still managed to graduate. This was his moment of glory after years of academic strife. By the evening, he'd have hundreds of dollars. With the dropout rate being as high as it was and my grades as low as they were, I knew that, if I managed to make it that far, I'd be in the running for the anchorman among my own classmates.

CHAPTER VIII
YOUNGSTER CRUISE

The new third classmen were given a choice between Hawaii and Europe for their six-week summer cruise. I chose the European cruise that would visit the ports of Portsmouth, England, and Hamburg, Germany. It began with a week of waiting spent at the Norfolk Naval Base. Among the hundreds of midshipmen there, Gus Hovedo was the only mid I met from the twelfth company which resulted in our spending a great deal of time together.

We were billeted in an old decrepit barracks that allowed no privacy. It was in two parts, barracks A and barracks B. To access B from the front of the building, the mids had to walk through A first and then through one end of the lavatory since it was a room perpendicular to the flow of traffic. In addition to this, the soda machine was in barracks B. There was a continual flow of pedestrian traffic between the barracks with the lavatory being a kind of innocent victim. The toilets were in two parallel rows of fifteen each, with no stalls, walls, or partitions separating any of them from the rest of the room and the traffic. To defecate was literally pulling your pants down in public. Decorum was maintained where the passers-by ignored their compatriots sitting forlornly on their thrones who, nonetheless, felt terribly exposed.

Until the arrival of the two troop transport ships that were to take them overseas, the mids had nothing to do. Gus and I spent our time eating at the officers' club and going to the officers' beach. From there we'd take long walks that led us to the civilian part of Virginia Beach. These jaunts proved to be a little difficult for me. The civilian beach

152

seemed to go on forever. It seemed so interminable that I felt infinitely small. Black specks in the distance turned out to be people. It was one thing to know that I was a single, unimportant speck in an immense universe; it is was another thing to see the physical proof of it and to be struck emotionally by that truth. I looked out over the water and that, too, seemed endless.

In contrast to this was the officers' beach. It was small and enclosed on all sides by a semicircle of bushes whose ends grew to the water's edge. I also found the houses along the civilian beach comforting. Both served to limit my view, at least in that direction, of what seemed to be infinite.

One sunny day, Gus and I went to the officers' beach. We sat awkwardly on our towels with our thin arms and legs hanging out all over the place. Short ocean waves slapped at the shore while Gus berated me for having run away from him when we were walking along the beach the previous evening. "I mean, Mike, if you don't want me around, say so. You don't have to run away. Tell me to bug off and I'll leave on my own."

"It had nothing to do with you, Gus. I wanted to be alone."

"Why do you want to be alone all the time? The world is a lonely place to begin with and you want to make it worse."

"Yeah, but I wanted to meet people."

"Oh, I see. You couldn't meet people with me there."

"That's not it either. People are easier to meet when you're alone. Last night I met two lifeguards and we spent the night on the beach avoiding the shore patrol—the Rat Patrol they called it—and telling stories."

"You couldn't do that with me there, right?"

"You're not that kind of person."

"How do you know what kind of person I am?"

"Then, after we split, I met these two good looking girls. It was kind of funny because I kept hinting that I had nowhere to sleep and I kept hoping one of them would invite me to her room, but it was a no go."

"That's nice, but don't do it again. I mean, I felt like a fool standing on the beach with my best friend running away from me like I had the plague."

"Okay, I won't do it again. I didn't know you'd get this upset."

"Well, I *did* get upset."

"Okay, I'm sorry."

Two teenaged girls sat down near us. They were long and slender with small, budding breasts. Gus, wanting to prove his worth, turned toward them and said, "The water's beautiful, just like a bath."

The blonde replied, "Oh really?" The conversation dropped like a pound of lead, when a few minutes later the blonde said, "Are you with the group of midshipmen that we've heard so much about?"

Gus answered, "Well, I don't know exactly what you heard, but I guess so."

"My name is Joyce, and this is Donna."

The girl with the long auburn hair smiled. "Hi."

Instinctively, we coupled up, with Gus facing the blonde while I turned my attention to Donna. During the afternoon, the couples talked mostly about themselves. While making small sand piles along the edge of their blanket, the girls told us that their fathers were Naval officers. They were delighted when Gus told them that we completed plebe year and that in three years we'd be Naval officers like their dads.

I picked up a handful of sand and let it sift through my fingers. Donna informed me that she was a model, which automatically had me inspecting her body. I didn't mean to be so obviously rude, but it was a first reaction. Then she held up a plastic bottle of suntan lotion and asked, "Do you want to do the honors?"

"Sure." I filled my hand with the warm, white cream as she turned onto her belly. I spread it smoothly, evenly over the lightly muscled, already tanned back. I had often seen scenes like this in the movies and had visions of Burt Lancaster rolling in the sand with Deborah Kerr. It was idyllic. It was perfect. I intuited what she was going to say and how I would answer. It was like an eternal recurrence, performed many times before an unseen audience, a life relived over and over until there were no errors. This time, I hoped, I would get it right.

When the afternoon sun became so hot that it was worth getting chilled just to cool off, I suggested that we take a dip. I stood up and offered my hand to Donna. She took it gently but firmly, and we ran into the water amidst a great deal of laughter and splashing. Gus and Joyce, who weren't interested in one another, walked separately to the water and waded quietly to their friends. Donna and I were wrestling with the usually reserved midshipman, me, holding her, protesting, in my arms. I dunked her screaming, laughing form and felt how wonderfully warm and soft she was. I had never felt anything so tender and responsive to my touch. I saw myself as the tough, muscled Marines watching from the beach must have seen me: a scrawny little boy. Why would a beautiful girl like Donna want to be with such a paper tiger? But she didn't seem to notice the other men.

After the swim, the girls had to go home, so addresses were exchanged and goodbyes said. The girls had a ride waiting for them and left before we did. When they were gone, Gus said, "You were in good form today."

"That's 'cause I'm in love."

"Seriously, I've never seen you come onto a girl like that before."

"Why not? We'll never see them again. What harm could it do?"

"How do you know we'll never see them again?"

"Because we won't. Life doesn't work that way. They're both young and beautiful. I'm destined to marry someone that's ugly."

"But I saw you give Donna your address. What about that?"

"I gave her my address because it was the thing to do. I guarantee that we'll never see either one of them again."

As we were slipping our clothes over our now dry bathing suits, I noticed that my trousers seemed a little light. I checked my pockets and discovered that something was missing. "Hey, my wallet's gone!"

"Did you drop it?"

"No, I don't think so. I had it when we first sat down." My mind caught the image of some young boys I'd seen eyeing our clothes. "I think some kids stole it."

"How do you know?"

"I remember some kids checking us out."

"How do you know *they* took it?"

"I don't know, but it's likely them."

"We'll have to report it to shore patrol. Was your ID in it?"

"Yeah."

"So now you're a man without a name. You have no identity; you've ceased to exist, and you know something? You deserve it."

155

"Cut the crap! I'm not in the mood to be badgered!"

"Aye-aye, sir."

We reported the incident to the shore patrol, then went to the officers' club for supper with me signing in as Hovedo's guest. We were due to ship out the next day and I was worried about how I was going to get by without my ID. However, when we returned to our barracks, the wallet was waiting for me. One of the lifeguards had found it in a trash barrel. The money was gone, but the ID was there. I held up the wallet and waved it in front of my friend. "See? I exist; I've got my identity back."

* * *

Youngster cruise began with five hundred new third classmen moving onto the two troop transports that were to carry them across the North Atlantic. Gus and I were pleased to find that we were assigned to the same vessel, although we were in different compartments. Each compartment contained fifteen midshipmen who formed a small microcosm like that of a single cell in a much larger body. My group was assigned to the aft most and lowest of all the compartments, which effectively cut us off from the rest of the ship. A routine developed of classes, watch, and card playing, except that I exercised with a set of springs while the others played poker. Plebe year boxing had taught me the value of staying in shape.

The ocean air got progressively colder, and the water became rougher, darker, and more menacing the farther north we traveled. We hit two days of rough weather during which I had the comfortable feeling of being rocked like a child in my mother's arms. I was the only mid in my compartment not to get seasick. The others took turns running to the head.

Early in the cruise, I was pulling starboard watch just as it was getting dark and stood outside on the bridge in a baggy, green field jacket. A pair of large Navy binoculars rested on my chest as I watched the large swells roll and collide in endless turmoil while the ship behaved like a bit of flotsam, thrust aside, ignored, by huge, clashing forces. My eyes settled on a black buoy bouncing in the water about seventy-five yards from me. I keyed my phone and was about to call it in when I realized that the water must be at least two miles deep. No buoy cable was that long, and what would a buoy be doing out here in the first place? Fixing my binoculars onto the object, I watched it bubble up and down in synchronous motion with the swells. It still looked like a buoy but then it opened its mouth and I saw two rows of large, gleaming, white teeth. *A spy-hopping whale! A sperm whale!* I caught my breath. My pulse quickened its pace as the vessel came within fifty yards of the creature. Again, I keyed my phone to call it in when I caught myself. I thought, *why should I share anything with them?* I pictured the ship, its mids and officers, and behind them I saw Budge and Bancroft Hall. No, I wouldn't call it in. Whether it was my imagination or not, the whale seemed to have seen me. It was looking at me in a friendly way, smiling at me. *Is it personification?* I could swear, as the whale bobbed in his vertical position and watched the ship pass, that it was wishing me farewell.

As the sleek gray metal of the sister ships cut through the North Atlantic, I tried to imagine what was on the other side of the outermost bulkhead: cold, black water so deep that a man's courage would fail should he fall overboard. He would freeze to death before he could drown or be rescued. I liked the idea of sleeping in comfort below the water's surface, encased in a metal shell, an embryo in its mother's womb.

If I had to describe the voyage, "metal on metal" would be the best description. There were metal bunks, metal bulkheads, metal ceilings, and metal floors. Even the food and coffee had a metallic taste. If a fire broke out in a neighboring compartment, especially the one above us, we would all fry like eggs.

A mid caught stealing in another compartment was given a blanket party by wrapping him in a blanket so that his head was covered. Then, as a group, the other mids beat him. It was the kindest punishment they could have given him. He must have been well liked.

The shipboard classes had become a matter of routine. The primary duty of the midshipmen was pulling watch at the various duty stations. Though boring, it was necessary for the operation of the vessel. Watch cut into our sleep since a good deal of it was night duty. Yet, it encouraged fraternization among the mids as the darkness forced us to pair together, and the smooth, rumbling drone of the ship forced us to talk to one another to stay awake.

One night I pulled watch in the engine room with a youngster named Bradford Smith. We met in the ship's cafeteria shortly before duty to fill ourselves with the black Mississippi mud that passed for coffee. Thick and rich, it was designed to keep watches awake, a bit of reality in the unfamiliar world of shipboard life.

We went down several ladders, found the engine room, and talked with the seaman on duty who sat before a panel full of circular gauges. He explained to the mids what each gauge meant and what to watch for that would indicate trouble. An ensign showed up and gave us a small tour of the area, cautioning us about pinhole leaks from steam pipes that could cut off a man's hand before he was aware of it. Soon, the officer left us and wasn't seen for the rest of the night. We returned to the seaman, but he was reading a paperback. We stood near him, uncomfortably waiting for him to respond to our presence. The sailor was so involved in his book that he either didn't see us or chose not to see us.

When we realized that we were going to be ignored, we left the sailor sitting before his gauges and started a half-hearted inspection of the engine room. After a little diverse wandering, we settled on some metal gratings. Neither of us had a book with him, so sitting on the grating with our legs dangling from it, we did our best to talk in the surrounding noise and heat. Dirty bilge water sloshed from one side of the rolling vessel to the other side. In the half dark, we saw the large steel piping of the turbine rods that changed the steam into the mechanical force that drove the ship over vast seas.

Because of the isolation and inactivity, the conversation took an immediate turn toward intimacy. Brad was the talker and told anecdotes from his high school years. He told how he'd been class president and valedictorian of the senior class, receiving a standing ovation at graduation as he received his diploma. He had also dated the same girl throughout his high school career.

I admitted that I had done none of these things. "In fact, I wasn't very popular at all. I never felt as though I belonged there. I'd go to basketball games and try to be enthusiastic, but it seemed ridiculous to me to get frenzied over a group of people chasing a ball. Then I made a tragic mistake. I told the truth. I made an oral presentation in a class loaded with cheerleaders about how horrid Saturday and Sunday afternoons were because of all the baseball and football games on television. I made the case that most viewers had no interest in these games. The football team tried to show me the error of my ways. It didn't work. I spent a good deal of time avoiding them and their friends. This was in junior high. By the time we made it to high school, they couldn't care less what I thought."

I noticed a smudge of rust on my blue jeans. I tried to rub it off with my hand, but seeing that it had no effect, I decided that it would be better to change uniforms and send this one to the laundry. I continued, "I used to wonder what was wrong with me, then one day I got to thinking and I started to wonder what was wrong with *them*. Either way, I never fit in no matter how hard I tried."

Brad said, "Well, I wasn't *that* popular. Like I said, I went out with only one girl all that time. I don't know whether I should be ashamed of myself or not—well—no—I'm kind of proud of it. I'm still a virgin."

I gasped at the boldness of the assertion. Instinctively, furtively, I looked about to see if anyone thus far unobserved was listening. My voice became confidential as I admitted, "So am I. What do you think it's like?"

As visions of a mysterious paradise raced through my mind, my partner said, "I don't know what it's like, but I don't think that it's all that it's made out to be." Brad modestly lowered his eyes and sat with the composure of an icon saint. He lacked only the halo to make it complete.

I stared at the sloshing bilge water, then said, "I think you're probably right."

Soon, the conversation reverted to Academy and shipboard gossip. Brad said, "The best thing I ever did was to go out for fencing. I wasn't an athlete in high school, and I had to do something to get onto the team tables. A black guy suggested it to me, and I took his advice. I pity those suckers that had to eat with their companies."

"Yeah, so do I. I was one of them."

When the watch ended, I went on deck for a breath of fresh air. I had never seen such blackness before and felt with my feet to find the steps of the ladder. My arms were stretched out like tentacles searching for bulkheads. As my eyes became accustomed to the dark, I could pick out a couple of clearly shining stars that only served to accentuate the darkness.

I heard a retching noise like the sound of a dog vomiting as only a dog can vomit, with its whole body curved in an upside-down *u*, mouth agape like Mammoth Cave, and two inches from mother earth. Cautiously, I approached and saw an indistinct shadow leaning over the guardrails in an arc pointing toward the water. Getting closer, I could barely distinguish the ghostly white face of a youngster. He turned his head briefly in my direction, then snapped it back toward the water and vomited from the depths of his soul. When he came up for air, I hooted and said cheerfully, "Hey, that's pretty good!" In the placidly bovine eyes that turned upon me, I detected a threat. The mid lunged at me but swung away in midstride to puke over the side again. I couldn't help but laugh as I made a discreet retreat and hoped that my laughter wouldn't be redeemed later.

* * *

After a month at sea, the troop transports pulled into the harbor of Portsmouth, England. As the vessels were docked, all ship personnel not on duty dressed in whites and stood in formation to honor such a staunch ally. The sun was unusually hot while the vessels seemed to be unusually slow in getting to their berths. Midshipmen and crew fidgeted under the strain of immobility. Finally, to everyone's relief, they were dismissed. All the mids were granted a three-day leave, but since the first day was spent in docking and the last day would be spent getting underway, it was really a one-day field trip.

Early the next morning, dressed in the "uniform of the day"— a sports coat, white shirt, and tie—Gus and I hurried to the train station to exchange dollars for pounds and to buy two tickets for London. The wait for the train wasn't very long. Soon we were racing through "Lassie Come Home" country seated opposite an elderly couple. I saw myself, the returning war hero, coming back to the woman and dog I loved. I saw myself running through the beautifully green, thick grass that grabbed at my knees while my dog pranced happily about me and a fair blonde woman in a white dress and hair in a bun ran toward me with outstretched arms. I caught her, swinging her madly about out of the sheer joy and exuberance, when the elderly couple disturbed my epic reverie.

Looking as though they should be riding in a horse and buggy, they introduced themselves as Mr. and Mrs. Baker from the Isle of Wight. Gus, always the gentleman, introduced us and was interested when they told him that they had been visiting relatives and were going to London to see a play. He wanted to know about the play: what is its name, what is it about, where is the theater, how much are the tickets, and how hard are they to get. The Bakers were obviously pleased that Gus took an interest in them.

Mrs. Baker asked me, "Are you both from the United States?"

"Yes, I'm from Rhode Island." When I saw the look of bewilderment on their faces, I added, "Near Boston."

"Oh, that's nice." Mrs. Baker turned toward Gus. "And where are you from, young man?"

"Chicago."

The Bakers visibly recoiled from Gus as the woman said, "Oh, Chicago. Gangsters."

Their reaction upset him, and he asserted that Chicago had no more gangsters than any other place.

Unconvinced, Mr. Baker asked, "What about Al Capone? You have people like that there."

"That was a long time ago. Al Capone lived in the 1930s. It's not like that anymore. A lot of nice, decent people live in Chicago. You can't believe everything you see in the movies." Despite his efforts, the couple remained unconvinced. The conversation died in the silent reverberations of the Tommy gunfire from over forty years ago.

When the lush green countryside gave way to small brick buildings with compact, rich gardens appended to them, we knew that we had reached London. Saying goodbye to the elderly couple, and with great expectations, we entered the streets so well known to world history.

We took the obligatory tours of the Tower of London and the surrounding museums, always ending up in the weapons section. It was fascinating to see the instruments designed to take life. A thrust of this knife might have preserved the life and culture of its owner while sending an enemy's soul into eternity. It seemed hard to believe that such things happened, are happening right now, that whole armies and peoples exchanged death, that this knife and that sword were a part of that exchange.

In one room, we found a long, thirty-foot metal arm with a spring assembly at one end. A nearby guard explained, "It's a protective device. The arm was set at knee level. When a lever was pulled, it released the spring you see there and the arm, under the force of the spring, cut a circular swathe through the enemy forces."

Gus said, "These weapons weren't made to kill; they were made to mutilate."

At one point during our round of tours, a well-dressed, stout, middle-aged man sporting a well-trimmed beard and a bowler hat accosted us. "Are you gentlemen looking for a good time?"

Immediately suspicious, I answered for us, "No, thank you."

As the Englishman retreated from us, my friend asked, "What do you think he wanted?"

"I don't know. Maybe he's a pimp or maybe eccentric. You know how the English are supposed to be."

"Yeah, but you should have let him talk. Now we'll never know what he wanted."

As the day wore into the evening's darkness, the street people came to life. Attracted by the bright lights and photographs of the performers to be seen inside, we mids entered our first strip tease, standing room only. Neither of us had ever seen a naked woman before and we both were anxious to have our first glimpse of paradise. Several attractive women presented themselves on stage, went through their routines, and departed. My mind voyaged to other worlds where, perhaps, many men had been before, wondering at the bountiful bliss that must be found there by the lucky adventurer to those shores.

A heavyset woman who bantered with the audience performed the most interesting routine. She was dancing to a song about spacemen. As she disrobed in time with the music, it became apparent that her undergarments were a bright, fluorescent purple. As she danced, she made the purple tasseled knobs on her nipples rotate first in one direction, then in the other direction. Her dexterity was further demonstrated when she rotated her breasts in opposite directions so that one breast rotated clockwise while the other rotated counterclockwise. Then she stopped and rotated each breast in the other direction. The audience loved it, hooting at her as she smirked while I stood amazed by the contradiction of the physical laws of inertia such movement demanded. *How does she do that?* The culmination of her performance was when she flipped off her g-string and marched off stage.

The last show that we watched was that of a young woman, tall and thin, who made the audience audibly gasp when she stepped onto the stage. Everyone was spellbound. Her dark brown hair was long and thick. Her movements had an athlete's grace to them. Her breasts were hard and firm, yielding nothing to gravity. Desire rumbled through the audience. She seemed unapproachable, untouched like a virgin goddess, an earthly Diana. She still had dignity even when totally nude.

My friend and I stood in the back where it was darkest. A strong gripping sensation settled into my groin that grew stronger with every bit of clothing the woman tossed aside. Then, without warning, I felt indescribably sad. I didn't know its source and was confused by my own reaction. When the show was over, much to my relief, we left. As we re-emerged onto the streets, we saw the strippers leaving by another door. I was surprised that, once fully clothed, nothing distinguished them from the other people on the street.

Late that night, we met two blond youths who offered to show us all of London. The four of us walked the streets and talked. We knew that we were being "taken," yet neither of us minded since we both relished the walk through such a foreign, captivating world. We all agreed that Americans and Englishmen were brothers. The most outspoken youth compared American and English "birds," but interrupted his discourse by saying, "There's one place that every visitor to London must see. If he doesn't see it, then he hasn't been to London. And that place, my friends, is Trafalgar Square. Gents," he stopped to sweep his arm before him, "this is Trafalgar Square." I saw a dark statue looming up from the night shadows of the surrounding buildings. Except for we four "brothers," the square was eerily lifeless. Not even a pedestrian disturbed the silence. The speaker continued, "You do know who Lord Nelson was, don't you? He was the greatest British naval officer—no—the greatest naval officer in the whole world who ever lived."

After that statement had time to settle into mine and Gus' minds, the young men led us to the train station, casually mentioning that, sometimes, Americans gave them money. I counted out the equivalent of five dollars for them, but Gus reached into his pocket and indiscriminately gave each a handful of "funny money," delighting the recipients.

When we were alone, I asked, "Geez, Gus, why'd you give them all that dough?"

"We've got no use for it. Besides, they need it more than we do."

We caught the train for Portsmouth where we spent the remainder of the night in our bunks and shipped out the next day.

* * *

The ship pulled into Hamburg like an unwanted guest. The midshipmen and the crew lounged on the deck in marked contrast to their arrival in Portsmouth. I was standing next to a couple of senior officers and heard one of them say, "See that blond guy standing on the dock?" I saw a platinum blond man standing to one side of some officials. The officer continued, "He was a U-boat commander during World War II. I'm having supper with him tonight." I took another, more careful look. The German was dressed in neat civilian clothes that gave no hint of his military past. He looked like a young man. Making a quantum leap with my imagination, I placed the German at the periscope of a sleek, steel fish hunting Allied shipping, deeply and silently, through lightless, black water.

After the sister ships were docked, the mids and crew were given six days of leave. Again, I teamed up with Hovedo to visit zoos and parks during the day and to wander the seamier side streets at night. Once we saw a strikingly beautiful German girl. I asked, "Did you see that girl?" Gus nodded yes. I continued, "We'll never see her again for the rest of eternity."

"You can't say that."

"Sure, I can."

"How do you know?"

"Look! She's gone already."

"I think you have a screwed-up way of looking at things."

"Good. I like being screwed up."

The red-light district filled us with wonder. Women sat in display windows while groups of well-dressed mids and poorly dressed nondescripts said clever and obscene things to them. Some of the women were overweight and old, wearing scant clothing that allowed their obesity to bulge in all directions. Others were young and sweet like the girl next door that you want to marry. My sister, Cora, could have sat with them and not have looked out of place.

At the ends of the streets were groups of Germans holding Bibles above their heads and calling into the crowd. Gus asked, "What are they saying?"

"I don't know, but I'm sure it's something about us sinning or that this is a place of sin or something like that."

With each passing day, the prostitutes became more and more of an attraction. One night, after failing to find Gus after evening meal on board the ship, I went ashore alone. Desire led me to the domains of love. I had decided that the women in the display windows were a little too shopworn for my tastes, so I tramped the side streets until I found a small hotel with an enclosed courtyard. Here was ecstasy, ready for the buying.

Standing in the courtyard with my fisted hands inside my pockets to hide my erection, I debated with myself. Even though it was legal in Germany, there was still something dirty and criminal about it. I had always regarded sex as sacred, the union of two people in both the physical and spiritual plane. It had to be unique and to be unique precluded free love and prostitution. It was a private and special act.

Yet, I was nineteen and still a virgin. I was haunted by a documentary that showed tombstones of English soldiers who had died at El Alamein during World War II. One of the dead had been seventeen years old when he was killed. I asked myself, *what could that boy have known about life?* I also knew that I'd be lucky to make it through third class year. Plebe year had taught me that I was not midshipman material; I did not belong at the Academy. Besides, a pattern of failure had been set and the mathematical and scientific foundation I should have had was not there. Failure meant Vietnam and Vietnam, to my feverish imagination, meant death. I asked myself, *what do I know about life?* It was this question that determined me to bed a prostitute.

I joined the milling crowds and tried to be inconspicuous. Unfortunately, I attracted the attention of a small, wiry, black-haired Italian woman of perhaps thirty years of age. She called, "Hey, you, sonny boy, come with me." She added a few words in German, which made the other women laugh. "Only ten dollars and you have all you want." She caught my arm and stroked it. "I'll teach you real good. The other girls will rob you." I broke away from the laugher of the women and jumped into the crowd.

Then I saw a goddess: young, voluptuous, the stuff of dreams. Since I was self-conscious, I didn't want to appear to be just another guy wanting to get laid. I thought that I might impress her if I appeared to be an intellectual and that required conversation. When she turned her electric blue eyes on me, I asked, "Do you speak English?"

"No."

"Oh," and I walked away. I stopped within sight of her and tried to screw up my courage for another assault on her virtue. My groin ached and I was afraid that I might have an orgasm right there. I decided, *It's now or never.* Purposefully, I walked toward the goddess, but was cut off by an old, dirty, decrepit man, recently exhumed from his crypt and rife with disease. I heard them mumbling together and the two took the elevator and ascended toward heaven. The scene was revolting, and my throat tighten.

Then I saw another woman who looked very much like the goddess, only ten years older. Her tight skirt was so short that I could see the bottom of her butt as she jiggled by me. I knew I had found El Dorado. I asked her, "Do you speak English?"

"Yes, do you want me?"

"Yes."

I followed her to the elevator and thought of all the intellectual things I could say, how this could be a part of a sociological study, then decided that it would only make me look stupid.

She asked, "Are you with the boat of midshipmen at the pier?"

"Yes."

"What's your name?"

"Michael."

"My name's Mary."

The elevator stopped at a neat, clean apartment with modern furniture and a Swiss couch. She asked, "Would you like a drink?"

"Okay."

"Do you mind if I have one too?"

"No."

"What would you like?"

"A soda."

"I'll have a scotch and water. The drinks are two dollars and fifty cents apiece."

"Okay."

Mary brought the drinks and we sat on the couch. She said, "For ten dollars, I lift my dress and we do it that way. For fifteen dollars, I take off all my clothes, and for fifty dollars, we see a movie, I give you French love, and then we make love. What would you like?"

I didn't know what French love was and was afraid to find out, so I opted for the fifteen-dollar thrill. "I'll take it with all your clothes off."

"Nothing else?"

"No."

"Including the drinks, that'll be twenty-five dollars."

I noted the error in her math but kept quiet about it and gave her the money. Immediately, she walked to the wall and dropped the bills into a chute like a mail slot. She slipped out of her clothing. She had a nice body. However, I felt as though I was another person, as though I was watching myself from another location. Ever since I stepped out of the elevator, I was disassociating myself from these events. I was numb and dazed as the prostitute pulled down my trousers and slipped a condom onto my penis. Then she lay down and opened her pearly gate. I was upon her, had penetrated the forbidden zone, and came before I took two breaths. Masking my reaction, I maintained my erection and did my best to play the man. In less than a minute, Mary started to persistently ask, "Did you cum yet? Did you cum yet?" I kept shaking my head no, but on an upstroke, she slid from beneath me and I plowed into the fabric of the couch, my poor penis banished from paradise. Sitting up, surprised, I asked, "Is that all?"

As I zipped up my fly, Mary showed me to the door. Although I didn't see anyone, I knew that if I protested, I would be severely beaten by her unseen pimp. As the door closed behind me, I thought, *I should have beat off.* Paradise had failed me.

* * *

During the remainder of the week, Gus and I had several small adventures. We took city buses and stayed on them throughout their entire routes. In that way, we saw all parts of the city.

As the friendship between us grew, Gus attempted to guide his lost friend. His tone was reasoning, almost pleading. Once, Gus, impressed, pointed to a Mercedes that passed our bus. I shrugged my shoulders and said, "So what?"

With evident shock, my friend exclaimed, "So what? That's what I like about you, Mike. You're ignorant of anything that's common knowledge and you say, 'So what?' And that's it. You don't even try to fit in."

"So what?" Gus fidgeted irritably.

To relieve the tension, I added, "So how am I supposed to learn about cars? Become a mechanic?"

"It's more than cars. What about sports?"

"I like to work out, and I like some sports, but team sports don't interest me. I don't care who wins, and I can't get excited over something as impersonal as a moving ball. I have never played a game of baseball, football, or basketball, not once. I've never even watched a single ball game, any ball game, on TV, not once. I don't care about cars and to assume that I'm abnormal because I don't have the right attitude towards them is wrong. I don't relate to them. The fact is that most of these things don't," I searched for the right words, "speak to me."

"Then what does speak to you?"

"Nature, the woods, philosophy, dogs, a thousand other things."

"Can you drive a philosophy book or a piece of the woods? You might know a hell of a lot about dogs, but who else in the world, *your* world, knows about dogs?"

"They're alive."

"Philosophy is alive?"

I smiled. "Metaphorically speaking." I chuckled, but Hovedo wasn't buying it. I continued, "How can anyone relate to a machine or get excited over people chasing a ball back and forth on a court like –a—a—yo-yo?"

"They're a part of life too. It's part of our culture. You relate to other people by knowing the things that bore you so much."

"Okay, so what am I supposed to do? Change my whole personality?"

"All you have to do is to pick up a magazine and read it. Pick up a magazine about cars or sports and read it from front to back, even the stuff you don't understand. If you're confused, ask questions, or look it up in the library. That's all you have to do. Then, when someone talks about these things, you'll know what they're talking about."

"Gus, I like the way I am."

"It's fucked up, if you ask me."

"Fine. I like being fucked up."

An old man sitting opposite us wiped his forehead with a handkerchief and leaned toward us. He said in broken English, "I was here during the war. It was a terrible time. Everybody was afraid. Thirty American girls were here. They were told to leave, but they didn't. Hitler tortured them to death." Gus and I looked quizzically at each other. The old man sat back and silently watched the street traffic. He got out at the next stop.

When the bus completed its circular route, we resumed our meandering on foot. We paused before a building that bore a sign reading "Academe Philosophic." I said, "See? A school of philosophy. I'm not the only dummy in the world."

* * *

The final adventure for the two of us was a tour of East and West Berlin. The first part of the morning was spent walking the busy streets of the West. The buildings were tall and the newness of the articles in the store windows along with the brisk activity of the pedestrians made West Berlin seem like a huge Toyland. Gus and I were with a group of mids when an elderly German woman stopped us. She gripped Gus' arm and said in English, "I want to thank you for saving us from them! I want to thank you for saving us from the Russians! Thank you, thank you so very much!" She left us gazing at her retreating figure.

I swelled with pride, but Gus said, "That makes me feel stupid. I haven't picked up a gun and stopped the Russians from doing anything."

In defense of my own feelings, I said, "But you could have, and you might."

We found our tour bus and were joined by a young German man who accentuated everything he said with a sardonic smile. He was to be our guide for West Berlin. As the bus worked its way through the congested streets, he pointed out the appropriate sites and added his own comments and jokes. "In Berlin," he said, "we have a King's Street, but no king; a Reich Street, but no Reich; and a Virgin's Street." Later he said, "When you go to East Berlin, they will take you to a park made by Russian soldiers to honor Russian soldiers and they will show you monuments made by Russian soldiers to honor Russian soldiers. They have a huge statue of a Russian soldier with his arm pointing toward the ground. He's unable to lift it because of all the German watches he's stolen." He then went on to describe the brutal Russian occupation immediately after World War II.

The transition point between East and West consisted of parallel rows of barricades straddling the road while at either end of the border sat a matching set of guard shacks. At the West end, a US Army captain stood at the front of the busload of midshipmen to brief them about life at the edge of civilization. He said that although most defections are from East to West, there are also defections in the opposite direction. The difference between them is that the West to East defections are almost all soldiers. He pointed out that there are nice German girls but that they are hard to meet. From the defensive tone of his voice, I speculated that the captain must be dating a German girl. He described the methods used to escape from East Berlin. The most original was a man who scuba dived his way to freedom. The most daring was a man who drove a sports car beneath the barriers, dropped his wife off, and then went back to successfully bring out his mother. Ironically, the hero's first name was Adolf. The most common escape route was hiding in unlikely places in a car.

After the captain left, the guide added, "This is the last time I'll be seeing you. I want you to remember that there is only one thing that we give to the East Germans and their allies: that's our sewage. I think that means something. Have a nice day."

Our bus maneuvered through the barricades and was stopped at the East Berlin barricade. A uniformed Soviet woman, a true James Bond villain, entered the bus. She was hard and unsmiling and reeked of discipline, brass knuckles, and barracks life. She walked down the aisle to count heads and to check the luggage racks. Meanwhile, a team of her compatriots was checking beneath the bus with mirrors and checking the baggage compartments below. The hermaphrodite left to be replaced by an equally unsmiling East German tour guide. We were very much the enemy.

Once in East Germany, we were startled by the lack of humanity on the streets, especially after all the activity in the West. It was as if the whole city was under the spell of a mythical wicked witch. Even if the whole population was working, there still should be some signs of life. As foretold, we visited parks and statues made by Russian soldiers to honor Russian soldiers. On the way, we saw innumerable ruins left over from World War II with trees growing out of the skeletons of bombed buildings, sometimes two and three stories up. That was another thing I hadn't seen in the West.

Whenever the bus stopped to let the mids visit a site, I had a cloying feeling. We were too carefully watched and not given enough time to walk around the block had we chosen to do so. At one stop, a mid changed buses. Immediately, he was missed, and the East Germans were in a panic until the next stop when he was found and returned to his original bus.

There was very little to be seen or was allowed to be seen. The highlight of the tour was a new housing development, a high rise. We were allowed to stand in its lobby for a couple of minutes. When the tour ended, we sighed with relief. The soldier woman again boarded the bus. Heads were counted, baggage compartments inspected, and the bus's belly subjected to mirrored scrutiny. We passed through the gate and soon free soil was beneath our feet.

We dismounted and waited for another bus that was to take us to the airport for the return flight to Hamburg. While waiting, we wandered to a small observation post fifteen feet from the infamous wall. Directly opposite us and within easy spitting distance was an East German observation post. Two East German guards sat there and seemed to be embarrassed while they ignored us. Not once did they look at us, but kept their eyes averted. A mid said, "Those are AK-47s they're carrying. Supposedly, only half of the guards shoot to kill when someone makes a run for the wall."

On the other side of the East German guards was a minefield about the width of a football field. The cinderblock wall was twelve feet high and was topped by a pipe that ran down its entire length. Should any German miraculously reach the wall and jump for its summit, the pipe was designed to roll back in his direction and throw him back onto East German soil. I turned toward the mid who commented upon the probability of getting shot at by the guards and asked, "Hell, would *you* try to get over this thing?" The question summarized what each of us was thinking.

* * *

The return cruise was accomplished in two quick weeks as opposed to the month it took to reach Europe. Both ship and crew were in a hurry to reach stateside where life could resume its normal course. We arrived at Annapolis at 0400 hours and were stunned by the heat and darkness as the midshipmen were ferried landward by the ships' launches.

Once ashore, two other Rhode Island youngsters and I searched the parking lot until we found Buddy standing next to my mother's large, boxlike Mercury. My brother agreed when I asked if it was all right to give my friends a ride home. Buddy then pulled a wad of keys out of his pocket, tried several of them on the trunk, giggled, and said, "Bigs forgot to give me the trunk key."

I said, "Figures," but the others were not concerned at the inconvenience. My brother and I sat in the front while the other two sat in the back, crushed by the luggage. Before leaving, I excused myself and returned with four cans of orange soda and passed them out. Buddy started the car and, as I touched the soda can to my lips, hit the accelerator. My head jammed onto the headrest of my seat as the soda spilled onto my clean white uniform. I yelled, "What the hell did you do *that* for? Are you nuts?" Buddy giggled while the mids in the back laughed. Then I laughed too.

CHAPTER IX
SUMMER LEAVE

Upon my return to Meantacut, I quickly resumed my old habit of reading while slowly sipping a cup of coffee and having Baron post guard at my feet. A week had passed when one day in the early afternoon, the dog alerted, and I was pleased to see Buddy walk through the front door. I stood up to greet my brother and, on the spur of the moment, thought to impress him with my boxing skills. Raising my fists, I challenged, "Want to fight?"

The words barely formed themselves when suddenly, my head was forced back with Buddy's palm jamming my nose as the fingers of that hand pressed into my eyes. His other hand gripped me by the throat and strangled me mercilessly as my body was lifted off the ground and slammed onto the floor. He increased the pressure at all points of contact until I whispered, "Okay, okay, I give." All this happened in a matter of seconds and would have gotten Buddy bitten, but I caught the dog immediately upon my release and soothed, "It's okay, Baron. We're just playing."

As soon as I was on my feet again, I asked with a lot of hurt in my voice, "Why'd you do that?"

"You wanted to fight."

"I wanted to box."

"You didn't say that. You said that you wanted to fight."

"All right, but you didn't give me a chance. I wasn't ready."

"That's the whole idea. You've got to learn that there are no rules in a fight. You either win or you lose. Period."

"Yeah," I assented sulkily, and then asked, "What brings you to this neck of the woods?"

"I wanted to see if you want to go to a movie tonight."

"To see what?"

"*Easy Rider.*"

"Sure."

That night I watched the Christ-like Peter Fonda bike across America. The ever wise, silent Peter traveled roads that I might one day travel. It was significant that Fonda's nickname was Captain America since that had been my nickname in high school. The commune scene captured my imagination. Free love. Sharing. A way to learn about the world; a way I'd miss at the Academy. Desire set into my heart as I watched Peter's experiences of the road less traveled. I, too, wanted to be silent and wise and decided to buy a motorcycle. After the movie, I asked Buddy to help me.

Two weeks later, my brother and I stood in a bike shop whose owner had a reputation for honesty. We talked to the short, squat, solid man with stubby, thick fingers and arms streaked with grease. He looked at my slender build, considered the price range, and led us to a sleek, light blue 250cc Triumph. He said to me, "This is the bike for you. It's in good condition, is easy to handle, and is a good bike to learn on."

I was immediately taken by it, but Buddy intervened, "It's too small." He then pointed to a greasy, grimy, black and green monstrosity and said, "This is the bike *you* want. You want something that'll make people look up, that'll make them know that a real biker is going by. The Triumph is nice, but can you see yourself going down the road making a buzzing noise like a bee in heat and having everyone laugh at you? Yesterday I saw a big guy on a small bike, and we all laughed at him. What made it even worse was that he was riding next to a 650."

The shop owner maintained his stance. "If this is his first bike, the young man should take the 250. The 650 BSA isn't near as good and the 250 will last a lot longer. Besides, he wants the 250 and that means a lot."

I joined in. "Bud, the 650's too big for me. I don't know how to ride the thing. I think I should start with something small."

"I'll teach you everything you have to know. Look, if you want to impress people, take the 650 BSA."

"I don't want to impress anyone."

"You're going to look like a fool on that toy over there."

I made an impatient move as though I wanted to walk out on the whole business and looked about me disappointedly. Finally, I conceded to my brother's will. "All right, I'll buy the damn thing, but I think you're wrong."

"You'll love it, Mike."

"Yeah, sure."

I looked at the monster I was buying; it looked like death with nothing between me and the asphalt but this beast. But then, death wasn't so terrible. After all, it might be a solution to all my problems. I remembered a poem I had read, "To an Athlete Dying Young." If I died now, the world would grieve the loss of such a promising treasure, never knowing what the Academy seemed to know so well—that I was a fuck-up. However, that was for destiny to decide. I saw no sense in courting death.

Training began the next day. In the summer haze of afternoon heat, my brother took me to the summit of a hill, newly flattened with all its life bulldozed away. The hill itself would have been flattened into nonexistence, but it was too large for the developer's equipment. The bleak desolation was drawn and quartered by the intersection of two newly paved roads. Buddy explained the mechanics of a motorcycle, took a short spin on his own 500cc Triumph, and returned to me. He handed the bike to me. "Now you try it."

Straddling the Triumph, I headed for the intersection where I'd have more room to turn around. While riding, I wondered how, if the accelerator and the brake were under the same hand, a biker could do one without doing the other. At the intersection, I started to make my circle, decided I couldn't make it, and turned the bike onto an artery going downhill.

Instead of braking with my fingers, I cocked my wrist back, causing the bike to accelerate while I was braking at the same time. Without thinking, I slammed my left foot onto the pavement in a futile effort to cause drag. The bike was internally hemorrhaging. A neighbor's car passed with startled, bulging eyes blanketing its windows. Buddy began a fast run to try to catch up. When he reached me, I was at the bottom of the hill, straddling the stalled motorcycle.

As I stood dazed, I noticed that my left foot was a lot warmer than my right foot. Looking at the sole of my left shoe, I found that it was almost worn through. A few minutes later, after Buddy caught up, he asked me, "Is everything okay?"

"Sure."

All movement stopped as the two of us paused, dumbfounded by what had happened, then we burst out laughing. Buddy said, "I'll take us back."

That was the extent of my training. The next day, I drove my mother's car to Providence and, by applying for a license from the right man, identified by word of mouth, I was able to get it without taking a driver's test. On lonely afternoons, I would sneak out of the garage on my monstrosity and ride for an hour or two.

* * *

The long summer days allowed me to observe Beth and to try to figure out the urgency in my mother's phone calls. Often, she sat in her room, hour upon hour, talking to herself. Not once did she burst into the rages of violence that she displayed when we were growing up together.

As was to be expected, my biggest joy and greatest comfort was my daily walk in the woods. I bathed in the solitude that I had come to love and let my imagination, curtailed at the Academy, run away at will. I followed small streams, thinking of them as great rivers. I tossed twigs into the flowing water, and they became ancient triremes venturing into unknown lands, the *Argo* into the Black Sea. Rain puddles became huge lakes while rocks became mighty cliffs.

Once during my walks, Baron and I passed a parked car on a dirt road. I heard the crack of a .22 so I snapped into a jog to keep my dog from having the time to investigate and possibly get shot. The dog followed, but soon fell behind, so I stopped, turned, and found a man with a rifle chasing us. I took a belligerent stance, hands tightened into fists and muscles knotted in anger. Although I hadn't heard the whine of the bullet, I might have been shot at. Our pursuer stopped, pointed to the car behind him, and said, "That's my car." I stood stiffly while Baron, between us, looked at the stranger with idle curiosity, jutting his nose toward him and trying to get a scent. The stranger scratched his head in obvious confusion, then walked to his car. Without a word, I turned and continued my walk.

Well into my leave, my brother again visited me. He said, "I dropped by to tell you that I sent for some tickets."

"For what?"

"For Woodstock."

"What's that?"

"It's a town in New York where they're going to hold a three-day open-air concert. All the biggies are going to be there: Joan Baez, Jefferson Airplane, Janis Joplin, the whole works. Do you want to go?"

"Okay."

"Good. How's the riding coming along?"

"I'm still alive if that's what you're asking. How much do I owe you?"

"My treat."

The tickets arrived within two weeks. Buddy, who had been the motivating force, gave me his ticket and said, "I've got some bad news. I can't make the trip because of conflicts with work and my grad courses, so I gave my ticket to Ed next door. I hope you don't mind going with him." Ed and I had been childhood friends until the age of puberty when the fuzz on Ed's upper lip and his deepened voice far outdistanced my delayed manhood. We remained cordial, but a distance that was never bridged sat between us.

I still held a little resentment toward Ed, and my reservations were further increased when I saw him for the first time in three years. I was standing in my mother's driveway under a scorching sun and was about to go inside when I heard someone calling to me. Turning, I saw Ed wave and start walking toward me. He took small, mincing steps as though he was walking through a field covered with plover eggs. He seemed to be consciously graceful. Tumblers clicked in my mind, but nothing took solid form. Wonder turned into suspicion, yet the words and images refused to develop. Ed said, "Long time, no see."

We shook hands. "How ya doing, Ed?"

"Good. How's things?"

"You know that I'm going to the Naval Academy?"

"So I heard. How do you like it?"

"I don't but try to tell *them* that." Ed grinned as I nodded my head toward my mother's house. I asked, "What have you been up to?"

"Right now, I'm studying architecture in Boston. Before that I was in computers but gave that up. And before that I was a ski bum in New Hampshire."

"Sounds like you've been having a good time."

"I try. I'd like to stay here and talk, but I've got to meet someone at five. I came to find out when you want to leave."

"Anytime."

"Good. Tomorrow afternoon at four?"

"Sure."

"Later."

"Yeah, later."

My eyes followed Ed as he walked back to his own home. They were arrested by the jaunty swing of his hips.

* * *

The next morning, I took The Beast, my name for the motorcycle, out for a spin. I raised the garage door, straddled The Beast, then hurtled into the bright sunlight. After a mile of suburb turnings, I reached a main thoroughfare. Now the riding would be much easier. Every corner was a source of concern since I had previously discovered that the bike tended to stall whenever fully stopped. Once it stalled, I would have to wait five to ten minutes before I could get it going again. The wait was both embarrassing and aggravating.

As I approached an intersection, I saw a car coming from my left. Tempted to pull out, I decided against it and stopped. The bike stalled, and the car took a right turn. The car's driver, a fat, white haired, old woman, hadn't used her directional. The motorcycle died just as the old woman sailed blindly past me, totally oblivious of the trouble she had caused me and apparently oblivious to the rest of existence as well. I knew that I shouldn't have stopped. Now, I would have to sit beneath the hot, glaring sun until The Beast was cool enough to allow me to start it again.

After the requisite ten-minute wait, I was again racing down the open road, a free soul, Captain America, experiencing life. I saw before me a stop light and all the frustrations of the last half-hour made me race a little faster to catch the light, but to no avail. The light turned red before I reached it, forcing me to stop, which caused the bike to stall. Again, I wheeled it to the side of the road. I heard a disembodied voice ask from one of the many windows of nearby houses, "Why don't you get yourself a real bike?" Humiliated, I waited my ten minutes, this time under some cool maple trees, then I hit the road.

Alas, my trials had yet to reach a climax. I was ripping down a straightaway, feeling a communion with The Beast, wind whipping at my clothes and asphalt whizzing by, when I saw before me a stop sign. This time, however, I was determined that no fat old lady was going to have me roasting in the hot sun by the side of the road. I'd run the stop sign. I hit the accelerator and the Beast lurched at my touch. I saw a car coming from my left. Without thought, I went faster, took a left turn a little too sharply, and felt the bike hit the curbstone.

In the next instant, I was flat on my back, sliding down the sidewalk and watching the tree branches pass overhead. Luckily, I wore a helmet and my head bounced as I turned it to see the Beast traveling a parallel course in the gutter. The two of us slid for forty feet before friction brought us to a stop. Quickly, I stood up in embarrassment, wobbling back and forth. A car driven by an elderly man pulled up. "Are you alright?"

I checked to see what damage I had done to myself and found a small scrape about the size of my palm on my right hip. I answered, "I guess so." The old man shook his head back and forth condescendingly then drove away.

Next, I checked the bike. Its left pedal was pushed up. I noticed that a few other parts were a little askew, but all in all, it seemed to be in good shape. I wheeled the bike to the nearest telephone booth half a mile away. Once there, I called Cora, who, fortunately, was at my mother's house, to come and pick me up.

She arrived as quickly as possible. As she pulled into the parking lot of a small country store, I saw how much older and careworn she seemed, as if she had aged ten years since last spring. She was getting beefy and hard. I thought it odd that I should notice this now. We decided that I should go back to our mother's house, take a shower, and change clothes. When that was done, she drove me back to the bike where I straddled it again to ride it home. Cora followed me all the way and said, once safely there, "It took a lot of guts to get back on that thing."

My Easy Rider career ended with a shrug of my shoulders.

* * *

That afternoon, I took a large brown paper bag and tossed enough underwear in it to last three days, one pair per day. Next, I went into the kitchen for food. I reasoned that three cans of Campbell's Pork and Beans, one per day, ought to be enough to keep me alive. However, when Mom saw the meagerness of my preparations, she insisted on making a lunch that filled the rest of the bag.

She asked, "Do you know where you'll be staying?"

"I guess we'll sleep in the car."

"I'll put a blanket in the car for you."

At the appointed hour, I stepped outside in time to see Ed tiptoe across the lawn. He carried a large brown suitcase sufficient for the siege of Stalingrad and a gallon milk bottle full of water. In a soft, floating voice, Ed asked, "Ready to go?" I noted how beautiful Ed's large, green eyes were and felt uncomfortable under their gaze.

I did all the driving while Ed did all the talking. He told about his life's experiences and the things that he'd learned from them. "The women in New Hampshire are the horniest broads in the world. I don't know what it is, whether it's the isolation or what, but I never got laid so much as when I was working at a ski lodge up there. And the women of Boston only screw married men. I was having it rough until I was told to get a wedding ring. So I bought one and, sure enough, I started getting laid like you wouldn't believe. I experimented too. Once in a while, I'd take the ring off to see what would happen and I dropped into nowhere land. I'm telling you, if you go to Boston, wear a wedding ring."

I said, "I think that says a lot about our society."

"Yeah, all the women like to fuck."

I chuckled. "What about integrity?"

"What about it?"

I shrugged. Ed put an understanding hand on my shoulder and said, "You'll learn."

180

"Thanks." I smiled.

In the late evening, after a couple of hours of driving, we found ourselves in a long line of glittering headlights forming a thick, slow moving, diamond necklace leading to Woodstock. Gossamer voices picked at the darkness while blue-jeaned hips and legs walked between the cars, the upper portions of the bodies unlit and invisible in the night. Parking would have been impossible to find, but miles of waving flashlights pointed out where to go and led us to a field of thick, green grass. The summer night was cool and fresh.

I parked the car, turned off the ignition, and was so tired that I decided to sleep right then and there. I rolled my jacket into a ball to use as a pillow just as it started to rain. The last thing I remembered was Ed asking me if I wanted to check out the concert to see if anyone was performing. *No.* He then disappeared into the subdued turmoil of disparate voices and slamming car doors.

I awoke to a bright, clean day. I stayed where I was, crinkled up on the front seat, enjoying the settled-in comfort. After pleasantly musing on the events of the day to come, I decided to look at the scrape on my right hip. To my dismay, I found that the blood had formed a scab of which my pant leg had become a part. Too late, I thought that I should have bandaged it and became determined to peel my trousers off in case I had to defecate.

Ed snapped awake in the back seat when he reached for the milk bottle that held our drinking water. I asked, "Was anybody at the concert?"

"Yeah, Joan Baez."

"What was she like?"

"Revolutionary kitsch. Oh, by the way, I think we've wasted our eighteen dollars. They're letting people in for free. Give me your ticket and I'll see if I can sell them." After a moment, he asked, "Do you mind if I grab something to eat?"

I shook my head no. Ed reached into my paper bag and asked, "Do you want anything?"

"Yeah, the cinnamon rolls."

"The whole pack?"

"Well, you can have one if you want. No, I'm kidding; grab what you want, but they might not be there later."

Between mouthfuls, Ed said, "There are three broads in that tent."

I saw three dumpy, unkempt women preparing breakfast over an open campfire. Ed said, "I'm going to scout about a bit," and left me to myself. After making sure no one could see me, I pulled my trousers down as far as they would go. There was no going beyond the scab. Pressing my shoulders against the back of the seat and straightening my legs, I propped myself up as best as I could. Alternately, I poured water onto my wound and peeled the trousers down half an inch at a time, then poured more water. The ordeal was painful despite the care and time I put into it. Half an hour passed before my leg was free. Seizing the moment, I rushed to the portable latrines nearby to move my bowels. When I returned to the car, I put some salve onto the wound but was unable to find anything to use as a bandage. Instead of improvising, I accepted the situation and unconsciously set myself up to undergo the same ordeal the following day.

When Ed returned, I was sitting on the hood of the car with my back against its windshield. He was followed by three men, all uniformed, like nearly everyone else, in dirty blue jeans, T-shirts, and sneakers. Ed asked me if I could open the trunk of the car. Without moving his suitcase from the trunk, he opened it to reveal rows of plastic bags filled with pot and a variety of pillboxes. I stood with them for a couple of minutes, but the strange terminology and confident knowledge of the others confused me, made me an outsider, so I returned to my seat on the hood.

When their business was concluded, I returned to the group. The five of us left for the concert grounds, each carrying a blanket over his shoulder. One of the newcomers carried a gallon jug filled with tea. Another walked with his arms wrapped about a huge watermelon. I carried the lunch prepared by Mom. Halfway to the concert, we stopped to eat and shared everything.

The road was filled with a milling crowd of pilgrims. The jubilant laughing and talking was exciting as the dust rose in small clouds and the police ignored the pot smoking. A stream of clear water cut a swathe through a field that was well below the level of the road. Nude bathers were there where the dust couldn't reach them. A full-bodied woman moved along the stream's bank, her dark triangle pointed toward the good earth, rich with fertility and growth. The woman's long, dark hair reached her waist in a thick braid. Her body oozed with images of warmth and softness, tender comfort, and quiet calm. The mystery, the otherness of women, impressed itself again into my mind.

The five of us found a clear spot about halfway up the hill from the stage where we placed our blankets. One asked me, "Want a joint?"

"No," I said and was surprised when no one hassled me or tried to pressure me into smoking it. They had accepted me, and I had the unique pleasure of being a member of a group instead feeling like a pariah. The tea made its rounds, passed from hand to hand. Whenever someone bought sodas or hot dogs, he bought enough for all of us.

The stage was bare except for the crew who looked no bigger than match sticks. Yet, the acoustics were magnificent. We could have been sitting in a living room, listening to a stereo. Hearing the music would be no problem.

The master of ceremonies called from the stage, "You people are the finest people in the world." He repeated this so often that it became aggravating.

A small poster found its way to me. It was a stark black and white print showing a soldier firing an M-16. A stanza from Bob Dylan's "Like a Rolling Stone" flashed across its belly:

Nobody's ever taught you how to live out on the street
And now you're gonna have to get used to it.

I folded up the poster and slipped it into my pocket. It would be a good memento.

The American flag was everywhere, especially in the small camps nestled among the copses of maple trees. It dangled from poles made from young saplings that were cut down for that purpose. A voice that noticed the same thing lifted above the crowd, "I thought these people were supposed to be communists!" When a man walked by wearing the flag like a skirt, I wondered, *should I feel outrage*?

The master of ceremonies said, "There are four hundred thousand of you fuckers out there." Then he reminded them how they were the finest people on earth.

The concert got off to a slow start with vast spaces of time sitting between the sounds of acid rock guitars ripping through the air. Incense burned in competition with fresh breezes to dominate the scene, making a perfect contrast so that the air seemed fresher and the incense seemed more captivating. Between performances were large gaps of silence clogging the long wait beneath the broiling sun, filled by a watching crowd busy watching one another. Ed said, "I've never seen so many freaks."

I thought, *why do they all look so much alike?*

The master of ceremonies said, "You people are great!" Desultory hand clapping answered him. He continued to warn them that the brown acid being passed out was not good. "Of course, it's your trip, man, but I'd be careful." Then he introduced Richie Havens whose pleasantly raspy, sandpaper voice carried his message of freedom throughout the multitude. The concert rolled onwards, picking up momentum with less and less time between performances.

Man is a territorial animal and each person's blanket became that person's territory. I nearly got into a fight over my own blanket. I had gone to the hotdog booth where I was served by a young lady with the kindest amber eyes I had ever seen. Her lithe, poetic movements added to her mystique. When I returned to my blanket, I found a sixteen-year-old boy with a foot-long bayonet stuck in his belt sitting on its edge. As I sat down, the boy tried to yank my blanket away from me. Angered, but not intimidated by the weapon, I jerked it back, ready to fight. The boy sensed the fury in my movement and left.

The MC: "Don't go to the hotdog booths on the top of the hill. They're charging a dollar for a hotdog. The booths farther down are charging only a quarter."

Jefferson Airplane showed up and the concert took off. For the umpteenth time the MC said, "You people are wonderful. You're the finest people in the world."

A young girl nearby asked in annoyance, "Why does he keep saying that?"

Groups of performers came and went in a frenzy of musical delight. Night and day became confused in the continual fluster of activity on the stage. Jimi Hendrix played the "Star Spangled Banner."

I was asked, "Want to try some acid?"

"No, thanks."

Country Joe McDonald performed with abrasive, antagonistic cynicism as he gave a spelling lesson. "Give me an F."

"F."

"Give me a U."

"U."

"Give me a C."

"C."

"Give me a K."

"K."

"What does that spell?"

"Fuck!"

"What does that spell?"

"Fuck!"

"What does that spell?"

"Fuck!"

"What does that spell?"

"Fuck!"

Country Joe then sang about how Uncle Sam "got himself into a terrible jam way down yonder in Vietnam."

The song disturbed me, especially since everyone around me knew all the words. Kenny, who was currently serving in South Vietnam, and my brother, Buddy, would see this as a betrayal, as ridiculing and making meaningless the deaths and sacrifices of them and their friends. They would see it as sending a message to North Vietnam, "Hang in there and we'll see that you win." I wasn't sure where I stood, but I didn't sing the song.

In the evening, during a break in the music, I took a small walk and returned to my blanket to find that it was again occupied, this time by a guy and a girl. They were lying on it, their bodies facing one another and their faces nearly touching. Their torsos were separated enough so that I could sit between their legs. They were immersed in conversation, and I could hear their slightest whispers.

The man: "When did you get here?"

The girl: "This morning."

The man: "What'd you think of it so far?"

The girl: "It's all right."

The man: "How'd you get here?"

The girl: "My mother dropped me off."

The man: "Are you staying for the whole concert?"

The girl: "No. My mother is going to pick me up later."

Silence.

The girl: "I'm only seventeen."

The man: "That's all right."

The girl: "How old are you?"

The man: "I'm twenty-four. Do you smoke?"

The girl (A note of fear in her voice): "Sometimes."

The man: "I got some really good stuff in my tent. Do you want to try it?"

The girl (Afraid): "I'm only seventeen."

The man: "What has that got to do with it?"

Silence.

The girl: "All right."

Their dark figures disappeared into an even darker night.

* * *

Three o'clock in the morning, I awoke to hear Janis Joplin singing, "Baby! Baby! Baby!..."

The MC: "Somebody's passing out bad acid. It's purple and it's fucked up a lot of good people! If you see any acid that color, don't take it! As for the guy who's passing it out, mother, you better never let me get my hands on you!"

A man crawled by on his hands and knees.

Before his performance, Arlo Guthrie gave a monologue. "Yeah, it's far out, man. I don't know if you, I don't know—uh—like, how many of you can dig how many people there are, man? Like, I was rapping to the fuzz, right. Can you dig it, man? There are supposed to be a million and a half people here by tonight. Can you dig that? New York State Highway is closed, man. Yeah. Lot of freaks! Ha, ha!" Then he sang a song about smuggling dope from Mexico.

Two guys were about to fight, but the pleading of the people about them quelled their anger.

Crosby, Stills, Nash, and Young sang their cryptic songs, portions of which stuck in my mind and became distorted even as I listened to them. I sang, "I am yours. You are mine. I am what you are. I feel fine." After a few lines passed, I sang, "You've got to tell it like it is. What've you got to lose?"

A woman had a child. No fights were reported.

Sly and the Family Stone performed. "I want to take you higher!" and with each "'higher" arms were raised in time with the music.

I saw the most beautiful face I had ever seen. She had gently tanned, fine features haloed by straight, well-groomed, brilliantly shiny hair. This was a woman I could fall in love with. I changed my position to see her better, the view of her body having been totally blocked by the intervening people. Quickly, I looked away. The young lady was a man.

Joe Cocker sang a song about needing someone to love.

During the night, an entertainer had the audience light matches. It was dark until the effulgence of light covered the field with thousands of earthbound stars.

Sporadically, it started to rain, and I joined in the chant, "No rain! No rain! No rain!" The will of the masses was ineffectual against nature. The chant struck me as being absurd, futile, and enchanting. A mudslide was made, down which people belly flopped for hundreds of feet, careless of their clothing.

The overused porta johns became foul. To urinate, I stood on the seat of the commode since the floor was too slick with excrescence to stand on. I prayed that I wouldn't have to move my bowels again before we left.

The rain intensified as the concert ground to a halt. The multitude dispersed as quickly as it had appeared, leaving behind their waste and small pockets of die-hard humanity. Some were busy cleaning up the area. Others were sitting in small groups, smoking pot. One clot lifted a large American flag over its collective head to ward off the rain. I searched within myself to see if I felt outrage. I didn't.

An army helicopter hovered overhead. A voice said, "I don't believe it! They're dropping dope!" They were dropping daisies.

The five of us eventually decided to leave and return to our cars. The field had become muddy, and we knew we'd be lucky to get out. I sat behind the wheel of my mother's Mercury and hit the gas while the others pushed. The car screamed and the others grunted, but the car didn't move an inch. Opening the car door, Ed asked, "Do you have it in neutral?"

"Yeah."

Without comment, he reached down and released the emergency brake. The car was freed.

Now it was my turn to push. Taking my stance at the rear of the other car, I pushed with all my might only to discover myself being sprayed with mud from the spinning tires. Hoping no one had noticed, I changed my position. Again, we struggled to move the car, but the vehicle refused to budge. One of our companions said, "Don't worry. We'll get the farmer's tractor to pull us out."

We all shook hands and Ed and I left for home.

By then it was night. Figures loomed along the roadside, thumbing to be picked up. Occasionally, we'd hear, "Hey, Rhode Island," but we kept going and made excuses to one another that we hadn't seen them in time to stop. Finally, Ed said, "Let's face it, Mike, the concert is over, and I can't risk being stopped by the police because of a carload of hippies."

* * *

As my leave drew to a close, I spent more and more of my time following the small streams and rivulets familiar to me since childhood and letting my imagination course along with them. Hovedo had sent me an invitation to spend the remainder of my leave boating with him and a newly found girlfriend in Illinois. However, I preferred staying in my native element eating blueberries, wild cherries, and wild grapes.

During my rambles, my mind wandered further than my body ever could. Sometimes I saw myself as the first man on the moon. At other times I saw myself as a great lawmaker on the order of Solon, distributing wealth as fairly as possible while keeping the initiative of capitalism alive. I saw myself as the great spokesman against privilege, standing on a dais with lifted fist in conjunction with massive applause. Every adult would have fourteen acres of tax-free land, like the Spartans. It would be hereditary, always going to the first-born man or woman.

Vast areas of land would be set aside to preserve animal species and to give children an opportunity to see life without glass and asphalt. Realizing that I was on the edge of a totalitarian state, I tried to think of a system whereby free thought and action might be preserved. Maybe cities of sanctuary could be set up like in the Bible. After several hours of similar musings, I reminded myself that I shouldn't daydream so much, especially once I returned to school.

My walks were blighted by the absence of bob white quails. For years I had cut through these fields and been thrilled by the sudden flush of a dozen birds. They always startled me no matter how much I expected their panicked flight. Something had either killed them off or driven them away. I was unable to find even a single straggler. Even the crows were gone.

I spent a lot of time observing Beth. Seeking answers to the problematic phone calls that assailed me at school, I frequently asked my mother what the "story" was when Beth was either sleeping or taking a bath. Finally, after numerous evasions by Mom and in total frustration, I slammed my coffee cup onto the kitchen table and said, "Look! It doesn't help any to leave me to guess what's wrong. It's unbearable the way you keep me guessing. Can't you see what it's doing to me? Why don't you give me a break for a change and be honest with me, if only for this one time, okay?"

She hesitated, then, "I think something happened to your sister."

"Oh good, something happened to Beth. That really relieves my mind now that I know the whole story."

"I think Peter next door had sex with her or is having sex with her or something like that."

"What would Pete want with Beth?"

"You have to remember that Beth is not unattractive. You don't see her as being attractive because she's your sister and you have to remember that Pete is a bit retarded too."

"No, I don't think he's retarded."

"Slow then."

"Why do you think it's him?"

"Because Buddy saw them sitting downstairs together on the couch. Pete had his arm around her."

"Yeah, Buddy told me about that. He told me he was coming into the house one afternoon with a bag of groceries when he looked into the cellar window and saw them. That means that he put the bag of groceries down, got onto his hands and knees, put his head into the window well, and saw them. I know Buddy wouldn't lie to us, but why would he do that?"

"You know that he's psychic. He probably had a hunch."

"Okay, so he has a hunch and is at the window. Even then, how could he see inside? Even with the cellar lights on, how could he see inside well enough in daylight to see what was going on? Besides, I don't think you *can* see the couch from *any* of the cellar windows."

"What are you saying?"

"I'm not saying anything. It just seems physically impossible to me that he saw them. If it was anyone else but Buddy who said this, I wouldn't believe him."

"Well, that's what he saw."

"So you think Pete is pooning her?"

"Mike, this is your sister."

"Okay, do you think Peter is still having sex with her?"

"I'm not sure."

"I'll tell you what. I see him in the yard almost every day. I'll see if I can catch him."

"How are you going to do that?"

"You'll see. Oh, by the way, knowing Buddy as well as I do, I'm surprised that he bought groceries for you. Somehow, I find that hard to believe."

"Well, he did."

* * *

A couple of days later I was sitting in the kitchen picking ticks off Baron. Already I had three of them in my hand. The dog kept his ears pinned to the sides of his head. I pretended to be lavishing affection on the dog who knew that I was really looking for the telltale lumps that would reveal other ticks. Forlornly the dog looked down as though he was being punished.

Mom said, "I think I'll go see Buddy and Anne. Pauline next door gave me some hand-me-downs for the kids."

"How long will you be gone?"

"Most of the day. Why?"

"Is Beth going with you?"

"I don't know." She called into the bedroom, "Beth, are you coming to Buddy's with me?"

"No."

"Okay." She turned toward me. "Why do you want to know?"

I pinched another tick from Baron's forehead. "Because I think I'll spend the day fishing."

I watched Mom flutter through the house. After a lot of hustle and bustle, she seemed only to have put on her coat. Then I walked to the bathroom after having to wait fifteen minutes because my mother had reached it only seconds before I did. I heard the garage door being lifted. Then the Mercury gave a roar, and my mother was on her way.

Lifting the toilet seat, I tossed the four ticks into the bowl. The two fat, green ones sank immediately to the bottom, but the lean ones struggled on the surface. I was a god. Pursing some saliva on my lips, I let it drop into the bowl, aiming it at a tick. I barely missed my target. The next time, I took more careful aim, hit the tick dead center, sending it to the bottom. I thought, *this is cruel*, and flushed the toilet, then questioned, *can ticks survive in the sewers? They're tough little bastards.*

I walked to the door of Beth's room and stood watching her. She looked as though stranded on a beach. I said, "Ed and I are going fishing. We're using his mother's car. I'll be leaving in a couple of minutes. Okay?"

"Yep."

"You'll be all right?"

"I'll be all right."

"Okay. I'll see you in a couple of hours."

Softly, I opened the cellar door and called, "Ed's here. I'm leaving. Bye."

"Bye."

I opened the outside door and slammed it shut, then I slipped into the cellar. Since I didn't want any loose boards to betray me, I took a full fifteen minutes descending the wooden stairs. I tried to control my breathing which seemed so loud. Once my feet hit the solid cement floor, I took a deep breath and relaxed. Apprehensive that Beth might come downstairs to see if I took my fishing gear, I hid it behind some boards in a corner of the cellar. Sitting in an old chair, I prepared myself for a long wait and regretted that I hadn't brought something to read. One hour passed, then two. I waited for Pete to knock on the door and invite himself in. I waited for Beth to dial the phone to let him know that she was alone.

Pete came into the backyard to spend half an hour hitting stones with a stick as though they were bat and ball. I watched him from the small cellar windows and waited for him to move toward the door. Nothing. Pete went into his own home.

Another hour passed and I was about to give up, thinking that either Pete or Beth must know that I was hiding when I heard the creaking of the springs in my sister's bed. I heard a couple of heavy bounces and listened as she ran across the kitchen floor. I heard the rasping of a window being raised when she screamed at the top of her voice, "Basteh! BASTEH! GOD DAMNED BASTEH!" I was stupefied. Certainly, the neighbors must hear her. What did they think? More windows were raised as she screamed, "BASTEH! BASTEH! GOD DAMNED BASTEH!" then the windows slammed shut. Beth was in a frenzy. *How long will it go on?* "GOD DAMNED BASTEH, YOU BASTEH!"

Was she yelling at me? Did she know I was here? What's a basteh? Finally, I said softly to myself, "What the hell," and slipped to the head of the cellar stairs. I waited until I heard her run into her bedroom, then quickly, quietly, I left the cellar, opened the outside door and called, "Beth, I'm home."

"Hi, Mike."

I went through the house and noticed that nothing seemed disturbed except that Baron was sitting in a corner of the living room with eyes as large as silver dollars. I looked into Beth's room. She didn't seem to have moved at all. She was exactly in the same position as she had been when I "left" hours before. She looked up impassively. I asked, "How was your day?"

"Okay."

"Did you do anything?"

"No, I was just thinking."

"About what?"

"Oh, nothing, just thinking."

"Ed and I went to Sneech Pond, but we didn't catch anything." I tried to read the expression or lack of expression in her eyes but couldn't decide exactly what had happened.

That evening after Mom made supper, I sat reading in the living room and waited for Beth to go to bed. She had watched television for a couple of hours, but when darkness settled in, she returned to her room. When I thought that she might be asleep, I whispered to Mom, "I've got to talk to you."

She sat on the couch next to me. "What is it, son?"

I told her what I had witnessed, then added, "You know that she has violent tendencies. When I was growing up and you and Dad weren't around, I used to have to fight her off, literally, when she'd go into one of her rages."

"Your Dad and I never knew that."

"Well, you know now. Anyways, I'm not sure if you're safe with her. What if she turns on you?" A thought formed in my mind. "She's not beating on you, is she?"

Mom anxiously answered, "No. No. She's not."

I thought a moment, then asked, "What's a basteh?"

"I don't know." After a moment's thought, she said, "I keep thinking of your grandfather. You remind me so much of him. He was such a kind man. There was a badly beaten horse in the neighborhood. He'd been beaten so badly by his owner that he had bitten halfway through his tongue because of the pain. It hated people and attacked everybody but your grandfather. He used to give it apples and sugar whenever he passed through its pasture. Finally, your grandfather bought it, poor as we were, and took good care of him, not even using him to do any work, until the horse died."

"He should have killed the owner instead. That's the only way to handle people like that."

"Your grandfather used to steal coal from the railroad. He'd jump onto the moving train and throw chunks of coal along the tracks. I was only a little girl and I'd follow the tracks to put the coal into a burlap bag. We'd use it to heat the house."

"What are you trying to tell me?"

"Oh, I was just talking."

Again, I paused in thought, then said, "By the way, a month ago I bought three new shirts and I can't find them. Do you know what happened to them?"

"You must have misplaced them; they'll turn up."

* * *

Buddy arrived at Mom's house the morning that I was to leave for school. Anne and their two daughters were with him. I said, "You're a bit early, aren't you? The plane leaves at three and it's only ten o'clock."

Buddy said, "I promised Mom that I'd take her shopping at the mall."

"You're not going to make me late, are you?"

"No, we'll be back in plenty of time."

Beth, Buddy, and Mom soon left, leaving Anne behind to take care of the children. As usual, I sat on the couch to read when I was joined by Anne who sat next to me. When I looked up, she asked, "Have you read Sigmund Freud?"

"No. I haven't."

"Do you know who he is?"

"Not really."

"He was a famous psychoanalyst. He wrote in the 1930s." She edged closer to me. "He believed that, ultimately, everything is based on sex. Do you believe that?"

Uncomfortable, I wanted to leave the room but didn't want to appear rude. "I don't know."

Anne leaned toward me, putting a hand on my knee, casually, as though by accident. She asked, "Do you think everything is based on sex drives?"

"I—I don't know. I haven't thought about it."

She continued, "He divided the mind into three parts: the ego which is the 'I' of the personality, the person's self; the superego which represents parental authority; and the id, which is unbridled passion, freedom." Anne rubbed her hand up and down the length of my leg. "If I

194

tell you something, do you promise not to tell anyone, especially Buddy?"

"O—okay," I stammered.

"When I was a teenager vacationing on Cape Cod, I used to strip naked and run through the woods. It was wonderful. I was so free! Don't you think that in today's society, the passions are too restricted?" She leaned against me so that her breasts pressed against my arm. "Don't you think we all should be free?"

She was about to kiss me on the cheek when I lunged up, left the room, and called, "Baron!" Without seeing anything clearly, I ran into the woods with the dog.

An hour later, I returned to the house and found Buddy and the others waiting for me. I tried to sense if anything had happened while I was gone, if Anne said anything. It seemed the same. My sister-in-law was full of smiles that gave hints of collusion and deep secrets between us. *Why did Buddy leave us alone?*

He drove me to the airport, smirking, when I complained about "that hellhole," and said, "C'mon, it's not *that* bad. Give it another try. What've you got to lose?"

"My sanity. Don't believe the crap you read in the papers or see in the movies. The place stinks!" Yet, I admitted to myself it would be good to see my friends again, people who had gone through a similar experience and understood what I was saying.

Buddy said, "You remind me of a masterpiece, Mike. What I see is incredibly beautiful. You're almost a perfect piece of art, but there are gaps. You're like a masterpiece with portions of it left unpainted, as though there were pieces missing. I keep wondering what you would be like if they were filled in. I think that's why you screw up so much."

"I sometimes think there's something missing, too."

Buddy dropped me off at the front entrance of T.F. Greene Airport. Dressed in my white uniform, I picked up my white Academy duffle bag and started a struggling waddle to the check-in counter when I saw a group of college students. Among them was a small, fragile, college-aged man wearing blue jeans, a blue working man's shirt, and a red bandanna tied about his neck. His long, brown hair reached to his shoulders. Although he had neither buckteeth nor puffy cheeks, he still reminded me of a chipmunk. As I was passing, the youth lifted a small, hand printed sign that said, "ANARCHY IN THE USA." He jauntily popped up one of his hips, stood as defiantly as possible, and threw me the finger.

I was neither angered nor alarmed but experienced a kind of passive curiosity. Then I heard a laugh that attracted my attention to a young woman standing next to the chipmunk. She smiled at her hero, then looked directly, judgmentally, at me. Although her light brown, soul searching, eyes were gentle and her features soft, I couldn't help but think that she hated me. She was stunning with a dark complexion, a rich, fully developed body, and long, thick, chestnut-colored hair. Looking from her to her partner, then back at her, I noticed her hand rubbing the young man's buttocks and assumed that I was meant to feel envy. It worked.

After the check-in, I went to the waiting area and became aware of two Army privates about my own age sitting near me. Casually, I glanced at them and started. One of them had a brilliantly livid, jagged, scarlet line running down the center of his face. Our eyes met. The soldier looked quickly toward the floor while I just as quickly looked away. Vietnam. I had to look again. I saw the scar as the soldier, likewise, saw me looking. Again, we both turned away. Despite all my efforts, my eyes kept straying to that unwanted sight. The soldier seemed embarrassed and behaved with the shyness of a cornered animal. Vietnam. *Is that what I can expect if I flunk out of the Academy?*

A little girl wearing sneakers, a T-shirt, and shorts had been sitting with her young, composed, stately mother, but became bored and started doing cartwheels between the rows of chairs. After half a dozen performances, she stood before the soldiers and said proudly, "I got first place in my gymnastics class!" The soldiers smiled. Then she bluntly added in alarm, pointing to the soldier with the scar, "What's that on your face?"

The adults jumped in their seats. The scarred soldier turned away and seemed about to cry. The mother said sternly, "Janet, don't bother the gentlemen! Sit here next to me and behave yourself!"

CHAPTER X

THE BEGINNING OF THE END

YOUNGSTER YEAR

I was happy to set foot on Academy grounds. I missed Hovedo, Boatman, and the other mids with whom I felt a certain camaraderie. It would be good to see them again. I hoped that before long I could come to love the Academy in the same way as a son still loves an abusive father, that I would want to be there as much as I wanted to be with my friends. Miracles do happen; I hoped that I would have a change of heart.

The upperclassmen rushed from one room in Bancroft Hall to another to exchange tales of summer leave. Room assignments had already been agreed upon from the previous spring and I was to room with John Boatman. The hang-dog Southerner shook my hand and asked, even before I put my bag down, "How was summer leave?"

"Good."

His next question was, "Who's rooming with Valdres?"

"Hovedo."

"You mean Easy-going Gus?"

"Yep."

John lit up with joy. "Sle." I remembered his habit of brief, noisy inhales for emphasis. "He won't be so easy going once Valdres gets through with him. I give Hovedo a week before he's in here complaining."

"John, I admit that Bob was a bad roommate, but he wasn't *that* bad."

"We'll see. Remember, one week from today."

From our fifth deck window, I could see Chesapeake Bay to my left. Directly below were the roofs and walkways of the library and dining hall. To my right stood the marble bastion of Memorial Hall.

John said, "We have a mandatory event at the field house after evening meal."

I turned from the window and started to unpack. "What's that?"

"Sle, the super's going to address the Brigade."

Youngsters were allowed record players, so John unpacked a small battery operated one that fit snugly on his desk. Then, he put on an album of Paul Revere and the Raiders.

I asked, "Have you seen the new plebes?"

"Not yet."

"I'm sure they'll be a bunch of bimbos."

"Why don't you meet them first?"

Just then we heard, "Sir, you now have ten minutes to evening meal. Sir, the menu for evening meal is..." and the routine recommenced. I stuck my head out of the doorway to look appraisingly at the plebe, who seemed nervous. His eyes were a bit too open, his forehead a bit too furrowed as his mouth tried to keep up with what his mind was telling it to say. I walked into the corridor, hands on hips, to stare at the plebe. Beads of sweat formed on the plebe's forehead; small rivulets ran down the sides of his temples. *Had I looked that worried when I had given chow call?* When it ended, the plebe stood expectantly at attention. He glanced at me, so I asked sharply, "What are you looking at, mister?"

The plebe was caught. "Nothing, sir."

I resisted the temptation to ask, "Are you calling me nothing?" Instead, I said, "You better use these few minutes to square away your uniform. GO!" The plebe ran to his room.

The youngsters arrived at formation shortly before the new second classmen. By tradition, the youngsters befriend the plebes, help them to break into Academy life, and try to prevent their getting fried too often by the second class. The four plebes in my squad stood at the end of the squad line. While checking their uniforms I asked each one where he was from: Texas, Nebraska, Indiana, and New Jersey. Already, I knew that the plebe from Indiana would have fewer problems than the others. Plebes from Ohio, Indiana, and Florida seldom had trouble. They were too well adjusted, too cosmopolitan in outlook, to be suitable targets for upper class ire. The problem children came from highly sectionalized areas of the country. Too often they were unable to conform and be reshaped into good midshipman material.

I was in line when John rushed up, giving the plebes a big smile, straightening a tie that I had just straightened, then getting into line. The other third classmen in the squad were Matt Helmsley and Fred Meade. The first and second classmen were, fortunately, people I had no dealings with during plebe year.

Roll call was taken, then the companies marched to the chow hall, and the mids stood at their places at table while waiting to be seated. No one was taking an interest in the plebes, so I decided to ask them their rates. "Gaut, five articles from the newspapers."

"Aye-aye, sir," and he gave a short summary of current events.

"Ryan, why didn't you say 'sir'?" The plebe rattled off the formula.

"Butrus, the football team."

"Sir, the football team is, sir…" and off he went.

"Austin, the team captains."

I was pleased to see that the plebes knew their rates. They seemed to be a sharp group. I waited for the second classmen to begin their hazing, but nothing developed. Suddenly, all the plebes at all the tables were granted carry-on. The third classmen were struck dumb and couldn't believe what they were seeing. It seemed like a bizarre joke perpetrated by the new firsties, the class of '70. We were outraged. We had spent months proving ourselves before we had been granted our first carry-on. The upperclassmen ate in sullen silence, wondering just how easy the Academy was going to be for this new class of plebes.

After evening meal, the whole Brigade marched to the field house. The Brigade of midshipmen stood at attention during the National Anthem after which the midshipmen, according to custom, yelled, "Beat Army and the command "seats" was given. The superintendent was the first to speak. He stood at the rostrum in the arrogant, eminently successful way that I detested.

"Gentlemen," he said, "it's good to have you back with us. You young men are the finest the world has to offer. It is an honor and a privilege to have you here with us tonight. As you know, this summer has been one of considerable dissention among the American populace. The anti-war demonstrations have increased. Anti-military, anti-American behavior has run rampant. It has come to our notice that some midshipmen sympathize with these people. Some midshipmen have attended the concert held at Woodstock, New York. You know who they are. The Academy has no room for people like that. I want these Woodstockers *out of here!*"

I was sitting next to Hovedo, nudged him, and said, "I guess he means me."

Gus, who was intently listening to the superintendent, responded with an absentminded, "Huh?"

"Nothing." I was no longer paying attention and started to look at the mass of white uniforms and youthful hopes surrounding me. My ear caught stock phrases that told me that the super was looking forward to a good year. When the super reiterated his belief that the mids were the finest group of young people on earth, I thought of the same refrain heard endlessly at Woodstock. I wondered who was right. Either way, I was in both camps, or, seen from another perspective, I was in neither camp.

The next speaker was Commandant Green of the US Marine Corps. Attention quickened when this solid, compact man marched to the microphone, every inch of him exuding sharpness. He said, "Men, as the representative of the Marine Corps, I have often been asked exactly what is it we do? I'll tell you what we do. We fight this nation's enemies. So far, ninety five percent of the personnel of the Marine Corps has had a tour of duty in Vietnam and the other five percent are going." A prideful murmur ran through the ranks of listeners. He continued, "The Naval Academy has always served us well, giving us some of our finest officers. We're all proud of you." He then walked off the platform amidst the silent admiration of all the midshipmen.

With the termination of ceremonies, the Brigade started its trek to Bancroft Hall. Hovedo and I entered the dark, sultry night. The glare of the fieldhouse lights made the night that much more impenetrable. The darkness at the edge of the ocean seemed always deeper, more profound, than that of other places. Here, the lamplight was ineffectual, like isolated points stressing futility. Hovedo asked, "Why didn't you come see me during leave?"

"I don't know, Gus. I just didn't. You know how I am."

"I've told everybody I know about you. My parents wanted to meet you."

"They have."

"I mean that they really want to meet you, not for only two minutes on a busy street. They want to get to know you. After all, you're my best friend."

"Gus, I promise that the first chance I get, I'll go to Illinois with you to visit your folks."

"Sometimes I think you don't give a shit about anybody."

"That's not true."

"Well, damn it, the way you behave is enough to drive me up a wall."

"Okay, okay, okay, you've made your point. I've already promised to see your folks and that's that."

"Sometimes I wonder about you. Other than not answering my letter or accepting my invitation to visit me, what did you do this leave?"

I recounted my summer and lent willing ears as Gus told his own stories.

* * *

The final unpacking was done the next morning. There was the usual room inspection, but since John and I were upperclassmen, we weren't overly concerned about it. Our room did not need to be as spic and span as a plebe room. I had taken care to spray an extra coating of floor wax in our doorway so that when the inspector arrived, he'd see the shiny the floor, making a good impression on him. Instead, our inspector, First Classman Roderiques, stepped into the room and slipped with his arms flailing for balance and support. His clipboard went flying across the room and crashed against a locker with a loud bang, but he was lucky enough not to fall. After he recovered his poise and collected his clipboard, impressed, he said, "You guys pass," then he left.

It was also the day the different classes of the company held their first meetings. John and I heard the plebe watch from the hallway. "There is a third class meeting being held right now in Midshipman Third Class Bemes' room, sir!"

Bemes had been assigned as third class company commander. The first sight that struck my eyes as I entered the room was Larry with one foot on a chair, arms folded and resting on the raised knee, body leaning slightly forward as though he was in the con of a ship during heavy seas. I thought, *what class!* and was proud to have him in the company. His intelligent, composed eyes scanned the group of youngsters before him. He asked, "Where's Calhoun?"

A voice answered, "He's got watch at Batt. Ops."

"Okay. Somebody, you Bill, get word to him about what went on in the meeting, okay?"

"Sure."

Bemes' eyes swept over his classmates. "How was your summer, Mike?"

"Good."

"Listen up, men. I talked to the new company commander, Lieutenant j.g. Dimwiddie. He seems like an okay guy. The word is that there's going to be a few changes around here. From now on, it's the third class who are going to run the plebes. The first and second class get to skate. We do all the work." The youngsters grumbled. Hazing was a lot of work. Only a handful of upperclassmen enjoy it. Effective hazing requires distance. That distance was lacking between youngster and plebe year.

Matt Helmsley asked, "Is that why the plebes got carry-on last night?"

"Yeah. I'm not supposed to tell you guys this, but they're going to have it easier than we did, a lot easier."

Helmsley then said, "I talked to some second classmen who were here during the summer, and they said that the plebes were always getting carry-on." Bitterly, he added, "And for nothing. They were rewarded for doing things that were expected of them in the first place, rewards that we had to work our balls off for! I think it's another Academy 'good deal' that our class has always been getting!"

Charley Bragg joined in, "Harrington and Roebuck were the second classmen for the first half of the summer. I heard that Roebuck turned to Harrington at meal and said, 'I can't stand this,' then granted them all carry-on!"

Paul Carnevale added the final sting. "A plebe told me that the work-outs were so easy during the summer that he actually got *out* of shape."

An unsettling movement ran through the group of youngsters. Bemes said, "I have no doubt that all you've said is true, but there's nothing we can do about it. I think our best bet is to follow the tide." Larry glanced down at the palm of his hand. I could barely make out the edges of a notepad. He continued, "Sunday evenings we're going to be tested on current events, so read the papers, men."

Unexpectedly, I had a strong sense of brotherhood with the mids in this room. I was pleased to be included in this select group and admired the way Larry tossed off the word "men" so casually and effectively. He continued, "That's pretty much all I have to say. Would anybody like to add anything?" Larry scanned the group of curious faces. Nothing. "Fill out these forms that I'm passing out. They're for general info." After the cards had been handed out to the youngsters, Larry asked, "Mike, do you think you can stay out of trouble this year?"

There was a soft, affectionate twitter that ran through the group. I was happy that my friend noticed me. I smiled, "I hope so." The meeting then broke into casual conversation. I felt so much closer to these men than to my own family. They had become a dominant force in my life.

As I was leaving, I overheard Gus Hovedo and Fred Meade arguing. Gus said, "The range of the *Phantom II* is twenty-three hundred miles."

Meade replied, "It's twenty-eight hundred miles."

"No way. You're thinking of the *Intruder*."

Meade reiterated, "The range of the *Phantom II* is twenty-eight hundred miles."

"You're wrong." Turning to me for support, Gus asked, "Sores, what's the range of the *Phantom II* jet?"

Stunned, I stopped in my tracks. "You guys know better than to ask me a question like that. Give me a break."

* * *

The first time I met Dimwiddie, the officer was strolling up the middle of the corridor where the plebes were required to chop whenever they were in Bancroft Hall. Upperclassmen, by tradition, walk along the sides of the corridors. I saw a heavy set, beefy man with ruddy, thick cheeks that made him look like a fat, happy, little boy. Dimwiddie's eyes had the inquisitive innocence so often seen in plebe eyes. As our paths crossed, we whipped salutes to one another. The officer glanced at my nametag and asked, "How are you, Mr. Sorensen?"

I stopped at attention. "Fine, sir."

He faced me. "I've heard a lot about you. How's the running?"

"Fine, sir."

"You *are* running this semester?"

"No, sir."

"What sport are you playing?"

"Squash, sir."

"Oh, I see. And how does this year look in terms of your classes?"

"I think I'll do all right, sir."

"How many credits are you taking?"

"Twenty, sir."

"Do you think you can handle it?"

"Yes, sir."

"We'll see, won't we?"

"Yes, sir."

"Carry-on."

"Aye-aye, sir."

We again exchanged salutes. While this was going on, I could see Dave Husaby standing in his doorway like the village gossip and listening to the conversation. As soon as the officer left, my friend motioned for me to join him. He said excitedly, "Dimwiddie knows who you are! I bet that except for Bemes, you're the only youngster he knows by name! That's a real honor!"

"Dave, he knows me for all the wrong reasons. He knows me because I'm a fuck-up."

"Still, he does know who you are."

"I wish he didn't."

"It's still an honor."

"I got to go, Dave. See you later."

"Sure enough."

I was on my way to classes before seeing Dimwiddie. I intuited that I'd be seeing a lot of him, and I didn't like the idea. My course load included physics, naval engineering, navigation, and general management, as well as gym class and naval skills such as practical experience with yard patrol craft, all taught with Naval Academy efficiency. As I saw it, I had two major drawbacks. First, I lacked the sufficient background information from my science and math studies because of successful efforts to keep me from studying. Secondly, I despised the Machine. *How can I ever work in a system I hate so much?*

In addition to this, I became aware of a change in my worldview. Except for the last couple of months of plebe year, I had never been midshipman sharp. Now, however, I found that I was becoming somewhat absentminded. It went beyond my daydreaming and superficial philosophy. Cynicism and disillusionment were certainly a part of the change, but now I seriously, profoundly, began to doubt about the meaning behind everything. Simple charts took on a complexity that seemed unfathomable. I'd become preoccupied, not by the useful information yielded by the charts, but in questioning how they were made and by whom. Who took these soundings and exactly what did the charts represent? What kind of animals lived there? What were the people like? What history did that part of the globe experience? That fragment became a whole world that stretched from the past into the future and what part I might have in that future. I was stupefied by the wealth of knowledge behind each idea, each measurement, each chart and graph presented to me. I knew, or thought I knew, that there was something very deep and important here that the students and professors were missing, something much more integral to life than the material taught in the classroom.

The same day as my accidental meeting with Dimwiddie, the officer attended noon meal formation and inspected my platoon. He ambled down each of the three rows representing the three squads. Briefly, Dimwiddie stopped before each mid. He passed without comment until he reached Matt Helmsley. He asked, "Mr. Helmsley, did you shave this morning?"

"No, sir."

Kirk, who was the platoon commander, glared angrily at Matt. The officer passed on to the next man. "Mr. Sorensen, did you shave this morning?"

"No, sir."

Again, Kirk gave his hateful look, this time at me. Dimwiddie completed the inspection. When the attending midshipmen returned to their places, Kirk leaned a little from the squad line. He said, "Helmsley, Sorensen, bring around a Form 2."

We answered in unison, "Aye-aye, sir."

Once the formation broke up at the chow hall, Matt and I looked at one another, chagrinned. "Hell," I said, "I don't need to shave. One miniscule whisker and *he* spots it!"

Matt muttered beneath his breath so only I could hear it, "The asshole!"

* * *

Within days of the beginning of the fall semester, Easy-going Hovedo burst into my room. He ripped off his cap and gripped the back of his head for lack of enough hair to pull. With no introductory remarks, Gus faced me and yelled, "How did you stand it? How did you stay with Valdres a whole year? I swear I'll kill him!"

I smiled while John asked, "What did he do?"

"Do? That's just it! He doesn't do anything! Remember the room inspection we had last Saturday morning? He didn't do a freaking thing! *I* did everything! I waxed the floor. I cleaned the blinds. I did everything but make his bed for him! I couldn't move him! He's the most stubborn idiot I've ever met! How did you take it, Mike?"

"I thought it was a personality conflict between him and me. I thought this might happen, but I wasn't sure."

"You're a saint, Mike."

"Yeah, I'm a saint all right."

Gus rushed out of the room as quickly as he had entered it. He was no sooner gone than John gave a little joyful hop. "Yippee! Now Valdres is in for it!" I was both pleased and surprised when John added, "You thought it was your fault, didn't you?"

"Yeah, I did. I feel vindicated, or somewhat vindicated, but it wasn't all his fault."

"How long has the Brigade been back?"

"About a week. Why?"

"Exactly a week from today. I told you that Gus would come screaming in here, didn't I?"

"You sure did." I decided since I wasn't getting any studying done to take a shower. I stripped down, wrapped a towel about my waist, and picked up my regulation soapbox. I opened it, then held up the soap for my roommate to see. It was covered with a thick layer of black pubic hair. I said, "I let Matt borrow my soap. I guess this is his idea of a joke." John chuckled while I took my bayonet and carved away the hair.

* * *

Before very many weeks had passed, John and I had developed the bad study habits that would leave me with low grades and sleep filled eyes for nearly the whole of the coming academic year. The real problem was that we had a tremendous liking for one another. When we should have been studying, we were doing little more than amusing ourselves. A typical study night began with each roommate sitting at his desk opposite one another, intent on the text in front of him, when John said something like, "Izzie friend or foe? Wazzie?"

"What?"

"It says here that when the Interrogation, Friend or Foe Radar System was first developed, the operators called it 'Izzie Friend or Foe' and when it didn't work and the unidentified target got away, they added 'Wazzie?' Get it?"

"Yeah, I get it."

Not to be outdone by my friend, I asked, "Do you know what the Battle of the Pips is?" After five seconds of silence and my roommate's blank stare, I continued, "During World War II some radar operators picked up an unidentified fleet off the Aleutian Islands about fifteen miles away. All night the Americans bombarded the enemy fleet to discover the next morning that there was nothing there. They figured the pips were coming from some mountain peaks sixty-five miles away. That's why it's called the Battle of the Pips."

John was delighted. I then asked, "Do you know what the best weapon against a battleship or destroyer is?" I paused for effect. "A rowboat."

"How do you figure that?"

"Wood absorbs radar waves. Get a wooden rowboat, put a torpedo in it or some high explosives, row up while the ship is in dock, and blow it up. The rowboat wouldn't be detected by radar."

"Impossible. There's no way you're going to sink a destroyer with one torpedo."

"Why not?"

"It's too big to be sunk by one torpedo. Today's ships are compartmentalized with waterproof doors. If you blow up one end of the ship, the other end will still float."

"You know as well as I do that hatches aren't kept closed all the time. The ship would sink before they had time to respond."

"There is no record of a destroyer being sunk by one torpedo."

"How do you know? I would think that there must be dozens."

"Name one."

"I can't."

"See?"

"That doesn't prove a thing except that I'm not up on Naval history."

"Sle, take my word for it. Your plan wouldn't work."

"I think it would."

"I know it wouldn't."

"I know it would."

The two of us returned to our reading, both a little disgruntled, when five minutes later, John asked, "Did you hear the latest about the Midshipman Brigade Commander, the black guy? He wrote a youngster up yesterday. It was during noon meal formation. He was inspecting and told a youngster that he needed to work on his shoes. The youngster, a white guy, said, 'Where *I'm* from, *you'd* be shining them.'" John laughed wholeheartedly.

I sat pensively, a little embarrassed that a white man should say such a thing. I asked, "Have you ever met him, the Brigade Commander, I mean?"

"No."

"I have. He seems like an okay guy. It's too bad it was said to *him*. What happened to the white guy?"

"Class A offence."

"Good, he deserves it."

* * *

Another major distraction was the record player. John loved pop music and spent hour upon hour listening to it. He always asked me if the record player disturbed me. To please my roommate, I always answered no, but it did disturb me. Only one thing disturbed me enough for comment. Generally, he played half a song, then switched to another song without finishing the first. I asked, "Why do you listen to only half a song?"

He answered, "Once I hear the first half, it reminds me of the second half which I already know and because I already know what it's going to sound like, I don't have to listen to it."

I considered this for a moment then said, "Do me a favor. If you play any of the songs that *I* like, play the whole thing, okay?"

"Sure."

* * *

I called home. "Hi, Mom."

"Hi, son," and the love oozed through the telephone.

"How's everything?"

"A little hard with your sister and all."

"Why? What happened."

"She's really been carrying on."

"Like how?"

"Screaming. Talking to herself."

"Is that all?"

"Mostly."

"What do you mean, mostly?"

A pause. "I've got some bad news for you." Another pause. "Your dog died."

"How?"

Bitter: "Anne killed him. She had her dog over to the house and she let both dogs out. Her dog started chasing cars and Baron, who never did this before, joined her and got hit by a car. Then Anne called the vet, had him pick the dog up, and told him to put Baron down. I was at work, and she never thought of calling me nor did she call Cora. She just had Baron put down." Furious: "I don't think Baron was seriously hurt!"

"Didn't she call Buddy?"

"No, not that I'm aware of."

"Really? She never does anything without his okay."

"She didn't call him."

I heard her sniffling. "Are you crying?"

"Your sister's so hard on me. I can't control her."

"Mom, I can't do anything from here. What about Cora and Buddy?"

"Cora helps out. We go grocery shopping once a week and she cuts the lawn, but she lives too far away to help with Beth."

"What about Buddy? Can't *he* do something?"

"He has his own family."

Now I heard her full-bodied crying. My heart dropped beneath me as I was overwhelmed by a sense of helplessness. I wanted to give up, go somewhere, anywhere, but where I was.

"Mom, I can't handle these phone calls. Maybe I shouldn't call anymore. It's too tough." I could hear her crying like a child.

"But they mean so much to me."

"I call home every weekend and you end up crying all the time. I'm depressed the rest of the week and then I call home and it starts all over again. I can't handle it, not with everything else that's going on. Maybe we should just cut back a little and I'll call you every other week."

"But your calls mean so much to me. I look forward to them all week. Promise me that you'll call next week."

Resigned, I said, "Okay, another promise. I'll call next week."

* * *

Death was a common feature at Meantacut Hospital where I worked parttime as an orderly while in high school. During my two years there, I had taken five bodies to the morgue. Since I didn't know the people, it was easy to maintain distance as I helped to lift the bodies off the bed and onto the stretcher and from the stretcher onto the movable, metal tray pulled out of the refrigeration unit at the basement morgue. I noted how easy people were to move while they had a speck of life in them and became as difficult to move as a cement bag when that speck passed away. Fortunately, I did not know them.

The problem came with the people I befriended. During the school year, I worked on weekends. One weekend I would be talking to a patient and the next weekend, I would find an empty bed or another patient in the room, the original patient having died.

One patient was an elderly woman I befriended. She had been an English teacher and kept asking me, "Do you know how this poem goes, 'two ships passing in the night?' What words come after that line? I can't remember and I used to know it so well. Do you know it?" I thought that it might be a poem by Longfellow, but, although I was vaguely familiar with it, I couldn't quite place it. One weekend we talked poetry and the next weekend I walked into a room with an empty bed. She had died during the week while I was at school.

Another patient was a total paraplegic, an immigrant from Belgium. I took care of him during the summer, and he said only one thing to me the whole time I was with him. He said, "I was a trouble shooter during the war." Suddenly, I saw him as a young man, raiding German lines during the night, blowing up bridges. One day I came into his room, and he was crying. The tears flowed freely down his face, and he was unable to wipe them away. I went to the nurses' desk to ask what had happened. His grandson had been killed in Vietnam. One day I went into work and his bed was empty too. I had not seen either death so there was no immediate reaction. How do you grieve emptiness?

There were other deaths and with each death I experienced an indescribable hollowness, as though I was an empty jar with its outward form still there but with its contents gone. That hollowness gripped me when I called home and found out that Baron was dead.

Later, John Boatman found me in our room, sitting at my desk, blankly staring at a textbook. He asked, "What's up?"

"My dog is dead. He got run over by a car."

"I'm sorry to hear that."

"I know it sounds stupid, but that dog was really close to me."

"Oh, you mean more of a friend than a pet."

"Exactly, and that bitch of a sister-in-law had something to do with it."

"Was she driving the car?"

"No, but she let him out of the house and after he got run over, she called the vet and told him to put him down. The only problem is that my mom seems to think he wasn't that hurt. No one else was there at the time, but Anne didn't bother to wait to see what the others would say. She just had him put away. What gets me though, is that she never does anything without my brother giving her the okay. He's the boss man in their house. I can't believe that she didn't call him first."

"Maybe your dog was really hurt."

"Well, something's going on at home. She never does anything without his okay and I'm even suspicious about the pass she made at me last summer. Remember? I told you about it."

"I don't know your brother, but maybe he's the kind of guy who'd kill a dog, or maybe have his wife kill a dog, for revenge or jealousy. Didn't you tell me that he tried to get into the Academy but failed the entrance exam?"

"Yeah, but he became an officer through OCS. Besides, you're wrong. There's no way he would ever put Baron down since he loves dogs, and he would never hurt me. How could he possibly be jealous? He has so much more than me. He's the guy who was a Marine Corps. captain, not me. He's a research scientist working towards a doctorate, not me. He's everything I want to be. What could he possibly be jealous of? I admit that he might not be perfect, but it was Anne who killed Baron. Although," I shook my head back and forth in disbelief, "I can't see Anne doing anything like this on her own."

* * *

One afternoon right after classes, I found a chit waiting for me on my desk. It was from Lt. Dimwiddie ordering me to his office ASAP. It had to be bad news. At his office, I sounded off, "Midshipman Sorensen, 721260, sir, reporting as ordered, sir!" I saluted and received one in return.

"At ease, Mr. Sorensen, have a seat."

"Aye-aye, sir." I sat down, alert.

"How is everything, Mr. Sorensen?"

"Fine, sir."

"And your studies?"

"Fine, sir."

"My records tell me that you had some trouble last year."

"Yes, sir."

"What about this year? How does it look to you?"

"Fine, sir."

"Really?"

"Yes, sir."

"I hope so. That'll be all, Mr. Sorensen."

"Yes, sir." I snapped a salute and left.

* * *

As the school semester worked its way into the fall, I continued to follow the habits I had developed during plebe year. I still jogged with Carnevale, went drinking with Matt and Danny on Saturday evenings, and skipped church. Because of my new status as a youngster, I rated an occasional weekend leave that I often took with Husaby and Carnevale. The three of us visited D.C. museums and art galleries. As a rule, I was unable to relate to modern art and questioned the value of art that failed to reach its audience. However, I also recognized my lack of culture and made the effort to understand the works before me. The Sunday morning phone calls home and my mother's consistent weeping were also resumed.

Early in the semester it was evident that I would have trouble with my grades. The study habits that Hooker tried to graft onto me had failed to take root. Although I had made it through plebe year, I made what was possibly a self-fulfilling prophesy that I might not make it this time. I didn't understand the material in the texts. Homework was relegated to fifteen minutes of scratching on a piece of paper to show the professor that, yes, I was trying. When I went to the library, I no longer went to the magazine rack. Instead, I often went to the sound booths with Carnevale and Matt to listen to albums. Matt, who had an IQ of 160, often brought math puzzles for the three of us to solve. Invariably, I was the first one to solve them. Eventually, each of us got lost in thoughts of home, life, and the future while quietly sharing in each other's company.

My classes proved to be a repetition of the horrors of my first year. With few exceptions, I didn't like my professors. My naval engineering class began on an especially bad note. Its focus was metallurgy and the structural stress placed on ships. The instructor, an ensign not much older than the mids themselves, had the boyish look of Mower and, like Mower, had the habit of blinking dozens of times in a row, especially when making a point. On the first day of class the ensign entered the room, and the class was called to attention. Ensign Halleck said, "At ease, gentlemen." We all sat as the blinking juvenile eyes scanned the room to finally settle on me while I sat in a comfortable slouch. Halleck stared expectantly at me, and I knew that I was expected to sit up in proper midshipman fashion. I didn't move. Halleck said, "Mr.—ah—Mr.…."

"Sorensen, sir."

"Mr. Sorensen, don't you think you should sit up like an officer and a gentleman? After all, Congress has declared that all midshipmen are officers and gentlemen and we don't want to disappoint them, do we?"

I sat up. "No, sir."

"This might be a classroom, but it is still a military organization."

"Yes, sir."

"Now that we have *that* settled, my name is Ensign Halleck. I'll be your instructor this semester."

* * *

I received my worst grades in navigation even though I liked the work. The professors were Naval officers and were oddly human for that species of animal. I liked them a lot, especially when they told humorless jokes such as not confusing a winch with a wench.

Navigation classes were held in Luce Hall. Every class day I saw a plaque that read, "My country, right or wrong" at the bottom of the ladder. In the dysfunctional atmosphere of the Vietnam era, I questioned the validity of such a blatant statement of patriotism. My stomach turned a little as the emotional issues of the day reached out and gripped me. Each day the anti-war protest marches increased in number and intensity and each day brought me closer to active duty.

Class was held on the second deck. It was a large room running the length of the building and was decorated with many thick hemp ropes tied in an impressive number of Gordian knots. Like McDonough Hall, it smelled of dusty comfort and exuded an aura of seamanship. I always arrived early so that I could stand at the window nearest my desk. I stood with my back to the room and listened as it slowly filled. Once the room was full, I turned around and greeted the three or four mids I'd come to know by their first names.

One morning, as I stood at the window, I saw the two most beautiful waterfowl I had ever seen. They were a pair of distinctly marked black and white ducks. Images flashed through my mind as I searched for a name. I was certain that I had seen this species before or most likely a photo of it. I let my mind float, hoping that it would land on the right spot. I saw ice burgs and cold, black water. An Arctic species. I looked for a name. *Eider ducks, I think they're eider ducks. I wonder what they're doing here.* I watched as the ducks dove into the purples, blues, reds, and greens of the water's surface covered with spilled gasoline. A Styrofoam cup and a beer bottle floated in the corner of the dock area. Behind me, I heard a pencil drop. With a loud bang, an unknown mid slammed his text onto his desk. I thought of the day's exercise, a cruise to Australia, and sighed. Somewhere in the South Pacific I'd strand my vessel on reefs. I'd rather watch the ducks.

In conjunction with the navigation classes, we were required in the fall and spring to cruise the Chesapeake Bay in the yard patrol craft (YPs). Generally, this was just another hassle where we'd pretend to be sailors while the real sailors, the enlisted men below decks, worked the vessel. An officer on board saw to it that the mids did no irreparable damage to the craft.

My own attitude toward the YPs was ambiguous. I didn't like the thick, oily fumes or the rasping gasp of their engines. Nor did I want to find myself in a position of command where I could only prove my incompetence. Yet, I loved it when the small craft bucked against the waves, the salt spray slapping my face and the surge of the sea swelling inside me. My imagination, which I was gradually learning to control, became recalcitrant and lost me in Viking raids, English corsairs, and Portuguese explorations. Theme songs from the epic "Victory at Sea" raced through my mind as images of aircraft carriers and submarines danced in the vibrant up-reach of the music. Of course, I was the captain, a watchword of fear among all enemy vessels, but a word of prayer to friend and ally.

Despite my many disasters on the plotting boards, I had an instinct for the real thing. The instructor, himself an inconspicuous figure and, as such, well liked, turned to the group of midshipmen on the open bridge where I tried to disappear. I looked down at my feet as though I was deeply involved in profound thought. Then, I looked into the distance as though I wasn't aware of the instructor's searching eyes. When I heard, "Mr. Sorensen, would you like to take the con?" my heart jolted in panic. The officer continued, "You'll have to dock the craft for us."

My eyes, showing intense dread, met the instructor's laughing eyes. I answered, "Aye-aye, sir," and thought, *why me?* Then, I set about my task. I said into the voice box connecting me to the helmsman, "Helm right thirty degrees," and prayed that I did not make a fool of myself.

The helm repeated, "Helm right thirty degrees."

Instead of waiting for the vessel to settle, I said quickly, in response to the craft swinging past its intended position, "Helm left ten degrees."

"Helm left ten degrees."

Now the vessel swung the other way. We were going in too fast. "Cut engines to quarter speed! Helm right ten degrees!"

"Engines to quarter speed! Helm right ten degrees."

"Helm left ten degrees!"

"Helm left ten degrees."

The vessel started swinging back and forth. I thought that we were about to crash. I panicked. "Helm right ten degrees!"

"Helm right ten degrees."

The vessel kept swinging past the intended position. Back and forth. Back and forth. *How can I stop it? What can I do?* Then I saw Beth trying to stuff a turkey into a Tupperware container. *I'm behaving like Beth!*

I paused, collected my thoughts, and waited for the YP to settle. I said calmly, "Helm left five degrees."

"Helm left five degrees."

"Reverse engines."

"Engines reversed."

"Helm right three degrees."

"Helm right three degrees."

"Cut engines."

"All engines stopped."

The craft touched the dock with the gentleness of a mother tucking in her baby. The instructor complimented me, "Excellent work, Mr. Sorensen."

I knew that I'd done well. "Thank you, sir."

After class, I sat on a docking butt. My identity with Beth during my moment of crisis disturbed me. *Am I really like Beth?* I remembered my pleasant surprise when I was twelve and had taken out a library book only to discover that Beth had taken out the same book two months earlier. I remembered my feeling of kinship with her. I thought, *Maybe I'm not so much different from Beth after all and, maybe, these other mids aren't so much different than I am.*

* * *

My physics class was cataclysmically boring and on the liveliest day tasted like dry dust. The instructor was always pleasantly calm and never inflected his voice. I fell frequently into a trance like that created by constantly repeating a mantra. The mass of formulas and equations thrust onto the black board was as dense as any dwarf star.

In such an atmosphere, I developed the habit of watching the other students. They listened so intently that I could barely control my sense of irony. I could almost see the concepts winging into the skulls of my compatriots and ricocheting off the thick bone like electrons off condensed atoms. They were so serious. Did they really understand the material? Despite my valiant efforts to be calm, my sense of humor sometimes overpowered me. I covered my face with my hands as though resting my eyes, but the convulsions of laughter gave me away. The instructor, so deadly pleasant, once said, "Perhaps if Mr. Sorensen would let us in on the joke, we all could laugh with him." I shook my head "no" and doubled my efforts at composure. I got my best grades when absurdity overcame me.

It was during a physics lab that I received a graphic illustration of the nature of trauma. It occurred on a bright, shining autumn day that had me humming to myself with the joy of being alive. The exercise was going smoothly, and I had nothing to do except to enjoy the moment. As I waited for the result of an experiment, a wandering finger touched the top end of a fluorescent lamp that sat near me. I felt a pleasantly tingling sensation tickling the tip of my finger. With the same finger I felt the opposite end of the lamp and felt the same tickling sensation. *What would happen if I touched both ends at the same time?* Tentative fingers stretched forward. WHAM! A tremendous shock racked my body and nearly knocked me off my stool while I rocked back and forth. Suddenly, I was tired, so very tired. I fought to stay awake during the rest of the class while my eyes begged for rest. After class, I walked slowly back to my room, too tired to talk to anyone, putting one foot before the other, and barely conscious of my surroundings.

All effort exhausted me, but I forced myself to undress. While doing so, two figures, one wearing a skeleton mask and the other a witch's mask tried, unsuccessfully, to startle me. They jumped at me after entering my room through the window from the three-foot-wide gutter outside of it, but I was too familiar with Danny and Bragg not to recognize the outlines of their bodies. They told me of the success they had frightening a couple of youngsters taking an afternoon nap. Then they climbed back out the window to search for more victims.

I went to bed and slept until the plebe chow call for evening meal. Ryan woke me up telling me that I had ten minutes for evening meal formation. I rolled over in a sleepy stupor. Again, the plebe came into the room to tell me that I had five minutes to evening meal formation and was about to leave the room when he asked, "Mr. Sorensen, sir, are you all right?"

I noticed the concern in the plebe's voice and appreciated it. "Yeah, I'm okay."

"You've got five minutes, sir."

"Thanks."

In a sleep-laden daze, I dressed, passed through formation, and ate supper. Vaguely, I noticed that Gaut was wearing white gloves and remembered when I was made to do the same thing. The tip of my right finger had been blackened from shining shoes and Budge had decided to humiliate me that way. Gaut's second classmen were so excited that, even in my oblivion, I was aware of it. I looked at the plebe and saw that his face was screwed up as though he was about to cry, but I was much too tired to take an active interest; I'd talk to the plebe tomorrow.

After meal, I wandered to my room to lie down again, sinking deep, deeper, into nothingness, into escape. I slept and when I awoke the next morning, I was still tired, but not as exhausted as the night before. I added up the hours to discover that I'd been asleep for the last sixteen of them.

* * *

One sunshine Saturday, I was sitting at my desk, reading my mail. I had just finished a letter from Mom and was about to open the one from Cora when I happened to look up and had to swallow my heart back down. The windows of the fifth deck of Bancroft Hall, its topmost floor, are bordered by a copper rain gutter, the same gutter that Danny and Bragg had used to try to frighten me. This time I really was frightened; I saw John Boatman run along the gutter in front of our window as though he was jogging through a park. When my roommate crawled through the window a couple of minutes later, I yelled, "Are you crazy? That's at least a seventy-foot drop out there! One slip and that's it!"

"Does it make you nervous?"

"No, John, that's why I'm sitting here shitting my pants; because it doesn't bother me!" My groin tightened as I tried to imagine what such a fall must feel like. I said, "That must be a horrible way to die. The fall must last forever."

"A few seconds."

"Forever to the poor sucker it's happening to. Look, if you want to kill yourself, don't do it in front of me, especially by falling a thousand feet."

"You're exaggerating, but sle, okay, I won't run in the gutter when you're in the room." John took off his sneakers and tossed them into a corner of the room. "What are you going to do in the spring when the upperclassmen are sunbathing out there?"

"I won't look. Anyone who'd fall asleep next to a drop like that is an idiot. What if he rolls over in his sleep or when he first wakes up and is disoriented and he steps off the ledge?"

"Wheeeeeee!"

"Yeah, wheee."

John sat on his bunk. "I saw a strange thing out there. I looked into Meade's room, and he was standing in front of his mirror, the full-length mirror, buck naked and looking at himself. Sle, what do you make of that?"

"Nothing. He was looking at himself in the mirror. I don't think he's queer if that's what you're asking."

"Neither do I. I just wanted to see what you thought of it. How'd the recital go?" John was referring to an organ recital to which Danny and I had been ordered to attend as ushers.

"All right. We didn't have anything to do but show people to their seats and collect money."

"Get much?"

"No, a couple of bucks. Fortune was there. He was the only mid in the audience. I couldn't figure out what middie-puke in his right mind would want to listen to the fugues of Bach. There's something wrong with the boy. Ever notice how he walks with his head down like he's afraid to meet people eyeball to eyeball?"

"No, I haven't."

"John, are you blind? He's headed for trouble, just like Gaut."

"Gaut?"

"Yeah, he's another one. The next time we go to formation, check out his eyes. They look like those of a puppy that's been hit for something it didn't know it did."

"Sores, you sound like a mother hen. You have your own problems to worry about. These guys will make it the same as you and I did. Besides, they're not getting run nearly as hard as we did."

"I'm not so sure about that. At any rate, I'm going to have a talk with Gaut. Maybe I can save him some hassle."

Buns McMunn, followed by Mower, both in the regulation gray sweat suit and breathing heavily, interrupted the two of us. Buns was carrying a pair of expensive track shoes which I had bought when I ran on the high school cross country and track teams. He said, "Thanks, Sores, for letting me borrow your track shoes. They're beautiful. Where'd you get them?"

"A shoe store in Providence, Rhode Island."

"Those are quite a pair of shoes."

"I know. They're made of kangaroo leather."

The first classmen felt the texture of the material. "What do you want for them?"

"They're not for sale."

"I'll give you twenty bucks for them."

"No, thanks."

"Thirty."

"Nope."

"If you ever want to get rid of them, you'll let me know?"

"Sure."

When the firsties had left, I faced John and asked, "Whoever heard of buying someone else's track shoes?"

"Maybe they want something to remember you by."

"Not likely."

"I'm surprised you let McMunn borrow them. I thought you hated those guys."

"I do. Don't even doubt that."

"Then why do you let them borrow your stuff?"

"Why not? If I said no, it would only cause resentment." My voice became a harsh monotone. "I don't know why they bother to come around here! They must know that I hate their guts! They could read my mind when I was a plebe; why can't they read it now?"

"Maybe they come here to bust your balls."

"I don't think so. I think they really wanted to buy my shoes. Why, do you think that's what they were doing?"

"No, but it's worth considering. Remember, humility builds character."

"Yeah, but what kind of character?"

As John started his shower, I finished reading my letters from home. As my roommate was drying himself, I said, "My sister seems to be under the impression that I had an affair with my sister-in-law."

"Did you?"

"No, but you don't think she's running around telling people that I banged her, do you?"

"Nobody would believe it."

"Unless they wanted to believe it."

After John left for town, I decided since there were a couple of hours before evening meal that it was a good time to study. A *Time Magazine* sat next to my physics book. I briefly thumbed through the textbook, thought, *I'll have plenty of time later to study,* then delved into the magazine.

Hours later I still hadn't begun to study. I was hungry and wanted to know what was for evening meal. In conscious imitation of McMunn and knowing the impression I was about to make, I burst into Gaut's room. The plebe, who was sitting comfortably at his desk, leapt to his feet and sounded off while from my right came the sound of another plebe, Fortune, sounding off. I turned from Gaut to stand nose to nose with Fortune, a plebe visiting from another squad. My voice rasped with threat in it. "Evening meal, mister!"

Fortune looked worried. "Sir, the menu for evening meal is Salisbury steak, sir." The plebe paused.

"What else, mister?"

Beads of sweat formed on his forehead. "I'll find out, sir."

This was what I wanted. Inwardly, I was overjoyed, but outwardly, I appeared furious at plebe incompetence. I raged, "What do you mean you'll find out? This isn't a girl scout camp! You're supposed to know your menus two meals in advance, and you don't even know the next one! Do you think you're on vacation? That you can bag it because it's Saturday night?"

"No, sir. I wasn't expecting to be asked, sir."

"What kind of crap is that? Do you think a VC only attacks when a GI is expecting him?"

"No, sir."

Fortune was a red head and I remembered how Roark used to address Bemes during plebe summer. Like Roark, I said, "Look, you red-headed piece of shit, I want you in my room in five minutes with the next three meals memorized! Got that?"

I stared angrily at the frightened plebe. I couldn't believe I was having such an effect upon another human being. Why should Fortune be so worried? I was about to leave when I caught the startled expression on Gaut's face. Harshly, I asked, "Mr. Gaut, you're not taking any of this crap personally, are you?"

"No, sir."

"Good." *Did I look like these two when I was a plebe?* Once in my room, I noted the time. In exactly five minutes, Fortune requested to come on board. Granted. After the plebe sounded off, I asked, "Well?" Fortune rattled off the menus. I asked him to repeat the deserts as I had been made to repeat the deserts when I was a plebe. He did so. I asked, "Are you sure?" and considered going into the hall to find a plebe to verify the deserts.

I couldn't believe how much I was enjoying myself. I could see how an upperclassman could get caught up in the game. More to stop myself than anything else, I decided to spoon Fortune. As I held out my hand, the plebe's head snapped back in surprise, then he shook my hand. It was unspoken tradition that upperclassmen who had been run hard as plebes ran their own plebes as hard as they had been run. I decided that I would break that tradition. I was enjoying myself far too much. I asked, "I scared you, didn't I?"

"You sure did."

"I don't want to be a hard ass, but I had to find out how it feels."

"How does it feel, sir?"

"The name's Mike."

"How does it feel, um, Mike?"

"Great!"

Although at Saturday evening meals there weren't designated company areas, I noticed that Gaut was sitting with two of the second classmen from our squad. It was unusual to have two second classmen in Bancroft Hall on a Saturday evening, but I remembered how my own demoniacs sometimes stayed behind to bear bait me. The plebe looked weak and frustrated, which reminded me to make a point of having a long talk with him. I heard a second classman say, "Gaut, how did you get in?"

"Sir?"

"How did you get in? Political pull?"

"I'll find out, sir."

"Are you a jock?"

"No, sir."

"Are you something special?"

"No, sir."

"They must have been hurting to let you and some of your classmates in, right Gaut?" The plebe swallowed. A beaded tear formed in either eye. The upperclassman pushed for an answer. "Right, Gaut?"

"I'll find out, sir."

"You do that."

* * *

That evening, Danny Calhoun and I went drinking without Matt and found ourselves sitting in the back room of the Pizza Palace. It was comfortably dark. The television, which neither of us was watching, was casting its messages of consumption and the good life of bikinis, tits, and beer. Both of us were drunk but not so much so that we couldn't enjoy one another's company. Each was lost in his own isolated, floating dreams when four youngsters sat at a table near us. One of them called, "Hey, you guys got the time?"

Danny glanced at his watch. "Nine thirty."

There was a slight stir among them when another one of the mids called over, "Then fuck you."

Danny started, "Huh?"

"I said, 'Fuck you.'"

Immediately, Danny's slouch turned into an erect, wary, sitting posture on the edge of his seat. He returned the courtesy by saying, "Fuck you yourself."

Instantly, everyone was on his feet. I saw defeat before us, perhaps a severe beating. Not only were Danny and I outnumbered four to two, but we could barely stay on our feet. I stood near my friend, quietly, not quite conscious of what was being said. The mannerisms and tones of voice told me that people were arguing. Whenever the noise level lessened, the smallest mid among the four interrupted by saying, "Okay, guys, that's enough. Let's go. We've all had our say."

There was more noise. I saw the small mid pulling at his larger companions, talking in a low undertone. The four mids started to leave but couldn't resist turning around at the door to hurl a few last invectives. My only comment throughout the whole episode was to raise my middle finger to pop them the bird. There was an instant reaction at the door. One of the mids pushed through the restraining arms of the small mid and rushed up to me. He pushed me and I pushed him back. The mid said, "Let's go outside."

My senses were gradually returning, but I still didn't have enough control to trust myself to respond, so I remained mute. My opponent was bigger, taller, stronger, and more intense than me. He knew I would lose, as did I. The small mid forcefully gripped his buddy's arm. "C'mon," he said. "Let's go. Let's not get into any trouble."

"Let's go outside," repeated the big mid as the small mid pulled at his arm. He jerked his arm away and squarely faced me. "You're white trash, just white trash." The small mid finally succeeded in pushing his partner to the door. As they looked back, I popped them another bird. A tremendous stir ruffled the doorway. My stomach turned as I thought that my opponent was about to return. I hoped I could take my beating without showing cowardice. However, the small mid prevailed and the four youngsters vanished into the street.

Danny had quietly watched this last episode. I turned to him to ask, "What was *that* all about?"

Danny shrugged his shoulders. "Beats me."

It was nearly time to sign in at Bancroft Hall, so we left the Pizza Palace to return to our rooms. As soon as I walked into my room, I pulled out my *Lucky Bag,* the school's yearbook, to search the photographs for our would-be assailants. I found a photo of one of them and ran to Danny's room with the book. "Look," I said, "I found a picture of one of those jerks! He's in the twenty-third company. Here's another one!"

"What do you want to do about it?"

"Find their rooms and jump them while they're sleeping. They'll never know what hit them."

Danny objected, "We can't do that."

"Okay, we'll cut up their shoes or do something like that."

"Why don't we challenge them to fight us in the ring?"

"Why? We might lose. Why don't we give them the same chance that they would have given us, which is no chance at all!" There was a moment of silence as we realized that we would never be able to agree. Then, "Good night, Dan."

"Good night, Mike."

* * *

That Sunday the Academy went from summer whites to winter blues. Now, the small rectangular marching columns of the church parties were in black instead of white. Danny, Husaby, and I still deserted church formation whenever we could, but I was the only one who managed to skip it every week. Both Danny and Husaby had moments of flagging courage and ended up kneeling weak kneed in a pew while I made my escape. A Class A offence for me would not be as devastating as it would be for my friends.

This weekend it was Husaby who had successfully braved the first and second class gauntlet guarding the church doors. We marched back to the Academy in a formation of two. Bancroft Hall was in sight when we were unexpectedly stopped by the officer of the day, derisively nicknamed Jo-Jo. He was a hard liner with an Academy-wide reputation for frying midshipmen. The officer smiled pleasantly as he pulled up next to us in a black Navy sedan. The three of us exchanged salutes as Jo-Jo's eyes scanned us impassively like a radar dish. With his thick glasses and slimy smile, he looked like the movie stereotype of a Gestapo interrogator. He asked, "What church party do you belong to?"

Husaby answered, "To the St. James party, sir."

"Aren't you a rather small party for out-in-town church?"

"No, sir. We're a small group anyway, but some of the other midshipmen like to go to the meetinghouse for coffee and donuts after the service. We're the only ones who decided to come back."

"But you *did* attend the service?"

"Oh, yes, sir."

"Very well. Carry-on."

"Aye-aye, sir."

We saluted. Throughout, I had remained silent. Husaby had just blatantly committed an honor offence for which he would have been dismissed from the Academy. For all my hatred of the Machine, I would not have lied, although I admitted to myself that I was both thankful and relieved that Husaby had done so. We blithely walked away from Jo-Jo as if nothing had happened.

That morning offered yet another surprise. It was one of those rare mornings when visitors were allowed inside Bancroft Hall. After breakfast, I slipped out of my uniform and into my blue bathrobe. When I stepped into the hallway, I recoiled back into my room when I saw a second classman with his girl. I then remembered that it was visitor's day and hurriedly changed into my uniform. I cursed the delay in my trip to the head when there was a knock on my door. John, who was nearest to it, said, "I'll get it."

Budge stood on the other side with a small, demure young lady with flowing brunette hair standing next to him, her arm looped lovingly in his. By way of introduction, he said, "Sores, I want you to meet Miss Brooks, my fiancée. I've told her a lot about you, and I wanted her to meet you."

As the lovers entered my room, my guts started roiling. The lips of my anus puckered. A dragon wanted out, but I tightened my buttocks and forced it back into its lair. Affably, I smiled, "I'm pleased to meet you." I held out my hand. As Miss Brooks shook it, I prayed that no untoward events, such as unwanted squeaks and pops, would occur.

Budge said, "This is the guy I had in my squad last year."

She said, "Yes, I remember you telling me about him."

Budge held out his hand. As we shook hands, he said, "We've got to get going. I wanted her to meet you. I thought you'd like that."

Continental shelves rumbled and shifted in my guts. I answered, "Yes, very much so."

The couple left. As soon as the door closed, John hopped and said, "Surprise! Do you forgive him now?"

I expelled a long stream of flatus, "Brbrbrbrbrbrbrbrbrbrbrbrbrbrbrbrbrbrbrb," while at the same time verbally emitting, "Ahhhhhhhhhhhhhhhhhhh. That felt good!" Then I answered John's question, "Hell no, but it *was* nice of him to do that. I simply don't understand how he could expect us to be friends."

"You *did* share your most glorious moments together."

"Yeah, but it was all *my* glory," and I left for the head.

* * *

As the semester worked its way toward midterm exams, I noticed that the expressions on the faces of Gaut and Fortune were troubled. Gaut had been haunting my thoughts, so much so that I was determined to talk to the plebe to exorcise whatever demons were bothering him. When I went to Gaut's room, I found his roommate there. Ryan snapped to attention and sounded off.

I said, "Carry-on." Ryan sat back into his chair while I sat on the edge of the desk and asked, "What's the story with Gaut?"

"What do you mean, sir."

"He's acting strange, well, not exactly strange, but there's something wrong. You can see it in his eyes."

"I don't know what it could be, sir."

"No family problems?"

"None that I know of, sir."

"Anybody been hassling him?"

"No more than anyone else, sir."

"I *know* there's something wrong." There was a long pause while the two of us ruminated. "What about Fortune?"

"Oh, Fortune. He's being run out, sir."

"Is he midshipman material?"

"Yes, sir."

"So why is he being run out?"

"Sir, can I speak to you confidentially?"

"Of course."

"There's absolutely nothing wrong with Fortune. He's intelligent, athletic, knows a hell of a lot about a lot of things; I mean that he's A-1, sir. At the beginning of plebe summer, he was as sharp if not sharper than anyone else in the company, but do you know what happened, sir?" I lifted my chin slightly to indicate that I was listening. "He believed them, sir. When they called him a no-good piece of shit, he believed it. And from there things got worse. The more he believed them, the more he fucked up. The more he fucked up, the more bullshit they gave him which made him fuck up all the more."

I was staring at the floor. "That's too bad. I wish there was something I could do, but he's not in my squad. I can't break protocol." I took a deep breath. "Okay, I got to go. See you at evening meal."

Ryan stood up, "Sir? Shall I tell Gaut to see you?"

"Does he have come-around tonight?"

"I think so, sir. I'm pretty sure he does."

"No, don't bother. I'll catch him some other time."

"Aye-aye, sir."

I mulled over what Ryan had told me. There must be some way to short circuit the monster that the Academy had become for me. My attitude towards the school was becoming ambivalent. At times, I dreamt of seeing it raised to the ground, granite block by granite block. Yet, I knew that I would willingly die to defend it. It was like the loyalty that wives often showed to abusive husbands or the love that children had toward abusive parents. I wasn't sure that I'd want to change the Academy even if I could. Yet, I might be able to kick its heart of stone.

That evening meal I stood at the table fidgeting much as I remembered my own third classmen fidgeting when I was a plebe. Boatman was playing with his silverware while the rest of the upperclassmen stood in comparative silence. I watched as the plebes filled the glasses of the first and second classmen as was required of them. The third classmen were expected to fill their own glasses. This time, however, when the plebes were done, I looked up and pretended surprise. I exaggerated my mannerisms and facial expressions to attract the attention of the plebes. They were confused. In imitation of dozens of motorcycle movie heroes, I sneered. Butrus and Ryan smiled while Gaut looked worried. Austin was on team tables. I snapped my fingers and looked meaningfully at my glass. Butrus caught on and hurriedly passed the milk to Gaut. I looked angry, snapped my fingers forcefully, and Gaut exchanged the milk for tea. Like a kindly saint, I looked on as Gaut filled my glass. Then the plebe put a spoonful of sugar into my tea. I snapped my fingers, and a second spoonful was added. The mixture was carefully stirred. Casually, I glanced at the plebes. They were all smiling. My newly created game and subtle ridicule of the Academy had relieved a lot of the tension among them. However, the first and second classmen were not amused and showed their displeasure by a studied silence. I was afraid that they'd retaliate against me, but I was willing to take the chance.

The brigade was ordered, "Seats, gentlemen." The food was passed around in descending order of rank. Continuing my Chaplinesque routine, I snapped my fingers without looking up after I had eaten my corn. Immediately, the corn was passed to me. I finished both the corn and the potatoes and snapped my fingers. The potatoes were passed to me. I looked at Gaut with a startled, harsh look on my face, putting enough exaggeration into my expression to let the plebes know that I was mocking their superiors. The potatoes disappeared to be replaced by the corn. The plebes joined wholeheartedly into the game. I was pleased that I received much better service than anyone else at the table. What pleased me most, however, was that Gaut was smiling, and his eyes were sparkling.

As the days passed, the plebes became more proficient at second guessing my wishes. At each meal, I waited for an upperclassman to say something to make me stop my pantomime. Their brooding expressions darkened, and I knew that it upset them more and more. With each meal, the silence became more profound. The first and second classmen milled at the ends of the table, looking at the floor or at the tabletop, wanting to say something, but unaccountably restraining themselves. After a couple of weeks, I decided to stop the game. Gaut was smiling again although the first and second classmen grew far more sinister. I knew that I hadn't hurt the Academy by any means, but I had gotten a little satisfaction by slapping its face.

* * *

One day I received a letter from Donna, the girl from Virginia Beach. I ripped open the envelope and the letter and a photograph dropped out. The photo showed Donna wearing a bikini that showed how well-proportioned she was.

I turned my attention to the letter. She was still at Virginia Beach with her parents. As I knew from the summer, her father was a Navy lieutenant stationed at Norfolk. At night, under a full moon, she walked disconsolately along the shore, listening to the hush of the breaking waves, dreaming only of me. Unconsciously, I turned around in my room to see if she was talking about someone else. I took another, more careful look at the photo. I studied every groove and curve of her body. With a couple of leaves and dances coming up, I thought that I should ask her out. I returned to the letter. She was pining for me. The night spoke to her of our love. Every star was a wish that she might see me again.

I finished the letter, then sat looking at the photo. About a month ago, Matt had come into my room and waved his middle finger back and forth under my nose. It had a strong musk odor that was unfamiliar to me but the source of which I could guess. I had leered knowingly at him as though the odor was as familiar as smog. Now was my chance to do the same thing to Matt. I wrote Donna a long letter inviting her to the youngster dance scheduled for the end of the month. Matt would be with his townie, Carnevale would be with his girl, and both had wanted me to triple up with them if I could find a date.

On the night of the dance, the six of us, all coupled, met in the rotunda of Bancroft Hall. A mid was playing "Shenandoah" on the piano in Memorial Hall. The song floated hauntingly to the young people. I had never heard anything so beautiful. Donna's parents were there but stayed only long enough to meet their daughter's date before walking away, arm in arm, like lovers. I had been civil but could no longer produce my catalogue smile.

Matt introduced his date, Alicia, to the group. She was a short, dark, squat girl with rough edges like the girls found in the mills of New England. Immediately, I knew that Matt would never stay with her; yet I found her to be a lot of fun, more so than my own date. Carnevale introduced his date, Lauri, to us. She was an extremely attractive blonde with large, sightless eyes. Paul hadn't told me that his date was blind, but Matt seemed to have already known. I took my cue from the other two mids. Since neither Matt nor Paul was condescending, neither was I, especially since I was taken with her pleasantness and genuine good will.

We all went to the dance. The music was so loud that it hurt our ears, and nothing could be heard except the trilling of electric chords. We gyrated to the beat, and I pretended to be an Indian on the warpath, throwing spears and tomahawking people, looking for all the world as though I was really dancing. At times I'd break out laughing because I'd wonder how the dancers would look if suddenly the music stopped, and we found ourselves in the presence of God. How ridiculous we'd look! Donna wanted to know what I was laughing about, but I couldn't be heard above the music. Ridiculous or not, I was having an awfully good time.

Toward the end of the evening, we went into town for ice cream. It was an enjoyable walk. The weather was a little brisk, but it accentuated by its clarity the brightness of the city lights. On the way, Paul described everything to Lauri, who was pleased when he told her how Matt and I were dancing like wild men. Now we were dancing arm in arm like Greeks. We turned and were now doing a waltz together.

At the ice cream parlor, I tried to tease Donna by scooping the cherry off her sundae. Instead of fighting me for it, she said, "I want that." I replaced it. Matt did the same thing to Alicia who demanded her cherry back. She jabbed him in the ribs as he held it aloft like a trophy. When he was about to jam it down his throat, she jumped at his arm and a small wrestling match ensued. Quickly, Alicia grabbed the cherry, licked it, and then offered it to her date. Matt said, "Yummy!" then shoved it into his mouth. Donna beamed at him.

The table conversation was an almost unbearable trial. While Matt was wrestling with Alicia and Paul was busy describing it to Lauri, I was left on my own to talk to Donna. I hemmed and hawed, searching for words to say, but nothing clicked. On the way back to the Academy, I hugged her and told her that I was a bear that mistook her for a pot of honey. Her response: "Uh huh." I found it increasingly embarrassing to be with her and I was afraid of what my companions might be thinking.

Soon, we were saying goodnight to our dates. Paul walked Lauri to the bus station. Alicia and Donna left together, the former to her car and the latter to her parents who, as previously agreed, were waiting for her.

As Matt and I were walking back to Bancroft Hall, I said "We've got ten minutes to sign in."

Matt responded, imitating Donna, "Uh huh."

"Okay, Matt, cut me some slack." We walked a little way when I said, "Do you know what I think is weird?"

"What's that?"

"Paul's girl. I think she's happy. I think she's really happy, not just pretending to be happy."

"Why shouldn't she be happy?"

"How can a blind person be happy? Think of all she's missing."

"What do you expect her to do, crawl into a hole and die? Let me ask you a rhetorical question. Who's your favorite singer, you know, the guy you listen to all the time when John is out of the room?"

"Jose Feliciano."

"Precisely." After a while Matt asked, "Did you ask Donna to the Army-Navy game?"

"Yeah. It's that damn body of hers. There has to be *something* in there!" Besides, I didn't want to be the only mid there without a girl.

* * *

The Saturday evening before exams, Matt, Danny, and I went into town. I suggested that we go to a movie, but there was nothing playing that we wanted to see. Danny bitterly suggested that we go to D.C. and join a protest march.

I asked, "Do you really think they hate us?"

Matt asked, "Who?"

"The war protesters."

"Of course, they do! They hate everyone in uniform!"

Danny savagely inserted, "Or does the media make it appear that way?"

I said, "Some of them must be sincere. Ideally, they're right. They want world peace."

"My ass! For some of them it's a collegiate event and the rest are just cowards!"

"You don't know that."

"You're right; I don't know that. I don't know if the organizers of the war protests are Soviet *agents provocateurs*, but they might as well be. But I can tell you one thing that I *do* know: I *do* know that the war protests are perfect psyops for the North Vietnamese and their ally, the Soviet Union, the enemy I might remind you! You can bet your ass that the commies cream their jeans when Ivy League undergrads chant, 'Ho, Ho, Ho, Ho Chi Minh, the NVA is going to win!'" Unexpectedly, he cried out, "MY BROTHER LOST HIS LEG IN VIETNAM!"

Silence settled onto us. No one knew what to say. Moments passed that seemed endless. Subdued, Matt finally said, "Let's do something besides bitch about the news. What do you want to do?"

No one had any innovative ideas, so we decided to follow our normal ritual of getting drunk. We gave our money to a young black man with a gold earring hanging from his left ear. After waiting fifteen minutes for the black to return, Danny went into the package store to investigate. The store owner told him that the young man had left by the back door. When Danny returned to his friends, we pooled our money and found a much older black man to buy booze for us. He returned with three pints of rum.

Again, we roamed the streets, mixing our rum into the sodas we bought at a fast-food hamburger chain. When we were finished drinking, we found another hamburger joint to rest in. Here, we ate a meal and drank coffee.

I reached for a napkin and accidentally knocked the sugar bowl over, spilling its contents in Danny's direction. I placed the sugar container onto its base and scraped the spilled mess off the edge of the table with my hand. Danny pointedly picked up the sugar bowl, poured some sugar onto the table, then scraped it off onto my lap. Both Danny and I tensed up, fists clenched, seething with anger. The slightest remark from either of us would precipitate a fight.

Matt broke in, "Cut it out, you guys! Jesus Christ! It's getting so's I hate going out with you two! You're always scratching at each other like a pair of cats!" We calmed down, sitting back into our chairs, and pretended that nothing had happened. Later, on the way back to Bancroft Hall, we almost apologized to one another.

* * *

Midterms arrived with me in my usual state of unpreparedness. Instead of staying up until 0100 hours in the morning talking nonsense with John, I now stayed up until 0400 hours in the morning, ostensibly studying, but in fact, goofing off. The exams were often at 0800 hours so I would only get two or three hours of sleep when I should have been well rested. It was almost like plebe year where I was so exhausted that I lost the will to study. The difference now was that the exhaustion was self-inflicted and came from a lack of sleep instead of coming from muscle fatigue due to the manic behavior of upperclassmen.

When the grades were posted, I found the appropriate computer listings taped on the walls of the lower decks of Bancroft Hall. I'd slink up to one of the sheets with a sinking heart and prayed that life wouldn't be as hard as expected, but it always was. I'd find my ID number on the roster and, hoping that the mids surrounding the grade sheet weren't watching, slip my finger horizontally to the grade opposite. Once I saw my grade, I'd look at the other grades to see if anyone had scored lower than I did. Generally, there were one or two lower grades, but that was little consolation in a class of from twenty to thirty people.

Whenever a classmate asked, "How'd you do?" I answered, "All right" and then walked with a jaunty air as if I had the world in my pocket. After I collected my grades, I returned to my room. John was sitting in his skivvies, feet on the desk and reading a newspaper. His skin tone and general hairlessness reminded me of frozen chicken. He greeted me with his customary, jovial smile and asked, "How'd you do?"

I sat on the edge of my bunk. "Bad, and you?"

"I'll get a 3.0 this semester."

"Your study habits are as bad as mine. How'd you do it?"

"Luck, I guess. How bad did you do?"

"Bad."

"Bad enough for an academic board?"

"Yeah."

"You still have a couple of months before the end of the semester to pull your grades up."

"I suppose." I spotted a chit on the desk telling me to report to Dimwiddie. "I see the fat man saw my grades." I picked up the chit and threw it into the trash. "By the way, John, I seem to have lost my Cross pen, the gold one with my name engraved on it. You haven't seen it, have you?"

"No. Where'd you lose it?"

"I don't know. Maybe the library."

"Maybe Valdres clipped it when you were moving out."

"Valdres is a lot of things, but he's not a thief."

"Sle, Valdres or not, do you think you'll ever see it again?"

"Why not? It has my name on it. It can be traced through the Academy roster."

"That's not what I mean."

"Oh, I see. You think that whoever finds it is going to keep it, but I think you're wrong. Midshipmen are a pretty trustful lot. I don't think anybody will keep it. In fact, I'd be surprised if it *wasn't* returned to me."

"You can expect a surprise then."

"John, you've got to learn to trust people."

"I do. I trust you."

"More people than just me."

"Yeah."

After a year at the Academy, I had learned to get the unpleasant over with as quickly as possible. At the company commander's office, I sounded off, then saluted and held it until the officer returned the salute. Dimwiddie told me to sit down. I sat apprehensively while the officer sat in a long, profound pause of consideration. "Mr. Sorensen, have you seen your grades?"

"Yes, sir."

"What do you think of them?"

"They're pretty bad, sir."

"Horrible, wouldn't you say?"

"Yes, sir."

"Can you tell me why they're so bad?"

"I'll find out, sir."

"Give me a real answer."

"I don't know, sir."

"Do you like it here?"

"Yes, sir."

"Do you want to stay here?"

"Yes, sir."

"So, what's the problem?"

"I don't know, sir."

"Do you have any family problems?"

Yeah, right, as if I was going to tell my family problems to another representative of the Academy Machine. I remembered Kristin's "if you think you can use your father's death as an excuse to bag it, you're wrong." I didn't want to hear that from Dimwiddie, so I answered, "No, sir, nothing that I can't handle."

"Is it the Vietnam War?"

"No, sir."

"What about the protest marches? Do they bother you?"

"Sometimes, sir."

"Do you think those people are right?"

"Sometimes I do, sir, and sometimes I don't. I really don't know, sir."

"Would you like to join them?"

"No, sir."

"That's the only way you could find out if they're wrong or not."

"Yes, sir."

"Mr. Sorensen, I can't help you if you don't tell me what the problem is."

"I don't know, sir. I don't seem to be learning anything."

"What do you mean?"

"I'm not learning anything that's important, about life I mean. I feel like a caged animal, a caged lion. I'm learning a lot of math and science, but the real world is passing me by. There's so much of the world to see, and I'm not seeing it as a midshipman."

"You have your whole life ahead of you to learn about the things that you think are important. The Academy is also a part of life, a part of this mysterious world you've posited. You can learn just as much about life here as anywhere else."

"I don't know that, sir. I want to understand what's happening in the world."

"What's there to understand?"

"I don't know, sir. That's what I'd like to find out."

"Mr. Sorensen, get your grades up. We'll talk more about this later."

"Aye-aye, sir."

"You're dismissed." We exchanged salutes and I left for my room.

That night, for the first time since I'd been at the Academy, I heard "Taps." John and I had gone to bed early with our window opened a crack. In the cool air that floated into the room came the sadly haunting

237

notes from the bugler at Memorial Hall. The tune carried past our room to the far shores of the Chesapeake and into the night sky. The bay's waves lapped at it; the ionosphere threw it into space. The notes drifted into the deepest parts of the ocean and the farthest reaches of the universe. They defied time and would float forever past listening midshipmen who have lost their way.

CHAPTER XI

DECEMBER SURPRISES

YOUNGSTER YEAR

I was sitting in my room listlessly thumbing through a textbook, thinking how endless every book and assignment seemed, when George Verga entered my room. George was a first classman with whom I had little contact. The firstie sat down without invitation and started talking to me in a confidential tone. "I heard you went to Woodstock." I nodded yes while wondering what could have possibly brought Verga into my room. The firstie's eyes were glowing and a smile played on his lips. He said, "I'm tripping. I took some acid." I waited for the inevitable question of whether I had ever tripped, but the firstie assumed that I had. George continued, "The first time I took acid it felt as though a wave washed over me and all my inhibitions went with it. Man! I feel great! Woodstock was great, huh? Did you read in the papers about a dealer who was walking through the crowd like a fruit vendor calling, 'Grass! Quaaludes! Amphetamines!' and followed by a hippie calling, 'Apples! Pears! Plums!'?" I remembered the article and nodded. George continued, "The hippie was me. I wore these funky jeans, a T-shirt, and hadn't washed in days. It was great. Look, man, any time you want a hit, come over to my room. If I don't have what you want, I'll get it for you. I've got all kinds of contacts in town. See you around, man!"

"Sure."

Other than one or two brief comments, the firstie had never spoken to me before. Now his mannerisms and tone of voice implied that we were on intimate terms, good pals. I had never liked George since he always impressed me as being weak. Despite my desire to be "cool" and "with it," I hoped that he would leave me alone.

I rummaged through my physics book for the tenth time that day and knew that I should study but was too tired to do so. Exhaustion was constantly gripping me. I was aware of this but knew neither its cause nor how to deal with it. I thought of my mother and sister. The crying over the phone and the panic in my mother's voice had increased. Yet, it had been going on so long that my weekly bouts with depression had become more of a habit. As far as I knew, they didn't explain my deep craving for sleep. My grades were bad, and the protest marches had increased, becoming more aggressive, but I learned to live with this also. I undressed, felt the cool comfort offered by my sheets, and was soon fast asleep.

Hours passed when I awoke to the babbling of the plebe chow call for evening meal. As I lay in bed, I watched John get ready when Ryan popped his head into the room. "Ten minutes, sir." The head vanished, but immediately reappeared. "Mr. Sorensen, you've got ten minutes to chow, sir."

Quietly, I answered, "Thanks." When I sat up, I felt the blood rush to my head. I had just enough time to put on my uniform and make the third class bell. At formation, I walked down the rank of plebes and stopped in front of Gaut. The plebe's eyes were glassy and had that hurt look in them again. "Gaut."

"Sir."

"Everything all right?"

"Yes, sir."

"You look tired."

"I had to close upper class windows at five this morning, sir."

"Well, I had to do the same thing. You're alternating with your squad members, aren't you?"

"Yes, sir."

"Is there anything else wrong?"

"No, sir."

For the hundredth time, I made a mental note to talk to the plebe when I got the chance. Maybe with just the two of us, Gaut would open up.

At the table, I found that the seating had been changed. Instead of being at his usual place, Gaut was sitting at the table behind me. At the first class end of my own table sat Dimwiddie. To make room for him, a plebe had been ordered to float. I noticed how beefy the officer's jowls were, as if he had never missed a meal in his life. For no apparent reason, there was a lot of excitement and swirling activity among the mids. I speculated about the cause and noticed that the plebes were getting an unusual amount of harassment.

Again, looking behind me, I saw Gaut wearing his white gloves just as I had worn them a year ago. The hurt look in the plebe's eyes was more intense, making me wonder if I had looked so hurt when I was in the same boat. My attention shifted to Dimwiddie, immersed in conversation with the first classmen. Although he was seeing everything about him, the officer seemed oblivious to it. He was smiling despite the inferno about him, and I knew that he was a happy man.

A sudden rush of noise forced me to glance behind me. Gaut was standing in the middle of the aisle with his fists raised in a boxer's stance. I looked at Dimwiddie who seemed unaware of what was happening. Again, I glanced at Gaut. The plebe was about to cry. A grinning second classman pretended to correct his stance. The plebe tensed, lunged past the second classman, pushing him out of his way, and said in his flight, "Fuck you!" Then he ran out of the mess hall.

I was enraged. Had Gaut been near me, I would have punched the plebe and forced him to sit down. I saw that my crime would again become the focus of unwanted attention, that I would again be subject to derision, if only by comparison. Hadn't anybody learned anything? Surely, Gaut and the other plebes must have known what I had gone through. Was all that torment for nothing?

Dimwiddie sat stiffly upright with a startled look on his face. When the mids were given "Seats, gentlemen," the atmosphere relaxed, and the officer was smiling again.

In an emotional tither, I reviewed the incident and thought of what I should have said to Gaut. "Look!" I'd grab him by the shoulder. "Don't let these clowns get to you. They're no better than you are. They're garbage, don't you know that? They're scum. Real men wouldn't play these games." Now it was too late. Gaut was a fallen angel.

The commotion in the cafeteria resumed in the halls. Small pockets of upperclassmen formed to discuss the latest event. I walked through them, careful not to look either way and invite comment. John, already in the room when I arrived, asked with his characteristic intake of breath, "Sle, what do you think of our man Gaut?"

"He's a fool."

"Does that mean that you were a fool, too?"

"Yeah, but he's a bigger fool. He should have known what's going to happen to him."

"What do you think will happen to him?"

"Not as much as happened to me, but if it ever gets that bad, I'll figure out a way to help him."

At that moment, Husaby glided in. "McMunn said a real nice thing about you, Mike. He said that you're a real man and that what Gaut did wasn't in any way like what you did. He told everybody that he really respected you, that Gaut could never do what you did, you know, take all that punishment."

"I don't know about that, but thanks for telling me, Dave."

"Sure enough," and Husaby glided out of the room.

I said to John, "Buns might respect me, but that and ten cents will get me a cup of coffee."

It took three days for Gaut's Form 2 to be processed. During that time, I waited to see what would develop. Nothing. I waited another week. At times I'd see Gaut in marching gear or gym gear on his way to E.D., but the upperclassmen left him alone. In fact, all the harassment of the plebes almost came to a complete halt.

One day Gaut was on his way to E.D. when I happened to be in the corridor. The plebe had on his white leggings, bayonet belt, and carried his M-1 at parade rest, telltale signs of his destination. As we passed, the plebe gave me a collusive smile as though we were conspiratorial allies. I didn't return the smile and thought, *you've got it easy. Why is it that I was treated so severely while you're being handled like a little girl?* I was careful never to look at or talk to Gaut ever again. The plebe had ceased to exist.

* * *

Ensign Halleck entered the classroom, giving the mids immediate carry-on. As we all settled in our seats, Halleck said, "Today, gentlemen, we're going to discuss metal fatigue." Looking pointedly at me, eyelids fluttering like a fleeing moth, he said, "Mr. Sorensen, why are you sitting in a slouch like that? I've been watching you since the beginning of the semester. One would hardly think you were in the military. Your shoes are never shined (not true), your brass is never polished (not true), and your schoolwork is inferior (well, that *was* true)."

I tensed. When the instructor had first addressed me, I slowly moved into a more upright position, but soon rolled down into my slouch again just to annoy him. I tried to appear cool, calm, and indifferent, but I felt butterflies in my stomach.

The ensign continued, "A child could do this work which seems to have you so stumped." The ensign paused, then spit out, "Look at you! You don't have an ounce of military bearing, sitting like that with your legs wide open like a slut."

I was burning and tried to maintain my indifferent attitude, but I knew that I must be a bright red. The ensign paused, blinked, and faced the class. "Now, to get back to metal fatigue..."

I sat through the rest of the class, brooding, wondering what the rest of my classmates thought of the incident. After class, another youngster who had taken a dislike to Halleck said to me, "I met that guy on summer cruise. I was in a bar with a midshipman buddy and his girl when I saw Halleck in a crowd of officers. He came over and tried to snake my buddy, pulling that 'Come with me; I'm an officer' bullshit!"

"Did she go with him?"

"No."

"Good for her."

As I was walking to another class, I saw a monument with a large cannon perched on top of it. The plaque beneath it stated that its sister cannon had blown up at its first firing, killing a Secretary of State and a handful of other dignitaries and their wives. Bitterly, I hoped that the Secretary of State had been like Halleck. Although I fought the impulse, I experienced a certain satisfaction that some of the elite had been destroyed. Knowing how very wrong I was, I still thought, *good, that's one for our side.*

* * *

The afternoon was one of relative freedom in that no mandatory events were scheduled and no required sports needed to be played. A good squash match would do me a world of good, so I decided to find a partner with whom to play. I tried Carnevale's room, but he was out, as were Danny and John. I went into Matt's room to find him the focus of a dozen admiring youngsters. Standing, arms crossed, he leaned his butt against the edge of his sink and was saying, "Every once in a while, my nose bleeds for no reason at all. It just starts up." I saw that my friend had a nosebleed. As the blood dribbled from his nose, Matt rubbed his hands beneath it and over his face to completely cover it with blood. The youngsters gave humorous groans of distress. He continued, "My body needs the release of excess blood. Like cum. I beat off at least once a day." Many of the youngsters shifted their postures in obvious discomfort. The mid was talking taboo; no one ever talked about masturbation. They'd have to torture me on the rack before *I'd* ever admit to it. I tried to judge whether Matt was joking or telling the truth, but he maintained a calm, informative demeanor. Of everyone in the company, only Matt was secure enough in his manhood to admit such a thing. No one doubted his sexual prowess, and all admired his strength of character.

When there was a lull in the general conversation, I asked, "Anyone for a game of squash?" There weren't any takers, so I returned to my room, changed into my gym gear, and left for the courts alone. As I was walking down the corridor with my ball and racket, Dimwiddie, who was strolling down its middle, called, "Hello, Mr. Sorensen, are you going to the library to study?"

I didn't see any irony in the officer's face, nor did I pick it up in the tone of his voice. The officer seemed to be asking a serious question. I responded, "Good afternoon, sir. I'm going to play a little squash, sir."

"By yourself?"

"Yes, sir."

The court area was always dark except for the courts themselves. As a rule, they were empty unless the intramural teams were holding a competition. I heard the echoing slap of a ball hitting the court walls, but it could have been coming from any one of a dozen courts. The solitary slapping served to accentuate the silence of the area and its desolation. Soon, the slapping ceased, and I was left the only occupant of that part of the building. Of the many courts on Academy grounds, the ones in Mahan Hall were my favorites. They had no windows or balconies for spectators. Once the door to the court was closed, the rest of the world was irrelevant, nonexistent if the athlete so chose.

I started to hit the cold, hard ball against the court wall. In a little while, the ball became soft, readily responding to the racket's touch. I started hitting it harder and faster! WHAP! WHAP! I didn't like Halleck. WHAP! The ball was Halleck's head. WHAP! And Budge's head. WHAP! A low-cut right into Budge's knees. WHAP! I got him in the knees again. WHAP! What if I'd been a Viking? WHAP! Then the racket would be a sword. WHAP! A low strike would cut into an enemy's leg. WHAP! A high strike would cleave an enemy's skull. WHAP! A slashing motion and the head toppled off. WHAP! A head. WHAP! A knee. WHAP! If the ball got past the racket and hit me, then I was wounded. WHAP! I'd have liked to have been a Viking. WHAP! Then I could have hacked Halleck, Budge, Buns, and Mower into a thousand pieces. WHAP! WHAP! WHAP!

* * *

John was sitting at his desk when I returned to the room. Only moments before, my roommate had come back from the pool where he'd been practicing some of the swimming tests which he needed to pass to graduate. As he was drip drying with his hair wet and curling, John thumbed through a magazine. He said, pointing to a photograph, "I hate this."

I looked at the photo accompanying a magazine article. It showed Norman Mailer with a group of people standing before a pit that contained an engine block. "Why? What's wrong with it?"

"They're burying an engine block."

"So?"

"They're protesting the use of technology, right?"

"Yes, that seems to be the gist of the article."

"How do you think they got the engine block there in the first place? By hand?"

"John, I think they're protesting against the abuse of technology, not against its use."

"I think they're a bunch of lousy hypocrites."

As I took off my sweat-soaked gear in preparation for a shower, John hooted, "Look at this!" My eyes followed the line of John's finger. "See the hard hat beating up the protestor?" Instinctively, like a child hugging a favorite teddy bear, I warmly approved of the laborer's action. He continued, "Check out the old guy in the background." I saw an elderly, well-dressed businessman. John laughed, "Did you ever see such a shit eating grin?" I smiled.

After the shower, I sat on the edge of my bunk. There was a little over an hour before evening meal. I decided to take a short nap. I sighed; I was so tired.

* * *

A plebe dance was being held in the armory. The darkness was almost palpable as though an immense, undefined monster was sitting upon my shoulders. A balcony surrounded the dance floor from which the upper classmen were able to watch their inferiors. After walking disconsolately along the sea wall for half an hour, I decided to watch the fun and was soon seated twenty feet above the plebes, resting my arms on the railing, my chin on my crossed arms.

A huge curtain, where the midshipman watch was posted, bisected the dance floor. The girls stood calmly on one side of it while the plebes were at the doors of the room on the other side of the curtain. When the midshipman officer of the day waved his arm, the plebes ran to the curtain while a handful of stragglers remained behind. I thought the running, stamping, and fuming of the plebes was undignified, reminiscent of a herd of stampeding cattle. I would have been with the stragglers. Once at the curtain, the watch arbitrarily paired the mids and the girls so that each girl, and not just the good-looking ones, would have a beau for the evening.

As I watched the proceedings, I felt a tug on the hair of the back of my head. Looking up, I saw Paul Carnevale's kind smile as he asked, "How's it going?"

"All right. There are some real horror shows down there."

"I know."

"I was thinking how I wished they were all naked. Then I could take a BB gun and shoot any plebe with a hard-on right in the head of his dick. If I had the power, that's what I'd do."

Carnevale sat down next to me. "My, my, bitter, aren't we?"

I shrugged, "I suppose." I was surprised to see Matt Helmsley walking toward us. He sat down on the other side of me. "Hi, guys."

The three of us watched the activity below. Matt asked, referring to the evening after the Army-Navy game, "How was your date, Mike?"

"All right."

"Did you get anything?"

"Yeah, I got something."

"What?"

"I took her to the hotel room."

"And then what?" Seeing that I kept quiet, Matt asked, "Did you fuck her?"

"Not exactly."

"Either you jumped her bones, or you didn't. Did you, or didn't you?"

"I didn't lay her if that's what you mean."

"Then what did you do?"

"I got some tit."

"You mean you took off her blouse and felt her up."

"Well, not exactly."

"You left her blouse on."

"Yeah."

Paul gushed out a breath of air and started chuckling, causing me to become even more defensive. Matt continued, "Did she have her bra on?"

"Yeah, she did."

"You reached under her bra and felt her up."

"Well, no." Carnevale chuckled harder.

"Then what did you do? Feel her tits through her clothes?"

"Yeah, that's what I did."

Carnevale's laughter was uncontrollable. Matt said, "Hell, that's nothing."

Paul interrupted, "Mike, do you mean to say that that's all you really did?"

"Yeah, that's all."

Carnevale curled up with laughter, saying, "All along I thought that *you* were the one pulling *Matt's* leg."

Matt asked, "How long you been going out with her?"

"A couple of months."

"And you haven't laid her yet?"

I answered sulkily, "No."

"Then tell her to get on the ball. Nail that nag, Mike."

"Sure." Embarrassed, I added, after standing up, "I got to go. See you guys later."

Both Matt and Paul sat up sharply with the former asking, "I didn't scare you away, did I?"

"Naw, I got things to do."

"I'm sorry if I did. I didn't mean to."

"No, really, I got things to do," and I made a quick escape.

* * *

The week of that semester's final exams was upon us. John and I spent interminable amounts of time talking and memorizing material that should have been learned months ago. It was a repeat of the midterm cramming except that I stopped taking No-doze and being miserable throughout the rest of the night. I knew I did badly, but when final grades were posted, I didn't rush to the first deck to check my grades. In due time, I would learn my grades. I reasoned that I would be contacted, officially, with all the needed details if I was to go before an academic board.

* * *

For Christmas leave, I packed my dress blues for midnight service and left my full-dress blues behind. I also packed some books but knew that I wouldn't even glance at them. Shortly before leaving, I found out that Budge's girl had left him and hoped that I had something to do with it; that maybe Budge's stories about his abusive behavior toward me had scared her off; that somehow, through me, she had divined his true nature. I hoped the firstie was taking it hard.

Buddy picked me up at the airport. While waiting for my luggage, I was a little disconcerted by seeing a teenaged girl wearing the American flag like a skirt. On the drive home, I didn't mention Baron's death. I could only be bitter and accusatory, which would serve no purpose, and I was too upset to talk about it.

The approach to Meantacut from T.F. Greene Airport in Warwick was through the woods and fields of one-time dairy farms now neglected and overgrown. As the car turned onto a road bisecting Lauman's farm, I started. Before me sat acres and acres of bulldozed land. "My God!" I exclaimed, "it looks like a World War I battlefield!" Not a tree was left standing; not a single stone wall survived the onslaught.

I asked Buddy to stop the car. The bulldozers had bypassed a plot of ground reserved for a little league baseball field. On one side of the plot sat a small, wooden barn hundreds of years old. On the opposite side were the furthest reaches of Walnut Hill Plat. As we sat in the car, we watched two lines of people who, like leaf cutter ants, were moving from the houses to the barn and then back to the houses. Women, children, whole family groups were part of the movement. In holiday spirit, the returning throng carried various items in their arms.

I asked, "Do you know what's in that barn?"

"No."

"Antiques. Bobby Greensweit and I got in there when we were kids. There was an old Model T Ford, lots of furniture, and I remember seeing a grindstone that you pedaled with your feet. I found some McKinley election buttons. There was a whole pile of them, so I took some." We watched as a little girl struggled under a particularly heavy load. Her father stopped to help her shift it onto her shoulders. "I felt guilty and returned the buttons a week later."

The suburbanites behaved as though they had struck gold. Voices were loud and high, mannerisms quick and excited. Buddy said, "What a betrayal! I hope Lauman's son is proud of himself."

Buddy put the car into gear and completed the small journey home. As we pulled into Mom's driveway, my brother said, stressing his words to add significance to them, "Anne's pregnant."

I said, "Congratulations," and wondered at the tone of his voice.

Another comment that didn't quite fit occurred when Cora visited me to take me to Ye Olde English for fish and chips, a treat we enjoyed together when I still lived in Meantacut. While there, Cora stated, "There's something going on with Beth. After you went to the Academy, I found Beth wandering around outside next to the garbage cans. Mom was at work and the dog was in his pen. At first, I thought she was going through the garbage, looking for something, you know how she does, but then she wouldn't go into the house. I had to practically drag her in. I didn't think much of it at the time, thinking it was some weird quirk, but now, I don't know. Something happened and I'm not sure what."

I then told her of what I saw last summer when Beth thought that I went fishing. I asked her, "What's a basteh?"

"I don't know. Bastard? Something's not right. I hope Buddy didn't do anything stupid or mean."

"C'mon, you know better than that. Sometimes he's thoughtless, that's all."

"You were probably too young to remember this, but the only time Mom ever hit any of us was when Buddy tried to light a tenement house on fire. She took a coat hanger to him. This was when we lived in the projects. There were seven families in that house."

"I find that hard to believe. Besides, if it's true, he was only a kid and didn't know any better."

"I find it hard to believe, too, but it's true. Ask him about it. I asked him and he admitted to it, giving me that giggle of his. He was lucky Mom caught him instead of the cops."

As we were eating our lunch, Cora became lost in thought, then said, "Mike, I want you to remember one thing." I lifted my chin slightly to show that I was listening. "Beth can be programmed."

"What's that supposed to mean?"

"Just that. She can be programmed."

Confused, I asked, "Why are you telling me this?"

"I'm not sure."

"Oh, good. Another mystery."

* * *

I missed Baron. No one mentioned him or told me what had become of his body.

* * *

What I termed as my Cryptic Christmas Leave was an anticlimax to my first Christmas leave. With every passing day, I found myself wishing more and more that I was at the Academy and frequently, though unintentionally, referred to it as home. Although I hated the institution, I missed the quiet desperation of Matt and Danny, or having Boatman and Hovedo asserting that this was the best of all possible worlds. Increasingly, I became frustrated in my efforts to tell people exactly what the Academy was like. Their world view forbade the translation of the institution into anything bad. Budge was always identified as a boyish, mischievous imp over whom I would laugh years from now. Whenever my mother talked about the school, a proud lilt entered her voice and she'd have a wholehearted smile on her face. No matter what I said, the reactions were always the same. I was thankful when my leave ended, and I could return to people with whom I identified, more so than the people at home.

The journey back to school was accentuated by my seeing two "incidental" people. The first was a young woman in Baltimore who stepped out of her chauffeur driven limousine as I was walking the two blocks from the airport to the bus station. The black machine stopped before a bank and the young lady, wrapped in furs, beauty, and smiles, cascaded out of it. She was gorgeous and I stopped in my tracks to watch her run into the bank. She was from another world with glories and privileges that I could only suspect and of which I would never be a part.

With this image fresh in my mind, I walked the remaining block to the bus station and passed a row of benches filled with nondescript men with vague, remote pasts. They were all dirty, tired, and in need of adequate clothing. None of them appeared to be the eccentric millionaire so famous in urban legend. In my clean, sharply pressed uniform, I walked briskly past the last bench where one of the nondescripts looked me squarely in the face and asked, "How's it going?"

I said, "Good, and you?"

The old man shook his head back and forth, sadly saying, "Not so good. Not so good."

Reaching into my pocket for change, I waited for the extended hand, but the tramp kept his hands on his lap and repeated, "Not so good. Not so good."

I quickened my pace, feeling a conglomeration of sadness, shame, guilt, and embarrassment. I also felt fear. I knew I could never be an American prince. I also knew that it would be far too easy to become a homeless old man sitting on a bus station bench.

* * *

At the Academy the frenetic activity so characteristic of midshipman life resumed. As expected, my final grades were bad, but I wasn't called before the academic board. John was safe with all passing grades. Together, we heard the names called over the intercom like the voice of doom, soft and sinister. The corridor seemed so much emptier and hollow with each name called.

John was telling me about a joyride he and a friend had taken during leave. "I spent most of my time driving around town with a pal from high school. One day we saw a black boy walking along the side of the road and my buddy rolled down his window and winged an apple at him. He got the black square in the back, and you would've thought he got shot. His whole body bent back, kind of wiggling." An inner glow lit John's eyes as he told what was to him a humorous story. "Then we pulled into a gas station and a white couple, old folks, pulled up next to us and gave us a funny look." John's affable, pleasant voice that I loved listening to changed into righteous indignation. "Sle, they stared at us, and we could see them talking. After gassing up, we hit the road again and the first thing we knew, a cop was pulling us over. He asked us if we were the two guys who threw the apple at the black. We figured that he had our license plate number, 'cause why would he have stopped us if he didn't, so we said yes. The cop told us that he talked to the black who was just back from Vietnam. We felt kind of bad until later when we got to thinking. Sle, the cop wouldn't have had enough time to talk to the black and stop us too. We figured it was the white couple who turned us in."

"Did the cop do anything?"

"No, only talked to us."

John's sense of outrage toward the white couple was so pronounced that I asked, "You don't see anything wrong in throwing the apple at the black?"

"Why?" John seemed genuinely confused that I should have asked such a question.

"John, you're a good guy. You don't see anything wrong about what you did?"

"Why?"

"Look, just think about it, okay?"

We sat quietly together, both being comfortable with the other's silent companionship, when John asked, "Has anyone returned your Cross pen?"

"Nope."

"You see how honest midshipmen are?"

"I refuse to let my belief in the basic honesty of midshipmen to be undermined by a few bad eggs."

"Live and learn."

The plebe watch entered the room. "Mr. Sorensen, Lieutenant Dimwiddie wishes to see you, sir."

"Right now?"

"Yes, sir."

"Very well."

As I hurriedly slipped into my uniform, John said, "Looks like trouble."

"So, what's new?"

I walked quickly to Dimwiddie's office, entered, and sounded off. We exchanged salutes and I accepted the offer of a seat. The officer began, "Mr. Sorensen."

"Sir?"

"I assume you've seen your grades."

"Yes, sir."

"Well, I'm happy for that."

"Yes, sir."

"What's the problem?"

"No problem, sir."

"My records tell me that you've changed majors three times already."

"Yes, sir."

"Can you explain that?"

"Yes, sir."

"Well?"

"Well, sir, I started off as an engineering major because I thought that once I got out into the civilian world, I could get a good job and make a lot of money. Then I decided to go into management because the courses seemed easy, and I figured that I could at least graduate that way. Finally, I decided to go into political science because I thought it'd be good to find out who's running the whole show and that's pretty much it, sir."

"Exactly what *do* you want?"

"I don't know, sir."

"Let me put it this way. What do you want to do with your life?"

"I don't know, sir. There's so much *to* do that I can't make up my mind."

"What about the protest marches? Do they bother you?"

"A little, sir."

"Explain."

"Did you see the article in the *Washington Post* about the candlelight march in Washington, D.C.?"

"I'm familiar with the event."

"Did you see the photograph of the young girl they took, putting a candle on the fence?"

"I didn't happen to notice it but go on."

"Well…when I saw the photo I thought, 'What a lovely girl!' Then I thought, 'She hates me.' *Then* I wondered why they took that particular photo of that particular girl."

"For effect, of course. Image is more important than substance."

"It stinks of dishonesty and manipulation, sir."

"What do you want for fifteen cents?" The officer thought a moment. "If it makes you feel better, I can assure you that the American people are behind their servicemen more than ever. We've had more applicants for the Naval Academy this year than in any previous year." There was a pause as though he had come to a startling conclusion. "Mr.

Sorensen, I still don't understand you." We stared at one another as though stunned. Finally, Dimwiddie said, "That'll be all, Mr. Sorensen."

"Aye-aye, sir." We exchanged salutes.

At my return, John asked, "How'd it go?"

"I'm still alive."

John was surprised to see me putting on gym gear. "You're not going to study?"

"Why bother? I'm a doomed man, John."

"What are you going to do?"

"Play squash."

"By yourself?"

"Yep."

John smirked. "That's what I like about you, Sores. You're so consistent even in your inconsistency."

CHAPTER XII

BAD NEWS

Deep winter and the gray slate of the Chesapeake looked cold and forbidding, powerful, with short white caps tearing its surface. Snow had fallen in soft, white purity. It lay a couple of inches thick but wouldn't hinder midshipman activities. Steam leaked through the yellow brick walkways between Mahan Hall and Bancroft Hall, oozing from the underground heating pipes and passageways as though a city of Morlocks worked furiously beneath them.

I was dressed for town so I could treat myself to an ice cream sundae. Calling over my shoulder, sounding defeated, I said to John, "It's time for my weekly punishment," then left for the phones on the first deck. As I passed the watch desk, the plebe on duty straightened himself from his writing to say, "Sir, this message is for you."

"Thank you." The note said that Donna was waiting for me in the visitor's lounge near Memorial Hall.

Once on the first deck, I went to the phones to call home. I heard my mother's voice say, "Hello?"

"Hi, Mom."

"Oh, hi, son, I knew it was you." Right away she collapsed into tears. "I'm having such a hard time with your sister and all. It's so difficult keeping the house going."

"Do you need money?"

"Well, no, but I'm having a lot of trouble with Beth. I've been taking her to a psychiatrist."

"Okay. What's wrong?"

"We don't know."

"I see. And the crying is going to help?"

"Son, don't be so heartless."

"Okay, I'm sorry, but you seem to think that I can wave a magic wand to make your problems go away." My voice swelled with frustration. "Well, I don't, and I *can't* get rid of them! There's not a thing I can do from this hellhole!" I was consumed with guilt as the weeping intensified at the other end.

Mom asked, "What do you want me to say?"

"I don't know. You're never honest with me. You only tell me bits and pieces from which I must guess the rest. The only thing *that* does is make me worry even more."

By now the weeping had stopped and both of us were talking in calm, exhausted voices that betrayed the real love we had for each other. Mom asked, "How are things going with you, honey?"

"All right. I've been sleeping an awful lot, about ten hours a day. I don't know what it is. I'm always tired no matter how easy my schedule is."

"Maybe it's the calm after the storm."

"I don't think so. I can't seem to get myself motivated. No matter what I do, I can't get enthusiastic about anything, even the stuff I like. I'm always tired."

"You'll get over it."

"Yeah. What's been happening with Beth?"

"She's okay. She's doing a lot better."

"Better as compared to what?"

"Now don't you worry about a thing."

"Just level with me for once. What's going on back there?"

"Nothing you have to worry about." Without further comment, Mom changed the subject. "What are your plans for today?

"I'm going into town to enjoy myself for a change, if only for one day. By the way, I made an interesting discovery last weekend. For the last year I kept hearing about the Subbase and spent a lot of time trying to figure out where it was, thinking that there was a submarine base somewhere in the area. Then I find out that it's a place that makes grinders, what they call submarine sandwiches around here. I have yet to go there."

"Today's your chance."

"I don't know; I'd rather eat a hamburger and fries."

We talked for another twenty minutes about the Canada geese returning to Rhode Island in increasingly large numbers and how cardinals and opossums were extending their ranges further north into the state. I joked about how opossums, according to what I'd read, tasted like pork and some roadkill might be good to eat the next time I was home.

Finally, I said, "Mom, I've got to go."

"You'll call next week? It means so much to me."

"Sure, okay."

In my progress toward the main gate, I ran into Gus Hovedo who rushed up to me and said, "I've been looking all over for you." He reached into his pocket and pulled out a fistful of change. "I found this in a telephone booth right after church formation, two dollars and thirty-five cents. Do you think I should hand it in?"

"To who? The telephone company? Batt. Ops.? Keep it."

"I feel guilty though."

"Of what? Is that why you were looking for me? To tell me that you're rich?"

"No. I wanted to catch you before you left. Donna is waiting for you in the visitor's lounge."

"So?"

"Aren't you going to see her?"

"No."

"What do you mean 'no'? She came all the way from Virginia to see you."

"Not to see me, Gus. To see a midshipman. Any midshipman will do, just as long as it's a midshipman. She won't want me; I'm flunking out. I can only disappoint her."

"You mean that you're not going to see her?"

"That's exactly what I mean."

"You're not going to leave her waiting there."

"Why not? How is she going to know whether I got the message or not? She'll get tired of waiting, then she'll leave."

"Sores, I don't believe what I'm hearing. You don't do things like that."

"That's exactly what I'm going to do."

"Boy, you've got problems, you know that?"

"Good. I like to have problems."

"I mean, you're really fucked up."

"Excellent. I like being fucked up."

"Well, I'm not going to leave her stranded like that. I'm going to see her for you."

"Fine."

"I just might tell her what you've done."

"That's all right by me."

Gus shook his head back and forth in disbelief. "Sometimes I wonder about you."

I shrugged. "Sometimes I wonder about myself, too, but that's the way things are."

Gus turned around to head for the lounge. He called, "Later."

"Yeah, later," and I went into town.

* * *

The plebe watch knocked on the door and informed me that Dimwiddie wanted to see me. Turning to John, I asked, "Now what?"

When I reached the company commander's office and got through the formalities, the officer said, "Mr. Sorensen, I thought that now would be a good time to talk while the semester is still young."

"Yes, sir."

"You look tired. Is there anything wrong?"

"No, sir."

"Are you sure?"

"Yes, sir. It's just the day, sir."

"How are your classes looking?"

"Fine, sir."

"Good. How many credits are you carrying?"

"Twenty-two, sir."

"Do you think you can handle it?"

"Yes, sir. I'll try, sir."

"I've been doing a lot of thinking since our last discussion, and I can't help but feel a certain hostility that you have toward the Academy."

"It's not hostility, sir."

259

"Then what is it?"

"I don't know, sir."

"Sometimes I think that you think that we're all inferior in some way."

"Not inferior, sir. All the midshipmen are in good physical shape and they're all intelligent."

"But...?"

"They lack something, sir. I don't know what it is, but there's a definite lack."

"Mr. Sorensen, did it ever occur to you that maybe *you're* the one who is lacking? After all, you're the one getting bad grades, not the other midshipmen."

"Yes, sir."

"Look at me when I talk to you!"

I stiffened to attention. "Aye-aye, sir."

"I seriously suggest that you stop evaluating the Academy and start evaluating yourself and your study habits!"

"Yes, sir."

"That'll be all."

"Aye-aye, sir."

I thought about telling him about the phone calls home, but what could I say to a member of the Machine? It would be interpreted as weakness to let family problems, unspecified family problems based on hints and intuitions, interfere with my duties as a midshipman. Didn't Kristin say as much when he found out about my father's death?

Dimwiddie and I saluted, and I returned to my room. As always, John wanted to know how it had gone to which I answered, "All right," then added, "I'm awfully tired. I can't seem to stay awake. I'm going to rack out until evening meal."

"Will the record player bother you?"

"I don't think so, not if you keep it low." I took off my uniform and lay on my bunk. The weather was cold and damp and accentuated the contrasting warmth of my bunk. Soon, I was falling when I landed at Macdonough Hall.

* * *

I am *wearing gym gear and am carrying my squash racket when I become afraid and start to run for the squash courts. A huge, terrible beast, dark and formless, is running behind me, trying to catch up. I run faster and faster toward the safety offered by the courts, but the beast is gaining on me. The closer the beast comes, the more I become frightened. It is a horrible death that awaits me should I be caught. I am sprinting for all I'm worth. I see the dim lights of the courts and know that I will be safe there. I am twelve feet, nine feet, six feet from the comforting closeness of the squash courts. Three feet and the beast catches me!*

* * *

Startling into a semi-conscious state, I am aware of John sitting near me. I try to call, but no sound issues from my mouth. I try moving, but my body starts to convulse, or, more accurately, I think I'm convulsing. Frightened, I struggle to move which causes more convulsing. Finally, after what seems to be hours, I make a valiant effort and manage to move my hand. This releases me.

I sit up and ask my roommate, "Did you notice anything right now while I was asleep?"

"Like what?"

"Did I make funny noises or move funny in any way?"

"You slept like a baby."

"You didn't notice anything?"

"Nothing at all."

I lay down again into the comfort of the afternoon. My last wakeful thought was, *There must be a God somewhere. Why isn't He helping me?*

* * *

The brigade marched by company to Mahan Hall to listen to a series of presentations by Navy pilots. These presentations were generally enjoyable. Not only did they break up the monotony of Academy routine, but the pilots were often mavericks and real personalities with interesting insights. As the mids herded through the main corridor, the battalion watches were busy writing up those mids foolish enough to leave their caps on the heads of the busts decorating the foyer.

During the first presentation I fell asleep but was woken up by an officer kind enough not to give me a Form 2. What surprised me more was to have Bragg visibly upset and casting me looks of contempt because I had broken decorum. There would have been some justification for this reaction from one of the studs like Bemes or Meade, but to have a bagger like Bragg react that way was almost more than I could bear.

After an hour and a half of listening to the various presentations, the last of the young pilots stood at the podium. He said, "Good evening, gentlemen. I've been requested by your superintendent to tell you about the life of a pilot. I honestly don't know what to tell you. My predecessors have already amply covered the training a pilot receives at Pensacola and elsewhere. The requirements to become a pilot have already been discussed. I suppose I could tell you about the good life, wine, women, and song, but I'm sure you know more about that than I do, or you soon will know more. So, I've decided to give you a few anecdotes which, I'm sure, will set some of you to thinking."

The pilot talked about American air power in Vietnam. With a wickedly bemused smile, he told of how he'd been fired upon by missiles from "one of our own bases." He said that initially he had seen some dots approaching him that transformed themselves into missiles the size of telephone poles. He managed to avoid them. The mids laughed when he told of a North Vietnamese aircraft expert ejecting himself from a downed, nearly intact, American aircraft. There were nods of approval and chuckling when he mentioned the air superiority maintained by the US aptly proven when a missile loaded destroyer asked permission to fire a practice missile and downed MiG that had been airborne for five minutes.

However, the presentation shifted gears when the pilot focused on his carrier experiences. He compared landing on an aircraft carrier to landing on a moving postage stamp, how a pilot's heartbeat quickened even more upon landing than it did in combat, and when he maneuvered on the flight deck, he would sometimes look to the side of his aircraft and see nothing but water below him. Then he mentioned how on take-off, some aircraft plunged into the water directly in front of the carrier. The image caught me as it did most of the other mids. Sinking into that horrible depth of water, how could a man *not* panic? The water—impersonal, deadly, seeking a way into the cockpit to kill—would be swirling around the windows, caressing the glass, licking it, looking for a way in. Supposedly, the pilot waited to see the screws of the carrier pass overhead before he ejected himself to the surface. *Could this be true or is this the equivalent of an urban legend? Could I wait so patiently with death only inches away?* I saw myself in the cockpit, waiting forever for the screws to pass as the distance to the surface seemed to increase to eternity while the water became a progressively deeper, murkier green. The pilot answered the question foremost in every midshipman's mind, "Yes, sometimes pilots panic. Some have even ejected from their aircraft while it was upside down, smashing themselves right into the ground."

The pilot became lost in his own thoughts and stood before the podium for three heavily awkward minutes of silence. A few officers in the front row stood up, about to go onto the stage, while a subtle roar of mumbling escaped from the mids. Finally, the pilot said, "I hope I'm not being unfair, but I'd like to show you that being a Naval officer isn't all glamour. Of course, there's a lot of danger involved, but the real danger is much more insidious than most people realize, and, in a way, it applies to everyone. I would like you first to see a film taken during the recent disaster on the *USS Forrestal*, then I'd like you to listen to a tape recording of a pilot who is about to crash."

The audience watched the film and saw the *USS Forrestal* engulfed by flames. Knowing the heat convection properties of iron made the mids appreciate how deadly the fire really was and the burning hell that the ship must have been. They saw flames eating up the sky and ineffective, running men, looking very small, trying to contain those hungry flames. A puff appeared in the middle of the deck. The officer asked, "Did you see that puff? An ensign tried to cool an explosive with a fire extinguisher. When it didn't work, he tried to carry the explosive to the edge of the deck to throw it overboard and it exploded on him. Let's play that again." The scene was played again, and I thought of the fragility of human life. At one moment a young man was alive and at the next, he no longer existed. In a hundred years he'd be completely

263

forgotten, like most people, like a politician thinking he'd be remembered forever by leaving some lamely bloviated legacy.

Next, the audience listened to a tape recording. A pilot was talking to ground control in a casual, matter of fact way when he said that something was wrong with his guidance. The pilot's voice quickened to the speed of a plebe giving chow call. The words were still distinguishable though an edge of panic could be heard in them. When the pilot lost total control of his aircraft, he tried to eject, but, tragically, the ejection mechanism either didn't work or the pilot didn't have enough composure to save himself. The audience listened to the pilot's words being jammed together as terror took control. As the aircraft plummeted toward the earth, the voice rambled faster and faster until the words were no longer distinguishable. Soon, only syllables slammed together were heard until the voice sounded exactly like a tape recorder on fast forward. I wondered how a human mouth could move so fast as I tried to imagine the terrible, gut-wrenching fear behind it.

The tape ended. The speaker stared briefly at the surface of the podium while some agitated movement among his peers in the audience showed how nervous they were becoming. The speaker continued, "I suppose what I'm trying to point out is that, as Naval officers and as pilots, you must face these types of situations. If you panic, you lose. The problem is though, how does one keep from panicking? Can anyone be cool all the time?" The speaker paused, reaching for a thought. "I wonder if death is all that terrible. I don't think so, but I don't know. Perhaps if I found myself in the same situations as those other men, I would behave in exactly the same way. It's easy to theorize about death with a full belly and a clean place to sleep, but when you can't escape him, what then?

"My experiences in Vietnam were the focus of death. Yet, as a pilot, I was somewhat divorced from the whole thing. You knew that when you looked in the papers and saw the rubble of bombed out buildings, there were bodies beneath that rubble. You knew you were killing people, but you never saw the bodies. What I think I'm trying to say is that there's a certain unreality to being a pilot. At times, I felt like I was in a surrealist painting. Nothing seemed quite real. Do you understand?

"Well, that about wraps up what I have to say. I hope I have given you some food for thought and I hope that I haven't offended anyone or made myself sound too ridiculous. Thank you."

An officer from the front row walked to the podium and called, "Attention!" The whole audience stood as the front row of officers made their exit through a side door. Then the officer said, "Dismissed."

As the midshipmen clustered in the dark of a late winter's afternoon, a burst of opinion sounded from the seemingly disembodied shadows. There were few lights in the area and the black uniforms made it seem darker. A series of comments arose.

"He's one of our top aces, second or third or something like that."

"That guy was *great!*"

"I think he was a jerk."

"It was a good speech, but it didn't help his career any."

"Sle, what career?"

"It sounds to me like he's reached some kind of limit."

"He sounded like you, Mike. 'Is death really that terrible?'"

"You mean that I'm a jerk."

I felt a warm hand on my arm that gave me a friendly squeeze. "I mean he's off the wall, like you are."

Another voice came from behind me. "I think Mike is more like that Bronson guy on TV."

I had never watched *Then Came Bronson* so I didn't know what he meant. Although I questioned whether I was even remotely like "that Bronson guy," I was pleased by this friendly bantering. I belonged here in this place and time with these men. Sometimes, with my friends chiding me, the Academy through them seemed like home, as though I was a part of a great tradition.

Unfortunately, the camaraderie I'd been feeling was doomed to be shattered. During evening meal formation, Lackning slithered up to me and said in a condescending voice, "Sorensen, do you have the plebe reports finished?"

"Yes, I do." Ebullience sounded in my voice, a rich happiness that Lackning was quick to notice.

"You signed them and all that?"

"Yep."

"Have them on my desk after meal."

"All right."

"I'm interested in how you evaluated the plebes."

"Aye-aye."

"That's good, Sorensen. You say 'all right' to my orders and then say 'aye-aye' when I make a comment. That's very good. One would think a youngster would know the correct responses." With a smug smile, Lackning ambled away while I seethed with anger. I'd been humiliated and reprimanded not only in front of my peers, but also before the plebes. What little fellowship I had been developing toward the Academy died in that instant. I knew I was still in Bancroft Hall.

* * *

I had yet to go before an academic board. My grades were bad enough to warrant such action, but perhaps there were mids with even worse grades than I had. My courses for this semester were a sorry continuation of the frustrated struggle of my previous three semesters. Although my study habits had always been atrocious, that art had almost fallen into nonexistence. I was no longer a student. Instead, I went through the form of being a student.

Of my six professors, three were relegated to the ranks of anonymity since they were neither good nor bad. The other three, all Naval officers, stood out because of their personalities or lack thereof.

The first deserving comment was my economics professor, Lieutenant Hughes. He was a solidly built man with flaxen hair, brown eyes, a light, ephemeral skin tone, and thick, black glasses. Never did he raise or lower his voice. Nor did he ever smile. He was as colorful as lead and as engaging as asphalt. I felt the same kind of dread before this man as I had felt before Earling. There was a void there more profound than the deepest reaches of space. Hughes was pure business, the perfect man to cram two semesters' worth of work into a one-semester course. Everyday a new economic formula was thrown onto the board and explicated with as much dash as a slab of cement. The very thought of Hughes parched my throat while sending chills up my spine. To attend one of his classes was like listening to a teletype machine or drinking sand. There was absolutely no juice at all to be found in such a desert.

Because of my almost innate dislike of Hughes, I was careful to listen to his every word just to find fault and discredit this man. The officer said that he disliked authors since they'd often collect unemployment while writing their books. I decided that if I ever wrote a book, I'd be sure to collect unemployment (not true). Hughes stated that he thought the government should tax unused land. In that way, the owners would be forced to develop it. I had already seen first-hand what development was doing to Rhode Island. Thus, my nickname for Hughes became "The Disciple of Destruction." I half expected Hughes to support the paving of the whole of Pennsylvania as a parking lot for the new shopping mall, New York State.

At the other extreme was Lieutenant Castiglione, my psychology professor. He was a personable Italian American who colored his classes with stories from his own personal experiences. He had a soft, gentle voice that matched the pleasing informality of his classes. I did my best work for him and was always prepared for his classes. It was important to me that I not appear inept to the professor and to the other students of this class. When the class lagged or Castiglione asked a question which no one ventured to answer, I always responded and voiced an opinion to help the officer out. My lowest grade for the whole semester, excepting a C on the final exam, was an A-.

The final Naval officer worthy of note was my navigation professor, Lieutenant Biron. He was a short, solid man with a blond crewcut. He also had dozens of stories to tell, mostly about his own midshipman days. I neither liked nor disliked Biron. What singled him out for me was his frequent suggestions to the me to go to him for E.I. He'd hand me a corrected quiz scarred with a flaming red F and say, "Isn't it time to get some E.I., Mr. Sorensen?" I now avoided using aye-aye and answered, "Yes, sir," then I'd let the suggestion die of inertia. The officer prodded me on an almost daily basis, but all to no purpose. After dealing with Halleck, I wanted no part of E.I. It was better to flunk. Even when the youngsters were assigned a massive project to plot a course from San Diego to Japan, I sought help from neither classmates nor instructors. The ordeal was immense and not worth the effort. I knew that I would only navigate my ship onto some rocks when approaching Japan, providing I didn't destroy the vessel somewhere in mid-ocean. I thought how appropriate it would be if I flunked navigation.

* * *

The weather was chilly which aptly fit the mood that I was in. I traversed the streets of Annapolis feeling the weight of my heavy black overcoat pressing on my shoulders. I kept my hands jammed into my pockets and hoped that I wouldn't run into anyone I knew. I wandered through the small shops characteristic of the town, not looking for anything in particular, but wanting to buy something to cheer myself up. In one shop I found rows of pillboxes filled with variously colored beads. In high school I had sometimes worn a single strand of beads like those worn by Paul Stookey and Peter Yarrow on one of their album covers. Perhaps I would start wearing them again, albeit surreptitiously. I bought a couple of boxes of blue and black beads along with some dental floss with which to string them. Then I returned to Bancroft Hall.

I was surprised to find Fred Meade standing in my room, one leg propped on a chair in the old sea dog style of Larry Bemes. Fred looked as though he'd been waiting a long time. I wondered what Meade was doing here alone and in this room of failure. Fred was at the top of his class and seemed destined to become Midshipman Brigade Commander. It seemed incongruous that he should be here. It was dark in the room, the only light coming from the window, so I hit the light switch. My friend said, "Hi, Mike, I've been waiting for you."

"Hi, Fred, what's up?"

"I thought I'd drop by and talk, that's all."

As I took off my coat, I watched Fred out of the corner of my eye, trying to think of any reason that could have brought this man to this room. Meade seemed to be a bit embarrassed as well as disoriented. The sharpest of all midshipmen, Meade looked about the room, then at the chill afternoon resting outside the window, then at the room again. Finally, he said, "This cold weather, this day, reminds me of Montana. It's beautiful there with the rivers and mountains. My folks own a ranch."

In the pause that followed, I waited for what I believed would turn into a confession of some sort. Meade's talking of home bordered on taboo. Fred asked, "Have you ever been to Montana?" I shook my head no. "You'll love it there. The ranch is right next to Yellowstone Park. It's gorgeous. If you want, we can hunt jackrabbits there this summer." I was stunned. The best of the brigade was asking the worst to visit his home for the summer. The thought that Meade might have a sister passed through my mind, but he would have mentioned her. "I think you'll like it. We have elk and bear." There was no reason here. "The air is incredibly brisk. It's paradise to camp and wake up to that first cup of coffee." I felt violated, as if a customary law was being flagrantly broken, as though an unclean beast, me, had been left on the altar for the gods. "You wouldn't believe how peaceful it is. No one hassles you." Briefly, I thought about accepting the offer. After all, Meade was the one being defiled, not me. Then I thought of the hunting. I envisioned myself shooting hundreds of rounds and not bagging a thing while the hunters about me had full game pouches. I would only shame myself. He continued, "There wouldn't be any problems with my parents. They'd love to have company." Fred stopped and waited for a response. To me, the whole thing was improper. Didn't Fred know that I was flunking out? For me, there would be no "next summer." I decided to let the offer hang fire. An embarrassed silence ensued that lasted for a couple of minutes, then shifted into eternity. Neither of us knew what to say. Finally, Fred said, "You might think about my offer."

"Sure," and he was gone.

I undressed to take a nap before evening meal. As I composed myself for sleep, falling peacefully into the dream state, I started, or thought I started, to convulse. I shook violently and made muted, strangled efforts to scream. The strain was unbearable when, suddenly, I snapped out of it and sat up in bed. I was exhausted and found it odd that John never noticed my struggles.

I lay down again and floated into sleep.

* * *

I am at my mother's house. It is unusually dark, and the walls are made of oaken beams that continually sift dust onto the dirt floor. It is more like a cellar with a maze of small rooms through which I wander apprehensively. Stepping from one small room into another, I see Dimwiddie. Automatically, I recoil and ask bitterly, "What are you doing here?" The officer has been expecting me and shows no reaction. Undemonstratively, he lifts an arm and points, saying, "She's in there." I run into the room and see Mom sitting in bed, wrapped in a long, winding, white shroud. She looks exhausted and bedraggled. Throwing myself into her waiting arms, I hide my face in her lap, weeping uncontrollably. In an agonized cry I sob, "You're going to break my heart!" and I wake up.

* * *

After evening meal, I stood in the doorway of my room watching the plebes march up and down the corridor in mock procession. The lead plebe, wrapped in a white sheet, was goose stepping in a very solemn, portentous manner. His arms were extended straight out before him and supported a pillow on which sat a red brick wrapped in toilet paper. The procession was chanting, "Who gets the brick? Who gets the brick?" The brick was given by the plebes to the upperclassman who had the worst date on any given weekend. The procession seemed interminable, and I was getting impatient when the lead plebe led his followers into Roderigues' room. There was a commotion at the door, and I saw, briefly, the slim figure of Roderigues rise, head and shoulders, above the surge of plebe bodies before it was submerged. I knew the rest and smiled when I heard the shower of Roderigues' room and the cheers of the plebes as the firstie was thrown, fully clothed, into the cold water.

* * *

Time was nibbling away at me, an ocean slowly eroding a beach. There was nothing for me to do but wait and maybe a miracle would happen. Maybe my attitude toward the Academy would change, that it would become everything that it promised, and, in a valiant spurt of energy and effort, I would save my future.

With spring came a last-ditch effort to motivate myself. Often, I sat at my desk, reciting the mantra, "Yes, I like it here. I belong here. The Academy is a great place," and hoped that I would come to believe my own lies.

Unknowingly and in desperation, I reverted to primal urges. A shower became a cleansing ritual. Lathering my body, I thought, *I'm washing away my impurities and sins. I'm washing away my*

270

despondency. When I step out of the shower, my day, my life, will begin anew. It will be as if my past failures had never existed. As was to be expected, the cleansing ritual was totally ineffectual. My frame of mind was already too embittered to change.

With my newly acquired beads, I made single strand necklaces with famous sayings, written in Morse code, such as "when the going gets tough, the tough get going" or "the best revenge is success." I wore these hoping that somehow I'd imbibe their messages. The conjuring tricks didn't work anymore than it worked for South Sea Islanders chanting magical names before French cannons. This life I was living had already died; nothing worked to inspire me. My lethargy became more profound.

I loved to stare out the window at the world outside. However, I no longer saw the Severn below me nor the Chesapeake Bay. Now, I was looking four stories down at the hard pavement. A moment's desperation could plummet me over the edge of the gutter and a few seconds later, all would be ended. I thought of the fall and the intolerable rush in the guts. The few seconds spent in such a fall must be excruciating. No, I didn't want to die that way. If only a tragic accident happened, leaving family and friends to mourn the loss of such a bright star on the horizon. No one would ever know what a loser I really was. Then I thought how Budge, Lackning, Kristin, and the others would see suicide as proof that I wasn't midshipman material. That idea was simply unacceptable, and I dismissed any further consideration about taking my own life.

Once, when I was thus musing, John burst into the room. Without turning around, I said, "You know, John, I wish I was never born. I know it's a terrible thing to say, but this is a horrible world we live in."

* * *

My grades in navigation continued to plunge. The class exercise, a voyage to Japan, was a catastrophe. The immensity of the chore was staggering, and my consistently bad results made any effort seem futile. I thought, *why should I plot a course, the results of which would be nebulous at their best?* Already, I was too tired to take the first step necessary for any long journey. I decided to do nothing and wait for something to happen of itself. It did. Biron soon realized that his student was in trouble. He gave me a direct order to see him for E.I.

A day later, I roamed the lower portions of Luce Hall and found the cubicle that served as Biron's office. I stepped inside and sounded off.

"At ease, Mr. Sorensen. Do you know why you're here?"

"Yes, sir."

The officer sat down. "Please be seated. It is evident to me that you're having a great deal of difficulty with the work we're covering in class. Your quizzes are consistently bad."

"Yes, sir."

"What's the story?"

"I'll find out, sir."

"Come on. I want a real answer."

"I don't know, sir. I don't seem to be learning anything. I can't get interested in anything. It's all floating by me, and I can't seem to catch it."

"I see. How is that special assignment coming along?"

"Fine, sir."

"How much have you done?"

I hesitated. "I haven't started it, sir."

Biron sat up stiffly in his chair. "You haven't started it?"

"No, sir."

"Why, that's incompetent. Why haven't you started it?"

"There's no sense to it, sir."

"Come again?"

"There's no sense to it. I'm flunking out anyways, so why bother starting such a long project?"

"You can't give up like that. Don't you like it here?"

"No, sir."

"You'd like to graduate, wouldn't you?"

"Yes, sir."

"Well, you've got to do something. From now on, I want to see you at least once a week and we'll see what we can do."

"Aye-aye, sir."

Faithfully, I kept the weekly appointments. At first, I'd bring my books and open them at the sections that were being covered that week, but Biron was little inclined to go over the work with me. Instead, he said, "Navigation isn't your problem. You have other problems. Let's sit down and talk a while." I came to like Biron and, for the first time in my Academy career, really talked to a superior. The officer asked, "Do you have problems at home?"

"Yes, sir."

"What kind of problems?"

"I'm not sure, sir. Something is going on back there, but I don't know what it is. Every weekend I call home and there's a lot of crying, but no one tells me anything. I have to guess what's happening."

Biron nodded as if he knew exactly what I was talking about. I knew that he couldn't really understand, not fully, but I appreciated Biron's concern. I didn't feel so alone.

After some time, the officer asked, "Do you still think you're not learning anything?"

"Yes, sir, or at least nothing important."

"Navigation is not important in the Navy?"

Normally, I would either be intimidated by or antagonistic toward an officer, but Biron seemed really interested. I answered, "The books, the courses, they don't," I searched for words, "they don't seem relevant to me."

"Why don't you find something that does have relevance? Don't you think that's *your* responsibility? You must find your own way. Even the Academy with all its courses and regulations can't tell you where to find meaning. If you really want to learn, you must do that yourself. There's nothing keeping you from going down to the Severn, taking a drop of water, and looking at it under a microscope. You might be surprised at what you'd find. You might even discover a new organism. You might discover meaning. But *you're* the one who must do it, not the Academy. The responsibility is yours."

I answered, "Yes, sir." Although I knew that at this point I had no hope, the professor did his best to offer it, if not for the present then for the future. I clung to that straw and was thankful that Biron had given it to me.

* * *

The full resurgence of spring was signified by the return of the birds, buds, and mud. The midshipmen had not yet changed from their winter blues to the lighter summer whites. I liked the dark uniforms since they seemed to be more comforting, easier to hide in. The whites were associated with swimming and plebe summer and meant hours of marching in the dust and sun of fair weather. At odd moments, I was pleased to be a part of the long, weaving lines that snaked their way to and from classes.

One afternoon, I found my roommate sitting on the edge of my bunk looking at a small cup of seeds which he held in one hand while the fingers of the other explored its contents. John said, "I think we got some poison here. Sle, for the mice. Want some?" He proffered the cup.

I picked up a coated seed and, while carefully inspecting it, asked, "What kind of seeds are they?"

"Wheat, I think. It'd be an easy way out of here." John smiled.

"Don't give me any ideas; I just might try it. Do you think they'd grow?"

"Maybe."

"Do you mind if I take the box?"

"Not at all. There's another one beneath your bunk, too."

That same afternoon, Danny and I attended a lecture on naval engineering. I told Danny of my idea of trying to grow the seeds and how I needed dirt. After the lecture, the two of us found a dirt mound destined to cover an exposed steam pipe. I pulled out a small, plastic bag from my pocket. Since we were still near the dark lines of midshipmen, we milled about trying to remain inconspicuous. Finally, Danny said, "Go ahead, Mike, it's all clear."

Without moving, I said, "What am I going to say if we get caught? 'Sir, I'm getting mud to grow rat poison, sir'?"

My friend said, "Oh for crying out loud," grabbed the bag, thrust his hand into the mud, and threw a large clod of dirt into the bag. Then he picked up a dirty rag lying on the ground and wiped his hand. Presenting his palm to me, he said, "See? It's as good as new," and he chuckled.

I carried the bag cupped in my hands, trying to keep it from prying eyes. At Bancroft Hall, we parted company with me returning to the company area. Seeing me from his doorway, Dave Husaby said,

"There you are. I was coming over to get you. There's a Bob Dylan song on the radio." He led me into his room where we listened to "Lay, Lady, Lay."

When it ended, I said, "It's a nice song, but why did you want me to listen to it?"

"I know you're a Bob Dylan fan, or I think you are. You're definitely a Bob Dylan type and I thought this song fit you."

"Well, thanks."

He pointed to the bag. "What've you got in there?"

"Dirt."

"For what?"

"John found some poisoned seeds in our room and I'm going to try to grow them."

"Why?"

"Out of curiosity, I guess."

"I'd be careful of that stuff if I were you. Some of these poisons localize themselves. If the seeds grow, the poison might work its way into the new seeds. Then, if any birds eat them, they'll die or won't be able to lay fertile eggs or something like that. Some of these poisons don't break down either."

"Dave, that doesn't make sense. Why would anyone use a poison they couldn't get rid of? Besides, there must be laws against that kind of stuff. The United States government simply wouldn't allow its use."

"I think you're wrong."

"God knows that it wouldn't be the first time, but I'm not going to let anything be poisoned in my room. I want something to grow in this place. I want to take death and turn it into life."

As I was leaving, he scoffed, "Keep dreaming, Sores, keep dreaming."

* * *

In psychology class I waited to see what Lt. Castiglione would do with the two blocks of wood which he held in his hands. One was a square foot while the other was a third of that size. The officer said, "A lot of things you see and learn have to do with perspective. Unknowingly, a person engaged in any kind of evaluation might already have preconceived ideas. Things aren't always what they seem to be. I'm going to pass around these blocks of wood. As they reach you, tell me which one you think is heavier."

Castiglione bypassed the mids in the front row and gave it to me. Using my arms like a balance, shifting the blocks thoughtfully up and down, I couldn't feel any weight difference, but I liked this professor and gave what I thought was the expected answer. "The larger one weighs more." Among the twenty mids in the class, all of them followed my lead while only two stated that they thought the smaller one weighed more.

The prof took back his blocks and said, "They weigh the same. The answer you should've given is that the smaller block weighs more because its weight is contained in a smaller volume, making you think it's more condensed and, therefore, heavier."

I wished that I'd said that they weighed the same, but I was only trying to help.

After class, I returned to my room having first picked up my mail at the watch's desk. I sat at my desk and opened a letter from Kenny Sadler. A photograph had come with the letter. My eyes ran over every feature of Kenny's person and the flat, barren landscape behind him. My friend was standing in a trench surrounded by sandbags and smothered in the hot, glaring tropical sunlight. His eyes were nearly closed, his skin a deep brown. An M-16 was held casually in his arms, and it looked more like a Mattel toy than the killing machine it really was. The photo forced me to face the same question that I faced when Buddy was in Vietnam. How would I respond should my friend be killed or taken prisoner? The question was always in the back of my mind. I didn't know what I would do. It was impossible for me to know before the fact.

John came into the room and slammed his books onto the desk directly in front of me. I jumped, startled, and a flare of anger flashed through me, but then I calmly said, "John, I wish you wouldn't do that."

"Okay. What've you got there?"

"A letter from my friend in Vietnam. Here's his picture." I handed it to him.

"He's black?"

"No, he's a white guy."

"Sle, he looks like he needs about ten years of sleep."

"Yeah, I know. He doesn't seem to have a handle on what's happening to him there."

"That's understandable. No one seems to have a handle on it."

"I know." The photo reminded me of a Korean War veteran, one of the incidental people I met at the bus station, who referred to the men and women fighting in Vietnam as sacrificial lambs. "That whole thing pisses me off."

"I know, Sores, I know."

* * *

Midterms came and went as all the exams did. There was the last-minute cramming and total exhaustion exactly when I should have been most alert. A long weekend was coming up during which the exam grades were to be posted. Upperclassmen were allowed to take a short leave, so I decided to take advantage of this reprieve from Academy routine. I had no intentions of waiting a day to find out how I had done, nor would I check my grades upon my return. They would be bad and nothing I said or did would change them. Without telling a soul, not even John, I packed my overnight bag to go to D.C. I wanted to be alone and to have three days for myself.

I caught a bus for the city and hired a taxi as soon as I arrived. I started to reminisce about my first two visits to D.C. when my parents and I travelled here on our way to Quantico, Virginia, to see Buddy graduate from Officer Candidate School. We stayed in the Ambassador Hotel. Feeling nostalgic, remembering the good, sweet times when my parents and I had walked these streets, I told the driver to take me there. With dismay, I discovered that there were no vacancies. The taxi driver explained that there were several conventions in town and that it would be unlikely for me to find a place to stay. However, he drove me to a couple of hotels he thought might have a room. They, too, were full.

In desperation, I decided to find my cousin, Denise, who lived in Georgetown. Mom gave me her address for just such an emergency and now I decided to use it. It was awkward since I did not really know Denise. Although my aunts and uncles frequently met, the cousins were too numerous and dispersed to have all of them on intimate terms.

I gave the driver her address. Traffic was thick and slow, and I was impatient. When the driver said that we were in Georgetown and had only a couple of blocks to go, I decided to walk the rest of the way. After I paid the driver, I left the relative safety of the taxi. As I stepped onto the sidewalk, I saw a gas station and thought about changing out of my uniform in the rest room. I dismissed the idea because I thought it would be too much of a hassle to change in a small and smelly men's room for a fifteen to twenty-minute walk. I could avoid the balancing act I would have to perform if there was urine on the floor.

As I started my walk, I wondered what I would find. She said that she was a secretary, but family rumor had it that she was a call girl. But that was rumor. The only certain fact was that she lived with another woman. I hoped that my sudden, unexpected intrusion into her life would be accepted with grace and without too much inconvenience. It would only be for three days, then I need never see her again if she so chose.

The street was a main thoroughfare. Its sidewalks were crowded and lined by restaurants serving Northern Italian cuisine and designer coffee. As I walked down the street, I became aware of the sullen hostility of nearly everyone I saw. When I met their eyes, I saw deep loathing, a profound hatred, directed toward me. For the first time that day, I wished that I had changed out of my uniform. The turning heads and staring eyes told me that I was much too conspicuous. I felt besieged by these longhaired, drug breathing hippies, scions of well-to-do families, their beautiful, irresponsible women, and their rich, leftist, intellectual friends. This was a world of which I could never be a part; I didn't have enough money, nor could I worship them from afar. My back was toward the traffic as it moved past me. During that short walk I had two half-full beer cans and half a dozen lit cigarettes thrown at me, probably with my white cap as a bullseye, from the windows of passing cars. They missed my head by inches. The beer cans landed with heavy thuds about six feet in front of me. I saw the hot, glowing flashes of the cigarettes pass at eye level and didn't know if any others hit me in the back. Because I was uncomfortable, my walk was stiff and quick. I was a hunted animal. Never would I forgive Georgetown and all it represented, just as I would never forgive Budge.

Upon inquiry, an older man gave me directions to the street where Denise lived. More than anything else, I wanted to take off my uniform and join the ranks of the anonymous. I blushed as I tried to look strong and hard, knowing full well how foolish I looked when I did so. Turning onto a side street, I was overwhelmed by relief at its quiet darkness. Here, any hate-filled eyes would be met on more equitable terms. The comforting shadows swallowed me as I floated along the rows of apartment buildings. Soon, I found a small cottage-like building that matched the given address. Upon ringing the bell of the darkened door, a couple of small dogs started yapping at me, then silence. I rang again, heard the dogs and what seemed to be a shuffling noise from invisible clothing, then silence. Peering into a window, I saw a dimly lit stairway but nothing else. I rang a third time, waited, then concluded that Denise and her girlfriend must be out. Now I had to decide what to do next. I sat on the curb with my satchel next to me. I stretched and relaxed as I noticed how pleasant and cool it was. Should I wait or face the good citizens of Georgetown? I waited for fifteen minutes, picked up my bag, and, with bated breath, re-entered the horrors of Georgetown courtesy.

The antagonisms of the previous half hour returned with my emergence into the garish lights of the busy street. The only good thing was that now I was facing the on-coming traffic and no more beer cans were thrown at my back. I began to think about returning to the Naval Academy. No one need know the failure of my solitary expedition to escape being a midshipman if only for a weekend. After a few minutes, I saw a young man waving at me from across the street and tooting the horn of his car. I recognized a youngster from one of my classes but couldn't remember his name. The first thought that ran through my mind was that it was against regs for a youngster to drive a car on local leave. I was relieved though to find a kindred soul among the hostile masses about me. The youngster wore civies and had a fragile looking young lady with him. The youngster asked, "Where ya going?"

"I don't know. Anywhere, I guess."

"You don't have a place to stay?"

"Nope. I tried all the hotels and they're full."

"I'd invite you to stay with me, but the place I'm staying at isn't my house and I wouldn't want to impose."

"That's okay."

The youngster rubbed his chin in thought. "I know a place where you could probably stay. It's for military guys and run by civilians. It's a barracks and you won't have any privacy, but it's a place to rack out. It's only two fifty a night, too."

"I've got nowhere else to go. I might as well try it."

"Hop in."

The girl slid to the middle of the seat as I got in. She was wearing a light gossamer dress that ended well above her knees. Her legs were as slender and delicate as those of a doll. She hardly seemed real as she mutely sat between the two of us. The youngster asked, "Why are you still in uniform? Didn't you feel a bit weird wearing that stuff in Georgetown?"

"You bet I did, but I had nowhere to change."

"You should have tried a gas station."

Soon, the youngster had me at a well-kept brick building. He said, "This is the best I can do for you."

"Thanks, I really appreciate it."

"Sure. Anytime."

As I was leaving the car, I took a quick look at our silent companion. For a moment I wondered what she was like and what kind of relationship the two of them had. It was strange that he never introduced the girl and that she never uttered a single word.

While listening to the car pull away, I faced the building. Pausing briefly in doubt, I entered the structure. Once through the door, I found a clerk's desk to my left and a reading/television room to my right that consisted of several armchairs and couches mixed with coffee tables splattered with magazines. Against the wall nearest to me was a bookcase housing dozens of war and science fiction books. At the far end sat a group of loud, young GIs cheering their television heroes.

Turning toward the clerk's desk, I saw that I was being watched by a chubby, pink-skinned, white haired old man who asked, "What can I do for you, son?"

"Um, I need a place to stay, and I was told I could get one here."

"You're in luck. I have one spot left. For two dollars and fifty cents, you get a bunk, a locker, and a lock."

"Great."

He showed me to a room with thirty cots lined up in two rows. Tall metal lockers were against the walls. I was taken to an end bunk.

"This here bunk is yours, son, for as long as you want to stay. It's not much, but it's a place to sleep."

"Believe me, it's a real blessing."

I sat on the bunk, unpacked my bag, then put on my civies. It was about ten in the evening, so I thought that I'd take a walk and find a coffee shop in which to sit and read. I jammed a magazine that I picked up at the bus station into my back pocket and left the premises.

Although winter was barely over, the weather was such that light short sleeved shirts sufficed. Even though I was gun-shy from my jaunt in Georgetown, the weather and the excitement of nighttime D.C. conspired to perk me up and revive my spirits. The walk was an expression of the indefinable joy of the moment. I never found a coffee shop, but I found pleasure in the simple act of sitting on a bench and watching the other pedestrians under the calm, restful streetlights that made the buildings and monuments glimmer. At one in the morning, I wandered by the Washington Monument and noticed how thick and green its park-like lawn had already become. I was surprised to still find tourists at its base.

At two, while considering my chances of being mugged, two Caucasian gentlemen approached me. One was a good looking blond with a slight build. The other was dark and somber with a solid build that offered no leniency. He frowned in inverse proportion to the smiles of his friend. The smaller man did all the talking while his more robust companion stood nearby, silently watching. The blond said, amiably, "Hi, there."

I responded, "Hello," and was about to pass them when the blond stepped directly in my path. Looking at my feet, he said, "Sneakers. How gauche!" Spotting the magazine sticking out of my back pocket, he made a successful grab for it. Holding it in his hands, he said, "*Mad Magazine*. My, my, my, you *do* need help." I shrugged my shoulders, very alert to the dark man's eyes eating into me. The blond asked, "How would you like to go to my place?" The dark man tensed while I noticed that his mouth was a perfectly straight line.

I answered, "No, thanks."

Cajolingly, the blond smiled, "You coward. Why don't you try it just once? You might like it."

"No, thanks. Look, it's late. I've got to get going." I retrieved my magazine and walked away, my thoughts preoccupied by the strangeness of the second man.

At three in the morning, I returned to my bunk and enjoyed a deep, dreamless sleep.

* * *

The next day boasted a fine morning. I awoke to discover that I was nearly the sole occupant of the barracks room. A few bodies were engulfed in blankets, so much so that the bunks looked empty except for the rhythmical rise and fall of the blankets in conjunction with the breathing of the GIs. It was quiet and still. I dressed and ate a bacon and eggs breakfast in a greasy spoon. Since I hadn't any plans for that day, I returned to my temporary abode to fiddle with the magazines and indulge in my favorite pastime of reading over a cup of joe.

I had been there for half an hour when an elderly, energetic man barged through the outer door, calling, "I got a bus waiting outside for anyone who wants to come with me to the zoo!" I was filled with a good, pleasant envy at the happiness that filled the bus driver. I wished that I, too, could face life with such overwhelming joy. The driver entered the main part of the building as I listened to his progress through the walls. "Free ride to the zoo for anyone who wants to go! Free ride to the zoo for anyone who wants to go!" A few minutes later, the driver was back in the reading room and getting himself a cup of coffee. He said to no one in particular, "My bus is gassed up and ready to go so I might as well get gassed up, too, while waiting for the sleepy heads." He looked at me, "You going to the zoo, bub?"

"Yep."

An answering smile. "Good."

There were about twenty GIs, so everyone had his own seat. I saw that they were all in their late teens or early twenties. None of them had the hard frowns and bitter mouths so common among the older, more experienced Vietnam vets. All of them were well dressed, clean, and born to live long, healthy lives. I sat in front. When I looked back at the young men, I wondered how many of them would still be alive within a year.

The driver decided to take us on a small tour. He explained what the different buildings were while his youthful guests talked excitedly with romance and adventure in their voices. Once at the zoo, the driver told us when and where to meet him when he returned to pick us up. The bus subsequently drove off as the young men split into three groups to one of which I loosely attached myself. Within five minutes, I was by myself.

The zoo was always an emotional experience for me. The nervous pacing of the canines filled me with dismay. I avoided the monkey house since I had no desire to look into the accusing eyes of fellow primates and to have the resultant sensation of kinship and guilt.

When I entered the cathouse, I heard a loud roaring. In turning a corner, I surprised a small, thin, bespectacled man teasing a large male lion with a stick, poking at the animal like a mischievous little boy. A woman was next to him, and both were giggling at the caged animal. As soon as they saw me, the man dropped the stick, giving me a weak smile, and the couple left the area. I remembered Cora once telling me that I had the same greenish-brown eyes of a lion. After studying the caged animal, I decided that she was right. I picked up the stick, placed it against my knee, and broke it in two.

As I weaved my way further into the cathouse, I was stunned by a magnificent, sprawling, Bengal tiger. A slender, well-dressed young lady about my age stood as if mesmerized before the animal. She had long blonde hair reaching down to her waist and had an athletic build. She and the tiger stared at one another. They seemed to be a single, solitary unit and were very much alone despite the encircling spectators. They were like a perfect poem. I walked stealthily by them.

By now it was well into the afternoon and the groups had come together to wait for the bus. We saw the bus working its way through the traffic a couple of blocks away. We started walking toward it. Gradually, the walk became a jog, the jog became a run, which in turn became a race. Two blocks away the bus stopped and waited. Another man and I took immediate leads and ran nose to nose. When we were almost at the bus, I put on an extra spurt of speed and barely beat my challenger. I knew that I was in the peak of condition and was surprised to have won by such a small margin.

Once on the bus, we returned to our quarters, exhausted and happy, and disbursed into our separate existences, each man being essentially alone.

* * *

That night I was again on the streets but this time I looked for a bar. A short distance from my sleeping quarters, I found one packed with GIs. I sat alone at the only empty table and ordered a Bud from a young, heavyset woman wearing a tight bunny outfit with a mean-looking stiletto held in her garter. Her virulent customers kept her busy and she'd often take breathers at my table. At first, I thought that she might be coming onto me, but then decided that she wanted a little peace and quiet, whatever the moment could give her. I said hello but didn't pursue her.

After my third beer, a black man in his fifties sat down opposite me. Having finished his own drink, he picked up my glass, poured its contents into his mouth, then spit it back into the glass. Then he gave me a sullen, fierce, challenging look. I waited for him to push me or to do any number of aggressive moves. Instead, he only stared at me. I knew that the other man was drunk so I wasn't worried by any physical threat he could offer. I ordered another beer and a clean glass and decided to ignore the whole situation.

It was then that I noticed three white GIs sitting at a table behind the black. One of them pointed at the man, held up four fingers, then one finger, and mouthed the words, "Four to one." Unobtrusively, I nodded in agreement, pleased by the fact that, for once, I was a part of the pack instead of its victim, but I also knew that I would never gang up on anyone.

When my beer arrived, I was careful to keep my hands on my glass and bottle. The black still glowered at me, but I felt confident in the difficult situation and relaxed despite the possibility of a fight. The black, not getting a response from me, soon left and I left half an hour later.

* * *

My heart turned to lead the morning I had to return to the Academy. The reading room looked so comfortable that I spent the greater part of my remaining time in it. The bus driver rolled in with a booming, "Good morning!" He looked at me, saying, "I'm going to the Smithsonian today. You going along?"

I shook my head no.

"You're going back to your outfit?"

Unhappily, I nodded yes.

The driver said sadly, "Good luck."

"Thanks."

I watched as the GIs gathered at the front of the building. All of them seemed so young and handsome. Like a pall, the almost visible specter of Vietnam loomed over them. I signed out and caught a cab to the bus station.

Once there, I bought a ticket and sat in one of a long line of dirty, green, plastic chairs. While I was waiting, a white-haired lady with the wildest eyes I had ever seen sat next to me. As soon as my eyes landed upon her, she glanced about suspiciously and dramatically whispered, "They're after me!" I looked at her with mild wonder. She continued, "The popes are after me. They call them popes because they work for the pope. They wear white jackets. They kept me for years, but I finally got away."

"I see." While she rambled on and launched into an involved story including President Johnson as a coconspirator, I thought, *even if every word was the absolute truth, who would believe her?*

I caught half of a sentence. "...might send an ambulance for me."

"I see. You'll have to excuse me. My bus will be here any minute."

I walked to a group of midshipmen waiting to be taken to Annapolis. They were telling one another the events of the weekend when one of them said, "You'll never believe what I saw in Georgetown Friday night. A middie-puke. I couldn't believe it. He was striding down the main drag in dress blues." I met the speaker's eyes. *Is it me he's speaking of? Did he recognize me?* The speaker continued, "I couldn't believe my eyes. There he was, strutting down the street like the town marshal." The mid imitated the walk he claimed to have seen, exaggeratedly swinging his arms and taking gigantic strides. The midshipmen laughed. Wanting to be inconspicuous, I laughed, too.

* * *

That evening, I sat in my room and thought of my future or the lack thereof. *Where will I be a year from now?* My hand touched the beaded necklace that I had made. I thought of its Morse code message, took it off, and threw it into the trash. I found the other necklaces and threw them away too.

It was time for my weekly call home, so I went to the telephone room. I thought it was odd that the rows of wooden telephone booths looked so much like upended caskets. I dialed and when the ring was answered, said, "Hi, Mom."

"Hi, son, how's everything?"

"Bad. I'm flunking out."

"Can't you get your grades up?"

"I don't know. I suppose I could, but why bother? I'll get kicked out one way or another."

"Buddy said that your grades aren't that bad, that you might be able to pass."

"What do you mean Buddy said that my grades aren't that bad? Have you been showing him my grades? That's my business, not his! He's not my father!"

Crying on the other side. "I'm sorry, son. I didn't think you would mind."

"It's bad enough to flunk out without everyone knowing how bad it is. I don't snoop into his affairs. Why does he snoop into mine?"

"Will you be going back to work at the hospital?"

"How can I? They gave me a going away party and here I am flunking out."

"It's all right, son. I've been telling everybody that you're going to resign just in case you do flunk out."

"Are you ashamed of me? You don't know what it's like here! I've done nothing wrong. I've nothing to be ashamed of."

"You're not trying. You've given up."

"I put up with a lot of crap, and now it's over! Plebe year did me in; I hate this place too much to even WANT to try."

"I was trying to protect you."

"Why should you protect me? Why should I be ashamed of not graduating? Bragg is going to graduate, and he's used a townie for the last two years, four by the time he leaves! Those guys who made Boatman jam a squash ball up his butt are all going to graduate! Budge is going to graduate! McMunn is going to graduate! Mower is going to graduate! They're the ones who should be ashamed, not me!" Even as I went into this tirade, berating the Academy as much as I could in my emotional turmoil, I still saw the school as being right in its judgement of me. The Academy was a virgin that could never be soiled.

I heard more crying on the other side. "Son, don't be so hard on me. I can't do anything right. I've been having a horrible time with Beth." There was a long pause. "Did Cora tell you how she came home and found Beth in the yard, that she didn't want to go back into the house?" Another long pause as I listened, afraid of what I would hear. "Your sister was raped."

My heart collapsed. I sagged in the booth, asking softly, "Do they know who did it?"

"No. Some guy selling magazines. He knocked on the door and when your sister answered, he realized the situation and came in. He was with a group of people that camped on the power line off Old Wrentham Road, on the right-hand side as you go up the hill."

I didn't know about any group of campers on the power line. I had walked Baron along that power line hundreds of times and knew that area intimately. I envisioned the area. It had a dirt road so narrow that cars were unable to turn around. The land on either side was so uneven with bushes, rocks, and trees covering all of it that even a pup tent had no room for placement. I just couldn't see it, but I had heard enough. My sister was raped.

Mom continued, "It came out during psychoanalysis. She was behaving so badly that we took her to a psychoanalyst and now she's under his care. The rapist chased her…"

"I don't want to hear anymore."

"… around the kitchen table, then into your room."

"Okay, that's enough."

"He threw her onto your bed…"

"I don't want to hear anymore."

"…and raped her. He held a knife to her throat and told her that if she told anyone, he'd kill her."

"Okay! Okay! Okay! I've heard enough, okay? I don't want to hear anymore!"

"Son, I thought you should know.

"Okay, now I know."

"Your sister's been terrible."

"Is she beating you up?"

"She blames me for the rape. I should have been there to protect her."

"She's been beating you up, hasn't she?"

A long silence, then, "No, she hasn't"

I leaned against the wood and glass of the telephone booth's door. So, this was what they'd been hiding from me. "Mom, I'm tired. I'm going to my room to catch some zees. Bye."

"Goodbye, son."

I return to my room to crash into sleep. *I am walking through a field of bright yellow and red flowers. They bloom as I pass through them. The motion becomes progressively faster and the flowers bloom so quickly that they become violent slashes of red and yellow, looking like deep, garish, gaudy wounds.* I awaken with a start and am horribly depressed. I look about the room, realize where I am, and drop off into the sound sleep of the dead.

CHAPTER XIII

THE BITTER END

The academy changed to whites. The long, black, weaving lines of midshipmen going to class turned into white shimmering streamers. With the better weather came the Wednesday afternoon p-rades and an increase in anti-war protests. The mids were told to hang onto their M-1s should any protesters among the spectators grab for them. Like all the military, the mids were ordered not to fight back. They were to hold valiantly onto their rifles and let events take their course.

I started walking to class with a midshipman stud named Jacob "Jock" Schein. We shared two classes: economics and physics. Jock was everything a midshipman should be: handsome, intelligent, strong, and a member of the football team. Since we were often headed in the same direction, it seemed natural that the two of us, who also enjoyed one another's company, should walk together.

As the spring deepened toward summer, we frequently passed through the red tiled patios of Bancroft Hall where sunbathing was allowed. One day, I said, "I think sunbathing is dishonest."

"How's that?"

"A tan is associated with outdoor activity. When you see someone with a tan, you think they got it water skiing or swimming or from some activity like that. Instead, these guys are lying around like a pile of dead fish, cooking themselves and making everyone think how athletic they are."

Schein laughed with amusement touched by a little annoyance. It was a laugh that I often heard from him. He replied, "This is the way I

289

look at it. If you're handsome and strong and would get a tan anyway, or should have a tan, then you should sunbathe. I sunbathe all the time. It makes me look good and, let's face it, I've got the stuff, so why not flaunt it?"

Despite his egotism, I liked him immensely, as he did me. When the Sharon Tate murder was having wide media coverage, my friend said, "I feel so bad for Sharon Tate, and I feel especially bad for her husband. She was so young and beautiful. The fact that she was pregnant makes it even worse. What a horrible crime!"

I spurted out bitterly, "What's so horrible about her getting murdered? She was beautiful, rich, and famous. I feel sorry for the kid since he never had a chance to live, but plenty of people die every day and they barely get a condescending fart from the news!"

"That's a lousy thing to say! No one, I don't care who, should be murdered like that. The fact that she had everything to live for makes it that much more tragic."

I retorted animatedly, "There are guys dying right now in Vietnam," and I intuited, oddly, that I might've been talking about myself, "who've never had anything except to get spit on. I suppose that's not tragic." I stepped into a plebe room we were passing, saying, "Plebe, got a paper?" I returned to Schein and thrust the paper at him. "Two hundred guys died this week. Where are their names? We've got a number, but where are the *Newsweek* and *Time* articles on them? They don't have fame. They don't have money. They've got nothing!"

We walked in silence for a couple of minutes, then Schein asked, "What sign are you?"

"Scorpio."

"That's you all right. You're just full of poison." When that comment settled, he added, "Mike, I know you really don't feel that way, at least about the Sharon Tate murder. You're a good guy and something's hurt you."

The next day Schein was again at my room and the two of us walked to class.

* * *

I was sitting in Dimwiddie's office. The officer's uniformed opulence seemed to oppose my thin intensity. An insurmountable wall sat before us. Language was mute. The officer asked questions to which I answered, "I'll find out, sir," or "No excuse, sir." What little dialogue we had was now dead. We both knew the futility of my being in that room. The company officer wanted a revelation of some sort, an awakening that would lead me to accept the system, what I called the Machine. I only wanted to be free, especially from the long minutes spent in silent, hostile opposition to Dimwiddie.

* * *

Saturday afternoon, I staggered out of bed, not quite aware of my surroundings. I went to the window and saw the green of the trees in full leaf. To my left was the library, directly in front was the chow hall, and to my right was Memorial Hall. I slipped into a pair of white trousers, put on my bayonet belt, and positioned myself at the window with my M-1 carbine cradled in my arms. I waited until some tourists showed themselves on the balcony of Memorial Hall. They were indistinct at that distance, but they looked like an old man, a younger woman—perhaps his daughter—and a small boy.

The firing pin of the M-1 had been removed, making it a sterile weapon. I cocked the rifle, took careful aim at the old man, rasped in an off key, grating voice, "Truth can never be found," and, CLICK, I fired. I cocked the weapon, snuggled it lovingly against my cheek, aimed at the woman, rasped, "Justice does not exist," and, CLICK, I fired. Again, I cocked the weapon, aimed at the boy, rasped, "Honor is outmoded," and, CLICK, I fired. In my mind's eye, I scored three hits. They left the balcony and were replaced by other tourists. CLICK! I fired and cocked the rifle. CLICK! CLICK! CLICK!

Fifteen minutes passed when John came in, stopped in evident surprise, and asked in confusion, "Sores, what are you doing?"

"Killing tourists." CLICK!

John stood next to me to see what I was aiming at. He said with a sibilant intake of breath, "Sle, some of them might see you."

CLICK! "How can they? I can barely see *them*."

"You know how these things work."

CLICK! "Yeah, I know."

John placed his right index finger next to his temple and moved it in circles while saying, "COO-coo. COO-coo. Mike, your acting coo-coo. Cut it out."

"Yeah, I guess you're right." After I put my rifle and bayonet belt back into the closet, I sat on my bunk while John remained standing next to his desk. "I keep thinking about the mills in Meantacut and the Vietnam War. If I flunk out, that's where I'm headed. First the mills, then Vietnam. My buddy's back from Vietnam. He's getting married and I think it's a copout. He'll get married, get a job, and pay taxes to support a nation that betrayed him. Then he'll have kids so that they, too, can go to war, get shot at, and come back to be called baby killers. Like my working in a mill. I'll work my balls off so somebody else's kid can go to Harvard without ever having worked a day in his life. And *I'm* the one they'll consider inferior. We ought to tell them to go fuck themselves!"

"Who?"

"Everyone."

"Mike, what's the matter with you?"

"What do you mean what's the matter with me? I'm on a one-way train to hell and you're asking me what's the matter with me? Hey, I've got a joke for you."

"What?"

"Nobody's above the law."

"Where'd that come from?"

"Read the papers."

John smiled mischievously. "A youngster I know told me that he laid his girl in Memorial Hall, right on the table where they signed the Japanese peace treaty."

I took an immediate interest, wondering if there was some way I could do an equivalent feat. "No kidding? Do you think it's true?"

"I don't know. Maybe. I think it's possible."

"I'm surprised he didn't get caught. If it's true."

Boatman opened his lock box for his wallet. He said, "I'm going into town. Want to come along?"

"No, I don't think so. I'm going to stay here and catch some zees."

"Hell, I'd think you were getting enough sleep to last a lifetime."

"I know."

"How much do you sleep now?"

"About fourteen hours a day. That's because I'm so happy. What I can't figure out is why I'm still so tired."

"Maybe you're chasing Donna in your dreams."

"I doubt it."

"No more true love?"

"There never was. She didn't want me. She wanted a midshipman. Anyone would do. Now that I'm flunking out, I'm sure she'll have nothing to do with me."

"You didn't give her a chance."

"You mean I didn't play the game."

"Whatever. Oh, did you hear the latest?"

"Okay. What's the latest?"

"The first and second classmen are staying in tonight. They're having a meeting with fearless leader Dimwiddie about the leadership ability of the third classmen. Sle, anyone not up to snuff is getting the boot."

"You'd think they'd get tired of porking us."

"What if they nail Valdres?"

I shrugged my shoulders. "Then they nail Valdres. I don't wish it on anyone."

"I'm leaving. Need anything in town?"

"Nothing you could bring back."

"See ya later, Sores."

"Yeah, later."

I laid on my bunk, afraid that I'd slip into one of my fits, or nightmares, or whatever they were. I suspected it was nervous tension, but I was not a doctor and suffered quietly. I relaxed and fell into a sleep lasting for hours but seeming like minutes.

* * *

I dream that I am standing in the middle of an immense auditorium, enclosed by profound darkness. Gradually, it starts to brighten. I hear laughter and the brighter it gets, the louder and more brazen the laughter becomes. I see faces, thousands of them. When the noise becomes unbearably loud, I see that the faces belong to midshipmen and that they're laughing at me. I ask, "Why are you laughing at me? What have I done? Why are you laughing at me?" The laughter intensifies and I stand with my head hanging in shame. The laughter changes. Although it's as loud and arrogant as previously, it comes from two gigantic heads that replace the thousands of midshipmen. I recognize the anarchist and his girlfriend from the airport. I ask, "Why are you laughing at me?" I feel dirty.

* * *

I awakened when John came in to make evening meal formation. He wore a jaunty smile and had spring in his blood. He asked me if anything had happened to which I answered, "I don't know. I've been asleep." I couldn't believe how nonchalant John was about the whole thing. I had mentally made a tally of the third classmen and had picked out myself, Valdres, Husaby, and Mandvik as the likely candidates to be dismissed. None of us were midshipman material. Except for the youngster studs like Schein, Meade, and Bemes, none of us were safe, including my roommate.

After evening meal, John again went into town in a holiday spirit that I found appalling in the present circumstances. I sat at my desk and remembered the many Saturday nights I had done this same thing during my restriction. There was movement in the somberly quiet corridor. Featureless figures, members of the two ruling classes, filtered past my room. Indistinguishable murmurs sounded as though they came from the inner environs of a deep cave. Although I had eaten with them almost every day for the last two years, they seemed like strangers, more like nameless instruments than human beings. I realized that if I was one of the chosen, it would be another humiliation in a long line of humiliations that I would have to bear. Being voted out by fellow midshipmen struck me as one more unbearable insult.

In a short period of time, but what seemed like a millennium, the figures started moving from the first class rec room where the meeting had been held. A second classman paused at my door. He asked, "Where's Boatman?"

"In town."

"You're all right, Sores. Your name didn't even come up." He was telling me that, according to the senior midshipmen, I made the grade, I was midshipman material, but I didn't see it that way and neither, I suspect, did the Academy.

I appreciated his kindness. "Thanks."

"Sure thing." He moved off.

That night when John returned from town, he asked me how the meeting had gone. "All right, I guess. I only know that I'm not one of the ones getting the boot." I was amazed by his casual confidence that he had not been chosen.

He said, "That's good. I was worried about you."

The results of the meeting became known on Sunday evening. The midshipmen were called individually to Dimwiddie's office to hear sentence. Valdres, Mandvik, and Boatman were to be discharged. Husaby was to stay. I saw Boatman come into the room with his eyes blistering in tears. Keeping his eyes fixed on the floor, he said, "I'll always remember the midshipman motto: humiliation builds character." He glanced briefly at me before his eyes resettled on the floor.

I murmured, "Sorry, John," and I left the room. My roommate would want to be alone.

The next day, John was gone. He didn't say goodbye, nor did he leave behind his address.

* * *

It was always stressed during boxing class that one should find a partner within ten pounds of his own weight. I had followed the suggestion, not quite believing that ten pounds could make any difference. After the warming up exercises, the class was told to find sparring partners. I approached a mid who seemed much bulkier than I was but who, according to the mid, outweighed me by only ten pounds. We agreed to be partners although the other mid expressed reservations about our disparity in weight. I said, "What difference can ten pounds make?"

When we fought, we faced one another in the ring, parrying one another's jabs. Suddenly, my partner threw a strong right. I caught the punch using the proper form with my left glove, but the force of the blow jammed my own fist into my face. Immediately, my arms dropped while I saw stars circling about my head. I thought, *it's exactly like in the Bugs Bunny cartoons!* I stumbled about the ring, not wanting the disgrace of being knocked out. I saw the concern on the face of my partner who was kind enough not to come in for the kill. A firm hand gripped my shoulder and Captain Courage asked, while waving his hand before my face, "How many fingers do you see?"

"Two."

"Follow them with your eyes." I did so. "You're okay." Captain Courage left the ring with me being much more cautious, dodging punches rather than catching them with my gloves, even with the correct form.

The class days dragged, almost forever.

* * *

On a Saturday afternoon, Gus Hovedo asked me if I'd like to go sailing. It was a beautiful day that begged to be enjoyed. We went to the small craft area where the docks were lined along the water's edge with sailing craft on one side and brand new sports cars owned by the first classmen, soon to be ensigns, on the other. This was the sign of success for which every mid lived.

The two of us signed for a dinghy and were soon bouncing atop the warm, sunlit waters of the Chesapeake. Gus was the real sailor, so I imitated him, leaning in the direction that my friend leaned and letting my companion handle the rigging. The sky was so clear and the air was so fresh that it was hard to imagine that a war was being waged in another part of the world.

Suddenly and unexpectedly, our craft was overwhelmed by a surge of water coming from the wake of a small motorboat. The motorboat paused, swung about, and made another run at us, barely clearing our bow and soaking us in the waves of its wake. Again, it paused, staggering long enough for the us to see, partially standing, a blond, red-faced youth about our own age. He made another soaking rush at us, and I asked, "What is he doing?"

"I don't know. Get his registration number."

The young man paused before another run. I had never seen anyone so devoured by hatred. His appearance and mannerisms were so violent that they verged on madness. I thought, *how do you fight such rage?* I said to Gus, "He seems to hate us. Why?"

"I don't know. Maybe because we're mids or maybe because of the Vietnam War. You have to remember that we're part of the military-industrial complex, whatever that is."

As the motorboat came at us again, I looked for something to throw at him, but the dinghy offered nothing that would serve the purpose. I then said resentfully, "What does *he* have to worry about? He must be rich or he wouldn't be riding that thing."

When the motorboat left for other pursuits, I asked, "Did you get his number?"

"Yeah."

"Are you going to turn him in?"

Gus shook his head no, then asked, "Would it do any good?"

* * *

In preparation for my last fight, I scanned the group of midshipmen for a partner. Not wanting to reenact the disaster from my last class, I sought a mid my weight or within a couple of pounds of it. Spotting a mid slightly smaller than myself, I asked, "How much do you weigh?"

"One eighty."

I answered truthfully, "I weigh one eighty-nine. Do you want to be partners?"

"Sure."

Warm-up was easy enough. My partner was quiet and unassuming. When we got into the ring, we jabbed and parried, looking for weaknesses in the other man. I threw a hard right and clocked my opponent directly on the nose. He held up his gloves in the proper manner but didn't respond to my attack. Since my fist was already past his defenses, I pulled it back a couple of inches, making sure not to pull out of the small pocket formed between my opponent's gloves and his face. I hit him again and again and I kept count: "One, two, three, four, five, six." My opponent still didn't respond, and I saw a small trickle of blood wending its way from the nose and down to the mouth of my foe. Six punches were more than enough, and I didn't want to be cruel. I stopped hitting him while at the same time I was submerged in a warm glow of pleasure. *There's one middie-puke down.*

* * *

At the end of the semester, when I knew that I was at my last E.I. session with my navigation instructor, the officer told me, "I'm going to give you an F for the course. I can't give you anything else and be fair to the other students. How are your other grades?"

"Bad, sir."

"Will you be going before the Board?"

"Probably, sir."

"Let me know when it's going to be held. I'll write a letter to them, or better yet, I'll make a personal appearance to explain the situation to them."

"Thank-you, sir."

* * *

I did no cramming for the final exams and was well rested when I took them. Oddly enough, I seemed to know the material, yet I was certain that I would flunk.

When exam week was over, Danny Calhoun and I rented a car and left for Ocean City where the mass of the company's youngsters had agreed to meet. Danny did the driving while I sat shotgun.

We arrived in midafternoon and hit the beach to look at the women and to find our friends. The idleness of people lying motionless on the sand bothered us and, for some unknown reason buried in our personalities, we became anxious, as though we and our friends should be doing push-ups or building a house or doing anything constructive, anything but lying there like mollusks.

We found Matt Helmsley in a group of youngsters that included Husaby and Carnevale. Sitting down with them, we watched the tumbling of the ocean and listened casually to the desultory conversation of our peers.

Matt said, "Look at this." Cautiously, so as not to awaken him, he lifted the elastic waistband of Carnevale's bathing suit. Underneath the band was soft, white flesh that contrasted sharply with the reddish brown of Paul's exposed skin. Barely controlling himself, Matt said with relish, "He's gonna be a hurting puppy tomorrow. Look at the burn he has already." Carefully, he replaced the band. Dan and I fidgeted a few minutes longer, neither of us being very comfortable, when Danny said, "Let's go," and the two of us left the beach.

We returned to the car to drive about town for an hour, feeling the freedom of motion. Danny went into a liquor store and came back with a case of beer, two pints of rum, a quart of soda, two large bags of potato chips, and a can of peanuts. We found a vacant lot and parked the car on the street next to it. The nearest houses were two large, burley houses opposite one another half a block away. Although it was still a bright afternoon, we began drinking. Neither of us spoke to the other. It was as though words would be meaningless and couldn't convey the same messages as effectively as our mutual silence. Occasionally, I pulled out a harmonica, my latest acquisition, to play a few simple tunes.

As the afternoon faded into evening and the evening faded into night, my mind faded into a semi-aware fog. More like a vision than an actual event, Danny borrowed my harmonica, sat on the trunk of the car, and played a series of incoherent notes under a newly risen full moon. Throughout the night, we watched nondescript young men and women sneaking between the houses at the far end of the street. Sometimes they hid in the bushes for their clandestine assignations. What surprised us both was that there were so many, and we realized that everyone must be cheating on everyone else in both houses. Danny said, "Why don't they all have group sex and get it over with." Eventually, we fell asleep.

I awakened in the early morning and reached into the backseat for a breakfast of potato chips and peanuts. Danny woke up so we shared the repast, neither of us saying a word.

An emaciated, bearded hippy was walking his unleashed Pembroke Welsh corgi next to the nearest house. The hippy went in one direction and the dog in the other. Abruptly, the hippy turned around, fists clenched, and yelled with every fiber of his body convulsing with the effort, "Arthur! Arthur! You get back here!" The Buddhist indifference of the dog approached the sublime. He ignored his master, and the hippy furiously followed the dog out of sight.

A couple from one of the buildings strolled by arm in arm. Upon their return a few minutes later, they stopped at the car. The guy asked, "What are you doing here? You've been parked here all night." The comment failed to evoke a response, so the couple continued their walk.

The morning aged. Neither of us talked until Danny asked, "How long have we been parked here?"

Looking at my watch, I made a mental calculation and said, "Eighteen hours,"

"I guess it's time to find the others."

We rejoined the beach group in their futile efforts to meet women. The attitude was that if Matt was unable to find a woman, what hope was there for the rest of us? Carnevale was frowning deeply, the look of a man about to kill. He was in pain and I was surprised not to hear him complain. The group of us played Gameland games at the boardwalk well into the night. At one o'clock in the morning the whole group was sitting at a table in an overnight diner. With my companions talking animatedly about the day's lackluster events, I crossed my arms before me on the table, then rested my head on them. Amidst my joyful friends, I fell soundly asleep. The last I heard was the young waitress. She shook my shoulder and pleaded, "Oh, please don't! Please wake up! You can't do that in here! I'll get into trouble! Oh, please wake up, wake up, okay?"

CHAPTER XIV
THE FINAL NIGHTMARE

I receive my final grades. I get the expected 'F' in navigation and think, *how appropriate*. However, when I see the C in psychology, I'm flabbergasted. I had expected an 'A or at the very least a B. I had counted on that grade to save me. It doesn't seem fair to have a whole semester's worth of good 'A-quality work destroyed by a C in the final exam and the resultant C as a final grade. Tomorrow I'm going before the Board. I need to have that grade changed, not as a favor, but because I deserve a better grade.

Hurriedly slipping on a uniform, I dash out the door and head for Luce Hall where several professors have their offices. Luce Hall is directly behind McDonough Hall with only Dewey Field and Santee Basin, the small craft docking area, between it and the Severn River. As I march in subdued anger toward Luce Hall, I couldn't help but notice what a beautiful day it is. The sun is warm and comfortable, the Severn calm, and the tree line across the river green and inviting.

Entering the shadows of Luce Hall, I turn left at the plaque stating, "My country, right or wrong," and try to find Lt. Biron to tell him that the Board is meeting tomorrow, could he show up? Unfortunately, Biron is out, and I think, "I'll catch him later, on my way back."

I find the office of Lt. Castiglione which is in the same building one flight up. The lieutenant isn't there. It's imperative for me to see him to have my grade changed. Otherwise, I won't have a chance before the

Board. In a neighboring office sits Lt. Castiglione's youthful, attractive, charming secretary. She asks, "May I help you?"

"Yes, I'm looking for Lt. Castiglione."

"What do you want to see him about?"

"About a grade for a course."

She snickers and says, unconvincingly, "Lt. Castiglione is in the hospital with ulcers." Again, she snickers, and I assume that she's lying.

I walk away and try to find Lt. Biron. He's not there and I decide to catch him tomorrow morning before the Board convenes.

* * *

I am again staring at the waters of the Chesapeake. In the immediate distance I see a narrow, green point cutting into the bay. It looks soothing, comforting, and I wish that I was meandering along its edge. It's 0800 hours, too early for the sailing craft and their pristine white triangles to be on the black water. It's also too early for me to find my navigation professor. I had been ordered by Dimwiddie the night before to be ready at eight. My last hope is gone.

I lean over the window's gutter to view the pavement four stories below me. I try to imagine the sharp thrill that must rip through the guts in such a fall. I pull my head quickly back into the room. Death might be easy, but not that way. I am in my dress whites, waiting to hear my name over the intercom and am so expectant that I have not gone to the head despite the increasing demand. Finally, I plunge into the corridor and almost run into Larry Bemes, who stops in sudden amazement and says, "Mike, you've grown so tall. I never noticed it before." I realize that I'm looking down at Larry. During plebe summer, Larry had been much the taller of the two of us.

Upon my return to my room, I again station myself at the window. Over the intercom I hear my name accompanied by a room number and my stomach thrills at the words. At my arrival I find a small room with a handful of comfort chairs and a couch occupied by midshipmen. A second classman asks me what my cume is. "I don't know." The second classman asks another youngster who answers, "Point nine six."

The second classman asks the youngster, "Where do you intend on going to school?"

The University of Maine unless my gimmick works."

"What gimmick?"

"I'm going in there doing a sailor's jig." He gets up, humming a traditional Navy tune, and dances grotesquely to the laughter of his audience.

Another youngster says, "I'm going in there walking like Popeye." He juts his butt out and swings his arms like the cartoon character. I smile sadly, not quite believing the levity of these men. An ominous silence descends upon the room, punctuated by an occasional joke, as its early occupants sift out the door into the boardroom and are replaced by other midshipmen.

Dimwiddie passes through the room to go into the boardroom. He shows no awareness of my presence. A minute later, he's at the door and says, "Mr. Sorensen?"

I hop to attention. "Sir?"

"The Board will see you now." Dimwiddie holds the door open for me so that I can precede him. My confidence deserts me and in uncertainty, I recoil back onto the officer to ask what I already know, "Do I sound off?"

The officer starts in surprise and nods yes. That's my last call for help.

I sound off and look at the Board which consists of two admirals and a civilian sitting on three sides of a large table so that only one of them faces me. The superintendent sits on my left. He glances briefly at me before riveting his gaze onto the tabletop in front of him. He says, without looking up, "Mr. Sorensen, you are being considered for dismissal from the United States Naval Academy because of your grades. Your cumulative average is point nine eight. Do you have anything to say for yourself?"

I stare at the floor, thinking of what I might say. I want to tell them about my mother and sister and the telephone calls that torment me. I want to tell them of their stifling approach to education, particularly science, and how it kills all imagination. Above all, I want to tell them that their midshipman system in Bancroft Hall fosters creatures like

Budge. There is so much to say. Keeping my eyes lowered, I say, "No, sir."

"Please wait in the next room."

I am readmitted into the first room of waiting mids and wonder how long it will take for my fate to be decided. Upon the Board's decision hangs my continuance at the Academy with its concomitant "golden road to success," or my return to Meantacut with its mills and, perhaps, Vietnam. A lot depends on them.

Thirty seconds later, Dimwiddie is again at the door. After sounding off, I stand before the three men who are all looking at the white sheets of paper before them. I intuit that they hate this as much as I do. None of them meets my eyes, not even the superintendent who tells me, "It is the decision of this Board that you are to be discharged, as of this moment, from the United States Naval Academy for academic deficiency. You'll be 1A. Your local draft board will be notified of your new status. The secretary on your way out will tell you what to do."

"Aye-aye, sir."

Resentfully, I snap a salute and leave when it is returned. These are great men. I expected more than, "You'll be 1A. Your local draft board will be notified of your new status." No one said, "Good luck, draft bait," or "Goodbye, hope you don't get killed." I had expected thoughtful insights, words of wisdom, from such men, but in their defense, I refused to explain myself to any representatives of the Machine such as Budge, Mower, and McMunn, and now to these men. No matter how badly I want to graduate, I am unable to overcome my hate.

I am breathing heavily, fighting back the tears as I listen to the young lady. She gives me a long list of signatures that I'll have to get before leaving. I am anxious to get away and ask, "How long will it take?"

"About two days, a day and a half if you're lucky."

I pause in the corridor after leaving the secretary's office. It's totally deserted and the lack of decorations of any sort makes it seem empty, a great void. The walls are pale green and remind me of the isolation I envisioned while staring at the patches of woods across the Severn. Looking down the emptiness before me, I see myself abruptly cut off from all hope of a successful and happy future. I'll be 1A and not in college and I won't run away.

In the next two days, I'll have five meals during which I'd be the focus of attention among the company's midshipmen. With this idea haunting me, I hurry from office to office, trying to get the required signatures. Throughout the ordeal, I am filled with a bitter disappointment that no one on the Board had asked me searching questions about my home life and Bancroft Hall, that the truth hadn't been torn from me. A congested, burning sensation fills my heart.

Here, at least, luck is on my side. Everywhere I go, the individual I am looking for is in. A secretary would tell me that, say, Mr. Soals will be out of the office for the next two hours, and that very person would step through the door before her sentence was completed. One secretary, another young woman, smiles sympathetically when she sees me and says, "Cheer up. It's not the end of the world." I know better.

When I see the battalion commander, the lieutenant turns away from a bookcase to confront me. With a huge grin, he shakes my hand. "You know, Mr. Sorensen, you could have resigned. I know flunking out on purpose is one way to get out, especially in some situations where resignation is looked upon as quitting, but resigning would have been easier. You should have made that choice yourself instead of letting events choose for you." He then signed my list.

During my odyssey, another secretary asks me, "Were you recruited for any athletic teams?"

"No."

"Are you sure?"

"Yes."

"We had a midshipman leave who was recruited for a team, but he didn't tell us. It caused a lot of trouble. Are you sure you're not recruited for a team?"

"Yes, I'm sure," and secretly I hope that I had been, if only to cause them a little trouble.

At noon meal I sit at my usual place. All the mids know what is happening. I try to catch Carnevale's eyes, but my friend refuses to look at me. I see Dave Husaby cutting through youngster alley, the end space between two tables, to speak with me. Husaby has always been a sensitive and thoughtful man, so, when Dave rests his hand on my shoulder, I expect words of solace. Instead, he whispers, "If you'd been black, you'd still be with us." He then returns to his place at table. Again, I try to catch Carnevale's eyes, but am disappointed in my efforts.

After lunch, I continue with my out-processing. I must go to the book annex next, so I wrap my naval engineering textbooks in my arms and carry them to the gruff old man that I dislike so much. I dump the pile of books onto the old man's desk, expecting the cynical, sarcastic sneer I'd seen so often before. I present the index card containing the list of books that I am to return. The old man looks at the list, then at me, then at the list again and pointedly rips the list into pieces. The old man looks inconceivably sad. Not a word is exchanged between us, but I know that the old man is letting me keep the books. The gesture almost makes me cry.

By the middle of the afternoon, the list is complete except for Dimwiddie's signature. I enter the company office and sound off, handing the officer the list of signatures. Dimwiddie looks at his watch and asks, "Ready so soon?"

"Yes, sir."

"That was quick."

"Yes, sir."

Dimwiddie looks over the list. "Are you going to appeal?"

"No, sir."

"What are you going to do?"

"I don't know, sir."

"Well, I hope everything turns out all right for you." The officer holds out a friendly hand that I am reluctant to accept. He says, "Mr. Sorensen, I still don't understand you."

I want to spit at the proffered hand. I certainly don't want to shake it, but, after some hesitation, I grasp it. "Thank you, sir."

I start packing as soon as I'm in my room. I pick up a mug that I had bought as a plebe. It has engraved on it, "Mike Sorensen, Class of '72." Carrying it into Danny's room, I ask him, "Do you want this?"

"What do *I* want with it?"

"What should I do with it?"

"Destroy it."

I toss the mug onto the floor, and it shatters into thousands of pieces. Danny snickers, and I say, "I'll clean it up."

"That's not necessary. I'll do it."

"No. That's okay. I'll do it." I then sweep the floor.

While I'm cleaning up, Dan asks, "You flunked navigation?"

"Yeah."

"Who was the prof?"

"Biron. Why?"

"Some of the guys are talking about beating him up."

I smile sadly, "Why? He was the best prof I had."

Soon, I am again in my room and packing as quickly as possible. Holmes stops by to offer to buy some of my uniforms. I tell him, "Take what you want," and continue to pack.

Hovedo comes in after Holmes leaves. He asks, "Are you going to appeal?"

"I don't think so."

Gus looks hurt. "Why not?

"Because I don't want to."

"C'mon, Sores, appeal. You'll get back in. You can't just give up."

"I can't, huh?"

Hovedo sits on the edge of the stripped mattress that had once been Boatman's bunk. "Please, Mike. Appeal. We all want you to stay."

"I've had it with this place. I want out."

"Think about it, okay? Promise me you'll think about it."

"Okay, I'll think about it, but the answer will still be no."

Gus watches me indiscriminately cramming my bags with whatever touches my hands. He asks, "Is there anything I can do for you?"

"No, thanks."

"They're buying used textbooks in the library. Why don't you let me sell your books and I'll send you the money?"

Our eyes meet. "Sure, Gus, thanks. Could you do me one more favor?"

"Of course."

I go to the window and pick up a cookie tin from the gutter. In it is dirt covered with a blanket of young, green shoots. I say, "Those wheat seeds started growing. Could you take care of them for me?"

"Sure."

Gus offers to help me carry my bags to the ground floor, but I insist on doing it myself. I call a taxi and wait outside, still in my dress whites. The sun is a little strong, and the smell of spring and the antics of a mockingbird give the scene an aspect of life. Taking a deep breath, I let my eyes wander along the fifth-floor windows. Hovedo is there waving. I wave back and Gus is gone.

Moments later, Budge comes around the nearest corner of that wing of Bancroft Hall. He stops short, as though in surprise, to ask in a small, sweet voice, "Sores, what are you doing here?"

"I'm waiting for a cab."

"Why?"

"Because I flunked out."

"Geez, that's too bad." He chuckles, "You know I graduate in a week." I watch the gloating, strutting figure of Budge as he walks to the nearest entrance of Bancroft Hall. My eyes seem to be playing tricks on me. With every step, Budge gets smaller and smaller. Although the entrance is less than fifty feet away, Budge seems to be, literally, no larger than an insect. Briefly, I question whether that meeting had really been an accident or the triumphal march of a worm. It occurs to me that, should I be killed in Vietnam, for an ungrateful nation no less, Budge would have succeeded in murdering me.

Two years ago, when my father died, I didn't weep since that was unmanly. Instead, I quit track although I was a star athlete and my grades plummeted from a straight A student to Bs and Cs. By then I had already applied to and been accepted by the Naval Academy. My acceptance to the Academy was the happiest day of my life. I held the letter in my hand, dancing and singing, and ran around the house with unfettered joy. I called all my family and friends. I had something to live for, a new meaning, a new purpose. Now, I'm returning to poverty and what I see as a hopeless future. I think of this as I wait in the parking lot.

When the cab arrives, the driver, a wizened black man, gets out. "How ya doin', youngblood?"

"All right."

"You the guy waitin' for the cab?"

"Yeah, that's me."

The driver opens the trunk and would have helped me with my bags, but I thrust them into the trunk myself. Once we are on our way, the driver asks, "Where to?"

"I don't know. Home, I guess. The airport."

When we pull onto the highway and into the hurrying scuffle going to Baltimore, the driver says, "It's always busy this time of day."

I watch the traffic and brood quietly. Suddenly, I slip to the edge of my seat and say intensely, as though to myself, "You know, I used to watch the traffic and wonder about all the people in all the cars. I used to think that they had something important to say or something important to do, but then I thought a long, long time and you know what? I came to the conclusion that they have nothing to say and that they're all rushing to nowhere!"

The driver is startled by my mannerisms. "Say what?"

I heave a huge sigh and sit back in my seat, very composed. "Nothing. Just get me to the airport—please."

THE END

AFTERWORD

This is a semi-autobiographical novel. I attended the US Naval Academy from June 1968 to May 1970. It was a traumatic experience for me. When I was in my early thirties, I sat down to write my story. It was pure catharsis. I had to get it out of my system. Initially it was 150 pages long, but soon it took on a life of its own.

I let a couple of members of the class of '72 read the rough draft. Their responses were very supportive. One suggested that I don't change anything in my story, and I got the impression that he wanted to preserve our lives there as much as possible, a kind of historical document to show that we existed and lived those lives. However, the draft did not work as a novel, and I ended up rewriting the whole thing.

Another suggested that I write this afterward since no one would believe that the events described in it are true. He had met Navy officers who graduated from the Naval Academy even a couple of years after us who had not gone through anything like we experienced, that they would think that the whole thing was made up. He suggested that I write this afterward while the aging members of the class of '72 are still around and can verify the truth of the harassment and the Naval Academy culture at that time. As my friend said, "What can you expect when a bunch of nineteen- and twenty-year-old men make life changing decisions for seventeen- and eighteen-year-old men?"

When I was stationed at Camp Navarro in the Philippines in the summer of 2008, I found myself sitting at lunch with an Army captain and a Navy ensign who had graduated from the Naval Academy that year. If nothing else, life is ironic. He was from my old company at the Academy. I described some of the harassment which my class experienced. The captain asked him, "Did you experience anything like that?" He shook his head no. Other members of the class of '72 have confirmed that the Academy of today is not the same Academy that we had attended

The Twelfth Company as described in this novel never existed. The company number is totally arbitrary, and the characters are largely fictional. However, the separate events, including the hazing, are all true.

The pilot's speech at the end of the novel is anecdotal. He says a lot of things which I was told by Navy pilots throughout my military career, but I don't know how much of it is accurate. I did watch a film of the fire on the *USS Forrestal* and the professor did point out the officer who was blown up. I also listened to a tape of a pilot about to crash, and it sounded as I describe it. The musings about life and death are mine.

Plebes were required to memorize the answers to the questions listed below. The answers can be found in *Reef Points 1968-1969* by the United States Naval Academy. There is no copywrite page.

What's up?	Page 196
How's the cow?	Page 196
Why didn't you say sir?	Page 196
What's an Irish pennant?	Page 184

ABOUT THE AUTHOR

Tom Doughty graduated from high school in 1968 during the Vietnam War. He attended U.S. Naval Academy from July 1968 to May 1970 when he was discharged, which is the subject of this novel. The following December, he enlisted into the U.S. Air Force and later found himself a security guard at the North American Aerospace Defense Command (NORAD), the subject of his novel, *Childe Roland.* Six months later, he was stationed in Athens, Greece, for three years as a security policeman – law enforcement - as described in his novel, *Heaven's Door.* After his discharge from active duty, he earned a bachelor's degree as well as a master's degree in English and found work in an environmental agency for 26 years. During the first Gulf War he enlisted into the National Guard to serve19 years in that capacity to achieve the rank of master sergeant. He is currently retired, has two wonderful daughters, and is living with his wife of more than 35 years.

The Psychologist's Shadow

The
Psychologist's
Shadow

LAURY A. EGAN

Enigma Books

First Edition, Enigma Books, 2023

Cover design: Laury A. Egan/Andrew May
Cover illustration: iStock photos
PhotoShop enhancement by Vicki DeVico

Discover more thrilling books at www.enigma-books.com

THE CAST

Dr. Ellen James Haskell, clinical psychologist
Dr. Ken Haskell, archeologist, and Dr. Myra Haskell, art historian
(parents)
Nick Ianni, Ellen Haskell's cousin's husband

CLIENTS
Lucas Constantine, classical guitarist, NYC
Greta Graf, potter
Carson Kendricks, painter
Robert Gabriel Fleet, stockbroker
Samantha Cosgrove, writer, high school student
George Durst, university maintenance supervisor, sculptor
Lloyd Baskins, philosophy professor
Dolly Bordella, writer
Denise DiNicola, sculptor
Steve Clayton, communications; Sharon Clayton, artist (married couple)
Mei-Ling and Chang Lee, engineers (married couple)
Marguerite Fleury, concert pianist
Mary Brown, antiques dealer
Albert d'Auberge, Mary Brown's son and assistant

POLICE
Sergeant Wilcox, New Jersey State Police
Sergeant McFadden, Princeton Borough Police

OTHER
Dr. Adrienne Barrow, clinical psychologist, NYC
Herbert Longfellow, literary agent
Martie Tyron, tennis pro photo

I've been searching for so long. To find the One, and finally I've found you. The last time I felt this way, it was all wrong—I was wronged—but not now. Now I'm sure. As you asked, I will prove my loyalty.

Dear Ellen, I'm waiting and watching for your signal.

THE OCTOBER FOG was oppressive. Unlike the poet's description, it didn't move on little cat's feet but in dense curtains of white, slicking every surface and thrusting its damp fingers down the collar of my trench coat. As I approached my office, I stared at the gift from my mother, a new brass plate: "Dr. Ellen J. Haskell, Clinical Psychologist." I smiled at her kindness, used my keys to unlock the outer door, and climbed upstairs, feeling that the weather was being ushered in with me. In many ways it was, because my mood was as heavy as the air outside. It was on a foggy day such as this, six months ago in the spring, as the dogwoods were blossoming in New York City, when my confidence as a psychotherapist was severely shaken.

Lucas Constantinou was a gifted classical guitarist, tall, slender, and strong, with virile dark looks. Perhaps it was his heritage, but he reminded me of a Greek warrior-athlete. Lucas had begun counseling after falling down a flight of icy steps and breaking his right wrist and four fingers when he had thrust his hand forward to protect his face. The other bruises healed, but despite two surgeries, his fingers and wrist would never regain the dexterity needed to play the guitar at a professional level. Thus, a year after a glorious debut and dozens of performance opportunities in America and Europe, Lucas' career was finished. He found work as an instructor but making music was his joy, his life's singular passion. Lucas had been in therapy with me for three months with very little improvement in his depression.

Despite my strenuous efforts to maintain a professional distance, I was attracted to Lucas, miserably so. In fact, fearing that I could no longer remain impartial, I had planned to refer him to another therapist, though I didn't intend to reveal the reason. I was in the process of devising an explanation when the unthinkable occurred.

Like this Wednesday morning, the fog had erased the sun. I remembered watering the purple hyacinth on my window sill, noting the cheerfulness of the hyacinth's color even in the gray light. Lucas was my first client. Knowing he was probably sitting in the outer room, waiting, filled me with pleasure. Already my intention to terminate our professional relationship had wavered.

Promptly at ten, I opened the door and there he was, smiling, but with tears in his eyes.

He rose to his feet. "I'm sorry, Ellen."

"Lucas, what's wrong?"

Just as I asked the question, I smelled it—gasoline—and saw the gallon container behind his chair. Before I could say a word, Lucas flicked a cigarette lighter into flame, and with it, himself. He shrieked in agony and fell to the floor.

"No!" I screamed. "No!"

Horrified, my brain froze. Then I rushed into my office and pulled the rug from under the coffee table. I ran back and smothered his writhing body, smelling his charred flesh and the stench of gasoline and hearing his heart-rending cries.

A receptionist from a doctor's office appeared in the doorway, her eyes huge. "Oh, my god! I'll call for help!"

By the time NYFD and an ambulance came, a janitor had grabbed an extinguisher and doused the flames, including those on the carpet and nearby chairs. When the medics hurried in with a stretcher and removed the rug from Lucas' face, I lost consciousness.

He lived but with terrible burns that required countless skin grafts. I visited him in the hospital, but Lucas wouldn't speak to me or to anyone. Eventually, his family brought him home to Voula, on the coast south of Athens, hoping their care and the sea air would be restorative.

My left hand was singed and required treatment, but the real wound was inside, a guilt and torment only partly relieved by the efforts of my therapist, Adrienne Barrow. Hordes of questions keep assailing me: why did Lucas try to kill himself? Why select such a painful and horrific method and why do it in my office, in my presence? To prove how desperately he hated his life? Because he wanted to die near someone who cared about him, or was he angry about something I'd said? No matter how I analyzed his intentions, I felt responsible. Although Lucas had been more unstable than his words and behavior indicated, I believed my personal attraction had blinded me, and I'd been professionally negligent.

I took a three-week hiatus and resumed my practice in a rented room because my office was badly damaged due to the fire and smoke. By August, I decided to leave Manhattan, hoping a new location would end the frequent flashbacks and offer a fresh start, yet I worried my failure and the visions of Lucas were too deeply imprinted to heal so soon.

———

After this tragic event, my parents begged me to live in Princeton. Six years before, they had built a new house about eleven miles from campus, on the outskirts of Hopewell. My father, Ken, originally a professor at New York University, had been hired by the Department of Art and Archaeology at Princeton in 1976 and was now professor emeritus; my mother, Myra, an art historian, had also transferred to the faculty and was retired. Although I had been raised in the city, I enjoyed the town's academic tone and the country's natural beauty, so when my father found a commercial lease beginning last month—September 1992—until September 1994, I readily accepted.

The second-floor space featured a private entrance, anteroom, sunlit main office, and a small bathroom. Starting a new practice was a financial challenge, although I had savings and received modest royalties from two books. Spreading word that I was open for business was another big issue. In addition to announcements in local media, I'd scheduled lectures at Rutgers University, Trenton State and Rider Colleges, and had participated in two workshops in order to attract new clients. Princeton University's director of counseling had also offered to make occasional referrals, especially for creative people—my specialty. Until I could afford an apartment, I was staying at my parents' home, a cedar-sided contemporary on six acres of woods. While the three of us were in residence, the house had been crowded, but my parents had recently left for Greece, to go off "wandering," as my father described their travels.

Now, as I looked through my office's half-circle window at the iron-grille gates of Princeton University, I missed the sunlight that usually spread through the room from its southern exposure, but with three lamps on, the office was pleasantly lit. It featured a high ceiling supported by dark beams that imparted an Elizabethan air, as if the Bard himself should be sitting at my desk, quill in hand. Built-in bookcases were across from the window, with a filing cabinet adjacent, on top of which sat a hotplate. Opposite the coffee table, couch, and two armchairs, my collection of Venetian Carnival masks were hung on the wall behind the desk. On the table sat a box of tissues and a vase of flowers—white chrysanthemums and sprigs of purple asters remaining from a television interview taped here last week, a "Welcome to Princeton" program. Amid the clutter of phone, fax, computer, pens, calendar, and open folders, a few photographs rested on my desk, one of which I examined: a picture taken last April with my parents on the deck of their house, in celebration of my thirty-sixth birthday. At five-foot-nine, I was five inches taller than my mother, though perhaps the difference in height was greater now, because at sixty-seven, her posture had developed a slight stoop. We looked much alike, with straight

7

noses, wide-set brown eyes, and athletic builds. My hair, cut just above my collar, was unruly like my father's and the same color: dark gold with casts of brown, though his hair had mostly turned gray. In the picture, he stood to my left, still tall and straight-backed at seventy-one.

As I stared at my mother's image again, I realized we looked comfortable with each other, whereas in earlier photos—during my teenage and young adult years—we appeared disconnected. During this period, we'd had some feisty disagreements, but perhaps this was true of most mother/daughter relationships. I recalled a time in 1978 when she was impatient for me to read Nancy Friday's *My Mother/My Self*, insisting that it would be edifying. I was twenty-two and ignored her, especially after she handed me her copy which had been underlined and copiously notated, the implication being that I should attend to her perspective. Later, when the paperback was published, I bought my own book and found it very interesting, though I didn't mention my opinion then. When we finally talked about Friday's ideas, the discussion opened a new era of mutual appreciation. In fact, after my move to Princeton, my mother and I had become even better pals: playing tennis, going for long walks, and seeing films.

I missed my parents, especially because I knew almost no one in the area. It had only been a short while since I closed my office on West 68th Street and, though I intended to make friends, starting my new practice had required a lot of time as had recovering from Lucas' catastrophe. I still battled with memories and was beset by doubts about my psychological steadiness and my competence as a therapist.

As I laid down the photograph, the phone rang.

"Good morning. This is Ellen Haskell."

No response. Faint breathing.

"Hello…is anyone there?"

Whoever it was waited a few seconds and then hung up. Odd. A wrong number?

I shrugged and reached into my files for the folders relating to today's clients. I'd met most of them at least once. Many were artistic, attracted by themes in my two books. The first title, an expansion of my doctoral thesis, *The Effect of Day Care on Creativity*, raised the point that decreasing time alone during childhood limited opportunities for imaginative play and removed the impetus to self-entertain through creativity. Although I credited the "day care children" with other strengths: the ability to share, compromise, and feel more connected to a community, I maintained they might be artistically impoverished and exhibit less independent motivation. I made parallels to the studies of only children, who spent more hours by themselves, versus middle or youngest children, who were in the daily company of siblings.

The second book, *The Loner's Crusade*, dealt with the effects of social, emotional, and psychological isolation throughout life's various stages. Building on the premise of the first title, it proposed that a certain amount of separation was conducive to the growing artistic temperament but too much could be damaging. In both publications, my inspiration was personal—I was an only child and had been a somewhat lonely one because both of my parents worked and frequently traveled. At an early age, I began writing poetry to express feelings and to entertain myself. Although I seldom wrote poems now, I became fascinated with what caused some people to construct things through imagination. My current project, *The Creative Life*, cited biographies of successful painters, writers, musicians, sculptors, and dancers—not all famous—and proposed a set of influences that forged the artistic personality.

Today's first appointment was with Greta Graf, whom I'd met

last week and thought would make a good case study for my new undertaking. Greta was a fifty-four-year-old divorced woman of German descent, a talented potter—I'd seen her work in a local gallery. Though she was of average height, she gave the impression of having Valkyrian strength: a raw-boned frame; large, blunt hands and heavy legs; and a short neck that tilted her head forward, as if she might be a hard of hearing. She wasn't attractive in the standard sense, but Greta's green eyes were alert and intelligent. Her speech was usually straightforward, but she eagerly popped the balloon of anyone who held himself up too highly or whose opinions she disdained. An earthy woman, Greta reminded me of the dense red clay she formed into surprisingly graceful shapes. According to her initial explanation last week, she had initiated counseling because she was living alone and drinking more heavily due to depression.

As I always did before beginning sessions, I turned off my answering machine's ringer to avoid interruptions. I then showed Greta into the office. She was wearing a shapeless burgundy wool skirt, an ochre-colored linen blouse covered with a leather vest, and Birkenstock sandals over thick rag socks. Baroque red and gold beads tumbled down her ample chest, and her graying hair was gathered in a ponytail, none too neatly. I offered my hand and had it crunched.

We exchanged pleasantries. I usually allowed my clients a few minutes to shake off the outside world and to limber up for the conversation ahead, but Greta was frugal with her fifty minutes.

"I've been thinking about ways to meet people," she began.

"That's good, Greta. What did you have in mind?"

She gave me her mystical smile. "I could join a church."

Was she teasing me? With all the neutrality of a Swiss diplomat, I said, "Yes, you could."

Her smile drew wrinkles back from her eyes. "Actually, I'm an atheist. I don't think that would be a wise idea."

"No, I suppose not." Greta's sense of humor was disconcerting as was her tendency to employ "gotcha" set-ups, laid like small traps to catch those who fell in with banal opinions. Greta induced a kind of low-grade wariness, causing me to keep watch so as not to make a pedestrian remark.

"I also thought about a book group or joining the Y."

I had difficulty imagining Greta exercising or evenhandedly analyzing the prose of some writer she detested, chosen by a group's democratic voting. "Either or both might be a good place for you to start. Do you know of any reading circles?"

"No," she replied, again giving me the feeling of having stubbed my toe.

"Well, the Y offers a number of physical activities. One might make you feel better."

"Get those endorphins going?"

I nodded.

She looked at me with amused forbearance. "I'm not doing those silly yoga or modern dance classes. You know, middle-age ladies contorting themselves into pretzels or young go-go girls jumping all about."

I suppressed a smile and avoided glancing at her large feet shod in the heavy leather sandals. "I can understand why those programs might not appeal to you. What about swimming?"

"That's more what I had in mind. Yes, all right," she agreed. "I'll try the pool."

"Good. What else?"

"Perhaps a singles dance."

I wasn't going to get caught again. "The only singles groups I know about are at two churches. Would that be a problem?"

11

She frowned. "I suppose not. I don't think they mention God or anything, do they?"

"No, particularly not at the Unitarian Church. You might even forget you're inside a church altogether."

"I would always remember that. Probably the attendees wear those little gold crosses banging around on their sweaters."

I couldn't help laughing. "I don't think everyone touts their religious beliefs on their sweaters."

"I certainly hope not. Do you know I watched a few minutes of a baseball game last night? I couldn't believe it. The shortstop was wearing this silver chain with an enormous cross. Every time he threw the ball, the thing would fly up in his face. I thought he was going to lose an eye. Imagine! Religion as advertising. So very offensive." Greta recounted this with some pleasure, as if the thought of injury by an errant cross was due payback for religiosity.

I steered the conversation to the singles dance. "I believe there's an over-fifty night once a month."

"Yes, I saw that in the paper. Most likely a bunch of old geezers with canes and walkers who've lost their significant others along with their marbles."

I smiled. "It might not be like that. There are a lot of interesting people in this town—retired professors—"

"I know, I know," she cut in impatiently. "We have as many Einstein impersonators as Las Vegas has Elvis Presley reincarnations. I doubt I'll have a good time, but maybe I'll try it."

Though encouraged by her willingness, I didn't have high expectations for success because her sardonic nature would tag along. "Could you tell me how you feel about going?"

She gave a short bark of laughter. "Ah, one of your 'how do you feel' questions." Greta passed a casual hand over her head, more to indicate the comment wasn't meant to sound critical rather than to fix any stray hair.

I smiled again. "Yes, it is. You caught me."

"Well, I've never been a joiner," she stated. "I've always hated anything too organized, too clubby or communal."

"I can sympathize with that."

Greta studied me for a second. "Yes, you probably aren't fond of groups, either."

"I think you need to grow up with siblings to like groups."

"Or spend formative years in day care centers," she said, slyly acknowledging my book. "I think you make some excellent points, by the way."

"Thank you," I replied. "Greta, we haven't talked much about your ex-husband. How did you meet him?"

She laughed, showing large, strong teeth. "Heinrich dropped a volume of Shakespeare's plays on my foot. In the library. My freshman year in college."

"Did he do it intentionally?"

"He never told me. I think he was just clumsy."

"Do you miss him?" I asked, inserting the question quickly.

Greta looked past me, lost in a moment of remembrance. "Yes."

This admission changed her slightly, as if a glimpse of her true self had peeked through.

"When is the hardest?"

"Saturday nights. We often went to movies and ate dinner out. Or Sunday mornings having coffee, reading the *Times*. Heinrich would get lox and bagels and the paper. That was nice."

"I would be sad to lose those moments. Perhaps it's trite to say, but weekends are difficult times to be by yourself." I knew this from personal experience.

She nodded but remained silent.

"Maybe you should plan an activity for Saturday evening or Sunday morning? Perhaps go to the Y?"

"I really can't see being at the Y on a Saturday night, but I could try Sunday...or later in the week."

We spent the last part of the session talking about her husband, who had been an English professor. They had met young, dated no one else, but after thirty-one years of marriage, Heinrich had suddenly announced he was tired of Greta, bored with teaching, and was moving to Greenwich Village. He gave her the house and most of its contents, taking only his books, clothes, desk, and favorite chair. At first, she believed he had a lover, but eventually Greta realized this wasn't the case. They had maintained a phone friendship, but shortly after their divorce, Heinrich died of a cerebral hemorrhage.

Though his death may have muted her feelings of rejection, Greta didn't blame Heinrich for leaving her, even expressing the opinion that it was his right, an attitude consistent with her adamant individualism. Even so, I suspected his departure made her feel cast off as well as afraid of entering the dating market, which she had never really experienced during her youth. I tried to explore these territories with her, but her guard was now firmly up.

As she was leaving, I extended an appointment card. She accepted it and stared at my left hand.

"How did you get those scars?"

I disliked being asked. "I tried to put out a fire."

"That's what firemen are for," Greta remarked.

She left and I sat at my desk, feeling nonplussed by her tart response. I made some notes and then checked my messages. An incoming call, a pause, a click, and silence. Since my office number was new, I assumed it had once belonged to someone else, yet it was strange that the caller didn't ask for whomever owned the old number.

I leaned back in my chair, feeling unnerved. I'd received quite a few of these hang-up calls over the last few days.

Once, there was another love, an unfaithful one, and I was betrayed. But now you have chosen me and everything will be different. You will always be true, and I pledge the same to you. We will be very happy together.

You are so beautiful—with your gold-brown hair and large dark eyes—and so intelligent. At night, I think about us and wonder if I'm worthy, but then I hear your voice telling me I am, that you have a secret plan for us. You say our union will be a revelation and send me blessings in the rain that falls. Rain is your secret sign—that I'm special.

I like today's weather. Fog is so mysterious, so easy to hide in. Early this morning, I went to Lake Carnegie, where the fog was thick, and gathered raindrops from the leaves, as you asked. The air was chilly, but I felt good knowing I was doing something that will please you. I saved the rain in a jar and will get more because I must never run out. This is very important if we are to find Rapture.

On Saturday, I bought this dark blue notebook stamped with gold letters: "The Journal 1992." You've told me to write in it every day and tell our story so everyone will know how the miracle happened. I also bought a red fountain pen made in Venice (our city). As you instructed, I will write only in red ink, like the blood that flows from your heart to mine.

MY ONE O'CLOCK appointment, Carson Kendricks, was the only client from my Manhattan practice—most of them didn't own cars, and no one else wanted to make the trip to Princeton by public transportation. Carson, however, had formed an attachment, crediting me with a renewal in his creative productivity and was willing to drive, as he had been willing to wait during my time away after Lucas's attempted suicide.

Last March, on a windy afternoon in New York, Carson had turned up for his first session, his blond mane-like hair twitching over the upturned collar of his navy pea jacket. He sprawled on the sofa and announced he would never paint again because he felt drowned in malaise. We worked on his inability to start a new series of canvases, discussing his sex life with some concentration because Carson linked his lack of success with one as having an immediate effect on the other. I wasn't sure if this had precipitated the creative block but gamely tried to follow him through the explanations he offered as to why women weren't flocking to his bedroom and why he was so artistically uninspired. Though Carson had been a client since late winter, because of my two interruptions in his therapy and his cancellation of several appointments, we hadn't accomplished much.

With high cheekbones divided by a large beaky nose and small coffee-colored eyes, he gave the impression of a bird of prey, a falcon or hawk. His paintings, which I'd seen at Razz, a brash SoHo gallery that represented Carson, were studies of death and destruction, some bearing a resemblance to roadkill, with generous dollops of blood red and hot orange dominating the canvases. Even though he was only twenty-eight, Carson was already considered a promising painter, a role he played like a flush hand when he was in a self-promoting mood. And it was in just such a confident mood that he had agreed to participate in a two-man show opening next January. Yet when he faced the reality of the commitment, the deadline initiated panic and moved him to start therapy. In addition to these reasons, Carson had unresolved issues about the death of his sister, a fraternal twin, who had been killed in a mafia-related street massacre, which he had witnessed at age twelve. I suspected memories of the bloody scene might be fueling some of his artistic imagery, as he tried to wrestle with guilt regarding his failure to protect his sister and other complex emotions he refused to discuss.

Eventually, after my hiatus due to Lucas' tragedy, Carson had picked up a brush, perhaps stimulated by newspaper accounts of the violence in my office, which might have emotionally connected to his own history. Or was he inspired by staring at my Venetian masks? Though I hadn't seen any of the finished canvases, Carson had shown me several lurid pastels featuring armies of people with masks, their mouths fixed in hysterical smiles that were in chilling contrast to the war-like scenes. In one unforgettable drawing, white-gowned Pierrots pranced crazily through a welter of bodies pierced with swords, axes, and knives and past men and women who were crucified on crosses. The images were disturbing, sadistic, and cruel. While I couldn't imagine hanging his art on my wall, the gallery owners were reportedly excited by his efforts and were encouraging him to finish the ten paintings he had agreed to exhibit.

This afternoon, as he entered my office for the first time, Carson examined the room with care, studying the familiar masks on the wall. He removed his leather jacket and red scarf and sat, angled toward the windows, legs crossed, as if he had dropped in for a social visit. I asked how his painting was progressing.

"Awful. I hate everything," he exclaimed. After a sheepish glance, he shook his head. "I have five done. Well, maybe five and a half."

"Four and a half to go?"

He smoothed a long hank of yellow hair and sighed. "Yes, exactly. You better work your magic soon, Ellen, or I won't be ready for the opening."

"Carson, you know I have no control over your painting—"

"Nonsense! Why do you think I drive down to this little nest of academia? Because I'm fond of ivy?" He sniffed in disgust. "No, Ellen, I'm not letting you out of my sight—metaphorically speaking—until I have accomplished ten pieces. And I need to gaze at your masks. They give me ideas."

I smiled at him. "If the masks interest you, why not buy your own?"

He wagged a finger at me. "You know it's you *and* your masks—the combination—that are inspiring. Besides, if I had to look at these all day, I'd go nuts."

I turned toward the wall behind me. My mother had begun my collection with a Casanova mask that featured a black tricorn hat and a gold, tan, and black diamond face—a beautiful creation I had hung in the center. Next to it was a Pierrot, a traditional *commedia dell'arte* design, with full white face, a black tear on the cheek, and a black and gold skullcap, a mask Carson had already included in one study. The Harlequin beside it was a three-quarter face split in red and black with the typical diamond pattern. I also had two plague doctor's masks, each with long beaks. These interested me because of their history: a doctor who wore such a mask was supposedly immune from disease. A small *Gatto* or cat mask was near a Fool's mask in purple, black, and white; its lips were lavender while the cap had the requisite three dangling gold balls. Two *I Bellini* masks in blue, white, and gold were placed by a red and black *Baute* mask, with its lower section jutting outward, and an elegant Columbina mask with musical notes painted in gold on the ivory scrolled cap. A pair of Comedy and Tragedy masks, in opposing black and white, with mouths twisted respectively in a manic grin and a woeful frown, completed the group.

"Which is your favorite, Carson?" I asked, turning to him.

"It depends. I like that you chose classic designs without a lot of feathers and sequins."

I wondered about the psychological linkage between the masks and his gruesome imagery and how his art channeled underlying hostility, which I hadn't noticed in person.

He closed his eyes halfway, observing the wall beyond my shoulder. "I find it interesting that their mouths are fixed, as if the person wearing the mask is stuck with its expression."

"And if the wearer's mood is in conflict with the mask's?"

Carson gave me a wily smile. "Then they would be hiding how they feel."

There was something strange about the way he said this. "To disguise their faces and their emotions?"

"Perhaps."

"Sometimes my clients select a mask from the wall and use it to act out a role. Do you know what I tell them? I quote Oscar Wilde: 'A mask tells us more than a face' or 'Give him a mask, and he will tell the truth.' So, Carson, how do you travel from the mask to the scenes you depict in your paintings?"

He laughed. "You mean, where does the blood come from? The death and dying? Or what truths I'm telling in my work?" Carson examined my face carefully. "What do you think?"

We were fencing. Carson enjoyed this sport. I didn't.

He stroked his chin. "Okay. Well, maybe sex leads to pain? Love leads to misery or death?"

I hesitated, then asked, "Do you have fantasies about hurting people?" I had attempted this discussion before, but he had always deflected the topic.

"Only when I paint."

"Art is a balance between emotions and intellect—the translation of non-visual feelings into forms, colors, textures, and shapes that communicate moods as well as ideas. Carson, can you describe how you experience this transfer of your feelings?"

He regarded me like a lion in tall grass watching its prey. "It's very immediate, very intimately tied together."

"So there's only a little space between how you feel and what you put on your canvas?"

He nodded and looked pleased. I couldn't get past the unpleasant sense that he was toying with me.

"Could it be that the reason you've felt unproductive and unable to paint is because of the disturbing nature of your emotions? The ones that emerge in your work?"

"If my paintings depict the cruelty of mankind, mixing revelry with aggression, well, I suppose I'm getting my point across, aren't I? That's how I feel. Whenever something is too perfect, too beautiful, it will be broken, smashed, ruined."

I sighed. "That makes me feel sad for you."

He was silent for a moment. "I think you get what I mean."

I shifted in my chair. "I'm not suggesting you don rose-colored glasses, but I hope we can find a way toward a more hopeful outlook. It would be interesting to see you paint an entirely different scene with these masks. One in which a little joy suffused the people—"

"Hah! What next? Large-eyed children? Charming little English cottages under blue skies?"

"You misunderstand what I'm saying."

He threw me a sour look. "I will consider it."

We then discussed a young woman Carson had slept with over the weekend. My impression was that she was close to adolescence, probably a drug-user, and perhaps hypersexual. Did his selection of late-teenage girls represent a subconscious wish to reunite with his twin sister, who had died at age twelve? If so, had he harbored feelings for her that extended beyond the love of a sibling? I reminded myself that Carson had also mentioned affairs with a series of wealthy older women who had elicited sex in return for introductions to influential gallery owners, a kind of prostitution Carson believed necessary for his advancement. These women used him and moved on, as he did to them. Whatever his reason for selecting inappropriate people, the most recent relationship might be another bad choice, a woman who would disappear like the others.

—

I made notes in Carson's file and prepared for my next client, a twenty-six-year-old stockbroker, Robert Gabriel Fleet, who worked in town for a brokerage firm. Like his namesake, Gabriel, Robert wasn't hesitant about horn-blowing, though his career had failed to rise to the heights he felt were commensurate with his ability. A slim, three-piece-suit type, he was convinced of his judgment in all matters financial and many matters outside this arena. Robert wasn't above self-denigration, but I realized at our first appointment that he used this as a ploy to elicit praise. When I failed to react accordingly, he became more down on himself and tried to manipulate compliments. His primary complaints arose out of his ambitiousness and frustrations with his manager, who hadn't promoted him at the pace Robert deemed appropriate, and with fractious peer relationships.

At age twenty-two, Robert had married Debby, a beautiful woman who he portrayed as an ideal wife. They bought a new house, part of a development erected on the former farmlands east of Princeton. It was a stone-fronted monster with a porch, a huge marble foyer, and bathrooms and closets that were larger than many bedrooms. Robert had shown me photos of his home during our first session, causing me to muse upon the similarity between the false façade of Robert's house and his personality. With the huge mortgage and two expensive cars, Robert and Debby's finances were in the red, though he blamed his misfortunes on external sources. Robert himself was perfect—except when it suited him to pretend otherwise. Of all my clients, he was the least endowed with creativity.

This afternoon, he was punctual, though apologetic for being late, a gambit that implied scheduling our appointments was logistically difficult because he was so busy. Immediately, Robert launched into a description of a morning staff meeting, one he related in detail. The upshot was that he hadn't received a coveted account and was annoyed with his manager's reluctance to provide him with lucrative opportunities. Robert sighed often and crossed and uncrossed his legs to mark each paragraph of commentary.

I let him talk for ten minutes, nodding, listening, and giving him the close attention he probably didn't receive from many people. As with other clients, I said little until the person ran out of steam, which Robert finally did, having spilled his cup of unhappiness in my lap.

"I'm sorry you didn't get this recognition," I told him. "That must have been very disappointing." I paused, to let this hover in the air. "Just so I understand, please explain why this account was so significant and why the decision was unfair to you?"

Robert rarely made direct eye contact, but he glanced at me, as if my questions were imbecilic. He then began a financial exposition on the client's business, net worth, and the commissions such an account would bring to the chosen broker. When he came to the end of the litany, Robert hadn't answered my second question.

I tried again from another angle. "Robert, did the woman who was awarded the account feel pleased?"

He shrugged, but his expression relayed suspicion, as if he were trying to detect the ambush.

"Did she work hard to earn it? I'm not saying you didn't work as hard, but perhaps she's a competent person who also deserved the account."

Robert didn't buy that idea, but he admitted she was competent.

"A minute ago, I used the word 'awarded' when I described the assignment of the client. Does 'awarded' sound like she earned a prize or a gold star? A recognition? Something you didn't receive which implies you didn't get the gold star or win a competition?"

Robert tipped one shoulder forward and flicked his forefinger on an invisible speck of dust on his trousers. "In a way."

"How do you feel about that?"

"Not happy."

"Do you feel judged by your manager? That this was a sign of his disapproval?"

Robert frowned. If he said "yes," it was an admission the boss disapproved of him. If he said "no," the reply might be a lie.

"I suppose I did regard this as an indication."

"Of what?" I asked, quietly insisting on a complete answer.

He sighed. "Of not being the right broker for this particular client."

"Robert, if you had been awarded this account, would your colleagues congratulate you?" I waited for his nod. "Did you congratulate your colleague?"

He fidgeted with the tassel on his loafer. "No, I had to leave for lunch and then came directly here."

I studied him. "Would you feel comfortable returning to the office and saying something complimentary to the woman who received the account?"

"I suppose I could."

"How do you think she would react if she heard this from you?" I imagined his honest response would be "surprised," but he wasn't going to admit this.

"I guess she would feel appreciated."

A significant concession, though Robert sighed again, as if he had been herded into a corral.

"I think you're right. It would make your colleague feel good...and would make her like you."

He always perked up if anyone confirmed he had been correct. "Okay. I'll do that." Robert gave me a thin smile.

This seemed to close off the "business" side for the session. "How are things at home?"

"Not great." His head, usually held high, lowered a notch, and he began itemizing minor problems that had transpired between his wife and himself. Finally, Robert folded his arms in a defensive posture. "I think Debby is having an affair."

Was he making a false accusation in order to elicit a sympathetic response? "Why do you think so?"

"Well, she didn't come home until ten on Tuesday night. Then she took a shower—which she never does before bed. She was also gone most of Saturday. I don't know where."

"Did you have an argument on Monday, Tuesday, Friday, or before she left on Saturday morning?"

Robert looked uncomfortable. "Not really. I worked late on Monday and Friday."

"Did you call and tell her?"

"Yes. I phoned about eight."

"Was Debby disturbed? Perhaps because she had already prepared dinner?"

"No, of course she wasn't."

I suspected Robert was shading the truth. "Could your wife have feelings of resentment about your late arrivals? Debby works all day, too, doesn't she? Perhaps she was paying you back in kind. I'm not suggesting this is a satisfactory way to get a point across..."

"I should say not!"

"Does she feel appreciated? By you and also at her office?"

Robert didn't hide a belittling snort. "She's a secretary. Debby has a much easier, less stressful day than I do."

"Perhaps it's sufficiently stressful for her. Have you ever discussed how she feels?"

"Occasionally."

We compared Debby's job to his, the fact that she put in eight-hour days, ran the house, did the shopping and most of the cooking. Considering their young age, I was surprised how role-bound they were, or at least how stuck in a traditional male role Robert was.

"Does your wife want to work?"

"Not particularly. She doesn't really have a career."

I felt irritated with him. "You might not consider that being a secretary is a career, but secretaries are often the glue that holds an office together. Besides, many graduate to more responsible positions."

"That won't happen. Debby's just filling in until we pay some bills, and I make more money, which will be soon."

"Do you think she resents having to work? Didn't you tell me it was her idea?"

"*I* resent that she needs to work," Robert corrected.

"Maybe, like your colleague, it might be nice to appreciate her contribution. Talk to her about what she's providing you and your marriage," I said. "Obviously, you care about your wife, so although your day was disappointing, perhaps you can create a nice evening for her and for yourself."

His face brightened. "I'll get a bottle of wine. And flowers."

"Okay. Now, do you really think Debby's having an affair?"

He shook his head. The idea that his wife could prefer some-one else to him was difficult for Robert to imagine, even though he had cast that aspersion himself.

After the session ended, I speculated whether Robert lay on the sociopathic spectrum, the high-functioning side, because of his low-empathy behavior, but categorizing him was premature.

[THE JOURNAL]

I carry my journal to keep you close. I'm afraid of how much I'm beginning to feel. But you know this, don't you? You know everything. Sometimes I worry because I'm not good enough, but then you don't let me think that way for long. Soon I hear your voice in the sky, from the trees, in my room, and you tell me everything is fine. That we are fine.

This is all so new. I have so much to learn about us.

I POURED a glass of water and looked through the window at the busy scene below. The breeze had dispelled the fog and was whisking red and gold leaves from the trees, creating an impressionist painting on the green grass. Students, wearing sweaters or light jackets, hurried across diagonal pathways to classes. Most were with others, talking and laughing. Their camaraderie made me think about Greta and her attempts to overcome loneliness, which, in turn, connected to my own predicament. I needed to make friends or else I might find myself in my client's shoes.

The exterior door shut. Plodding footsteps on the stairs. Samantha Cosgrove was in the waiting area.

Sam, as she preferred to be called, was a seventeen-year-old girl whose parents contacted me because she had lost interest in school, though all testing and previous grades indicated she was exceptionally bright. Sam refused to go to clubs or other activities, loathed sports, didn't date, and was exhibiting depressive episodes. Seeing a psychologist wasn't her idea, and on occasion, Sam felt righteously resistant; at other times, her natural curiosity emerged. I never knew which mode I would encounter, nor for how long. Whether her mercurial personality was being abetted by teenage hormones or whether she had a chemical imbalance that might be corrected with medication, I wasn't sure.

I opened the door and Sam slumped in—her mode of walking, sitting, and standing. Slung over her right shoulder was a heavy backpack of books. She dropped it on the floor near the couch and extricated herself from a black leather jacket, a man's biker coat perforated by metal studs. Underneath, she wore a baggy black turtleneck and jeans, which were too long at wrist and leg, even though Sam was tall. Her ears were pierced with silver hoops that snagged in her dark brown hair, a tangled mass of curls that appeared to have been cut by a blind man and often obscured her brown eyes, forcing Sam to frequently brush back errant locks. Her nose was prominent above small pursed lips. Altogether, she wasn't the most presentable young woman. And surprising, too, because her parents, who I'd met before Sam's first appointment, were well-groomed and dressed with conservative care, both handsome. Sam's greatest attributes were her creativity and sharp mind, the latter sometimes a detriment when she felt disdainful, in which case her remarks could be scathing. Most often, she hid her intelligence behind silence or monosyllabic responses.

Sam sprawled against my tan couch and fiddled with a black leather band tied above her knee. My experience with current teenage fashion was dusty, but the band caught my attention, as perhaps she intended. I asked her about it.

She shrugged and threw me a quick glance. "It's to remind me."

"Remind you of what?"

She twisted the band so the knot was to the outside of her leg. "Someone."

I waited for a second because occasionally Sam would anoint her laconic replies with more information.

"Someone at school," she added.

"A friend?"

Sam stared at me before glancing toward the Venetian masks behind my shoulder. "Just a guy."

"What do you want to remember about him?"

She wrenched her mouth to one side. "Like, he's dead. Isn't that a good reason to remember him?"

"Yes," I agreed, trying not to look surprised. "What happened?"

After rolling her eyes, she focused on the view through the window. "Blades."

"Razor blades?" I asked, aware that I might sound a little slow.

"Yeah, like, he slit his wrists. Got the job done."

30

I teetered between showing sympathy for the loss and trying to adopt some of her laissez-faire attitude. I went with the former. "That's really sad, Sam. I'm sorry."

She glanced at me, as if my response was a trick. "He did the right thing."

"Do you believe that? That suicide is a solution?"

"Yeah. Sure. I mean, like, whatever. He wanted to be out of here and he is. That's cool."

Which way to go first? Her flat affect didn't provide direction. "Tell me about him."

Sam tossed her hair over her shoulder. "He was okay. For a guy."

"What was his name?"

"It doesn't matter to you." Her voice was tinged with hostility.

"It matters to you, doesn't it?"

She was silent and then replied, "Jake."

"Was he in some of your classes?"

"Yeah."

I was beginning to feel like a dentist pulling teeth. "Which ones?"

"English, French, and American History."

"What was he like?"

"Like no one, like everyone." Sam accompanied this statement with a shrug.

"Did you ever go on a date with Jake? Or see him outside of school?" I asked, keenly aware of the nineteen years difference between us.

Sam grimaced. "I saw him, you know, like, around. I'm not into the dating thing. It's so boring."

She then volunteered that Jake wrote free verse. Mostly, I suspected, on dire topics, poems he shared with a small following of friends, a group she described as modern-day Beats. Because Sam was also a poet, I wondered if she was close to this group? Had they influenced her choice of dress, appearance, and attitude?

"Are his other friends wearing a leather cord?"

"Some are. Some aren't."

I asked the obvious question. "What caused Jake to kill himself? Was it a reaction to something that happened?"

Sam stared at me for a second. I had the feeling that if one of her parents had asked the question, they would have been treated to theatrical groaning. At least I had graduated from the lowly caste of pseudo-parent.

"I don't know. I guess he had nowhere to go."

The simplicity of the statement matched my directness. Still, I was taken aback by the remark. "Do you want me to say that everyone has somewhere to go?" I asked, hoping my question didn't make me sound like a Pollyanna.

"Whatever."

"Didn't Jake have a future? If he was a writer, didn't he have a responsibility to write?"

Sam lifted one eyebrow and quickly lowered it. "Well, like, who knows? I mean, I doubt anyone would've published his stuff, if that's what you're saying."

"Did you read any of his writing? Was it any good?"

"Yeah, some of it…but it was sort of not-for-everyone."

I straightened in my chair. "I need to know how you feel about suicide, Sam."

She gave me a moody look. "It's an option."

"When you have nowhere to go?"

"Like then, yeah."

"Do you sometimes feel that way?"

Sam nudged the coffee table with her knee. "Yeah." She glanced at me with subtle defiance. "Who doesn't?"

"When do you feel that depressed or upset?"

"Different times."

I felt like the dentist again. "Describe to me one of those occasions, Sam."

"Like, different times. Why does it matter to you?"

"You know it matters to me," I told her quietly.

She silently stewed over this. "At night, late. That's the worst."

"When everyone is asleep?"

"Yeah."

"Tell me more about it."

"Sometimes I can't stand being in my room. I mean, it's just...too...much." She emphasized the last three words as if they were small separate islands. "That's when I leave. Walk around by the lake, in the woods, wherever. Or I take my car, but mainly I like to walk, particularly in the rain. Rain makes me feel better." She threw me an odd glance that I couldn't interpret.

"Do your parents know you're out?"

"No. Their bedroom is in another wing of the house. I think that's why they bought the place. So they could be separate. But I don't care because I can come and go as long as I'm quiet."

Were the Cosgroves aware of Sam's nightly outings? I couldn't reveal this information to them unless Sam was in imminent danger. "I also enjoy being by the lake. There's a lovely spot I know. A willow tree by the shoreline. Wild violets grow there in the spring."

Samantha smiled. "Yeah. I like to go there."

"Did you ever meet Jake when you're walking?"

"Yeah. A couple of times we hung out. We read some stuff we'd written—did a joint—talked."

I ignored the marijuana use. "It sounds like you enjoyed being with him."

"Yeah, I did."

I thought for a moment. "Sam, when you're gone during the

night, why do you come back home?"

Her eyes widened for a second, but then she scrunched her shoulders as if the room had become cold. "I return when I feel like it. It's okay being at the house sometimes. When I'm listening to music or writing."

"I know you like to write—you mentioned that last week," I said. "You certainly don't have to do this, but would you show me something you've written or a new piece?"

She was silent, her arms across her chest. For a minute, I thought I'd been too invasive, but a glimmer of interest lit her brown eyes. "Yeah, okay. If you want."

I felt as though I'd won a minor skirmish because she was willing to share something important to her. "Good. Perhaps you could write about Jake?"

"Like a memorial?"

"Yes. Do you think he would've liked that?"

She nodded. "Probably."

The issue of suicide still hung in the air between us. I weighed the value of re-approaching her on the subject against the danger of making it too important, as if my concern might make Sam more inclined to consider it as a viable option. Nevertheless, I was worried.

"Sam, you didn't tell me exactly how you feel about suicide. That's something we need to talk about, don't you think?"

She ran her top teeth over her lower lip and didn't answer.

"To be honest, I want you to know that I'm concerned. Just to relieve me, could you promise to call if you ever feel that bad? In fact, you can call at any time if you're really down. I can't always answer the phone, but if you leave a message, I'll reply as soon as I'm free."

Although Sam avoided my gaze, she shrugged by way of acknowledgment. We then discussed the problems she was having in math class: how the teacher didn't like her and how irrelevant she thought math was. This led into a conversation about her falling grades, a topic her parents were eager for me to pursue, yet one I believed was less of a core issue and more of a symptom of her depression.

"Sam, you know your parents are pretty upset about your grades."

"Yeah." Her voice was flat.

"They're probably worried about your future. And what kind of college you'll go to and what kind of job you'll get and what kind of future you'll have." I made a joke out of it, exaggerating in order to bridge the gap between them and Sam, placing me somewhere in the middle or preferably nearer to her.

"They're really on me about that stuff. I wish they'd just go back to their golf games and bridge club meetings. It's my life."

"Maybe you could compromise. Tell them you'll work on your grades, but they have to get off your case."

She uncrossed her legs and set them on the floor askew. Her hair fell down across her eyes. "I'm just not, like, into school."

"It's probably too easy for you."

Her head jerked in surprise. Then she replaced her reaction with a bored expression. "Yeah, maybe."

"I understand how you feel about math, but why don't you talk with your parents? If you prefer, you can have them attend a session or part of one—"

"No. I don't want them here."

This indicated she was establishing a therapeutic connection with me and assumed I was with her rather than aligning with her parents. A small but significant step. We spoke until our session was over. I reminded her to bring her writing at the next visit.

I had an hour before my next appointment. After locking the exterior door, I went around the corner to Nassau Street. The sidewalk was crowded, townspeople mixing with gowns-people and the ubiquitous tourists who were unperturbed by paying premium prices. I walked inside the building's front entrance and unlocked my post box. As usual, there was little mail except for some flyers and one bill for my office's telephone service. Personal mail from my previous address was being forwarded to my parents' house.

I bought a coffee at a nearby deli, returned upstairs, switched on the phone's ringer, and found a message from George Durst, saying he couldn't make his appointment because of an accident at work. The last-minute cancellation was inconvenient, but I assumed it was unavoidable. I drank my coffee, worked for half an hour, replaced the files in the cabinet, and was leaving when the phone rang. I set down my briefcase.

"Hello. This is Dr. Ellen Haskell." No response, only breathing. "May I help you?" Click. Was this a potential client vacillating about asking for a session?

After I left the office, I bought a salmon fillet at the fish store and a baguette and some fresh salad greens next door. On my way home through the rolling hills of Hopewell Valley, the setting sun glistened on millions of raindrops hanging from the branches of black trees.

Your smile lights up my heart. At first, I wasn't sure of you, what the messages you were sending me meant. Now I know. Every night, before I sleep, as you command, I'll put one raindrop on my tongue and another on my forehead so that you may bless me and make me pure. It better rain again soon.

I began to read The Loner's Crusade. *You understand me so well. No one has ever understood me before.*

I hope it will always be just the two of us. Maybe that's why you've chosen me. So we will never be alone again?

You shine like the sun while I must remain in the shadows, waiting.

As I drove to Hopewell, I thought about my parents. In August, they had given in to their usual restlessness and leased an apartment on Corfu. The location was a geographic compromise between the two countries that fascinated them, Greece and Italy: the island was Greek but the Venetian influence was significant.

My father had officially terminated his regular teaching schedule several years ago, but he could still be enticed to deliver a lecture, write a symposium article, or serve as a consultant for the department, particularly concerning excavations, which have claimed his fascination for decades. His digging days were done, much to his regret, because his knees had succumbed to arthritis after years of kneeling in the dust of ancient civilizations. Although somewhat slowed, he liked nothing more than to pack a suitcase and head for the airport, as did my mother, an art historian who specialized in Italian Renaissance painters. Over her career, she had made many lengthy sojourns to Europe and preferred poring over a new tome on Titian instead of attending to the house, my father, or, when I was a child, to me. Sometimes, when I was younger, I accompanied my mother or father on their travels, but mostly I spent hours on my own at home, trying to understand who I was and why my life felt so different from others my age. This pursuit of self-analysis made psychology a logical professional choice.

After my undergraduate studies at Cornell University, I completed my master's degree and Ph.D. there, then did a three-year internship. As I was beginning my practice, I did what most clinical psychologists do: find an older, more experienced therapist as a guide through the treacherous process of understanding my demons, blind spots, and shortcomings. This began several years with Dr. Adrienne Barrow, a caring woman in her early fifties, who greatly improved my interpersonal skills, sensitivity, and also assisted me through several low periods. Whenever I circled over another one of those quicksand moods, the skills learned during therapy improved my ability to avoid the morass, though not entirely.

Without my parents' cheerful presence these last weeks, the house felt solitary, yet it was a pleasure to return there after a day of sessions and experience the quiet repose of the forest that shimmered with maples, pin oaks, and silver beech trees. Below the house—a cedar and glass construction—was the curving Stoney Brook. The stream had many personalities. Shy and parched in times of drought, it could swell mightily during winter snows or spring melt, enlarging its boundaries and treacherously stealing earth from the saplings that struggled to grow along its edges. Huddled on the banks were numerous gray boulders that resembled a herd of slumbering hippopotamuses.

I stopped on the road for the mail, drove the car down the driveway, opened the free-standing garage, parked, and entered the three-story house. The first level was an above-ground basement. I climbed the interior staircase to the main floor, which featured a great room with a cathedral ceiling and a stone fireplace. Prow windows brightened the area and flowed onto an extensive deck accessible from two sliders or, from the outside, by steps ascending from a walkway near the front door. Opposite the great room was a dining table, pass-through, and modest kitchen; behind it was a library containing glass cabinets crammed with treasures found on digs as well as bookcases stacked with publications and research materials. My parents' desks faced each other and were laden with clippings, notes, and articles. Beyond the library, down a short hall, was a bathroom and two bedrooms.

The third story filled the back section of the house and was accessed by stairs and fronted by a short balcony overlooking the living room. To the left was a bath and to the right was my parents' loft bedroom, where I had been sleeping since their departure—they told me to use it because it was more spacious than the second-floor bedrooms.

After shedding my coat, I felt the house's welcoming presence and smiled. I poured a glass of red wine and imagined Greta doing the same. Musing at my hypocrisy—do as I say, not as I do—I kicked off my shoes, sat on the couch, and looked at the mail. Mostly bills and catalogues, though not the monthly phone bill, which should have arrived days ago. My father kept a ledger to record household expenses, and the water, electric, and phone bills were always paid at the same time. If I didn't receive it soon, I'd report the bill missing. At the bottom of the pile was an airmail letter from my parents. I rushed to open it.

The envelope contained a single page from my father, in his meticulous hand, and a three-page letter from my mother, in her more generous script. Both were waxing euphoric on the beauty of Corfu, how they were eating a variety of fish, sampling local wines, and taking long walks. My father was excited about their plans to rent a car and drive to Paleokastritsa on the western side of the island, where the eighteenth-century Monastery Panagia Theotokos was located. He quipped that Myra would have to forgo her shorts in favor of more demure attire. My mother, as if in response to his comments, said that while he was examining the monastery's "Story of Creation," she might opt for a swim at the beach. They both sounded in fine spirits and mentioned a Canadian couple they had befriended.

I returned the letters to the envelope and went into the kitchen to design a Caesar salad, one with anchovies and plenty of Parmesan cheese. I broiled the salmon fillet and poured another glass of wine, and because the house was damp and I hadn't turned on the heat, I made a fire. When dinner was ready, I sat at the table with my glass and plate and watched television. From the news, I migrated to a movie, and at eleven, I climbed the stairs to the loft, changed into pajamas, slipped under the comforter, and fell asleep.

—

I awoke feeling stuffy from the wine and annoyed when I saw that it was 2:35 a.m. After a visit to the bathroom, I resettled into bed. A few minutes later, for some reason, I opened my eyes. On the balcony outside the door, a strange light was forming. At first, I thought it was an odd trick of moonlight but then realized there was no moon, nor was it a light from the street because the house was too far from the road.

I sat up, trying to decide whether to investigate or to give into my tiredness. As I hesitated, the light congealed into a white, wispy, vertical figure. With a start, I realized I was looking at an eerie semblance of my mother, a milky translucence hovering in the open air above the living room, as if the ghost—for that's what I thought it was—couldn't make up her mind whether to come in.

The manifestation seemed benign, but because I identified it as my mother, I was frightened about what her presence meant. I stared while she approached the foot of the bed. A noticeable coolness accompanied her.

"Mother? Is that you?"

The apparition moved across the room, paused, and slowly dissipated. I stood and went to the spot where it had last been and noticed the faint smell of cigarette smoke. This struck me as peculiar because my mother had given up cigarettes a year before my parents built the house. It hadn't been an easy addiction to break, and to the present, she often sighed and said she craved a cigarette. Because my mother's temptation was so strong, however, she couldn't tolerate anyone smoking inside, but now, quite distinctly, the scent was in the bedroom. I rose and walked onto the balcony. The acrid smell was obvious there but not on the staircase or at the bottom. I walked through the living room, searching for anything amiss and found nothing disturbed. After a few minutes, I returned to bed, shivering with apprehension. Had it really been my mother's ghost? If so, why and how had she appeared? For an hour, I waited, silently imploring my mother to communicate with me again, but she never did.

—

I had scheduled a free Thursday after my busy week, a relief because I was exhausted and frazzled by my agitated night. Downstairs, I poured a glass of orange juice and a mug of coffee. On a plate, I set three slices of buttered baguette and brought everything to the table. As I ate breakfast, I glanced over the woods and stream, noting the thousands of colored leaves flying from their summer homes, and felt an omnipresent anxiousness, as if a predicted storm was on the horizon and I had no way to avoid the coming disaster. When the phone rang, I knew the call was the one I was anticipating. Mechanically, I walked over, lifted the handset, and said "hello."

In carefully constructed English sentences, a man introduced himself as the captain of the police department in Kerkyra and then corrected that to Corfu Town. He told me my parents had been in a car accident, and my father was in the hospital with a concussion and a broken foot.

"And my mother?" I asked him, already sure of his response.

"Miss Haskell, I regret that your mother did not fare well," he replied, pausing. "She went through the windscreen and broke her neck. She died immediately. I am very sorry to give you this sad news."

I collapsed on the couch, clutching the cordless phone, my

thoughts spinning. The air seemed incredibly dense.

"Miss Haskell, are you there?" the policeman asked.

"Yes, I'm sorry," I replied, unable to remember his name. "Is it possible for me to speak with my father?"

"Soon, Miss Haskell. He is in surgery for his foot. When your father is awake, he will call you." He described the circumstances of the accident and provided his name and number as well as those of the hospital, which I wrote on a pad of paper.

After turning off the phone, I sank against the sofa cushions, suspended in the frozen ether of shock. I had no idea how long I sat there, but then, as if some switch had been flipped, tears started falling furiously down my cheeks and words came out of my mouth, though they seemed to come from someone else. The warm sunlight, flooding through the prow windows, fell on my face, but its warmth went unappreciated.

Sometime later, the phone rang again. I answered it.

The voice on the other end was weak. "Ellen?"

"Yes? Dad?"

"Hi." He was quiet for a moment, then asked," Did the police call and tell you what happened?"

"Yes, they did."

"Your mother...I am so sorry...so sorry," he said in a choked voice. "This is all my fault! If I hadn't rented that damned car!" He paused to catch his breath. "I didn't have a decent map—we were just trying to get to the other side of the island. Somehow I must have made a wrong turn, and when Myra told me to continue on the main road, I didn't." My father coughed and let out a labored sigh. "We started out fine and then the road became really steep and the pavement was full of ruts with a lot of loose gravel. Myra wanted me to turn around, but like a pig-headed fool I kept telling her we were close to the top and the road had to get better. Next thing I knew, the front tire blew, and I lost control of the steering."

43

His voice trembled with emotion. "It all happened so fast, Ellen. The car slid and flipped over twice. I banged my head on the steering wheel, the door buckled into my foot and broke my ankle." He inhaled with effort. "Sorry, Ellen, my breathing isn't so good." He was silent for a moment before continuing. "Your mother—you know how she never wears a seatbelt—well, she crashed through the windshield and fell down the cliff. I was knocked unconscious for a while and then managed to get out of the car. There was all kinds of glass everywhere, but I crawled to Myra, who was lying next to some olive trees."

For some reason, my father described these trees in great detail, their silvery green leaves and dark twisted trunks. I asked more about his condition and learned that his foot was in a cast up to his knee, his face and hands were bandaged where shards of glass had cut him, his ribs were bruised, and he had a headache from the concussion. Although he didn't complain, he was obviously exhausted; the drug, trauma, and sorrow sapping his energy. Suddenly, he began crying. I'd never heard him do this before.

I offered to fly to Corfu, but despite his distraught state, my father was firm that I shouldn't make the trip. I told him I would call the next day, and he agreed we would discuss arrangements at that point. He ended the conversation, saying he was tired. Next, I phoned the hospital and spoke with one of his doctors, who reassured me that my father would be fine and was in no danger from his injuries. I provided my house and office telephone numbers and thanked him.

After ending the call, a sharp photographic image of the accident came to me. I could picture the overturned car on the hill, my father beside it, the glinting shards of glass, the olive trees, and the blue sky. Everything was clear, but my mother was absent.

Slowly, I broke through my shock long enough to consider practical matters. I had bunched my clients to allow for a four-day weekend, which was my plan until I had too many sessions to book. Because today through Sunday was unscheduled, I had time to pull myself together. After that, depending on how I felt, I could cancel appointments if necessary, though I didn't have much to do because there was no immediate funeral to organize. In some ways, the usual arrangements necessary after a death would have been helpful, a kind of anesthesia of busyness.

I stood and threw the half-eaten toast in the garbage, poured the remains of the cold coffee down the sink, and wandered around, crying and talking to the room. Finally, I took myself in hand and found my parents' address book and began the unpleasant task of relating the news. Several of their Princeton friends asked me to dinner, but I thanked them and refused.

After notifying my parents' attorney, I sat on the couch, held a large pillow to my chest, and stared blankly at the mesmerizing leaves. Tears welled up in my eyes as the horror of my mother's death struck again. Sometime later, I fixed a bowl of soup; for dinner, I heated some two-day-old leftovers. Eventually, night blackened the house except for the light above the kitchen stove. I thought about watching television or listening to music, but like the nullifying effect of darkness, silence suited my fragility. Shortly after ten, I headed upstairs. As I stepped onto the balcony, the smell of cigarette smoke emanated out of nowhere, disappearing as I went into the room. I stopped and retraced my steps, wild with hope that the smoke was a harbinger of my mother's return, her ghost's return, but it wasn't.

I changed, climbed into bed, and remembered my mother's story about seeing her father's ghost after his death, hovering over the casket in their parlor. Though she never espoused a theory, I knew she believed in an afterlife. I was agnostic on the subject, but we shared a kind of mental telepathy that often astonished me. Almost every time she called on the telephone, I was sure it was her, and if I called my mother and the phone was busy, she would phone back, sensing I was trying to contact her. While I didn't regard either one of us as psychically gifted, I gave credence to the possibility that some form of communication might exist. As a psychologist, I understood the wish many people had to contact beloved people who had died, a desire that could abrogate someone's ability to be rational, thus creating a ripe atmosphere for seers who described heaven, hosts of white-winged angels, and a beautiful light flooding the passageway for the soul as it departed the body. Even though my parents and I didn't harbor any religious beliefs and didn't attend church, I had always kept an open mind about other realms and states of consciousness. Now, with what I'd witnessed the night before, I felt positive the apparition had been my mother, stopping on her ethereal journey.

[THE JOURNAL]

My thoughts are always with you and know yours are always with me, even when those crazy people sit on your couch and waste your time.

I read more of your book. Although we hadn't met when you wrote it, you have magical powers and must have known me somehow. It was thoughtful of you to alter my name to protect my identity so no one will know about us—at least not yet. That time will come.

When I was very young, I wasn't like other children. I had to do chores so my hands were always dirty. Dirty Hands! That's what my mother called me. How I hated that!

It's easy to get carried away writing to you because you understand everything. It's time for the raindrops. See, I haven't forgotten. I never forget you—ever.

I SPENT Friday morning at my mother's desk examining her scrapbooks, photographs, and correspondence, including a number of letters from me written during college and shortly after. These I read with trepidation because a few contained critical remarks that I'd tossed her way like so many tiny, destructive, hand grenades. During my years in therapy with Adrienne, I dealt with a number of issues that involved disagreements with my mother such as about my choice of a career, one she worried might place me in contact with unstable people. Unfortunately, at the time, I didn't possess the skill to communicate my feelings with sensitivity and now found these attacks very painful to re-visit. It was additionally distressing that she had kept the letters instead of throwing them away. My inclination was to destroy them, but they were part of our history, a sad reminder of how unkind two people could be, for though she had never written me in the same vein, she had spewed some barbs that had been tough to forget. Nevertheless, my mother—and my father—had always been consistent supporters, the people I depended upon most. After I finished reading the letters, I moved them into my suitcase so my father wouldn't come across them.

As I browsed through correspondence from her friends, I came to appreciate the role she played in their lives. Perhaps because of the essential narcissism in the child/parent relationship, it's difficult for the parent to see the child as a separate entity and the child to see the parent as a person apart. Perusing these letters and poring over her college yearbooks, I formulated a view of my mother as a distinct self with her own unique attributes, a successful social and professional life, and some artistic talent that was never fully realized.

A little before eleven, I phoned the hospital and received an update from the nurse on duty. My father was doing well, was still on morphine, and was reporting that his headache had lessened.

She transferred my call, and he answered, sounding sleepy. As we spoke, he gathered clarity and thanked me for contacting his attorney and other relations and friends. After a bit, he returned to the accident, as if its magnetism was a constant pull. He described the olive trees again—they seemed to be imbued with symbolic value. I let him talk, thinking it was better for him to remember the trees rather than my mother lying bloody and twisted at their feet. He told me he had stayed with her body for almost two hours before a boy from a local village had come upon the accident and run for assistance. My father didn't relate anything about this period, which must have been extremely painful for him physically and emotionally, nor did I ask him about it. I would wait until he was ready, though knowing his innate reticence, that day might never arrive.

We spoke about how he was being treated and about the kind help he had received from the Maillarts, the Canadian couple with whom my parents had been spending time before the accident. Jacques Maillart owned a jewelry shop near the Liston, an arcade built by the French. He and his wife, Catherine, had lived in Corfu for nine years. They had negotiated the return of the damaged rental car and had ensured that my father had been seen by the best specialists on the island.

I was uncomfortable questioning my father about funerals or other arrangements. Finally, to my relief, he suggested it might be best to cremate my mother's body there rather than deal with transporting a coffin, particularly since he wouldn't be able to travel for some time because of his condition. I agreed with this proposal, remembering that my mother once said she preferred cremation. He promised to bring the ashes home and asked me to write an obituary for the newspapers.

With this part of the conversation over, he seemed to lose energy. Again, I offered to come to Corfu, but again my father refused, saying there was little to be done. I suspected he wanted to deal with his grief in private. I could sympathize with that. In many ways, we were alike, both reserved. I promised to phone him on the following day and hung up. Then I checked my office answering machine. No one had left a message, although there were calls in which breathing had been recorded. It was strange that someone kept losing nerve before leaving a name and number.

I decided to take a walk and slipped on a green suede jacket. Exiting through the sliding glass door, I stepped onto the cedar deck and descended the leaf-slick stairs. The air was pleasantly cool, colder near the stream. Although the summer had been dry and hot and had done its best to evaporate Stoney Brook, the stream had been nourished by some heavy September rains and was moving briskly, with brilliant white highlights winking in the swirling water. Along the banks, sections of the loamy topsoil were eroded, exposing the clay underneath, which colored rocks and tree roots a sickly olive-brown.

I sat on a bench by the bank and stretched my legs. The seat had been a Christmas present I'd given my mother. At my request, the woodworker had carved "Peace and Silence" in flowing letters across the back. I knew my mother came here often, sometimes carrying a book or a mug of hot tea. It was impossible to think she would never sit on this bench again, never tuck up her feet and let the sun shine on her face. Above my head, I noticed she had pruned several branches so the light could beam down unimpeded. I smiled at her desire to make this spot perfect.

As much as I tried, I couldn't fathom the final reality of her death. I wanted to pick up an astral phone and speak to my mother. Yet, if I hadn't been deceived by a quirk of light, she had materialized in front of me soon after her death.

Frustrated by my inability to contact her, I kicked some leaves.

As I did, I noticed an empty brown candy wrapper. A Heath Bar, with goldish-yellow type. What was it doing here? I didn't like toffee and neither did my parents. The bench was too distant from the street for the wrapper to have been carried by the wind, and no one would trespass on the property, especially this close to the house. I shook my head and placed the wrapper in my pocket.

—

Sometime during the afternoon, the phone rang. I was surprised to hear Nick Ianni, my cousin Katie's husband, on the line. He expressed his condolences, saying my uncle in California had passed word about my mother's accident, and then invited me to dinner either tomorrow or Sunday. Nick explained that his wife and their children were visiting friends, and he was on his own over the weekend. Something about this set off an alarm, perhaps because Nick had overstepped the bounds of family relations on two occasions when Nick and my cousin were newlyweds. Recently, no issues had arisen, but there had been no opportunities. Nick and Katie lived near Freehold in a pseudo-mansion much like the house of my client, Robert Fleet. Nick was a successful sales executive for a company with multiple car dealerships throughout the state, rising fast despite a troubled upbringing and receiving only a high school education.

Trying to stall him, I said I wasn't up for a long drive. He then offered to meet in Princeton, at the Alchemist & Barrister, a friendly restaurant that featured a pub bar as well as more formal rooms. I hesitated, feeling I was too emotionally uneven to be around people. Bouts of tears had come and gone all day, interspersed with a deep, dragging sadness. I told him no, but Nick wasn't to be deterred and sounded concerned, suggesting some company might take my mind off my sorrow. I thought about the empty house, the nearly empty refrigerator, and reluctantly accep-

51

ted for Sunday evening on the understanding I might leave if I became upset. We agreed to meet at seven, at the restaurant. As soon as I hung up the receiver, I felt an overwhelming urge to cancel, but I couldn't muster the energy to find his phone number.

The solitary afternoon and evening loomed ahead. Since I had already spoken with my mother's financial advisor, I turned my attention to tasks such as canceling her magazines and memberships. After finishing, I strolled to the end of the driveway to get the mail. The late afternoon sun sent long shafts of gold light through the forest, illuminating motes of dust and intensifying the leaves' autumnal colors.

To my surprise, the phone bill wasn't there. I shrugged, gathered the letters, and returned to the house, made coffee, and tried to listen to a CD of one of my mother's favorite singers, but the music made me sad so I turned it off. The sudden silence felt surreal. As if to ground myself, I touched the mahogany table, following its tight reddish-brown grain with my finger. Then I glanced around the room at mementos of her travels, some from trips alone and some with my father: a rectangular brass tray from Egypt, etched with rows of ancient pictographs, served as a table between two armchairs; a tall silver pitcher with matching cups resided on an old rosewood chest in the corner; and worn Oriental carpets lay in haphazard rectangles here and in other rooms, with little concern for color harmony. The place looked lived-in, loved, and comfortable. It also seemed intensely quiet, as if my presence made no impression.

I was grateful no one had called—here or at the office. If it hadn't been for my father, I would've taken the phone off the hook. Sometime after dark, I dumped some canned tuna fish into some pasta and turned on the television.

—

I ran several errands on Saturday. Cleaned and vacuumed the house and cried in between. That night, I saw a rented video of *Prince of Tides* with Nick Nolte and Barbra Streisand—a decent movie that made me forget my situation for a while. On Sunday morning, after breakfast and still in my bathrobe, I walked to the street for the *New York Times*. As I leaned over for the newspaper, I noticed a dark blue car parked on an adjacent road, which was odd because of the early hour and the fact that there wasn't a house near it. I was tempted to check in case someone needed help but felt silly wandering around in my pajamas and robe.

Inside, I read the paper and then called my father. He sounded alert and explained he would be released the next day. The Maillarts had offered a ground-floor room in their house while he recovered. He said he would be on crutches for some time and was still adamant that I should stay home. I mused upon the kindness of strangers and was happy that his friends were being helpful.

Lunch was a bowl of chili, which bit the lining of my stomach. I chewed an antacid and soldiered on, doing two loads of laundry and some ironing. I then watered my mother's tumultuous array of plants, which were suffering serious thirst from my neglect, and sat down to work on her obituary. This took more time than I expected, and before I knew it, I needed to dress for my dinner with Nick, though I was skeptical about the wisdom of going. Nevertheless, I went upstairs and slipped on Black Watch plaid wool pants and a black blazer and turtleneck. After dressing, I brushed my hair, fastening it with a tortoiseshell barrette, and added eyeliner, shadow, blush, and a salmon-hued lipstick. With my trench coat in hand, I went outside to the garage. I was using my mother's silver Audi Quattro sedan whose leather seats were beginning to crack but was otherwise in fine shape—my father's car was on loan to an impoverished graduate student who was doing research for him in return.

After dropping off the video, I drove to Princeton through the broad valley, which was darkening as the sky cooled to a dusty lavender. I kept alert for bands of roving deer until I reached the outskirts of town. On Witherspoon Street, I turned into the public lot and parked my car in my designated place by my office. It was a short walk to the restaurant.

Nick Ianni was standing in the alleyway near the pub entrance, examining a container of russet and yellow mums in an adjacent flower shop window. He hurried to give me a hug and a kiss. Nick was tall, over six feet, handsome, dark-haired, and in fine physical condition from playing basketball, his twice-weekly addiction. He was impeccably dressed in a starched white shirt, cherry-red cashmere sweater, navy wool trousers, and shined shoes. After he opened the door to the pub, we were shown to a tiny table, a tight fit, but it was set in the corner where the noise from the bar—now at a surprising roar for a Sunday night—would keep our conversation private. The room was paneled in dark brown wood and was filling with cigarette smoke and a second tier of standees at the bar, who were leaning in to place drinks' orders. When the waiter came, I asked for a glass of white wine, and Nick ordered a double Jack Daniel's.

Nick reiterated his condolences and then inquired about the accident and how my father was doing. I told him the details, keeping my account as neutral as possible because it wouldn't take much to start tears rolling, and I wanted to spare Nick and myself a scene. As soon as I could, I turned the conversation to him, asking after his wife and children. He was a proud father and his descriptions of his children's accomplishments continued until the waiter arrived to recite the specials. We both opted for the Irish lamb stew, and Nick chose a bottle of Beaujolais, which was brought before we had finished our drinks. Nick tossed off his Jack Daniel's, while I drank my white wine so the waiter could pour the red. As I held the glass, Nick asked how I'd hurt my hand.

"An accident."

"Why didn't you have some kind of cosmetic surgery or something? You're so pretty. It's a shame to have—"

"It's fine, Nick." I placed my hand in my lap.

He tucked in his chin. "Okay…whatever…"

I was relieved when the lamb stew arrived and conversation became sporadic. However, halfway through our meal and the bottle of Beaujolais, I noticed Nick was observing me closely. I asked what he was thinking. He took a swallow of wine and began.

"Ellen, perhaps this isn't the time to bring this up, but whatever happened to that guy you were dating. I don't remember his name."

I didn't want to discuss my private relationships. "His name was Drew."

"Yeah, that's right. Drew. I kind of liked him."

"He kind of liked you," I replied.

"So are you still together?"

"No."

"Really? Why?"

I sighed, slightly annoyed by Nick's curiosity. "Well, after two years, Drew realized he was gay."

His eyes widened. "Gay? Really? I couldn't tell."

"He's a great guy," I replied, avoiding Nick's prejudiced remark. "We had a lot in common."

Nick's expression turned into a frown, as if he were imagining Drew and speculating about telltale signs of gayness he'd overlooked. "Funny, he didn't come on to me or anything."

"Why would he?" I felt protective of Drew, sensitive to signs of homophobia.

Nick shrugged and took a bite of lamb. "So, did he just tell you one night or did you find out? Oh, my god, he didn't have AIDS, did he?"

I shook my head. "No, he didn't. I became aware of his orientation shortly before we ended things. Drew really wanted to be heterosexual, to have a wife, and to appease his parents, who weren't very liberal. When I first brought up the subject, he denied any interest in men, but later he admitted he hadn't been truthful. I encouraged him to discuss how he felt and supported him in his choice. We're still friends."

"That must have been hard."

I wasn't sure where he was going with this. "Hard?"

"Well, knowing he wasn't satisfied with the sex you had with him."

My face stiffened. "I didn't look at it that way. I was glad for him. Drew was much happier afterward."

"That's very understanding," Nick poured himself another glass of wine. "So have you been seeing anyone since?"

"Recently?" I thought about Lucas. "No."

"Someone after Drew?"

I was wondering why he was stuck on this and realized his smile had become lacquered with charm. Alcohol and candlelight glazed his eyes. "I dated a few people in the city," I explained. "Since then, I've been occupied by making the move from Manhattan, establishing my new office here, and working on another book." I hoped one of these activities would catch his interest, but Nick was fastened on my social life for reasons that were beginning to worry me.

"It's great you're doing so well with your practice, but it seems like a lonely life. I mean, living in the house by yourself."

"I don't mind, Nick. I'll make friends."

He hung his head for a second and tried a sheepish look that came across as practiced. "You know, Ellie, my wife and I have been having some problems..."

"I'm sorry." I disliked being called "Ellie."

"Yeah, she's been away a lot. All I do is work long hours and play a little basketball. It's boring being alone." He studied his half-empty glass and generously re-filled it. "I guess you and I are both flying solo." A lop-sided, rueful grin accompanied this admission. "It's tough kicking around at home with no one to eat dinner with, no one to wake up next to."

This was heading in a predictable fashion. Under normal circumstances, I was adept at parrying this kind of manipulation. Tonight, with my emotions so close to the surface, his sexual innuendoes felt insensitive, if not offensive.

"Nick, I regret things aren't going well for you," I said. "I hope you and Katie work everything out." I wiped my mouth with the corner of my napkin, making deliberate eye contact with him. "And I apologize if this is an incorrect assumption, but it sounds like you're coming on to me. If you are, this isn't appropriate. You need to talk with your wife and resolve the differences between you and decide what your future together will be." By transforming the conversation into a more professional mode, I hoped to insert some space between us.

He leaned forward and tried another smile. "I agree, but damn, I've always liked you, Ellie. You know that."

"I like you, too, Nick, but not in that way."

His seductive smile disappeared. "So you're going to tell me that you're like your pansy friend Drew? Gay or something?"

I gave him a sharp glance. "I don't appreciate your bigoted remark about Drew, nor is my personal life any of your business." I felt like adding that his heterosexual affairs were hardly admirable and making a few other comments, but I didn't want to start an argument. I reached into my pocketbook, pulled out two twenties and a ten, and placed the bills and my napkin on the table. "Nick, thank you for the invitation, which I'm sure was kindly intended, but perhaps it wasn't a good idea for me to have dinner tonight." I stood up. "Please give my love to Katie and the children."

I made it out the door before I fell apart. As I walked to my car, tears began coursing down my face. When I shut the Audi's door, I was sobbing, upset about my mother and infuriated with myself for going out before I was ready and with a man I didn't really like. I was also irritated for misreading Nick's invitation and with him for trying to take advantage of my emotional frailty.

The drive home went by in a blur. I parked the car in the garage and unlocked the front door, feeling unnerved by the dark house. Upstairs, I resisted the irrational urge to search all the rooms and closets, though I had the curious feeling of not being alone. I considered pouring myself another glass of wine, but the effect so far had been depressive. I didn't want to feel worse.

I called to check the messages on my office answering machine. Quiet breathing and two hang-ups. Who the hell was doing this? Muttering to myself, I climbed upstairs, and as I did, I smelled smoke again. Must be my imagination or more likely the odor from the restaurant on my clothes.

I threw my slacks over a chair, grabbed my nightgown, and went to bed.

[THE JOURNAL]

I can hear your voice if I listen hard, but I wish you would give me a clear sign about what to do. I'm waiting, ready, though I understand it's necessary to be patient because you know what's best. I tell myself this over and over.

I've only had one serious romantic relationship before but that wasn't really love. Not like I love you and you love me. You are so wise. You have it all figured out and will explain everything soon.

ON MONDAY, I faxed my mother's obituary to the funeral home after explaining the situation and giving details to them on the phone. They promised to send the notice to the area newspapers and provide estimated costs for different types of memorial services. Then I called Corfu and learned my father had checked out of the hospital. Because I didn't have the Maillarts' number, I hoped he would telephone. Nevertheless, I felt worried and had to fight the impulse to book a flight to Greece.

My poor judgment about seeing Nick was still bothering me. I'd failed to listen to my inner voice, and although I counseled myself not to be self-critical under the circumstances, one of my mantras warranted repeating: psychologists aren't emotionally infallible. In fact, at the moment, I felt acutely unsteady and buffeted by human frailty. Looking around the living room, it seemed that even the house had changed, had lost its joy and lightness just as I had. The last thing I wanted to do was to drive into town, go to the library, and hold sessions, but I needed to make headway on my research, and consistency in my practice was essential, especially with clients in the early stages of counseling. Besides, staying home and watching the rain slide down the trees wasn't an attractive alternative.

Through my father's influence, I had received a special pass to use Firestone Library on campus, a fine resource to have at my disposal. An hour later, I walked through its doors to the periodical section, where I began reading recent articles in psychology journals, a task I assigned myself once a month. After copying several pieces relevant to my research on creativity, I followed the professorial stream to The Annex, an old restaurant that had witnessed decades of poor geniuses and hungry students. For the most part, the food was Italian, inexpensive, and resolutely untrendy. I ordered salad, lasagna, and a glass of iced tea, all of which were accompanied by slices of Italian bread in a plastic basket. I doubted the menu or the presentation had ever been altered.

—

George Durst was my first client of the afternoon. During our initial meeting, he had reported feeling dissatisfied with his life and wanted help to change it. Although he had canceled last week's session because of an accident, I heard him trudging upstairs promptly at two o'clock. Though he wasn't tall, George was built like a boxer, with a stocky body and thick legs. For the last year, he had been employed by the university as a maintenance worker and had previously worked at a plant near Trenton. George made an effort to change into clean work clothes before coming and to scour his hands and face, but the grease and oil were worked deeply into his skin and cuticles, beyond the reach of soap. His hair was jet black and curly, cropped close. Something about him made me uneasy, though he had always been polite.

George lowered himself onto my couch, gave me a shy smile, and waved a bandaged wrist in the air. "Cut myself on some steel."

"I bet that hurt. I hope not too much."

"No, a few stitches is all. It's rough work, what I do. Got to expect these kinds of thing now and then."

"Are you back on the job?"

"Yeah. I had the rest of Thursday off and Friday. Gave me a chance to pay some bills, do the laundry, send letters."

"Who did you write?"

"My mother. She's in Berlin for several months. On a retreat."

"Are you considering a trip to see her?"

He shook his head. "She's with a women's group led by several nuns. Anyhow, I can't take a vacation, what with winter coming and the heat starting up. Lots of maintenance problems to deal with. Besides, I may have a reason to stay around."

"Oh? What's that?" I asked.

George's face colored. "Well, as you know, I haven't been married. Had to take care of Mom—she was ill for many years. Didn't have time for making friends or dating, so I never found the right girl."

"And you think maybe you've met the right girl now?"

He nodded. "Maybe. She seems to like me."

"And you like her?"

George nodded again. "Oh, yeah. I do."

"Have you been out on a date?"

"No, not yet. Haven't asked her, though maybe I might soon. I want to be sure she'll say yes."

"Well, don't wait too long. Give it a try."

He gave me a shy smile and then began describing the landscaping business he was starting—a first step in his improvement plan. Though I was sure he was a hard worker, I was less sure that he could handle the accounting side of such an endeavor. George was a hands-on man—probably could fix anything set in front of him—but as for paperwork and keeping records, I was less sanguine about his aptitude for detail. However, he surprised me.

"Yeah, I know it's a lot with a full-time job," he said, "but I have a file box for my receipts and got myself a ledger. I divided it up like my friend Ben told me to—he does the accounting for a company in Lawrence. I even bought a mileage book."

"Good for you, George. I'm impressed you're being so careful."

He looked happy. "'Slow and sure' is what my mother always tells me."

George explained what he was doing for his new clients after work and on weekends—mostly preparing lawns for winter and trimming tree branches. I let him speak for a few minutes because he was so enthusiastic. Then he reverted to the earlier topic, and his expression darkened when he mentioned a man who might be interested in the girl he wanted to ask out. He shook his head and wrung his big, stiff hands together. "Maybe I'm mistaken about him. I just saw her with this guy. It's probably nothing. Never mind."

"Are you sure you don't want to talk about it?"

His body bristled with tension. "No, I don't."

A menacing tone had suddenly crept in—not aimed at me— but at whomever George perceived as his potential rival. I could easily picture his hands around someone's neck, choking them to death. He reminded me of a pit bull—once on the attack, unyielding and deadly. Yet as swiftly as the black mood came upon him, it vanished. His hands relaxed and cupped his knees.

"Nothing to worry about, Ellen. I'll take care of things."

Despite a glimmer of a smile, this sounded like a vague threat. I was struck by the changeable nature of his emotions. Did more serious mental illness lurk behind his introverted demeanor? Before I could consider this, George began discussing his job at the university.

"My boss said he trusted me to hire a new maintenance man. I have to write an ad and show it to him before I place it. I hope this means my boss likes me. I'm not quick, mind you, but I get the work done."

"It's great that your ability is being recognized. He must be a good person to deal with."

"Oh, yeah. Very fair. He even lets me off to do errands. I like being on my own. Being responsible for planning my day."

We ended the session on a positive note, though what remained was the memory of his dark side and the speed with which his demeanor altered. I sat at my desk and scrutinized the self-portrait he had drawn at the first session, a task I usually set before my new clients. His drawing was rough but intricate, featuring a convoluted machine with all kinds of gray pipes and hoses next to him. George had pictured himself wearing his tan work clothes, his body in profile at the right of the paper. In his left hand, the only one visible, was an object that looked like a wrench, but it could have been any kind of implement from a stick to a knife. His head was large on a squat torso, with a face that didn't convey any emotion—the mouth was a straight line as was the single eyebrow. The left eye was a brown dot drawn in the center of another short line. I was struck by the rigidity of his expression and the attempt to make his figure resemble a solid block. In comparison to his portrait, which seemed semi-inanimate, the machine was depicted with flowing shapes and curves. Overall, my impression was that George considered himself unimportant and joyless. It also occurred to me that his pictorial containment might reflect his powerful desire to inhibit his emotions, emotions that he might experience as volatile.

I closed George Durst's folder and slipped it into the hanging file.

—

My next client was a sixty-two-year-old Parisian who had moved to Princeton with her husband fifteen years before when he was hired to teach music history at the university. Though Marguerite Fleury never made any solo commercial recordings, she was a concert pianist of some renown, performing with the New Jersey Symphony, the Philadelphia Orchestra, and at New York City venues. During our first meeting, she explained that her husband, Louis, refused to let her accept offers in Europe or any place that meant an overnight stay away from him. The exception was when he was doing summer lecture tours, in which case she booked performances at festivals near his university gigs. Marguerite was diminutive in size, a bit over five feet tall, but with long hands that she used to mesmerizing effect in conversation, probably much as she did on the keyboard. She was cheerful yet at the moment was teetering between her innate optimism and despondency over the rheumatoid arthritis stiffening her joints, especially her knees—walking up my stairs was a trial—and, of more concern, her fingers. It was sad to see such a joyous woman succumb to the painful realization that her career was winding down.

Louis was not providing much support and seemed ambivalent about his wife's career. He wanted her home and continued to restrict her schedule, thus stymying her opportunities, yet he also understood how much pleasure she received from performing and had been attracted to Marguerite because of her talent. Though she hadn't expressed much resentment about Louis up to now, I was waiting for her to explode. I liked the woman a great deal and found her charming, resilient, and admirable.

We began the session with a discussion of the medical treatment she was receiving and what the prognosis was for her condition. Already, Marguerite explained, she could hear a change in her playing, though she admitted it was subtle and would be noticed by only the most discerning critics. As she told me this, tears formed in her eyes.

"How is your husband responding?" I asked.

She shrugged and reached for a tissue. "I don't think he hears the difference."

"How does that make you feel?"

Her hand tossed up some air. "Feel? Eh? It makes me feel terrible! He is busy now, you know, with the students, his book that he writes. He tells me to take aspirin or not to practice so much." She shrugged again in frustration. "Louis does what he wants. I mostly do what Louis wants." Marguerite gave me a shrewd glance. "But now, perhaps I will not do what Louis wants. Perhaps now I will revolt."

"How, Marguerite?"

"I might make a recording. With the Baltimore Symphony. The Maestro has been asking me for years. Perhaps I can do it before things get worse."

I expressed encouragement. "What music would you select? And how long would it take?"

Her eyes brightened and she smiled. "Chopin. My dearest Chopin. The time would depend if it's taped in a studio, with the full orchestra or a smaller ensemble, or if they want to schedule a live concert. I would much prefer the studio, as you can imagine, because mistakes can be re-recorded. I would be afraid to do it live."

"And Louis would object to this?"

"Yes, he would." She gestured as if she were bestowing a curse. "He is so selfish!" Marguerite sighed. "I help him in everything he does. I cook. I shop. I entertain."

"Have you talked with Louis about your RA and what it means?"

"He tells me I'm fine. When he is being nice, he fixes me tea or rubs cream on my hands. But he is so preoccupied. Only if I stopped playing altogether, then maybe Louis might notice. Although that might make him happy. He would have no competition for my attention."

"And how would you feel if—"

"I would die!" she told me with surprising heat. "You understand? I would die. I am a pianist!" she said with pride and a flash of anger.

"When did your husband begin exerting so much control?"

Marguerite looked at me sadly and recounted her first months with Louis in Paris, where he had been a visiting professor. Before their marriage, he would do anything she asked; afterward, he insisted they move to America, his home, and the relationship changed drastically, rendering Marguerite almost powerless. We discussed the situation, and by the end of the session, she had regained her smile, even though I suspected she was still upset.

After she left, I looked at my calendar and hoped my Monday schedule would be filled over the coming weeks because the office's rent and my insurance were hefty expenses. I'd also offered to pay the utilities on the house as a contribution. When my father returned, would I continue to live with him or move to an apartment? Although I wanted privacy, particularly if I began dating again, I might need to prolong my stay until he recovered from his injuries and the loss of my mother.

I drove home and found four no-message calls on the answering machine. What the hell was going on? Was someone trying to reach my mother or father? If so, why didn't the person leave a name? Or had my unknown caller at the office learned my parents' home telephone number? How? It was unlisted. At least he or she didn't know where I lived.

Your father sounds very dignified on the recorded message. His voice makes me feel calm like yours does. I don't know what kind of job he has, but maybe he works at Educational Testing Service or the university or is retired, if he's old enough. I know you are thirty-six, so your parents could be in their late fifties or as old as seventy. I hope they like me, though mostly we'll be by ourselves. I don't want to share you. In fact, I won't.

It's raining! I was worried I would run out of rain. I went to the woods and filled most of my jar using leaves to catch the drops. The wind was blowing your message though I didn't understand it until I sat beside a tree and listened. You say that I must be like the lion that guards the palace in Venice and watch over you. I went to the library and looked at pictures of St. Mark's Square in a book.

I will be there for you always.

ON TUESDAY morning, I met with my parents' attorney, John Strauss, to begin the process of procuring a death certificate from Greece. The Maillarts, ever helpful, had contacted their lawyer on Corfu and asked him to act as go-between with the authorities and Mr. Strauss—my father had provided them with his attorney's phone and fax number. It was fortunate I had been named my mother's executor, because if my father had, matters would have become very complicated.

After seeing Mr. Strauss, I drove to the office amid torrents of rain, noted two incoming calls without messages, pounded my desk, and swore at whoever kept phoning. I could think of no way to prevent this exasperating behavior, so I took a deep breath and ate a sandwich I'd brought from home. Before my first appointment was due, I reviewed his folder.

Lloyd Baskins was a fifty-two-year-old philosophy professor at Princeton, who had been referred by the head of the university's counseling center. Lloyd wanted to consult with someone off campus because he was afraid of being discovered seeing a therapist. After reading my first book and determining I was gay-friendly, Lloyd had called for a session with his lover, Peter, who had abandoned Lloyd, with whom he had lived for nineteen years. Peter, a landscape architect, now resided in a cottage with a young nurseryman who worked for him. Lloyd and Peter were wrangling over ownership of their house; their dog, Bibby; and a host of mutually purchased possessions. Lawyers were involved, and the situation had deteriorated into an acrimonious situation.

On my first day in the office, Peter and Lloyd had arrived together, but it was obvious Peter was no longer invested in Lloyd. His main purpose in agreeing to the sessions was to ease Lloyd's feelings of rejection and thereby facilitate agreement about material items. But with Peter's excitement about his new relationship barely contained, his participation made Lloyd feel worse. After a stormy session, Peter announced he didn't need therapy and bolted from my office. Lloyd continued with individual appointments.

He was a few minutes early so I brought him in. Lloyd was dressed for his teaching duties, though more stylishly than many of his peers. He was wearing a camel-colored jacket, ivory shirt, tan-and-black paisley tie, and a plumed handkerchief in his breast pocket. A heavy gold bracelet peeked from French cuffs. His thinning brown hair was artfully arranged and coifed to maximize what thickness it still possessed, though the battle was turning regardless of his efforts. He had a neat mustache, probably aided, as was his hair, by some darkening assistance from a bottle, for no gray was in evidence. Lloyd was slender, neat-featured, and nervous as a cat, tending to speak in bursts that were offset by measured silences. His humor was wry, alternating between self-deprecation and theatrical pronouncements.

"Good afternoon, dear Ellen."

I smiled. I liked Lloyd. "How are things?"

"Oh, just hunky-dory. You would *not* believe what Himself is up to now!" he said. "He wants to have equal custody rights over Bibby. Can you imagine such a thing? The poor little dear would be so, so confused with such an arrangement! Bibby is already upset as it is."

Lloyd tended to view his dog's feelings as equivalent to those of a human's, as well as habitually transferring his own feelings to Bibby. The dog in question was a prodigiously pedigreed Boston Terrier.

"What does your attorney say?"

Lloyd sighed. "Well, since Bibby was bought by both of us, the lawyer wants to ask for her in trade. Isn't that awful? Or to grant Peter equal time."

"Is Peter able to care for Bibby? Is he home to take her for walks?" I caught myself in the trap of thinking of the dog as if she

70

were a child.

"Heavens, no! I return from work every day before three, and he doesn't get home until after six. When he works late hours during the summer, he says he's going to hire a dog walker. Really! Can you imagine? Some stranger who doesn't know her little habits."

I opted to steer the conversation away from the dog. "How are you doing…being by yourself?"

Lloyd flattened against the couch and crossed his leg neatly at the knee. His well-shod foot twitched. "Oh, all right, I guess."

"Have you seen any friends?"

"I had dinner with William and Malcolm and another couple on Saturday, but it's so hard to go out by oneself, particularly when everyone else is together. You know how that is."

I did know but tried to keep my social life off the table, though Lloyd had inquired last week whether I was a "hetero" or "homo." I had gently veered away from answering.

"I know it's uncomfortable, particularly after so many years together," I said. "Are most of your acquaintances mutual friends, yours, or Peter's?"

Lloyd leaned forward. "Mainly ours. And, of course, it's embarrassing because everyone knows Peter left me."

"Is there any way to meet new people?"

I meant finding new friends but realized Lloyd might interpret my question as a suggestion to find a replacement for Peter. This worried me because Lloyd needed to work through a period of adjustment. Peter had only recently departed their house—according to Peter this action had been taken to alleviate pressure he felt living with Lloyd. According to Lloyd, Peter's paramour had been delighted to nurse Peter through his stress and to have a free place to live, a cottage Peter rented.

"Someone new? Oh, dear. At my age it's not so easy."

"Surely there must be someone in town—"

"Ellen, darling, we *know* all the girls in town!"

"At the university?"

"Some pipe-smoking-type? Oh, my! And one must take care with one's reputation," Lloyd said. "I thought about going to the piano bar in New Hope, but so many of our friends are regulars there. Of course if I met someone, it doesn't have to be an 'I do' kind of thing."

"No, it doesn't. Finding people who share your interests might be a start," I suggested. "Lloyd, perhaps we should talk more about what happened with Peter first?"

"Yes, certainly. I intend to go over all of that with you, dear Ellen, but I'm not a nun, although two years ago at Halloween— my favorite holiday—well..." he gave me an owlish look, "...I wouldn't mind a little companionship."

"What about an advertisement in the paper?" I asked, despite my misgivings about encouraging him to begin a new relationship.

"Pul-lee-ease. A personal ad? My god, everyone would know who placed it. Simply everyone."

"How about running a personal ad in the *Village Voice* or the *New York Review of Books*?"

Lloyd rested his chin on his hand. "Hmm. But what would I say?"

"Would you like to write an ad?" I asked, amazed by the speed of my capitulation. He thought about this and nodded. I handed him a pen and a pad. "GM to start, right? What are you looking for? What interests and traits?"

"A hunky twenty-year-old with a..." Lloyd thought better of the rest.

"Seriously."

He sighed, unhappy to be dissuaded from his fantasy. "Oh, all right. I suppose I'm looking for someone who is twenty-five to thirty years old."

"Maybe forty-five to fifty-five years old?"

Lloyd sighed again. "Well, if you insist. Forty to fifty." He jotted this down.

"Interests?" I prompted.

"Theater, opera, books, lifting weights."

"Lloyd?" I raised an eyebrow.

He wrote the first three. "Okay. How about this? 'Princeton area man seeks charming guy for nights at the theater and a place by the fire.'" He giggled at this. "Must love Boston terriers."

I smiled. "You do have a fireplace, don't you?"

"Oh, is that what you meant?" he replied coyly. "Yes, I have a fabulous fireplace with a very fine Berber rug in front of it."

"Good. Why don't you try the ad and see how it goes?"

He nodded. We discussed Peter for the rest of the session. Lloyd was still in love with him, which led me to wonder if the purpose of the personal ad was to make Peter jealous. At the end, Lloyd remarked that at the next appointment he wanted to learn more about me—where I lived, why I'd moved to Princeton, and—again—whether I liked men or women. I smiled but made no commitment to respond.

—

My two o'clock client was late. Dolly Bordella had approached me after a lecture at Rutgers University and had asked whether I had a private practice. When I opened my Princeton office, she was one of my first sessions.

I heard Dolly came up the stairs at a near run. I waited for her to recover, but she was still breathing heavily when I opened the door. Dolly was thirty-five, slightly above average height, and slender. Her eyes were large and pale blue, her hair long and flaxen and precisely parted in the center. Dolly had married briefly and then, after seeing a performance of Ibsen's *A Doll's House*, had inexplicably walked out on her husband. To her, the decision was as simple as Nora's in the play. Dolly was highly emotional, cried easily, often arrived in disarray with red-rimmed eyes, and manifested mildly paranoid behavior. My preliminary diagnosis was an anxiety disorder, though her symptoms were prolific, including phobic and panic reactions. Something was clearly not right with Dolly.

When she entered the room, she checked the corners and behind the couch as if someone lurked there. Dolly reported fear of bridges, high places, crowds, and a cluster of other things that multiplied at each session. Today, she was wearing a Victorian frock dress printed with a pink floral pattern and edged with a lace collar and cuffs. Although her usual demeanor was one of innocence, sometimes she drew her brows together into a tragic expression. We began by discussing her flight from her marriage, a topic we had touched upon previously.

"Oh. Yes, that," she said, as if she had forgotten all about it. "I went to the play."

"And what about it disturbed you?"

"Everything." Dolly wasn't always prone to fulsome answers.

"Can you be more specific?"

"I just identified with Nora. Like we were the same."

"In what way?"

She checked behind the couch and then clasped her hands together. "Nora was finished with men at the end. I know it."

"Are you finished with men?"

"Oh, yes, I think so."

This kind of mental dental work reminded me of Samantha, though I couldn't imagine two more disparate personalities. "Can you talk more about this?"

"Well, as the book says: women are from Venus and men are from Mars. They don't understand each other."

"That may sometimes be true," I agreed, trying to cajole Dolly into a deeper revelation. "But don't you think some men are capable of understanding women? Of being kind and thoughtful?"

She shook her head emphatically. "No, I don't."

"What about women?"

"Are you asking if I like women? Or am attracted to women?" She furrowed her well-lined forehead.

"Yes, I suppose. As a friend…or perhaps as a sexual partner."

"I don't know. It's possible."

"Which is possible? Have you ever been drawn to a woman?"

Dolly gave that some thought. "Yes. In college. To my roommate."

"Did anything happen?"

"No."

"Did you want something to happen?"

"Maybe." Dolly stared out the window. "She had beautiful hair." She turned and studied me. "Sort of goldish-brown like yours, only it was longer. And dark blue eyes. She was very gentle."

"Was she attracted to you?"

She chuckled and folded her hands together. "Probably not. I was pretty shy."

"Do you regret that nothing occurred?"

"No. I don't think I could've dealt with it then."

"And now? Have you thought about it?"

Dolly shrugged noncommittally. "Hasn't every woman?"

This switch from the specific personal to the general was a device she used in order to give herself maneuvering room.

"I don't know if every woman has thought about it," I replied. "I suppose if they're very honest, they would answer 'yes.'"

"It's strange, when you think about it," Dolly observed, apparently more comfortable with a philosophic conversation. "I mean, there are only two sexes, and yet nature is designed to accommodate all kinds of various combinations."

I smiled at this. "That's very scientific. But it doesn't tell me much about you."

She dipped her head in agreement. "No, it doesn't. I haven't made up my mind."

"Are you telling me that you feel bisexual or perhaps asexual?"

Dolly laughed. "Ah, the labels! I have no idea what I am." She nibbled at the edge of a well-bitten fingernail. "But I might like to be with a woman. Once. Just to see what it's like."

"Have you ever seen a lesbian film or read a gay book?"

"I read *The Well of Loneliness* a year ago."

"A bleak story. Anything else? Can you describe an actress you find interesting?"

"Marlene, of course. When she wore a top hat and tails and kissed the woman. I can't recall the name of the movie."

"*Morocco*," I said. "Anyone else?"

"Garbo in *Queen Christina*. At least in the first part of the movie when she was dressed in men's clothes. She'd been having an affair with one of the women who attended to her. Before she fell for the guy. I hated the ending."

"Garbo was very magnetic as was Dietrich. They played women who were in control, who went their own way."

"Until they fell in love with a man."

I nodded.

"I wish they would make a movie without men. Of course, that would have been unthinkable then."

"Probably true," I replied. "Dolly, you're a writer. Have you considered creating a story about a woman? Maybe re-write one of those movie plots to concentrate on the parts you liked?"

"So the heroine meets the man and goes back to the woman?"

"Yes. Something like that."

"No, but it is an interesting idea." She seemed to have forgotten about the space behind the couch for a moment.

"It's just something to think about," I said. "Could you talk a little about some of the men you dated before your husband?"

Dolly was reluctant to move into this territory but finally told me about two brief affairs she'd had before her marriage, both with older married men. Dolly was definitely drawn to no-win arrangements or detonated others that might work, such as the relationship with her husband. Even her interest in women might give her an out because of the inherent social difficulties. In general, she avoided situations where she might succeed and was hedged in by anxieties, requiring her to stay strictly in the middle, perched on a psychological balance beam, a narrow path that was nearly impossible to walk upon. The two powerful women, Greta Garbo and Marlene Dietrich, would be attractive to her because they were polar opposites of Dolly; they played characters who acted decisively, as she hungered to do. Instead, her fears were sapping mental and emotional energy and leaving Dolly to flounder in a cloud of disorganization and the inability to make choices, so that most attempts to move forward quickly self-destructed. I had no idea how she managed to make out a simple grocery shopping list, much less deal with more complicated matters. However, one notable area of accomplishment was her writing—several distinguished journals had published her short fiction. Dolly explained that her goal was to complete a novel, but so far she hadn't mentioned whether a long work was in process.

I decided to try a different avenue. "Dolly, if you could, would you quickly say a word that most often describes how you feel?"

She thought about this for a second. "Scared."

"Scared," I echoed. "Can you tell me what you're frightened of?"

"I don't know..."

"Say the first thing that comes to mind. Fear—"

"Fear...darkness."

"Were you afraid of the dark when you were a child?"

Dolly nodded and twisted a button with her fingers. "Yes. Very."

"Are you still afraid of the dark?"

"Yes. I keep the hall and bathroom lights on at night. With my bedroom door nearly closed."

"Did anything upsetting ever happen to you in the dark, Dolly? When you were a small child?"

Her eyes grew large. "I had a lot of nightmares."

"What were they about?"

"I don't remember very well. I think there was a man in them."

"Did you know who the man was? Your father, an uncle?"

"No."

"A neighbor? A family friend? Someone you knew?"

Dolly's eyes widened even more. "Yes, maybe."

"Were you afraid of anyone specifically?" I asked. "Did anything occur that could explain this fear?"

She closed her eyes tightly.

"Perhaps something did happen, or you thought something might. Can you tell me why you're feeling so fearful right now? You seem frightened."

"I was afraid of Mr. Vanderhoek—he was a butcher. He owned a shop down the street from our house. My mother made me go there to get things. Every few days."

"Can you describe Mr. Vanderhoek?"

"He was very big. With big hands. They were all red with blood. He wore an apron. It was red with blood, too. He sold rabbits. They had blood on their fur. There was blood everywhere..."

I noticed she was beginning to hyperventilate. "Dolly, I want you to stop and take a deep breath and slowly let it out. Can you do that for me?"

She did as I asked, though the exhalation was light. I requested her to repeat this three more times. She obliged and slowly the color returned to her face. "Everything is okay."

She nodded, still practicing her breathing.

"Now, let's take this more slowly. Did Mr. Vanderhoek ever say or do anything that upset you?"

"Yes," Dolly answered in a small voice. She glanced behind the couch and into the corners of the room before settling her focus on me again. "Once, he asked me to come around the counter…into the storage area. Where he kept the meat in refrigerators. It was very, very cold. He had a big cleaver in his hand. It had blood on it."

"Why did you go back there with him? Was there a reason?"

Dolly drew in her shoulders, crossed her arms over her chest, and tightened her hands into fists. "He wanted to show me something. I don't remember what."

I had stumbled into a traumatic event with five minutes left in the session. Often the iron-clad time period was useful, but now it wasn't.

"Dolly, there's nothing that can harm you. What you experienced as a child was a long time ago."

"It doesn't feel like it," she whispered.

"I understand. Your memories and feelings probably seem very immediate. Remember you're all right. That's important," I replied. "We'll talk more about this in detail next week."

She nodded and unclenched her hands, but her forehead was lined with apprehension.

I considered and then added, "Dolly, it might be helpful if you bought a sketchpad and some crayons or colored pencils. When you have time, perhaps you could make a few drawings of Mr.

Vanderhoek. Maybe in his shop alone and also one with you. The artistic quality doesn't matter. Just put down whatever comes to mind without thinking too much before you start. Afterward, set the sketches aside until you see me, all right?"

"I really can't draw," she said, "but okay."

"One other thing. I always ask my clients about their general health. You already filled out the form, so I know you're not taking any medication. Have you had a recent physical?"

Dolly looked stricken. "I don't like doctors. I had a very bad experience with one. And, besides, they're always giving you needles. I hate needles."

"Do you have an internist or G.P.?"

"I did but I don't now. If I'm sick, I use natural remedies."

I sympathized with her but suggested that a physical might be worthwhile. I explained the importance of having complete bloodwork and an evaluation done.

Dolly grimaced, as if I might be implying she had a deadly disease. I quickly reassured her, trying my best to make my request casual, and finally she agreed to make an appointment.

After she left, I made careful notes about Mr. Vanderhoek, wondering what her artwork would illustrate.

[THE JOURNAL]

I saw you on television again. On "Welcome to Princeton." I called the station to find out when your program was going to be repeated so I could record it. I've now seen the tape six times. I want to play it over and over because each time you smile at me. You look so beautiful in your suit. So dignified and smart.

I've decided that I love you more than I've ever loved anyone. Maybe you doubted me? Soon I'll come to you. Very soon. I promise.

LAST WEEK, due to some confusion over dates, Denise DiNicola and I met for only ten minutes between clients, though I spoke with her on the phone prior to that. During our conversation, she admitted to feelings of depression but didn't expand on the causes.

Today, Denise was on time and waiting, her foot tapping. She greeted me with a smile, showing irregular teeth. Her face was pleasant but plain, with a curtain of brown bangs that slipped loose from a barrette which gathered her hair in the back. She wore a gray turtleneck under an orange and black Princeton sweatshirt. Her jeans were spotted with old paint or plaster and worn near the pockets and knees. Denise kept in shape by walking, she said, and by her apprentice job at the Marble Studio, where she packed sculptures for shipping, ordered supplies, cleaned, made deliveries, and sometimes was allowed to do work of her own, using leftover chunks of marble or pieces of wood. The position didn't pay well, but she reported that her needs were simple, and the hours were flexible. Denise was forty-one, unmarried, with no children or siblings.

After adding details to the questionnaire she had filled out last week, I asked if she had ever been to a psychologist or a psychiatrist before. I already knew from her short medical history that no prescription drugs, including psychiatric medications, were listed.

Denise frowned and shook her head.

"You mentioned you were depressed. Is this recent?"

"Not really." She glanced at the scars on my left hand, as people often did. "I kind of feel down a lot."

"Do you feel down at the moment?"

She smiled. "No, not right now."

"Is there anything in particular upsetting you? Your job, a relationship, family?"

"My job is fine. It's tiring sometimes, but I like the work. I'm learning a lot, but I wish I'd gone to art school to study sculpture. I've only taken a ceramics class at the community college. Too bad the teacher and I didn't get along." Denise paused here, as if she had forgotten the rest of my question.

"What about family? Are your parents still alive?"

"Yeah, but I don't see them. They live in Florida. Papa's retired."

"Do you have a good relationship with your mother and father?"

Denise rubbed the faded denim stretched across her knee. "Sort of. I don't hate them or anything."

I thought the word "hate" was a noteworthy choice. Usually people say that they love their parents, whether they do or don't. "Not hating" them made me instantly feel that she might, in fact, hate them. Her demeanor didn't clarify this. "How about friends?"

Denise looked uncomfortable. "I kind of keep to myself, though there's someone I like." She blinked, as if embarrassed.

"A friend?"

"Yeah. Maybe more than that." She paused and then added, "But mostly I see people at work. Sometimes we have lunch at the studio, though I also go for walks or drive around by myself. You know, get some fresh air after all the dust in the workrooms."

"Have you ever been involved in a primary relationship, Denise?"

"A couple times." She slipped her hands in her pockets. "The last one? He wasn't a good guy."

"I'm sorry to hear that."

"It's okay. I'm over him."

"How long did the relationship last?"

"Two years. It wasn't a big deal."

She didn't seem interested in discussing the matter, so I returned to her presenting issue—depression. "Denise, can you say a little more about your sadness? When do you feel that way?"

"I get blue at different times during the day but mostly at night." Denise brushed a sheath of bangs from her eyes.

"Has your mood affected your sleeping habits or appetite?"

Denise twisted her mouth, considering. "I don't sleep much."

"Do you take any over-the-counter sleeping medications?"

"No. Maybe I have a glass of wine or two. That helps."

"Do you have wine every evening?"

Her brow knitted together. "I have a few glasses with dinner. Not every night." Denise thrust her hand in her jeans' pockets again.

I didn't think she was being truthful about the amount or the frequency, but her discomfort level seemed to be rising. I would return to her alcohol use at a later time.

"Denise, I often ask my clients to do a drawing during their first session—a self-portrait. You can surround yourself with whatever environment you like or with other people. It's up to you." I placed a sketchpad and a box of crayons on the table in front of her.

She recoiled imperceptibly. "Sorry. I'd rather not do that."

I gave her a sympathetic smile. "Could you please try? It doesn't have to be a masterpiece."

Denise heaved a sigh and finally acquiesced, though she darted several suspicious glances at me. She took the materials and backed against the arm of the couch. Holding a brown crayon stiffly, she started with her head, as most people do. When she noticed I was observing her, she tipped the pad so I couldn't see what she was drawing.

This allowed me a few minutes to study Denise. The clothes she needed to wear for her job precluded fashionable attire, so I had no idea how she would dress after working hours. Her ears were pierced with round silver studs, and an inexpensive watch with a leather strap was on her left wrist. As she drew her portrait, her concentration was intense. Vertical lines grooved between her eyes.

At last, she laid the sketchbook on the table between us.

"May I look at what you've drawn?" I asked.

"Yeah, I guess so."

The pad of paper was eleven by fourteen, large enough for detail, small enough so that the space wasn't intimidating. Denise, however, had been intimidated. Her figure was only five inches high, placed so the torso was cut above the waist by the bottom edge of the page, with no stomach, legs, feet, or hands visible. Her head was proportionately smaller than the body, and her arms were pressed to her sides. Denise had drawn her hair in brown, carefully delineating the bangs. Her eyes were round expression-less circles; the nose was a simple "U" sprinkled with some freck-les—an accurate rendition. What struck me most was the mouth: a straight red line curved slightly upward at the ends, as if the smile were forced or tentative. Her blouse was colored dark green, and its collar was buttoned to the top. Beyond the figure, the back-ground was empty white paper. The usual blue sky and sun that many people included were missing. She had also been parsimo-nious with the colors, restricting herself to green, brown, and a small amount of red.

I thanked her for the drawing and raised the sketchbook so she could view it. "What do you see in what you drew?"

She stared at the portrait for a long time, as if she had never set eyes on it before. "I don't know. I should have added more. A house or trees or something." Denise switched her gaze from the sketch to me. "Do you have to keep it?"

I noted she hadn't said anything specific about the portrait or asked my opinion. "No one else will look at it, I promise. Maybe in a few weeks you can do another one that you might like more."

With this, she relaxed and even produced a half smile, a more cheerful one than in her drawing. "Okay."

We discussed her depression. She believed that once her sculptural work was appropriately recognized, she would feel better. Her plan was to be represented by a gallery in Philadelphia or New York, which Denise thought was possible in two or three years. I encouraged her endeavors, though I had no idea how talented she was. Mostly, I felt sympathy for Denise.

—

I was grateful for my break. I admitted to myself that canceling appointments for a few days might have been sensible, but it was too late to do that now. During the session with Denise, I kept visualizing my mother lying in a freezing-cold morgue—a disturbing image that wouldn't retreat. Because my father hadn't called, I didn't know what was going on—if her body had been cremated and if he was okay. I assumed he was exhausted from the move and from the adjustment to the Maillarts' house.

After selecting an apple from the bowl on my desk, I took a stroll on campus. It must have been during a class change because the pathways were crowded with students and professors on foot and on bicycles. To add to the activity, small service trucks plied between buildings. When I finished eating my apple and tossed the core in a wire trash can, I approached Nassau Hall. The sun was shedding pale lemon light across the paws of the two bronze tiger statues in front of its entrance. I sat beside one and was instantly flooded with grief, remembering when my mother and I were here during my freshman year at Cornell. I was home for a long weekend, and we had gone clothes shopping and planned to meet my father for lunch at Prospect, the faculty club. Since we were early, we talked for a few minutes about my professors and classes. I didn't tell her how homesick and unhappy I was. Because my grades were excellent, I was dating and had made some friends, my mother assumed I was doing well. As I thought back, I recalled fighting tears and putting up a good front. Now, the tears were shed.

—

Fearing my eyes were red, I applied drops and then hurried to my office where Sharon and Steve Clayton were standing by the door, regarding each another with wary distrust. Couples counseling was often frustrating—usually because by the time two people sought help, one had decided to vacate the relationship and the other was hanging on in a futile attempt to make things work. The opt-out partner made an effort to appear kindly and willing at first, as compared to the other partner, who was stuck holding the emotional bag and was suffering, prepared to beg or—failing that—ready to inflict some damage. Eventually, the situation combusted, which either caused healing or termination. At this point, Sharon and Steve were still being polite with each other—just barely. This was our second session.

I showed them into my office and mentally reviewed their family situation. They had two children, a boy and a girl, who were in the process of throwing fat onto the fire, acting out their hormonal imbalances in true teenage fashion. Manipulations were rife: the daughter twisted the father, and the son twisted the mother. Whenever those methods proved ineffective, the parents were set against each other by one or by both children.

Steve appeared untroubled and assumed a paternal and controlled air. He was an upper-level communications specialist, thirty-nine, average height, fit, and dressed in a jacket and loosened tie. However, under that polished exterior lay resentment. Steve was pressuring himself at work—or allowing his boss to pressure him. This behavior spawned a desire for the opposite lifestyle, one unattached to responsibilities.

Sharon sat on the sofa, her hands placed quietly in her lap. Originally a brunette, she was negotiating the subtle transformation into blondness via highlights that made her hair lighter. Every inch a Princeton townie, today she was well-coordinated with pressed tan khakis, a cream blouse, and a butterscotch-colored cardigan adorned with a gold lion's head pin. Her sleeves were pushed above the wrist to exhibit a cluster of gold bangles. Sharon was an active volunteer at the Art Museum and helped with fundraising for several charities. What gave her the most pleasure, however, was her watercolor painting. In addition to exhibiting, she was considering a partnership with a friend interested in opening a gallery. From what I had observed up to now, Steve wasn't enthusiastic about her plans. At thirty-eight, Sharon was feeling stifled and also worried about her relationship with her husband and his increasingly distant behavior.

The positions of husband and wife were set like opposing forces in a classic battle. My job was to re-align them on the same side—a tall order. I asked Sharon to begin, which she did with well-prepared verve. She complained that her husband was working late and not calling, was never around on weekends until it was time for dinner or a party, and he didn't spend time with the children. Throughout the litany, Steve remained silent, a wan smile on his face. When Sharon had aired all of her grievances, I asked Steve how the week had been for him.

He smiled. "Fine, Ellen, thanks for asking. I had a hectic several days, as a matter of fact. A delegation of Japanese businessmen was visiting, which was why I had to work several nights." Steve draped his leg over his knee, taking up more than his share of the couch. "I played some golf on Saturday—my boss told me to entertain the Japanese. You know how they love golf."

"Yes, and he missed our son's track meet and our daughter's

horse show. They were very disappointed!"

Steve was prepared for this and put a large hand on his wife's shoulder. "Come on, Sharon, I explained the situation to the kids. They were okay."

"That's because they could rely on me, Steve. What would happen if I wasn't around?"

"Well, we would manage. But you are around, and you do a great job with them." His tone was mildly placating.

This was not what Sharon wanted to hear, or rather it was what she was used to hearing. She countered with more accusations. Steve stopped smiling and withdrew his hand from his wife's shoulder. The tension in the room rose. Stepping into the fray, I asked them to mirror what the other partner had said about their week. Neither could do it with any success, although it was a rare couple who listened well, empathized, and accurately relayed what they had heard from their partner. I tried another therapist's technique.

"Sharon, would you face Steve? Imagine what kinds of feelings and problems he encountered at work—some of which you just heard—and play Steve. Steve, in this transaction, please play your boss, who is asking you to work overtime."

They agreed. Steve, as his boss, sounded demanding. Sharon, as Steve, tried to appease him and to steer a professional course, but he defied her at every turn. When we finished, I asked Sharon how she felt being her husband.

She tossed Steve a glance before returning to me. "I felt like I was on a hot stove. If I presented reasonable answers, his boss would ignore them or throw up roadblocks."

"Did you feel valued?" I asked.

"No, not very much," she admitted. "I felt like I was expending a lot of energy unnecessarily. It was frustrating."

"You know Steve's boss, don't you?"

She nodded. "Leonard comes to some of our dinner parties, but we only invite him when we include Steve's colleagues."

"Did Steve represent him accurately?"

"A little more stubborn than he probably is."

I looked at Steve, who was smiling faintly. "And how did you feel playing your boss and dishing it out to Steve here?" I pointed to his wife.

"I didn't feel comfortable with Leonard's critical attitude…his assumptions."

"Did Sharon portray you well?"

Steve placed his hand on her forearm. "Yes. Actually, she might have been braver than I am." He chuckled. "Maybe Sharon should ask for my next raise."

They exchanged smiles. We then had Steve play his wife in a conversation with their daughter, played by Sharon. After the scene was over, Steve admitted it hadn't been easy to discipline his daughter. Because he was rarely home to fulfill this role, he had deferred much of the child-raising to Sharon, who resented his absentee approach.

By the end of the session, some emotional heat had been aired. Playing roles was an effective technique to use with the Claytons. Listening to each other without the "script" might be another matter.

———

A young couple, Mei-Ling and Chang Lee, were next. Chang was first-generation Taiwanese, born in New Jersey, and Mei-Ling had emigrated from Taipei when she attended the Stevens Institute. The two met there—both engineering students—and married after graduation three years ago. Surprisingly, Mei-Ling was far less inclined to support traditional roles than her American husband. Even though he had first encountered her as an equal, he was now displaying a chauvinistic attitude—according to Mei-Ling. However, they were both intelligent and thoughtful people who genuinely cared for each other. A lengthy course of therapy wasn't likely.

—

Shortly after 7:30, I headed downstairs. Near the bottom was a small gold package of Godiva chocolates. No note. I love chocolate, but I left the box in case it had fallen from a client's purse or briefcase and he or she came looking for it when I opened the office tomorrow. I locked the door and walked to my car, thinking the package didn't look like it had been accidentally dropped.

[THE JOURNAL]

Dearly Beloved,
I wanted to leave you a present to show I'm thinking of you. I like chocolate and hope you do, too.
Your Lion

DURING the morning at home, I read journal articles, though my concentration was scattered. When the phone rang, I was relieved to hear my father's voice. He assured me he felt better, though navigating with crutches around the Maillarts' crowded house was challenging. He had made arrangements for my mother's cremation on the island and suggested we plan the service once he returned to Princeton. I asked when he intended to leave Corfu, but he explained that the leg cast would remain on for more weeks and elevation was required to prevent swelling, making travel difficult.

After an early lunch, I drove into town, parked my car, unlocked the office door, and saw the Godiva box on the steps. Besides myself and my clients, only the owner had access, and he was seldom around. I kept the outside door unlocked as usual and picked up the chocolates because clients would be using the stairs. As I carried the box to my office, I was tempted to eat one chocolate, but then I recalled the mysterious Health bar candy wrapper by my mother's bench and felt strangely repelled. I placed the box in my desk drawer.

Greta Graf was a few minutes late, giving the perennial Princeton excuse—no parking. She sat down heavily, settling an overstuffed Guatemalan bag beside her. She was dressed in earth colors: olive, eggplant, and gold and in a long skirt, billowing blouse, and vest.

"How did last week go, Greta? Did you get to the Y?"

She gave me her world-weary smile. "As a matter of fact I did. I went on a tour and took out a membership. I used the pool once, but a class was going on. Too many children."

"I'm glad you signed up. Maybe you can find out when the pool is scheduled for adults."

"Yes, I might."

"And what about the singles dance? Did you go?"

"Friday night."

93

She didn't offer more. "How was it?" I asked.

She shrugged. "The music was loud." Greta's face puckered with disgust. "Not to my taste."

"Anyone there you knew?"

"I ran into one of Heinrich's friends from the English department. His wife died eleven months ago. Breast cancer."

"I'm sorry to hear that."

"We only saw her and her husband at a few university gatherings, that sort of thing."

"What's the man's name—the one you met?"

"Stanley Hoffman." Greta shifted on the couch. "He's a little older than I am. Sixty or so. He has a house off Faculty Road."

"What's he like?"

"Intelligent, interested in classical music, literature, art, and theater. Plays the violin."

"Did you make any plans to see Stanley again?"

"Yes and no," she replied slowly. "He invited me to lunch."

"How was it?"

"I didn't go."

I wished Greta would be more forthcoming. "Didn't you want to?"

"I had a doctor's appointment. I told him I'd call."

"Will you?" I was fighting to subdue my exasperation. Greta always seemed two beats slow.

"I might."

"Maybe you could ask Stanley for Sunday brunch," I suggested. "You mentioned that Sunday morning was a lonely time."

Greta mulled this over. "I'll think about it."

Feeling I had scored a minor victory, I moved on to other things: her work, places she might meet people, how much she was drinking. We proceeded like the hare and the tortoise, covering little ground before we reached the session's end.

—

Greta's late arrival had reduced my time between clients. I felt fatigued after expending so much effort propelling the dialogue with her, but when I heard Carson Kendricks in the waiting room, I showed him in. He was dressed in black jeans, a commando-style sweater with shoulder patches, and suede desert boots. Under his arm, he carried a large tie-string portfolio, which he opened a few minutes later. Inside were sketches for his next painting—more details of costumed Carnival-goers, though one drawing featured a gory image of a Joker running a silver dagger into the naked breast of a woman wearing a *Gatto* mask and little else. Her body was draped over the curved rail of a Venetian canal bridge, with blood trickling into the green lagoon below. It was an abhorrent depiction, one meant to shock. Was this Carson's main intent? To repulse the viewer? Or was he illustrating a dark pathological urge, one that bubbled onto the paper?

"Carson, can you explain about the origin of this scene?" I asked.

He smiled, as if the grisly image spread in front of him was a cheerful landscape. "I like the juxtaposition of the Joker and what he's doing. The grin on his face and the evil that's undoubtedly beneath the mask. It's, well, meant to say we never really know anyone, at least from their superficial looks."

"The drawing is chilling," I told him, "though very well executed." It was. Carson was a master draftsman. "Did you think more about what we discussed last week?"

"About some kind of happy scene? Yeah, but it doesn't work for me. Not my thing. Or what the gallery wants."

"Don't you think it would be interesting to compare one with the other? Contrast the violence with its opposite?"

As Carson pondered this, he rubbed his unshaved chin, the blond hairs ticking against his fingers.

"I see what you're getting at, Ellen. Maybe it would be worth one canvas."

I wasn't persuaded that Carson would paint any jovial scenes. And the more I thought about, would doing so have any effect on his state of mind? If his state of mind was reflected in his current work?

"You mentioned last week that you only had dark thoughts when you were painting. Were you being honest?"

He smiled. "More or less."

"How were you being dishonest?"

"I have dreams like what I create. Last night, for example. I was in some kind of medieval war. All of a sudden, these men in enormous black helmets ran out of the forest. They were carrying pointed pikes, and they formed a line and attacked. I grabbed a spear but it was too short—or at least shorter than theirs. I woke up in a sweat, worried about how to defend myself."

As a non-Freudian, I refused to comment on the phallic imagery. Instead, I asked if Carson felt under siege in real life.

"I don't know. There was a break-in next door to me. That happens a lot in the city—you lived there so you understand. And, growing up, my family's apartment was in the Lower East Side, a rough neighborhood."

"Where your sister was killed," I added.

Carson nodded but didn't respond. After a moment, he said, "Actually, I was thinking about finding a place around here. A studio where I could get away to paint. I visited a few short-term rentals last week. Near Lambertville."

"A nice area, Carson. A lot of artists in town," I replied. "But before we talk about that, could you say more about being afraid of someone?"

"Afraid of others?" He laughed. "Or my very evil self?"

"Are you really so evil?" I tried to match his odd humor and yet maintain course.

As if enjoying the conversation, he leaned against the sofa, his leering expression reminiscent of the Joker's mask. "I am very, very evil, Ellen. You know that."

We had returned to the fencing of the previous session. "So which are you, Carson? The evil predator or the one being attacked by evil predators?"

"In my painting, I can be both. The man thrusting the sword, and the woman being stabbed."

"Have you ever physically assaulted anyone or been assaulted?"

His eyes narrowed. "I'm not sure I should answer that."

The response made me nervous. "Please do."

Carson stretched both arms above his head and clasped his hands behind his neck. "Oh, you know, the usual childhood scraps. I didn't exactly get along that well." He recounted several incidents of being bullied in grade school but said this had ceased when he was a teenager.

"And have you ever assaulted anyone?"

"Once or twice in high school." He stared through the window and smiled at a private thought. "And maybe a few of my sexual adventures might have crossed the line a little." He glanced at me, his mouth curled with amusement.

"Can you tell me what happened?" I tried to sound composed though his admission was unsettling.

"I wanted to. She didn't want to. We did."

"Are you telling me you forced a woman to have sex with you against her will?"

"I guess she changed her mind. I can be very persuasive."

"Was your 'persuasion' physical?"

"You mean rape?" He brought his arms down and crossed them. "No, I didn't rape anyone."

"Have you ever wanted to rape a woman?"

"Sure. What man hasn't? It's a basic male fantasy."

"I'm not so sure about that, Carson."

"That's because you're not a man. But you know what, Ellen? I bet even you have had fantasies about being raped. Look at women's romance novels. Isn't that in every bodice-ripping plot? And the gallery owner who will show my work. She's a woman, and she's really hot to exhibit my paintings and loves the sexual and physical aggression."

We were running out of time. "Good luck with your apartment search, Carson. And I hope you consider a more positive approach to your painting, even if it's just as a counterpoint to the work you've already done." I hesitated and then added, "We'll discuss the subject of sexual coercion next week."

He tied the portfolio case, stood, pulled his wallet from a back pocket, and stepped within two feet of me. "Ellen, don't worry about what I told you. I made it all up." He gave me a flirtatious smile and handed me a check. "See you soon."

I was startled. Had Carson really fabricated the incident? Or had he raped a woman or come close to using force? Even if nothing had occurred, Carson was obviously fascinated with the idea. Or was he mentioning this because he fantasized about such a scene between us? I didn't think so, but why had Carson encroached on my physical space at the end of the session? I recalled the attraction I'd had for my client, Lucas, and how it had blinded me to what was going on inside him. I needed to take care that I didn't make inaccurate reverse assumptions about Carson, imagining he was interested when he wasn't, and to remain alert for any transferences that might develop.

—

Robert Fleet was in the waiting room. When I opened the connecting door, he was fussing over a spill on his blue silk tie and removing the tie from around his neck. We greeted each other, and he said he'd need to leave a few minutes early to buy another tie before returning to work. He sat and began a fast-paced recital of work-related irritations. After a while, I asked how his colleague had reacted to his congratulations. His face reddened.

"I'm sorry, Ellen. I should have spoken to her after our session. I just got angry again when I returned to the office. That was really terrible of me."

His apology was a sham. "Do you think you could tell your colleague that you admire her work? I'm not suggesting an overblown compliment. Maybe after your weekly meeting, if she makes a comment that strikes you as intelligent." I wasn't sure Robert was paying attention. He rarely did when the focus veered away from himself.

"Well, I suppose I could say something to Susan…"

It was tempting to be more emphatic, but it was better to work with the client rather than against him. I asked about his home life instead.

"How did things go with Debby? You planned to have a conversation."

"I gave her some flowers, though I think she was suspicious. You know, about why I brought them. Maybe Debby thinks I'm having an affair and felt guilty."

"There's always a danger of being misunderstood unless you also spoke with her that evening. Did you?"

"Some. I asked her about her job, but she didn't say much."

"Perhaps Debby isn't used to talking about herself. People tend to keep things to themselves unless discussions happen regularly with their partners. Do you think you could try again, Robert?"

He looked at me as if doing so would be an imposition. "I guess. But really, Ellen, what's so interesting about typing and faxing and filing and copying papers all day?"

"I'm sure not everything Debby does is routine. She has insights into the business, her co-workers, and how she might advance with the company. If she doesn't like her job, maybe she can address that. You tell her about your day, don't you?"

"Every night. But what I do is different."

"You may have a more challenging career, but let's try an experiment. Ask Debby a few questions every evening about work or something she did and see how she reacts."

He nodded and smoothed his suit jacket. The gesture seemed designed to erase the previous dialogue. Promptly thereafter, Robert began a discussion of his financial worries that occupied us until the end, whereupon he handed me a check and left for a nearby men's shop.

—

When Samantha Cosgrove arrived, she placed her backpack on the floor and walked to my Venetian collection. After removing the Casanova mask, she examined it and then hung it carefully on the wall. Without saying a word, she took a seat on the sofa.

"Do you like that one, Sam?" I asked, pointing to the mask she had been studying.

"Yeah, maybe. It's pretty far out."

I smiled at her description. "It's one of my favorites. Do you know about Casanova?"

"He's sort of like Don Juan, right?"

"Yes. He was a renowned or, perhaps I should say, a notorious womanizer in Venice during the eighteenth-century. Are you familiar with Venetian Carnival?"

Sam nodded hesitantly. "Everybody gets dressed up in costumes and goes around trying to fool everyone about who they are."

"Right. It has a long tradition. Noblemen and commoners,

the beautiful and the ugly, the young and old, men dressing as women, women dressing as men—they're all transformed by their chosen disguise. It's an interesting idea. Having the opportunity once a year to be someone completely new, someone of your own choice and imagination."

"I'd like that," she mused.

"Who would you be?"

Samantha was silent for a moment. "I like Casanova there. The black hat and all."

I asked her if she wanted to try the mask on. I could tell she wanted to do so but was probably too embarrassed. I stood and brought it to her. "Just hold it up, Sam. No need to tie the ribbons."

The mask looked perfect for her, as if she had dressed in anticipation with her black clothes. Perhaps it was my imagination, but it seemed that she was sitting straighter on the couch.

"How do you feel as Casanova?"

She thought about this. "I feel like, I don't know, like powerful. Like I could do anything I wanted."

"Invisible?"

"Yeah, like no one can see me."

"That's what most people say about wearing a mask. It's amazing how little it takes to make a person feel differently about themselves."

Sam lifted the Casanova mask away from her face. "Oh, is that the moral to the story?" she asked with a trace of annoyance.

I laughed. "Yes." She gave me the mask which I returned to the wall. "At the risk of belaboring the mask-wearing discussion, I think it serves to illustrate how mutable our self-images can be. How we can change merely by covering our faces or moving to a new place or meeting someone new."

Sam didn't respond and seemed preoccupied. I let her have a

moment and then asked if she had brought her memorial to Jake. After a brief hesitation, she removed a piece of paper from her jacket pocket.

"Sam, do you want to read it?"

She shook her head and chucked the paper on the table. "Go ahead," she said, gazing out the window, distancing herself from her writing.

I picked up the paper. Folded in quarters, the text was typed.

To Jake: You left. Your choice. I understand your leaving. Most people will never understand, but I do. I wish you were still alive so we could talk, go on walks, be night people together. I am a night person. You were a night person. Your dreams were nightmares. I know because mine are nightmares. Darkness forever. I will never forget you.

"Sam, sorry, but I can't quite read the last sentence. It's typed over white correction fluid."

She took the paper and read: "Whenever I walk in the rain, you will be with me." She handed it back.

I looked the paragraph over again. "I can't speak to the literary quality, though I like the use of night. I guess that's the word that stands out, one you attach to Jake," I said. "You mentioned the two of you went for walks?"

"Yeah. I wish we'd done it more often. When I used to go by myself, before Jake and I did, I'd think about him."

I returned the paper to her. "Was he aware of how you felt?"

She played with a silver ring on her index finger. "Maybe."

"What did he say?"

Tears formed in her eyes, but she fought them down. "Does it matter? It didn't make any difference, did it? Like, what difference does anything make?" she asked, suddenly rebellious. "Nothing matters. This means nothing." She crumpled the memorial and thrust it into her pocket. "Jake had the right idea."

I thought that she was about to run out of the room, but slowly she calmed down, crossing her arms defiantly and pushing her foot against the coffee table as though she wanted to get as far away from me as possible.

"I think what you're really saying is that you didn't make a difference."

She sniffed and wiped her eyes.

"Sam, it always makes a difference—how we feel about someone. But sometimes our feelings don't weigh in strongly enough. Sometimes our caring can't overcome powerful feelings of depression, futility, or sadness in a person who is special to us. And, too, we're learning that chemistry can affect our emotions. It's likely that Jake was overwhelmed by forces he couldn't control without pharmacological intervention."

"Like tranqs and stuff?"

I nodded. "Or anti-depressants. We'll never know why he did what he did. The second Jake cut himself, he might have regretted it, but he isn't here to tell us. His death will always be one of those terrible events that can't be explained. All those he abandoned— his parents, friends, and you—share a sense of guilt because you didn't foresee or prevent what happened. Unfortunately, Jake left you very confused, trying to understand why he was so upset." I knew this all too well because of Lucas.

She was silent. I couldn't read her mood. "Sam, I think we need to address your feelings about suicide. We spoke about it last week."

"What's there to say? I mean, like, it's a valid option."

"Do you think about it often?"

"Sometimes," Sam admitted. "I'm not going to do the blade thing, if that's what you're worried about."

"I'm relieved to hear that. But I'd like to know if you've imagined a plan. How to do it."

She bit her lip. "No. Not really."

I felt relieved to hear Sam hadn't formulated a method. That was a positive indication, though suicide couldn't be ruled out.

"If you consider how you feel about Jake now that he's gone…how sad you are…well, a lot of people would feel the same way about you if you killed yourself. Think about how you're feeling, and how you wouldn't want anyone else to feel like you do."

Sam was quiet, assessing what I'd said. "No one should feel this way."

"No. It's very painful. Do you believe we have a responsibility to people who care about us? I'm not saying we always have to act with them in mind, but in the case of something irreversible like suicide, our family and friends are reasons to fight depression and these kinds of thoughts. I know several people who have lost someone. They're never the same after. Never."

My vehemence surprised her. She crossed her legs the other way. "I get that."

"Good. Jake may have believed that how he felt was how he would always feel in the future. However, in most cases—particularly in younger people—depression passes and is replaced by a more optimistic outlook as they become engaged with others and achieve goals that are important to them. Perhaps we can change the way you're thinking by concentrating on what makes you feel happy," I said. "Can you give me a list?"

With a air of teenage derision, she tucked up the side of her mouth. "Happy? Not much."

"There must be something…"

"My writing."

"That's important. What else?"

"My dog. Walking at night. I like my music, my car. And chocolate," she said with a faint smile. "Yeah, I like chocolate!"

Had Samantha left the Godiva box? If she had, I hoped I would be sufficiently sensitive to behavioral changes that would indicate she was developing an infatuation. I decided to stay on topic and not question her about the candy, yet I examined Sam with more care, wondering why I kept thinking my clients might be attracted to me.

"Anything else?" She shook her head. "Well, keep adding to that list. Whenever you feel good about something or someone, pay attention to the moment and remember it. At times, we get into a negative mindset and only notice our sad reactions. Let's try a week of the opposite."

She shrugged. Whether she was agreeable to this request, I had no idea.

"Sam, our session is about up. If you need to call me, pick up the phone," I told her. "And let's keep positive, okay?"

"Yeah," she replied.

"One more thing. Could you do some more writing for me? On the subject of night?"

"Yeah, maybe."

She stood and handed me a check from her mother.

"Have a good week, Sam."

I saw the video nine more times. Every time I see it, I learn more about you. How you have such presence and authority, how you tilt your head to the side when listening. I also heard the hidden messages you send which express your devotion. Soon, we will share everything...just like we shared the chocolate.

I wish I knew all the things you like besides our magic city, Venice—I only know about that because of your masks. Maybe someday soon we'll go there and walk by the canals and ride in a gondola. I borrowed three books from the library and think of us in St. Mark's Square with all the pigeons flying around.

I've ordered some presents that you will like. I hope they will be a surprise.

AFTER inserting Samantha's file, I opened my desk drawer and stared at the gold Godiva box. My resistance to the chocolate had disappeared, replaced by a craving for a sweet. I untied the ribbon and lifted the top. Instantly, an icy shiver shot down my back. One candy, a chocolate-covered cherry, was half-eaten, the sticky red liquid interior oozing onto its white wrapper. Repulsed, I shoved on the lid and threw the box and ribbon into the trash. Who could have left such a sick present on my stairs—if it was, in fact, intended for me?

I thought of all of my Tuesday clients. The only person I could imagine accidentally losing a box of chocolates was Dolly. If this had been a gift, however, the giver could have been someone who wasn't on the schedule that day, such as George Durst, who mentioned interest in a new woman. Of course, it was possible the culprit was unknown to me or some lothario had mistaken my door for one that led to another office or apartment, though my name was on the plaque outside. I shivered again. It was difficult to believe this second explanation.

I was eager to go home, away from my mysterious suitor, and hurried down the stairs. As I closed the outside door, I saw an envelope taped to it, my name printed in red ink. The envelope contained a travel magazine article, "The Beauty of Venice," which featured photographs of St. Mark's Square with millions of pigeons, the Rialto Bridge crammed with tourists, and a café alongside a canal with a man and a woman eating an intimate meal. Above, the sender had drawn six red hearts.

Was this from one of my parents' friends? Only a few knew where my office was and that I loved Venice. I swallowed hard. I was avoiding the frightening reality. The article and the chocolates were from the same person, who also persisted with silent calls—two of them today.

—

Thursday morning dawned clear and fresh. Invigorated by the cool air, I ate a quick breakfast and then took the blower to tackle the leaves in the driveway. My father was always of the opinion that they would eventually settle to the sides, swept by cars coming and going, but I wanted to be outdoors and this provided a good excuse.

A jittery breeze was riling the yellow leaves on the beeches near Stoney Brook. The smell of the humus soil, damp from an overnight rain, permeated the air as I untangled the orange electrical cord, plugged it into the exterior outlet, and attached the blower, which I switched on and began to sweep the turn-around area and the entrance to the house. This took longer than I expected, and because the power cord only reached a short way down the driveway, I had to finish the rest with a rake. By the time I was standing on the street, I was tired and perspiring. Although delivery rarely came this early, I leaned the rake against the mailbox and checked the mail. Inside, I found the phone bill. Its envelope had been slit open and then taped closed. Was that how my suitor had learned my parents' number? If so, this confirmed that he or she knew where I lived. And had followed me home. Or lived nearby and had followed me to my office, although because the hang-up calls began in Princeton, it was likely the activity had originated there. Unless this was Nick.

I cursed, grabbed the rake, and sprinted toward the house, glancing left and right, worried I was being observed. The breeze was turning into a more persistent wind, and I noticed some of my handiwork was already undone as leaves blew across the gray gravel.

—

On Friday, I drove to Hopewell and checked two newspapers for my mother's obituary and found it in both. I purchased copies, continued into Princeton, and began reviewing chapters in my "On Creativity" file. A half hour later, the phone rang. It was Nick. He started to apologize for the previous Sunday, but I cut him off.

"Nick, I won't get involved with you. For one thing, you're married—"

"Oh, Ellie…I'm only half married. Katie is still gone. I'm all alone, wandering around by myself."

I took a deep breath. "Even if you were divorced, I wouldn't be interested."

"You can't mean that! We'd be great together!" he protested.

I was wondering what I had to say to get rid of him. "Nick, we have nothing in common."

"Like you and Drew?" he asked, a hint of nastiness in the comment.

"I won't discuss Drew. Just because you're Katie's husband, that doesn't give you permission to be invasive."

"Oh, come on. Can't we do lunch? I'm in town and can be there in a minute."

"No."

"Come on. A burger and a beer—"

"No."

"Okay, okay. Maybe another time."

I couldn't believe his obstinacy and the depth of anger I felt. "There'll be no other time. Goodbye, Nick." I dropped the receiver and exhaled with relief. As I was about to leave to get a sandwich, I realized that he knew the location of my office and might have called from a phone booth nearby. Better to wait an hour, I thought, returning to my manuscript.

—

I skipped lunch and kept working. About three, I ate a granola bar, but by six, I was hungry. I closed the anteroom door and began descending the stairs when I noticed a bouquet of red carnations lying on the second step. The same step where the chocolates had been.

Staring at the flowers with disgust, I then looked for a note. None. Once again, there was no way to identify the sender. Nick? Was this his apology? The thought that the flowers came from him was really annoying. If Nick hoped I'd call to thank him, hell would freeze over first.

I tucked the carnations under my arm and opened the exterior door. The wind was chilly, coming from the north, and dusk had fallen. The streetlights lit the parking area, which was full of cars owned by Friday evening bar-goers and diners at restaurants. I scanned the lot for Nick or for anyone suspicious and rushed to open my car, telling myself the bouquet, article, and chocolates were probably presents from him. If this were true and he was being a jerk, why was I so rattled? Or was I just angry that he was disregarding my feelings? I shuddered to think what he might do next. If these "gifts" were from Nick.

I drove to my favorite take-out Chinese restaurant, ordered sesame noodles and a crispy duck entrée, and sat on the ledge by the window to wait, my eyes smarting from the peanut oil smoking in the woks. When my order was ready, I paid the cashier and returned to the car, checking both sides of the road. As I pulled out, I noticed a dark sedan leaving at the same time. The driver was too distant and the car was nondescript, but I doubted it was flashy enough for Nick. I accelerated, ignoring the 25 m.p.h. speed limit, and executed a few unnecessary turns until I lost the car. This was silly, of course, because Nick had been to my parents' house as had whoever placed the phone bill in the mailbox. Nonetheless, I felt relieved to see darkness in the rearview mirror.

When I reached the driveway, I stopped for the mail before continuing to the garage and parking the Audi. The house and grounds were unlit because I'd forgotten to reset the timer on the outside lights. Cursing my foolishness, I neared the front door, and as I did, the wind slid into an uneasy moan. I was so nervous, my key ring slipped through my fingers. I picked it up and muttered, "God, you're ridiculous! Nick is just being aggravating. Don't respond and he'll stop."

I entered and turned on the hall lights. Upstairs, all was silent except for the whir of the refrigerator, however the answering machine was blinking. Two calls, no messages.

I clenched my teeth in irritation and filled a vase with water and stuck the carnations in, though I was tempted to throw them away because their cloying scent smelled toxic. Instead, I grabbed the containers of Chinese food and a glass of water and sat at the dining table. After turning on the television, I ate and viewed *Dark Victory* with Bette Davis, which was overly melodramatic.

[THE JOURNAL]

Friday is here at last. I can spend more time thinking about you. I saw the obituary for your mother in the paper. It didn't mention a service, probably because your dad is still in Greece—a car accident in Corfu was given as the cause of death. This means you're alone in the house because no brothers, sisters, or husband were listed, though I know you're not married because you don't wear a ring. Besides, your car is the only one at the house.

I wish I could be with you. We should be together during your time of grief, but you haven't given me permission. I know you have a reason. I watch the video to find out, but it doesn't help. This is up to you, of course, because you're wiser about these things than I am. To be honest, I'm beginning to feel frustrated, which is not good. I also worry what will happen when your father comes home. Maybe he's really hurt from the accident and will never return. That would be best for us.

I went shopping to find something to cheer you up because of your mother. The flowers are at the bottom of your stairs.

ON SATURDAY, I drove into Manhattan, to the International Center of Photography. Their exhibit wasn't to my taste: snapshot-style black and whites with little emphasis on composition. Disappointed, I treated myself to a nice lunch and a glass of white wine and then resolved to resurrect my opinion of photography by driving to a gallery in SoHo that only exhibited images using palladium, gum bichromate, and other traditional printing processes. The place was restorative: worn oriental carpets on honey-colored floorboards and bird of paradise flowers in a crystal vase. A recording of *La Traviata* with Beverly Sills was playing, her voice soaring in the large room. The photographs on display were handsome still-life arrangements captured on square-format film.

Afterward, I visited several other galleries but began having flashbacks about Lucas greeting me in the office, his strange smile, and then the whoosh of orange fire. Suddenly, I was desperate to leave the city, to outrun my memories. In the car, my hands clutched the wheel as I struggled to negotiate the thick traffic. When I entered the Lincoln Tunnel, claustrophobia assaulted me, and I felt sick as the noxious fumes seeped through the shut car windows. After exiting into the brightness on the other side, I raised the volume on the classical station so the music would drown my thoughts.

By the time I arrived on Stoney Brook Road, it was dark and I felt calmer. The house blazed with lights and illuminated the front entrance. I parked, went upstairs, and noticed the flickering signal on the answering machine. Five clicks. No messages.

"Damn it!" I cried. This constant provocation was making me crazy, but what could I do to end this invasive behavior?

After heating the leftover Chinese food, I listened to the news. Shortly before ten, the phone rang. No one called this late unless there was an emergency. Instantly, I was alert.

"Hello?"

I heard breathing. Someone was on the line.

"Who is this?" I asked.

The caller disconnected.

I turned off the TV and listened to the noises in the house, then told myself I was scaring myself for no reason because whoever called couldn't be on the phone and on the property at the same time. Still, if this was my mysterious suitor, they now knew they had reached me and that I was home. And if the person had seen my mother's obituary in the papers, he or she could deduce I was alone.

Of course, Nick had my parents' number, had visited the house, and knew my father was on Corfu. He could be harassing me because I'd rejected him, but had he also stolen the phone bill or was its opened envelope just a coincidence? Unable to sort out the mystery, I went upstairs and changed into pajamas in the bathroom because I felt exposed by all the bedroom windows, none of which had curtains or blinds. If someone was out there, the interior lights would illuminate me clearly. This had never occurred to me before because the house was set a long way from the road, with acres of trees acting as a screen. I examined the windows. I would buy blinds tomorrow.

The sheets were cold as I slipped between them. I didn't sleep well.

—

After eating a mushroom omelet and toast, I retrieved the Sunday *New York Times*, completed the crossword, and drove to Home Depot, where I purchased white venetian blinds. Returning to the house, I realized I'd forgotten to check yesterday's mail and now did so. Thankfully, nothing worrisome lay in wait, only the usual bills and catalogues, so I went into the basement for tools and then climbed the stairs to install the blinds in the bedroom.

114

While I was in a handywoman mood, I replaced the burned-out lightbulb in the kitchen and tightened the screws on the security bolt attached to the downstairs' door. Once all of these tasks were finished, I lay on the sofa and began reading a Josephine Tey mystery, a book inscribed with my mother's signature in faded blue ink. When I realized no one had touched the paperback since she had, I let out a long breath. So many things reminded me of her.

As the afternoon shadows were lengthening and an orange light filtered through the western trees, the telephone rang. This time I let the machine take it. Another click. Nick was carrying this too far. I was tempted to call and give him a few forthright comments regarding his behavior, but I didn't want to encourage him, even though it would have eased my mind to know it was Nick rather than someone else.

The house was silent except for Tchaikovsky's "The Swan Lake," which floated through the room via four speakers. I returned to my novel, aware of the oppressively sweet smell of the carnations.

—

The phone rang early Monday morning. After a moment of hesitation, I answered it and was happy to hear my father on the line. He reported he was becoming adept with crutches and was seeing the orthopedic doctor at the end of the week and would have a new set of X-rays taken of his foot. He sounded in good spirits and asked what I had been doing. I told him about the gallery visit to New York, the progress on my book, and paused, tempted to mention Nick's phone calls, candy, and flowers. Because there wasn't anything my father could do, I resolved not to upset him and instead nattered on about the weather and how much I was enjoying the house. He liked to hear these things, as mundane as they were, and seemed content with the exchange. I didn't ask about his plans to return, and he didn't raise the subject. He suggested I call him in a few days because he didn't like using the Maillarts' phone. I said I would.

After the conversation, a heavy sadness passed over me. Tears pricked my eyes, but I refused to cry. I needed to keep busy, I told myself, so I called my tennis pro, Martie Tyron, and scheduled a lesson at ten. Quickly, I threw on my navy warm-up suit and white sneakers and made the short trip to the club, where Martie was waiting, her usual amused smile on her face.

I liked Martie, as had my mother, who introduced us six years ago during one of my first visits to my parents. Whenever I was home, I scheduled sessions with Martie and occasionally played doubles with my mother and some of her friends. Martie was tall—an inch taller than me—large-framed, and, if there was such a thing as a kindly curmudgeon, she was that. Her tennis form was classic—no two-handed backhands. Though I'd never competed against Martie in a real match, we often played points during a lesson. After surviving her first serve, there was almost no chance to keep the ball away from her as she rushed the net, towering over it like an impenetrable wall and swatting crisp, non-returnable volleys.

"I was sorry to read about your mother, Ellen," she said, standing.

"Thank you," I replied, uneasy with condolences.

Martie studied me for a moment. To avoid questions, I changed the topic to tennis.

"If we could, I'd like to work on my backhand."

"Ah, the perennial backhand problem! Sure." She gave me a big grin. "Not your serve?"

I laughed, knowing she was teasing me. "No, I'm comfortable with that for now." My serve was outstanding, a weapon that won points, and Martie knew it.

She reached for her racket and headed down the steps to the court, held the netting for me, picked up a ball carrier, and stood at the service line. I trotted to the opposite side of the net.

"Fifteen volleys on the deuce court. Fifteen on the ad court," she explained. "I hope that won't tire you out too much?"

We worked on this drill for about ten minutes until I had to pick up the tennis balls. Next, Martie did a refresher instruction on backhands and forced me to hit only those, running side to side beyond the baseline. I knew she would keep at it until we ran out of balls or I ran out of gas—most likely the latter would happen first.

The hour went by quickly, though after forty minutes, I was exhausted and had started various stalling techniques. Martie took pity and let me chat while my lungs recuperated. Then I took the carrier to retrieve the balls, and she stowed it in the storage closet.

"How about going for a beer and pizza this evening?" she asked.

This was the first time Martie had ever suggested a social interaction. "Not tonight," I said, "but thanks. Let's get together soon."

—

At home, in the shower, I questioned my decision. It would have been pleasant to have company for dinner, but I felt on edge, aware of negative energy surrounding me. The more I considered the situation, the less I believed Nick was responsible for what was happening. Was Carson Kendricks my admirer? He was roaming around the area, searching for a rental. George? Samantha? Greta? Dolly? Others? Or was it Martie? My home address and two phone numbers were on the club's membership form. It would be easy for her to learn the location of my office.

I stepped out of the shower, exasperated, and kept berating myself for my inability to identify my tormentor. After toweling off, I dressed in a brown tweed skirt, gold turtleneck, and a rust-colored sweater. When I walked downstairs to one of the living room windows, I was still worrying about the stalker and about my safety.

From the house, the road was almost invisible, but I had wide views of the woods, yet anyone hiding behind trees, bushes, or the garage could observe me, especially at night when the interior lights were on. Conversely, after dark, unless the person stepped into an area illuminated by the spotlights, it would be difficult to see them.

Should I move to a hotel for a week? I rebelled at the idea of spending money for probably no reason. After all, there wasn't any evidence that my unknown admirer's intentions were dangerous. Other than the strange phone calls, the candy, chocolates, and flowers were gifts a guy with an infatuation would send. Though this was the first time I'd ever received such anonymous attentions, I remembered two of my high school crushes and my own adolescent behavior. This led me to think of Samantha. Or could it be someone who attended my lectures? Or a merchant who saw me around town? The friendly guy at the shoe store or the one at the deli? Whoever it was, I needed to resolve this mystery soon before anxiety influenced my therapeutic relationships. While I always kept notes after each session, I would write more details, including subjective impressions. Then I considered the wisdom of leaving the exterior office door unlocked. However, running up and down between sessions would be a terrific nuisance, nor would it be fair to ask clients to wait outside in bad weather. I decided the door would stay open even if it granted access to the wrong person. Of course, he or she probably already had that access.

I ate lunch and drove into the office.

[THE JOURNAL]

I hope you liked the carnations. They are a small token of my love.

I followed you home again to your beautiful house, although I guess it's your parents' place because it has their name on the phone bill and your dad is on the answering machine. I know you want me to have your telephone number so I can call and keep track of where you are—that you're safe at home or at the office. Don't worry. I'll keep visiting.

Every night before I sleep, I put a raindrop on my forehead and on my tongue, as you instructed me to do. It makes me feel like we're merging, that I'm at one with you more and more. Soon, our souls will flow together like rivers. Our hearts will beat at the same time, though I believe they already do.

The Lion Watching Over You

I HAD just arrived upstairs when my office telephone rang. Perhaps it was one of my two afternoon clients calling to re-schedule. Or it was my elusive, annoying caller.

"Hello, this is Ellen Haskell..."

"Hi, Ellen. This is Marguerite Fleury."

"Hello, how are you?"

"Well, not so well. I'm in a flare—that's what the doctor's call it."

"I'm sorry to hear that."

"Yes. It is a particular nuisance because I need to practice this afternoon, and, of course, we have an appointment at three. If it isn't too much trouble, could we reschedule for next week?"

"That's fine. Shall we keep our usual time on Monday?"

"Yes. Thank you for being so kind."

After we ended our conversation, I walked to the deli to buy a coffee. On my way, I passed a community notice board and was surprised to see my photograph on a poster, announcing my Friday lecture at the university. How nice! Probably there were quite a few plastered across town and campus.

—

George Durst was prompt for his two o'clock appointment. The bandage on his wrist was still present, tinged with dirt. On his left forefinger, white adhesive tape wrapped around a piece of gauze. I asked him about both.

"The hand is better. And the finger's just a scratch."

Because George was disinclined to say more, I inquired about his week, and when he began to talk about the woman he was interested in, I listened carefully.

"I haven't asked her out yet. I want to."

"Can you tell me something about her, George?"

His head lowered so it almost rested on his chest. "I thought she liked me, but now I'm not sure."

"What makes you say that?"

He raised his hands. "Look at me. I'm not the kind of guy girls like. I'm not one of those dandy types, all pressed and neat and proper."

"Not everyone is looking for a fashion plate. Many women value loyalty, gentleness."

"Would you go out with me?" he asked. He blushed and added, as if to indicate his question was only rhetorical, "I mean, any gal could count on me to be faithful. But gentle?" He shook his head. "I try to be careful, but I break things. The more I try not to, the clumsier I get."

I couldn't see George handling Waterford crystal. His hands were meant for hammers and chisels. However, it was his first question that snagged my attention. Did he really wish to know if I would be interested in him? I stayed on subject.

"George, tell me what you can offer a girlfriend. What are your best qualities? Brag on yourself a little."

His eyebrows raised in surprise. "My good points? Well, like I said, I wouldn't ever stray. I work hard. Don't make a lot of money, but it's solid work, work that takes skill." He thought for a minute. "I try to keep up, like with visiting the library. I go every two weeks, regular. Read magazines. Bring in two books, take out two."

"What do you like to read, George?"

"About other countries, history. Wars and battles. I was in Vietnam, you know."

"No, I didn't. I suppose it hasn't come up."

"I don't talk about my experience much. I try not to think about it."

"Army?"

He nodded. "Yeah. I've seen things like, well, like no one should ever see. The worst you can imagine."

121

"Do you have nightmares?"

"I did for a long while. I've gotten kind of used to them, but they still make me jumpy. I find that the less I talk about 'Nam, the better I feel."

"I can sympathize with that, George. And I respect your wish to put the war behind you as much as possible. It must have been a horrible time that affected you deeply. However, if you're still suffering from nightmares, maybe we should discuss how you felt at the time and how the experiences are upsetting you now."

"Let's wait. I'm not ready."

"I understand. Whenever you wish." I paused, in case he changed his mind, and then continued. "Okay, let's return to your attributes. What are some other things that you'd want someone to know?"

The tension in his face relaxed now that the subject of Vietnam had been dropped. "Hmm. I'm strong. I can fix all sorts of things. My place is neat. I make my bed every morning, corners square. I cook a little—nothing gourmet. Things like goulash and sauerbraten that I learned from my mom. And I go to church every Sunday."

"Good, George. Anything else?"

"I've saved some money. Enough for a down payment on a house. For when I settle down and we have kids."

Did he mean a generic "we" or, specifically, us? "It sounds like you're prepared for a future. Have you ever had a girlfriend? Someone you saw for a length of time?"

"I've dated a few girls, but no one ever took to me, or I didn't take to them."

"Tell me more about the woman who's caught your fancy now."

His eyes lit up. "Ah, she's a real beauty. Wise. Kind of serious, with a nice smile."

"How did you meet?"

"Ah, we just met, sort of."

"What's her name?"

George looked embarrassed. "I'd rather not say right now. I feel kind of funny talking about…well, you know what I mean."

"Like if you told me, she would disappear?"

He shrugged. "Yeah, like that."

I nodded. "You haven't asked her out, but maybe if you did, you'd know where you stand."

He winced. "Yeah, that's true, but if she says no, then I'll be sorry." He examined his blackened palms. "And I need to get myself spruced up if we go on a date. With my work, I have to deal with grease and oil and dirt all day."

We talked about how he might buy new clothes and get his hair styled. This amused him to the point where he suggested a manicure would help. I laughed and agreed that it might. I gave him some positive feedback along these lines, and he seemed pleased.

As George was about to leave, my suspicions rushed in when he asked me to follow him downstairs. He wouldn't say why. With some trepidation, I did as he requested. He opened the outside door and pointed to my car. On the trunk, someone had drawn a large red heart in lipstick. An arrow pierced it at left and right— the typical Cupid design. In the middle was written "I AM YOURS."

Stunned, I glanced nervously at George.

He chuckled. "Guess you've got an admirer."

I was sure my face had gone pale. "Seems so."

"Well, time to get back to work. See you soon."

He left before I could ask him how he knew the Audi was mine, though George probably had seen the sign indicating that the parking spot was reserved for my office suite. Still, I felt unsettled by his behavior and upset about my car.

After running upstairs to get paper towels and liquid soap, I returned to scrub off the lipstick, embarrassed as several passersby looked on and smiled. Because the cleaning was imperfect, it was necessary to go to the car wash later.

Once seated at my desk, I pondered George's odd comments during the session and whether George Durst could be responsible for the lipstick heart. He had opportunity: an afternoon appointment, a job that allowed him to move freely within walking distance of the parking lot, and his reported interest in a woman that he refused to name—someone he'd seen with another man. Was that other man Nick? When we met for dinner? George had demonstrated hostility toward this assumed rival, which brought to mind a character, Jud Frye, in *Oklahoma!*, a loner fixated on a woman. When she rejected him in favor of another man, Jud turned violent. Had I connected the two because George resembled Rod Steiger? I reminded myself that George was a client who deserved my professional consideration. I didn't know what raged inside of him, but I knew that if he became frustrated or angry, George—a trained soldier and a very powerful man—would be physically formidable.

No other clients were scheduled for the day, and my annoying caller had temporarily ceased cluttering my answering machine. Despite the distraction over the lipstick-scrawling fanatic, I worked on my book and printed the completed chapters. After tucking the stack of paper in my briefcase, I went downstairs and surveyed the parking lot. The businesses surrounding it had rear service entrances, with their main doors on Nassau Street. It was unlikely any shopkeepers had seen my suitor write on my car, but I asked several. No luck.

I drove to the car wash and then felt relief knowing the repellent sentiments had been removed. Then I went grocery shopping.

—

On Tuesday, Lloyd Baskins arrived at one, dressed in a handsome tweed jacket, green and white tattersall shirt, and khaki trousers. His brown hair was a trifle wispy, the wind having overpowered the glue of mousse and hairspray. He patted his head at the back, where the bald spot was conscientiously trying to make itself seen, and edged behind the coffee table, arranging himself in the corner of the sofa and folding his hands in front of him like a parishioner in church.

"Tell me about your week, Lloyd."

"Oh, dear Ellen, thank you for asking! Bibby and I had such a time with Peter. You can't imagine! Absolutely hideous!"

"What happened?"

"Well, Peter came over for a few tools that he left in our shed. You know, drills and wrenches and things like that," he explained, frowning in disdain. "Herself would never touch such nasty things, of course," he said as an aside. "When he came into the house, he told me he intended to take dear Bibby with him. I said no, but he was *so forceful*!"

"Why did he think you should give him Bibby?"

"No reason whatsoever! The lawyers are still fussing and fighting and sending each other letters and nothing has been resolved. So, anyhow, I told him Bibby was not leaving the house. And can you imagine? He tried to pick her up!"

"What did you do?"

"Oh, my, god, Ellen, it was quite a scene! As you know, Peter is such a big boy, but I had to protect Bibby, so I threatened to phone the police."

"And did this have any effect?"

"Sort of. He got very angry, but I held my ground. Finally, he left after calling me all kinds of horrible names." Lloyd's face fell, still disconsolate at the memory.

"You must have been upset."

"I was." His shoulders sagged. "I don't think he cares anymore. That chippy little nurseryman must be satisfying him."

"Do you think Peter will come back to you?"

Lloyd pursed his lips, drawing a finger across one of the horizontal lines in his forehead. "I suppose the answer is that he won't." He pressed harder on his head, as if trying to avoid the tears that appeared on the periphery of his blue eyes.

Though I was tempted to hand him a tissue, I waited to see which way he went: tears or self-control. With a lengthy drawn-out sigh, he reached for the tissue himself and wiped the dampness.

"Lloyd, I know how unhappy you are. You and Peter have been together for so long. It never seems fair that one person goes off after years of emotional investment—"

"And a house and a dog and paintings and a Steuben collection and…a lot of things. I thought we would grow old together." Lloyd said this with deep sorrow, touching the tissue to fresh tears.

As commonplace as sadness was in my office, it sometimes felt incredibly difficult to alleviate. I asked Lloyd to tell me more about how he felt. Mostly, he was miserable, shocked, lonely, and above all, wounded. I encouraged him to write a note to Peter saying it would be a comfort if Peter would cede his claim to the dog, since Peter had moved on to someone else. At first, Lloyd believed this would be too pathetic, but I suggested it could be written with dignity. We then discussed the personal ad, which Lloyd had posted in the *Village Voice*, and as he was leaving, Lloyd took my hand and expressed his sympathy over my mother's death.

I thanked him and said goodbye.

[THE JOURNAL]

It was kind of weird buying the lipstick. The salesgirl kept giving me odd looks, which made me embarrassed, but I stuck to it because it was important to pick the right color. Everything I get for you matters and has to be perfect. My message on your car was an avowal of my feelings and marks the next stage in our relationship. I'm ready to be closer. I know you are, too.

AFTER Lloyd's emotional session, I wrote notes, all the while wondering if Lloyd could be my nemesis caller. He was an unlikely candidate, but the fact that I was even considering him as a possibility meant I was becoming distracted by my personal situation. I turned my thoughts to Dolly Bordella, my next client, mused over her sexual ambivalence and odd manner, and determined to focus on therapy and not detective work.

I glanced through her file and stared at the self-portrait she had completed during her initial appointment. A multitude of obsessively drawn flowers, reproduced in pastel colors, studded a yellow meadow and crowded the page around her diminutive figure. Dolly had drawn more flowers on her dress so there was little separation between Dolly and her surroundings. Her blue eyes were drawn as large circles, giving the impression of astonishment, and her torso was an androgynous rectangle, with arms stiffly flanking each side and fingers reproduced as sharp sticks, like the nails of a Chinese mandarin. Did Dolly view herself as invisible amid the flowers yet able to flash claws if confronted?

I opened the door to the outer room and found her waiting. She was wearing another floral dress, this one printed with violets and bluebells, an outfit more appropriate for June rather than October, though Dolly had added a pale pink mohair sweater. She entered the office and folded herself into the arms of the couch, but only after a peek behind it.

From an old leather briefcase, Dolly withdrew a sketchpad, flipped the cover, and gave it to me. "I did one drawing—not both."

After my recent study of her self-portrait, I was surprised to see this new sketch. As light and summery as the first depiction had been, this drawing was ferociously dark, with black and red used liberally. Dolly had drawn Mr. Vanderhoek, the butcher, in what I assumed was a back room or cold locker. The walls were outlined in black and tilted with a skewed perspective. The butcher was a huge presence on the page, with a massive head on an imposing body. A bloody apron was tied around his thick waist, and his right arm was raised in a threatening pose with a big bloody cleaver clutched in his fist. Blood dripped into a red puddle on the floor. The effect was terrifying and seemed to accurately convey the nightmarish memory she had previously related to me.

I looked at her. Her eyes were oddly dilated and her hands were shaking, but the upset expression had been erased, as if she had departed her body.

"Dolly," I said gently, "could you tell me how you felt doing this drawing?" I hated to ask because she seemed so far away.

A sad smile formed and she sighed. "I don't remember."

"When did you make the sketch?"

"One evening," she replied in a drifty voice.

"This is Mr. Vanderhoek, the butcher? In his shop?"

"Yes."

"He's very frightening. Is this a scene that happened, Dolly?"

"I don't know. Maybe."

"He probably wore an apron," I prompted.

"Yes, he did."

"And there was usually blood on the apron?"

She began to look behind the sofa but stopped halfway, then stared out the window. Her voice was distant. "Yes. Blood on the apron. And all around. Rabbits hanging from their ears. Pigs' feet with red hooves."

"Do you know how old you were in this scene?"

Dolly turned to me. "Not exactly. Maybe seven. Not older."

"Was there a reason your parents sent you on an errand like this when you were so young?"

"I had lots of little jobs. I had to be responsible," she told me, as if repeating what her parents told her. "To help out."

"Dolly, this seems like a scary experience for a child, don't you think?"

She didn't answer, though her eyes widened by way of response.

"Did you stop going to Mr. Vanderhoek's at some point?"

"Yes. My mother went instead."

"Why did she decide to do that? Do you recall?"

"No."

Obviously, something had occurred between the butcher and Dolly, though at the age she had been, it was possible that the suggestive nature of the shop—with the blood, gore, and animal parts—would have been sufficient to produce fear without anything untoward happening. I doubted she would say more, probably because she was incapable of doing so.

"Dolly, if it's okay with you, could I keep this drawing? Unless you have anything to add, maybe we could talk about it again during another session?"

She nodded. The color returned to her cheeks, and she seemed more present.

"Could you tell me about your last few days?" I asked.

"I did some writing."

"Good for you. What about?"

"A story. I don't want to say much until I'm sure about it."

"A writer's privilege?"

She liked that. "Yes, I suppose so."

"What else?"

"I went to the store and bought flowers. Lots of them. I love flowers!"

"What kind did you buy?"

"Yellow and gold mums. Asters. Roses. Carnations. And some coxcombs."

"What color were the carnations and the coxcombs?"

Dolly smiled as if I'd asked an idiotic question. "Red, of course. The coxcombs, though, are more of a dark pink." She looked at her hands folded in her lap. "I shouldn't have spent money on them, but sometimes one has to do that sort of thing. To show appreciation."

This last comment startled me. "Appreciation?"

She gave me a forbearing look. "One should always appreciate beauty in the world, don't you think?"

"Yes, you're right."

"You love flowers, too, don't you, Ellen?"

"I do. Very much."

"Good. I couldn't like anyone who doesn't love flowers."

I inquired whether Dolly had made a medical appointment for a check-up, and she replied that she would call in a few days. I wasn't sure if she was telling the truth, however seeing a doctor didn't seem to induce a phobic response, even if the objects of her fear were difficult to predict. We then discussed her plans for the weekend, which sounded solitary. I proposed trying some activities that would bring Dolly into contact with others, where she might make some new friends.

"I have a friend," she told me quietly. "I just don't see her very often. Not as much as I would like. She lives out of town."

I tried to ascertain information about this person, but Dolly wasn't forthcoming. We parted and I made notes: "blood, violence, unknown trauma with Mr. Vanderhoek at 7 yrs. +. Disassociation when confronted with memory. Secrets. Writing a story. Has a friend, won't discuss."

———

When I heard Denise DiNicola enter the waiting room, I took a drink of water and showed Denise in. As she seated herself, I noticed she was wearing new clothes and shoes: a red-and-white-striped blouse, navy wool pants, and Clarks black suede shoes.

"You're dressed up, Denise. You look very nice."

She blushed. "Thanks. I went shopping today."

"Did you go with anyone?"

Denise looked surprised by my question and shook her head, causing a lock to fall over one eye. "I went by myself." She loosened her barrette and fixed the errant hair, swearing under her breath as she did so.

"I see. Well, it's always good to buy new clothes," I said. "So, Denise, how have you felt this week?"

"A little better. Not all the time."

"When were you unhappy?"

"When I'm alone."

"That's understandable. How can you meet new people?"

"I have friends," she insisted.

I let the subject drop. "How is work? Are you starting a new project?"

"Yes, sort of. I was given a piece of marble. A large piece, though it's irregular."

"What are you going to do with it?"

"A portrait."

"Of whom?"

"I'll decide soon," she replied, smiling. "Of course, the position of the head will depend on the marble. It's faults and flaws."

I observed how Denise's face had brightened. "That sounds like a challenging project. One you're excited about."

"Yeah. I can't wait to get started."

I nodded and asked if anything else had happened over the week.

"Not really."

Though I was hesitant to inquire, I asked if she was still drinking as much wine.

Her mood changed abruptly. "What's that got to do with any-thing?"

"I'm just concerned about you. Alcohol can increase depres-sive thoughts. So when you're feeling a bit rocky, moderation might be helpful."

"If you want me to stop, I will," she said in a sullen voice.

"It's not that I personally want you to stop. The things you do, Denise, you do for yourself. To benefit your health and well-being."

Denise was now scowling as she had during the last session when I brought up the topic. As much as it was important for her to reduce the deleterious effects of alcohol, I had to tread gingerly.

"Perhaps you could you try a little less wine this week and see how it goes."

She dipped her head in concession. "Okay, I guess."

After an uncomfortable silence, I returned to questions about her work as a means to put a positive spin on our conversation. Denise explained that her employer, Victor, had been pleased with a section of flowers she was carving at the base of a statue commis-sioned by the City of Trenton.

"I'm only doing a small area. The centerpiece is a child play-ing in a field. Victor is carving the figure and another apprentice and I are doing the ground. The sculpture will be installed in one of the parks."

"That's exciting, Denise. Congratulations!"

She grinned. "It's the first time I've had a chance like this. On something important."

"You must be quite talented. It sounds like Victor is confident in your work and trusts you."

Denise shrugged, as if embarrassed. People probably didn't praise her often. I also suspected that past relationships, particu-larly familial ones, had been problematic. Though we only had ten minutes left, I ventured into that territory.

"You have no brothers or sisters, right?"

She frowned. "Well, actually, I had a baby brother, but he died."

"Younger than you?"

"Yeah, I was five. He was about a year old."

"How did he die?"

"I think he fell out of his crib, but I don't remember." Denise placed her hands in her pockets.

"That's very sad. How did your parents handle his death?"

"I don't know. After it happened, my parents sent me away, to stay with my mother's sister. I didn't like her. She used to hit me with a belt. Said it was good for me."

"I'm sorry, Denise."

"I was really scared the whole time I was there. Sometimes my aunt would have too much to drink at the bar downstairs—she and my uncle owned a tavern. I used to hide to get away from her."

Alcoholism ran in her family. Were her parents also heavy drinkers? "How long did you stay with your aunt and uncle?"

"A few months. I went there before Christmas."

"Did you ever tell your parents about her behavior?"

Denise snorted. "What for? They were just as bad."

"They punished you, too?"

"Yeah. For nothing. They made me do all sorts of things. I always had a lot of jobs, so I didn't have much time for my schoolwork, and then they'd yell at me, complaining I was stupid because my grades weren't good."

"You must have felt angry at them," I suggested.

"Angry?" Her eyebrows rose. "Oh, yeah, I did," Denise said, as if recalling a long-forgotten feeling. "But that's the way it was. When things were tough, I stayed in my room or went into the woods. To a hut I'd made with tree branches and bunches of dried grass tied together for the roof." After a second, she added, "I'd take food from the refrigerator. You know, for when I had to be gone for a while."

"That sounds very lonely. How old were you?"

She thought for a minute. "Probably about eight but this stuff continued for years. Sometimes I brought a blanket, in case I had to sleep outside all night."

Her additions were beginning to seem fabricated, though the story was plausible.

"Weren't you frightened sleeping in the woods by yourself? That required bravery."

Denise was silent, either wrestling with the unaccustomed commiseration or trying to devise other embellishments—I wasn't sure which. I thought of Dolly Bordella and noted some similarities between her experiences and Denise's.

"I don't remember," she said.

"I'm glad you had a safe place. That's important. Though this room is probably unlike your apartment, I hope you'll come to feel safe here, too."

She examined the office as if for the first time and nodded. "I do."

"Good," I replied. "Denise, our time is up for today, but I'd like to talk more about some of these things at the next session. I hope you have a good week."

"You, too."

She thanked me and left, though she seemed disinclined to go. I felt we had established a connection and was optimistic that working on the sculpture and a reduction in alcohol might help improve her mood.

[THE JOURNAL]

I'm not getting much done—not like I should—but it's difficult to think about anything else when all I can think about is you. You must have trouble concentrating on your clients because you're dreaming about me. I know you need the money, but I wish they would find another therapist. I don't like that you spend so much time with them. I hate it. But we'll be together soon, and you won't see them anymore. In the meantime, I'm getting frustrated.

I STAYED in the office during my break. At five, the Claytons were in the waiting room, looking steamed. As soon as Sharon touched down on the couch, she exploded because Steve had promised to meet a client at the train station and had to leave halfway through our session. I knew this signaled more than job interference and was emblematic of how he used professional excuses to avoid their personal interactions. I could understand why Sharon was angry, but my difficulty lay in trying to value her feelings without alienating Steve.

"There wasn't anyone else who could go?" I asked him.

He was uncomfortable with my question—Sharon had undoubtedly been peppering him with the identical one. "Not really. It's part of my responsibilities at work."

"Nonsense!" his wife interrupted. "You could've sent your secretary or any of a half-dozen people. By the time we finished here, you would have been at the office in time to have your meeting. Besides, why do they have to schedule it at 6:30 p.m.?"

"That's not up to me, Sharon. That's the way it was arranged."

Hostility flushed her cheeks. "I bet."

Though I agreed with Sharon, I had to stay balanced. "Maybe you feel as though it's essential for you to be present?" I asked Steve. Sharon shot me a dagger, as if to say, "whose side are you on?"

He gave me a wan smile. "I know I should be here, but this was important."

I didn't believe him. "For therapy to work, it's vital that everyone commits to the time we have together. I'm sure you realize this, Steve, and I'm equally sure this was an unavoidable situation."

Sharon crossed her legs away from her husband, indicating disagreement.

"And Sharon, I understand why you feel frustrated. The reason you wanted to come into couples' counseling was to have more primary involvement with Steve. Cutting short his participation today must be most upsetting."

"It is! I'm tired of being last!" she retorted. "And my kids are tired of it. We don't rate at all."

"How do you feel about this, Steve?"

He cast his eyes downward, as if teetering between guilt and grievance. "I don't know."

"Sharon, how do you think Steve is feeling right now?"

She turned to look at him. "Guilty. And annoyed at me because he feels that way."

Her perspicacity was rewarded with an impatient grunt from Steve. "Guilty? I don't think so. Someone has to pay the bills. Someone has to work ten-hour days so you can buy an art gallery that will go bust in a month."

Like a cornered beast, he was becoming aggressive. For him, this was unusual behavior.

"Steve, I think Sharon isn't wrong when she says you feel guilty but perhaps saying you feel badly might be more accurate. Badly because you have so little time to spend with your family."

I was tossing him a life preserver, and though he wanted to grab it, he was cautious. "Yes, of course I want to be home more. I don't enjoy working so much overtime."

His wife sniffed.

I leaned against my chair and observed Sharon and Steve. "It could be that this has evolved into an entrenched pattern for the two of you. Here's the transaction as I see it. First: Steve works late because he believes it's necessary in order to keep his job secure. Result: Sharon feels the job is more important than the children and her and accuses him of neglect. Second: Steve feels some legitimate remorse. Result: Sharon senses this and turns his remorse against him. Third: Steve becomes angry with Sharon, resents her lack of understanding, and feels alienated from her. Instead of communicating these feelings, he removes himself and begins to manufacture excuses to create distance. He also avoids resolution of his frustration at work. Result: Sharon becomes angrier with him, feels deserted and rejected. She also doesn't communicate clearly and swings between behaviors that are retaliatory and demanding."

"Are you saying this is all my fault?" She sounded astonished.

"No, I'm not laying the fault at anyone's feet. You're both extremely sensitized to each other and may be repeating the same detrimental reactions. As you can imagine, if you expect certain rote behaviors and responses, that's what you'll notice. If Steve has to work late, he knows how you will react and starts to feel resentment before he even discusses the matter with you. In other words, he's already placed himself in a pre-determined mental and emotional position and belabors his reasons for the overtime hours or for canceling family plans. His explanation sounds phony to you, Sharon, as in some ways it is, but not because he's being intentionally deceitful. He's trying to avoid your response, the one he expects. In the end, Steve creates the reaction that he dreads most." I paused for a minute to see if this made sense to them.

"So how do we fix this mess?" Steve asked.

"It isn't easy. We have to re-wire the circuits and change your habitual behaviors so you're more aware of exactly how you feel before you speak or act. Shall we try a short transaction? Sharon, please play your husband. You have to tell your wife that you must work on Thursday night rather than go to a party with her as planned. Instead of telling her the way you believe he would, tell her how you would like to be told yourself. In a way that would transform your resentment into understanding and acceptance. Steve—you're Sharon."

With some prodding and direction, they created a semblance of the dialogue I had in mind. Though it was only a modest success, Sharon and Steve appeared to be more relaxed with each other.

To my surprise, Steve asked to use my telephone to call the office and find someone to go to the station for him. Afterward, we did a short drama with Steve playing himself, facing Sharon—played by me. I asked him to re-imagine the earlier scene in my waiting room, when he told his wife he intended to leave mid-session. I studied Sharon's face as her husband had trouble telling me about his intentions.

"Sharon, what I said earlier about the dynamics between the two of you is partially incomplete. It makes it seem as though you become difficult when Steve has job-related extra hours. In fact, a significant part of the equation has to do with Steve's inability to set boundaries—at home and at work. He displaces his resentments and has trouble standing up for himself. He may also have trouble verbalizing his feelings about you and the children—both his positive feelings and the negative ones. One way people cover this is by activity. It might be easier for him to run away and be busy. You, on the other hand, want him to stand and deliver. Ultimately, you desire the same outcome, but your approaches bring you into conflict. This week, I'd like both of you to make written records of conversations that fall into the transactional categories we've discussed. Please don't discuss what you've written with each other. At our next session, we'll reconstruct the scenes."

—

Mei-Ling and Chang Lee came in, upset. Mei-Ling's parents and sister were arriving from Taiwan. Though Mei-Ling was excited, Chang seemed divided between respect for her family and logistical and financial concerns. Mei-Ling only saw his lack of enthusiasm about the visit and began the session in polite, but frigid silence.

After a few minutes, Chang interrupted. "How are we going to put up three people for a month, Mei-Ling?"

"If it were your parents, this wouldn't be an issue!" she retorted.

"My parents live twenty minutes away. It wouldn't happen."

"Yes, and we see your parents several times a week. No matter how busy I am at work or how tired, I have to prepare elaborate meals. You never ask if I want to cook or if they can come. You just invite them." Mei-Ling slapped her hands together. "Just like that!"

Chang was taken aback by this outburst. "I thought you liked my parents, Mei-Ling?"

"That may not be the problem, Chang," I explained. "Did you listen to what Mei-Ling said?"

"She said my parents come over too much, and she doesn't like it."

Mei-Ling shook her head, but remained silent, jabbing her toe against the leg of the table.

"I think she's trying to make the point that you have constant access to your family. And you don't consider how much effort it takes to prepare dinner. Both of you work very hard at your jobs and put in the same number of hours. Is that true?"

"Yes," he said.

"So, while Mei-Ling is willing to entertain your family sometimes, she isn't always happy to do so and not without discussion before an invitation is extended. Perhaps you can take more responsibility when you wish to see your parents. Arrange to go out for dinner without her, for example."

Chang looked unhappy. "But they'll think something is wrong if Mei-Ling isn't there."

"The wife must always be at her husband's side?" I asked.

Mei-Ling gave me a little smile.

Chang was displeased. "Yes. That's the way I was raised."

"But you were brought up in America," Mei-Ling protested. "It's not like that here."

"Chang, maybe you can explain to your parents how busy

your wife is, what an important career she has, and that she can't always be with you. Tell them how much she values them as family—Mei-Ling, that's part of what you need to do, too," I said, turning toward her.

"I'll try."

"And Chang, if you can ease Mei-Ling's participation in some of your family gatherings, eventually she may arrive at a comfortable level of engagement."

Though he didn't look entirely agreeable, he said he would think about it.

"The second part of this is about your parents," I told her.

Chang immediately stepped in. "That's the real trouble!"

As Mei-Ling glared at him, I replied, "Chang, I think the order of the problem is correct as we've discussed it. When was her parents' last visit?"

"I don't know. Maybe a year ago," he replied.

"Almost three years," Mei-Ling corrected. "We were still in our studio apartment then."

"So they come infrequently. This time must be very valuable to your wife," I said to him. "Chang, can you explain what the husband's role is in situations like these?"

He stared at the floor. "Like that of the wife in relation to her in-laws."

"Is it fair to say you both feel straight-jacketed by traditional expectations? You, Mei-Ling, want to have more equal say in matters that concern your husband's family. And you, Chang, want the same thing in regard to your wife's family."

They both looked at each other and nodded.

"Mei-Ling, where will your family stay?"

"My sister will go to a cousin's house. Because we have a slightly bigger place now, my parents will be with us. They'll use our bedroom, and we'll sleep on the sofabed in the living room."

"That displaces you and Chang. Maybe he's not happy about that."

Mei-Ling thought for a minute. "I have an idea. Our neighbors will be out of town for the first week my parents are here. We could ask them if my parents can use their apartment."

"That sounds like an excellent solution."

They agreed to investigate possible accommodations. By the session's end, I felt like we had resolved a small fracas at the United Nations.

[THE JOURNAL]

I took the photograph of you from the back cover of your book and copied it at a 200% enlargement and then did that one at 200%. I also took a photo of me and enlarged it and taped it next to yours, our heads touching. Just to be safe, I tacked posters over us so no one can see our pictures. Have to keep our secret!

Pleasant dreams.

No MORE hang-up calls were on the answering machine, and nothing was on the stairs when I left the office. The parking lot was crowded with cars and diners flocking to the restaurants on Nassau and Witherspoon Streets. As I approached my Audi, however, I was shocked to see a long-stem, red rose tucked under the windshield wiper and even more horrified to observe a trail of red along the car's silver side. Paint? I looked carefully and shivered. No. Blood. Should I call the police? But what if this had been done by Nick? I had to be sure before I reported a family member. If he was the perpetrator, he needed counseling and not by me.

I pulled tissues from a box on the backseat. Using them, I freed the rose and carried it to a nearby waste container, taking care with the thorny stems and thinking that an accidental jab couldn't have caused the amount of blood on the rose and car. As I wiped the windshield and metal surfaces, I concluded this was a symbolic display. The pricking of fingers was sometimes done to exchange blood, as a pledge of devotion, so the bloody rose might serve as a vow of loyalty, in the belief that pain is required to prove faithfulness. Similar to a connection Carson had made. And hadn't Dolly bought roses as well as other flowers?

These reflections made me shudder. I wasn't interested in playing Juliet to a lunatic Romeo. No bowers for me and no pricked fingers.

I stopped at the video store and rented *Oklahoma!* because I wanted to study Steiger's portrayal of Jud, to analyze why the character reminded me of George. Thinking of George tripped an image of the gauze on his finger. Had he purchased the rose the day before and cut himself? I reminded myself that George handled a lot of sharp objects and probably had been injured at work. But his odd question also kept resurfacing in my mind: "Would you want me?"

From the store, I drove home quickly, checking the rearview

mirror and feeling paranoid. But paranoia was a reaction to imaginary foes. In my case, my arrivals and departures at the office had been observed by a real person, someone sitting in the parking lot in his or her car or monitoring my movements from a hidden vantage point, such as from an adjacent business or the Princeton Public Library. And, too, it was likely that my house was under surveillance.

As I unlocked the front door, I focused again on Nick. Though I dreaded calling him, I was determined to learn if he was behind the gifts. If it was Nick, it didn't explain why my phone bill had been tampered with, unless a neighbor had received it and accidentally opened the envelope.

I ran upstairs, noting two more clicks on the answering machine, and checked my cousin's number in my parents' address book and dialed. Katie answered. She sounded pleased to hear from me, then expressed her sympathy over my mother's death. I thanked her and asked how long she had been home. She was surprised that I knew she'd been away and said she'd returned two weeks ago. So much for Nick's lie about her absence. After a few minutes, I asked to speak to him, even though Katie might think it was unusual. He came on the line from another room.

"Hi, Ellie. This is a nice surprise."

Was his wife within hearing range or still on the phone? "Hi, Nick. Do you have a minute?"

I heard the click of Katie's receiver and Nick close a door.

"So you've changed your mind?" he asked with a trace of sarcasm.

"No, I haven't changed my mind, but I'd like to ask you about some odd things that have been happening."

"We could have drinks after work. Maybe at the Peacock Inn?"

The Peacock Inn was a small hotel with a bar and restaurant. The sexual suggestion was glaring.

"Nick, please, will you listen to me? Did you put some flowers on my office stairs?"

"Oh, so now you think I gave you flowers?" He laughed. "Maybe I did."

I had no idea if he was teasing or telling the truth. "I'm serious. I need to know."

Nick chuckled again. "Perhaps you should send me some flowers."

"Look, someone is leaving me carnations and chocolate and—earlier today—a rose. Did you or did you not do that?"

"Ah, so you have a gentleman fan! Hey, I'm jealous!"

This was not proceeding as I'd hoped. "Please…just tell me."

"Maybe Drew's come back? He's realized he's not gay and you're the one for him."

"Don't talk about Drew."

"Oh, Ellen, dear Ellen. What can I say? Call the florists and the candy stores."

"Don't make fun of me, Nick. I've also had quite a number of phone calls. Hang-ups after the message has played. At the house and at the office."

"Gee, that would be a little frightening, particularly at home. That big place with all the great big windows. You all alone… those dark woods."

I couldn't discern whether he was putting me on or whether he was enjoying my predicament. His tone fell somewhere on the scale between pique and spite with a hefty dose of innuendo, as if my phone call was an engraved invitation to my bedroom. No matter how I asked the questions, Nick didn't give me straight answers. Even if he had patched up things with his wife, he was still only interested in one thing.

I tried again. "Can you please tell me if you're giving me flowers and calling?"

A loud guffaw greeted my question. "Poor little therapist," he finally managed through his laughter, "come to me for help!"

"I don't need your help, I need you to answer!"

"Somebody has the hots for you...I wonder who?" he half-sang.

Furious, I slammed down the phone, tempted to throw the damned thing against the wall. I felt almost as dirty as if I'd actually had sex with him.

What should I do next? I would either have to catch the person, figure out his or her identity, or call the police. If I called the police, I would be stuck in no-man's-land between my clients' privacy and my need to have intervention. At this point, I hadn't been threatened, nor had any real damage occurred. I decided to wait until my admirer came forward, or I could catch Nick—or whomever it was—in the act.

—

After dinner, I slipped the video of *Oklahoma!* into the VCR. It had been many years since I'd viewed the movie, but I knew the score well and immediately remembered the plot. When Rod Steiger appeared, I was amazed by the resemblance between George Durst and Steiger's Jud, the surly and menacing farmhand. Even Steiger's heavy-shouldered posture and brooding demeanor were eerily similar to my client, as were his dirty clothes and hands. Jud was a solitary loner, who represented the dangerous side of love, a side that I hoped my shadow lover wouldn't cross.

The film did nothing to alleviate my fears. When it was over, I double-checked the locks and went upstairs, eager to be out of the great room with all the windows. The blinds in the bedroom were still lowered from the night before, which made me feel less vulnerable as I changed into a nightgown. Climbing into bed, I wished

I could be downstairs in my room with my parents asleep up here. I considered calling my father in the morning and begging him to come home. If I told him what was happening, he would be on the next available plane. I also knew I wouldn't ask him. He needed to regain his health, mental and physical. It would be selfish to deprive him of the time he required. This was something I had to handle, even if I was growing more and more anxious.

—

The next morning arrived too soon. All night, I had tossed and turned in frustrated anger at Nick, devising questions that would have forced him to admit he was harassing me. George made a brief appearance, too. Hulking in a dark hallway, waiting. My stomach was churning as I came into the kitchen for breakfast. I poured a bowl of cereal and skipped coffee.

After dropping off the video in the before-hours slot, I drove into Princeton. Two clicks were on the answering machine. Aggravated, I paced the room, trying to relieve the tension. Finally, I sat at my desk and began working on the lecture scheduled for Friday evening at the university. The topic was creativity, with a presentation followed by a Q&A session. Because I'd given this speech twice before, all I needed to do was insert some ideas from recent weeks of research.

—

Greta Graf turned up at ten in an olive, cable-knit cardigan missing a wooden button. An orange and brown bead necklace was caught around a remaining one, making a comma shape across her chest. Instead of her Birkenstocks, she sported a startling pair of turquoise and white running shoes.

"New sneakers?" I asked.

She turned a thick ankle to admire a shoe. "I needed them. I've joined a walking program. We get together near the lake."

"Good for you, Greta! So you've met some people?"

"Yes, I suppose, but I don't know if I'll be able to keep up with the younger ones. They're very spry, athletic types."

"Surely there are others who aren't so vigorous."

"One or two."

I realized today's "gotcha" game was milder than usual. I hazarded a guess. "Your friend, Stanley, wouldn't be one of them, would he?"

She smiled. "Yes, as a matter of fact he mentioned the group to me. But there's also a woman I know slightly, a weaver who shows her work at the same gallery I do. Anne Ainsley. A nice gal."

"Wonderful news. Exercise and new friends."

"Well, I wouldn't quite say 'friends' yet. Acquaintances, more like it."

"Acquaintances, then. How often does everyone meet?"

"Depending on the weather, Tuesday and Friday afternoons. Attendance is optional. I like that."

We were silent for a moment. "So how are you and Stanley getting along? You were considering the possibility of asking him for brunch."

"I know. I was thinking of doing that but maybe including Anne, so it would be less like a date. Anne is a widow, by the way. Lives near me in a house off Harrison Street. She plans to visit my studio."

I was pleased. It was astounding what social creatures we were—how deprivation led us into swamps of misery but making new friends could magically lift us up. Although Greta was depressive by nature, I believed that an accurate view of reality was sometimes a justifiable cause for mild depression. It was also my opinion that depression and creativity often went together, one chasing after the other, in a kind of up/down stair pattern. As long as one was productive and enthused about a project, the depression disappeared. When 'writer's block' or an analogous creative impediment struck, depression returned, as Greta had recently experienced.

I explained some of this to Greta and asked if this resonated with her experience. I was curious about her perspective because of my analysis of creative people.

"I agree with you, Ellen. When I'm full of ideas, I feel fine. It's when I'm not, well, that's another matter. It's worse since Heinrich left. He always wanted to know what I had accomplished when he come home at night. He was a perceptive critic and supporter."

"Having a relationship with someone who appreciates what you're doing is extremely important for an artist. And rare to find." I thought of Drew and suddenly felt overcome with nostalgia for our time together.

"Yes, it is," she agreed, studying me closely. "I think that's one reason I feel comfortable with you. You share some of the same feelings."

I smiled at her recognition. "Thank you, Greta. I'm happy you feel that way."

We chatted until the end of the session. As she was leaving, Greta gave me a friendly smile, which was both a surprise and welcome.

[THE JOURNAL]

I can't sleep. I left you a perfect rose, perfect as we are. It's comforting to know you will get my beautiful flower and realize it came from me, the one you've chosen. My blood is a pledge to be yours forever. One day soon you'll give me your blood as a pledge to be mine. When that day happens, I will possess you completely, and I will be yours completely, blessed and pure and clean.

I can see you on the wall. The moon lights your face and tells me things about you, secret things, inside things that only I am allowed to know.

I BOUGHT a chicken salad sandwich, carton of milk, and two oatmeal cookies for lunch. Bag in hand, I returned to the office and laid the food on my desk, just in time for another call. I answered, heard breathing, and a click. My stomach turned over. I pushed away the sandwich and fell back against my chair. Who could this be? Nick was still at the top of my list, but his flirtatious evasiveness during our conversation had prevented any enlightenment. So while Nick was a possibility, others were, too, including people I might not have met or might not know well. Shopkeepers or waiters in places I frequented; dozens of people, many with a low profile on my mental radar. I even wondered if one of Lucas' friends or relatives blamed me for what had happened to him and had designed this torture as a kind of crazy revenge. The harder I tried to narrow the field, the larger the field became.

Determined to eat something, I forced down half of the sandwich and the container of milk. I placed the cookies in my briefcase to take home, tidied up the crumbs on my desk, and sat looking through the window, thinking.

—

Carson needed to come at one instead of noon, so we had scheduled for then. When he arrived, he was sporting his jaunty red scarf and was wired with excitement because he had sub-let the first floor of a Victorian house in Lambertville. The apartment had large rooms and high ceilings that would allow him to tackle bigger canvases. He proceeded to enthuse about the town's restaurants, the artistic community, and a New Hope disco, where he had successfully met some women. That brought us back to last week's topic.

"Carson, could we talk more about your comment? That you persuaded women to have sexual intercourse with you? Do you recall what you told me?"

"Sure. And then I said that I'd made the story up."

"Yes, you did," I replied, "but the conversation caused me to wonder why you would portray yourself as an aggressor and afterward tell me the story was fiction."

He ran his fingers over his mouth. "You don't have anything to worry about, Ellen."

Meaning what? Was he speaking in general or to me specifically? Whichever the case, I had heard enough.

"I know it's in vogue to create sexually shocking work…and that with each additional increase in depicted violence, the public seems willing to raise the bar another notch. However, I'm not comfortable with this tolerance of sexual and physical aggression. It denigrates people, both men and women, pouring them into molds of either an attacker or a victim, removing their individual attributes, their complexities. I apologize for the lecture, but I'm concerned about your self-myth-making, even if you've recanted your story. Whether you did or did not behave this way, you sound like you're dehumanizing women. You've often said you desire the companionship, love, and caring of a partner. If you do, then perhaps we need to work on your fantasies because I'm not convinced you've acted in a loving manner in the past, even if you believe your actions fall within the boundaries of acceptable conduct."

"My god! What set you off?" He laughed and unwrapped the scarf from around his neck. "Someone must have gotten out of line with you."

I didn't like his attitude or his personalization. "Carson, I'm committed to helping my clients achieve healthy relationships, but how are we going to achieve that when you equate sex with aggression?"

"What's wrong with aggression? We're animals. Males are expected to attract females by proving their physical prowess."

I was surprised by his tenacity and that his feelings hadn't been so plainly expressed before. Perhaps since he had started painting again, his libido had become re-awakened.

"We aren't gorillas swinging from trees. This attitude won't wash with me. I'm sorry."

He moderated his stance. "I'm exaggerating, Ellen. You know that."

"You may be exaggerating. I hope you are," I said. "Maybe we should begin by talking more about your family, about the relationship between your parents, your grandparents. I know we've touched on some of this last spring."

Carson sighed and then reiterated his background, providing more detail. He came from a lower-middle-class family with a working father and a stay-at-home mother. He didn't remember his grandparents well, most of whom had died before he was born. The Kendricks lived in New York City's Lower East Side throughout his childhood and suffered a number of financial scrapes due to his father's frequent unemployment. The death of his twin sister created a rift between his parents, and as Carson's artistic interests became more pronounced, his father began criticizing him and insisted he pursue a practical career. Although I knew some of this information, he now mentioned a closeness with his father's brother, a jazz musician. After some prodding, Carson admitted that his uncle had encouraged him to have sex at an early age, even arranging for a prostitute to initiate him. He maintained there was nothing unethical about what happened.

"Did your uncle have a wife?"

"Harry? Yeah...well, when he was young and on the road he married some gal. Have no idea what the hell happened to her. He often turned up with someone new."

Was this callous attitude Carson's or his uncle's? "Do you admire him?"

"Harry died a few years ago, but sure, he was fun to be

around. He also liked my painting—he bought one of my first nudes for $200. A lot of money back then. He also helped me get a scholarship to art school and introduced me to some cool hipster artists."

"How did your uncle get along with your parents?"

"They tolerated him. Dad was a bore by comparison and despised the guys Harry hung out with, calling them commies, hippies, atheists, scuzzballs. It didn't matter that Harry made decent money playing in clubs—more than my father did at his different jobs. And Mom? I don't know whether she liked Harry or not. I never saw them together without my dad."

"Was there a reason for that?"

Carson squinted his eyes. "Harry was sometimes on the make. He liked the ladies."

"Did you ever overhear a conversation that led you to believe your mother wasn't at ease with your uncle or that he had made advances?"

He shrugged. "I recall one night, after I went to bed. I heard Dad shouting at Harry. To keep his hands to himself. Something like that."

I leaned against my chair. "I hate to say it, Carson, but it's possible your uncle wasn't the best role model for you."

Carson studied his fingernails. "I don't know about that. He certainly knew how to have a good time."

"He probably was an interesting person. Even so, his attitudes toward women don't sound very respectful."

"Never thought about it much." He considered for a moment. "Though one time Harry made a pest out of himself with one of my girlfriends. I went out to buy beer, and when I came back, she was waiting downstairs, mad about something he'd done. I thought she'd overreacted."

"Did that end the relationship with your girlfriend?"

He nodded. "Yeah, as a matter of fact."

"So you took your uncle's side?"

Carson looked at me, an odd expression on his face. "Yes, I did."

It was my turn to nod. "I think we need to discuss this more, Carson, don't you?"

"Maybe."

"This may come across as strange, but will you draw a picture of your girlfriend and your uncle? A quick sketch for next week?"

He shot me a quizzical look but agreed to do so.

"We'll talk more then, okay? And good luck with your new place. I hope it's a productive environment."

He thanked me and left in a somber mood, a considerable contrast to the boisterousness he'd displayed in the beginning.

As I sat at my desk, adding to his file, I kept wondering about his sudden decision to rent an apartment in Lambertville. Lambertville was only a few minutes from my house in Hopewell. A coincidence? And what about the violence depicted in Carson's artwork? Benign artistic fantasies or aggressive expressions of desire?

———

Robert Fleet came in as if he had been blown up the stairs by the wind. Breathless, he related a story about how he had garnered a large commission as a result of a purchase by one of his wealthiest clients. I congratulated Robert and listened to his detailed account. Then, with some embarrassment, he confessed that his colleague, Susan, had praised him.

"That was very nice of her. Did you say anything to Susan during the week? Like we spoke about?"

He lifted his shoulders. "No."

"How does that make you feel?"

"Well, not good."

Finally! Progress! "Susan sounds like a gracious woman."

Robert's mouth ruffled with displeasure, perhaps noting the tacit comparison between her behavior and his. "I guess I need to compliment Susan," he muttered, focusing on the Venetian masks. Then he faced me. "But, hey, the commission will improve my chance for a bonus."

"I hope so. That would be a real accomplishment."

He beamed, sat straighter, and smoothed his red silk tie. "It would."

"Your wife will be very pleased for you."

"Yeah." Her opinion didn't seem important to him.

"How are things at home, Robert?"

The subject held little appeal, consumed as he was with his career triumph. I tried to steer the dialogue to marital matters twice, but Robert refused to stick to any discussion involving Debby. As I was beginning to wonder if something was going on, he changed tacks.

"I don't know how to say this, Ellen, but I think Susan is attracted to me."

From being jealous of her to interested in her made me alert. Susan had commended him, and in Robert's mind, that equated to attraction.

"Why do you think so?"

"She asked me to lunch tomorrow. To celebrate."

"That was thoughtful, but why do you think she's interested in more than a collegial lunch? If a male co-worker invited you, would you think he was attracted?"

"No, of course not."

"So why is Susan's invitation different?"

He chuckled. "Men know this kind of thing."

I thought of Nick and suddenly felt irritated. "Is she married?"

"I think so."

"Robert, at the risk of sounding old-fashioned, I'd say you might be heading down the wrong road for several reasons."

"I haven't done anything yet!" he protested.

"No, you haven't, but if Susan is married, as you are, then entertaining these thoughts isn't a good idea, don't you think? And if you've misunderstood her intentions, you might jeopardize your working relationship with Susan if you flirt with her. She could take offense and lodge a complaint with your employer."

He looked uncomfortable with my objection. Robert didn't tolerate correction well. "All right, all right. Maybe I'm wrong about her."

This was as close to an admission of fallibility as I would hear from him. "Accept the lunch offer—she's made a friendly gesture—and keep things professional."

Robert looked surprised by my vehemence, but after a short pause, he began nattering about ways to spend his commission, none of which involved his wife or paying down the debt on his credit cards. I tried again to ask how they were doing, but I couldn't shift the conversation in that direction. Finally, he left. Not one of my more successful sessions.

[THE JOURNAL]

I left you a valentine. I wanted you to know I was thinking of you. When I touched the car, I felt your energy flowing into my fingers, down my arms, and through my body. I have never felt this way before. I don't know how you arranged for that to happen.

This afternoon, as I was walking in town, I saw your face on a poster—an announcement of a lecture. Because I knew it was for me, I took it. And then I saw you on a telephone pole, on the side of a mailbox—you are everywhere! Every poster I saw, I brought home.

Is this the message I've been waiting for? Are you trying to tell me to come to you or to come to your talk? (Of course I'll be there!)

I CLOSED Robert's file when I heard Samantha enter the waiting room. After pouring a glass of water and setting it on the table by my chair, I opened the door. Attired in her usual black clothes, Samantha gave me a bleak smile as she sat on the sofa. Her eyes were bloodshot, and she'd made unsteady attempts at applying thick eyeliner.

"You look like you didn't sleep well, Sam."

In a morose voice, she replied, "Like, not much."

"Were you out walking last night?"

"Took my car."

"Where did you go?"

"Around."

"Were you by yourself?"

"Yeah. It was late."

"How late?"

She gave me an aggravated look. "Late."

"Did your parents know you were out?" I asked, instantly regretting my espousal of the parental viewpoint.

She shrugged, determined to be uncommunicative.

"How about the writing? Did you try anything this week?"

Samantha looked out the window. "Yeah."

"Did you bring it with you?"

With this, she reluctantly pulled out a sheet of paper, folded as before in quarters. She opened it and placed the paper on the coffee table. "It's not any good."

I reached for the typewritten poem and began to read:

NIGHT
Night is blackness.
Blackness is night.
Night is when things die.
Death is the blackest night,

161

a night that is forever,
a blackness that is darker
than anyone can imagine.
Death smothers light,
death smothers day.
Night is for wandering,
exploring the eternity
of death, its miracle
of painless ending.

"Wow! That's really well written, Sam. Some great lines and it's tied together beautifully, using repetition and short, powerful phrases."

Her frown turned to a smile. "Thanks."

I paused and then added, "The poem is also pretty intense. A lot of emotion comes across." When Sam made no response, I continued. "My guess is no one else knows how you feel. Unless Jake did?"

She twisted her mouth. "I didn't say much to him."

"Do you wish you had shared more of your feelings?" Perhaps I needed to address the big issue. "Or if you had been more open, do you think you could have prevented his death?"

Sam didn't answer, but her eyes flickered.

I tried again. "In some way, do you blame yourself for what occurred?" Another shrug. "Okay, let me be clear. You aren't at fault for what happened to Jake." While she considered this, I re-read the poem again. "Sam, are you worried you'll plunge into the same blackness as he did? 'The painless ending' you write about?"

She stared through the window, her face growing tight as she struggled to hide her emotions. A single tear slipped down her cheek. When more fell, I handed her a tissue which she accepted without looking at me.

"Sam, it's okay to cry."

"It doesn't help anything," she said with little inflection.

"I'm not sure about that. When people cry in my office, it means something deep has been touched, something sensitive. That emotional openness can be cathartic, even for those who don't like crying. People like you, perhaps." I paused. "Will you tell me more about how you're feeling?"

She wiped her eyes, removing a good amount of dampness and makeup. "Like, out of it. Like I'm in some kind of spiral."

"A downward spiral?"

"Sort of. Sometimes I don't think I can stand it any more."

"What would make you feel more hopeful?"

"Probably nothing."

"I don't think that's true."

Sam considered. "Maybe if I wasn't alone. If someone was around who I could talk with, do things with." She glanced at me. "I mean, someone like you, only someone not like you."

"I think I understand. You'd like a friend to confide in, who would be supportive. Maybe read your writing or let you read theirs."

"Maybe someone more like you than not like you," she admitted, with the ghost of a smile.

"Well, thanks. That's nice of you to say. At the risk of sounding trite, I'm here for you. Please know that."

"I do."

"Good," I said. "Is there anything else that could happen? That might alter the spiral from downward to upward?"

"Like, my parents could go on a six-month vacation or something."

I smiled at her. "I think you might miss them after a few days."

She pursed her lips, as if doubtful.

"What about if something you wrote was published?"

163

Her eyes widened. "How?"

"There's a journal that holds an annual poetry and story contest for high school students. I believe the deadline is in mid-December, but I'll check it if you like. Have you ever had anything published?"

"Yeah, sort of. In the school literary magazine. Three poems. A story."

"Want to give it a try?"

"I suppose so."

"Do you have an English teacher who would read and edit your work before you submit?"

"Yeah. I could ask Mrs. DeGornio from freshman year." Sam scraped her fingers against her palm and glanced at me. "Would you'd look it? You're written books."

"Yes, but only non-fiction. However, I'd be delighted to see whatever you plan to send, but not for the literary aspects. I'll leave that to your teacher. Next week, I'll bring in the guidelines."

"Okay," she agreed and began telling me about the plot, one that was obviously based on a relationship that went beyond the one she and Jake had shared. As with the memorial, I thought writing about him would be therapeutic, particularly if she could control the ending.

At the end of the hour, my concern about her depression hadn't eased. "Sam, I know this is a painful time for you. You know that if you need to—"

"Call you. Yes, I got that and I will." She smiled, somewhat amused by my seriousness and perhaps comforted by it.

"Thank you very much for bringing in your poem. It was a privilege to read it." I returned the paper to her and then, as she was leaving, drew her into a brief hug.

—

It was well after sunset by the time I arrived home. I considered sitting on the redwood chaise on the deck, but a chilly dew had settled in. Instead, I arranged wood in the fireplace and lit the kindling, then placed a chicken in the oven after dousing the bird with lemon juice and inserting sprigs of rosemary in the cavity. I opened a bottle of Pinot Grigio, poured some in a glass, cut several slices of cheddar cheese, and set them on a plate with crackers. As I sat on the couch, the fire was beginning to catch. The spotlights were on, and as I looked outside, a black bat cut a big, swooping line on his way to Stoney Brook before disappearing into the dark forest.

I sipped my wine and thought about my practice, my father, and myself. Thirty-six-years old, unmarried, without a home of my own, no one to call for a friendly dinner, no dates, and no one interested except my omnipresent suitor and Nick. When I compared my life to that of some of my clients, I had to admit mine was as dreary. I had work I loved, accomplishments of which I was proud, some money in the bank, and by many measurements, I was a success. Yet here I was alone with a glass of wine, a romantic fire, and the inviting smell of roast chicken suffusing the house. I should follow some of my own fine advice and try to meet someone.

—

The next morning, I phoned my father in Corfu, mostly because I wanted to know how he was, but also to make a connection with him. We didn't talk long because he and the Maillarts had dinner plans. I omitted any mention of my problems and told him everything was fine. It was up to me to make it so.

After lunch, I drove to the office to use my computer and work on my lecture. I spent two hours editing and printed the pages in 14-point type so I could read it easily. As I was closing the office, the phone rang. I answered, giving my name.

"Hi. Am I speaking with Dr. Haskell?"

I had already stated my name. "Yes, it is. How may I help you?"

"Well, I would like to make an appointment. My name is Mary."

"Sure. Thank you for calling me, Mary. Could you tell me what prompted you to see a therapist?"

"Oh. I'll explain when we meet, if that's okay."

"That's fine," I replied. "Let me check my calendar." I opened the book and asked when she would like to come in. "I have Monday available next week. At 1:00 or 4:00 p.m."

"One o'clock, please."

"May I have your last name and a number where I can reach you?"

"Er...Brown." She gave me a telephone number.

As I wrote the information in my calendar, I wondered whether she had fabricated her name. Sometimes people were secretive about seeing psychologists. After mentioning my rates, I offered directions to my office, but Mary said she knew the location already. Was Mary my unknown caller, timidly hanging up without leaving a message? Before I could ask more about her, she said goodbye. Though her behavior was odd, I was delighted to expand my client list, especially on Monday, my short day.

I grabbed my briefcase and left, relieved to find no objects on the stairs. Outside, my car was untouched. Perhaps I was going to have a suitor-free evening. I drove home, checking cars behind me, though everyone peeled away outside of Hopewell. At the end of the driveway, I stopped for the mail. A lot of bills and catalogues. But then, at the bottom of the pile, was a squarish white envelope with my name printed in red ink, the style similar to the writing on my car and the envelope containing the article about Venice. A sharp stab of fear shot through me.

In my car, I scrutinized the handwriting, but the block capital letters could have been written by anyone, of either sex. There was no return address, nor was there a stamp, which meant the letter had been placed in my mailbox—his or her fingers touching it last before I did. I swallowed my loathing and lifted the unsealed flap. The card was a children's valentine depicting a small dog giving a heart to a kitten. The front said: "Happy Valentine's Day." The inside read: "I'm Yours, Be Mine!" Below, in red ink, was printed: "YOUR LION."

Although the handwriting was unfamiliar, I would check my files to compare the style with the information sheets my clients completed during their first sessions. Then I wondered where someone could purchase a valentine in October. Was it from a packet of assorted cards sent by charities in order to solicit donations? Or was "my lion" a frugal shopaholic who bought items on sale after the holiday, keeping them for the following year, or did he or she live with a parent or roommate who did? George Durst owned a house near his mother and would have access to any stash of cards she owned.

Inside the house, I decided it was wise to record these occurrences. On a pad of paper, I wrote today's date and described the card and then notated my other gifts and communications. Unsettled, I walked to the window and gazed through the woods. The spotlights illuminated only about two hundred feet into the trees and didn't extend to the street.

I tucked the card in my briefcase.

[THE JOURNAL]

I stare at your photos and know your every feature by heart. You are so beautiful with your gold hair and brown eyes, your warm smile. I touch your cheek and can almost feel its softness. On the video, your smile is for me. You know I'm watching.

I hope you liked the valentine's card. I'll put a "Graduation" card in your mailbox. I know it's not exactly right, but I want to congratulate you on your talk tomorrow night. I don't know if you'll get it before you go, but it will be waiting for you after. I plan to attend. Thank you for inviting me.

My life has changed so much. I can't explain it to anyone because no one else would understand except you. I've become special. Like I matter because you love me. One day this journal will be read by the world, and then the world will know what love really is.

I PRACTICED my speech and then read some of the Josephine Tey mystery. During the early afternoon, I pruned bushes around the garage because branches were scraping the paint. As I was piling debris on a tarp, I glimpsed a dark sedan near the mailbox. I couldn't see the car well, and by the time I stepped into the driveway to get a better look, it was gone. I set down the clippers and hurried to the street, dread increasing with each step. Slowly, I lowered the mailbox door and looked inside. Damn it! Another card!

I peeled off my lambskin work gloves and opened the envelope, noting "ELLEN" written in red ink on the front. Inside was a graduation card with an owl holding a diploma on the cover and "Congratulations" in metallic letters. My sender had written "GOOD LUCK ON YOUR TALK, LOVE, YOUR LION." The card was cheap, much like the valentine.

My suitor knew about tonight's lecture, which was open to the public. Would he or she attend and would I be able to spot an obsessive person in a crowded hall? It was likely some of my clients might come as well as a few of my parents' friends and colleagues, though their advanced age probably eliminated them as suspects.

As I walked to the house, I reconsidered my initial belief that my gift-giver suffered from a harmless infatuation. I no longer thought this. The person had developed an intense compulsion. A *Fatal Attraction*? I hadn't seen the movie—I was in Venice at the time—but certainly knew about it. Glenn Close and Michael Douglas. I decided to rent it over the weekend, though I was sure the movie was an unrealistic thriller.

After eating some leftover chicken, I showered. My hair, which needed a trim, would have to do with careful blow-drying. I then dressed in a brown and charcoal-gray suit jacket and skirt, black silk blouse, gold earrings, and a gold Florentine necklace my mother had given me. I slipped on a pair of low-heeled black shoes and left for the university.

—

The hall was already congested even though the doors were still open. Sixty people were present, maybe more. As I fidgeted with my notes and poured water into a glass, I noticed some familiar faces from the art and archaeology department, who probably came to see if I measured up to my parents, though I hoped some were interested in my topic. Of my clients, Greta Graf sat toward the front, talking with a woman who might have been Anne, her new walking companion. The Cosgroves were with Sam. Her parents were well-dressed and dignified; she wore black and slouched in her chair, angled away from them. Had the Cosgroves insisted on coming or had it been her idea? At the far left, I saw Dolly Bordella, looking anxious, perhaps working on a case of agoraphobia. Behind her, Denise DiNicola was sitting alone. I smiled at both. Dolly gave me a little wave, and Denise returned my smile. The Lees were together mid-way and nodded, and although my view was partially blocked by three tall men, I thought my tennis pro, Martie, was sitting in the last row. How did she learn about the lecture? Perhaps she'd seen a poster in town or an announcement in the paper.

The head of the counseling center introduced me. When I began speaking, I saw George Durst, neatly dressed in a jacket and tie, standing along the side wall toward the rear. He appeared ill at ease, but when he noticed I was looking at him, his face relaxed. After that, I concentrated on my speech, trying to evenly divide my attention across the audience. Though I made eye contact, I had little memory afterward of anyone who stood out as odd. The Q&A at the end was active, always a positive sign. A comic touch usually provided a good chaser to a serious discussion, and I tried to leaven my answers accordingly. At the end, there was solid applause, which I scarcely heard.

The University Store had brought several cartons of my two books to sell. Judging by the number of copies I was signing, we were doing brisk sales. Though I hadn't seen him earlier, Lloyd Baskins came to the table and requested a signature on my second book.

"Ellen, my dear! Smashing lecture! And, oh, what a divine suit. Simply fabulous! Didn't you wear that in your television interview?"

"Yes, I did. Glad you came, Lloyd."

"The pleasure is all mine."

I returned the signed copy. "I hope you enjoy it. Let me know what you think."

"Oh, Bibby and I might stay up all night and read it!" he exclaimed as he made way for the next person in line, a forthright woman who wanted to tell me about all the psychology books she had read in college. When she left, Mei-Ling and Chang passed both of my two titles for signing. They were enthusiastic about the talk. Several psych students were next and then George Durst asked me to endorse copies he had previously purchased.

"It was thoughtful of you to attend, George."

He gave me a sheepish smile. "I learned a lot."

"You look very nice tonight."

He touched the soft wool of his new blue sports jacket. "Yes, for the occasion."

"I'll see you next week," I said, handing him the two books.

As George left, a shy woman in a tightly buttoned blouse and an old-fashioned sweater vest approached. Large silver-framed glasses dwarfed a snub of a nose, though the eyes behind the glass were bright.

"I'm, er, Mary."

"Mary Brown?"

"Yes." She dipped her head several times.

"Thank you for stopping by tonight."

"Well, yes. I wanted to see you again."

I couldn't recall encountering Mary Brown before. "You have me at a disadvantage, Mary. Perhaps it's my poor memory, but when did we meet?"

She looked at me with surprise, then glanced left and right, as if someone were listening. "Oh," she said in a whisper, "It was in August. At Rutgers. Your lecture."

"Yes, I gave a talk there. That's right."

"And at Trenton State, too."

I had participated in a forum discussion in September.

The woman pushed a copy of *The Loner's Crusade* toward me, her gray eyes darting around the room. I signed and returned the book. "Thank you. I'll see you on Monday, Mary."

"Quite, quite," she replied, tucking the hardcover under her arm and daring one last peek before disappearing into the crowd.

I began to gather my things, though some people were still milling around, making comments and asking questions. I wished I'd surveyed the rear of the hall more carefully—there had been some latecomers standing by the door, but they would have been the first out—possibly with Martie—if the woman in back had been her.

I was pleased with the evening from a professional perspective. At least thirty-five books had been purchased, judging by the number brought for my signature, and several people had asked for my card and said they might call for appointments. I was less happy about progress on my detective assignment for the evening. The clients who had attended were, for the most part, the ones I would have expected. No one acted strange or not unusually so. I was surprised the Cosgroves hadn't spoken to me, but I surmised

Sam was embarrassed to be seen in public with her therapist. Greta wasn't the type to make a public show of congratulations, and Dolly and Denise were probably intimidated by the crowd. As for Martie, I might have been mistaken about her. If she had come, I was fairly sure she would have said hello.

My thoughts then drifted to Mary Brown. A peculiar sort, in her fifties, though she was one of those women who probably had looked old in the cradle. By her own report, she had been following my career for at least two months. Had she been following me home, too? Though it stretched the imagination to picture her drawing a lipstick heart on my car, she might buy cards on sale and stash them away. If my suitor was Mary, other than dealing with the inappropriateness of her behavior, there was no cause for concern.

George Durst had taken pains with his appearance. What had he said about buying new clothes? We had discussed that during our last session, but in terms of the woman he wanted to ask out. Was I that woman? As I drove home after the talk, keeping an eye on the rearview mirror, the thought of George Durst gnawed at me.

—

I slept late on Saturday, exhausted from the lecture and unenthusiastic about the stormy day: rain and wind, with tormented clouds streaking across the sky. I pulled on my green terrycloth robe and stumbled downstairs, yawning, wishing a pot of coffee was already made. After toasting a bagel and spreading it with cream cheese, I stood at the pass-through, sipping orange juice and sluicing hot water through the coffee filter.

I had nothing planned for the weekend. A dismal thought that perfectly matched the weather. Should I clean my mother's closet? The task would undoubtedly fall to me because I doubted my father would want to do it. After eating breakfast, I went upstairs, half-opened the blinds, and walked to my mother's closet where she had crushed her clothes together in the back so I had room for mine. Although most of her winter wardrobe was downstairs in the guest room, her favorite old clothes were here, the ones that evoked the most memories.

As I slid open the closet door, the scent of Chanel No. 5 emanated from the confined air. Without hesitation, I grasped a chamois shirt she often wore with her glasses peeking from the breast pocket. Threadbare at the elbows, its tawny color reminded me of faded deerskin. I held the shirt to my face, inhaling the enduring perfume, and tears began falling. This connection to my mother was too important to lose, so I returned the blouse to the closet. Several dresses and suits evoked less nostalgia. I inserted these and some blouses, skirts, and pants into a garbage bag, which I'd drop off at a charity. Then I looked at her shoes. The dress heels were stored in boxes in the rear, but her beloved English pigskin Oxfords were set at right. I lifted one shoe and wondered why she had left them behind but remembered her saying they were too scuffed for the trip. I caressed the beige leather and decided to keep them. Feeling overcome, I lay on her side of the bed and reached for a tissue. The day had cleared and the sun slipped through the blinds and spread a pattern of stripes across the comforter. An hour passed, and I still had no urge to rise. I felt hypnotized by grief, by the whir of memories clicking like an uncontrollable slide show. The phone rang three times. I let it ring. I didn't care. I wanted the call I would never receive, the one in which someone would say my mother had survived the accident and was coming home.

Finally, I walked to the balcony and surveyed the view through the prow windows of the stream muscling around the rocks. The stillness inside and out reinforced my loneliness. Realizing I needed to improve my mood, I called the tennis center for a lesson, but Martie was unavailable. I reviewed the people I knew in Princeton, who I might call to meet for dinner, and rejected each. It was too late to drive into the city, and a trip to the mall held no appeal. I went downstairs, made a ham sandwich, poured a Coke, and observed the bubbles pimple the black liquid with amber. I considered phoning my therapist, Adrienne, but it had been months since we'd spoken, and though she would want me to contact her if I felt like this, inertia beset me.

After tightening my bathrobe's belt, I grabbed a tea towel, opened a slider, and walked onto the deck. The rain had stopped several hours ago, but the redwood chaise was damp. I dried it with the towel, laid down, and absorbed the warmth of the sun, watching tongues of yellow light flicker between the tree trunks and branches.

I fell asleep. Sometime later, I was awakened by rustling in the woods. I came to my feet and shaded my eyes but couldn't see what was causing the noise. Probably a deer or a dog. Apprehensive, I stepped inside, closed the slider, placed the dowel in the track, and chided myself for being nervous. Regardless of whether I had cause for alarm, it was time to quit being lazy and get dressed, if only to fetch the mail.

Wearing jeans and a sweatshirt, I trudged down the driveway. Inside the mailbox were two condolence notes containing the awkward phrases that illustrated how uncomfortable people were when speaking about death. After tucking them under my arm, I saw it: "ELLEN" was written on the front. I held the envelope between my thumb and forefinger, as if it contained poison. Suddenly, I remembered the disturbance in the forest earlier. Had my suitor deposited the envelope and then observed me as I slept? I looked around, feeling exposed so far from the house, and ran for safety. I locked the door, rushed upstairs, and removed the card.

"THINKING OF YOU" with "THE LION WATCHING" printed inside. Had my lion just done exactly that—watched? I wrote the date on the envelope and placed the card in my briefcase.

Twenty minutes later I drove to the video store. It was time to see *Fatal Attraction*.

Your speech was so good! I was very proud! I hope you received my card and liked it. It's important for us to support each other. You will do the same for me.

I came home and looked at the tape of you again. I've seen it nineteen times. I keep count. You wore the same suit tonight. It's my favorite.

I have the whole weekend to think of you and maybe to visit with my camera.

—

I just drove to your house to leave a reminder that I was there. When I saw you lying on the deck, I thought you looked so beautiful asleep, like an innocent golden angel. Dreaming of us together, your voice said through the trees. I longed to kneel at your feet until you awoke, but I took photographs instead, to honor you. I will enlarge some and might send a few.

I hope you're not sick. You were still wearing your bathrobe.

SEEING *Fatal Attraction* was a disastrous idea. The plot was extremely frightening, even if the story and my own situation weren't similar. In the film, a brief romantic relationship existed between the two main characters, whereas there was no relationship in my case—or not a close one.

As I read the Sunday newspapers, I thought about Glenn Close's Alex, who was so persistent and obsessed, characteristics Alex and my suitor had in common. However, the transformation from attraction to jealous outrage to maniacal violence hadn't happened in my case. Or hadn't happened yet. I took the cards from my briefcase and spread them in front of me. Up to now, all were adoring and immature, expressing the sentiments of someone in love for the first or second time, possibly an adolescent or an inexperienced lover. What else did I know? My suitor owned a car or had easy access to one and also had flexible time during the day and night. Someone with a rigid work schedule wouldn't be able to leave gifts during the afternoon. Unfortunately, these characteristics fit most of my clients. I eliminated Robert Fleet from the list—he wasn't the type—and the Lees, the Claytons, and Marguerite Fleury were unlikely. Lloyd Baskins was an improbable suspect, because he was so absorbed by the situation with Peter, and, well, I was fond of Lloyd. Though I couldn't picture Greta Graf going to all the devious trouble, I couldn't rule her out. There was something strange about her, though perhaps I felt this way because of her social awkwardness. George Durst was a serious possibility as were Dolly Bordella and Denise DiNicola. Samantha Cosgrove had to be considered even if the style of the cards and gifts were dubious choices for her. Sam would favor bleak and cryptic notes, though she might send blatantly saccharine gifts to be ironic. And she owned a car. Carson Kendricks was a definite prospect. He had maintained a relationship with me despite my move to Princeton and was now intending to live nearby. Martie had made a friendly overture about dinner, but her behavior had always been appropriate. Nick was still in the running, and then there was Mary Brown, who might fit the profile. It would be interesting to see her tomorrow, when I would also bring the cards to the office and compare handwriting with the forms completed by my clients.

—

On Monday, after returning the video, I parked in the lot and was disgusted to see a card taped to the door of my office. I snatched the envelope and ran upstairs to open it. "Get Well Soon!" was its emphatic message, illustrated by a nurse rabbit checking a thermometer. A baby bunny was in bed, ailing. The card was signed in red ink: "THE ONE WHO LOVES YOU."

I tossed the card and envelope angrily on my desk, heard two breathy silences on my answering machine, and erased them. Opening my briefcase, I removed the other missives and then unlocked my files. From the shortened list of clients I'd devised, I selected their dossiers to study each person's handwriting. Unfortunately, each sample was in longhand, and no comparisons could be made with the capital letters printed on the cards, whose slant was stiffly upright. The squat style was unlike Dolly's lofty script, though people's printing was often different from their cursive. The only noteworthy trait was a few horizontal strokes similar to George Durst's handwriting and not unlike the writing of Greta, Carson, Denise, and Robert. I had no sample from Samantha because I had completed her form during my conversation with her parents, and the two pieces of writing she had shown me during sessions were typed. Lloyd's sheet contained only a few words written by him as he and Peter had launched on their narratives before finishing, causing me to enter his information via questions asked during the appointment. I had never seen Nick's or Martie's handwriting.

My sleuthing had only produced more frustration. I dated today's card, stuck it in my briefcase with the others, and tried to concentrate on my book, but my mind bounced around as I kept analyzing the meaning of each gift.

An hour later, the phone rang. I answered and heard the brusque voice of my literary agent, Herbert Longfellow. Herb was in his sixties, a grizzled pro who didn't waste anyone's time, much less his own.

"Ellen, are you free for drinks? I'm arriving in Princeton on the 4:30 train."

I laughed. "On the Dinky?"

"Yes...whatever the connection is called."

"And you need a ride from there to where?"

He chuckled. "Got me. Yeah, I'm meeting with Jonathan Markowitz."

"Aha, so you have bigger fish to fry than me."

"Yeah, but I'll buy you two martinis before you take me to his house."

"Not three?"

"Nope. Two's your limit. And mine. See you soon."

I was always pleased to see my agent, but I could finally report progress on my manuscript, not that this news was of much consequence compared to the delivery of a completed novel by Herb's prize author. Herb wouldn't venture out of Manhattan unless the bait was substantial, and I didn't provide much incentive, except we had hit it off from the beginning, at one of my speaking engagements in the city, one that dealt with the material I was gathering for *The Loner's Crusade*. To my astonishment, Herb asked to represent me and my project—a rare offer for a semi-academic writer, particularly because his agent's commission would be small. Ever since, Herb had been an enthusiastic advocate and had arranged speaking engagements that brought in some income and promoted sales.

—

I heard a timid rap on the door. Mary Brown. After inserting a new information sheet on a clipboard, I invited her in.

"Welcome, Mary. Have a seat." I pointed to the couch. "I always ask new clients to answer a few questions. I hope you don't mind?" I gave her the clipboard and a pen.

When Mary finished, she hesitated to pass the form to me but finally did. I read that she was fifty-one years old, on hypertension and ulcer medications, divorced, with an adult son. She owned an antiques shop in Kingston and lived above the store. Her writing was in cursive and couldn't be matched with the printing on the cards.

After reading her details, I glanced at Mary. For some reason, she was bobbing her head up and down, as if agreeing with something. Her gray eyes were pale as was her face; her graying hair was collected in a French twist. As at my lecture, Mary wore the same large silver glasses, their prominence diminishing her tiny doll's nose. Attired in a blue knit dress, she was of average height, a few pounds overweight. Not a woman who would catch your eye, but on closer inspection, she was moderately attractive.

"What is your specialty?" I asked. "In the antiques business?"

"Restoration of furniture and mirrors, particularly *Louis Quatorze*. I love to do gold-leaf painting…so I'm a bit creative."

"That's very interesting. Your work must require patience."

"Yes, it does. I like the artwork from that period, too, though I'm not an expert."

"So, Mary, why did you decide to see me?"

Her eyes grew sad. "May I call you Ellen?"

"Yes, of course. I should have said so earlier."

"Well, Ellen, I'm concerned about my son, Albert." The name was pronounced with a French accent. "He's grown but he's still living with me. This summer, he said he wanted to return to school. To Chicago, to study art. While I have nothing against pursuing one's education, he keeps flitting about, attending one college and another. He even entered a seminary for a year. Now, he's changed his mind about Chicago and wants to stay home. Which I suppose is fine because I really can't afford to pay his tuition any longer." She let out a long breath. "Ellen, I don't understand him. He's a different sort of boy—man. He's always been artistic, you know, and not very masculine, so I thought he might be homosexual, but Albert says he's been seeing a girl recently. I suppose he's telling the truth, yet she's never come to the house or telephoned. Forgive me for doubting him, but I think he's making her up."

"I see. How can I help?"

"I want to understand my son. He's all I have," Mary said. "My husband abandoned us when Albert was seven—at least with enough money for me to get by reasonably well. I will credit him for that." She sighed again. "Marcel comes from Burgundy where his family owns a big manor house that dates to the eighteenth-century. In fact, that's how we met. I was studying art history at the Sorbonne, and he was in Paris to catalogue his family's collection of furniture. Marcel isn't handsome, but he has charm and sophistication. I never did understand why he became interested in me, nor do I believe his people were pleased to include an American in their midst, despite my appreciation of their country's art. Still, one thing led to another, and we married. Marcel had it in his head to own an antiques company in New York City, so we moved there shortly before Albert was born and opened a shop on the

Upper East Side. As the baby took less time, I began to do more and Marcel began to do less. He was always running off to Europe, chasing some magnificent piece that he insisted we have. On one of these trips, he found more than a chair, if you know what I mean. After a few months, I realized he was having an affair. I confronted Marcel and asked him for a divorce, to which he agreed. He promised the store would be mine along with some investments that would cover Albert's education. Soon after Marcel flew home to France, I sold the business because it was too challenging to run a Madison Avenue shop by myself and believed a simpler life, in a less hectic environment, would be better for my son. We came here seventeen years ago."

"So your son is in his mid-twenties?"

"He'll be twenty-four in February."

"Albert was raised more or less without a father? As an only child?"

"Yes. I've never re-married."

"Have you been involved with anyone since?"

Mary Brown smiled. "Not really. I have some male friends who are colleagues. Mostly gay. They're delightful company, but being of that persuasion, they wouldn't consider me as a suitable romantic partner. And I see my priest on Sundays." Here she laughed. "Though he doesn't count."

I nodded. "Returning to Albert…what was he like growing up? Was he social?"

Mary clasped her hands together. "Oh, Albert always had a few friends among the artistic crowd—he loved to draw and paint and still does. He never participated in sports during school or attend football games."

"When he was a teenager, did he date anyone?"

"Not exactly. He went to his school prom, but she was only a friend who wanted to go."

"And at college?"

Mary thought about this. "I'm not sure. He mentioned a few girls, but Albert seemed to spend most of his time alone or with one or two male friends."

"I see. You expressed a concern that your son might be gay. Why do you think so?"

"Oh, little things. He's a big man, but he's not athletic. And, as I have just told you, his interest in girls seems slight, though Albert might be keeping his social life secret. Or he could be bisexual."

"I should mention that not being athletic doesn't indicate he's gay," I said. "Do you think Albert is distressed about his sexuality?"

"Partly. That and, well, he has his little obsessions."

"Obsessions?"

"Shortly after Marcel left, Albert began collecting things. Childhood toys at first, then, later, some items of value as well as those with personal meaning for him. I'm not allowed to touch anything in his room, which is crammed. There isn't an inch of space left on the walls, either. Now he won't let me inside ever since he flew into a rage because I had moved one of his dozens of notebooks."

"Do you have reason to believe your son is upset or depressed?"

"I think so but he doesn't talk with me often. He was all ready to go to Chicago and then decided against it without explaining. Recently, he referred to a girl. I have no idea who she is, and when I asked, he became angry and left the room. Of course, I hope Albert is seeing someone."

"Does he visit his father? Are they close?"

"Albert absolutely adores Marcel, but Marcel rarely phones. Since the divorce, he's come here a few times but invited Albert to France only twice. He's always promising Albert trips to Paris and then cancels. If Marcel understood how much Albert loves him…well, to be candid, I don't think Marcel really cares."

"So he's been essentially absent in your son's life?" I made a mental note of this.

"Yes, he has." She nodded, her expression downcast.

"Do you think Albert would like to speak with me? I couldn't relate what is said in the sessions, but perhaps you would feel relieved if he had an outlet. It doesn't sound like he has many people in which to confide."

Her eyes brightened. "Interesting that you should suggest this. I was hopeful that Albert might make an appointment on his own because he was the one who had urged me to call you. We went to your talks, and Albert was very impressed. Which is very unusual because he's quite critical."

"I don't recall seeing him with you last Friday."

"Oh, he was too shy to say hello, but he was fascinated with what you said about creativity. He read your first book and is now on the new one I bought."

"My goodness, a fan!" I said, smiling at her.

She nodded enthusiastically. "Yes, he is. I think he might be willing to come in, however you must understand he's not very extraverted. Mostly, he writes things in his notebooks, his *Pensées*, as he calls them. He doesn't show them to me, but I've peeked over his shoulder now and then when he brings a book into the living room and is writing or sketching."

"I see. Well, if he's interested, please have him phone."

"I'll ask Albert. I think it would be a wonderful idea. It would make me feel better."

"I can see that, Mary. You've put a tremendous amount of energy into raising your son by yourself. It isn't easy being a single parent."

"No, it isn't. Even though he's all grown up, he's still at home, and in many ways, he's still my little boy."

I couldn't ascertain whether this thought made her happy or sad. I turned the subject to her as a separate person from her son and asked Mary to describe a typical evening and a usual Sunday and Monday, days the shop was closed. She explained that she was frequently by herself. When I inquired what Albert usually did, Mary replied that he was often out, many times until late at night, and that his work schedule was erratic.

"I don't know where he goes, Ellen. Albert sometimes takes adult education classes, but I don't think he turns in all the assignments or attends every session. Usually, I see him only at breakfast and dinner, if he's home."

Albert was beginning to resemble my stalker's profile, though I resented my increased hypersensitivity whenever anything arose that was vaguely connected to the suitor. More and more, the stalker was evolving into an invisible but pervasive presence, regardless of my effort to ban him from my client's fifty minutes.

"Do you have a picture of Albert?" I asked.

"Yes. It's a few years old. His high school graduation photo." She withdrew her wallet and handed me a dog-eared color snapshot, a head-and-shoulders portrait of Albert in cap and gown. His brown hair was long, almost an Oscar Wilde cut, and he had inherited his mother's gray, tiny eyes and wan complexion. It was difficult to tell how tall Albert was, but he looked stocky. His nose was small, like Mary's, set in a broad face, and his chin was weak. There was nothing engaging about Albert's expression, even on a celebratory day.

"His hair is a little shorter now, thank goodness. Albert has sort of grown out of that bohemian phase, although he still wears odd clothes." Mary frowned. "Unfortunately, he's gained a few pounds since then. My fault, I suppose."

"He's very nice looking," I replied, using a safe expression.

Mary Brown knew what I meant and nodded. "Albert is built like his father. I keep hoping my son will slim down."

"Does he use his father's last name or yours—I assume 'Brown' is your maiden name?"

"Yes, it is. Albert's is d'Auberge."

Checking the clock, I noted there was time for Mary to do a self-portrait. I asked if she would be willing to make a drawing, and when she reluctantly agreed, I handed her the sketchpad and explained about the exercise. She gave me a nervous glance and settled to work. Her portrait took considerably longer to complete than it did most of my clients.

"Not very good," she said. "I'm not an artist."

I smiled and accepted the sketch. Regardless of her humble appraisal, the drawing was well done. Mary had placed herself in an ornate chair amid a clutter of frames and mirrors.

"My favorite chair. With sheep's horn stretchers—a prominent feature of the Sun King's furniture."

"This is an elaborate portrait."

Mary Brown was pleased. "That's the way my shop looks."

She had drawn her face with a serious, yet enigmatic expression. Her hands were gathered in her lap—so Mary could showcase the chair's arms more precisely or because she felt timid? The size of her body was small compared to the regal chair, giving the impression of a dwarf within a cage. I mentioned that she resembled a queen of antiques and received a smile.

"Mary, can you tell me how you feel with your hands held like this?" I pointed to the sketch.

"Like a lady," she said with a nod. "That's how I was raised. Feet together when I sit, hands in my lap."

The shoes were touching each other in the drawing. That was a detail that I had missed.

We discussed the drawing until the end of the session. I thanked her for coming.

"You're welcome, Ellen," she replied, giving me a check. "I'll speak to Albert about an appointment."

[THE JOURNAL]

I hope you're feeling well enough to be at work and that my card didn't blow off the door. After watching you sleeping on the deck yesterday, I was worried you were sick. I can't wait to see the photographs and will shoot more, though I don't have many opportunities. I wish I could have you pose for me. Maybe take some of us together?

It feels right to be on your property. I like the trees and the stream and being near you.

GEORGE DURST arrived in a new black suit, explaining that he had attended a funeral for an aunt and was off work for the day. I expressed my condolences and asked after his relative, though George didn't seem sad about her death or inclined to give any information. Dressed nicely as he was, to my relief, George no longer resembled Jud as much.

At the first opportunity, he switched the discussion to my Friday lecture and complimented me on the presentation. I thanked George and asked what had specifically interested him. He appeared to be intimidated by the question and answered vaguely. After a brief silence, he began talking about some construction sculptures he was creating.

"Can you describe them?" I asked, curious.

Shyly at first, George explained that he saved odd pieces of metal and machine parts from work. "I really like the shapes, the textures, and I put them together using a blowtorch, by making metal collars, or fastening them with wires or screws. I scrub everything so the metal is shiny, sometimes in an acid bath. I just bought a decent camera and have been thinking about lighting. Maybe setting up a spotlight on my work to create shadows."

"That sounds very interesting, George. How many pieces have you done?"

"Hard to say. Several that are separate from each other, but sometimes I can't help myself, and I've stuck two or three together. They keep growing in size."

"Rather organic?"

George liked that description and smiled. "Yeah, exactly!"

This was the most animation I'd witnessed in our sessions. "Do you have any snapshots of your work? I would love to see what you're doing."

"Really? I'll take some pictures and bring them in for you.

We then discussed modern sculpture, a subject about which

George was surprisingly knowledgeable. He admired the work of Louise Nevelson and Alexander Calder, both of whom had installations on campus, and liked Nevelson's piece near Firestone Library, saying it was one of her first works in steel, most of her earlier constructions having been created from wood. He had visited the Guggenheim Museum to see her *Luminous Zag* and *White Vertical Water*, favorites of his. I asked about the Picasso in front of the Art Museum, but George confessed it didn't inspire him, that he liked more complex designs.

I was astonished George would try his hand at art and even more amazed he had ventured to museums in the city.

"How do you feel when you're creating your sculpture?"

"Like the world disappears," he admitted. "I work slowly because of the materials but also because I don't want to rush."

"Yes, I understand."

He chuckled. "Thought you might. That's one reason I knew you were the right therapist. That's why you chose me."

His remark sent off mental alarms. "I beg your pardon?"

"Oh, sorry. I meant, I chose you."

George was on my suitor short list. Had this truly been a slip of the tongue? "How are things going otherwise?"

"You mean...with my friend?"

I nodded.

"Well, I'm not sure. I hope she'll make a move. Give me a sign of interest or something."

"Why not take the initiative and ask her out?"

He shrugged. "I think she'll let me know soon. I cleaned up at home, just in case. The place was a mess, with machine parts everywhere. Sketches and stuff pinned on the walls." He looked at me. "I also bought some bottles of French wine. I think she likes wine."

"Good idea."

George looked reassured and then raised a problem with someone at work, one of the men he had recently hired who wasn't showing much diligence. We talked about the best way to inspire people to do better without criticizing them. I gave some examples, and we did a short role-playing exercise to practice. Throughout, George listened with care as I played his part.

—

Because my connecting door was open, I heard Marguerite Fleury climbing the stairs. She stopped twice along the way, her arthritic condition making the steps a challenge. Out of politeness, I closed the inner door and waited so she could compose herself before the session. This gave me a chance to jot down George's strange comment about my choosing him rather than the other way around and to make a note about his behavior: waiting for a sign from the woman in whom he was interested. Did my stalker harbor the same feeling? George seemed reluctant to discuss his girlfriend, which made me wonder about her identity. He had also been away from work today and would have had an opportunity to tape the card to my door. The same was true for the rest of the day and evening, should any more incidents occur. Was he really the embodiment of Jud? The quiet inferno of a man who loved deeply but was afraid to confront his love object? Until violence erupted out of compressed frustration and jealousy?

When I opened the door, Marguerite stood, trying to disguise her pain. She negotiated her way around the table and was seated.

"Are you feeling better?" I asked.

"Oh, yes, I am. Last week, ah, a disaster! I couldn't practice except a little over the weekend." She studied her hands, rubbing the knobby joints gently. They were swollen and looked tender.

"I'm very sorry this is happening to you. You must feel frustrated, not to mention uncomfortable."

"Very frustrated, yes. But after our last talk, I've negotiated the final details about a recording in Baltimore. Everything looks positive—even Louis is willing to take time to accompany me. That's unusual for him, as I've explained."

"Why do you think he feels differently?"

She gave me a dismissive wave of the hand. "Eh, who knows what goes through men's minds? They have dark caves up there!"

I chuckled. "I must remember that, Marguerite. That's often an apt description."

She smiled and then turned serious. "To be honest, I think Louis has become concerned. When I don't practice for a day or two, that might earn a comment. When it's longer, like last week, he noticed. Perhaps he's realizing my career is nearly over. Maybe he feels guilt because he's tried to control me so much. That I've never made a commercial recording because of him. I don't have any idea. A dark cave."

"Perhaps he's genuinely worried about you?"

"Guilty is more likely."

"At least he feels that. Some people only are inconvenienced by their partner's disability, or they worry about themselves and their own sense of mortality."

"Let's not put us in the grave yet, Ellen!" she protested, laughing. "But however Louis feels, it will soon be more difficult for me to travel. I don't know when things will become worse, though I admit I have pain all the time." She flexed her fingers.

"What about a change of climate? Some spot in Arizona?"

"*Impossible*! I couldn't live that far from civilization! Princeton is on the edge of civilization already!"

I was amused, particularly because Princetonians were famous for their chauvinism about the university and town. Someone once explained that Princeton had an inferiority complex from its inception because it was considered a country school compared to the more urban and sophisticated Harvard and Yale. "You may have something there, Marguerite," I agreed. "I'm finding it to be a challenge adjusting to living outside Manhattan."

"Do you have friends here, Ellen?"

"Not yet." I returned to her recording. "Will it be a studio or live taping?"

"In the studio, which is a relief. I hope Louis will be patient. He thinks he's being generous by accompanying me, but I wish he wouldn't. I'd do better without him there."

"Have you told Louis you would rather go alone?"

"Yes, I have."

"Tell him again. He doesn't have the right to impede your career. Not at this point, particularly," I said with unusual vehemence.

Marguerite was silent, pondering my remark, until she straightened her posture. "Ellen, I agree with you. I'll tell Louis that if he insists on coming to Baltimore, he can only drive me there and then must leave. Otherwise, I'll divorce him."

I was stunned. I hadn't expected such decisiveness after all of Marguerite's years of being subservient to her husband. "An ultimatum?"

"Yes, precisely. It's long overdue."

Though I approved of her determination, I was worried her husband might become angry and agree to separating. She would need help with her disability. I mentioned this, but Marguerite said she could manage without him if necessary. "I have money. I have friends. I can live anywhere I wish. Maybe I'll return to Paris or at least New York. Out of this provincial town. I'm only here because of Louis."

Her dignity and courage were impressive. I encouraged her to think the matter over before confronting her husband. She agreed to wait but also said she had already waited too long. We scheduled an appointment for the same time next week.

—

I selected the Alchemist & Barrister for drinks with my agent. Herb and I sat on stools at the bar, in the corner, near the table where Nick and I had been seated. He lit a Marlboro, took a deep drag, and ordered us two gin martinis, which were delivered promptly.

"So how are tricks, Ellen?" he asked, after a sip.

I explained where I was in the book and that I hoped to have the manuscript finished by the following spring.

"Early or late spring?"

I laughed. "Are you asking me if this is real time or academic time?"

He nodded.

"Real time, Herb. I don't have professorial luxury. Not if I have an agent."

"*Touché*. When can I see something? Contents? Proposal?"

"I sent you a proposal," I reminded him.

"Oh, yeah, Forgot. It's been crazy. You know how it is in publishing."

"If it would help, I can do an update."

"Yeah, okay, when you get a chance. We might wind up with the same editor and publisher. If they take it, maybe we can do a two-fer."

"So you think I have another book in me?"

"Absolutely." He swallowed the last of his martini and ate the green olive. "Another one," he told the bartender.

I still had half of my martini left, which I drank while he enthused about the new Markowitz novel he was about to receive.

His eyes gleamed when he talked about it, whether from excitement or greed or both. As he lit another cigarette, he surprised me by commenting that I looked tired.

"Trying to meet my *real* deadline." I smiled and then explained about my mother's death in a car accident, that my father was still on Corfu, and some strange events had been happening. After expressing his sympathy, he asked what was going on.

"Actually, I think I've acquired a stalker." This was the first time I had uttered the fearsome word out loud. I didn't like the sound of it.

"A stalker? Who is he? Some old flame?"

"No, I don't believe so, but I'm not sure who it is—whether it's someone I know or someone I don't know at all."

He puffed on his cigarette. "You're staying at your parents' house, aren't you? In the country? Alone?"

I nodded. "Yes, I am. I love the house. It's a beautiful spot but rather isolated. Several acres of woods and a stream."

"Sounds damned dangerous to me." This coming from a man who navigated the seedier bowels of Manhattan without the slightest concern.

"I'll be careful, I promise."

"You better be. I don't want anything to happen to one of my favorite authors." He tapped the ask off of his cigarette. "So, tell me, what's this stalker doing?"

"Sending flowers and chocolates. Calling and hanging up. Leaving cards in my mailbox at the house and at my office."

Herb chuckled. "Hey, when I was a kid I used to do that kind of stuff all the time."

"It's probably nothing to worry about."

"Probably not," he agreed, "but if you need help, call me, okay?"

I said I would. Herb gulped down his second martini, crushed his cigarette in the ashtray, and waited for me to finish my first drink. Once I had, he caught the bartender's eye, paid the tab, and we strolled to my car.

"You know this stalker stuff..." he began. "There's quite a lot of interest in that. It's in the news. Crazy husbands who murder their ex-wives. People are saying the laws don't protect victims. Might be an interesting next project for you."

"I don't think so."

"Okay. Just asking. Sure you're okay to drive?"

"No problem."

He directed me toward the western section of Princeton, to a handsome Federal-style house hidden behind dense rhododendron bushes. Herb thanked me for the lift and laughed when I offered to take him to the train later.

"No, Ellen, your chauffeuring duties are over for the night. Thanks. It was great seeing you. I'll look for the revised proposal."

I told him it was a priority.

"Over those nutty patients of yours."

"Clients, Herb. Clients."

"Yeah, whatever. Talk to you soon." He grabbed his briefcase from the back seat and briskly waved goodbye, his mind already on Jonathan Markowitz and the Great American Novel.

I was a quarter of the way home already. As I drove down Carter Road, I ruminated on the label "stalker." Had I misspoken? Though Herb was correct that stalking was becoming a high-profile crime, one garnering media interest, I wasn't sure where the dividing line fell between an infatuated admirer and an obsessed stalker, nor had I paid much attention to the recent cases of fans following movie stars or read much on the issue except as it related to domestic violence against women. Some research was definitely in order.

I made the turn on Stoney Brook Road and left the engine

running while I checked the mailbox. Nothing unusual. Relieved, I drove down the driveway and then saw a flicker of candlelight by the front door. I left the car inside the garage and rushed to the house. A tall glass cylinder held a half-burned black candle. Surrounding the glass was an autumn wreath constructed of wildflowers, leaves, and acorns; a dead pigeon lay on the doormat beside the arrangement, with a daisy tucked under one bloody wing. Above, on the brown door, a heart with arrows was drawn in lipstick, similar to the one left on my car.

I stepped backward, horrified. What did this sick, macabre arrangement mean? I whirled around to see if someone was in the woods. The spotlights were on, but no one was visible. After checking my watch to note the time, I blew out the candle, unlocked the door, and went upstairs.

Had my stalker seen me leave the office to pick up my agent at the station, followed us to the restaurant, and then driven to Hopewell to place the candle and dead bird by the door while we were drinking cocktails? The candle had been burning for some time, so that explanation was reasonable. Or had the trip to the house been made on chance, with the possibility of being caught providing additional excitement? If the thrill of risk was a component, was the stalker still somewhere on the property? I turned off the living room light and took my father's binoculars outside on the deck to surveil three sides of the house. Nothing amiss. Should I call the police? Cards and flowers and candy were one thing; vandalism and dead pigeons were another.

Regretting my two martinis, I phoned the state police and spoke with Sergeant Wilcox, who agreed to come to the house. After hanging up, I went into the bathroom, brushed my teeth, and gargled with mouthwash, feeling embarrassed to have alcohol on my breath, nor was I happy to involve the police, especially if the person was one of my clients. As a therapist, I had to maintain confidentiality of names and records. How could I help the police and still do that? They would respect my professional ethics but might not be sympathetic to the restrictions. I could hear the conversation now: "If you want us to catch whoever is bothering you, tell us who you think it might be." That meant turning over names, giving reasons why one person might be more suspect than others. I now wished I'd waited. But waited for what? Something serious to happen?

I grabbed a pad of paper, a pen, and the cards from my briefcase and reconstructed the timeline of gifts, cards, and phone hang-ups.

[THE JOURNAL]

I'm so excited about my "welcome home" present! It's not as grand as it should have been, but I didn't have time. The pigeon is to remind you of St. Mark's Square and where we'll go when we're together. (I hit the bird with a rock on one try—I always was good throwing things.) I hope the candle didn't blow out. It's a shining beacon of our perfect love.

I sent two rolls of film to be developed late on Saturday. They should be back tomorrow because I asked for them to be rushed. After I select the best ones, I'll have them enlarged for us.

I want to be with you. Why won't you let me? I have waited and waited and waited! I don't understand why you keep us apart. I come to your house, just to be near. I think you're wrong about waiting. Our love is pure. I want Us!

AT 7:10, a police cruiser arrived, and a handsome, broad-shouldered African-American man stepped out. I went downstairs and opened the door, which he was examining along with the tableau of adornments on the mat. Sergeant Wilcox introduced himself and said he would join me after making notes and taking Polaroid photographs of the scene. I left him to his documentation, and shortly after, he climbed the stairs and entered the living room.

"Nice house," he commented, surveying the large windows and deck.

"It's my parents' home. They're, well, my father is in Greece."

"And your mother?"

"My mother was with him. They had a car accident a few weeks ago. She died. My father is recuperating."

"I'm sorry. Please accept my condolences."

"Thank you."

"So you're minding the place?"

"Yes. I work in Princeton. Just starting a therapy practice in town." I explained the situation.

"Are you here alone?"

Something in the way he asked the question disturbed me. I wasn't comfortable with anyone knowing I was by myself, even a policeman. I silently reprimanded myself and tried to shelve this unhelpful attitude.

I nodded. "Would you like a cup of coffee or tea?"

He declined but thanked me. I suggested we sit, but he said he wanted to walk around first, to be sure the house was secure. I provided more detail than I had on the phone and showed him the cards and my rough approximation of what had happened, where, and when. I added that I'd checked my clients' handwriting against the cards and could make no connections. He asked if he could have a copy of my timeline of events, and I agreed, saying I would prepare it while he was outside. When Wilcox went downstairs, I heard some squawking from the patrol car's speakers and then saw him, flashlight in hand, as he began a systematic search.

I felt tired. The high from the martinis had worn off. I went into the kitchen, ate a few crackers, and returned to the living room to watch the progress of the policeman's flashlight through the trees and to copy my report. Finally, there was a perfunctory knock on the door, and Wilcox re-entered the house. I noticed some burrs had attached to his pants, and his well-shined shoes were muddy from the many tiny streams that crisscrossed the property. After sitting at the dining room table, he placed his clipboard in front of him.

"Dr. Haskell, do you have any idea about who might be acting in this manner?"

"Are you asking if I encouraged a person to behave this way?"

"Yes, even inadvertently. Any prior relationships with a guy who's still interested in you? Or are you currently in a relationship?"

"No to both. I've been busy with writing, research, and my practice. I haven't dated anyone for some time, and no one since I moved from New York to Princeton."

Wilcox looked me over. "I hope you don't mind this comment, Dr. Haskell, but you're an attractive woman…"

"And you find it implausible that I wouldn't be seeing anyone?"

He lifted a huge hand and smiled. "Not at all. I'm just trying to be sure there isn't some jealous man out there, someone from your past or someone you know casually, who's developed an abnormal attachment."

I shook my head. "No old boyfriends that live in the area—I'm not from here. You may be right, however, that my suitor—for lack of a better word—might be someone who observes me in town, yet I haven't noticed anyone acting strangely."

"I'm sure you would've picked up on anything unusual because it's your profession." He smiled again and the furrows on his lined face relaxed. Wilcox appeared to be a man who absorbed the tragedies he saw, yet also maintained his sense of humor.

I liked him better and smiled. "Sorry to report that my analytic powers have proved completely useless. But even though I haven't identified the culprit as a client, I'm bound by doctor/patient confidentiality, which complicates things."

"That's a problem in this case, Doctor," he agreed, pausing for a moment. "Do you feel frightened? I mean, do you think that whoever is doing this might become aggressive?"

I stared at him. "I have no idea and, yes, I'm scared. This all started with hang-up calls and things left at the office until attentions were also focused here—at the mailbox and now at the door. The person is obviously tracking where I am. Just so you know, I'm usually in Princeton on Monday, Tuesday, and Wednesday, though I occasionally am there to write. So my schedule varies."

Wilcox looked around. "This isn't an ideal place for you to be under the circumstances. Anyone outside can observe you, particularly at night. There's a lot of cover behind all the bushes and trees. Best to keep the blinds down."

"I know. I've added blinds in the upstairs bedroom, checked the locks, and set the timers on the spotlights. I don't know what else to do."

Wilcox stroked his chin. "I examined the locks. They're pretty good, but the one on the ground floor is only effective if you're in the house and have the bolt thrown. Otherwise, a determined individual could force it. Plus you have all the glass. It isn't easy to break a slider but not impossible, and there are windows in the basement."

This summed up my own appraisal of the house.

"You could add an alarm system or surveillance cameras on the corners of the house."

"Sounds expensive."

"Yes, it would be. And you might consider hiring a private detective. Someone to keep an eye on the house and your office. Maybe he could catch the perpetrator."

I thought about this. "Installing an alarm won't be a problem. I'll schedule an appointment tomorrow. And the detective? I'm not prepared to do that yet."

"I understand. For now, we can send a patrol car here at random times during the day and evening. Be careful if you go outside alone and leave your car locked, near the front door. Without an electric opener to keep the garage shut, someone could wait inside." He sighed. "I don't mean to upset you, Dr. Haskell, but I'm concerned. Also about the parking lot in Princeton. It's busy, but it's possible to hide behind cars. And returning to your house—even with the spotlights on—might be hazardous. Avoid being out at night."

"I'll try to rearrange my evening appointments, but I have to be available whenever it's convenient for clients."

Wilcox nodded. "Do the best you can." He handed me his card. "Also notify the police in town. I've put the pigeon and stuff in a trash bag so you won't have to bother with the mess. And, by the way, the bird didn't die a natural death. Looks like he was hit with something, and then his neck was snapped."

I didn't like the sound of that, but I gave Sergeant Wilcox the timeline, thanked him for his kindness, and promised to be careful. After he left, the house felt empty. My presence in the room seemed negligible, inconsequential, as if I had no mass or gravity. The thought of cooking dinner was unappealing. The best I could do was heat a frozen stroganoff dinner. Shortly after I went to bed, listening to the scrape of trees in the woods before falling asleep.

In the morning, I scoured the front door with soap and water, glancing around in case I had company. After finishing, I rushed into my car and locked it. How I hated this feeling! I was afraid to be home, afraid of damage to my car at my parents' house or in the Princeton lot, afraid to be in the office with the door unlocked—what was to prevent my suitor from walking up the stairs and attacking me? Or when I stopped in the driveway to get mail? There were numerous times and places where I might be vulnerable, with no way to protect myself. A gun? Should I apply for a license? It would take several weeks, and besides, this was no time to purchase a firearm. With my inexperience and overall jumpiness, I might shoot myself in the foot.

When I reached the office, there were four clicks on the machine and no messages. Maybe the person just liked to hear my voice on the tape? A creepy thought. This propelled me to call a surveillance company, but the soonest we could schedule a time was next Tuesday morning at nine. I shuddered to think what could happen in the meantime, particularly because Halloween was on Saturday. Surely an inspirational occasion for any stalker? After making some tea, I read, though my concentration wasn't admirable.

—

When Lloyd Baskins arrived, he was beaming with happiness and began to tell me why even before he was seated.

"You are *so* smart, Ellen! I called Peter about Bibby." He sat on the sofa, steadied his voice, and spoke distinctly. "I was very reserved, very calm. I told him that we had many differences and had bought a lot of things together we both wanted. I offered some of my prized possessions if I could have Bibby, which made him appreciate how much she means to me. Or maybe he just got laid and was in a jolly mood. Whatever. But he is giving up any claim to her. Isn't that wonderful?"

"I am so pleased for you, Lloyd. Your ability to negotiate an agreement with Peter is an important step."

"Yes, I agree. Maybe I'm beginning to get over him a little."

"It will take time. You've been together for so many years."

"I know," he said. "By the way, I had a few replies from the want ads. Some losers, but a few possibilities, especially one hunk who sent me his photo. Absolutely stunning!" Lloyd sighed. "Alas, he's too young for me."

I was startled. "Too young?"

"Yes. Probably eighteen." He hung his head in mock embarrassment. "Maybe."

"You have to be careful."

"Oh, I know all about that, Ellen!" Lloyd chuckled. "Still, a girl can dream, can't she?"

"Yes, I suppose. What about the others?"

"One dishy lawyer who lives in Teaneck. But, my goodness, does anyone really live in Teaneck? I mean, come on!"

"Did you call him?"

"Yes."

"And...?"

"He's driving to Princeton on Saturday afternoon."

"So you have a date?"

He nodded his head and covered a smile with his hand.

"Tell me more about him."

Lloyd leaned forward. "Well, he's forty-two—a bit old, but we'll let that pass. Six feet tall. No steady partner for several years. Says he's been tested for HIV and is negative, though one can never be sure they're telling the truth. He works on Wall Street for some big financial firm. I think he does very well."

"Good. What are his interests?"

Lloyd blushed so I knew that whatever he was thinking was not suitable for my ears. "Oh, let's just say he likes fireplaces, shall we?"

"Is he an opera fan?"

"No, unfortunately, that's a drawback. I'll have to educate him, but he enjoys classical music, although he might have said that to impress me."

"Are you going out for dinner or are you cooking for him?"

Lloyd rolled his eyes. "Good question. What do you think?"

I was beginning to feel like his high school girlfriend chatting about boys. "Perhaps it might be prudent to meet him in a public place. At least the first time."

"Yes, that would be sensible. But I do love to entertain."

"How long did you speak with him on the phone?"

"An hour. He didn't sound like a crazy person. And I could make such a dinner! Maybe a nice pear, pecan, and goat cheese salad and then *Coq au vin*. Some apple pie—he sounds like quite a boy. Like Himself. He loved pie. Me, *crème brûlée* or berries with whipped cream." He laughed merrily and clasped his hands together. "Besides, I enjoy showing off my little house!"

Lloyd's home, though I had never seen it, was described by him as a museum: full of Persian rugs, Japanese prints, a Steuben collection, and a conservatory of plants.

Though I was concerned about his safety, I had never seen Lloyd so happy. "Well, I understand you want to put your best foot forward."

He gave me a coy look. "I certainly do! And anything else I can put forward!"

I laughed. "Lloyd!"

"I take your point about the public place, Ellen," he said. "We plan to talk again before Saturday. If he doesn't seem like Jack the Ripper, I'll decide whether to meet in town or at the house."

"Fine. I'd feel better knowing you'll be careful." And I did, although I was still concerned when a sudden transformation occurred and clients jumped to replace a relationship before resolving the previous one. As a psychologist, it was a trade-off: see your client feeling positive or keep him chained in the chasm until he understood what happened and why. This was the dilemma of life. We rarely neaten up before we fall headlong into another mess. And, in a way, I had encouraged Lloyd in this behavior by suggesting the personal ad.

I wasn't above reproach on this matter. I hadn't resolved everything in my past relationships, either. With Drew, some of the issues were mine and had little to do with his homosexuality, though this was the primary reason for the split. However, I sometimes questioned if my attraction to him might have incorporated a subconscious awareness that he was "safe," even if he didn't tell me he was gay until two years later. And then there was the attraction to my client, Lucas, whose tragic suicide attempt still haunted me. At times such as these, I felt like a fake—giving advice to a client about his love life when my own was in disarray.

I steered my attention to the conversation. "If he comes to the house, I'm sure he'll be impressed. You'll have a fire in the fireplace. Some music, candles?"

"*De rigueur*, Ellen. How else does one entertain?"

"Lloyd, more seriously, don't get your hopes up too much. He sounds interesting, but you're still dealing with the loss of Peter."

"And Bibby might not like him. She doesn't take to just anyone, you know."

"Yes, that's always a concern. Did anyone else answer the ad?"

He told me about two other letters. One was from a man closer in age to Lloyd. I encouraged Lloyd to call him, though he was smitten with the younger fellow. Then he mentioned my university lecture and gushed over my suit, which he said looked "so dignified," and the second book, which he pronounced "fascinating." I thanked him and brought the discussion back to Peter, but Lloyd was so excited about his date with the stockbroker that not much therapeutic work was accomplished. He gave me his check and flew down the stairs on clouds of euphoria.

I'd rather be with you than where I am. How often have I thought this? All day and much of the night.

I'm growing restless, eager for our union, so I telephone in the hope of hearing you and confirming where you are, unless, of course, I see you in person. At bedtime, to feel your presence, to find peace, I place a raindrop on my forehead as you instructed, but I may not be able to stand this much longer. Yet when I see the tape, you smile and tell me to be patient.

I've started to collect leaves when I visit your house, especially the ones that match the color of your hair.

As always, I'm watching…

DOLLY BORDELLA was waiting in the outer office, looking slightly more wintry in a wool dress, though its gold background was sprinkled with the usual flowers. A Peter Pan collar made her appear girlish and innocent. I wondered how innocent she was. Though the handwriting in her file didn't resemble the writing on the cards, she might have disguised it.

She entered the room, checked behind the sofa, walked to the wall with the Venetian masks, and stared at the *I Bellini* pair worn by a man and a woman. She gave me a hesitant glance.

"Go ahead, Dolly. You can take one down."

With great care, she lifted an ivory, blue, and gold mask from its hook. The mask's expression was serene, neither a smile nor a frown, locked in unemotional stasis, and was elegant with intricate gold-leaf embellishments on the forehead and white ribbons trailing from the sides. I encouraged her to bring it to the couch, which she did, and asked her to hold the mask to her face. With her long yellow hair and gold dress, she looked very exotic with the mask. Her blue eyes staring through were unblinking.

"How do you feel, Dolly?"

She was silent, as if absorbing the mask's identity. "Oh, no," she began tentatively. "Not Dolly. I am...I am a courtesan!" she announced. "A lady of the night. That's who I am."

This flight of fancy was a stretch, considering Dolly's fearful demeanor.

"And as a courtesan, what will you do this evening?"

"I'll wait until it's dark. Very, very dark and then I'll walk through the city. Over the canals and down alleyways, past the palaces and cafés. I'll keep to the shadows." She intoned this like a sleepwalker, hypnotically, with a measured cadence.

"Are you afraid?"

"I'm never afraid. I'm a courtesan. I am powerful!"

This entire charade surprised me because it was so out of

character. I had no idea how to direct Dolly's fantasy. "Are you alone?"

She shook her head. "I have many friends and lovers."

"Men?"

"Yes," she replied solemnly. "Men and women. Old and young. Though they must be beautiful or rich to pay for my services. And afterward they would only want me."

I was nonplussed at the confidence the mask had given her. I almost believed I was witnessing multiple personalities.

"How do you like being a courtesan?"

She closed her eyes, as if experiencing memories. "I love the freedom. I can go anywhere."

"You can go anywhere without being a courtesan," I remarked, trying to give her a gentle tug back to reality.

Dolly's eyes flew open. "No, I can't, but now I'll dance until dawn. Make love to anyone, in rooms with thousands of candles and flowers, music playing, crystal glasses of wine, silver platters filled with pheasant and rabbit." Dolly laughed lightly, dramatically different from her usual constrained laughter. "I would bewitch my lovers forever."

I was unnerved. She seemed to be addressing her words directly to me. "As a courtesan, you would have that power. And as yourself, would you like that? To bewitch people?" I asked, hoping to separate Dolly from her inventions.

Though I couldn't see her mouth, I sensed she was smiling. "Of course. Who wouldn't want that power?"

"How would you use it?"

"To make men and women helpless. Slaves who would do anything I asked."

"What would you ask them to do?"

"Bring me joy and riches, bring me vengeance on those I hate."

The transformation was fascinating. "Who do you hate?"

"The butcher, of course."

Sensing that she had worked herself into an illusionary state, I asked her how she would hurt the butcher.

"I would tell one of my lovers to hack him to pieces or I'd do it myself, using his meat cleaver. Jam his head on a big hook," she replied with grim satisfaction.

"What did the butcher do that frightened you so much?"

With that, Dolly slowly lowered the mask and continued to stare at me, as if in a trance. Her body appeared to shrink. Finally, her blue eyes blinked twice, and she returned to the room, the office, and herself.

"I don't remember," she whispered.

I stood and reached for the mask, which she gave me with sleepy reluctance, and hung it on the wall. Taking my seat, I thought she seemed withdrawn, like someone coming off of a drug high. I let her re-acclimate for a moment, as I did with clients who had been under hypnosis. The effect of the mask on Dolly had been similar. When she turned toward the window, her expression lacked animation, and she showed no inclination to continue the conversation. It was time to gather the reins.

"Dolly, last week you mentioned a special friend. Did you have dinner or see each other?"

"Not dinner, but we spent time together." She still wore a dreamy expression when she faced me. "I love being with her."

"Does she feel the same way? Do you have plans to meet soon?"

Dolly nodded. "Yes."

"Does she have a name?"

Dolly laughed and covered her mouth. "Of course she does."

I wasn't sure whether this friend was imaginary or real. There was something other-worldly about the mysterious person unless the friend was me. If so, this would explain Dolly's amusement when I asked for the woman's name. Her strange behavior also made me wonder again whether Dolly suffered from dissociation.

"Can you say more about her?"

"She's wonderful! She's very intelligent and accomplished," Dolly said, staring at me.

"What does she do?"

"She works with people."

I had the sense that Dolly thought the question was unnecessary. "Is she a social worker or a doctor?"

"She gives people so much. Sometimes I worry if there will be enough left for me."

Again, her comment sounded personal. Before I could respond, Dolly abruptly announced she had finished a short story.

"Really? That's great. What is it about?"

For the first time since she'd sat down, Dolly peered over the couch. "It's a children's story about a beautiful little girl. Dina. She's five years old."

"What happens to Dina?"

"Her mean mother sends her to the store, but it's late in the afternoon and the sky gets darker and darker. Night falls and she loses her way. The streets look the same…all curled around. Dina runs, crying for help, but no one comes. Scared, she knocks on a big door with a giant brass knocker—a fox's head. After many minutes, the door slowly opens, and in the blackness, Dina sees a black bull." Here, her face contorted with fear, and she began speaking faster, her hands raised and gesticulating furiously. "The bull is angry at the girl for knocking on his door. He snorts and bares his teeth. His eyes are red, his long horns sharp. The girl flees into the deserted street, screaming. The bull chases her, his huge head lowered, his eyes flashing. Dina hears his hooves on the cobblestones, coming closer. Suddenly, the bull stops and moans in pain. The girl turns to see blood gushing from his neck. The blood pours down his chest and his legs onto the pavement. Everything is red. Then a voice from above says, 'The vengeance is mine. You shall not live, Bull, for you frightened the little girl!' and with that, a beautiful woman emerges. The sun rises, making the woman's hair gleam like gold, and she lifts Dina up. The girl climbs into the woman's arms and feels safe as they disappear into the sun."

I was stunned. While the story was about power, with a bloody, disturbing denouement, more significantly it implied a client/therapist transference, with me cast as the rescuing woman. The bull was clearly the butcher, Dolly's embodiment of malevolence and evil. His death was Dolly's deliverance from fear, her retaliation for whatever he had done to her.

As I observed Dolly sitting on the sofa, her hands now gathered in her lap, I wondered if Dolly had picked up the butcher's cleaver and attacked the man rather than the butcher doing something to her? Dolly had reported that she stopped going to his shop, and I had assumed the butcher had abused or scared her—unless the incident was a product of Dolly's childhood imagination. There was no doubt she was afraid of him, maybe with justification, but had she been the aggressor?

"That's quite a tale, Dolly," I said at last, when she made no move to break the silence. "Frightening and nightmarish."

"Yes, it is," she replied, gazing at me calmly, innocence shining from her pale eyes. Not the placid demeanor one would expect after describing such a ghoulish plot.

"Was your mother mean like in the story?"

With some reluctance, Dolly said, "She made me go to the butcher's when I didn't want to."

Dolly didn't seem interested in her mother, so I set aside the discussion for a later time. "Can you say who the woman in your dream is?"

"Ha! Can't you guess?"

I shook my head.

"What kind of shrink are you, then?" Dolly giggled.

My face colored. "The kind who likes to ask questions."

"Yes, you are."

Just then, I heard Denise DiNicola on the stairs and realized we were running late. We finished more quickly than I would have liked, but as Dolly turned to leave, she glanced at the mask. Then, mysteriously, she smiled at me and said goodbye, closing the door behind her.

I stood there, confused. More than anything, I wanted to be alone, to muse over the session and make detailed notes. Was Dolly the stalker? Or was she friendly with someone in a field related to mine? Or was this all make-believe? And the transference?

Her strange smile had been unsettling.

—

Though I wasn't ready to see another client, I opened the door to the waiting area. Denise was in jeans with a brown corduroy shirt buttoned over a black turtleneck, all lightly speckled with plaster. She took her place at the corner of the sofa, hands in pockets.

I asked about her week. Denise smiled and explained that her employer was giving her time to start preliminary sketches for her sculptural portrait.

"I love marble," she said. "It's alive and breathing."

I enjoyed hearing artists talk about their experiences and their attitudes toward their work. "Three-dimensional carving must be very challenging."

"Yeah. Most people can't see that way. It's not like drawing. Drawing is putting marks on flat paper. Paper doesn't have much personality, but marble has history and life and flows. Wood is similar. I've done more work in wood, but I prefer marble. You can really get completely lost inside it."

"When do you think you'll begin cutting?"

"Maybe later this week. I have to consider the sides and the back. Most people don't think about anything except the front."

"No, they don't. You're right."

"Great sculpture is beautiful from all angles. Kind of like you experience people from different psychological perspectives."

"That's an interesting observation."

Denise grinned. "Thanks."

"So, what else did you do this week? Something you enjoyed?"

"I took several long walks. It's very beautiful with the trees turning colors. It's my favorite time of year. Maybe it's because my birthday is coming up. I heard that people prefer the season in which they were born."

"A Scorpio?"

She laughed. "Yeah, watch out for the stinger."

I smiled. "Do you believe in astrology?"

"I do, sort of." Denise proceeded to explain the positions of her sun, moon, rising sign, and planets.

When she finished, I asked Denise to tell me more about her family. "They live in Florida, right?"

Her face, which had been alive with animation, suddenly clouded. "Yeah, ever since my father retired. Papa used to work in a warehouse, stacking boxes of automobile parts before he hurt his back. My mother is very religious. Catholic. She helped at the church, doing the flowers and running errands for the priests. When I was a kid, she also took in laundry and did some sewing, but Mama didn't get on with people well."

"Why is that?"

Denise shrugged. "She's got a bad temper. Especially when she drinks whisky."

"When you were a child, did your mother drink a lot?"

"Yeah, she did. Me? I never touch whisky. Makes me really sick, the smell of it."

I was interested in her answer, the connection between her mother and herself. "That must have been tough on you. What time did she start drinking?"

"It depended on if she had to go to church or whether she had shopping to do. But it usually began after Papa left the house and went on most of the day. That's why I didn't want to come home after school."

"What would happen when you did?"

"Usually, she'd be passed out in the chair. Then I could sneak in, grab something to eat, and do household stuff before going to my room."

"And other times?"

"If Mama was feeling like it, she made me drink with her. If there wasn't much left in the bottle, it was just one because she'd want the whisky for herself. Often, it was more. I hated when that happened because I couldn't do my homework afterward. When my father arrived, he'd start yelling that I was drunk. As if it was my fault. He'd take a belt to me. Mama, she'd laugh, if she was still awake."

I noted Denise's unemotional tone, as if these incidents had happened to someone else. "He never blamed her?"

"I don't think it mattered to him whether I was squiffed be-cause of Mama or because I'd helped myself. Either way, if Papa was in the mood, I was in line. Mostly, I think he just enjoyed hit-ting someone."

"Did he ever physically abuse your mother?"

"Now and then. She was about as big as he was, though. Mama gave as good as she got."

"Did your father drink?"

"Yeah. Mostly at the bar. To be with the guys and see football or baseball games."

"What would happen when he returned?"

"Nothing if Mama was asleep. But if Mama was still up, he'd get mad sometimes."

"Or if you were still awake and she wasn't?" I asked, thinking that her mother would have trouble staying conscious after a day abusing alcohol.

"Then I'd leave through the upstairs window and climb down the trellis. I'd sleep in my hut until the house lights went out and he was asleep."

"That's terrible, Denise. Didn't your school counselors know what was going on?"

"No. They just thought the bruises were because I was clumsy—that's what Mama told them. And that I was lazy. My teachers believed it was my fault that I wasn't getting good grades or doing my homework."

"Didn't you discuss this with anyone? What about your priest? He knew your mother."

She scoffed. "He's the last person who would've believed me. He thought my mother was a saint. Of course, he never saw her when she was tanked."

I felt sorry for her and said so. We spoke about the effects of emotional and physical mistreatment, a subject I promised we would continue next week. I also mentioned that it was okay to contact me if her depression returned. She said she would and added that my Friday talk really hit home for her. Though curious, I made a note to ask more during the following session.

—

I sat at my desk and rolled my shoulders to relax. Both of the sessions had been intense. In Dolly's file, I recorded her children's story and my impressions about her playacting with the mask. There were strong similarities touched on in both. The butcher/bull personifying evil, worthy of bloody punishment administered in one case by a fairy godmother—or by me—and in the other by Dolly herself, protected by a courtesan's invulnerability. In both tales, magic was employed in a gothic way. Her descriptions of thousands of candles and flowers were feverishly opulent, and the animal imagery harkened to her fascination and phobic reaction to the butcher's shop and its contents. Two of the animals—the pheasant and rabbit—were passive, unthreatening, and in her courtesan's version, available to be eaten by her if she wished. The fox, a more equivocal creature, literally opened the door to the bull, a ferocious animal and the symbol of the butcher, who Dolly needed an all-powerful presence to quell. Was I also the fox? Did she view therapy as the portal to that which she feared? Maybe I was pushing the imagery too much, but were there also sexual overtones in the description of the woman lifting Dolly up in an embrace?

How unbalanced was Dolly? I had been concerned about her impressionability after she told me about leaving her husband because of feelings engendered by the Ibsen play, and some of her reactions were definitely overwrought. Today's stories seemed like those produced by a mind trying to vanquish trauma by creating fantastical super-characters.

Could Dolly be my stalker, and if so, what risks did she pose? She was slender and didn't appear strong, though Glenn Close's Alex hadn't been powerful. If armed with a weapon, even someone of Dolly's physique could be dangerous. Had our "relationship" been going on in her mind prior to our first appointment? Begun at one of my lectures, unbeknownst to me? If Dolly wasn't my follower, I still detected an interpersonal issue arising.

Denise's depiction of her childhood was Dickensian. Was it

partly an invention? To make the family environment worse than it was as a means to enlist my interest and sympathy? I'd noticed a flat affect when Denise explained about her alcoholic parents and how she had abused liquor through the enforced camaraderie with her mother. Had Denise demonized them in the same fashion as Dolly had chosen the butcher as her stock personification of evil? What did ring true was Denise's recounting about being punished with a belt. I also didn't doubt that her formative years had been difficult, but her story about climbing in and out of windows at night required more detail for verification. I reminded myself that I could be wrong and needed to be both gentle and vigilant in how I questioned her.

Was Denise responsible for all the calls and gifts? If she was, why didn't she let me know? Because she had little experience in these matters and was unsure of herself? Then there was that comment about Scorpios having a stinger. Admittedly, this was a well-known trait of the sign, and the manner in which Denise had imparted it to me had been rather scorpion-like. Overall, the session had been unnerving, as had the one with Dolly, who'd seemed flirtatious or teasing at several points in the conversation. Why?

[THE JOURNAL]

The prints arrived today—of you sleeping on the deck. With the sun shining on your hair, you look very pretty. I fell in love with you all over again. After examining them carefully, I'm having four negatives made into 11 x 14 enlargements.

I still wonder why you chose me, though I think I know. You want someone who will always be there, who will never leave. We are bound together until the end.

Later, I'm going to gather more leaves. One day we will lie together and look at all the golden leaves, and you will know that I'll take care of you always.

I FINISHED my notes and opened the door. The Claytons were talking quietly to each other, a significant change from their hostile postures during the previous session.

"You two look like you've had a good week," I remarked after we were seated.

Steve, who sat close to his wife on the sofa, glanced at her with surprising tenderness and smiled. "Yes, I guess we have."

"Steve decided he's going to switch companies. He's realized his boss is too demanding and encroaching on our life."

"That sounds like an accurate assessment."

"After I saw the effect on my family," Steve began, "I knew Sharon was right. We went out for dinner and talked, really talked, for the first time in a long while. I explained how much pressure I felt being the breadwinner, particularly in my current job which reminds me of an octopus, with tentacles reaching everywhere. I think my resentment about work got turned against my wife and kids. I was so busy being angry at everyone that it completely blocked me from dealing with the real problem."

"The job, the boss..." I suggested.

"Yeah."

"Steve, I'm reminded of a sentiment people often express: 'he made me so angry' or 'she made me feel powerless.' Those expressions displace culpability onto a second person. As in your situation, your manager. Though I agree the boss was abusing you in the workplace and didn't respect where your private life began in comparison to your work responsibilities, ultimately drawing that line is up to you. To set your own boundaries between job and home even in the face of his inappropriate expectations."

"That's what I've been saying. Exactly what I've told you," Sharon said to Steve.

"Yes, Sharon, but some of this issue also applies to the space between you and Steve. Both of you need to negotiate boundaries.

Steve requires time away from you, away from the children, and away from work. Likewise, so do you. Your children need privacy and separation at times. Everyone does. A good relationship is both fused and separate—that makes for flexibility, and flexibility is essential for personal growth. Think about it like a moving joint. There has to be attachment but space to bend and flex. A successful marriage works best when we find joy within ourselves and also with our chosen partner, sometimes together, sometimes apart."

They took this in and nodded. Steve looked at his wife. "We hear you."

"Good."

They discussed the ideas I'd presented for a few minutes, then Sharon brought up the gallery she wanted to start.

"Have you talked with Steve about how much it will cost to get it running?"

"Some. He hasn't been very encouraging."

Steve squeezed her hand. "Actually, Sharon, I'd like to help."

"You would? Really?" Sharon gave her husband a big smile. "As a matter of fact, my partner and her husband will pay the rent. My costs will be splitting the electricity, heat, phone, and running expenses. I'll balance by spending more time at the gallery and coordinating publicity efforts with newspapers."

"That's reasonable," Steve replied. "I think we can afford to give it a try."

Sharon was delighted and eagerly reviewed her plans. Steve was thoughtfully appraising, and the lines of tension in Sharon's face dissolved. When I commented upon this, both of them stared at each other and considered how disintegrated their marriage had become. The awareness sobered them, and they seemed thankful to step back from the precipice. Then I asked Steve where he was looking for work.

"There's a small business in Lawrence that's advertising for an office manager, one who can make suggestions about improving communications within the company and also with their clients. I have an interview tomorrow, but they're already interested."

"So you might get to be the boss now?"

"Maybe, but I promise I won't act like my current one!"

We discussed the dialogues the two had written as part of their therapy assignment, but so much progress had been made that they were quick to correct their own errors. While a few sessions might be necessary to help them over the hurdles of new life changes, I doubted they would remain with me for long. I extended my best wishes for the job interview.

—

Chang and Mei-Ling came in, nodded hello, and sat nearer to each other than usual. It made me wonder if I might have a magic touch, if the Lees' week had been as harmonious as the Claytons'. We exchanged pleasantries about the weather, something we always did, and when I asked about the upcoming visit from Mei-Ling's parents, Chang smiled at his wife and said they'd had success in finding accommodations with the neighbors.

"That's terrific news."

"Yes," Mei-Ling agreed. "And Chang will be out of town on an assignment for several days during the last week so that will give me more time alone with my parents to do activities we like."

"Like shopping," Chang teased.

"I'm happy this arrangement will suit everyone. And how are things with your parents, Chang?"

"Very well, thank you. We're getting together tonight for dinner at an Indian restaurant. Mei-Ling has agreed to come."

"Fine. I hope you enjoy your evening."

I asked about their respective jobs. Then we hit a snag. Chang, though he hadn't mentioned it to Mei-Ling, had been offered a position in East Orange. He quickly explained that it paid almost twice his current salary, and he could commute by train from Trenton. Mei-Ling accused him of hiding this information until he was protected by me in the session. She edged toward the far corner of the sofa.

"Mei-Ling, I can see this is very upsetting for you. Can you tell me how you're feeling?"

She shook her head, pressed her lips tightly together, and threw a furious glance at her husband.

"Mei-Ling, I'm really sorry," Chang apologized. "I only heard about the proposal a few hours ago."

"I don't believe you!" Mei-Ling gave him another scathing look.

"Why would I lie?" he asked, exasperated.

"Because you're afraid," she retorted, crossing her arms tightly. "You're a coward."

I stepped in. "How much extra time would commuting take, Chang?"

He considered. "Maybe two hours or so each day. I'd be home about six-thirty or seven."

"And now?"

"Mei-Ling and I work near each other. I pick her up after work, and we're home by five-thirty."

"Do you drive, Mei-Ling?" I asked.

"No, I don't and I don't want to!"

"Mei-Ling," Chang argued, "everyone in America drives. You have to take lessons and learn. With the money I'll make, I can buy you a car."

She continued to glare at her husband. "I don't want a car. You wish to do what you want to do. You don't care if this is a big

226

inconvenience. And what will happen every night? I do the cooking all by myself, like a traditional woman, and have dinner on the table when you come home? I have the same degree as you. I even had better grades." Her face was red with anger.

Chang jumped from the couch. "This is unfair! Why can't you be an American? Why can't you drive like everybody else? Right now I always have to stop work even if I have more to do because you're waiting."

"Chang, please sit down," I told him gently. "I think we're getting into some of the same issues as we dealt with last week. Probably one of the main attractions Mei-Ling had in coming to this country was the freedom to be an equal and respected person, regardless of her gender. In opting for this opportunity, she's sacrificed much of her security—home, family, and friends. You have this security in place. For Mei-Ling, quite understandably, you've become an important part of her life, because she has no one else to rely on. This puts the two of you in an unbalanced situation which is the cause of many of your disagreements." I caught my breath and looked at them both. "I know you love each other. That's obvious. Are you familiar with the term 'parity' as it applies to people?"

"No," said Mei-Ling. "What is this 'parity?'"

"It's a simple concept. A contract in which partners have an equal say in everything that affects the relationship, so one person doesn't control the other or make all the decisions. It also grants some autonomy on individual matters, things that you do that have no effect on Chang or vice versa. The main point is that if Chang wishes to take this job, and you believe it will negatively impact the equality of your marriage, this needs to be discussed and a fair solution found that's acceptable to both of you. Not every decision can be perfectly fair, but that's the objective. In this situation, if Chang wants to move to a more challenging position, then something compensatory should be worked out so your needs are being met."

"How is this done?" Mei-Ling asked.

"Chang, do you have any suggestions?"

He glanced at his wife, annoyed. "No. If I don't accept the offer, then there's no problem, right?"

"And you'll resent Mei-Ling because you lost an opportunity," I told him. "And Mei-Ling will feel guilty because every time you're unhappy at your current company, she'll believe you blame her for keeping you there."

He frowned. "Yes."

"Marriage isn't made up of iron chains locking two people together in a static state. It needs to change and grow as the two partners change and grow. Whenever there's an opportunity for one and not the other, it causes significant stress on the relationship. Unfortunately, two people seldom get their opportunities at the same time. In addition to trying to achieve parity, we also have to be aware that sometimes parity isn't possible. In those instances, one partner gives up something because he or she loves the other. This is a conscious and generous act, one that shouldn't be automatically expected. If you, Mei-Ling, agree to let Chang take the new job, then Chang, you need to keep in mind her graciousness and compensate her whenever possible. Mei-Ling, if you agree to this arrangement, what can Chang do to make the situation feel more balanced?"

She thought about this. "He can do the shopping every Saturday, pay the bills, and cook meals several nights a week."

"Chang, is this agreeable to you?"

"Yes, I suppose. But what about her driving?"

Mei-Ling uncrossed her arms and sighed. "I don't want to, but maybe I'll take driving lessons." She threw a glance at her husband. "And if I like driving, you can buy me a Mercedes-Benz."

I smiled. We talked about her parents' visit, and when they left, Chang placed his arm around Mei-Ling's shoulder.

—

After I closed the office, I drove to the Princeton Borough Police Department. Turning the matter over in my mind, I couldn't understand why my stalker didn't declare his or her identity. The most obvious reason was that they recognized their behavior was abnormal, even if this awareness wasn't fully conscious, and were able to exert some control over their infatuation. If this were true, discouraging their affections or having the police tell them to desist, might make them stop—if we learned the person's identity. The other possibility was psychologically more complicated. Perhaps my stalker was under the impression that I welcomed the gifts and was a co-participant in the relationship. If so, the delusional factor increased. I knew enough about delusions to realize they were difficult to rationally dislodge because they served a critical purpose and satisfied a deep psychological need.

As it turned out, the State Police had already notified the Princeton police of my predicament and had shared details. I spoke with Sergeant McMadden, a tall, lanky man with large brown eyes and a friendly smile. He had dealt with two other stalkers over the last year. Both were more typical, insofar as I knew about such things. In one situation, a husband had followed his wife, who had separated from him. He had dogged her movements, made threats and annoying phone calls, and had hired an investigator to document her adulterous activities. When he finally had proof that she was having an affair with a mutual friend—a relationship that began after his separation from his wife—the man became unhinged, trashing her car, spray-painting "whore" and "slut" on the grass in front of the house, and eventually assaulting the boyfriend, who pressed charges.

The second case was similar, McFadden explained. A man, who had briefly dated a female bank teller, had become fixated on her. When she rejected him, the suitor began frequenting the bank and deluging the woman with flowers, letters, and telephone calls. In the end, he was picked up by the police in a cocaine sting, a fortuitous accident. McFadden said that if this hadn't happened, it would have been difficult to protect the woman because anti-stalking statutes didn't exist in New Jersey, though lawmakers were considering enacting legislation.

"Do you mean there's little that can be done legally? In circumstances like mine?"

"Yes. Unless the person breaks other laws—makes dangerous threats or commits forcible entry, vandalism, simple or aggravated assault, criminal trespassing, disorderly conduct—anything like that—we can charge them. However, most of these cases don't lead to incarceration."

"That's frustrating."

"It is. Sometimes a police officer can have a talk with the person and dissuade them from their activities. Usually that doesn't have much effect," he said. "Maybe you should move to California, Dr. Haskell. Anti-stalking laws are on the books there."

"We have trespassing and vandalism in this case."

"Yes, ma'am, that's true, but the acts fall into the nuisance category. Besides, you don't know who's doing this."

"I have some suspicions, but as I told the State Police, I'm bound by my professional ethics and can't discuss my clients."

"I understand that. However, if you determine that you're in physical danger, we can check to see if any of your folks have a record. Sometimes they do."

"You mean they may have previously stalked someone else?"

"Yes. Or they have a history of criminal behavior. When you're able to give me a list of names, I'll run them through the system."

"Thank you. I'm still uncomfortable doing that—at this point."

McFadden nodded. "Fine, but if you identify the perpetrator or something more serious happens, let us know. The dead pigeon on the doormat is a cause for concern."

"I agree. It may indicate that the person is having more violent thoughts. I'm sure you've considered this, but do you think fingerprinting items might help?" I asked, feeling a little awkward suggesting it before he did.

"Let's see what the person does next. Just keep everything together and put the cards in plastic bags in case we need to check them later."

I promised that I would. He then took information about my office address, my car, its license plate, and accepted a copy of the timeline of events. I wrote down his name and number.

—

Though I didn't like the idea of going home after dark, I drove to Hopewell, watching for anyone following me. No one was. The mail was just mail. The spotlights were on, and no new offerings were by the door. I went upstairs, feeling anxious. The machine held three hang-ups, a message from the State Police saying they were surveilling the house on occasion, and then, on the fifth message, my heart began beating faster. It was my high school boyfriend, Michael Larrimore. We had drifted apart during college—he attended the University of Washington. After graduation, he had remained in Seattle. Michael was handsome, sandy-haired, blue-eyed, kind, and smart. The great guy who got away. I'd always hoped we might reconnect. Quickly, I dialed his number.

"Michael, it's Ellen. How wonderful to hear from you!"

"Hi! When I received your card about the move to Princeton,

I've been meaning to get in touch." He paused and then added, "I've really missed you."

He sounded sincere, warm with interest. Perhaps more than interest, or was I misreading him because I felt hopeful for the first time in weeks?

Michael laughed. "So how is living with your parents? You had some issues with your mother when we were dating, though I guess things are fine now."

I exhaled a long breath. "Well, actually, they aren't. My parents left for Corfu shortly after I came home. They were in a really bad car accident, and my mother died. Dad is still on the island, using crutches and recuperating."

"Oh, my god! I'm so sorry, Ellen!"

I thanked him and explained what had happened. We then drifted into reminiscences about my mother, his parents, and our teenage days. He spoke about his life as an English professor, and I described my transition to Princeton. It was tempting to confide about my stalker, but before I could, Michael said he was planning to be in New York with his parents for Christmas and wanted to visit.

"I would love to see you!" I told him. "When?"

"December 28? I'll spend the holiday with them and then drive down."

"Great! Can you stay for New Year's?"

"Hey, I was hoping you'd ask!" Michael laughed. "It's a date! Now, I have to run, but I'm so excited to see you, Ellen."

When we ended the conversation, I realized I was grinning for the first time in days.

[THE JOURNAL]

I saw you eating dinner alone. How I wanted to be with you! Ellen, I don't understand why we can't be together yet. I paced and paced and looked at your video and your photographs, your face that smiles at me, and don't understand. I trust you but my patience is being tested. Maybe that's your point…that you're testing me, that I must prove myself by waiting, but for how long? I've gathered most of the things you asked me to buy. They weren't easy to find. Tomorrow I'll purchase the special object. I had to call all over to find one. Please…end this misery soon or else I don't know what I'll do.

I AWOKE with a sore throat and a cold. After I drank some tea with honey and ate some toast, I felt no better, no did I after my father telephoned and explained his doctor wasn't satisfied that the broken bones were healing at the predicted rate. This wasn't welcome news, but I sympathized.

"Getting lonely?" he teased.

"Sort of."

"Well, hang in there, Ellen. I'll be home in a few weeks, though when I'm able to travel, I might spend time in Athens. One of my former colleagues has a symposium scheduled in November and has offered an invitation to give the keynote speech. It's a nice honor for an old geezer like me."

"You're not an old geezer, Dad," I laughed, trying to cover my disappointment.

"At the moment I'm feeling like one." He chuckled. "Will you be okay?"

"I'll be fine." I described my university lecture and told him which of his friends had attended. He reminded me to get the furnace serviced for the winter and to shut off the water supply to the outside faucets. I promised to do both, though I couldn't help feeling abandoned.

—

Because I'd rescheduled Greta Graf for eleven, I had a little time before her appointment. I drove to Princeton and rushed to the university library, where I investigated articles on stalking in the *American Journal of Psychiatry*, the *British Journal of Psychiatry*, the *Bulletin of the Menninger Clinic*, and in some non-academic magazines. The work published in the 1980s was focused on "obsessive following" and dealt with situations in which the victim was partially connected to the victimizer. Toward the late 1980s, attention centered on "star stalkers" and their crazed fans, illustrated by the 1989 murder of sitcom actress Rebecca Schaeffer by a deranged admirer, Robert Bardo. He had hired a private   detective to find her and wandered the streets with her photo trying to locate anyone who knew where she lived. Finally, through the Division of Motor Vehicles, he discovered her address and rang her doorbell. When Schaeffer answered, he shot her. She died a half hour later at the hospital. There was no explanation as to the reason for his sudden attack.

Recent work, in which the term "stalker" was applied, dealt with the matter as a woman's issue—violence wrought by men on women who were in or had been in relationships with them. None of this was specifically pertinent to my dilemma. Then I found references to de Clérambault's Syndrome, or erotomania, a term for a monomaniacal obsession, and recognition hit. I copied several articles on the subject and the magazine piece about Schaeffer's murder.

As I was crossing Nassau Street on my return to the office, I was so upset about the Bardo article that I nearly walked in front of an oncoming car. My anxiety jumped another notch when I saw a missive pinned to my door. Furious, I tore off the envelope, charged upstairs, and took several deep breaths before opening it. Instead of a card, a letter was inside, written in capital letters, in red ink, on a white paper folded in quarters like Samantha Cosgrove did.

MY BELOVED ELLEN,
LAST NIGHT, YOU ATE DINNER BY YOURSELF. I WANTED TO COME TO YOU, BUT YOU'VE ASKED ME TO WAIT. I'LL BE PATIENT, BUT IT'S GETTING VERY HARD. I FOLLOW YOUR INSTRUCTIONS CAREFULLY, PLACING A RAINDROP ON MY FOREHEAD AND TONGUE EVERY NIGHT WHILE THINKING OF YOU, OF US TOGETHER. WE HAVE A

PURE LOVE. YOU'VE GIVEN ME CONFIDENCE BY CHOOS-
ING ME, THOUGH AT FIRST I DIDN'T UNDERSTAND.

I CAN'T SLEEP AT NIGHT, BUT YOU KNOW THAT,
DON'T YOU? YOU WANT TO TEST ME SO YOU'RE SURE I'M
WORTHY. I'M WAITING FOR YOUR MESSAGE, WAITING TO
UNITE WITH YOU. I HOPE IT COMES SOON. PLEASE MAKE
IT SOON.

LOVE, THE LION WATCHING

P.S. I BOUGHT THE THINGS YOU ASKED ME TO.

I collapsed into my desk chair. What kind of disturbed person
was this? I re-read the letter and was struck by the delusional aspects—the raindrops, the messages and communications supposedly originating from me. It was also frightening to realize I had
been observed last night, to think that he or she had been staring
at me as I ate dinner. On a third reading, the impatience began to
sound like a drumbeat. And what was the P.S. about? Buying what
things I asked? The corker was that this individual thought I had
chosen them, which seemed like an essential part of the fantasy's
construction. Suddenly, I recalled George Durst saying something
similar. I mulled this over for a moment, unsure whether he could
be my letter-writer, but whoever it was, someone had adopted me
as a love object and was now obsessively waiting for permission to
be united. I noted the letter contained no overtly sexual sentiments. In fact, the infatuation seemed non-physical and idealized.
The flowers, candy, and cards were traditional romantic presents—
not overly suggestive ones—and the tone was juvenile, although
an inexperienced older suitor might come across as immature and
young. But then what about the more ominious gifts: the dead
bird and blood-soaked rose?

Was this a male or a female? The blocky capitals had been carefully done, as if copied from a draft, and were unfettered with stylistic quirks except for a few horizontal slashes.

—

Greta Graf was attired in a puffy orange parka that would have been appropriate for the Arctic rather than a sunny day in the low 50s. After I said hello in a husky voice, she held up a hand like a traffic cop and told me to keep my distance, that she didn't need my cold. I didn't, either.

Greta reported her activities, including the walking program, which she was doing regularly, and swimming at the Y, which she had done once during the week. Greta had entertained her new friend, Anne Ainsley, on Sunday, and they were planning an art exhibit together. Greta's contribution would be a series of contemporary blackware pots inspired from the Greek Geometric Period—a radical change from her modern, free-flowing constructions. Anne was reprising the geometric motifs in wall hangings and using the same palette of colors: black, ivory, and red. After we discussed this project, I asked about Stanley.

"He's been away for the last several days."

"So you haven't seen him this week?"

"No, but he phoned before he left and promised to stop by Saturday for dinner, if he wasn't too tired from his trip."

"That's very nice. I'm delighted."

"I'll have to clean the house, but it needs cleaning anyway," she said, trying to disguise her pleasure. "I won't make a fuss. That's not my style," she said. "Maybe I'll cook beef stew."

"Sounds good. I hope he comes and you have a great time," I told her, commenting that she seemed less depressed. "Is that true?"

She smiled, though a shadow of sadness passed over her. "Yes, perhaps, but I keep thinking of Heinrich. I still miss him, miss talking with him. Stan is interesting, intelligent, thoughtful—many things that are important, but he's not Heinrich. The idea of being with someone else is complicated." She rotated the silver wedding band on her finger. "I suppose it's time to take this off."

"Are you ready?"

"I'll decide how I feel before he comes on Saturday."

"He's probably noticed the ring. If Stanley sees that you've removed it, he'll know why."

Greta gave me a wry smile. "That would be a signal, wouldn't it? He'll get the message I'm interested if I'm not wearing it, but he might conclude I'm not ready if I leave the ring on."

"That sums it up." I took a sip of water. "Regardless of the ring, at some point you'll know whether you're willing to consider a relationship that's more than friendly. Why not see how the evening goes? You might be content with a friendship, or you may find there's an attraction. Play it out."

"I've never been good at that," Greta admitted. "Playing things out."

"You're both mature people. No teenage hormones running rampant. I think you'll explore the way forward together. He's probably as nervous as you are, though he might not show it."

After she left, I noted that Greta's usual adversarial demeanor had mellowed, and she had smiled more. Greta would need support in the coming weeks, but I doubted she would continue if she and Stanley became involved. Sometimes, I felt more like a social director but encouraging connections was a part of the therapeutic process. At least with Greta, I wouldn't have to worry about impulsive behavior. In her approach to Stanley, she would be methodical, turning the relationship over and over like one of her pots. If there was a Stanley.

As soon as this thought crossed my mind, I shook my head,

irritated with myself. I sat for a moment and then checked my answering machine, which I hadn't done before Greta's arrival. Two hang-up calls and two messages, one from Carson Kendricks. He explained that his car wouldn't start, and he had to cancel his appointment. I knew he owned an old clunker, but his explanation didn't sound entirely honest. Was he too busy leaving cards and dead birds at my house? When I returned his call, I left a note that we could postpone until next Wednesday. While I was relieved to have one less client this afternoon, considering how sick I was, Carson's uneven attendance was becoming an issue.

The second recording was from Mary Brown. Her son Albert would be interested in starting therapy, but he wanted me to phone him to set the appointment. She provided his number.

Why hadn't Albert contacted me himself? Was he "waiting" for my message? Or was he too shy or embarrassed to contact a psychologist? For many people, initiating the first interaction was a big threshold to cross, an admittance they needed counseling. I wasn't sure what to do because I was beginning to feel apprehensive about seeing Albert. If he was my stalker, Albert was a large man, too big for me to handle if things went wrong. From his mother's description, he had to be on my list. On the other hand, if he wasn't the stalker, then I was turning away a client.

I called Albert. He answered and identified himself. His voice was baritonal and resonant. I explained that his mother had asked me to telephone him.

"I see. Yes. Mother."

I didn't know whether this was his manner or whether Mary Brown had fibbed a bit on the recording. "I wouldn't have called, except that it was my impression your mother had spoken with you."

"Yes, she did." The silence left at least one of us uncomfortable.

"If you would like to make an appointment, that's completely fine. If you would prefer to—"

"No, so long as you're agreeable…"

An odd thing to say. Without the benefit of visual clues, it was difficult to gauge his reactions. "When would you like to come in?"

He thought for a moment. "When would you like me to come?"

Strange phrasing again. "I have an appointment available at four this afternoon. Would that be convenient?"

Again, another silence. "Yes. Today is good."

"Okay. My office is located—"

"I know where it is."

I said goodbye, feeling unsettled. Did he know where my office was because he was the stalker or because his mother had given him the address?

Using the hotplate, I made another cup of tea. Eating a granola bar, I began re-reading the Bardo article.

———

Robert Gabriel Fleet wasn't someone I felt like listening to for fifty minutes. My throat was hot, and my thoughts about my personal predicament were circling around like a crazed squirrel on a caged track.

Robert sailed in and had scarcely landed before he began spewing slights. He came to a dead stop when I inquired about his coworker, Susan.

"Oh, well, you know I was right about her."

"How do you mean?" My voice was getting froggy. I noted Robert hadn't inquired if I was ill. I popped a lozenge to waylay a cough.

"Susan is really cold," he announced. "We went to lunch, and she droned on about a company ours does business with. I was all set for a little, you know, something on the side. I admit she's at-

240

tractive, but not pretty enough to listen to her opinions about work for an hour."

"Did you learn if she's married?"

"Yes. She is."

"Maybe she loves her husband?" I suggested with an irony too subtle for Robert.

"I wouldn't know. Frankly, he can have her. That's the last time we have lunch."

"Robert, I understand you're disappointed things didn't go the way you hoped, but don't you owe her respect as a colleague and as a married colleague at that?"

He looked at me as if I were nuts. "You don't understand men, do you, Ellen?"

This strategy was annoying. Then I remembered Marguerite's comment about their minds being dark caves and had to hide my amusement. "Though I'm not your gender, Robert, men and women aren't so different from one another. Making assumptions based on gender can be a superficial way of interpreting responses."

He frowned and thrust out his chin.

I changed gears. "How are you and Debby doing?"

Robert's annoyance slowly faded. "Well, as a matter of fact, Debby and I are thinking about having kids."

This took me by surprise. "Do you want children?"

"Maybe. We're the right age to start a family."

As was often the case, Robert was intent on fitting a profile of a successful man with the perfect job, house, wife, and now children. "That doesn't tell me how you feel."

He crossed his legs and ran a hand along his pin-striped trousers. "One might be okay. I don't care what it is, a boy or a girl." He sounded as if he was considering buying a hamster.

"Children are a big responsibility."

"Yes, I know. And Debby would have to quit her job. That would cut into our finances."

"She wouldn't have to stop working for a while," I replied. "Does she want a baby?"

He shrugged. "It was her idea."

Which was undoubtedly part of the problem. Anything proposed by someone other than Robert himself was doomed for disapproval.

"Perhaps we should include Debby in a session…to discuss this? It's an important decision." I was tempted to mention that their relationship wasn't built on the most secure bedrock and to remind him he had just been planning an adulterous roll in the hay. The thought of Robert as a parent was also a stretch, though I suspected Debby was more mature. But sufficiently so to counteract her husband's deficiencies? Overall, given the situation, I worried that having a child would destabilize their marriage, and Debby would find herself in a state of single parenthood soon after, with Robert free to re-marry and repeat the same mistakes.

"I would prefer not to have her here." He began listing Debby's flaws for ten minutes until I put my foot down.

"Robert, I'm sure your wife has traits that bother you, but it might be more productive to concentrate on both sides of your relationship. Important prerequisites for a good marriage are trust and loyalty. Do you think Debby is loyal to you? At the last session, you suspected her of cheating."

"I was wrong. Yes, of course, Debby has been faithful."

"If I asked Debby the same question, whether she believes you're loyal to her, what would her answer be?"

He narrowed his eyes, seeing the trap. "I'm sure she would answer the same way. That I'm a loyal husband." The lie stood between us as big as the coffee table.

"I'm relieved to hear it," I replied, after letting the repudiation remain unspoken.

"Even if I was thinking of a quickie with Susan, that doesn't mean I don't love my wife."

"What does it mean?" I was being sharper than usual.

"It means nothing."

"Unless I misunderstood, you were upset when Susan didn't respond at lunch."

"I was annoyed, that's all."

I considered giving him a piece of my mind but managed restraint. "If you were merely looking for a brief sexual liaison, you might feel good for a short while, but then you would have to deal with remorse and all the problems that would arise when you want to stop the affair or Susan does. Add in the complication that she works with you, and you might include career jeopardy." He was beginning to squirm on the sofa. "I know I am being hard on you—"

"Yes, you are." He weighed his situation and seemed to realize he wasn't in a position to argue. "I'm not altogether in favor of it, but I'll ask Debby about a joint session."

I nodded and accepted his check.

"And Ellen, you really should do something about that cold. You'll give it to someone." With this remark, he was off.

[THE JOURNAL]

My letter has been removed from the door. That makes me happy unless someone else took it, in which case I'll be angry. However, your car was in the parking lot, so hopefully you were the one who found it.

I hate that you spend hours with your clients instead of with me. They're a bunch of stupid losers and whiners who don't deserve you. I wish there was a way to get rid of them. At night, I make lists about how to do that, but it's too difficult. To calm myself, I concentrate on having pure thoughts. It's not easy.

I USHERED Samantha Cosgrove into the office and apologized for the state of my voice. As soon as she sat, I remembered that I had offered to give her contest submission rules. In the furor over the stalker, I had completely forgotten. Once again, I berated myself for being distracted and silently cursed the person responsible, whoever he or she was. I told Sam I would bring the information next week. She accepted this without much enthusiasm and appeared more sullen as the minutes passed. I asked her what was going on.

She shook her head. "Nothing."

"You don't seem yourself, Sam."

"It's my parents. They're being jerks." Sam blew out a breath. "After the last appointment, I tried to talk to them: 'You give me some space, I'll work harder at school.' Dad got mad and said I had no right to bargain about my grades. He threatened to ground me. You know, like take my car keys until my grades went up. They aren't that bad, except math. I mean, really, who cares about math?"

"I never liked it much, either," I agreed. "But maybe we should look at this from their perspective. They're concerned you might fail the class, and this could jeopardize your college applications."

"Yeah. I get that." Sam rolled her eyes.

"Well, that's an important consideration for you and for them."

"Whatever. They're also flipping out because I came in late one night and cut a few classes."

"Your parents might be worried about what you're doing— who you're with and why you aren't in school."

She glared at me, an expression she probably used with her parents. "They do what they want. I don't ask them what they're doing!"

This was a weak argument that didn't require a response. "Let's get back to the math grades. How bad are they?"

"I'm not failing…"

"But close?"

She nodded. "Yeah, like real close."

"Is there someone in class who might be willing to spend time with you each week?"

"Oh, hell, no! I wouldn't want anything to do with those nerds."

"You don't have to become fast friends. Maybe just try it for a while? Or perhaps the teacher could suggest a tutor—"

"No way! No tutors."

"If you don't get the math grade up—"

"Yeah, yeah, I know, it hurts my chances of getting into college. Who cares?"

"I think you care, Sam. If you want to be a writer, it's useful to go to a good university and have access to an excellent creative writing department."

She gave me a surly look. "A lot of writers don't get a degree."

"That may be true for some, but wouldn't it be better to have experienced mentors?"

"No."

I wasn't getting anywhere. As long as I stayed in the authority role, Sam would resist. She had that response down pat. "If your father follows through and takes your car keys, what will you do?"

"I guess I won't drive, will I?"

I sighed. "Sam, are you angry with me?"

"Not particularly."

"You realize I'm not one of your parents. It may be easy to react to them in a certain way, kind of like a habit. In fact, they may be stuck in roles just as you are. That doesn't mean they don't care about you or that you don't care about them. It means you're both maintaining battle fronts, that you've chosen them as the enemy. I don't think they're the enemy, do you?"

Sam shrugged.

"Then who is?" I asked.

She was silent for a long time, twisting a bracelet around her wrist. "I don't know."

"This may surprise you to hear, but I think you're the enemy. I think you're projecting your negative feelings onto your mother and father. Do you understand that concept?"

"Maybe."

"I'm not saying they're blameless and never do anything hurtful. Many of your grievances are probably legitimate. I'm only suggesting that your painful feelings about yourself have to go somewhere. They might be too overwhelming for you to absorb, so you displace your thoughts and feelings onto your parents and are upset with them rather than deal with all the anger and unhappiness you're experiencing…all the pain that's bottled up inside."

She glanced at me, a little shaken, and then stared at her bracelet again.

"I realize you're scared. You don't know what your future will be, whether you'll ever feel okay, whether your writing is good enough. You have one foot in childhood and one foot in adulthood. It's frustrating, I know." I studied her. She was silent but attentive. "Our job—yours and mine—is to work together to get these feelings out. To examine them and see them for what they are. Sam, I don't have magical powers of insight, but I know you can't outrun how you feel, no matter how often you escape at night and walk the streets or drive around. On the other hand— and some psychologists would disagree—I believe it's important for you to spend time alone, to mull over this complicated period in your life as it unfolds. Many people avoid self-confrontation. They clutter up their lives being busy, doing superficial things. You're different," I explained. "This may sound strange, but I think you're braver, and you have to be because of the unique challenges you face. Obviously, you're extremely bright and very talented, yet—as with many creative people—you feel separate and are more sensitive to the hypocrisy and shallowness in the world. While it's tempting to pull away and become isolated, I hope you'll keep searching for friends who will understand you. Look at the relationship with Jake, for example. You felt a connection to him—"

"And see what happened! He offs himself. 'Like, so who cares, Sam?' He might as well have said that!"

"What happened to Jake was very sad. My point is that you began to feel better knowing he was around, didn't you? Even if the ending was tragic?"

"Yeah."

"There will be others, I promise. And, in the meantime, we'll keep talking. We'll keep you from boiling over like Jake. Are you concerned about that?"

No response at first. Finally, she stopped torturing her bracelet and looked at me. "I guess you're right. I am worried about doing what Jake did."

"Okay. Thank you for telling me that, Sam." I took a sip of water from my glass. "So, let's talk about both of you. You and Jake shared similar interests and viewpoints. You related partially because you were different from your classmates. Jake was a valued person in your life and special—you don't have many people with whom you can share your thoughts and feelings or who share theirs with you. But you and Jake were also different, so let's separate him from you." I paused again. "Here's what I know: you're perceptive, thoughtful, and, yes, very uncomfortable with your parents and your peers. You have talent as a writer. Being a creative person is a lonely enterprise, and sometimes you may feel despair so don't expect the world is suddenly going to go all sunny and cheerful. It's my belief that there's a link between your feelings and the impetus to create, though creativity is more than just a valve to let off steam. Writing is its own accomplishment, a tangible thing you make, and maybe the greatest gift you'll give the world, a gift forged from an exploration of your self. From your pain, passion, and joy." I swallowed more water, studying Sam. "One thing I'm sure about. As you grow older and meet more people, you'll be appreciated for the wonderful person you are. But this takes time and a willingness to search for these perceptive individuals and connect with them. In the meanwhile, I hope you can find value in yourself because you are a very valuable young woman."

I was now hoarse. Samantha was stunned by my long speech. In many ways, I was talking to myself. I firmly believed in doing battle with inner demons. In my case, I had an outer demon, too. Could it be Sam? I didn't think so, but if my judgment was incorrect, she might construe my compliments as encouragement. Sam shared several key characteristics with my stalker. She also had opportunity, mobility, and a permissive schedule. But was she delusional? Was she suffering from more than teenage angst and the pain produced by an artistic personality?

I hauled myself back from my conjectures. "Do you understand what I'm saying?"

Sam nodded.

I laughed. "You know what I'm going to tell you next, right?"

"Yes. I will call you if I need to."

"Good. In the meantime, I hope you'll work on your story."

———

Albert d'Auberge was ten minutes late for his first session. I half hoped he wouldn't arrive because I was exhausted, but eventually, I heard ponderous footsteps on the stairs. After pouring a glass of water, I went to greet him.

Albert was average height, with a body undifferentiated by a waist and a thick neck joined to a round head topped with long brown hair, though it was cut shorter than in his graduation picture. His voice rumbled, as if we were in a huge theater and projection was necessary.

He took my hand in his large one and gave it a tiny squeeze. If it had been his wish, I guessed Albert could easily break my fingers. Then he strolled over to the Venetian masks and scrutinized each—I almost expected him to affix a monocle to his eye, since he seemed fashioned from an earlier era. Once he had examined them, I asked Albert to answer the questions on the information sheet, which he did slowly. After this was accomplished, I glanced at his cursive handwriting. There were some long horizontal flourishes, but I couldn't match the sample to my suitor's printing. For a moment, I considered requesting a self-portrait but feared Albert would take an hour to create a likeness that would pass his standards.

"I understand you work in your mother's antiques shop," I said.

"Yes. And I have done for some time," he replied, enunciating each word carefully.

"What do you do to help?"

"A little of this and a little of that. Sometimes, I take the van into the city to pick things up or use the car for deliveries."

"So you have flexibility in your working hours? That's always nice."

He exhaled a long breath, as if bored. "Yes, I suppose it is. I also do some gilding and retouching."

"Working with your hands must be rewarding." I paused, hoping he would amplify his statement, but he didn't. "So, Albert, why did you want to come for a session? Your mother implied that you were dealing with a few difficult issues."

He treated me to a mirthless laugh, as if what his mother thought was of little consequence. "That's not really an accurate assessment. To be forthright, my situation is neither happy nor sad. I'm merely waiting for inspiration."

"Inspiration?"

"Yes, quite. For the Muse to descend. I wait for her with great eagerness."

"Can you expound on that?"

"Surely you understand what a muse is?" Albert cocked one eyebrow.

"Yes, of course. But it might help if you explained more about what inspires you."

"What inspires me?" He chuckled. "No, it's more a matter of *who* inspires me. I wait for illumination from the one who grants the miracle of encouragement. I want to soar, to dream."

Albert was in love with his own voice.

"Your mother believes you have someone in your life. A woman? Is she the person you're talking about?"

"Oh, I will have a woman in my life, a muse, if she agrees to it." He smiled. "As I said, I'm waiting."

We were back to the start. Talking with Albert was an elliptical experience. "Do you have romantic expectations?"

He gave a small snort. "Oh, no, Ellen. I think not! She is not at all of that persuasion."

"Is she a lesbian?" I asked, feeling as though I was sawing off the branch upon which I sat.

He laughed heartily. "Oh, my, you have quite the wrong end of the stick!"

I had no idea which end of the stick I had and was growing more confused by the minute. "Well, what did you mean, then?"

Albert dabbed at his eyes with a colorful handkerchief and returned it to his pocket. "She is *not* a Sapphist. She is the embodiment of innocence and purity. If you must know, her name is Astraea."

A real person or a goddess? "Tell me more about her."

"Aha! I think my mother has asked you to find out about Astraea, hasn't she? That's a little roundabout even for her. Well, I can report I am entertaining Astraea today. I'll know more about the possibilities soon, though everything is up to her. More than this, I will not say. My mother will pester me otherwise, if things don't proceed accordingly." He winked. "But I am certain they will."

The wink felt uncomfortably inappropriate. Did Albert consider me a co-conspirator against Mary or was he signaling that I was Astraea? I rushed to clarify.

"Your mother didn't put me up to asking you questions. She's only concerned that you've found someone to care about. And besides, Albert, whatever you tell me remains between the two of us." I drank some water and reviewed his remark that he was waiting for his muse, a comment reminiscent of one made by my stalker.

After rebuking myself for having wayward thoughts, I took another approach. "Your mother said you're a collector. What do you like to collect?"

His response was vague. "Special things that I keep. In my room...and elsewhere." He sighed, looked over my head at the masks on the wall, and seemed disinclined to say more.

I felt frazzled. It wasn't obvious why Albert was seeking therapy. "I understand that you encouraged your mother to make an appointment. Is that true?"

He returned his focus to me. His eyes glinted with sudden interest. "Yes, as a matter of fact I did. She's a poor old thing. Not many friends—especially no romantic partners—and doesn't get out much. I think she's been despondent ever since my father left

252

her." He described his mother's life, a description similar to Mary's own account.

"Were you upset when your parents divorced?"

"Not particularly. Or rather, I wasn't surprised. My father is, shall we say, a *bon vivant*, an aesthete with the heart of a rover. Not the type to stay in a shop, even a very nice one in the city. He's not an American, you know," he added proudly.

"Yes, I understand he's French."

Albert nodded. "To answer more completely: I was distressed to see my father leave. Naturally, we keep in frequent touch. He plans for me to fly to France in the spring."

I made note of the disparity between Mary's report about her ex-husband seldom communicating or visiting with Albert versus his. "How did your mother react to the divorce?"

"Terribly. Father was above her in all things. She knew that she wouldn't find someone as worthy again."

Worthy? Hadn't my stalker used this word? Although I tried to concentrate, my mind was doing splits. Half of me was analyzing him as a client, but the other half persisted in analyzing him as an obsessed follower.

"Do you think your parents loved each other? At least in the beginning?"

"I have no idea."

I drank some water and decided to be direct. "People usually come here because they're experiencing a problem of some kind—they're depressed, frustrated, angry, or stuck in their lives. I'm trying to understand what is of concern to you and how I might help."

He pursed his lips together, leaned against the couch, and gazed at me. "I thought I told you. I'm worried about my mother."

"And she is worried about you."

"Rather circular, don't you think?"

I did. I felt like I was shoveling snow, but that it was falling faster than I could shovel. "Yes, it is. Perhaps you could share your goals for therapy?"

"My goals?" Albert laughed. "Sounds like a freshman English paper. Well, I wanted to meet you. I enjoyed reading your books and hearing your lectures, which fascinated me. And I'm not often impressed with what I read or hear. Most of it is drivel, claptrap of the worst ilk. In particular, I was interested in your analysis of the creative child. Your descriptions resonated with my own experience to a surprising degree."

"Really? How?"

"I spent a great deal of time alone as a child. My parents were in the shop or traveling, either apart or together. I was often in the care of sitters or left to fend for myself after school. Oh, it was safe enough—we lived in an apartment above the store both in Manhattan and here in Kingston."

"What did you do during all these long hours?"

"As I referenced earlier, I collected *objets d'art*. I also sketched and painted, read, made up stories. Activities of a solitary lad."

"Did you have any playmates?"

He shook his head. "Not really. One or two friends, but usually they weren't copacetic, if you see what I mean. I didn't like sports or mucking around in the mud, tormenting little animals. Things other boys did."

Or killing pigeons? "Did you have any girlfriends?"

"Again, one or two. I got along better with girls, at least until I was twelve or so. Then I began to find them unappealing."

"You're not physically attracted to women?"

He stared at me. "Not on that plane, no."

"So you're not attracted to women sexually, but you like being with them?"

"Yes, I suppose you could put it that way. But only certain

women interest me...those who are intelligent, sophisticated, admirable in all their attributes."

"Sounds like an idealized portrait of a woman," I remarked.

"Perhaps, but these women do exist."

He looked at me pointedly. Was I one of Albert's chosen ones? "And what about men?" I asked. "Are you interested in men?"

"Here, I can be more precise. Yes, I appreciate the male physique, the anatomy so glorified by Michelangelo. There is a divinity in the masculine form, a strength of line that's intoxicating. I don't, however, hold them up as emotional paragons as I do women."

"It seems like you're ambivalent in your attraction to both sexes."

"It's rather clear to me."

"Have you had sexual relations with a man or a woman?"

Albert lowered his chin, as if signifying this was an impolite question. "Yes."

"With whom?" His ambiguity was irritating. My voice was also nearly expired as was the time in the session.

"In my heart, both. In actuality, I did have brief affairs with a few young gentlemen while I was on the continent. Amorous flings, you might say. Nothing substantial."

"Are you intending to have a primary relationship with a man or a woman? In the future?"

Albert smiled smile. "*Mais, oui. Une belle fille.*"

"Astraea?" He didn't reply and appeared satisfied without saying more. "Albert, perhaps we can discuss this in more depth if you would like to come for another appointment?"

"Sure. Why not?"

"Next week at the same time? Is that okay?"

"Yes, that would be fine" He handed me a check written by his mother.

Between my illness and Albert, my head was spinning.

"Ta, ta!" he exclaimed, wiggling his fingers in the air as he headed out the door.

I was tempted to open the stalker's letter again, to compare its sentiments to those I'd just heard from Albert, which had set off alarms, but after writing his name in my calendar, I withdrew a sheet of paper from my desk and did a quick sketch of Albert. I'm a mediocre artist, but the drawing captured some of his character-istics. I made duplicates on my copier to give to the state and bor-ough police, if and when I was comfortable revealing any of my clients. However, if Albert was my suitor, he was a tantalizing psy-chological fit.

———

A few minutes before 5:30, I returned a phone inquiry from a potential client. The woman was unsure about paying my eighty-dollar fee, so I recommended she take time to consider or to call another therapist. I hated to be so business-like, but if I made excep-tions, it would get around, and I would be besieged by requests for financial clemency, which I couldn't afford.

Next, I called Sergeant McFadden and read the stalker's letter. He took notes and advised me to be careful. I didn't need remind-ing. After locking the office, I drove home, added wood on top of the andirons, and started a fire. I cooked lamb chops and some brown rice and ate lemon sherbet for dessert, which felt good on my hot throat. I washed the dishes and removed the articles about de Clérambault's Syndrome, a designation based on a 1921 treatise written by him. The term "erotomania" had become the current clinical diagnosis for this morbid infatuation, similar to other monomanias such as pyromania and some religious manias, which tended to focus the person's mind exclusively on one goal. In erotomania, the aim was directed at a target whose love and approval would compensate for the ego-deprivation and inadequacy the sufferer felt. The target was necessarily perceived as having a higher status, with attributes the erotomaniac desired to subsume. The force of this mania was considerable and, in most cases, unshakable, such as with a professor who had been hounded by a female ex-student for ten years until the professor relocated to the east coast.

I took a second to digest this bad news and then continued to read. Contrary to its "eroto" prefix, the fixation wasn't necessarily erotic. In fact, erotomaniacs often imagined a chaste and utopian relationship, in which sexual thoughts weren't integral to the delusion, so that the usual cross-gender attractions might not be based on physical interest. Or, in male-to-male or female-to-female "relationships," these could center around the transfer of status and not around homosexual attraction, though sexual delusion was present in other cases, either in heterosexual or same-sex stalkers. Reading this, I recalled Albert's "muse" and thought much of what he'd said coincided with this idealized description. Continuing on, I learned violence might erupt if the erotomaniac became blocked from achieving the desired union, which was a more common reaction with male erotomaniacs than females. In general, the infatuated person might appear more or less normal, though was usually a loner with impoverished social skills and minimal experience with relationships. In secondary erotomania, some suffered from hallucinations arising from pre-existing psychotic conditions such as schizophrenia.

I considered the implications as they pertained to my situation. If the person believed I loved him and had chosen him, then an elevation in good feeling would be psychologically transferred from me to the stalker, thus creating a relationship that became critical to the stability of the stalker's self-image. His core sense of well-being was now fused and dependent on my love; his self-esteem artificially enhanced by co-opting my identity.

From what I knew about delusions, their prominent feature was that people couldn't be easily separated from them because they believed the delusions were real. As a result, some of these patients proved resistant to treatment, causing incarceration in mental institutions or jails, depending on the nature of their abnormal behavior.

My suitor seemed to be unusual in that he or she had so far avoided identification. From the little I could ascertain from the journals, most stalkers felt entitled to their love object and didn't conceal their attraction. Why, in this case, had an effort been expended to skirt detection? Perhaps the explanation lay in the nature of the delusion itself, the part about waiting for me to give him the message to come forward. In a twisted way, the person may have evolved the delusion to become a test of his loyalty, worthiness, and love. It was also possible that the stalker was subconsciously protecting the delusion from exposure. One sense I got from the letter was that he was becoming frustrated, a grave concern. Though these monomaniacs were stubborn regarding their attachments, that didn't mean that the construct of the delusion was permanently fixed. The "message" might change. An imaginary green light could suddenly be switched on, giving him the go-ahead to approach me. If he intuited that he was being rejected at that point and denied his "fix," feelings of rage might be triggered, with an escalation into hostility.

I needed to determine the identity of my stalker and thus mold my behavior to minimize the danger. Or perhaps this was wishful thinking, the idea I could control this person. Again, I reminded myself that the psychiatric community gave themselves poor marks for treating these patients with medication, negative reinforcement, and talk therapy. I had a lion by the tail, or conversely, a lion had me by the tail.

The fire had disintegrated into scattered orange embers and the room was chilly. I went upstairs to bed, but sick as I was, I couldn't sleep because I kept ruminating about the psychological dynamics. Finally, I realized that the stalker's obsession was now obsessing me, and it might be wise to call my psychologist, Adrienne Barrow, to discuss erotomaniacs.

[THE JOURNAL]

As I promised in my letter, I came to your house—our house—tonight to be sure you were safe. The interior lights weren't on, but your car was in the drive. I tried to open the car's door, to sit in the driver's seat and feel your presence, but the door was locked. Then I walked around, staying in dark areas where the spotlights didn't reach, hoping to see you, but you were probably in bed asleep. After climbing the stairs to the deck, I lay on your chaise and looked at the stars and the moon until I got cold. I enjoyed being so close, though I obeyed your orders and didn't come inside. This afternoon, when I knew you were in Princeton, I also drove to the house and climbed onto the deck and looked in. The house is beautiful. We will be very happy living here, although when your father returns, we'll need to find a place of our own. Or maybe he'll move out and he'll give us this house when we're together. I love the fireplace and hope we'll have one. I love fires.

Now, back in my bedroom, I put the raindrops on my head and tongue so I can sleep and dream only of you. Tomorrow, the photo enlargements will come. I can't wait to see them.

I OVERSLEPT and awoke reeling from the aftershocks of a nightmare, one whose origin was obvious. I was in a zoo and in charge of dozens of snake cages. I had to throw live mice to the snakes through small slots in the doors, but some of the slots were too large and the snakes crawled through, hiding in shadows, behind rocks. Many of the snakes were poisonous, but I didn't know which ones were and which ones weren't. Hmm.

In addition to the nightmare, my throat was raw, my eyes were dry, and I had congestion and mild laryngitis. Good that no clients were scheduled today.

The morning didn't improve when I looked on the deck and noticed the redwood chaise had been turned around to face the house. This was no action by the wind—the chaise was too heavy and the wind too light. After double-checking all the locks, rooms, and the basement, I found no trace of anyone, yet I couldn't shake the fear that someone was inside. I drank orange juice and coffee and ate some toast and contemplated whether this incursion rose to the level of real concern. I decided it did and called the State Police and asked for Sergeant Wilcox. He was home with a cold— probably the source of my own malady. The dispatcher connected me to Sergeant Arroyo, who had been apprised of my case, so I didn't need to repeat my story. I read him yesterday's letter and reported that the stalker had been sitting on the deck during the night. Because I couldn't identify the person, he replied there wasn't much for the police to do except continue their twice-daily drive-bys.

"You could move out of the house for a week," he suggested.

"I might but I'd prefer to stay home. I'm responsible for my parents' house."

Who knew how the stalker would act if frustrated by my absence? And, though I didn't say so, I was in no mood to fuel my feelings of cowardice.

I thanked the policeman and then called McFadden in Princeton to update him about the chaise. He took down the information and promised to survey the Princeton parking lot. When I hung up, my voice was diminished. In the bathroom, I examined my throat—red with white splotches. After gargling with antiseptic, I showered, giving in to the urge to lock the bathroom door. I dried off and stepped into the bedroom, about to begin dressing, when the phone rang. I threw on my robe and hesitated until I convinced myself not to be so jumpy. I answered.

"Hi, Ellen. This is Martie."

She asked how I was, and I told her I was sick.

"Oh, that's too bad because I was wondering if you'd like to play for the club. In a day tournament being held here on Saturday."

Martie had never invited me for any tennis events. A coincidence? Or was she gay and interested? Or was she my stalker?

"Thanks, Martie, but I doubt I'll be feeling much better by then. I'd be honored to play at another time. Once I get rid of this cold, I'll be in touch about a lesson."

"Okay." She paused, as if wanting to say more, and then added, "Well, take care, Ellen. See you soon."

I disconnected and tried to parse Martie's tone and her intentions. Had this been a friendly call from a tennis pro who thought I was a good player?

I swore at myself for being mistrustful and muttered, "That's why you don't have a social life. Always analyzing."

I took off my robe, threw on my clothes, and went downstairs to confirm no damage had been done to my car or the property. Walking around the house, I saw nothing amiss, but footprints wouldn't register on the cement area under the deck or on the gray gravel paths or driveway. I couldn't vanquish the creepy feeling that I was under observation and was divided about whether to stay inside and hold the fort or leave. Because I was running low on cold medication, I finally drove to the pharmacy, where I purchased cough drops and decongestant. Next door, at the small market, I bought hamburger, green beans, and two cans of chicken noodle soup. After that, I came home and went to bed.

—

On Friday, I was still congested, but my throat wasn't as sore. Although I didn't feel like it, I drove into Princeton to work at my computer for a few hours. When I arrived, the outer door remained free of cards, and there were no hang-up calls on the machine. I opened my book file and then heard footsteps on the stairs and a loud knock.

"Dr. Haskell? It's Sergeant McFadden."

I opened the door, surprised to see him.

"Sorry to bother you, but I have a guy here who says his name is George Durst. Is he one of your clients?"

"Yes, though he doesn't have an appointment today."

"He told me that, but he's got an oversized envelope with him. Photographs…at least that's what he maintains. He refused to show them to me."

"I'll be right down."

I saved my book document and descended the stairs. About twenty feet from my door, McFadden was standing by his patrol car. George Durst, in work clothes, was next to him, casting furious looks at the policeman. When George saw me, his face colored even more. He started to step toward me, but McFadden restrained him.

"George, good morning. What's the problem?"

"I was just dropping by some pictures like you asked. I planned to leave them in the waiting room so I wouldn't bother you." He handed me the manila envelope.

How did George know I would be in Princeton? Was he observing the parking lot and my car? He already was aware that the Audi was mine. With some trepidation, I opened the packet and took out the prints, three of which had been enlarged. Photographs of George's constructions. I showed them to McFadden.

"Everything is okay. I asked George to bring these."

McFadden's expression remained skeptical. The scowl George aimed at the police officer conveyed dislike. Had uncivil words transpired between them?

"George, please go upstairs and have a seat. I'll join you in a minute."

He acquiesced but threw another antagonistic glance at McFadden before going inside.

"I think everything is under control," I told the policeman. "However, I really appreciate that you're monitoring the area."

"Just so you know, Dr. Haskell, we had a run-in with Durst some time ago. He got rowdy in a tavern. Too much to drink. The bartender reported him because he was annoying a female patron, who wasn't interested in his attentions. Then, when my partner and I arrived, a fight ensued with the bar owner. I tried to break it up, but Durst threw a punch at me—one I still remember," the policeman said, rubbing his cheek. "I'm sure you've noticed that Durst is a powerful guy. Wouldn't be surprised if he did some prizefighting in his day."

"Was he charged with anything?"

"No. I let the punch pass, and he apologized to the tavern owner and paid the damages. He even helped straighten up the mess. A strange guy."

"A vet."

"'Nam?"

I nodded.

"Too bad," he said. "A few guys have issues. Okay before they serve, but when they're forced into becoming killers for their country or see their buddies killed, they become different people. I can sympathize with soldiers coming home and trying to work at a quiet job after being under fire. One of my pals is a vet. He won't talk about it much, but his wife told me he still has bad nightmares." At this point, McFadden's radio summoned him. "Got to take this. Are you sure you're okay with him?"

"Yes. Sergeant, thanks for being so attentive."

I said goodbye and went upstairs. George was pacing in front of the coffee table.

"What was that all about?" His cheeks and neck were flushed bright red.

"Nothing really. I apologize about the confusion."

"Since when is walking around with an envelope a reason for a cop to stop someone?"

"Sorry, George, I've been having problems with an acquaintance."

He stopped and faced me. "Who's bothering you?"

"I don't know. But you remember the drawing on my car..."

"Yeah, I do." His mouth was tight with anger. "But that's no reason for a pig to hang around, hassling people."

"Well, there have been other things—"

"If you have trouble with anyone, call me. I'll take care of the guy."

Noting that his hands were bunched into fists, I quickly added, "Thank you for the offer, George. I really appreciate it, but everything is fine. Now, may I look at your photos?"

George still didn't look happy, but he unclenched his hands and nodded. "They aren't professional, but they should give you an idea what I'm doing."

Relieved that George had become calm, I spread the prints on the table and examined the snapshots. They were poorly focused, but the work was incredible. One construction was about five feet high—a complex arrangement of machinery parts; some elements were dark steel, some bright chrome. George had used different textures and shapes in a sophisticated way. The other assemblies were smaller.

"I may put these together." He pointed to two pictures. "The more I look at them, the more I think they should be linked."

I agreed with him and tried to imagine the compositions united.

George turned one photo to a vertical position. "That's how I would do it."

"Yes, I like that better. I'm very impressed."

"You are?" Suddenly, George grinned. "I haven't shown these to anyone."

"I think you should, but can you improve the focus and the lighting?"

"Yeah. I need to buy a tripod, but I wanted to get them to you right away because you matter. I mean, your opinion matters."

I smiled. "Thanks for saying that. It's a privilege to see these amazing sculptures. When you've upgraded your equipment, per-haps you can make some enlargements. If you do, bring them in. I also hope you'll begin searching for a gallery—one with a large floor space."

"Okay, I will."

After tucking the prints into the envelope, I showed him to the door. "And, George, I'm sorry about the police."

"Me, too. Just let me know if you need help. I'll be glad to watch out for you."

Interesting phrase. "See you next week."

This latest occurrence added to my jitters. Because of me, George was stopped by the police. This was no way to instill a sense of trust. On the other hand, George had made several statements that resonated with the stalker's letter, and he was a physically intimidating man and one with a temper.

I couldn't concentrate on my manuscript and was beginning to feel feverish. I drove home, gargled with hot salt water, took my temperature—100.5 degrees—and some aspirin, and read before falling asleep on the couch in the living room.

[THE JOURNAL]

I have the enlargements. They're not perfect, but I'm pleased to have them. When I go home tonight, after leaving a set of prints at your house, I'll follow your instructions exactly. You told me to hang these pictures on the wall opposite the posters from your lecture. I'm supposed to measure the middle point between them with a ruler, mark the spot on the floor, and stand there, first facing the posters and then the photographs. I'm to do this later, after an important investigation.

WHEN I WOKE from my nap, I realized I hadn't checked the mail. Although I didn't want to go outside, I pulled on a sweater and walked to the mailbox. Inside lay a large manila envelope similar to the one George had used.

Upstairs, I steeled myself to open the package which had been taped shut. Holding my breath, I removed a series of color enlargements of me asleep on the deck, shot from the side and from the front, with several angles in between.

I thudded my hand against my forehead and collapsed on the sofa. "You look positively angelic! How the hell could you sleep while someone was so close?"

The images were as poorly focused as George's, the handiwork of an amateur unaccustomed to handling a telephoto lens. Had he taken this series and enlarged them at the same time as his construction prints? Examining the angles, it appeared the first were from about seventy feet away, perhaps on the knoll beyond the garage because the position was almost even with the deck. The next ones were from a lower perspective, closer to Stoney Brook. Shot while standing on my mother's bench? Was the Heath Bar eater also the photographer? If so, how long had he or she been trespassing?

I examined the envelope and the pictures: no writing anywhere. I shivered and threw the prints and envelope on the table. The space between me and my suitor was narrowing, yet my pursuit of the person's identity hadn't advanced an inch, unless the coincidental timing of these photos with George's was pertinent. I wanted someone to confide in, but Drew was trekking in Alaska with his new boyfriend, and my other friends lived at a distance and were busy with families and jobs, unavailable to hold my hand while a stalker was terrorizing me. Besides, if the culprit was a client, I would be ashamed to admit I couldn't deal with them.

After dinner, I switched off all of the lights, went to the bedroom, and sat in front of the television, with half my mind on the show and the other half reviewing clues as to the identity of my abusive friend. The decongestant finally overpowered my alertness, and I turned off the set and went to sleep.

—

At 1:20 a.m., the phone rang. I jumped awake, pillows flying from the bed. Who was calling me at this hour? After three rings, I answered. It was the Princeton Borough Police, a sergeant whose name I didn't catch. He apologized for contacting me so late, but it had taken time to rouse my landlord and get my home number. The officer reported that my office had been burglarized at some point after nine o'clock, when the patrol car had driven by, and midnight, when a second car made the next round. There was damage to the outer door, which had been pried open. I took a deep breath and tried to steady my voice. "What's been taken?"

"Hard to say exactly, Dr. Haskell. Your file cabinet was broken into, and we think one of your masks was taken from the wall—there's an empty spot in the middle of your collection. Unless you have it."

"No. The masks were all there when I left earlier today. I don't have much of value in the office except the masks and my computer. Did anyone tamper with that?"

"Not that we can tell. You'll need to check everything in the morning."

I explained about my stalker. "He or she has been bothering me for weeks. Sergeant McFadden knows the story. He's been my contact in town and the State Police are also involved because I live northwest of Hopewell. Strange things have been happening here, too."

"I'm not aware of any of this. We were just driving around because it's mischief night. The kids are out even though they're not supposed to be," he said. "Your door has been secured with crime scene tape, but call us when you're coming in, and we'll meet you and open up. I'll leave a report for McFadden."

"Thank you, Sergeant."

"Don't worry. Everything will be okay."

How in the hell was I supposed to not worry? His prognosis of "everything will be okay" was pie-in-the-sky optimism. My stalker seemed to be warming up and willing to take more risks—the parking lot was an exposed location, even late at night.

I replaced the pillows on the bed and walked to the balcony. The living room was dark and quiet. The exterior spotlights were on, burning money by the minute. I couldn't wait for the electric bill. I couldn't wait to find out what the stalker's next move would be, either.

—

In the morning, I still felt stuffy and my voice was hoarse. I called Sergeant McFadden to tell him when I would arrive at my office and drove into town. After I parked my car, I joined the policeman and my landlord, who was sitting at the bottom of the steps, fuming.

"Hello, Dr. Haskell," said McFadden.

My landlord interrupted and asked me what was going on.

It was obvious from the look McFadden gave me that he had already wrangled with the man and was having little success alleviating the landlord's disgruntlement.

"Mr. Cheswick, I'm very sorry about the damage," I said. "Did Sergeant McFadden explain that an unknown person is following me?"

"Yes, he did." My landlord came to his feet and pointed an accusing finger at me. "When the wife and I learned the agency had rented the office to a psychologist, we thought some nut case

271

of yours would go on a rampage. Besides, we don't hold with all this psycho-babble stuff. People should turn to prayer to find purpose in life and to set one on the road to personal salvation."

I was in no mood for religious bromides. On the other hand, I couldn't afford to lose my rental. "Mr. Cheswick, we're trying our best to resolve the issue."

McFadden stepped in. "It isn't clear if this was a burglary or mischief caused by kids," he said to Cheswick. "Dr. Haskell needs to make a list of missing items, so if you'll excuse us, we'll do that now. When we have more information, we'll contact you. In the meantime, please have someone repair the door." Cheswick attempted to follow us, but McFadden prevented him.

Upstairs, the waiting room seemed untouched. The magazines were neatly stacked on the table, but in my office the file cabinet had been pried open, and the Casanova mask was missing, the one Samantha liked. I described the mask to McFadden and said one of my clients had been interested in it, though I had no evidence my client and the stalker were the same person.

"Would a man or a woman pick this mask?"

"Traditionally, it would be worn by a man. However, there was always a great deal of cross-dressing during Carnival, such as some do during Halloween," I explained. "One of the attractions about wearing a mask is that it empowers its wearer to assume a different identity and to act out of character. If a male selected it, becoming Casanova might transform him into an irresistible, dashing lover who captivates women, when, in actuality, his sexual self-image and relationships with women might be poor."

"And if a woman took it? Could she be interested in women? A lesbian?"

"Possibly, or the woman might be experiencing gender confusion. There are a wide range of orientations in this category, including a person who wants to change sex entirely. Or she might be heterosexual and take pleasure imagining herself as a male. Some women enjoy playacting in opposite sex roles."

"So, we're looking for a straight male who is a failure with women, a female who has gender confusion or might be gay, a transvestite or someone transitioning, or a woman who likes dressing as a guy?"

I sighed. "I'm sorry it's so hard to be precise. But whoever it is, the stalker seeks to fill a deep emptiness by consuming the positive qualities he or she believes I possess. The feelings may not be sexual, either. They could be emotional."

Sergeant McFadden scratched his chin. "Doesn't exactly limit the field, does it?"

"No, but from my research, the male or female will have a flawed self-image and will have been unsuccessful in relationships. If a lesbian, she may have submerged her feelings because her parents held strong homophobic beliefs and punished their children if they showed same-sex attractions," I said. "And a straight woman with an impoverished personality might be attracted to me because she wants to become me—in a delusional unification. It's also conceivable that a heterosexual woman who has been victimized by a man might choose a mask that represents her victimizer, Casanova being a perfect example of a victimizer of women. However, I doubt that a terrorized woman would incorporate this kind of stalking behavior into her psychological pattern and with me as the object." I thought of Albert. "There's also a chance that a gay male might feel erotic pleasure wearing a Casanova mask. If he has gender ambivalence, he might attempt sexual behavior that is at odds with his innate feelings."

"Wow! How many of your clients fit these descriptions?"

"Several of them. And a male relative might be in the mix or an unknown acquaintance."

"How many had opportunities to come to your office and

home at various hours of the day and night?"

"All of them." I opened the packet of enlargements taken of me on the deck and spread them on my desk. "Caught napping."

"I'd say." Sergeant McFadden couldn't suppress a smile. "I hope you're not lounging on the deck any longer."

"Not on your life. I even threw my robe in the trash."

"Have you shown these to the state police?"

"I will this afternoon. And I'll go to the photo shop to see if they know who ordered the enlargements."

"Good idea. At best we only have a vandal, thief, and voyeur," he said. "But you mentioned a male relative. You don't have to protect him, right?"

"No, but I'd rather wait before accusing him. One of my clients is more likely."

McFadden nodded. "And you won't give me their names?"

I shook my head. "I don't mean to be unhelpful, but if word got around that I'd made my clients' names public, it wouldn't inspire confidence and would be a serious breech of professional ethics."

"Well, I guess we wait. Just remember it's Halloween. If the stalker stole the mask to wear, he might approach you today or come to your house tonight."

I exhaled an uneasy breath. "I know."

"Will you check your files? Maybe there's a clue there."

I went to the cabinet and searched through each of my client's dossiers. Everything appeared to be in order, with nothing obviously taken from any of the individual histories, notes, or self-portraits, but it was difficult to be positive, as I told Sergeant McFadden.

"Perhaps my stalker wanted to read my comments but didn't object to what I wrote."

He nodded. "What about your computer?"

"It's password protected. Not much on it. A manuscript and some research," I said, booting up the computer. "I doubt anyone had success getting in. Besides, many of my clients aren't technologically savvy." I scanned my files. "Looks okay."

I powered down the computer, and McFadden and I checked the bathroom.

Lifting the trash basket, I told him some used tissues and paper towels were missing. "So are my toothbrush, comb, and soap." A wave of disgust flooded over me. "With all my germs, maybe my stalker will get sick."

"Serves him right if he does," the policeman replied as we stepped into my office. "One thing to add. Whoever opened the door and the files used a crowbar, perhaps a hammer. Any adult could do that, but a guy is more likely. Dr. Haskell, would your landlord install an alarm?"

I couldn't help laughing. "I doubt it."

McFadden smiled. "Okay. Well, if you notice anything else, let me know. Because this is a crime scene, we did a fingerprint analysis on several surfaces, but unless the perp is on record, this may only be useful later, though I hope your stalker stops his behavior. I'll call Wilcox at the state police and update him." As he was leaving the office, he turned. "And, Dr. Haskell, be careful."

———

I cleaned the fingerprint dust and any surfaces the stalker might have touched, locked the office, and walked to the photo store. After a short explanation of my predicament, I showed the least offensive enlargement to the owner. He shook his head and told me they didn't open packets of prints unless a client had an issue, nor did they make enlargements on the premises.

"They're reproduced by a service in New York. A carrier picks up from us and from some of the other photo stores in the area each afternoon," he said.

"Do you have a list of customers from the last several days?"

"Only credit card receipts and a few checks that haven't been deposited yet—usually we go to the bank daily. I can't show you these for security reasons. And quite a few folks pay with cash. As for customer's names, once the purchase is made, all of the identifying information goes with the form attached to the envelope containing the prints. Sorry."

"I am, too."

"Besides, there are a number of places in town and nearby that make prints, including drug stores, malls, and even private darkrooms, though this print doesn't look like a custom enlargement. And some people use direct mail services," the owner added.

I sighed and thanked the man. Leaving the store, I realized it would take me days to search every business in the county, and as a newcomer to the area, I didn't have any idea where all the places were. Besides, Carson could have ordered prints in New York or even in Lambertville, Mary and Albert were in Kingston and could trade in towns north along Route 1, Nick was in Freehold, I had no notion where Martie lived, and others were scattered all over. Plus, as the photo store owner said, my stalker might have used a mail service.

Discouraged and frustrated, I returned to my car and drove home. There, I ate lunch, and after cleaning the dishes, I walked to the street to check the mail. The sun was bright and the day was clear, but my mood was tainted by fear. Opening the mailbox had devolved into a frightening activity, as if I were about to get an electrical shock.

When there was nothing inside except bills and catalogues, I exhaled with relief and began strolling toward the house, thinking the leaves would be off most of the trees in a few weeks. Visibility would improve then, though the forest was young and low-growing trees and bushes were thick. I looked at a nearby cluster of maples, which were easy trees to climb. Curious, I walked through the underbrush to a tall tree on the east side of the garage. As I approached, I was horrified to see that the stalker and I had shared the same idea. The tawny grass around the tree was trampled like the nighttime nests deer make. Not a deer, however. My suitor had inscribed a note on the trunk:

ELLEN IS MINE

I AM ELLEN'S

The sentiment was etched within a heart pricked with arrows—the same design as on my car and the front door—and was freshly cut. Had my admirer borrowed a page from deer hunters: climbing a tree to wait and watch for their prey?

I drew in a fast breath. Although I felt dizzy, I needed to check what could be seen from a higher vantage point. I laid down the mail, placed my foot on the lowest branch, and hauled myself up until I was perched about twenty feet above the ground. It was possible to go higher, but the density of leaves and branches would negate the rationale of doing so. From here, I could see into the living room because my position was at the second floor level. At night, with the lights on inside, the stalker would have an excellent view. It was infuriating to realize someone had stood here, probably on this same branch, luxuriating in the pleasure of observing me. Armed with binoculars or a camera with a zoom lens, he or she could establish an intimacy between us that would feed a hungry desire for connection. I shuddered at the thought of all the times I had walked around the house, unaware of the fanatical attraction being fueled by my inadvertent compliance. Had the person become sexually aroused? This made me feel ill, as if the branches I held might be soiled with semen. Hurriedly, I descended, scratching my arms and nearly falling in my urgent wish to escape. When I reached the ground, I grabbed the mail and dashed to the house, locked and bolted the door, and ran up the stairs, out of breath, coughing, and trembling. I scoured my hands and took a swig of cough medicine and tried to calm down so that I could call the state police and tell them what had happened at the office and about the tree.

A few minutes later, I did exactly that but was disappointed Sergeant Wilcox wasn't on duty until the evening shift. The dispatcher promised to give him my message, though she said everyone was overextended due to Halloween.

After my conversation with the police, my anxiety didn't lessen. If anything, I was more frightened. The sun was setting, and I was alone in a house with too much glass. The blinds were already down in the library, but I also lowered them in the smaller windows in the living and dining rooms. This would impede the view from the tree, street, and driveway but not from in front of the deck or from the deck itself. I went downstairs to retrieve my father's stepladder and took his hatchet from the pegboard wall above the workbench, both of which I carried upstairs. Above the prow windows and over both sets of living room windows, curtain rods had been installed, but my parents had never hung the drapes they'd bought when they'd first moved in. After a search, I found the tan linen curtains in the guest bedroom's closet, climbed the stepladder, and added the curtains. The upper tier of the prow windows remained uncovered, but the stalker's view was blocked.

The effort to do all this brought on another coughing fit, so I sat on the sofa to rest, scanning the great room, which now felt claustrophobic without its expansive vistas. Instead of being in a beautiful house looking out on the world, I was enshrouded in a cage, at the mercy of someone who felt entitled to spy on me. Hopefully, the drapes and blinds would stymie his or her obsession, though they didn't hide my presence in the house, which was obvious due to the interior lights and my car in the driveway. I could move the Audi into the garage, but that held its own risk, nor did I wish to spend the evening in the dark, chewing my fingernails. As the police advised, I again considered staying at a motel, though how many days would pass before the stalker was apprehended? And how would I learn who it was unless I caught the person in a telltale act?

No, I wouldn't be scared out of my house due to the actions of a disturbed client. Leaving would be an admission of defeat, an admission that I couldn't manage someone who might have come to me for counseling. I was also frustrated that a client could hide behind such a well-constructed façade and that I wasn't sufficiently perceptive to spot an erotomaniac after several sessions of therapy, assuming it was a client. What kind of brilliant psychologist was I? One who was too embarrassed by my professional failure to run. I would stick it out, frightened as I was, though I wished my father would return from Corfu or my friend, Michael, was arriving sooner.

The decongestant I'd taken at lunch was making my mouth feel dry. I poured a tall glass of ice water and started to put on some music but didn't. I wanted to hear every sound the house made and to hear every sound that wasn't made by the house. Feeling jittery and trapped, I fetched a pair of high-powered binoculars, placed the hatchet near at hand, and sat on a stool by a window facing the voyeur's tree. With the blinds raised and the lights off, I could safely survey the forest between the house and the street. At the moment, nothing appeared suspicious, but I'd keep checking until I went upstairs.

I thought of the children who were running around the streets, wearing black pointed hats and big-nosed witches' masks or painted with green Frankenstein's faces, candy bars spilling from burgeoning trick-or-treat bags. I had always loved Halloween. In fact, this was the first year I hadn't been invited to a party. Though this was understandable because I knew few people in Princeton, it nevertheless sank my mood to an abysmal low.

When the telephone rang, I rushed to answer it. Sergeant Wilcox returning my call. Did I want him to come by the house? He sounded busy, but his deep voice conveyed concern. He said the Princeton police had faxed the report about my office break-in, and I explained about the photographs and the tree carving.

"I guess someone has set up camp," he said. "Pretty brazen. Coming close enough to take snapshots during daytime and carve hearts on a tree."

"Maybe the stalker no longer cares about being seen, but what worries me most is that the person is waiting for some kind of sign, one he or she might interpret as encouragement to come closer. A sign I might inadvertently give."

"Hmm." Wilcox considered this for a moment. "Well, I wish we could be more helpful, but our hands are tied unless the creep makes a documented threat or we catch him defacing your property. But even that probably won't net jail time. We're short-staffed today, but we'll send a car your way when we're able. Can't promise more. Stay in your house, keep the doors locked, and sit tight."

I sighed, knowing he was doing his best. Suddenly, I thought about calling local mental hospitals and asking them to check my clients against their list of persons with a history of admission. I would need to wait until Monday morning to do this, although I wasn't positive how far professional courtesy would extend and if administrators would cooperate. I mentioned this idea to Sergeant Wilcox, who thought I should try. He then asked me if there were any firearms in the house.

"None," I told him.

"That's too bad. Okay, well, don't panic."

I thanked him and ended the call, already missing the reassuring connection.

With nothing else to do, I returned to my lookout by the window. I didn't expect any trick-or-treaters. Not enough goodies per mile out in the country.

I was on my own for the evening. Alone with a deranged Casanova obsessing about me. I thought about his legend—the nightly forays over the rooftops of Venice to escape irate husbands or to rendezvous with his lovers. Or was a more modern interpretation accurate? That Casanova was breaking into bedrooms and raping women? Would the stalker imitate this behavior?

I read the notes in my file, hoping to learn how you felt or to see a message saying you were ready for us to become one. Most of what you recorded was what I'd said, though I'm still confused by a few of your comments. It gave me great pleasure to use your soap and hold the tissues and towels you touched. They gave me power, just as you do.

This afternoon, I went to buy the special item. It excites me to own it, to hold it.

In my bedroom, I wear the Casanova mask, looking at each of your portraits for exactly one minute, then moving to the next one, as you instructed. I must do this sixteen times before performing The Ritual at midnight. I've marked the floor with chalk and measured the distances twice because everything must be exact. I look at the photographs and want to be inside your heart and mind, to feel your love surrounding me.

It's time. I can hear midnight in my head—gong! gong! gong! gong! gong! gong! gong! gong! gong! gong! gong! gong!—twelve beats that match my heart. I'll now stand on the chalk, facing the posters.

I am risen in your power. Your blood is mine, running through my body. I hear your beautiful voice and am delivered unto you, into you, poured like water into a glass.

THE STEAK I cooked for dinner was too rare, but I forced myself to eat a little, felt nauseous, and scraped the rest into the trash. The phone rang twice—more breathing and no response. My stalker wanted to hear my voice and to confirm where I was. Though it occurred to me that I shouldn't answer because this might be perceived as encouragement, it also meant the stalker wasn't nearby. He knew where I was, and I knew that he wasn't here. A sufficient trade-off.

A half hour after the second hang-up call, I returned to the binoculars. Past the reach of the spotlights, blackness prevailed. If something large moved, I might see it, but could I discern someone in the surveillance tree? Maybe.

Although I hated to admit it, peering through the binoculars was becoming an obsession, as if the act allowed control in an uncontrollable situation, or I could ward off the evil presence by diligent observation. Rather like Dolly Bordella checking behind the couch? Of course, I might be facing the wrong way, and the stalker could approach from the west or from the back of the house.

This was all so crazy. I suddenly wanted to get in the car and flee, but I couldn't bring myself to go outside. I was too afraid.

Eventually, enough was enough and I went upstairs to bed, armed with a bottle of cough syrup and the hatchet. The Halloween fare on television was frightening, a hit parade of thrillers and scary movies. I soon gave up and tried to read a book. By 10:15 p.m., I was tired but acutely sensitized to every sound. After turning off the light, I lay there, unable to quiet my jangled nerves, and intermittently checked the digital clock on the side table, resenting its square red numbers as the minutes slid by. At 12:10 a.m., the phone rang. I didn't answer it. Then it rang again. And again. The sound echoed in the room, insistent and loud. There was a tiny chance it was my father with an emergency—it was morning in Corfu, but he knew what time it was in New Jersey. No one else would call except for the police or my fanatical suitor. The ringing continued.

When I could stand it no longer, I grabbed the phone and demanded to know who it was. Silence, except for respiration. Someone else wasn't getting much sleep.

"Whoever this is, listen to me. I don't know who you are or what you want, but the calls have to stop right now. Do you understand?" I was nearly shouting. "I'm not interested in your attentions. I don't want anything to do with you."

Still on the line.

I was incensed and trying unsuccessfully to keep my voice from cracking with rage and laryngitis. "The police have been notified. They're looking for you." I wasn't sure if this was smart to say, but I desperately wanted to keep the stalker away from the house.

A click and then air. A dial tone a few seconds later.

I banged down the receiver, swung my legs over the side of the bed, and blew out a hot breath of exasperation. "Oh, my god! You fool! What have you done?"

If the stalker believed I'd instigated this relationship and was now repelled by him, how would he react after what I'd just said? Erotomaniacs create the illusion of a relationship to fill a cavernous void, to increase their self-value by attachment to someone they admire. The shattering of this delusion would flood him with uncontrollable feelings of humiliation, and unmooring the person from the object to whom he had become attached—in this case me—could destroy his equilibrium. I thought of this scenario: "You made me love you. I did everything you asked. Now you reject me and treat me in this horrible way. I'm furious with you. I'll take revenge."

I turned this over, and no matter which way I viewed it, I had been incredibly reckless. The stalker wouldn't stop his pursuit because I said so. The case histories indicated that the sufferers had tremendous emotional endurance even when spurned. And some responded with assaults. Even though it felt good to express my anger, I had very likely raised the level of danger. If only I'd contacted a psychiatrist who specialized in erotomania and had talked through how to deal with potential situations! If only!

I groaned, fell back against the bed, and wished I could be any-where except where I was.

—

Sunday morning was foggy. A pre-dawn shower had dampened the trees, and the rain was starting to fall again. I brought the hatchet downstairs, checked the rooms, and looked through all the windows using the binoculars. No one was visible outside. Encouraged by an improvement in my throat and congestion and buoyed by the knowledge that I had survived Halloween, I made a mushroom omelet. After finishing my coffee, I took a shower and threw on old jeans and a Cornell sweatshirt. The *New York Times* was waiting at the end of the driveway, and I was determined to get it.

As I approached, umbrella in hand, I could see the newspaper's bright blue plastic wrapper shimmering in the rain. To my relief, the newspaper was just a newspaper, with no notes tucked inside. Though I chided myself for being optimistic, maybe I was incorrect about my concerns, and last night's harsh words would discourage the stalker. With the paper under my arm, I set a leisurely pace down the driveway, intent on enjoying the sparkling drops on the colorful foliage and the playful white mist that swirled in the low swales of the forest.

The stroll restored my proprietary custody of the land and—to an extent—my self-confidence. Inside the house, to alleviate my claustrophobia, I partly drew back the drapes. After brewing more coffee, I settled in with the paper, enjoying the house's silence, unbroken except by the occasional crackle of hot water sluicing through the baseboards. To my delight, the crossword puzzle was medium-hard, a worthy opponent. Once it was finished, I did laundry, read, and wiled away the afternoon, determined to forget my troubles.

The evening passed by without intrusion. I closed the drapes and went to bed early.

I was very confused after the phone call and didn't understand why you were angry. For a few minutes, I paced around my bedroom, swearing, throwing punches at the air, and kicking my desk chair. Was it all happening again? Were you—my great love—betraying me? Saying I wasn't good enough, and you didn't feel the same way as I felt about you? But no, this couldn't be true. You could never feel like that. You would never refuse the gift of my adoration. Not when you asked me to love you.

Then I realized the truth. You thought someone else was on the telephone. Some creepy old boyfriend or client who was irritating you. Once I figured that out, I sat on my bed and my spirits improved. You were yelling at him, telling him to quit bugging you. If I knew who the guy was, I'd take care of him so he would never upset you again. How dare he try to break up our special relationship!

I rose and stood in front of your photographs and knew you were sorry for the misunderstanding. Everything is fine.

Today, my love has been rewarded with rain. We are blessed! I left four bowls and three cups on my window sill to catch the drops. It would be easier to use a downspout, but you instructed me to collect the rain directly from the sky because it had to be pure. Gathering rain from leaves was okay because leaves are special.

In anticipation of how much we need, I found a large mayonnaise jar and washed it carefully. It's now half-filled, and it's still raining. I'll stay up so I can empty the bowls and set them out again. I am tired but renewed in my mission.

THE HARDWARE on the office door had been replaced, but not the door itself. Chisel marks remained and looked unsightly. My landlord had also left the door unlocked, which allowed free access inside. Irritated by his behavior, I climbed the stairs, imagining that he had probably snooped in my rooms. Everything looked undisturbed, however, and two sets of new keys were in a packet on my desk.

I slipped off my raincoat and checked the answering machine. Mary Brown had recorded a message requesting an appointment on Thursday, the day after Albert's session. Presumably, Mary wanted to hear my thoughts about her son, even though I'd told her his confidences wouldn't be shared. I called and left a time for Thursday and then researched mental health clinics and hospitals within a thirty-mile radius, placing calls to each, leaving seven names with the administrators, and requesting case information if any of my clients had been a patient. I explained that it was possible one of these individuals might become violent toward me, and therefore their cooperation was ethically appropriate and all information provided would be kept private. Though reluctant, they all agreed to review their case files, but it would take several days. I also inquired about psychiatrists who had specialized experience with stalkers, but no names were recommended. When I phoned Adrienne Barrow, my former therapist, a recorded message said she was away until the end of the week. Frustrated, I walked to the library to do more research.

Most articles described domestic situations: men and women who were married or in a relationship at one time and were separated or divorced. The stalker's goal was reunion with the spouse or partner, who was regarded as an extension of the stalker's self, a possession to which he felt entitled. When brought before a court, this type of victimizer maintained his right to behave as he had, stating that the sanctity of marriage vows or the holiness of the religious union justified his behavior. He staunchly denied any wrongdoing and exhibited no remorse or awareness that his conduct imperiled the well-being of his ex-partner. One situation was of a man stalking another man, a city mayor, although the suitor considered himself straight and had become outraged when the police suggested otherwise, saying, "We must be as one, but chaste."

Shortly after noon, I bought a ham sandwich and a Coke and returned to my office. There, I reexamined the suspects I'd provided to area mental hospitals: George Durst, Carson Kendricks, Dolly Bordella, Denise DiNicola, and Albert d'Auberge. Greta Graf was a "maybe" and had been included but not Samantha Cosgrove because her parents would have shared a record of psychiatric commitment. I was fairly confident that Lloyd, Mary, and Robert shouldn't be on my roster, and Marguerite, the Lees, and the Claytons weren't candidates. I hadn't inquired about Martie or Nick because they didn't seem delusional, though they remained on my tentative list. I couldn't think of anyone else.

—

I was apprehensive about seeing George Durst but told myself I had a duty to treat him. At two, he arrived wearing tan work clothes and gold leather boots. Everything was clean, including his hands, and his curly black hair was neatly combed. He showed me new 4 x 6 prints of his sculptures taken with better lighting and with the camera set on a tripod, which improved the quality. I enthused about each structure, and George beamed with pleasure.

"You're the only one understands," he said.

"Any sophisticated gallery owner would see the quality in your work, George. Have you investigated exhibition spaces?"

He nodded. "Was thinking about Educational Testing Service. I've also walked around town, but most of the galleries are in storefronts, without enough room. Once I get some of these shots enlarged, I'll try Lambertville and New Hope."

George then mentioned his mysterious woman friend. He still refused to divulge her name and looked askance when I asked.

"I might be seeing her tonight," he said. "Maybe."

I made a mental note of this comment and his guarded demeanor. Was George protecting himself in case the woman rejected him or was I the woman?

He turned his attention to my wall. "One of your masks is missing," he said. "And your exterior door is damaged."

I nodded. "The office was broken into on Friday night."

"Really?" George stared out the window and then stared at me. "Guess someone is upset with you, Ellen."

His tone was impossible to decipher. Ironic? Concerned? Amused? Guilty?

We discussed work for the rest of the session. After George left, I was struck by his quixotic manner and the unease I felt. "Definitely on the list."

—

Marguerite Fleury was the last appointment. She told me this was our final session, at least for now. She was excited about leaving for Baltimore to do her recording and had given an ultimatum to her controlling husband, who had—to her surprise—acquiesced to her trip and even become supportive. Although her fingers gave her pain, Marguerite was determined to succeed and willing to work at her marriage. I wished her well.

When she left, I made notes and worked on my book, becoming so engrossed that I failed to notice night had fallen. Cursing my stupidity, I hastened to my car. Despite the lateness of the hour, traffic was thick until I skirted Hopewell by making the left onto Crusher Road, which ran along a ridge above town and was noteworthy for old stone quarries that inspired its name. During the day, the road offered a Currier and Ives view of the valley.

After a short distance, I noticed a dark car behind me. This wasn't unusual, but I became worried as it came closer. Suddenly, two deer jumped into the street. I slammed on the brakes and swerved, just missing them. Giving me a wary eye, two more does stepped from the forest and ambled across the road. I checked the rearview mirror to ascertain the status of the dark car, which had stopped. I couldn't see the driver but decided not to tarry. At the end of Crusher Road, I turned left, as did my shadow, and made the right onto the lower section of Stoney Brook Road, a street that wasn't heavily traveled. The car followed.

I was now concerned. At Mine Road, I made a fast left over the narrow metal bridge and up the steep hill. The car did the same. If the driver lived in the Lambertville or Flemington areas, these maneuvers would be appropriate, but not if the driver lived in the direction of Pennington. On Route 31, I turned left, which would have taken me toward the road I had originally been on and thus was illogical. With a sigh of relief, I saw the car go to the right.

I circled around and headed toward my house, feeling shaken. After pulling onto the lip of the driveway, I checked the mailbox. Inside were bills and a Christmas catalogue whose cover featured a scene of a fireplace replete with a crackling fire and rows of stockings hung from the mantle above. Two cherubic children played with a train that circled a decorated tree. Though reminders of Christmas before Thanksgiving always annoyed me, I was especially upset to think about both holidays. Without my mother, they would be sad occasions, even if shared with my father. The bright spot would be Michael's visit over New Year's. A time chosen for a romantic renewal? Perhaps because he was moving east? The idea gave me a warm feeling.

I parked the Audi near the door and went inside. The house,

with its covered windows, seemed cold and unfriendly. Perhaps being reminded about fires from the catalogue, I thought one might help my mood. Grabbing the canvas carrier, I walked to the woodpile and gathered kindling and logs. On the road north of the house, a neighbor's beagles were howling, but beagles love to hear their own voices.

After locking the door, I carried the wood to the hearth, wrapped sticks of kindling in newspaper, which I stacked on the andirons, and then lit an edge of paper with a match. The fire started nicely, and a few minutes later, I lifted a log on top, closed the glass doors, and poured some white wine, ignoring my own advice about not drinking when depressed. I slipped two chicken breasts into the oven and made some rice. A second glass of wine got me through the cooking time and the preparation of a salad, and a third accompanied dinner, which I ate at the table. When I finished the dishes, I poured another glass, threw more logs on the fire, scanned my parents' opera collection, and selected Verdi's *Un Ballo in Maschera—A Masked Ball*. As the page, Oscar, began singing his aria, the wine was gone, and I opted for a snifter of Metaxa. In my present state, I soon fell into the abyss of melancholy, the alcohol providing an express highway to tears. I stretched along the sofa and gave in to feeling miserable.

At the conclusion of the second CD, I decided it would be prudent to go to sleep, though my behavior had strayed from prudent all evening. Ruing my inebriated state, I turned off the lights, trudged upstairs, and opened the blinds to see a sliver of new moon. Without considering the coolness of the room, I put on a sleeveless nightgown and laid on the bed, thinking that two days had passed without word from my stalker. Perhaps the phone call had discouraged him.

[THE JOURNAL]

I am exalted! No more waiting. No more watching. My patience will soon be rewarded. I have done all you've asked and gathered everything. I only hope I'm worthy and that you don't disappoint me. I'm sure you won't, Ellen, but I don't know what will happen if you do.

A HORRIFIC nightmare about my mother crashed me into consciousness. She had returned from the dead and was now alive and very frightened. "Get out of the house!" she shouted. "Blood and water! Blood and Water! Run, Ellen! Run!"

Her warnings were like live wires sparking bright red flares, electrifying me with fear. Trying to calm myself, I stared through the half-open blinds at the black sky and took several slow breaths. As I did, I became aware of moisture on my face. Had I been crying in my sleep? But I'd been terrified by the dream, not sad. I raised my hand and felt dampness on my cheeks but also on my forehead. How could tears roll upward?

Turning to the left, I was shocked to see my Casanova mask. I sprang back against the headboard and blinked, sure that I was imagining the black tricorn hat and its ivory, gold, and black diamond face. Yet two dark eyes glinted behind its oval holes, staring at me. The mask's lower section protruded into an angled beak that covered the wearer's mouth, and a black scarf was tied over the chin and neck. Below the scarf was a white wing-collar shirt and black cravat. The person was swathed in a black, floor-length satin cloak and stood beside my bed. Then the figure leaned forward, head cocked, as if waiting for permission to speak.

My heart was thudding in my chest; my mouth was dry. I wanted to bolt through the door and run, but the person was positioned to block my escape. Glancing down, I saw that my cotton nightgown was twisted high around my thighs, which were exposed to the stalker's scrutiny. Slowly, I inched my hand to the nightgown's hem in order to pull it down. With astonishing speed, the stalker encircled my wrist with a firm, black-gloved hand, preventing me. Did he want to remove my clothes himself? Was I about to be raped? Who the hell was this? I couldn't see his face, and the cloak's hood hid the back of his head so that no hair showed. I thought it was a man, but the person's size and gender were impossible to determine because the body was surrounded by the voluminous cape. All I knew was the grip on my wrist had been strong.

The figure released my hand and edged into the shadows without responding. I had no idea what the rules of this game were, but my words needed to be chosen with care.

"You've been very attentive," I said. "Thank you for the flowers and the chocolates."

There was no reply.

"And the photographs. You took them while I was asleep, didn't you?"

A nod.

I tried to sit more upright, but the stalker stepped forward and thrust a stiff hand against my chest, pinning me against the pillows. I swallowed nervously, wondering if I could overpower the person.

"Would you please remove the mask?"

The tricorn hat turned left and right, indicating a negative response.

"I want to see you."

The figure straightened slightly but kept his hand in place. I looked to the side. On the end table was an uncovered mayonnaise jar full of water or some kind of clear liquid.

"What's in the jar?"

More silence.

"Is it water? Did you put it on my forehead?"

Another nod.

With careful deliberation, while continuing to press me against the headboard, the person dipped a gloved finger into the jar and painted a wet line down my thigh to my knee. I shivered at the cold touch, frightened by the purposeful manner in which the finger moved. Had I been wrong about the "eroto" prefix? Was there sexual intent?

The stalker reached into the container a second time and sketched a liquid circle around my knee, raising gooseflesh on my leg. Quickly, I shoved his restraining hand away and attempted to spring from the bed, but as I did, the figure leaped forward and we met body to body. Whether because of an advantage of position or strength, the person forced me onto the mattress and fell heavily on top, crushing the sharp angle of the Casanova mask into my cheek. Frantically, I tried to free my arms to get leverage and push at the stalker's shoulders but only succeeded in shifting the person partially to the side.

Suddenly, the stalker disengaged and retreated around the bed to a space in front of the window, where his body formed an imposing black silhouette. Then I noticed it. Under the cloak. A red sheath dangling on a black belt.

When the person saw where I was focusing, he slid out the double-bladed dagger with a sensuous movement and clasped the knife like an object of reverence. The dagger was similar to one in Carson's drawings. Was it him?

"Wait a minute!" I cried, raising both hands and lowering my left foot toward the floor. "If you love me, if you've been patient and waited for so long, then we need to take this slowly. You're very special to me. You know that."

The dagger pointed down. I still couldn't tell who it was, whether it was Carson or a woman, whether it was one of my clients or some unhinged person off the street. "You're very special to me," I repeated.

The stalker's shoulders relaxed, as if the tension had been drained by my reassurance.

"But you know that, don't you?"

Another nod.

"And that I chose you…"

A dip of the head.

"Do you know why?"

The stalker tapped a finger on his heart.

"Yes. And you've done everything I asked, haven't you?"

A nod.

I tried to gauge how tall the person was. It was difficult to determine because I wasn't standing, nor could I see clearly in the dim light. Was Carson acting out his bloody fantasies? Oh, god, I hoped not! Or was this George or possibly Greta? The hands were strong enough for either of them. Denise? She had strong hands, from carving, as did Martie from playing tennis. Albert? The figure in front of me was disguised by the surrounding cloak, but recalling the weight of the person on top of me, I didn't think it was Albert. The figure was shorter than Nick. Samantha? She had shown interest in the Casanova mask, loved wearing black, and constantly spoke about roaming around at night. Had she been telling me all along that she loved me?

"Can we put on a light?" I asked, hoping to see better.

"No."

Whose voice was it? "Okay." I shifted my right foot closer to the edge of the bed.

The dagger's tip rose and pointed in my direction, motioning for me to return my legs onto the bed. That was the last thing I wanted to do because it placed me in a passive position. Then I recalled the hatchet. Where had I put the damned thing? Was it in the bedroom? No. I'd foolishly left it in the living room near the window.

The stalker came toward me, the dagger held in front. I edged away, trying to create space between us, but as I began to move, the person lunged forward and rammed me against the pillows, using his left hand.

"It's our night," the stalker whispered in a low, gruff voice. "To become one."

The night I would be violated or murdered? I ran through the strange imagery the person had assembled: the mask, cloak, and dagger, analyzing each for clues about the person's pathology. And the water in the mayonnaise jar? Was it intended as an anointment or purification before a rape or before my death? Did it have a religious connotation? Mary was Catholic, and because of their parents' Catholicism, George, Denise, and Albert might be, too.

"What do you mean?" I whispered. No response came. "I don't give you permission." This sounded inane, but I hoped that I had some leverage over what would happen.

The person hesitated, perhaps confused, but then the knife flew to my throat and pricked my skin. I gasped and the stalker quickly used the flat part of the blade to wipe the drops of blood trickling down my neck, acting as if the cut had been unintentional.

What would he or she do next? I lay there, my neck throbbing, and felt defenseless. With the dagger, the stalker gesticulated for me to place my arms by my sides. After doing this, I watched in frightened terror as the figure sat in a chair across the room, laid the knife on the table, pulled off boots and socks, and loosened the cravat, tossing it aside. Standing, the person parted the cloak and began to adjust a pronounced swelling at the crotch. His movements seemed slow and deliberate like George's. If it was George, how unstable was he? I concentrated on psychological dynamics, how I might manipulate and control him. He was too strong to overcome physically.

"George," I began quietly, let's talk about this for a little while."

The stalker jerked backward.

"Please, if we end this here, everything will be okay. We'll go downstairs, I'll make some tea, and we can talk. You can tell me how you feel, and I'll tell you how I feel. It'll be nice, like in the office." I tried to sound professional, but I was painfully conscious of the quaver in my voice.

"No!" came the barked reply.

Did the voice resemble George's? Maybe. I lifted myself onto one elbow, but the stalker grabbed the dagger, swiftly crossed the room, and forced me down. I sensed a change in mood, an angry heat, emanating behind the mask. Something was different. What had I said?

"Can we discuss this?" My words sounded desperate. More gently, I said, "Please, George."

A wordless scream of rage flew from deep within the person's throat. He swung the dagger in the air and punched my head with the hilt. I tried to block the next blow, but I was dazed from the attack and a second strike hit my temple. A third and a fourth followed and I was out.

—

It was still dark when I awoke. I hadn't been unconscious long, but long enough for the stalker to tie my hands to the bedposts with stockings from my dresser. My legs were free, and more significantly, my nightgown was still on, which made no sense if rape was the goal. I tried to analyze the situation, but my head ached, my ears were ringing, and my vision was blurry, not to mention I was scared. Really, really scared.

The stalker had unbuttoned his tuxedo shirt, though it was still tucked in, and the dagger was on the table. He approached, lifted the mayonnaise jar, and dipped a gloved finger into the water. With deliberation, he made the sign of benediction on my forehead and across the bare skin above the neckline of my nightgown. Although my skin was crawling, I remained still. What did this behavior mean and what was the purpose of the dagger? Was it only a weapon to force my participation or did it have special symbolism in this bizarre masquerade, charging its owner with erotic power? Would it be used? To coerce sexual assault or—please, no!—as part of the assault? Was I lying on my sacrificial bed? I thought of the years my mother had slept here. The image of being defiled and murdered in her room made everything worse.

"George, please. If you love me, stop."

He exhaled an angry breath and slammed the jar on the table. His hand tightened into a fist and slammed into my cheek. Instinctively, my legs came up, but they couldn't prevent another blow. I lay there, head bursting from the assault, and glared at the figure who was now standing across the room.

"Why are you doing this?" I thought about George's Vietnam experience, the mutilations, decapitations, and deaths he'd witnessed or perhaps committed. How did these tie in with the erotomanic behavior? Or had I become a figure of hope for George? The one person who could save him? If so, why was he hitting me?

"You don't mean to do this. You're acting against my wishes," I said with as much authority as I could muster. "Put on the light and we'll talk."

A low snarl, like that of a predatory animal, cut through the silence. He began pacing back and forth until finally he stopped. Staring at me, he loosened his belt and unzipped his black pants, revealing a dark protuberance.

"We must consecrate our wedding." A rough whisper.

"I can't be yours."

"No, you're George's, aren't you?" This uttered with venom.

Did this indicate a split in consciousness? Was George dividing himself so that part of him could commit rape and the other part could remain separate and innocent? A kind of dissociation that sometimes befell people who had experienced severe trauma. Or had I mistaken the stalker's identity?

I decided not to use George's name. "What do you mean?"

This was greeted with bitter, raspy laughter. The stalker came forward and stood above me. To my horror, he freed the bulge from his briefs and ripped it out and away, spraying a sock full of yellow-gold leaves and green acorns over my body. He began covering me with the leaves and acorns, as if driven to complete some prescribed task. Once this was done to his satisfaction, the person observed his work, nodded, and focused on me, as if unsure what to do next.

I thought about the fake protuberance. Was this George? Was this even a male? What did the acorns represent? Impregnating seeds? Would an inexperienced, delusional man behave this way?

"Are you pure?" he or she asked.

The voice might be a male's unless a woman had lowered her pitch. I was struggling to hear well because sounds were echoing in my ears as if I were in a deep cave, and the mask muffled his words. What was the safest answer? If I wasn't pure, would that mean I wasn't suitable for the consummation of sexual union? Or would a state of impurity require purifying? If so, how?

"Yes, I'm pure," I said, feeling disembodied.

"Have you lain with him or any other?"

Who in god's name was he talking about? "No."

"Am I the first?"

"Yes," I lied.

He sat on the bed, took my foot, and caressed it. "I'll be yours forever."

Although I felt like screaming, I managed to whisper, "And I will be yours."

The stroking continued up my legs. I wanted to kick his head, but one sideways, awkward strike wouldn't have much effect.

301

Though I didn't want to guess wrong, I continued with the dialogue.

"That's right. Show how you love me. You can do it better than anyone. You've waited and have cleansed yourself of all bad thoughts. You are worthy. There's no one else." I had no idea what I was saying, but I babbled on to delay an assault. Then it occurred to me how I might learn the stalker's identity. "Please, I want to see how pure your body is."

The cloaked figure stopped and inched away. His shirt parted to reveal white adhesive tape bound around his chest. Stunned, I inhaled sharply. My stalker was female!

"I must see you. All of you. It's time for us to be one," I said, trying to play the part of the virgin, a role I surmised was mine in this ritualistic enactment.

As if reassured, she came closer and began to draw strange patterns on my skin, scarcely making contact. As frightening as this was, at least the dagger was on the table, though within her reach. The woman seemed mesmerized by my body, staring at me from beneath the mask. Soon, she grew bolder, twisting my nightgown and kneading my abdomen as if to find the organs underneath. Her hands were relentless. Her attentions hurt.

"Gently," I whispered, but the stalker continued as if she hadn't heard.

"You're mine now," she said, digging forcefully above my hip and causing me to grunt as she probed and twisted. "I must know how you feel inside."

"I want to feel you, too. Release me so we can come together."

She continued her repetitive manipulations, chafing my flesh until it was on fire. I reacted to the pain by bringing my knees up. She pushed them down.

"I must do everything right," she hissed.

"I want to hold you. Please."

The woman hesitated. Finally, she stood and retrieved the dagger. What was she going to do with it? I was preparing for the worst, when she began to saw the stocking tied to my left wrist. When my arm dropped, I let it stay where it fell, pretending a passivity I didn't feel.

"You are so powerful," I said.

She went to the other side of the bed and sliced the other stocking. I let that arm fall, too. She gazed at me through the mask. I didn't move or speak and prayed she would lay the dagger down so I could leap to my feet and attack. Instead, the woman came nearer and sat on the mattress, her cloak covering the white bedsheets like a black wave.

"May I hold you?" I asked again.

A nod.

I placed my arms around her shoulders and felt her tense, but slowly she allowed me to draw her closer. I stayed in that position, smelling the sweat on her body and letting her become adjusted to the intimacy. Although she encircled me tightly with her left hand, she then raised her right and brought the dagger's tip to rest against my throat. We held that uncomfortable position for several minutes. Her breathing came in quick inhalations, as if she were extremely nervous. I tried to slow my own breathing, hoping to calm her, and spoke softly.

"We're together at last. I am yours."

"Yes. We are almost one." She sounded overcome with emotion.

If we weren't "one" now, how were we going to achieve that union? Was she waiting for encouragement? Was she aroused? No act had been overtly sexual, but still there was the dagger. I tried not to think about being stabbed, yet it was nearly impossible. With one quick shove of the knife, she could kill me. To avoid being hurt, I needed to use my wits. Suddenly, I realized that if I could see her hands, perhaps they might reveal the woman's identity.

"Oh, please…take off the gloves. I want to feel your hands in mine."

She gasped and held her breath. For a second, she sat there, frozen, but then she bolted to her feet, reeled violently backward from the bed, tripping in her haste and crashing against the dresser. Before I could move, she regained her balance, shook her head rapidly, and began to whimper. Low at first until the whimper slowly intensified into a wail of anguish. Louder and louder until it became a roar of pain.

"No! No! No!" she screamed.

I had no idea what tripwire had been sprung. Her earsplitting cries were deafening.

She continued to shake her head as if to deny some accusation. "No! You can't see! No, you can't!" As if to ward off some fearful demon, she outstretched her arm. "No! No! Dirty hands! Dirty hands! No! Don't touch with dirty hands! Don't touch!" she admonished herself fiercely, as an angry parent would reprimand a child. After inhaling a huge lungful of air, she shouted, "Never touch! Dirty!"

The woman was hysterical and began rocking on her feet, her mask twisting side to side.

"No, Mama! I didn't touch! Really, I didn't! Mama, I would never!" More head-shaking and a long, drawn-out sob of pain. "Mama said I'm not allowed! Only Mama can. Only Mama can touch!"

Her ravings filled the room with agonized remonstrations, shouts, and moans. I was alarmed, yet noted her last phrases. "It's okay," I said. "Your mother isn't here."

"No! You won't have me because of these!" Still clutching the dagger, she used her thumb and forefinger of her right hand to rip off the left glove, throwing it on the floor, and then switched the dagger and did the same with the right glove. Flailing her hands and the knife in front of her, she shrieked, "I am impure! I'm disgusting! Sinful! Mama says so!" Her voice cracked and turned into a guttural sob. "Oh, my god! I'm not worthy!" she repeated over and over. "I'm not clean! I'm not pure! Oh, dirty, dirty hands!"

I was scared but I now knew my stalker. "Your mother is wrong—"

Before I could say her name, she reared to full height, raised the dagger, and plunged its blade into her chest. She lurched two steps and thrust again. Howling in agony, she tried to stab herself one more time, but I rushed to my feet and grabbed her wrist. We wrestled, and the dagger grazed my left shoulder. I cried out, covered my wound, and then, horrified, saw her fall heavily against the wall and slip to the floor. Blood gushed down the white adhesive binding and her shirt. After she came to rest against the door frame, a gurgling sound escaped her lips.

Kneeling beside her, I lifted the Casanova mask and unwound the scarf. Denise DiNicola gazed at me; her mouth formed into an eerie grimace. She raised her bloody hand, as if to strike her heart again, but her arm went limp, and the knife skittered across the rug.

I pressed my palms against the wounds to stop the bleeding, but blood poured over my fingers and onto my bare knees and arms.

"Denise! Stay alive! Please!"

She gasped for air as her lungs filled. A thin red rivulet trickled from her lips. Her eyes were wide with panic. Should I call an ambulance? But First Aid would take too long to arrive—we were miles from Hopewell. I also knew that if I removed my fingers, she would die.

"I'm sorry, Denise! Oh, god! I should have known it was you!"

I kept imploring her to live, begging for her forgiveness. Then the intensity in her eyes faded as if she could no longer see. Her jaw slackened.

"No!" I screamed.

Denise stopped breathing. Her body became motionless.

I slowly raised my bloody hands and eased back on my heels, shocked by the silence. Dimly, I noticed light seeping through the window. Everything in the room appeared monochromatic except for one color—red. In a daze, I reached for the Casanova mask and stared into its empty eyes. I felt like Denise had vanished into their black void and I had, too.

Staggering to my feet, my body began to sway in a strange motion like a double-jointed doll. Tears streamed down my cheeks as I lifted the mask to my face and tied the black ribbons behind my head. Then my knees buckled and I collapsed onto the bed, where I lay, crushed by my catastrophic failure to help Denise and horrified by my abject blindness to the turmoil she had been experiencing.

"Oh, why, Denise? Why?" I sobbed.

The questions echoed against the walls, the tone turning more accusatory. Shivering, my teeth began to chatter and my body shook. I had never been so cold! Achingly cold. As I pulled the comforter tightly around me, I smelled cigarette smoke coming from the doorway into the bedroom. It lingered for a few moments and then dissipated.

[THE JOURNAL]

My beloved, I am coming. We are to be made one tonight, and death will not do us part. I have the rain water and will bathe you until you are clean and pure. I will place the leaves and acorns on your body so you will glow with golden light, and then I'll press the sacred blade into you until you fly to heaven, where I will follow. We will be united forever, and I will be clean and beautiful at last.

Items recovered in dark blue 1983 Toyota Corolla owned by
Denise DiNicola:

1: 8 x 25 Bushnell binoculars
2: Canon AE-1 camera with 80-200 mm lens
3: 1992 journal dedicated to Dr. Ellen Haskell, with 12 pencil portraits of her
4: 1990 journal titled: *To My New Love, Dr. David Burnfield*
5: Red fountain pen

EPILOGUE

I HAD treated Ellen Haskell before and after the suicide attempt of her client, Lucas. At the conclusion of her therapy, I felt sad to say goodbye. This morning, I was even sadder to see her in my waiting room looking so pale and shaken. Although I rarely make physical contact with my clients, I took her in my arms and held her for a long, silent minute. I couldn't have done otherwise, she was so changed.

We had spoken on the telephone three times after the tragic events early on November 3, although the first call wasn't really a conversation. Her father had connected me to Ellen while she was in the hospital because he—and the staff—hoped hearing my voice might pull Ellen from her semi-catatonic state. She did emerge a little, but it took a second call, once she was home, to have a more normal communication, and a third to establish she was capable of making the hour trip to the city, although I'd offered to drive to Hopewell.

Despite knowing some details of her harrowing experience, I wasn't prepared for Ellen's appearance. She was still bruised with purple and red discolorations on the left side of her face, and a bandage was on her neck. Her brown eyes, usually so full of animation and humor, were dull, and her handsome features seemed softer, with a vagueness I'd never seen before. Her bearing had altered, too, and she looked smaller, less able to command a presence in the room.

During our phone conversations, Ellen had related her hospitalization for concussion and the stitching of her shoulder and neck wounds, her mother's death in Greece, and in an abbreviated recounting, the suicide of her client, Denise DiNicola. Ellen's reticence to speak about that night indicated she was in a fragile state. Though I rarely exceed the fifty-minute hour, I had cleared the morning and told her so ahead of time, for which she was grateful. Also contrary to practice, I sat on the couch with her instead of in my chair. I did this instinctively because she seemed so delicate, as if she might collapse.

"Ellen, let's deal with medical matters first, if that's okay."

She gave me a smile that didn't reach her eyes. "I'm fine, Adrienne. The cuts on my shoulder and neck are healing, and the headaches are mostly gone. No permanent damage. I should be back to playing a bad game of tennis soon."

"That's good. As I recall, you're quite a fine player, aren't you?" I noted that Ellen didn't mention two days of semi-catatonia in the hospital.

She looked at her long hands and nodded.

"You've lost weight," I added.

"Some."

"Are you sleeping all right?"

Ellen glanced at me and shook her head. "No. Nights aren't easy."

"Are you re-experiencing what happened?"

Reluctantly, she said yes.

"Did your doctor prescribe medication?"

"Xanax as needed. It helps…"

"But not that well?"

She sighed. "No, but I'm not using it regularly. I prefer to get through this without being doped…as much as possible."

"I can understand that," I replied. "Nevertheless, I recommend you continue with the Xanax for a while. At least at night."

Ellen agreed to do so.

"And your father is home. I'm sure you're glad he is."

"Yes, I am. The state police found his number by the telephone."

She knew her father had contacted me once but was unaware

that we'd had several additional exchanges—he asked to keep these private.

"How is he?" I asked.

"The trip was an ordeal, but Dad is happy to be back. Well, he's not so happy about what happened." Ellen hesitated, rubbing her temple. "Once the forensic investigation was finished, we were allowed into the house. I'm sleeping downstairs, and he's in the room where..."

I noticed she kept massaging her head, as if it hurt, and decided to divert to another subject. "You told me a little about your mother's accident. How were you getting on with her before she left for Greece? We spent a great deal of time discussing your mother during our previous work together."

"Thanks to our sessions and an effort by my mother, we renegotiated our relationship and put it on a new track, which is one reason I moved to Princeton. When she and my father decided to go to Corfu, I was disappointed to see her leave because I was enjoying her company."

"Perhaps you could appreciate each other more as adults. And, too, some people become more mellow as they age. The sharpness wears off, and the mother/daughter competitiveness eases on both sides. It's even possible she sensed her time here was about to end."

Ellen looked at me with interest. "That thought occurred to me. She was always a bit psychic. Maybe she intuited her own passing."

"On the phone, you said her ghost appeared. The night before you received the call about her car accident?"

"Yes. I'm positive it was my mother," she replied. "Not only could I see her image, I could smell cigarette smoke. Though she'd given up the habit many years ago, she missed smoking. I have no doubt she would have reached for a cigarette at the pearly gates, once she didn't have to worry about lung cancer or annoying us non-smokers."

"And you also told me she came to you in a vivid dream. The night Denise broke in."

Ellen's expression turned more serious. "Yes. My mother yelled at me to get out of the house and kept repeating 'blood and water' over and over. Very insistently."

"A warning?"

"Absolutely. Probably during the dream, Denise DiNicola was entering the basement. She brought a jar of water..." Ellen paused, swallowing with difficulty. "And there certainly was a lot of blood...after..."

I put a steadying hand on her shoulder. "Why don't you tell me more about Denise?" I said gently. "I've done a little research on erotomania, but I'm not an expert."

Ellen sighed. "I only saw Denise a few times. My impression was that she was inexperienced in relationships and isolated. I should have realized how separate she felt after seeing her self-portrait. The background behind her figure was blank—just white paper."

"As if she was disconnected from the world?"

"Yes. The drawing illustrated the absence in her life, one she needed to fill." Ellen shook her head. "Alcoholism ran in her family and was accompanied by parental physical and emotional abuse. Denise was also struggling with drinking and poor self-esteem, though I often wonder what that means. Average intelligence, average in appearance. She dreamed about becoming a successful sculptor. I have no idea whether she was any good, or whether this was part of a fantasy. I didn't think Denise was delusional at all. I misread her completely."

"From my research, erotomaniacs may present as relatively normal people until their mania manifests itself and overwhelms their lives and the lives of others."

"That's what I've read, too. I didn't notice this escalation in the office, but it was becoming evident in the increasingly intrusive and proprietary stalking behavior."

"And as she became more aggressive, you probably became more anxious and obsessed yourself."

Ellen nodded. "I was trying to keep things together, but you're right, Adrienne. I was becoming obsessed, trying to figure out the person's identity, especially over the last week when I concluded the stalker was very likely one of my clients. And when I removed the mask and confirmed it was Denise, I was shocked that I'd missed the signs…that I hadn't detected the extent of her illness. If I had, I might have been able to prevent what happened."

"I don't think it was from lack of effort, Ellen. I'm sure of that."

"It reminded me of my failure with Lucas. I didn't see the warning signals then, either." Ellen pressed her fingers against her forehead and let out a long breath. "Although there weren't many clues, I should have attended more closely to Denise's descriptions of childhood suffering. Between us, Adrienne, I didn't entirely believe her. There was something distant about the recounting of her history, as if she were making up the stories or embellishing details."

"To get your attention? To make you interested in her?"

"That's what I wondered," Ellen replied. "I did notice she often seemed hesitant about leaving my office. Like she was hoping I would ask her to stay."

"She probably was."

"From the one letter Denise sent, it was clear she believed I had chosen her, and she was supposed to watch over me, waiting for my permission to be together."

"That's an interesting dynamic. Instead of coming forward

and making her identity known, as many stalkers do, perhaps Denise subconsciously incorporated a firewall as a protective device. Maybe because she was afraid of losing the positive feelings transferred from you to her—if you learned who she was and rejected her."

"Yes."

"And that psychological firewall was very successful. It kept her feelings for you, her compulsion, in check, at least in your presence. When she was by herself, I imagine she was more disturbed, more in the grip of her illness."

"It seems that was the case. The police said her apartment was filled with pencil sketches and photographs of me. Posters announcing my lecture and the picture on the back cover of my book and the enlargements of photographs she took." Here, she paused, gritting her teeth. "Oh, that was so awful, Adrienne! She walked up close to the house and photographed me on the deck while I was asleep in my bathrobe. After I saw those enlargements, I felt sick and threw away the robe. I couldn't stand to have in the closet."

"That was one of her violations of you. One of many."

Ellen glanced at me, fighting tears. "I never, never thought I could become a victim."

"No one ever thinks this kind of nightmare can happen to them. This is something you'll need to absorb and understand, insofar as possible. Let me say this: you are definitely not the type of woman who is easily victimized. You're strong, thoughtful, and self-actualized in many areas of your life. You don't place yourself in situations of this kind, situations that endanger your ability to handle events. That's important for you to realize. You didn't cause Denise to fixate on you. You didn't encourage her."

"I feel that something I said or did initiate her interest."

"That's an understandable reaction. We grow up with the

314

belief that relationships are created by two people, more or less in tandem. In this case, the relationship was started by Denise, nourished by her, and carried out according to the dictates of her exclusive needs. You were just a painted-in figure she used to counterbalance her devastating feelings of being unloved and unworthy."

"Rather parasitic."

"Yes, a very apt term," I replied.

Ellen turned to face me more directly. "I'm still wondering about her orientation. Her interest in me seemed platonic and idealized, as if she wanted to elevate herself by becoming close, to absorb the attributes she imagined I possess. In sessions, Denise never flirted or exhibited noticeable attraction. Even that night, when she might have physically taken advantage of me, she didn't. However, her fantasy was interrupted when Denise was confronted with a major trauma connected to her mother. Considering two significant phrases she said just before she stabbed herself, I think Denise was molested during her mother's frequent alcoholic episodes. So, in my opinion, I don't believe she was she repressing homosexuality in herself, just the incestuous abuse by her mother."

"That's complicated, but it makes sense."

"This viewpoint is further reinforced because the police told me Denise had stalked a male internist in Trenton. They found a journal dedicated to him, similar to the one addressed to me, but the first journal contained some sexual imagery."

"So that supports the likelihood that Denise wasn't a lesbian."

Ellen nodded. "And I've learned that two years before Denise attached to this doctor, she was an out-patient at a psychiatric hospital. Suffering from severe depression and alcohol abuse. An administrator there called to let me know this information shortly after I came home. If only I'd phoned the hospitals sooner, I might have received their report before the attack and realized Denise was my stalker."

"And to what effect? You told me her activities prior to November 3 weren't criminal except for breaking into your office. I doubt there were grounds to prosecute her or to issue a restraining order. Even if the authorities had, it's unlikely to have been successful. Denise would've remained free and fixated on you. From what I've read, erotomanic obsessions are very powerful. Confronting her might have ignited Denise earlier, and the outcome could have been worse for you."

"But maybe not fatal for her," Ellen replied.

"No, perhaps not." I paused, thinking we needed a small break. I placed a hand on her shoulder. "I'm going to make some tea. Would you like some, Ellen?"

"Okay."

I brewed two cups and returned, setting a mug in front of her. Shivering slightly, she clasped it with both hands.

"Getting back to the night," I began, "I know it's not easy, but are you able to tell me what happened in more detail? How she behaved?"

Ellen drank some tea and then fell wearily against the couch. "Everything keeps coming back in pieces, like so many frames of a movie sliced apart." She stared at me. "I don't even know where to start."

"You told me she dressed in a costume. A long, hooded cloak and your Casanova mask?"

"The mask was part of my collection. My clients face them when they sit on the couch. Sometimes I use the masks in sessions—"

"For role-playing?"

"Yes. Denise also wore a black scarf, ascot, pants, boots, and gloves, and a white tuxedo shirt. The dagger and the outfit were part of her Venetian-Casanova fantasy, a kind of wedding night invention in which she played the groom, and I was the bride, though her ideation didn't seem to include sex. One of the policemen read her journal to me which confirmed that."

"Maybe she was able to maintain her delusion because it was heterosexual, even if constructed in a twisted manner. A homosexual union may have been too close to what transpired with her mother. With the male doctor, Denise may have played a female part."

"That's quite a contortion."

"I know. Creating and sustaining a delusion requires psychological flexibility."

Ellen agreed and then was quiet for a long time, focusing on her hands, which she rubbed together. When she looked at me, her forehead was creased with worry. "Adrienne, I'm so ashamed. I might have heard Denise breaking in, but I drank a bottle of wine with dinner and then some brandy because I was depressed. By the time I went upstairs, I wasn't sober." She exhaled a tremulous breath. "I must have put on my nightgown and passed out on top of the sheets. That's how Denise found me."

"So you believe nothing would have happened if you had been in a different condition?"

Ellen hung her head. "I don't know."

"I really doubt that's true. Denise entered your house with a rigid, pre-conceived plan."

"Yes, but the nightgown's hem was hitched up…like I'd laid myself on a platter."

Though Ellen rarely cried during our years of counseling, she was battling to maintain her composure. She stared at the ceiling, trying to keep tears from falling. Unsuccessfully. I was ready with a tissue.

"What you were wearing or how you appeared probably didn't matter. She wasn't interested in a sexual relationship," I pointed out.

After shedding some tears, Ellen began again. "No, she wasn't. And she could have done whatever she wished. Denise was very strong—her strength made me think the stalker was my client, George Durst. I had no idea that it was a woman, otherwise—"

"Otherwise what? You told me Denise had a dagger."

"Yes, but…oh, I don't know. It's all a blur," Ellen said. "And there's the other strange element of the ritual. The water in a jar. She painted me with the water. Drawing symbols and crosses on my face…on my body. Like she was mimicking some kind of religious ceremony."

"Go on."

Ellen shut her eyes and more tears fell. "It was so degrading! I felt so cold. Very, very cold."

I put my arm around her shoulders and pulled her close. We stayed that way for a few moments as sobs convulsed her body.

Through clenched teeth, she whispered, "There was nothing I could do! Nothing. Adrienne, I completely blew the situation. I called her 'George,' which set her off. I can't believe I was so stupid. Unbelievably stupid! How could I mistake a woman for a man?"

I didn't answer. Moving apart from Ellen, I took another tissue from the box and handed it to her.

"Then she hit me several times on the head because she was furious. When I came to, Denise had tied my hands."

"You were completely vulnerable," I suggested quietly.

Ellen regarded me with tear-streaked eyes. "Yes."

"Thinking you were going to be raped or killed?"

"Yes," she said again in a small, broken voice.

"Tell me exactly how you felt, Ellen." It was important for her to verbalize this.

"I was very afraid." Ellen wrung her hands. "And, god…I don't know how to say this, Adrienne…"

"Tell me."

"When she was touching me…with the cold water…"

"Go on."

"I had…a sexual reaction. The feeling only lasted for a moment, but it was so humiliating!" Ellen shook her head miserably. "I couldn't believe that would ever happen."

I renewed my embrace and let her cry. "Ellen, our bodies become aroused in the strangest situations. Men who were prisoners of war sometimes admitted they had sexual responses to torture. Our physiological and nervous systems are complex and primal, sometimes perversely autonomous. Just because we experience fear and pain, we can still react in contrary ways." I leaned back and focused steadily on Ellen. "Once you knew the stalker was a woman, did you believe she was going to rape you?" She didn't answer, so I added, "Say what you're thinking."

Ellen looked at me with a tormented expression. "The dagger seemed to be significant."

"As a weapon or as a symbol of the male anatomy? Or was it part of the final act after becoming united? Because after achieving perfection, you both had to die?"

"I don't think the dagger was a sexual symbol, or she planned to use it as coercion to make me participate—Denise assumed I would go along because we were following 'my' plan. No, it was a tool to end everything, for both of us, which her journal implied."

I exhaled to release the tightness in my chest. When I reached for the mug of tea, my fingers were trembling. Ellen noticed and apologized.

"I'm sorry, Adrienne. This is painful for you to hear."

I stared at her in surprise. "Now, listen, don't give me any of that therapist nonsense, do you hear me?"

A glimmer of a smile. "Sorry, it's tough to stop the habit."

"One thing puzzles me," I said. "If the ending to her fantasy was a mutual death, what diverted Denise from this goal? You

319

began to explain why, but could you say more?"

"Yes." Ellen lay against the arm of the couch and dried her tears. "Accidentally, I tripped into a memory of one of the most internalized representations of her self-hatred."

"What was that?"

"Her hands. I thought that if I could see them, I might recognize one of my female clients. I already suspected Denise, but I had no idea that I would trigger such a powerful response. When I asked her to remove her gloves, she began screaming, 'dirty hands.' I'd noticed Denise's habit of hiding her hands in her pockets during our sessions, particularly when she felt tense or defensive. And in her self-portrait, her hands were hidden below the edge of the paper."

"A torso and head only?"

"Yes. I believe her mother either discovered her doing something sexual—perhaps touching herself—and then told her she was dirty, filthy. Or, after molesting Denise, her mother projected her own sinfulness onto her daughter. And, in reality, Denise's hands probably were dirty—Denise had to do household chores."

"So when you asked Denise to bare her hands, the request linked to a time when her mother caught her in the act of masturbation and shamed her, or when her mother derided Denise for performing incestuous acts—acts she forced Denise to commit against her will. Either of these would elicit feelings of deep humiliation and rage."

"Yes. And at the same time she was re-experiencing this, she was also becoming separated from the positive feelings that had accrued from her connection with me. Everything came crashing down at the same time. The partition between her normal and diseased selves collapsed."

"Causing Denise to destroy herself."

Ellen studied me carefully. "Yes. In her mind, she wasn't worth saving."

—

We met nine times during the following weeks and planned to continue after the Christmas holiday, which Ellen was unhappily anticipating because of her mother's absence. Only the planned visit with her friend Michael Larrimore relieved her grief. Each time we met, I arranged a double session because of the distance and because of her emotional state. I didn't want the terrible experience to fester or for her to bury memories. Ellen was sensitive to her situation and was willing to undergo rigorous self-exposure, determined to break through her usual reserve and tendency toward intellectual analysis into the depths of raw feeling. Often, when she left after a session, I was worried, knowing she had little support at home except for her father, who was still recovering from the loss of his wife and the shock of what had happened to his daughter. Even so, at each appointment, Ellen plowed through the pain without accepting much sympathy except in measured doses.

After the first visit, I counseled Ellen to continue postponing all of her own sessions in Princeton through January, but she insisted on a January 4 opening. After telephoning all of her clients, she was particularly anxious about Dolly Bordella, Samantha Cosgrove, and Carson Kendricks. I asked how each was doing.

Dolly, one of the most unstable, wasn't dealing well without Ellen. She had left several fearful messages, describing powerful phobic reactions to the dark and to crowds of people. Ellen, sensing her own frightening experience had spiked Dolly's anxiety, referred her to a psychiatrist, hoping Dolly would begin a course of medication, but she hadn't turned up for the appointment.

Samantha reacted to Ellen's call with sullenness. She had read the newspaper report, which had been carefully constructed by the police to minimize Ellen's involvement in the suicide. Nevertheless, Sam made connections to Jake's death and had become more depressed. Ellen explained to me that she had spoken with the Cosgroves, provided the literary contest information for Sam, and asked them to be kind toward their daughter until sessions could be re-started. Ellen felt terrible about interrupting Sam's therapy, which added to Ellen's regret.

Carson had also been over-reactive. He blamed Ellen for disturbing his painting and jeopardizing his exhibit. A day later, he called to apologize and requested an appointment as soon as she began seeing clients.

George Durst fared better. Finally working up his courage, he had asked his woman friend on a date. She accepted, liked the wine he brought to the restaurant, and was impressed with the pictures of his construction sculptures. When she reciprocated by inviting him to dinner, George was very happy. Two gallery owners had agreed to see his portfolio, and his freelance landscaping business was thriving.

When Ellen had telephoned Albert d'Auberge, his mother, Mary Brown, answered. She said her son had followed his muse to Chicago, transferring credits and enrolling in art school for the spring semester. Now on her own, Mary had set a goal of finding a partner. Greta Graf was making progress in her relationship with Stanley and the exhibit with Anne. The Claytons and Lees were coping well, Lloyd had seen his new boyfriend several times, Marguerite Fleury was in Baltimore, and Robert Gabriel Fleet was still Robert Gabriel Fleet.

—

After the fifth session, I received a thick envelope in the mail from Ellen: a copy of the detailed police report, which contained some redactions and deleted pages. A color Xerox of Denise Di-Nicola's body slumped against the door was stapled to the inside cover.

Reading through the folder, I learned that an alarm system estimator had arrived at the Haskell house a few hours after Denise's death. When no one answered the door, he noted the car in the driveway and began evaluating the building for the installation of surveillance equipment. He discovered the broken downstairs window and called the police. What Ellen would have done alone if no one had come to the house filled me with dread, particularly after reading the description of Ellen as the detectives found her: in bed; blood on her hands, arms, legs, and feet; shaking with cold; unable to speak; and wearing the Casanova mask.

A forensic statement and concluding remarks were also included. Denise's death was determined to be a suicide because only her fingerprints were on the knife, and the crime scene evidence supported Ellen's recounting. Denise's diary also revealed her murderous intentions.

How Ellen had managed to get hold of the file was unknown, though she said Sergeant Wilcox of the state police had been very supportive. What interested me was that Ellen had sent it. Unswerving honesty? Perhaps. Just as she wanted to explore her personal truth concerning the events of that night, it was also typical of her to provide perspectives other than her own so that I could formulate an independent view and ask her the necessary tough questions. Not for the first time, Ellen's conscientiousness impressed me, but I was also concerned she was being too hard on herself. Merciless might be a more appropriate description. She was deter-mined to hold her toes close to the fire, intent on castigating herself for her failure with Denise.

As I reviewed the report again, several details provoked questions, which I asked Ellen, yet her reason for donning the mask after Denise's death remained a mystery. I sensed it was best to delay addressing this issue until Ellen seemed more emotionally settled.

—

At our ninth session, Ellen looked trim in a charcoal-gray blazer and crisp blue-and-white-striped shirt. I wasn't fooled by the assured presentation because it was apparent that she'd lost more weight. When I inquired about her appetite, she insisted she was fine. She didn't look fine, though the bruises had faded and her color had improved.

I sat in my usual chair and Ellen chose the sofa. After considering options, I went with my instincts and began to walk Ellen through the events that initiated Denise's explosive reaction when she was asked to remove her gloves, even though we had already explored this. Once Ellen recounted the stabbing, I suggested she should describe what occurred next.

"I remember lifting the Casanova mask from Denise's face and dropping the mask on the floor." She stared at her hands. "I tried to stop her wounds from bleeding, but everything after that...is gone."

It was important to restore these memories, painful as they undoubtedly were. "Ellen? Are you willing to try some hypnosis? It may be too soon. Or we can wait...or not do it at all."

Ellen searched my eyes for reassurance and agreed. I stood and drew the blinds on the windows, darkening the room.

We had utilized hypnosis on several occasions over the years, so it was easy to achieve that state now. We went through various breathing techniques, and slowly the lines on her forehead lessened. I asked her to imagine a warm, happy place and gave Ellen time to experience a brief "holiday." After a few minutes, I did a countdown, so she would descend into a deeper level, and then led her toward the stabbing, leaving spaces for her to re-create the scene as it surfaced in her mind. The method I used was to set Ellen in the role of observer rather than as herself, the victim. Even so, just as the tension had evaporated initially, it now returned as traces of fear imprinted on her face, and her body began to tremble.

Had I been too insistent on the hypnosis? Was I taking a risk with Ellen by encouraging her to delve into a trauma she wasn't ready to re-experience? I fought down my doubts, though it hurt to see her struggle, locked into a dark place where I couldn't follow. I inhaled and exhaled quietly, trying to combat my anxiety, and stayed the course. Keeping my voice steady, I guided her through to the conclusion, allowing Ellen time to fill in the gaps between my minimal promptings and observing her shake like a plane passenger experiencing turbulence. After she was calmer, I restored Ellen to the pleasant, sunny oasis and let her linger there to stabilize before beginning reentry. When I asked her to open her eyes, Ellen did so with great reluctance. I remained silent while she adjusted to the reality of her surroundings. Then I raised the blinds, sat in my chair, and asked what had happened as she circled around the scene in the bedroom and looked down on herself.

Ellen closed her eyes, as if going under again.

"Ellen, tell me what you saw."

Slowly, her fingers raised to touch both sides of her face. "I watched myself holding the Casanova mask. There was blood on it."

"How did you—how did Ellen—feel?"

She opened her eyes. "Freezing cold."

"What else?"

Ellen swallowed hard and lowered her hands. "Terrified."

"What was frightening her? Denise was dead."

"True, but she didn't believe that. She thought Denise would begin breathing again, grab the dagger, and—" Ellen gave a long, drawn-out sigh. "Oh, Adrienne, she—I—wanted to disappear. To use the mask to hide from what had happened, to escape, to become someone else. That's what I felt a few minutes ago, under hypnosis. A sense of spinning through space and time, trying desperately to be free from my body—"

"A body in pain."

"Yes. A body in pain lying curled on a bed, on white sheets, with bloody hands, feet, and legs, wearing a bloody mask."

"And next?"

"My mother appeared. It was as if I had passed through the door to death, and together we were hovering above the room. We felt the heat, the torment emanating from Denise, so my mother opened a window for Denise's spirit to depart."

"Then?"

Her expression softened. "When I looked down at her—at myself—I wanted to lift her up like she was a small child."

"In many ways she was, Ellen," I said quietly. "Did you succeed?"

Tears rimmed her eyes but didn't fall. She gave me the kindest look, one that was deeply human, astonishingly intense. A look I'll never forget.

With surprising serenity, she replied, "Yes, I did. With my mother. Together, we rescued her."

There was an extended silence.

Finally, Ellen smiled. Tranquility suffused her features. "I will be okay."

She sat very still but didn't share her thoughts. Then she rose from the sofa and came to my side. I stood and she placed her arms around me—an enfolding embrace of amazing tenderness and strength, as if I was the one in need of consolation.

"Thank you, Adrienne."

Stunned by the transformation, I held her until she gently withdrew. Without another word, Ellen removed her navy blue overcoat from the chair and slipped it on. She turned and gave me one last smile and left the office. A moment later, I waited by my window to see her on the sidewalk below. With long, confident strides, her coattails blowing in the brisk winter wind, she crossed the street and slowly disappeared into the crowd.

"Find peace, my dear friend," I whispered. "I know you will."

ACKNOWLEDGMENTS

IT IS a great honor to have *The Psychologist's Shadow* chosen as the first title in Spectrum Books' new imprint, Enigma Books. Warmest thanks to Andrew May and his father, Carl, for selecting my novel and for the collegial relationship established during my premiere outing with Spectrum, *The Firefly*. They have been caring, responsive, enthusiastic, and professional partners. I look forward to future projects together with happy anticipation and toast "Cheers!" for the success of Enigma Books.

I'm also grateful to Alex Jones and Carl May for their excellent editing. Always appreciated!

Thank you to two special readers who reviewed an early version of the novel: Carol Oberle, a licensed clinical social worker, and Karla Linn Merrifield, an accomplished poet, who are longtime supporters. And, although she hasn't read the manuscript, Barbara Kleinrock Pollinger provided some of the techniques used by Dr. Ellen Haskell and Dr. Adrienne Barrow.

Vicki DeVico, as she has often done for previous covers, waved her PhotoShop magic wand over my still-life photograph of Venetian masks—thank you, Vicki! Andrew May and I collaborated on the cover typography—thank you, Andrew!

I am indebted to my many loyal readers and wonderful friends such as Beverly and Betty Harris, Julie and Tom Stewart, Mark Conover, Michael Ungs, Sandy Thatcher, Robin Miller Hardt, Shari Friedman, Jane Rundell, Nancy Borus Hart, Robert Starosciak, and Cynthia Bonner.

Photo by Vicki DeVico

ABOUT THE AUTHOR

LAURY A. EGAN is the author of eleven novels: *The Firefly, Once, Upon an Island, Doublecrossed, Wave in D Minor, Turnabout, The Swimmer, The Ungodly Hour, A Bittersweet Tale, Fabulous! An Opera Buffa, The Outcast Oracle, Jenny Kidd,* and a collection, *Fog and Other Stories.* Her poetry volumes include *Presence & Absence; The Sea & Beyond; Beneath the Lion's* Paw; and *Snow, Shadows, a Stranger.* She lives on the northern coast of New Jersey. Website: www.lauryaegan.com.

Excellent, gripping and exciting works of thriller fiction by
the most talented and unique authors.

Enigma Books

Mystery
Crime
Suspense
Action
Psychological
Historical
Horror
Supernatural
Political
Science Fiction

Visit us at
www.enigma-books.com

Or find us on Instagram
www.instagram.com/enigmabookpublisher